P9-DFH-893

KEN LIU

THE
PAPER
MENAGERIE

AND

OTHER STORIES

SAGA PRESS

LONDON SYDNEY **NEW YORK** TORONTO NEW DELHI

SAGA PRESS
AN IMPRINT OF SIMON & SCHUSTER, INC.

1230 AVENUE OF THE AMERICAS, NEW YORK, NEW YORK 10020

Previously published in *Lightspeed*: "Simulacrum" (2011), "The Bookmaking Habits of Select Species" and "The Perfect Match" (2012), and "The Litigation Master and the Monkey King" (2013); in *Polyphony 4*: "State Change" (2004); in *Strange Horizons*: "Good Hunting" (2012); in *Fantasy & Science Fiction*: "The Literomancer" (2010), "The Paper Menagerie" (2011), and "A Brief History of the Trans-Pacific Tunnel" (2012); in *Upgraded*: "The Regular" (2014); in *Asimov's Science Fiction*: "The Waves" (2012); in *The Future Is Japanese*: "Mono no aware" (2012); in *GigaNotoSaurus*: "All the Flavors" (2012); and *Panverse 3*: "The Man Who Ended History: A Documentary" (2011).
Cover art copyright © 2016 by Quentin Trollip.
"Origami Tiger" designed, folded, and photographed by Quentin Trollip.
Calligraphy for "The Literomancer" and "Mono no aware" copyright © 2016 by Mingmei Yip

Also available in a Saga Press hardcover edition.
The text for this book was set in Perpetua.
Manufactured in the United States of America
First Saga Press paperback edition October 2016
11 13 15 17 19 20 18 16 14 12
The Library of Congress has cataloged the hardcover edition as follows:
Liu, Ken, 1976–
[Short stories. Selections]
The paper menagerie and other stories / Ken Liu. — First edition.
pages ; cm
ISBN 978-1-4814-4254-1 (hc)
ISBN 978-1-4814-2436-3 (pbk)
ISBN 978-1-4814-2437-0 (eBook)
I. Liu, Ken, 1976- Bookmaking habits of select species. II. Title.
PS3612.I927A6 2015
813'.6—dc23   2014028362

CONTENTS

PREFACE

I started my career as a short story writer. Although I no longer write dozens of short stories every year since shifting most of my creative efforts to long-form fiction, short fiction still holds a special place in my heart.

This collection thus has the flavor of a retrospective for me. It includes some of my most popular works (as judged by award nominations and wins) as well as works that I'm proud of but didn't seem to get much recognition. I think they're a good, representative sample of my interests, obsessions, and creative goals.

I don't pay much attention to the distinction between fantasy and science fiction—or between "genre" and "mainstream" for that matter. For me, all fiction is about prizing the logic of metaphors—which is the logic of narratives in general—over reality, which is irreducibly random and senseless.

We spend our entire lives trying to tell stories about ourselves—they're the essence of memory. It is how we make living in this unfeeling, accidental universe tolerable. That we call such a tendency "the narrative fallacy" doesn't mean it doesn't also touch upon some aspect of the truth.

Some stories simply literalize their metaphors a bit more explicitly.

I'm also a translator, and translation offers a natural metaphor for how I think about writing in general.

Every act of communication is a miracle of translation.

At this moment, in this place, the shifting action potentials in my neurons cascade into certain arrangements, patterns, thoughts; they flow down my spine, branch into my arms, my fingers, until muscles twitch and thought is translated into motion; mechanical levers are pressed; electrons are rearranged; marks are made on paper.

At another time, in another place, light strikes the marks, reflects into a pair of high-precision optical instruments sculpted by nature after billions of years of random mutations; upside-down images are formed against two screens made up of millions of light-sensitive cells, which translate light into electrical pulses that go up the optic nerves, cross the chiasm, down the optic tracts, and into the visual cortex, where the pulses are reassembled into letters, punctuation marks, words, sentences, vehicles, tenors, thoughts.

The entire system seems fragile, preposterous, science fictional.

Who can say if the thoughts you have in your mind as you read these words are the same thoughts I had in my mind as I typed them? We are different, you and I, and the qualia of our consciousnesses are as divergent as two stars at the ends of the universe.

And yet, whatever has been lost in translation in the long journey of my thoughts through the maze of civilization to your mind, I think you do understand me, and you think you do understand me. Our minds managed to touch, if but briefly and imperfectly.

Does the thought not make the universe seem just a bit kinder, a bit brighter, a bit warmer and more human?

We live for such miracles.

I am forever grateful to the many beta readers, fellow writers, and editors who have helped me along the way. Every story here represents, in some measure, the sum of all my experiences, all the books I've read, all the conversations I've had, all the successes and failures and joys and sorrows and wonder and despair I've shared—we are but vertices in Indra's web.

I also want to thank everyone at Saga Press, my publisher, for helping me put together such a beautiful book. Among them are Jeannie Ng, for catching all those errors in the manuscript; Michael McCartney, for the lovely jacket design; Mingmei Yip, for accommodating unorthodox requests for calligraphy; and Elena Stokes and Katy Hershberger, for the thoughtful publicity campaign. I'm especially thankful to Joe Monti, my editor at Saga Press, for championing and shaping this book with his good judgment (and saving me from myself); Russ Galen, my agent, for seeing the possibilities in these stories; and most of all, to Lisa, Esther, and Miranda, for the millions of ways in which they make the story of my life complete and meaningful.

And finally, thank you, dear reader. It is the possibility of our minds touching that makes writing a worthwhile endeavor at all.

THE BOOKMAKING HABITS
OF SELECT SPECIES

There is no definitive census of all the intelligent species in the universe. Not only are there perennial arguments about what qualifies as intelligence, but each moment and everywhere, civilizations rise and fall, much as the stars are born and die.

Time devours all.

Yet every species has its unique way of passing on its wisdom through the ages, its way of making thoughts visible, tangible, frozen for a moment like a bulwark against the irresistible tide of time.

Everyone makes books.

It is said by some that writing is just visible speech. But we know such views are parochial.

A musical people, the Allatians write by scratching their thin, hard proboscis across an impressionable surface, such as a metal tablet covered by a thin layer of wax or hardened clay. (Wealthy Allatians sometimes wear a nib made of precious metals on the tip of the nose.) The writer speaks his thoughts as he writes, causing the proboscis to vibrate up and down as it etches a groove in the surface.

To read a book inscribed this way, an Allatian places his nose into the groove and drags it through. The delicate proboscis vibrates in sympathy with the waveform of the groove, and a hollow chamber in the Allatian skull magnifies the sound. In this manner, the voice of the writer is re-created.

The Allatians believe that they have a writing system superior to all others. Unlike books written in alphabets, syllabaries, or logograms, an Allatian book captures not only words, but also the writer's tone, voice, inflection, emphasis, intonation, rhythm. It is simultaneously a score and recording. A speech sounds like a speech, a lament a lament, and a story re-creates perfectly the teller's breathless excitement. For the Allatians, reading is literally hearing the voice of the past.

But there is a cost to the beauty of the Allatian book. Because the act of reading requires physical contact with the soft, malleable surface, each time a text is read, it is also damaged and some aspects of the original irretrievably lost. Copies made of more durable materials inevitably fail to capture all the subtleties of the writer's voice, and are thus shunned.

In order to preserve their literary heritage, the Allatians have to lock away their most precious manuscripts in forbidding libraries where few are granted access. Ironically, the most important and beautiful works of Allatian writers are rarely read, but are known only through interpretations made by scribes who attempt to reconstruct the original in new books after hearing the source read at special ceremonies.

For the most influential works, hundreds, thousands of interpretations exist in circulation, and they, in turn, are interpreted and proliferate through new copies. The Allatian scholars spend much of their time debating the relative authority of competing versions and inferring, based on the multiplicity of imperfect copies, the imagined voice of their antecedent, an ideal book uncorrupted by readers.

The Quatzoli do not believe that thinking and writing are different things at all.

They are a race of mechanical beings. It is not known if they began as mechanical creations of another (older) species, if they are shells hosting the souls of a once-organic race, or if they evolved on their own from inert matter.

A Quatzoli's body is made out of copper and shaped like an hourglass. Their planet, tracing out a complicated orbit between three stars, is subjected to immense tidal forces that churn and melt its metal core, radiating heat to the surface in the form of steamy geysers and lakes of lava. A Quatzoli ingests water into its bottom chamber a few times a day, where it slowly boils and turns into steam as the Quatzoli periodically dips itself into the bubbling lava lakes. The steam passes through a regulating valve—the narrow part of the hourglass—into the upper chamber, where it powers the various gears and levers that animate the mechanical creature.

At the end of the work cycle, the steam cools and condenses against the inner surface of the upper chamber. The droplets of water flow along grooves etched into the copper until they are collected into a steady stream, and this stream then passes through a porous stone rich in carbonate minerals before being disposed of outside the body.

This stone is the seat of the Quatzoli mind. The stone organ is filled with thousands, millions of intricate channels, forming a maze that divides the water into countless tiny, parallel flows that drip, trickle, wind around each other to represent simple values which, together, coalesce into streams of consciousness and emerge as currents of thought.

Over time, the pattern of water flowing through the stone changes. Older channels are worn down and disappear or become blocked and closed off—and so some memories are forgotten. New channels are created, connecting previously separated flows—an epiphany—and the departing water deposits new mineral growths at the far, youngest end of the stone, where the tentative, fragile miniature stalactites are the newest, freshest thoughts.

When a Quatzoli parent creates a child in the forge, its final act is to gift the child with a sliver of its own stone mind, a package of received wisdom and ready thoughts that allow the child to begin

3

its life. As the child accumulates experiences, its stone brain grows around that core, becoming ever more intricate and elaborate, until it can, in turn, divide its mind for the use of its children.

And so the Quatzoli *are* themselves books. Each carries within its stone brain a written record of the accumulated wisdom of all its ancestors: the most durable thoughts that have survived millions of years of erosion. Each mind grows from a seed inherited through the millennia, and every thought leaves a mark that can be read and seen.

Some of the more violent races of the universe, such as the Hesperoe, once delighted in extracting and collecting the stone brains of the Quatzoli. Still displayed in their museums and libraries, the stones—often labeled simply "ancient books"—no longer mean much to most visitors.

Because they could separate thought from writing, the conquering races were able to leave a record that is free of blemishes and thoughts that would have made their descendants shudder.

But the stone brains remain in their glass cases, waiting for water to flow through the dry channels so that once again they can be read and live.

The Hesperoe once wrote with strings of symbols that represented sounds in their speech, but now no longer write at all.

They have always had a complicated relationship with writing, the Hesperoe. Their great philosophers distrusted writing. A book, they thought, was not a living mind yet pretended to be one. It gave sententious pronouncements, made moral judgments, described purported historical facts, or told exciting stories . . . yet it could not be interrogated like a real person, could not answer its critics or justify its accounts.

The Hesperoe wrote down their thoughts reluctantly, only when they could not trust the vagaries of memory. They far preferred to live with the transience of speech, oratory, debate.

4

At one time, the Hesperoe were a fierce and cruel people. As much as they delighted in debates, they loved even more the glories of war. Their philosophers justified their conquests and slaughter in the name of forward motion: War was the only way to animate the ideals embedded in the static text passed down through the ages, to ensure that they remained true, and to refine them for the future. An idea was worth keeping only if it led to victory.

When they finally discovered the secret of mind storage and mapping, the Hesperoe stopped writing altogether.

In the moments before the deaths of great kings, generals, philosophers, their minds are harvested from the failing bodies. The paths of every charged ion, every fleeting electron, every strange and charming quark, are captured and cast in crystalline matrices. These minds are frozen forever in that moment of separation from their owners.

At this point, the process of mapping begins. Carefully, meticulously, a team of master cartographers—assisted by numerous apprentices—trace out each of the countless minuscule tributaries, impressions, and hunches that commingle into the flow and ebb of thought, until they gather into the tidal forces, the ideas that made their originators so great.

Once the mapping is done, they begin the calculations to project the continuing trajectories of the traced-out paths so as to simulate the next thought. The charting of the courses taken by the great, frozen minds into the vast, dark terra incognita of the future consumes the efforts of the most brilliant scholars of the Hesperoe. They devote the best years of their lives to it, and when they die, their minds, in turn, are charted indefinitely into the future as well.

In this way, the great minds of the Hesperoe do not die. To converse with them, the Hesperoe only have to find the answers on the mind maps. Thus, they no longer have a need for books as they used to make them—which were merely dead symbols—for the wisdom of the past is always with them, still thinking, still guiding, still exploring.

And as more and more of their time and resources are devoted to the simulation of ancient minds, the Hesperoe have also grown less warlike, much to the relief of their neighbors. Perhaps it is true that some books do have a civilizing influence.

The Tull-Toks read books they did not write.

They are creatures of energy. Ethereal, flickering patterns of shifting field potentials, the Tull-Toks are strung out among the stars like ghostly ribbons. When the starships of the other species pass through, the ships barely feel a gentle tug.

The Tull-Toks claim that everything in the universe can be read. Each star is a living text, where the massive convection currents of superheated gas tell an epic drama, with the starspots serving as punctuation, the coronal loops extended figures of speech, and the flares emphatic passages that ring true in the deep silence of cold space. Each planet contains a poem, written out in the bleak, jagged, staccato rhythm of bare rocky cores or the lyrical, lingering, rich rhymes— both masculine and feminine—of swirling gas giants. And then there are the planets with life, constructed like intricate jeweled clockwork, containing a multitude of self-referential literary devices that echo and re-echo without end.

But it is the event horizon around a black hole where the Tull-Toks claim the greatest books are to be found. When a Tull-Tok is tired of browsing through the endless universal library, she drifts toward a black hole. As she accelerates toward the point of no return, the streaming gamma rays and X-rays unveil more and more of the ultimate mystery for which all the other books are but glosses. The book reveals itself to be ever more complex, more nuanced, and just as she is about to be overwhelmed by the immensity of the book she is reading, her companions, observing from a distance, realize with a start that time seems to have slowed down to a standstill for her, and she will have eternity to read it as she falls forever toward a center that she will never reach.

Finally, a book has triumphed over time.

Of course, no Tull-Tok has ever returned from such a journey, and many dismiss their discussion of reading black holes as pure myth. Indeed, many consider the Tull-Toks to be nothing more than illiterate frauds who rely on mysticism to disguise their ignorance.

Still, some continue to seek out the Tull-Toks as interpreters of the books of nature they claim to see all around us. The interpretations thus produced are numerous and conflicting, and lead to endless debates over the books' content and—especially—authorship.

In contrast to the Tull-Toks, who read books at the grandest scale, the Caru'ee are readers and writers of the minuscule.

Small in stature, the Caru'ee each measure no larger than the period at the end of this sentence. In their travels, they seek from others only to acquire books that have lost all meaning and could no longer be read by the descendants of the authors.

Due to their unimpressive size, few races perceive the Caru'ee as threats, and they are able to obtain what they want with little trouble. For instance, at the Caru'ee's request, the people of Earth gave them tablets and vases incised with Linear A, bundles of knotted strings called *quipus*, as well as an assortment of ancient magnetic disks and cubes that they no longer knew how to decipher. The Hesperoe, after they had ceased their wars of conquest, gave the Caru'ee some ancient stones that they believed to be books looted from the Quatzoli. And even the reclusive Untou, who write with fragrances and flavors, allowed them to have some old bland books whose scents were too faint to be read.

The Caru'ee make no effort at deciphering their acquisitions.

They seek only to use the old books, now devoid of meaning, as a blank space upon which to construct their sophisticated, baroque cities.

The incised lines on the vases and tablets were turned into thoroughfares whose walls were packed with honeycombed rooms that elaborate on the pre-existing outlines with fractal beauty. The fibers in the knotted ropes were teased apart, re-woven, and re-tied at the microscopic level, until each original knot had been turned into a Byzantine complex of thousands of smaller knots, each a kiosk suitable for a Caru'ee merchant just starting out or a warren of rooms for a young Caru'ee family. The magnetic disks, on the other hand, were used as arenas of entertainment, where the young and adventurous careened across their surface during the day, delighting in the shifting push and pull of local magnetic potential. At night, the place was lit up by tiny lights that followed the flow of magnetic forces, and long-dead data illuminated the dance of thousands of young people searching for love, seeking to connect.

Yet it is not accurate to say that the Caru'ee do no interpretation at all. When members of the species that had given these artifacts to the Caru'ee come to visit, inevitably they feel a sense of familiarity with the Caru'ee's new construction.

For example, when representatives from Earth were given a tour of the Great Market built in a *quipu*, they observed—via the use of a microscope—bustling activity, thriving trade, and an incessant murmur of numbers, accounts, values, currency. One of Earth's representatives, a descendant of the people who had once knotted the string books, was astounded. Though he could not read them, he knew that the *quipus* had been made to keep track of accounts and numbers, to tally up taxes and ledgers.

Or take the example of the Quatzoli, who found the Caru'ee repurposing one of the lost Quatzoli stone brains as a research complex. The tiny chambers and channels, where ancient, watery thoughts once flowed, were now laboratories, libraries, teaching rooms, and lecture halls echoing with new ideas. The Quatzoli delegation had come to recover the mind of their ancestor, but left convinced that all was as it should be.

It is as if the Caru'ee were able to perceive an echo of the past, and unconsciously, as they built upon a palimpsest of books written long ago and long forgotten, chanced to stumble upon an essence of meaning that could not be lost, no matter how much time had passed.

They read without knowing they are reading.

Pockets of sentience glow in the cold, deep void of the universe like bubbles in a vast, dark sea. Tumbling, shifting, joining and breaking, they leave behind spiraling phosphorescent trails, each as unique as a signature, as they push and rise toward an unseen surface.

Everyone makes books.

STATE CHANGE

Every night, before going to bed, Rina checked the refrigerators.

There were two in the kitchen, on separate circuits, one with a fancy ice dispenser on the door. There was one in the living room holding up the TV, and one in the bedroom doubling as a nightstand. A small cubical unit meant for college dorm rooms was in the hallway, and a cooler that Rina refilled with fresh ice every night was in the bathroom, under the sink.

Rina opened the door of each refrigerator and looked in. Most of the refrigerators were empty most of the time. This didn't bother Rina. She wasn't interested in filling them. The checks were a matter of life and death. It was about the preservation of her soul.

What she was interested in were the freezer compartments. She liked to hold each door open for a few seconds, let the cold mist of condensation dissipate, and feel the chill on her fingers, breasts, face. She closed the door when the motor kicked in.

By the time she was done with all of the refrigerators, the apartment was filled with the bass chorus of all the motors, a low, confident hum that to Rina was the sound of safety.

In her bedroom, Rina got into bed and pulled the covers over her. She had hung some pictures of glaciers and icebergs on the walls, and she looked at them as pictures of old friends. There was also a framed picture on the refrigerator by her bed, this one of Amy, her roommate in college. They had lost touch over the years, but Rina kept her picture there, anyway.

Rina opened the refrigerator next to her bed. She stared into the glass dish that held her ice cube. Every time she looked, it seemed to get smaller.

Rina closed the refrigerator and picked up the book lying on top of it.

Edna St. Vincent Millay: A Portrait in Letters by Friends, Foes, and Lovers

New York, January 23, 1921

My Dearest Viv,—

Finally got up the courage to go see Vincent at her hotel today. She told me she wasn't in love with me anymore. I cried. She became angry and told me that if I couldn't keep myself under control then I might as well leave. I asked her to make me some tea.

It's that boy she's been seen with. I knew that. Still, it was terrible to hear it from her own lips. The little savage.

She smoked two cigarettes and offered me the box. I couldn't stand the bitterness so I stopped after one. Afterward she gave me her lipstick so I could fix my lips, as if nothing had happened, as if we were still in our room at Vassar.

"Write a poem for me," I said. She owed me at least that.

She looked as if she wanted to argue, but stopped herself. She took out her candle, put it in that candleholder I made for her, and lit it at both ends. When she lit her soul like that she was at her most beautiful. Her face glowed. Her pale skin was lit from within like a Chinese paper lantern about to burst into flame. She paced around the room as if she would tear down the walls. I drew up my feet on the bed, and wrapped her scarlet shawl around me, staying out of her way.

Then she sat down at her desk and wrote out her poem. As soon as it was done she blew out her candle, stingy with what remained of it. The smell of hot wax made me all teary-eyed again. She made out a clean copy for herself and gave the original to me.

"I did love you, Elaine," she said. "Now be a good girl and leave me alone."

This is how her poem starts:

What lips my lips have kissed, and where, and why,
I have forgotten, and what arms have lain
Under my head till morning, but the rain
Is full of ghosts tonight, that tap and sigh—

Viv, for a moment I wanted to take her candle and break it in half, to throw the pieces into the fireplace and melt her soul into nothing. I wanted to see her writhing at my feet, begging me to let her live.

But all I did was to throw that poem in her face, and I left.

I've been wandering around the streets of New York all day. I can't keep her savage beauty out of my mind. I wish my soul was heavier, more solid, something that could weigh itself down. I wish my soul wasn't this feather, this ugly wisp of goose down in my pocket, lifted up and buffeted about by the wind around her flame. I feel like a moth.

Your Elaine

Rina put the book down.

To be able to set your soul afire, she thought, *to be able to draw men and women to you at your will, to be brilliant, fearless of consequences, what would she not give to live a life like that?*

Millay chose to light her candle at both ends, and lived an incandescent life. When her candle ran out, she died sick, addicted, and much too young. But each day of her life she could decide, "Am I going to be brilliant today?"

Rina imagined her ice cube in the dark, cold cocoon of the freezer. *Stay calm,* she thought. *Block it out. This is your life. This bit of almost-death.*

Rina turned out the light.

When Rina's soul finally materialized, the nurse in charge of watching the afterbirth almost missed it. All of a sudden, there, in the stainless steel pan, was an ice cube, the sort you would find clinking around in glasses at cocktail parties. A pool of water was already forming around it. The edges of the ice cube were becoming rounded, indistinct.

An emergency refrigeration unit was rushed in, and the ice cube was packed away.

"I'm sorry," the doctor said to Rina's mother, who looked into the serene face of her baby daughter. No matter how careful they were, how long could they keep the ice cube from melting? It wasn't as if they could just keep it in a freezer somewhere and forget about it. The soul had to be pretty close to the body; otherwise the body would die.

Nobody in the room said anything. The air around the baby was awkward, still, silent. Words froze in their throats.

Rina worked in a large building downtown, next to the piers and docked yachts she had never been on. On each floor, there were offices with windows around the sides, the ones overlooking the harbor being bigger and better furnished than the others.

In the middle of the floor were the cubicles, one of which was Rina's. Next to her were two printers. The hum of the printers was a bit like the hum of refrigerators. Lots of people passed by her cubicle on the way to pick up their printouts. Sometimes they stopped, thinking they would say hello to the quiet girl sitting there, with her pale skin and ice-blonde hair, and always a sweater around her shoulders. Nobody knew what color her eyes were because she did not look up from her desk.

But there was a chill in the air around her, a fragile silence that did not want to be broken. Even though they saw her every day, most people did not know Rina's name. After a while, it became too embarrassing to ask. While the chattering life of the office ebbed and flowed around her, people left her alone.

Under Rina's desk was a small freezer that the firm had installed just for her. Each morning Rina would rush into her cubicle, unzip her insulated lunch bag, and from her thermos stuffed with ice cubes, she would carefully pull out the sandwich bag holding her one special ice cube and put it into the freezer. She would sigh, and sit in her chair, and wait for her heart to slow down.

The job of the people in the smaller offices away from the harbor was to look up, on their computers, the answers to questions asked by people in the offices facing the harbor. Rina's job was to take those answers and use the right fonts to squeeze them into the right places on the right pieces of paper to be sent back to the people in the harbor offices. Sometimes the people in the smaller offices were too busy, and they would dictate their answers onto cassette tapes. Rina would then type up the answers.

Rina ate her lunch at her cubicle. Even though one could go some distance away from one's soul for short periods of time without getting sick, Rina liked to be as close to the freezer as possible. When she had to be away sometimes to deliver an envelope to some office on another floor, she had visions of sudden power failures. Out of breath, she would then hurry through the halls to get back to the safety of her freezer.

Rina tried not to think that life was unfair to her. Had she been born before the invention of the Frigidaire she would not have survived. She didn't want to be ungrateful. But sometimes it was difficult.

After work, instead of going dancing with the other girls or getting ready for a date, she spent her nights at home, reading biographies to lose herself in other lives.

Morning Walks with T. S. Eliot: A Memoir

Between 1958 and 1963, Eliot was a member of the Commission for the Revised Psalter of the Book of Common Prayer. He was rather frail by this time, and avoided tapping into his tin of coffee altogether.

One exception was when the commission came to revise Psalm 23. Four centuries earlier, Bishop Coverdale had been rather free with his translation from the Hebrew. The correct English rendition for the central metaphor in the psalm, the commission agreed, was "the valley of deep darkness."

At the meeting, for the first time in months, Eliot brewed a cup of his coffee. The rich, dark aroma was unforgettable to me.

Eliot took a sip of his coffee, and then, in that same mesmerizing voice he used to read *The Waste Land*, he recited the traditional version that had infused itself into the blood of every Englishman: "Though I walk through the valley of the shadow of death, I shall fear no evil."

The vote was unanimous to keep Coverdale's version, embellished though it might have been.

I think it always surprised people how deep was Eliot's devotion to tradition, to the Anglican Church, and also how thoroughly his soul had been imbibed by the English.

I believe that was the last time Eliot tasted his soul, and often since then I have wished that I could again smell that aroma: bitter, burned, and restrained. It was not only the spirit of a true Englishman, but also that of the genius of poetry.

• • •

To measure out a life with coffee spoons, Rina thought, *must have seemed dreadful sometimes. Perhaps that was why Eliot had no sense of humor.*

But a soul in a coffee tin was also lovely in its own way. It enlivened the air around him, made everyone who heard his voice alert, awake, open and receptive to the mysteries of his difficult, dense verse. Eliot could not have written, and the world would have understood, *Four Quartets* without the scent of Eliot's soul, the edge it gave to every word, the sharp tang of having drunk something deeply significant.

I would love to have the mermaids sing to me, Rina thought. *Was that what Eliot dreamed of after drinking his coffee before sleep?*

Instead of mermaids, she dreamed of glaciers that night. Miles and miles of ice that would take a hundred years to melt. Though there was no life in sight, Rina smiled in her sleep. It was her life.

On the first day the new man showed up at work, Rina could tell that he was not going to be in his office for long.

His shirt was a few years out of style, and he did not take care to polish his shoes that morning. He was not very tall, and his chin was not very sharp. His office was down the hall from Rina's cubicle, and it was small, with only one window facing the building next to this one. The name tag outside the office said JIMMY KESNOW. By all signs he should have been just another one of the anonymous, ambitious, disappointed young men passing through the building every day.

But Jimmy was the most comfortable person Rina had ever seen. Wherever he was, he acted like he belonged. He was not loud and he did not talk fast, but conversations and crowds opened up places for him. He would say only a few words, but people would laugh and afterward feel a little wittier themselves. He would smile at people, and they would feel happier, more handsome, more beautiful. He popped in and out of his office all morning, managing to look purposeful and relaxed enough to stop and chat at the same time. Offices remained open after he had left, and their occupants felt no desire to close the doors.

Rina saw that the girl in the cubicle next to hers primped herself when she heard Jimmy's voice coming down the hall.

It seemed difficult to even remember what life in the office was like before Jimmy.

Rina knew that young men like that did not stay in small offices with only one window facing an alley for very long. They moved into offices facing the harbor, or maybe on the next floor. Rina imagined that his soul was probably a silver spoon, effortlessly dazzling and desirable.

The Trial of Joan of Arc

"At night the soldiers and Joan slept together on the ground. When Joan took off her armor, we could see her breasts, which were beautiful. And yet never once did she awake in me carnal desires.

"Joan would become angry when the soldiers swore in her presence or spoke of the pleasures of the flesh. She always chased away the women who followed soldiers with her sword unless a soldier promised to marry such a woman.

"Joan's purity came from her soul, which she always carried on her body whether she was riding into battle or getting ready to sleep for the night. This was a beech branch. Not far from Domrémy, her home village, there was an old beech tree called the Ladies' Tree by a spring. Her soul came from that tree, for the branch gave off a smell that those who knew Joan in her childhood swore was the same smell given off by the spring by the Ladies' Tree.

"Whoever came into Joan's presence with a sinful thought would instantly have that flame extinguished by the influence of her soul. Thus, she remained pure, as I do swear to tell the truth, even though she would sometimes be naked as the rest of the soldiers."

•   •   •

"Hey," Jimmy said. "What's your name?"

"Joan," Rina said. She blushed and put her book down. "Rina, I meant." Instead of looking at him she looked down at the half-eaten salad on her desk. She wondered if there was anything at the corners of her mouth. She thought about wiping her mouth with the napkin but decided that would draw too much attention.

"You know, I've been asking around the office all morning, and no one could tell me your name."

Even though Rina already knew this was true, she felt a little sad, as if she had disappointed him. She shrugged.

"But now I know something no one else here knows," Jimmy said, and sounded as if she had told him a wonderful secret.

Did they finally turn down the air-conditioning? Rina thought. *It didn't feel as cold as it usually did.* She thought about taking off her sweater.

"Hey, Jimmy," the girl in the cubicle next to Rina's called out. "Come over here. Let me show you those pictures I was telling you about."

"See you later," Jimmy said, and smiled at her. She knew because she was looking up, looking into his face, which she realized could be handsome.

Legends of the Romans

Cicero was born with a pebble. Therefore, no one expected him to amount to much.

Cicero practiced public speaking with the pebble in his mouth. Sometimes he almost choked on it. He learned to use simple words and direct sentences. He learned to push his voice past the pebble in his mouth, to articulate, to speak clearly even when his tongue betrayed him.

He became the greatest orator of his age.

•   •   •

"You read a lot," Jimmy said.

Rina nodded. Then she smiled at him.

"I've never seen eyes with your shade of blue," Jimmy said, looking directly into her eyes. "It's like the sea, but through a layer of ice." He said this casually, as if he was talking about a vacation he had taken, a movie he had seen. This was why Rina knew he was being sincere, and she felt as if she had given him another secret, one she didn't even know she had.

Neither of them said anything. This would usually be awkward. But Jimmy simply leaned against the wall of the cubicle, admiring the stack of books on Rina's desk. He settled into the silence, relaxed into it. And so Rina felt content to let the silence go on.

"Oh, Catullus," Jimmy said. He picked up one of the books. "Which poem is your favorite?"

Rina pondered this. It seemed too bold to say that it was "Let us live, my Lesbia, and let us love." It seemed too coy to say that it was "You ask me how many kisses."

She agonized over the answer.

He waited, not hurrying her.

She couldn't decide. She began to say something, anything, but nothing came out. A pebble was in her throat, an ice-cold pebble. She was angry with herself. She must have looked like such an idiot to him.

"Sorry," Jimmy said. "Steve is waving at me to come to his office. I'll catch up with you later."

Amy was Rina's roommate in college. She was the only person Rina ever pitied. Amy's soul was a pack of cigarettes.

But Amy did not act like she wanted to be pitied. By the time Rina met her, Amy had less than half a pack left.

"What happened to the rest of them?" Rina was horrified. She could not imagine herself being so careless with her life.

Amy wanted Rina to go out with her at nights, to dance, to drink, and to meet boys. Rina kept on saying no.

"Do it for me," Amy said. "You feel sorry for me, right? Well, I'm asking you to come with me, just once."

Amy took Rina to a bar. Rina hugged her thermos to her the whole way. Amy pried it out of her hand, dropped Rina's ice cube into a shot glass, and told the bartender to keep it chilled in the freezer.

Boys came up to try to pick them up. Rina ignored them. She was terrified. She wouldn't take her eyes off the freezer.

"Try to act like you are having fun, will you?" Amy said.

The next time a boy came up to them, Amy took out one of her cigarettes.

"You see this?" she said to the boy, her eyes flashing in the glow from the neon lights behind the bar. "I'm going to start smoking it right now. If you can get my friend here to laugh before I finish it, I will go home with you tonight."

"How about both of you come home with me tonight?"

"Sure," Amy said. "Why not? You better get cracking, though." She flicked her lighter and took a long drag on her cigarette. She threw her head back and blew the smoke high into the air.

"This is what I live for," Amy whispered to Rina, her pupils unfocused, wild. "All life is an experiment." Smoke drifted from her nostrils and made Rina cough.

Rina stared at Amy. Then she turned around to face the boy. She felt a little light-headed. The crooked nose on the boy's face seemed funny and sad at the same time.

Amy's soul was infectious.

"I'm jealous," Amy said to Rina the next morning. "You have a very sexy laugh." Rina smiled when she heard that.

Rina found the shot glass with her ice cube in the boy's freezer. She took the shot glass home with her.

Still, that was the last time Rina agreed to go with Amy.

They lost touch after college. When Rina thought about Amy, she wished that her pack of cigarettes would magically refill itself.

Rina had been paying attention to the flow of paper out of the printers next to her. She knew that Jimmy was going to move to an office upstairs soon. She didn't have a lot of time.

She went shopping over the weekend. She made her choices carefully. Her color was ice blue. She had her nails done, to go with her eyes.

Rina decided on Wednesday. People tended to have more to talk about at the beginning of the week and the end of the week, either about what they had done over the weekend or what they were about to do the next weekend. There was not so much to talk about on Wednesdays.

Rina brought her shot glass with her, for good luck, and because the glass was easy to chill.

She made her move after lunch. There was still a lot of work in the afternoon, and the gossip tended to die down then.

She opened the freezer door, took out the chilled shot glass and the sandwich bag with her ice cube. She took the ice cube out of the bag and put it into the shot glass. Condensation immediately formed on the outside of the glass.

She took off her sweater, picked up the glass in her hand, and began to walk around the office.

She walked wherever there were groups of people—in the hallways, by the printers, next to the coffee machines. As she approached, people felt a sudden chill in the air, and there would be a lull in the conversation. Witticisms sounded flat and stupid. Arguments died. Suddenly everyone would remember how much work was left to do and make up some excuse to get away. Office doors closed as she passed them.

She walked around until the halls were quiet, and the only office with its door open was Jimmy's.

She looked down into the glass. There was a small pool of water at the bottom of the glass; soon the ice cube would be floating.

She still had time, if she hurried.

Kiss me, before I disappear.

She put the shot glass down outside the door to Jimmy's office. *I am not Joan of Arc.*

She walked into Jimmy's office and closed the door behind her.

"Hello," she said. Now that she was alone with him, she didn't know what else to do.

"Hey," he said. "It's so quiet around here today. What's going on?"

"Si tecum attuleris bonam atque magnam cenam, non sine candida puella," she said. "If you bring with you a good meal and lots of it, and not without a pretty girl. That's the one. That's my favorite poem."

She felt shy, but warm. There was no weight on her tongue, no pebble in her throat. Her soul was outside that door, but she was not anxious. She was not counting down the seconds. The shot glass with her life in it was in another time, another place.

"Et uino et sale et omnibus cachinnis," he finished for her. "And wine and salt and all the laughter."

She saw that there was a saltshaker on his desk. Salt made the blandest food palatable. Salt was like wit and laughter in conversation. Salt made the plain extraordinary. Salt made the simple beautiful. Salt was his soul.

And salt made it harder to freeze.

She laughed.

She unbuttoned her blouse. He began to get up, to stop her. She shook her head and smiled at him.

I have no candle to burn at both ends. I won't measure my life with coffee spoons. I have no spring water to quiet desire, because I have left behind my frozen bit of almost-death. What I have is my life.

"All life is an experiment," she said.

She shook off her blouse and stepped out of her skirt. He could now see what she had bought over the weekend.

Ice blue was her color.

She remembered laughing, and she remembered him laughing back. She worked hard to memorize every touch, every quickened breath. What she didn't want to remember was the time.

The noise of the people outside the door gradually rose and then gradually settled down. They lingered in his office.

What lips my lips have kissed, she thought, and realized that it was again completely quiet outside the office. Sunlight in the room was taking on a red tinge.

She got up, stepping away from his grasp, and put on her blouse, stepped into her skirt. She opened the door to his office and picked up the shot glass.

She looked, and looked frantically, for a sliver of ice. Even the tiniest crystal would suffice. She would keep it frozen and eke out the rest of her life on the memory of this one day, this one day when she was alive.

But there was only water in the glass; clear, pure water.

She waited for her heart to stop beating. She waited for her lungs to stop breathing. She walked back into his office so that she could die looking into his eyes.

It would be hard to freeze salty water.

She felt warm, inviting, open. Something flowed into the coldest, quietest, and emptiest corners of her heart and filled her ears with the roar of waves. She thought she had so much to say to him that she would never have time to read again.

• • •

Rina,

I hope you are well. It has been a long time since we last saw each other.

I would imagine the immediate question on your mind is how many cigarettes I have left. Well, the good news is that I have quit smoking. The bad news is that my last cigarette was finished six months ago.

But as you can see, I am still alive.

Souls are tricky things, Rina, and I thought I had it all figured out. All my life I thought my fate was to be reckless, to gamble with each moment of my life. I thought that was what I was meant to do. The only moments when I felt alive were those times when I lit up a bit of my soul, daring for something extraordinary to happen before the flame and ashes touched my fingers. I would be alert during those times, sensitive to every vibration in my ears, every bit of color in my eyes. My life was a clock running down. The months between my cigarettes were just dress rehearsals for the real performance, and I was engaged for twenty showings.

I was down to my last cigarette, and I was terrified. I had planned for some big final splash, to go out with a bang. But when it came time to smoke that last cigarette, I lost my courage. When you realize you are going to die after you have finished that last breath, suddenly your hands start to shake, and you cannot hold a match steady or flick a lighter with your thumb.

I got drunk at a beach party, passed out. Someone needed a nicotine fix, pawed through my purse and found my last cigarette. By the time I woke up the empty box was on the sand next to me, and a little crab had crawled into it and made it its home.

Like I said, I didn't die.

All my life I thought my soul was in those cigarettes, and I never even thought about the box. I never paid any attention to that paper shell of quiet, that enclosed bit of emptiness.

An empty box is a home for lost spiders you want to carry outside. It holds loose change, buttons that have fallen off, needles and thread. It works tolerably well for lipstick, eye pencil, and a bit of blush. It is open to whatever you'd like to put in it.

And that is how I feel: open, careless, adaptable. Yes, life is now truly just an experiment. What can I do next? Anything.

But to get here, I first had to smoke my cigarettes.

What happened to me was a state change. When my soul turned from a box of cigarettes to a box, I grew up.

I thought of writing to you because you remind me of myself. You thought you understood your soul, and you thought you knew how you needed to live your life. I thought you were wrong then, but I didn't have the right answer myself.

But now I do. I think you are ready for a state change.

Your friend always, Amy

THE PERFECT MATCH

Sai woke to the rousing first movement of Vivaldi's violin concerto in C minor, "Il Sospetto."

He lay still for a minute, letting the music wash over him like a gentle Pacific breeze. The room brightened as the blinds gradually opened to the sunlight. Tilly had woken him right at the end of a light sleep cycle, the optimal time. He felt great: refreshed, optimistic, ready to jump out of bed.

Which is what he did next. "Tilly, that's an inspired choice for a wake-up song."

"Of course." Tilly spoke from the camera/speaker in the nightstand. "Who knows your tastes and moods better than I?" The voice, though electronic, was affectionate and playful.

Sai went into the shower.

"Remember to wear the new shoes today." Tilly now spoke to him from the camera/speaker in the ceiling.

"Why?"

"You have a date after work."

"Oh, the new girl. Shoot, what's her name? I know you told me—"

"I'll bring you up to speed after work. I'm sure you'll like her. The compatibility index is very high. I think you'll be in love for at least six months."

Sai looked forward to the date. Tilly had also introduced him to his last girlfriend, and that relationship had been wonderful. The breakup afterward was awful, of course, but it helped that Tilly had guided him through it. He felt that he had matured emotionally and, after a month on his own, was ready start a new relationship.

But first he still had to get through the workday. "What do you recommend for breakfast this morning?"

"You are scheduled to attend the kickoff meeting for the Davis case at eleven, which means you'll get a lunch paid for by the firm. I suggest you go light on the breakfast, maybe just a banana."

Sai was excited. All the paralegals at Chapman Singh Stevens & Rios lived for client lunches made by the firm's own executive chef. "Do I have time to make my own coffee?"

"You do. Traffic is light this morning. But I suggest you go to this new smoothie place along the way instead—I can get you a coupon code."

"But I really want coffee."

"Trust me, you'll love the smoothie."

Sai smiled as he turned off the shower. "Okay, Tilly. You always know best."

Although it was another pleasant and sunny morning in Las Aldamas, California—sixty-eight degrees Fahrenheit—Sai's neighbor Jenny was wearing a thick winter coat, ski goggles, and a long, dark scarf that covered her hair and the rest of her face.

"I thought I told you I didn't want that thing installed," she said as he stepped out of his apartment. Her voice was garbled through some kind of electronic filter. In response to his questioning look, she pointed to the camera over Sai's door.

Talking to Jenny was like talking to one of his grandmother's friends who refused to use Centillion e-mail or get a ShareAll account because they were afraid of having "the computer" know "all their business"— except that as far as he could tell, Jenny was his age. She had grown up a digital native, but somehow had missed the ethos of sharing.

"Jenny, I'm not going to argue with you. I have a right to install anything I want over *my* door. And I want Tilly to keep an eye on my door when I'm away. Apartment three-oh-eight was just burglarized last week."

"But your camera will record visitors to my place too, because we share this hallway."

"So?"

"I don't want Tilly to have any of my social graph."

Sai rolled his eyes. "What do you have to hide?"

"That's not the point—"

"Yeah, yeah, civil liberties, freedom, privacy, blah blah blah . . ."

Sai was sick of arguing with people like Jenny. He had made the same point countless times: *Centillion is not some big, scary government. It's a private company, whose motto happens to be "Make things better!" Just because you want to live in the dark ages doesn't mean the rest of us shouldn't enjoy the benefits of ubiquitous computing.*

He dodged around her bulky frame to get to the stairs.

"Tilly doesn't just tell you what you want!" Jenny shouted. "She tells you what to *think*. Do you even know what you really want anymore?"

Sai paused for a moment.

"Do you?" she pressed.

What a ridiculous question. Just the kind of pseudointellectual antitechnology rant that people like her mistake for profundity.

He kept on walking.

"Freak," he muttered, expecting Tilly to chime in from his phone earpiece with some joke to cheer him up.

But Tilly said nothing.

Having Tilly around was like having the world's best assistant:

—"Hey, Tilly, do you remember where I kept that Wyoming filing with the weird company name and the F merger from maybe six months ago?"

—"Hey, Tilly, can you get me a form for Section 131 Articles? Make sure it's a form that associates working with Singh use."

—"Hey, Tilly, memorize these pages. Assign them the tags: 'Chapman,' 'favors buyer,' 'only use if associate is nice to me.'"

For a while, Chapman Singh had resisted the idea of allowing employees to bring Tilly into the office, preferring their proprietary corporate AI system. But it proved too difficult to force employees to keep their personal calendars and recommendations rigidly separate from work ones, and once the partners started to violate the rules and use Tilly for work, IT had to support them.

And Centillion had then pledged that they would encrypt all corporate-derived information in a secure manner and never use it for competitive purposes—only to give better recommendations to employees of Chapman Singh. After all, the mission statement of Centillion was to "arrange the world's information to ennoble the human race," and what could be more ennobling than making work more efficient, more productive, more pleasant?

As Sai enjoyed his lunch, he felt very lucky. He couldn't even imagine what drudgery work would have been like before Tilly came along.

After work, Tilly guided Sai to the flower shop—of course Tilly had a coupon—and then, on the way to the restaurant, she filled Sai in on his date, Ellen: educational background, ShareAll profile, reviews by previous boyfriends/girlfriends, interests, likes, dislikes, and of course, pictures—dozens of photos recognized and gathered by Tilly from around the Net. Sai smiled. Tilly was right. Ellen was exactly his type.

It was a truism that what a man wouldn't tell his best friend, he'd happily search for on Centillion. Tilly knew all about what kind of women Sai found attractive, having observed the pictures and videos he perused late at nights while engaging the Just-for-Me mode in his browser.

And, of course, Tilly would know Ellen just as well as she knew him, so Sai knew that he would be exactly Ellen's type too.

As predicted, it turned out they were into the same books, the same movies, the same music. They had compatible ideas about how hard one should work. They laughed at each other's jokes. They fed off each other's energy.

Sai marveled at Tilly's accomplishment. Four billion women on Earth, and Tilly seemed to have found the perfect match for him. It was just like hitting the "I Trust You" button on Centillion search back in the early days and how it knew just the right web page to take you to.

Sai could feel himself falling in love, and he could tell that Ellen wanted to ask him to come home with her.

Although everything had gone exceedingly well, if he was being completely honest with himself, it wasn't *quite* as exciting and lovely as he had expected. Everything was indeed going smoothly, but maybe just a tad *too* smoothly. It was as if they already knew everything there was to know about each other. There were no surprises, no thrill of finding the truly new.

In other words, the date was a bit boring.

As Sai's mind wandered, there was a lull in the conversation. They smiled at each other and just tried to enjoy the silence.

In that moment, Tilly's voice burst into his earpiece. "You might want to ask her if she likes contemporary Japanese desserts. I know just the place."

Sai realized that though he hadn't been aware of it until just then, he did suddenly have a craving for something sweet and delicate.

Tilly doesn't just tell you what you want. She tells you what to think.

Sai paused.

Do you even know what you really want anymore?

He tried to sort out his feelings. Did Tilly just figure out what he hadn't even known he wanted? Or did she put the thought into his head?

Do you?

The way Tilly filled in that lull . . . it was as if Tilly didn't trust that he would be able to manage the date on his own, as if Tilly thought he wouldn't know what to say or do if she didn't jump in.

Sai suddenly felt irritated. The moment had been ruined.

I'm being treated like a child.

"I know you'll like it. I have a coupon."

"Tilly," he said, "please stop monitoring and terminate autosuggestions."

"Are you sure? Gaps in sharing can cause your profile to be incomplete—"

"Yes, please cease."

With a beep, Tilly turned herself off.

Ellen stared at him, eyes and mouth wide open in shock.

"Why did you do that?"

"I wanted to talk to you alone, just the two of us." Sai smiled. "It's nice sometimes to just be ourselves, without Tilly, don't you think?"

Ellen looked confused. "But you know that the more Tilly knows, the more helpful she can be. Don't you want to be sure we don't make silly mistakes on a first date? We're both busy, and Tilly—"

"I know what Tilly can do. But—"

Ellen held up a hand, silencing him. She tilted her head, listening to her headset.

"I have the perfect idea," Ellen said. "There's this new club, and I know Tilly can get us a coupon."

Sai shook his head, annoyed. "Let's try to think of something to do without Tilly. Would you please turn her off?"

Ellen's face was unreadable for a moment.

"I think I should head home," she said. "Early workday tomorrow." She looked away.

"Did Tilly tell you to say that?"

She said nothing and avoided looking into his eyes.

"I had a great time," Sai added quickly. "Would you like to go out again?"

Ellen paid half the bill and did not ask him to walk her home.

With a beep, Tilly came back to life in his ear.

"You're being very antisocial tonight," Tilly said.

"I'm not antisocial. I just didn't like how you were interfering with everything."

"I have every confidence you would have enjoyed the rest of the date had you followed my advice."

Sai drove on in silence.

"I sense a lot of aggression in you. How about some kickboxing? You haven't gone in a while, and there's a twenty-four-hour gym coming up. Take a right here."

Sai drove straight on.

"What's wrong?"

"I don't feel like spending more money."

"You know I have a coupon."

"What exactly do you have against me saving my money?"

"Your savings rate is right on target. I simply want to make sure you're sticking to your regimen for consumption of leisure. If you oversave, you'll later regret that you didn't make the most of your youth. I've plotted the optimum amount of consumption you should engage in daily."

"Tilly, I just want to go home and sleep. Can you shut yourself off for the rest of the night?"

"You know that in order to make the best life recommendations, I need to have complete knowledge of you. If you shut me out of parts of your life, my recommendations won't be as accurate——"

Sai reached into his pocket and turned off the phone. The earpiece went silent.

When Sai got home, he saw that the light over the stairs leading up to his apartment had gone out, and several dark shapes skulked around the bottom.

"Who's there?"

Several of the shadows scattered, but one came toward him: Jenny.

"You're back early."

He almost didn't recognize her; this was the first time he'd heard her voice without the electronic filter she normally used. It sounded surprisingly . . . happy.

Sai was taken aback. "How did you know I was back early? You stalking me?"

Jenny rolled her eyes. "Why would I need to stalk you? Your phone automatically checks in and out of everywhere you go with a status message based on your mood. It's all on your ShareAll lifecast for anyone to see."

He stared at her. In the faint glow from the streetlights he could see that she wasn't wearing her thick winter coat or ski goggles or scarf. Instead, she was in shorts and a loose white T-shirt. Her black hair had been dyed white in streaks. In fact, she looked very pretty, if a bit nerdy.

"What, surprised that I *do* know how to use a computer?"

"It's just that you usually seem so . . ."

"Paranoid? Crazy? Say what's on your mind. I won't be offended."

"Where's your coat and goggles? I've never even seen you without them."

"Oh, I taped over your door camera so my friends could come for a visit tonight, so I'm not wearing them. I'm sorry—"

"You did what?"

"—and I came out here to meet you because I saw that you turned off Tilly, not once, but *twice*. I'm guessing you're finally ready for the truth."

Stepping into Jenny's apartment was like stepping into the middle of a fishing net.

The ceiling, floor, and walls were all covered with a fine metal mesh, which glinted like liquid silver in the flickering light from the many large, high-definition computer monitors stacked on top of each other around the room, apparently the only sources of illumination.

Besides the monitors, the only other visible furniture appeared to be bookshelves—full of books (the paper kind, strangely enough). A few upside-down, ancient milk crates covered with cushions served as chairs.

Sai had been feeling restless, had wanted to do something strange. But he now regretted his decision to accept her invitation to come in. She was indeed eccentric, perhaps too much so.

Jenny closed the door and reached up and plucked the earpiece out of Sai's ear. Then she held out her hand. "Give me your phone."

"Why? It's already off."

Jenny's hand didn't move. Reluctantly, Sai took out his phone and gave it to her.

She looked at it contemptuously. "No removable battery. Just what you'd expect of a Centillion phone. They should call these things tracking devices, not phones. You can never be sure they're really off." She slipped the phone inside a thick pouch, sealed it, and dropped it on the desk.

"Okay, now that your phone is acoustically and electromagnetically shielded, we can talk. The mesh on the walls basically makes my

34

apartment into a Faraday cage, so cellular signals can't get through. But I don't feel comfortable around a Centillion phone until I can put a few layers of shielding around it."

"I'm just going to say it. You are *nuts*. You think Centillion spies on you? Their privacy policy is the best in the business. Every bit of information they gather has to be given up by the user voluntarily, and it's all used to make the user's life better—"

Jenny tilted her head and looked at him with a smirk until he stopped talking.

"If that's all true, why did you turn Tilly off tonight? Why did you agree to come up here with me?"

Sai wasn't sure he himself knew the answers.

"Look at you. You've agreed to have cameras observe your every move, to have every thought, word, interaction recorded in some distant data center so that algorithms could be run over them, mining them for data that marketers pay for.

"Now you've got nothing left that's private, nothing that's yours and yours alone. Centillion owns all of you. You don't even know who you are anymore. You buy what Centillion wants you to buy; you read what Centillion suggests you read; you date who Centillion thinks you should date. But are you really happy?"

"That's an outdated way to look at it. Everything Tilly suggests to me has been scientifically proven to fit my taste profile, to be something I'd like."

"You mean some advertiser paid Centillion to pitch it at you."

"That's the point of advertising, isn't it? To match desire with satisfaction. There are thousands of products in this world that would have been perfect for me, but I might never have known about them. Just like there's a perfect girl out there for me, but I might never have met her. What's wrong with listening to Tilly so that the perfect product finds the perfect consumer, the perfect girl finds the perfect boy?"

Jenny chuckled. "I love how you're so good at rationalizing your state. I ask you again: If life with Tilly is so wonderful, why did you turn her off tonight?"

"I can't explain it," Sai said. He shook his head. "This is a mistake. I think I'll head home."

"Wait. Let me show you a few things about your beloved Tilly first," Jenny said. She went to the desk and started typing, bringing up a series of documents on a monitor. She talked as Sai tried to scan and get their gist.

"Years ago, they caught Centillion's traffic-monitoring cars sniffing all the wireless traffic from home networks on the streets they drove through. Centillion also used to override the security settings on your machine and track your browsing habits before they shifted to an opt-in monitoring policy designed to provide better 'recommendations.' Do you think they've really changed? They hunger for data about you—the more the better—and damned if they care about how they get it."

Sai flicked through the documents skeptically. "If this is all true, why hasn't anyone brought it up in the news?"

Jenny laughed. "First, everything Centillion did was arguably legal. The wireless transmissions were floating in public space, for example, so there was no violation of privacy. And the end-user agreement could be read to allow everything Centillion did to 'make things better' for you. Second, these days, how do you get your news except through Centillion? If Centillion doesn't want you to see something, you won't."

"So how did you find these documents?"

"My machine is connected to a network built on top of the Net, one that Centillion can't see inside. Basically, we rely on a virus that turns people's computers into relaying stations for us, and everything is encrypted and bounced around so that Centillion can't see our traffic."

Sai shook his head. "You're really one of those tinfoil-hat conspiracy theorists. You make Centillion sound like some evil repressive government. But it's just a company trying to make some money."

Jenny shook her head. "Surveillance is surveillance. I can never understand why some people think it matters whether it's the government doing it to you or a company. These days, Centillion is bigger than governments. Remember, it managed to topple three countries' governments just because they dared to ban Centillion within their borders."

"Those were repressive places—"

"Oh, right, and you live in the land of the free. You think Centillion was trying to promote freedom? They wanted to be able to get in there and monitor everyone and urge them to all consume more so that Centillion could make more money."

"But that's just business. It's not the same thing as evil."

"You say that, but that's only because you don't know what the world really looks like anymore, now that it's been remade in Centillion's image."

Although Jenny's car was heavily shielded liked her apartment, as she and Sai drove, she whispered anyway, as if she were afraid that their conversation would be overheard by people walking by on the sidewalk.

"I can't believe how decrepit this place looks," Sai said as she parked the car on the side of the street. The surface of the road was pockmarked with potholes, and the houses around them were in ill repair. A few had been abandoned and were falling apart. In the distance they could hear the fading sound of a police siren. This was not a part of Las Aldamas that Sai had ever been to.

"It wasn't like this even ten years ago."

"What happened?"

"Centillion noticed a certain tendency for people—some people, not all—to self-segregate by race when it came to where they wanted to live. The company tried to serve this need by prioritizing different real estate listings to searchers based on their race. Nothing illegal about what they were doing, since they were just satisfying a need and desire in their users. They weren't hiding any listings, just pushing them far down the list, and in any event, you couldn't ever pick apart their algorithm and prove that they were looking at race when it was just one out of hundreds of factors in their magical ranking formula.

"After a while, the process began to snowball, and the segregation got worse and worse. It became easier for the politicians to gerrymander districts based on race. And so here we are. Guess who got stuck in these parts of the town?"

Sai took a deep breath. "I had no idea."

"If you ask Centillion, they'll say that their algorithms just reflected and replicated the desire to self-segregate in some of their users, and that Centillion wasn't in the business of policing thoughts. Oh, they'd claim that they were actually increasing freedom by giving people just what they wanted. They'd neglect to mention that they were profiting off it through real estate commissions, of course."

"I can't believe no one ever says anything about this."

"You're forgetting again that everything you know now comes filtered through Centillion. Whenever you do a search, whenever you hear a news digest, it's been curated by Centillion to fit what it thinks you want to hear. Someone upset by the news isn't going to buy anything sold by the advertisers, so Centillion adjusts things to make it all okay.

"It's like we're all living in Oz's Emerald City. Centillion puts these thick green goggles over our eyes, and we all think everything is a beautiful shade of green."

"You're accusing Centillion of censorship."

"No. Centillion is an algorithm that's gotten out of hand. It just gives you more of what it thinks you want. And we—people like me—think that's the root of the problem. Centillion has put us in little bubbles, where all we see and hear are echoes of ourselves, and we become ever more stuck in our existing beliefs and exaggerated in our inclinations. We stop asking questions and accept Tilly's judgment on everything.

"Year after year, we become more docile and grow more wool for Centillion to shave off and grow rich with. But I don't want to live that way."

"And why are you telling me all this?"

"Because, neighbor, we're going to kill Tilly," Jenny said, giving Sai a hard look, "and you're going to help us do it."

Jenny's apartment, with all its windows tightly shut and curtained, felt even more stifling after the car ride. Sai looked around at the flickering screens showing dancing, abstract patterns, suddenly wary. "And just how are you planning to kill Tilly?"

"We're working on a virus, a cyber weapon, if you want to get all macho about it."

"What exactly would it do?"

"Since the lifeblood of Tilly is data—the billions of profiles Centillion has compiled on every user—that's how we have to take it down.

"Once inside the Centillion data center, the virus will gradually alter every user profile it encounters and create new, fake profiles. We want it to move slowly to avoid detection. But eventually, it will have poisoned the data so much that it will no longer be possible for Tilly to make creepy, controlling predictions about users. And if we do it slowly enough, they can't even go to backups because they'll be corrupted too. Without the data it's built up over the decades, Centillion's advertising revenue will dry up overnight, and poof, Tilly'll be gone."

Sai imagined the billions of bits in the cloud: his tastes, likes and dislikes, secret desires, announced intentions, history of searches, purchases, articles and books read, pages browsed.

Collectively, the bits made up a digital copy of him, literally. Was there anything that was a part of *him* that wasn't also up there in the cloud, curated by Tilly? Wouldn't unleashing a virus on that be like suicide, like murder?

But then he remembered how it had felt to have Tilly lead him by the nose on every choice, how he had been content, like a pig happily wallowing in his enclosure.

The bits were his, but not *him*. He had a will that could not be captured in bits. And Tilly had almost succeeded in making him forget that.

"How can I help?" Sai asked.

Sai woke to Miles Davis's rendition of "So What."

For a moment, he wondered if the memory of the night before wasn't a dream. It felt so good to be awake, listening to just the song he wanted to hear.

"Are you feeling better, Sai?" Tilly asked.

Am I?

"I thought I turned you off, Tilly, with a hardware switch."

"I was quite concerned that you stopped all Centillion access to your life last night and forgot to turn it back on. You might have missed your wake-up call. However, Centillion added a system-level fail-safe to prevent just such an occurrence. We thought most users such as yourself would want such an override so that Centillion could regain access to your life."

"Of course," Sai said. *So it's impossible to turn Tilly off and keep her off. Everything Jenny said last night was true.* He felt a chill tingle on his back.

"There's a gap of about twelve hours during which I couldn't acquire data about you. To prevent degradation in my ability to help you, I recommend that you fill me in."

"Oh, you didn't miss much. I came home and fell asleep. Too tired."

"There appears to have been vandalism last night of the new security cameras you installed. The police have been informed. Unfortunately, the camera did not capture a good image of the perpetrator."

"Don't worry about it. There's nothing here worth stealing, anyway."

"You sound a bit down. Is it because of the date last night? It seems that Ellen wasn't the right match for you after all."

"Um, yeah. Maybe not."

"Don't worry: I know just the thing that will put you in a good mood."

Over the next few weeks, Sai found it extremely difficult to play his assigned role.

Maintaining the pretense that he still trusted Tilly was crucial, Jenny had emphasized, if their plan was to succeed. Tilly couldn't suspect anything was going on at all.

It seemed simple enough at first, but it was nerve-racking, keeping secrets from Tilly. Could she detect the tremors in his voice? Sai wondered. Could she tell that he was faking enthusiasm for the commercial consumption transactions she suggested?

Meanwhile, he also had a much bigger puzzle to solve before John P. Rushgore, Assistant General Counsel of Centillion, came to Chapman Singh in another week.

Chapman Singh is defending Centillion in a patent dispute with ShareAll, Jenny had said. *This is our opportunity to get inside Centillion's network. All you have to do is to get someone from Centillion to plug this into his laptop.*

And she had then handed him a tiny thumb drive.

Though he still hadn't figured out a plan for plugging the thumb drive into a Centillion machine, Sai was glad to have come to the end of another long day of guarding himself against Tilly.

"Tilly, I'm going jogging. I'll leave you here."

"You know that it's best to carry me with you," Tilly said. "I can track your heart rate and suggest an optimal route for you."

"I know. But I just want to run around on my own a bit, all right?"

"I'm growing quite concerned with your latest tendencies toward hiding instead of sharing."

"There's no tendency, Tilly. I just don't want you to be stolen if I get mugged. You know this neighborhood has become more unsafe lately."

And he turned off the phone and left it in his bedroom.

He closed the door behind him, made sure that the taped-over camera was still taped-over, and gently knocked on Jenny's door.

Getting to know Jenny was the oddest thing he'd ever done, Sai realized.

He couldn't count on Tilly to have made sure ahead of time that they would have topics to talk about. He couldn't rely on Tilly's always apropos suggestions when he was at a loss for words. He couldn't even count on being able to look up Jenny's ShareAll profile.

He was on his own. And it was exhilarating.

"How did you figure out everything Tilly was doing to us?"

"I grew up in China," Jenny said, wiping a strand of hair behind her ear. Sai found the gesture inexplicably endearing. "Back then, the government watched everything you did on the Network and made no secret of it. You had to learn how to keep the insanity at bay, to read between the lines, to speak without being overheard."

"I guess we were lucky, over here."

"No." And she smiled at his surprise. He was learning that she preferred to be contrarian, to disagree with him. He liked that about her. "You grew up believing you were free, which made it even harder for you to see when you weren't. You were like frogs in the pot being slowly boiled."

"Are there many like you?"

"No. It's hard to live off the grid. I've lost touch with my old friends. I have a hard time getting to know people because so much of their lives are lived inside Centillion and ShareAll. I can peek in on them once in a while through a dummy profile, but I can never *be* a part of their lives. Sometimes I wonder if I'm doing the right thing."

"You are," Sai said, and, though there was no Tilly to prompt him, he took Jenny's hand in his. She didn't pull away.

"I never really thought of you as my type," she said.

Sai's heart sank like a stone.

"But who thinks only in terms of 'types' except Tilly?" she said quickly, then smiled and pulled him closer.

Finally, the day had come. Rushgore had come to Chapman Singh to prepare for a deposition. He was huddled up with the firm's lawyers in one of their conference rooms all day long.

Sai sat down in his cubicle, stood up, and sat down again. He found himself full of nervous energy as he contemplated the best way to deliver the payload, as it were.

Maybe he could pretend to be tech support, there to perform an emergency scan of his system?

Maybe he could deliver lunch to him and plug the drive in slyly?

Maybe he could pull the fire alarm and hope that Rushgore would leave his laptop behind?

Not a single one of his ideas passed the laugh test.

"Hey." The associate who had been with Rushgore in the conference room all day was suddenly standing next to Sai's cubicle. "Rushgore needs to charge his phone—you got a Centillion charging cable over here?"

Sai stared at him, dumbfounded by his luck.

The associate held up a phone and waved it at him.

"Of course!" Sai said. "I'll bring one right to you."

"Thanks." The associate went back to the conference room.

Sai couldn't believe it. This was it. He plugged the drive into a charging cable and added an extension on the other end. The whole thing looked only a little odd, like a thin python that had swallowed a rat.

But suddenly he felt a sinking feeling in the pit of his stomach, and he almost swore aloud: He had forgotten to turn off the webcam above his computer—*Tilly's eyes*—before preparing the cable. If Tilly raised questions about the weird cable he was carrying, he would have no explanation, and then all his efforts at misdirection, at hiding, would be for naught.

But there was nothing he could do about it now but proceed as planned. As he left his cubicle, his heart was almost in his throat.

He stepped into the hallway and strode down to the conference room.

Still nothing from his earpiece.

He opened the door. Rushgore was too busy with his computer even to look up. He grabbed the cable from Sai and plugged one end into his computer and the other end into his phone.

And Tilly remained silent.

Sai woke to—what else?—"We Are the Champions."

The previous night of drinking and laughing with Jenny and her friends had been a blur, but he did remember coming home and telling Tilly, right before he fell asleep, "We did it! We won!"

Ah, if Tilly only knew what we were celebrating.

The music faded, stopped.

Sai stretched lazily, turned to his side, and stared into the eyes of four burly, very serious men.

"Tilly, call the police!"

"I'm afraid I can't do that, Sai."

"Why the hell not?"

"These men are here to help you. Trust me, Sai. You know I know just what you need."

When the strange men had appeared in his apartment, Sai had imagined torture chambers, mental hospitals, faceless guards parading outside of dark cells. He had not imagined that he would be sitting across the table from Christian Rinn, Founder and Executive Chairman of Centillion, having white tea.

"You got pretty close," Rinn said. The man was barely in his forties and looked fit and efficient—*kind of like how I picture a male version of Tilly,* Sai thought. He smiled. "Closer than almost anyone."

"What was the mistake that gave us away?" Jenny asked.

She was sitting to Sai's left, and Sai reached out for her hand. They intertwined their fingers, giving each other strength.

"It was his phone, on that first night he visited you."

"Impossible. I shielded it. It couldn't have recorded anything."

"But you left it on your desk, where it could still make use of its accelerometer. It detected and recorded the vibrations from your typing. There's a very distinctive way we strike the keys on a keyboard, and it's possible to reconstruct what someone was typing based on the vibration patterns alone. It's an old technology we developed for catching terrorists and drug dealers."

Jenny cursed under her breath, and Sai realized that until that moment, on some level he still hadn't quite believed Jenny's paranoia.

"But I didn't bring my phone after that first day."

"True, but we didn't need it. After Tilly picked up what Jenny was typing, the right alert algorithms were triggered and we focused surveillance on you. We parked a traffic observation vehicle a block away and trained a little laser on Jenny's window. It was enough to record your conversations through the vibrations in the glass."

"You're a very creepy man, Mr. Rinn," Sai said. "And despicable too."

Rinn didn't seem bothered by this. "I think you might feel differently by the end of our conversation. Centillion was not the first company to stalk you."

Jenny's fingers tightened around Sai's. "Let him go. I'm the one you really want. He doesn't know anything."

Rinn shook his head and smiled apologetically. "Sai, did you realize that Jenny moved into the apartment next to yours a week after we retained Chapman Singh to represent us in the suit against ShareAll?"

Sai didn't understand what Rinn was getting at, but he sensed that he would not like what he was about to find out. He wanted to tell Rinn to shut up, but he held his tongue.

"Curious, aren't you? You can't resist the pull of information. If it's possible, you always want to learn something new; we're hardwired that way. That's the drive behind Centillion, too."

"Don't believe anything he says," Jenny said.

"Would it surprise you to find out that the five other paralegals in your firm also had new neighbors move in during that same week? Would it also surprise you to learn that the new neighbors have all sworn to destroy Centillion, just like Jenny here? Tilly is very good at detecting patterns."

Sai's heart beat faster. He turned to Jenny. "Is this true? You planned from the start to use me? You got to know me just so you'd have a chance to deliver a virus?"

Jenny turned her face away.

"They know that there's no way to hack into our systems from the outside, so they had to sneak a trojan in. You were used, Sai. She and her friends guided you, led you by the nose, made you do things—just like they accuse *us* of doing."

"It's not like that," Jenny said. "Listen, Sai, maybe that was how it started. But life's full of surprises. I was surprised by you, and that's a good thing."

Sai let go of Jenny's hand and turned back to Rinn. "Maybe they *did* use me. But they're right. You've turned the world into a panopticon and all the people in it into obedient puppets that you nudge this way and that just so you'd make more money."

"You yourself pointed out that we were fulfilling desires, lubricating the engine of commerce in an essential way."

"But you also fulfill dark desires." He remembered again the abandoned houses by the side of the road, the pockmarked pavement.

"We unveil only the darkness that was already inside people," Rinn said. "And Jenny didn't tell you about how many child pornographers we've caught, how many planned murders we've stopped, or how many drug cartels and terrorists we've exposed. And all the dictators and strongmen we've toppled by filtering out their propaganda and magnifying the voices of those who oppose them."

"Don't make yourself sound so noble," Jenny said. "After you topple governments, you and the other Western companies get to move in and profit. You're just propagandists of a different ilk—for making the world flat, turning everywhere into copies of suburban America studded with malls."

"It's easy to be cynical like that," Rinn said. "But I'm proud of what we've done. If cultural imperialism is what it takes to make the world a better place, then we'll happily arrange the world's information to ennoble the human race."

"Why can't you just be in the business of neutrally offering up information? Why not go back to being a simple search engine? Why all the surveillance and filtering? Why all the manipulation?" Sai asked.

"There's no such thing as neutrally offering up information. If someone asks Tilly about the name of a candidate, should Tilly bring them to his official site or a site that criticizes him? If someone asks Tilly about 'Tiananmen,' should Tilly tell them about the hundreds of years of history behind the place or just tell them about June 4, 1989? The 'I Trust You' button is a heavy responsibility that we take very seriously.

"Centillion is in the business of organizing information, and that requires choices, direction, inherent subjectivity. What is important to you—what is true to you—is not as important or as true to others. It depends on judgment and ranking. To search for what matters to you, we must know all about you. And that, in turn, is indistinguishable from filtering, from manipulation."

"You make it sound so inevitable."

"It *is* inevitable. You think destroying Centillion will free you, whatever 'free' means. But let me ask you, can you tell me the requirements for starting a new business in the State of New York?"

Sai opened his mouth and realized that his instinct was to ask Tilly. He closed his mouth again.

"What's your mother's phone number?"

Sai resisted the urge to reach for his phone.

"How about you tell me what happened in the world yesterday? What book did you buy and enjoy three years ago? When did you start dating your last girlfriend?"

Sai said nothing.

"You see? Without Tilly, you can't do your job, you can't remember your life, you can't even call your mother. We are now a race of cyborgs. We long ago began to spread our minds into the electronic realm, and it is no longer possible to squeeze all of ourselves back into our brains. The electronic copies of yourselves that you wanted to destroy are, in a literal sense, actually you.

"Since it's impossible to live without these electronic extensions of ourselves, if you destroy Centillion, a replacement will just rise to take its place. It's too late; the genie has long left the bottle. Churchill said that we shape our buildings, and afterward our buildings shape us. We made machines to help us think, and now the machines think for us."

"So what do you want with us?" Jenny asked. "We won't stop fighting you."

"I want you to come and work for Centillion."

Sai and Jenny looked at each other. *"What?"*

"We want people who can see through Tilly's suggestions, detect her imperfections. For all that we've been able to do with AI and data mining, the Perfect Algorithm remains elusive. Because you can see her flaws, you'll be the best at figuring out what Tilly's still missing and where she's gone too far. It's the perfect match. You'll make her better, more compelling, so that Tilly will do a better job."

"Why would we do that?" Jenny asked. "Why would we want to help you run people's lives with a machine?"

"Because as bad as you think Centillion is, any replacement is likely worse. It was not a mere PR move that I made ennobling the human race the mission of this company, even if you don't agree with how I've gone about it.

"If we fail, who do you think will replace us? ShareAll? A Chinese company?"

Jenny looked away.

"And that is why we've gone to such extraordinary lengths to be sure that we have all the data we need to stop competitors as well as well-meaning, but naive, individuals like you from destroying all that Centillion has accomplished."

"What if we refuse to join you but tell the world what you've done?"

"No one would believe you. We will make it so that whatever you say, whatever you write, no one will ever find it. On the Net, if it can't be found by Centillion, it doesn't exist."

Sai knew that he was right.

"You thought Centillion was just an algorithm, a machine. But now you know that it's built by people—people like me, people like you. You've told me what I've done wrong. Wouldn't you rather be part of us so that you can try to make things better?

"In the face of the inevitable, the only choice is to adapt."

Sai closed the door of the apartment behind him. The camera overhead followed.

"Will Jenny be coming over tomorrow for dinner?" Tilly asked.

"Maybe."

"You really need to get her to start sharing. It will make planning much easier."

"I wouldn't count on it, Tilly."

"You're tired," Tilly said. "How about I order you some hot organic cider for delivery and then you go to bed?"

That does sound perfect.

"No," Sai said. "I think I prefer to just read for a while, in bed."

"Of course. Would you like me to suggest a book?"

"I'd rather you take the rest of the night off, actually. But first, set the wake-up song to Sinatra's 'My Way.'"

"An unusual choice, given your taste. Is this a one-time experiment or would you like me to incorporate it into your music recommendations for the future?"

"Just this once, for now. Good night, Tilly. Please turn yourself off."

The camera whirred, followed Sai to bed, and shut off.

But a red light continued to blink, slowly, in the darkness.

GOOD HUNTING

Night. Half-moon. An occasional hoot from an owl.

The merchant and his wife and all the servants had been sent away. The large house was eerily quiet.

Father and I crouched behind the scholar's rock in the courtyard. Through the rock's many holes I could see the bedroom window of the merchant's son.

"Oh, Hsiao-jung, my sweet Hsiao-jung . . ."

The young man's feverish groans were pitiful. Half-delirious, he was tied to his bed for his own good, but Father had left a window open so that his plaintive cries could be carried by the breeze far over the rice paddies.

"Do you think she really will come?" I whispered. Today was my thirteenth birthday, and this was my first hunt.

"She will," Father said. "A *hulijing* cannot resist the cries of the man she has bewitched."

"Like how the Butterfly Lovers cannot resist each other?" I thought back to the folk opera troupe that had come through our village last fall.

"Not quite," Father said. But he seemed to have trouble explaining why. "Just know that it's not the same."

I nodded, not sure I understood. But I remembered how the merchant and his wife had come to Father to ask for his help.

"How shameful!" the merchant had muttered. "He's not even nineteen. How could he have read so many sages' books and still fall under the spell of such a creature?"

"There's no shame in being entranced by the beauty and wiles of a hulijing," Father had said. *"Even the great scholar Wong Lai once spent three nights in the company of one, and he took first place at the Imperial Examinations. Your son just needs a little help."*

"You must save him," the merchant's wife had said, bowing like a chicken pecking at rice. *"If this gets out, the matchmakers won't touch him at all."*

A *hulijing* was a demon who stole hearts. I shuddered, worried if I would have the courage to face one.

Father put a warm hand on my shoulder, and I felt calmer. In his hand was Swallow Tail, a sword that had first been forged by our ancestor, General Lau Yip, thirteen generations ago. The sword was charged with hundreds of Daoist blessings and had drunk the blood of countless demons.

A passing cloud obscured the moon for a moment, throwing everything into darkness.

When the moon emerged again, I almost cried out.

There, in the courtyard, was the most beautiful lady I had ever seen.

She had on a flowing white silk dress with billowing sleeves and a wide, silvery belt. Her face was pale as snow, and her hair dark as coal, draping past her waist. I thought she looked like the paintings of great beauties from the Tang Dynasty the opera troupe had hung around their stage.

She turned slowly to survey everything around her, her eyes glistening in the moonlight like two shimmering pools.

I was surprised to see how sad she looked. Suddenly, I felt sorry for her and wanted more than anything else to make her smile.

The light touch of my father's hand against the back of my neck jolted me out of my mesmerized state. He had warned me about the power of the *hulijing*. My face hot and my heart hammering, I averted my eyes from the demon's face and focused on her stance.

The merchant's servants had been patrolling the courtyard every night this week with dogs to keep her away from her victim. But now the courtyard was empty. She stood still, hesitating, suspecting a trap.

"Hsiao-jung! Have you come for me?" The son's feverish voice grew louder.

The lady turned and walked—no, glided, so smooth were her movements—toward the bedroom door.

Father jumped out from behind the rock and rushed at her with Swallow Tail.

She dodged out of the way as though she had eyes on the back of her head. Unable to stop, my father thrust the sword into the thick wooden door with a dull thunk. He pulled but could not free the weapon immediately.

The lady glanced at him, turned, and headed for the courtyard gate.

"Don't just stand there, Liang!" Father called. "She's getting away!"

I ran at her, dragging my clay pot filled with dog piss. It was my job to splash her with it so that she could not transform into her fox form and escape.

She turned to me and smiled. "You're a very brave boy." A scent, like jasmine blooming in spring rain, surrounded me. Her voice was like sweet, cold lotus paste, and I wanted to hear her talk forever. The clay pot dangled from my hand, forgotten.

"Now!" Father shouted. He had pulled the sword free.

I bit my lip in frustration. *How can I become a demon hunter if I am so easily enticed?* I lifted off the cover and emptied the clay pot at her retreating figure, but the insane thought that I shouldn't dirty her white dress caused my hands to shake, and my aim was wide. Only a small amount of dog piss got onto her.

But it was enough. She howled, and the sound, like a dog's but so much wilder, caused the hairs on the back of my neck to stand up.

53

She turned and snarled, showing two rows of sharp, white teeth, and I stumbled back.

I had doused her while she was in the midst of her transformation. Her face was thus frozen halfway between a woman's and a fox's, with a hairless snout and raised, triangular ears that twitched angrily. Her hands had turned into paws, tipped with sharp claws that she swiped at me.

She could no longer speak, but her eyes conveyed her venomous thoughts without trouble.

Father rushed by me, his sword raised for a killing blow. The *huli-jing* turned around and slammed into the courtyard gate, smashing it open, and disappeared through the broken door.

Father chased after her without even a glance back at me. Ashamed, I followed.

The *hulijing* was swift of foot, and her silvery tail seemed to leave a glittering trail across the fields. But her incompletely transformed body maintained a human's posture, incapable of running as fast as she could have on four legs.

Father and I saw her dodging into the abandoned temple about a *li* outside the village.

"Go around the temple," Father said, trying to catch his breath. "I will go through the front door. If she tries to flee through the back door, you know what to do."

The back of the temple was overgrown with weeds and the wall half-collapsed. As I came around, I saw a white flash darting through the rubble.

Determined to redeem myself in my father's eyes, I swallowed my fear and ran after it without hesitation. After a few quick turns, I had the thing cornered in one of the monks' cells.

I was about to pour the remaining dog piss on it when I realized that the animal was much smaller than the *hulijing* we had been chasing. It was a small white fox, about the size of a puppy.

I set the clay pot on the ground and lunged.

The fox squirmed under me. It was surprisingly strong for such a small animal. I struggled to hold it down. As we fought, the fur between my fingers seemed to become as slippery as skin, and the body elongated, expanded, grew. I had to use my whole body to wrestle it to the ground.

Suddenly, I realized that my hands and arms were wrapped around the nude body of a young girl about my age.

I cried out and jumped back. The girl stood up slowly, picked up a silk robe from behind a pile of straw, put it on, and gazed at me haughtily.

A growl came from the main hall some distance away, followed by the sound of a heavy sword crashing into a table. Then another growl, and the sound of my father's curses.

The girl and I stared at each other. She was even prettier than the opera singer that I couldn't stop thinking about last year.

"Why are you after us?" she asked. "We did nothing to you."

"Your mother bewitched the merchant's son," I said. "We have to save him."

"*Bewitched? He*'s the one who wouldn't leave *her* alone."

I was taken aback. "What are you talking about?"

"One night about a month ago, the merchant's son stumbled upon my mother, caught in a chicken farmer's trap. She had to transform into her human form to escape, and as soon as he saw her, he became infatuated.

"She liked her freedom and didn't want anything to do with him. But once a man has set his heart on a *hulijing*, she cannot help hearing him no matter how far apart they are. All that moaning and crying he did drove her to distraction, and she had to go see him every night just to keep him quiet."

This was not what I learned from Father.

"She lures innocent scholars and draws on their life essence to feed her evil magic! Look how sick the merchant's son is!"

"He's sick because that useless doctor gave him poison that was supposed to make him forget about my mother. My mother is the one who's kept him alive with her nightly visits. And stop using the word *lure*. A man can fall in love with a *hulijing* just like he can with any human woman."

I didn't know what to say, so I said the first thing that came to mind. "I just know it's not the same."

She smirked. "Not the same? I saw how you looked at me before I put on my robe."

I blushed. "Brazen demon!" I picked up the clay pot. She remained where she was, a mocking smile on her face. Eventually, I put the pot back down.

The fight in the main hall grew noisier, and suddenly there was a loud crash, followed by a triumphant shout from Father and a long, piercing scream from the woman.

There was no smirk on the girl's face now, only rage turning slowly to shock. Her eyes had lost their lively luster; they looked dead.

Another grunt from Father. The scream ended abruptly.

"Liang! Liang! It's over. Where are you?"

Tears rolled down the girl's face.

"Search the temple," my father's voice continued. "She may have pups here. We have to kill them, too."

The girl tensed.

"Liang, have you found anything?" The voice was coming closer.

"Nothing," I said, locking eyes with her. "I didn't find anything."

She turned around and silently ran out of the cell. A moment later, I saw a small white fox jump over the broken back wall and disappear into the night.

• • •

It was *Qingming*, the Festival of the Dead. Father and I went to sweep Mother's grave and to bring her food and drink to comfort her in the afterlife.

"I'd like to stay here for a while," I said. Father nodded and left for home.

I whispered an apology to my mother, packed up the chicken we had brought for her, and walked the three *li* to the other side of the hill, to the abandoned temple.

I found Yan kneeling in the main hall, near the place where my father had killed her mother five years ago. She wore her hair up in a bun, in the style of a young woman who had had her *jijili*, the ceremony that meant she was no longer a girl.

We'd been meeting every *Qingming*, every *Chongyang*, every *Yulan*, every New Year's, occasions when families were supposed to be together.

"I brought you this," I said, and handed her the steamed chicken.

"Thank you." And she carefully tore off a leg and bit into it daintily. Yan had explained to me that the *hulijing* chose to live near human villages because they liked to have human things in their lives: conversation, beautiful clothes, poetry and stories, and, occasionally, the love of a worthy, kind man.

But the *hulijing* remained hunters who felt most free in their fox form. After what happened to her mother, Yan stayed away from chicken coops, but she still missed their taste.

"How's hunting?" I asked.

"Not so great," she said. "There are few Hundred-Year Salamanders and Six-Toed Rabbits. I can't ever seem to get enough to eat." She bit off another piece of chicken, chewed, and swallowed. "I'm having trouble transforming, too."

"It's hard for you to keep this shape?"

"No." She put the rest of the chicken on the ground and whispered a prayer to her mother.

"I mean it's getting harder for me to return to my true form," she continued, "to hunt. Some nights I can't do it at all. How's hunting for you?"

"Not so great either. There don't seem to be as many snake spirits or angry ghosts as a few years ago. Even hauntings by suicides with unfinished business are down. And we haven't had a proper jumping corpse in months. Father is worried about money."

We also hadn't had to deal with a *hulijing* in years. Maybe Yan had warned them all away. Truth be told, I was relieved. I didn't relish the prospect of having to tell my father that he was wrong about something. He was already very irritable, anxious that he was losing the respect of the villagers now that his knowledge and skill didn't seem to be needed as much.

"Ever think that maybe the jumping corpses are also misunderstood?" she asked. "Like me and my mother?"

She laughed as she saw my face. "Just kidding!"

It was strange, what Yan and I shared. She wasn't exactly a friend. More like someone who you couldn't help being drawn to because you shared the knowledge of how the world didn't work the way you had been told.

She looked at the chicken bits she had left for her mother. "I think magic is being drained out of this land."

I had suspected that something was wrong, but didn't want to voice my suspicion out loud, which would make it real.

"What do you think is causing it?"

Instead of answering, Yan perked up her ears and listened intently. Then she got up, grabbed my hand, and pulled until we were behind the buddha in the main hall.

"Wha—"

She held up her finger against my lips. So close to her, I finally noticed her scent. It was like her mother's, floral and sweet, but also bright, like blankets dried in the sun. I felt my face grow warm.

A moment later, I heard a group of men making their way into the temple. Slowly, I inched my head out from behind the buddha so I could see.

It was a hot day, and the men were seeking some shade from the noon sun. Two men set down a cane sedan chair, and the passenger who stepped off was a foreigner, with curly yellow hair and pale skin. Other men in the group carried tripods, levels, bronze tubes, and open trunks full of strange equipment.

"Most Honored Mister Thompson." A man dressed like a mandarin came up to the foreigner. The way he kept on bowing and smiling and bouncing his head up and down reminded me of a kicked dog begging for favors. "Please have a rest and drink some cold tea. It is hard for the men to be working on the day when they're supposed to visit the graves of their families, and they need to take a little time to pray lest they anger the gods and spirits. But I promise we'll work hard afterward and finish the survey on time."

"The trouble with you Chinese is your endless superstition," the foreigner said. He had a strange accent, but I could understand him just fine. "Remember, the Hong Kong–Tientsin Railroad is a priority for Great Britain. If I don't get as far as Botou Village by sunset, I'll be docking all your wages."

I had heard rumors that the Manchu Emperor had lost a war and been forced to give up all kinds of concessions, one of which involved paying to help the foreigners build a road of iron. But it had all seemed so fantastical that I didn't pay much attention.

The mandarin nodded enthusiastically. "Most Honored Mister Thompson is right in every way. But might I trouble your gracious ear with a suggestion?"

The weary Englishman waved impatiently.

"Some of the local villagers are worried about the proposed path of the railroad. You see, they think the tracks that have already been laid are blocking off veins of *qi* in the earth. It's bad *feng shui*."

"What are you talking about?"

"It is kind of like how a man breathes," the mandarin said, huffing a few times to make sure the Englishman understood. "The land has channels along rivers, hills, ancient roads that carry the energy of *qi*. It's what gives the villages prosperity and maintains the rare animals and local spirits and household gods. Could you consider shifting the line of the tracks a little, to follow the *feng shui* masters' suggestions?"

Thompson rolled his eyes. "That is the most ridiculous thing I've yet heard. You want me to deviate from the most efficient path for our railroad because you think your idols would be angry?"

The mandarin looked pained. "Well, in the places where the tracks have already been laid, many bad things are happening: people losing money, animals dying, household gods not responding to prayers. The Buddhist and Daoist monks all agree that it's the railroad."

Thompson strode over to the buddha and looked at it appraisingly. I ducked back behind the statue and squeezed Yan's hand. We held our breaths, hoping that we wouldn't be discovered.

"Does this one still have any power?" Thompson asked.

"The temple hasn't been able to maintain a contingent of monks for many years," the mandarin said. "But this buddha is still well respected. I hear villagers say that prayers to him are often answered."

Then I heard a loud crash and a collective gasp from the men in the main hall.

"I've just broken the hands off this god of yours with my cane," Thompson said. "As you can see, I have not been struck by lightning or suffered any other calamity. Indeed, now we know that it is only an idol made of mud stuffed with straw and covered in cheap paint.

This is why you people lost the war to Britain. You worship statues of mud when you should be thinking about building roads from iron and weapons from steel."

There was no more talk about changing the path of the railroad.

After the men were gone, Yan and I stepped out from behind the statue. We gazed at the broken hands of the buddha for a while.

"The world's changing," Yan said. "Hong Kong, iron roads, foreigners with wires that carry speech and machines that belch smoke. More and more, storytellers in the teahouses speak of these wonders. I think that's why the old magic is leaving. A more powerful kind of magic has come."

She kept her voice unemotional and cool, like a placid pool of water in autumn, but her words rang true. I thought about my father's attempts to keep up a cheerful mien as fewer and fewer customers came to us. I wondered if the time I spent learning the chants and the sword dance moves was wasted.

"What will you do?" I asked, thinking about her, alone in the hills and unable to find the food that sustained her magic.

"There's only one thing I *can* do." Her voice broke for a second and became defiant, like a pebble tossed into the pool.

But then she looked at me, and her composure returned. "There's only one thing *we* can do: learn to survive."

The railroad soon became a familiar part of the landscape: the black locomotive huffing through the green rice paddies, puffing steam and pulling a long train behind it, like a dragon coming down from the distant hazy, blue mountains. For a while it was a wondrous sight, with children marveling at it, running alongside the tracks to keep up.

But the soot from the locomotive chimneys killed the rice in the fields closest to the tracks, and two children playing on the tracks, too frightened to move, were killed one afternoon. After that, the train ceased to fascinate.

People stopped coming to Father and me to ask for our services. They either went to the Christian missionary or the new teacher who said he'd studied in San Francisco. Young men in the village began to leave for Hong Kong or Canton, moved by rumors of bright lights and well-paying work. Fields lay fallow. The village itself seemed to consist only of the too-old and too-young, their mood one of resignation. Men from distant provinces came to inquire about buying land for cheap.

Father spent his days sitting in the front room, Swallow Tail over his knee, staring out the door from dawn to dusk, as though he himself had turned into a statue.

Every day, as I returned home from the fields, I would see the glint of hope in Father's eyes briefly flare up.

"Did anyone speak of needing our help?" he would ask.

"No," I would say, trying to keep my tone light. "But I'm sure there will be a jumping corpse soon. It's been too long."

I would not look at my father as I spoke because I did not want to look as hope faded from his eyes.

Then, one day, I found Father hanging from the heavy beam in his bedroom. As I let his body down, my heart numb, I thought that he was not unlike those he had hunted all his life: They were all sustained by an old magic that had left and would not return, and they did not know how to survive without it.

Swallow Tail felt dull and heavy in my hand. I had always thought I would be a demon hunter, but how could I when there were no more demons, no more spirits? All the Daoist blessings in the sword could not save my father's sinking heart. And if I stuck around, perhaps my heart would grow heavy and yearn to be still too.

I hadn't seen Yan since that day six years ago, when we hid from the railroad surveyors at the temple. But her words came back to me now.

Learn to survive.

I packed a bag and bought a train ticket to Hong Kong.

•   •   •

The Sikh guard checked my papers and waved me through the security gate.

I paused to let my gaze follow the tracks going up the steep side of the mountain. It seemed less like a railroad track than a ladder straight up to heaven. This was the funicular railway, the tram line to the top of Victoria Peak, where the masters of Hong Kong lived and the Chinese were forbidden to stay.

But the Chinese were good enough to shovel coal into the boilers and grease the gears.

Steam rose around me as I ducked into the engine room. After five years, I knew the rhythmic rumbling of the pistons and the staccato grinding of the gears as well as I knew my own breath and heartbeat. There was a kind of music to their orderly cacophony that moved me, like the clashing of cymbals and gongs at the start of a folk opera. I checked the pressure, applied sealant on the gaskets, tightened the flanges, replaced the worn-down gears in the backup cable assembly. I lost myself in the work, which was hard and satisfying.

By the end of my shift, it was dark. I stepped outside the engine room and saw a full moon in the sky as another tram filled with passengers was pulled up the side of the mountain, powered by my engine.

"Don't let the Chinese ghosts get you," a woman with bright blonde hair said in the tram, and her companions laughed.

It was the night of *Yulan*, I realized, the Ghost Festival. *I should get something for my father, maybe pick up some paper money at Mongkok.*

"How can you be done for the day when we still want you?" a man's voice came to me.

"Girls like you shouldn't tease," another man said, and laughed.

I looked in the direction of the voices and saw a Chinese woman standing in the shadows just outside the tram station. Her tight western-style cheongsam and the garish makeup told me her profession. Two

Englishmen blocked her path. One tried to put his arms around her, and she backed out of the way.

"Please. I'm very tired," she said in English. "Maybe next time."

"Now, don't be stupid," the first man said, his voice hardening. "This isn't a discussion. Come along now and do what you're supposed to."

I walked up to them. "Hey."

The men turned around and looked at me.

"What seems to be the problem?"

"None of your business."

"Well, I think it *is* my business," I said, "seeing as how you're talking to my sister."

I doubt either of them believed me. But five years of wrangling heavy machinery had given me a muscular frame, and they took a look at my face and hands, grimy with engine grease, and probably decided that it wasn't worth it to get into a public tussle with a lowly Chinese engineer.

The two men stepped away to get in line for the Peak Tram, muttering curses.

"Thank you," she said.

"It's been a long time," I said, looking at her. I swallowed the *you look good*. She didn't. She looked tired and thin and brittle. And the pungent perfume she wore assaulted my nose.

But I did not think of her harshly. Judging was the luxury of those who did not need to survive.

"It's the night of the Ghost Festival," she said. "I didn't want to work anymore. I wanted to think about my mother."

"Why don't we go get some offerings together?" I asked.

We took the ferry over to Kowloon, and the breeze over the water revived her a bit. She wet a towel with the hot water from the teapot on the ferry and wiped off her makeup. I caught a faint trace of her natural scent, fresh and lovely as always.

"You look good," I said, and meant it.

On the streets of Kowloon, we bought pastries and fruits and cold dumplings and a steamed chicken and incense and paper money, and caught up on each other's lives.

"How's hunting?" I asked. We both laughed.

"I miss being a fox," she said. She nibbled on a chicken wing absent-mindedly. "One day, shortly after that last time we talked, I felt the last bit of magic leave me. I could no longer transform."

"I'm sorry," I said, unable to offer anything else.

"My mother taught me to like human things: food, clothes, folk opera, old stories. But she was never dependent on them. When she wanted, she could always turn into her true form and hunt. But now, in this form, what can I do? I don't have claws. I don't have sharp teeth. I can't even run very fast. All I have is my beauty, the same thing that your father and you killed my mother for. So now I live by the very thing that you once falsely accused my mother of doing: I *lure* men for money."

"My father is dead too."

Hearing this seemed to drain some of the bitterness out of her. "What happened?"

"He felt the magic leave us, much as you. He couldn't bear it."

"I'm sorry." And I knew that she didn't know what else to say either.

"You told me once that the only thing we can do is to survive. I have to thank you for that. It probably saved my life."

"Then we're even," she said, smiling. "But let us not speak of ourselves anymore. Tonight is reserved for the ghosts."

We went down to the harbor and placed our food next to the water, inviting all the ghosts we had loved to come and dine. Then we lit the incense and burned the paper money in a bucket.

She watched bits of burned paper being carried into the sky by the heat from the flames. They disappeared among the stars. "Do you think the gates to the underworld still open for the ghosts tonight, now that there is no magic left?"

I hesitated. When I was young I had been trained to hear the scratching of a ghost's fingers against a paper window, to distinguish the voice of a spirit from the wind. But now I was used to enduring the thunderous pounding of pistons and the deafening hiss of high-pressured steam rushing through valves. I could no longer claim to be attuned to that vanished world of my childhood.

"I don't know," I said. "I suppose it's the same with ghosts as with people. Some will figure out how to survive in a world diminished by iron roads and steam whistles, some will not."

"But will any of them thrive?" she asked.

She could still surprise me.

"I mean," she continued, "are you happy? Are you happy to keep an engine running all day, yourself like another cog? What do you dream of?"

I couldn't remember any dreams. I had let myself become entranced by the movement of gears and levers, to let my mind grow to fit the gaps between the ceaseless clanging of metal on metal. It was a way to not have to think about my father, about a land that had lost so much.

"I dream of hunting in this jungle of metal and asphalt," she said. "I dream of my true form leaping from beam to ledge to terrace to roof, until I am at the top of this island, until I can growl in the faces of all the men who believe they can own me."

As I watched, her eyes, brightly lit for a moment, dimmed.

"In this new age of steam and electricity, in this great metropolis, except for those who live on the Peak, is anyone still in their true form?" she asked.

We sat together by the harbor and burned paper money all night, waiting for a sign that the ghosts were still with us.

• • •

Life in Hong Kong could be a strange experience: From day to day, things never seemed to change much. But if you compared things over a few years, it was almost like you lived in a different world.

By my thirtieth birthday, new designs for steam engines required less coal and delivered more power. They grew smaller and smaller. The streets filled with automatic rickshaws and horseless carriages, and most people who could afford them had machines that kept the air cool in houses and the food cold in boxes in the kitchen—all powered by steam.

I went into stores and endured the ire of the clerks as I studied the components of new display models. I devoured every book on the principle and operation of the steam engine I could find. I tried to apply those principles to improve the machines I was in charge of: trying out new firing cycles, testing new kinds of lubricants for the pistons, adjusting the gear ratios. I found a measure of satisfaction in the way I came to understand the magic of the machines.

One morning, as I repaired a broken governor—a delicate bit of work—two pairs of polished shoes stopped on the platform above me.

I looked up. Two men looked down at me.

"This is the one," said my shift supervisor.

The other man, dressed in a crisp suit, looked skeptical. "Are you the man who came up with the idea of using a larger flywheel for the old engine?"

I nodded. I took pride in the way I could squeeze more power out of my machines than dreamed of by their designers.

"You did not steal the idea from an Englishman?" His tone was severe.

I blinked. A moment of confusion was followed by a rush of anger. "No," I said, trying to keep my voice calm. I ducked back under the machine to continue my work.

"He is clever," my shift supervisor said, "for a Chinaman. He can be taught."

"I suppose we might as well try," said the other man. "It will certainly be cheaper than hiring a real engineer from England."

Mr. Alexander Findlay Smith, owner of the Peak Tram and an avid engineer himself, had seen an opportunity. He foresaw that the path of technological progress would lead inevitably to the use of steam power to operate automata: mechanical arms and legs that would eventually replace the Chinese coolies and servants.

I was selected to serve Mr. Findlay Smith in his new venture.

I learned to repair clockwork, to design intricate systems of gears and devise ingenious uses for levers. I studied how to plate metal with chrome and how to shape brass into smooth curves. I invented ways to connect the world of hardened and ruggedized clockwork to the world of miniaturized and regulated piston and clean steam. Once the automata were finished, we connected them to the latest analytic engines shipped from Britain and fed them with tape punched with dense holes in Babbage-Lovelace code.

It had taken a decade of hard work. But now mechanical arms served drinks in the bars along Central and machine hands fashioned shoes and clothes in factories in the New Territories. In the mansions up on the Peak, I heard—though I'd never seen—that automatic sweepers and mops I designed roamed the halls discreetly, bumping into walls gently as they cleaned the floors like mechanical elves puffing out bits of white steam. The expats could finally live their lives in this tropical paradise free of reminders of the presence of the Chinese.

I was thirty-five when she showed up at my door again, like a memory from long ago.

I pulled her into my tiny flat, looked around to be sure no one was following her, and closed the door.

"How's hunting?" I asked. It was a bad attempt at a joke, and she laughed weakly.

Photographs of her had been in all the papers. It was the biggest scandal in the colony: not so much because the Governor's son was keeping a Chinese mistress—it was expected that he would—but because the mistress had managed to steal a large sum of money from him and then disappear. Everyone tittered while the police turned the city upside down, looking for her.

"I can hide you for tonight," I said. Then I waited, the unspoken second half of my sentence hanging between us.

She sat down in the only chair in the room, the dim lightbulb casting dark shadows on her face. She looked gaunt and exhausted. "Ah, now you're judging me."

"I have a good job I want to keep," I said. "Mr. Findlay Smith trusts me."

She bent down and began to pull up her dress.

"Don't," I said, and turned my face away. I could not bear to watch her try to ply her trade with me.

"Look," she said. There was no seduction in her voice. "Liang, look at me."

I turned and gasped.

Her legs, what I could see of them, were made of shiny chrome. I bent down to look closer: the cylindrical joints at the knees were lathed with precision, the pneumatic actuators along the thighs moved in complete silence, the feet were exquisitely molded and shaped, the surfaces smooth and flowing. These were the most beautiful mechanical legs I had ever seen.

"He had me drugged," she said. "When I woke up, my legs were gone and replaced by these. The pain was excruciating. He explained to me that he had a secret: he liked machines more than flesh, couldn't get hard with a regular woman."

I had heard of such men. In a city filled with chrome and brass and clanging and hissing, desires became confused.

I focused on the way light moved along the gleaming curves of her calves so that I didn't have to look into her face.

"I had a choice: let him keep on changing me to suit him, or he could remove the legs and throw me out on the street. Who would believe a legless Chinese whore? I wanted to survive. So I swallowed the pain and let him continue."

She stood up and removed the rest of her dress and her evening gloves. I took in her chrome torso, slatted around the waist to allow articulation and movement; her sinuous arms, constructed from curved plates sliding over each other like obscene armor; her hands, shaped from delicate metal mesh, with dark steel fingers tipped with jewels where the fingernails would be.

"He spared no expense. Every piece of me is built with the best craftsmanship and attached to my body by the best surgeons—there are many who want to experiment, despite the law, with how the body could be animated by electricity, nerves replaced by wires. They always spoke only to him, as if I was already only a machine.

"Then, one night, he hurt me and I struck back in desperation. He fell like he was made of straw. I realized, suddenly, how much strength I had in my metal arms. I had let him do all this to me, to replace me part by part, mourning my loss all the while without understanding what I had gained. A terrible thing had been done to me, but I could also be *terrible*.

"I choked him until he fainted, and then I took all the money I could find and left.

"So I come to you, Liang. Will you help me?"

I stepped up and embraced her. "We'll find some way to reverse this. There must be doctors—"

"No," she interrupted me. "That's not what I want."

．　．　．

It took us almost a whole year to complete the task. Yan's money helped, but some things money couldn't buy, especially skill and knowledge.

My flat became a workshop. We spent every evening and all of Sundays working: shaping metal, polishing gears, reattaching wires.

Her face was the hardest. It was still flesh.

I pored over books of anatomy and took casts of her face with plaster of Paris. I broke my cheekbones and cut my face so that I could stagger into surgeons' offices and learn from them how to repair these injuries. I bought expensive jeweled masks and took them apart, learning the delicate art of shaping metal to take on the shape of a face.

Finally, it was time.

Through the window, the moon threw a pale white parallelogram on the floor. Yan stood in the middle of it, moving her head about, trying out her new face.

Hundreds of miniature pneumatic actuators were hidden under the smooth chrome skin, each of which could be controlled independently, allowing her to adopt any expression. But her eyes were still the same, and they shone in the moonlight with excitement.

"Are you ready?" I asked.

She nodded.

I handed her a bowl filled with the purest anthracite coal, ground into a fine powder. It smelled of burned wood, of the heart of the earth. She poured it into her mouth and swallowed. I could hear the fire in the miniature boiler in her torso grow hotter as the pressure of the steam built up. I took a step back.

She lifted her head to the moon and howled: it was a howl made by steam passing through brass piping, and yet it reminded me of that wild howl long ago, when I first heard the call of a *hulijing*.

Then she crouched to the floor. Gears grinding, pistons pumping, curved metal plates sliding over each other—the noises grew louder as she began to transform.

She had drawn the first glimmers of her idea with ink on paper. Then she had refined it, through hundreds of iterations until she was satisfied. I could see traces of her mother in it, but also something harder, something new.

Working from her idea, I had designed the delicate folds in the chrome skin and the intricate joints in the metal skeleton. I had put together every hinge, assembled every gear, soldered every wire, welded every seam, oiled every actuator. I had taken her apart and put her back together.

Yet, it was a marvel to see everything working. In front of my eyes, she folded and unfolded like a silvery origami construction, until finally, a chrome fox as beautiful and deadly as the oldest legends stood before me.

She padded around the flat, testing out her sleek new form, trying out her stealthy new movements. Her limbs gleamed in the moonlight, and her tail, made of delicate silver wires as fine as lace, left a trail of light in the dim flat.

She turned and walked—no, glided—toward me, a glorious hunter, an ancient vision coming alive. I took a deep breath and smelled fire and smoke, engine oil and polished metal, the scent of power.

"Thank you," she said, and leaned in as I put my arms around her true form. The steam engine inside her had warmed her cold metal body, and it felt warm and alive.

"Can you feel it?" she asked.

I shivered. I knew what she meant. The old magic was back but changed: not fur and flesh, but metal and fire.

"I will find others like me," she said, "and bring them to you. Together, we will set them free."

Once, I was a demon hunter. Now, I am one of them.

I opened the door, Swallow Tail in my hand. It was only an old and heavy sword, rusty, but still perfectly capable of striking down anyone who might be lying in wait.

No one was.

Yan leapt out of the door like a bolt of lightning. Stealthily, gracefully, she darted into the streets of Hong Kong, free, feral, a *hulijing* built for this new age.

. . . once a man has set his heart on a hulijing, *she cannot help hearing him no matter how far apart they are. . . .*

"Good hunting," I whispered.

She howled in the distance, and I watched a puff of steam rise into the air as she disappeared.

I imagined her running along the tracks of the funicular railway, a tireless engine racing up, and up, toward the top of Victoria Peak, toward a future as full of magic as the past.

THE LITEROMANCER

September 18, 1961

Lilly Dyer anticipated and also dreaded three o'clock in the afternoon, more than any other moment of the day. That was when she returned home from school and checked the kitchen table for new mail.

The table was empty. But Lilly thought she'd ask, anyway. "Anything for me?"

"No," Mom said from the living room. She was giving English lessons to Mr. Cotton's new Chinese bride. Mr. Cotton worked with Dad and was important.

A full month had passed since Lilly's family moved to Taiwan, and no one from Clearwell, Texas, where she had been the third-most-popular girl in the fourth grade, had written to her, even though all the girls had promised that they would.

Lilly did not like her new school at the American military base. All of the other children's fathers were in the armed forces, but Dad worked in the city, in a building with the picture of Sun Yat-sen in the lobby and the red, white, and blue flag of the Republic of China flying on top. That meant Lilly was strange, and the other kids did not want to sit with her at lunch. Earlier that morning, Mrs. Wyle finally lectured them about their treatment of Lilly. That made things worse.

Lilly sat at her own table, quietly eating by herself. The other girls chattered at the next table.

"The Chinese whores are crafty, always hanging around the Base,"

Suzie Randling said. Suzie was the prettiest girl in the class, and she always had the best gossip. "I heard Jennie's mom telling my mom that as soon as one gets her hands on an American soldier, she'll use her nasty tricks to hook him. She wants him to marry her so that she can steal all his money, and if he won't marry her, she'll make him sick."

The girls broke out in laughter. "When an American man rents a house for his family outside the Base, you can imagine what the husband is really chasing after," Jennie added darkly, trying to impress Suzie. The girls giggled, throwing looks over at Lilly. Lilly pretended not to hear.

"They are unbelievably dirty," Suzie said. "Mrs. Taylor was saying how when she took a car trip to Tainan during the summer, she couldn't eat any of the dishes the Chinese were serving her. One time they tried to give her some fried frog legs. She thought it was chicken and almost ate them. Disgusting!"

"My mom said that it's a real shame that you can't get any decent Chinese food except back in America," Jennie added.

"That's not true," Lilly said. As soon as she spoke up she regretted it. Lilly had brought *kòng-uân* pork balls and rice for lunch. Lin Amah, their Chinese maid, had packed the leftovers from dinner the night before. The pork balls were delicious, but the other girls wrinkled their noses at the smell.

"Lilly is eating smelly Chinaman slops again," Suzie said menacingly. "She really seems to like it."

"Lilly, Lilly, she's gonna have a stinky gook baby," the other girls began to chant.

Lilly had tried to not cry; she had almost succeeded.

Mom came into the kitchen and lightly stroked Lilly's hair. "How was school?"

Lilly knew that her parents must never know about what happened at school. They would try to help. That would only make things worse.

"Good," she said. "I'm just getting to know the girls." Mom nodded and went back into the living room.

She didn't want to go to her room. There was nothing to do there after she had finished all the Nancy Drew books that she brought with her. She also didn't want to stay in the kitchen, where Lin Amah was cooking and would try to talk to her in her broken English. Lilly was mad at Lin Amah and her *kòng-uân* pork balls. She knew it was unfair, but she couldn't help herself. She wanted to get out of the house.

Rain earlier in the day had cooled off the humid subtropical air, and Lilly enjoyed a light breeze as she walked. She shook her red, curly hair out of the ponytail she wore for school, and she felt comfortable in a light blue tank top and a pair of tan shorts. West of the small Chinese-style farmhouse the Dyers were renting, the rice paddies of the village stretched out in neat grids. A few water buffalo lazed about in muddy wallows, gently scratching the rough, dark hide on their backs with their long, curved horns. Unlike the longhorns that she had been familiar with back home in Texas, whose long, thin horns curved dangerously forward, like a pair of swords, the water buffalos' horns curved backward, perfect for back scratching.

The largest and oldest one had his eyes closed and was half submerged in the water.

Lilly held her breath. She wanted to take a ride on him.

Back when she was a little girl and before Dad got his new job that was so secret that he couldn't even tell her what he did, Lilly had wanted to be a cowgirl. She envied her friends, whose parents were not from back East and thus knew how to ride, drive, and ranch. She was a regular at the county rodeos, and when she was five, by telling the man at the sign-up table that she had her mom's permission, she entered the mutton-busting competition.

She had held on to the bucking sheep for a full thrilling and terrifying twenty-eight seconds, a record that stunned the whole county. Her picture, showing her in a wide-brimmed cowboy hat with her tight ponytail flapping behind her, had been in all the newspapers. There was no fear on the face of the little girl in the picture, only wild glee and stubbornness.

"You were too stupid to be afraid," Mom had said. "What in the world made you do a thing like that? You could have broken your neck."

Lilly did not answer her. She dreamed about that ride for months afterward. *Just hold on for another second,* she had told herself on the back of the sheep, *just hold on.* For those twenty-eight seconds, she wasn't just a little girl, whose day was filled with copybooks and chores and being told what to do. There was a clear purpose to her life and a clear way to accomplish it.

If she were older, she would have described that feeling as *freedom.*

Now, if she could ride the old water buffalo, maybe she'll get that feeling back and her day would be all right after all.

Lilly began to run toward the shallow wallow, where the old water buffalo was still obliviously chewing cud. Lilly got to the edge of the wallow and leapt toward the buffalo's back.

Lilly landed on the back of the buffalo with a soft thud, and the buffalo sank momentarily. She was prepared for bucking and lunging, and she kept her eyes on the long, curved horns, ready to grab them if the buffalo used them to try to pry her off. Adrenaline pumped through her, and she was determined to hold on for dear life.

Instead, the old buffalo, disturbed from his nap, simply opened his eyes and snorted. He turned his head and stared accusingly at Lilly with his left eye. He shook his head in disapproval, got up, and began to amble out of the wallow. The ride on the back of the buffalo was smooth and steady, like the way Dad used to carry Lilly on his shoulders when she was little.

Lilly grinned sheepishly. She patted the back of the buffalo's neck in apology.

She sat lightly, leaving the buffalo to choose his own path and watching the rows of rice stalks pass by her. The buffalo came to the end of the fields, where there was a clump of trees, and turned behind them. Here the ground dipped toward the bank of a river, and the buffalo walked toward it, where several Chinese boys about Lilly's age were playing and washing their families' water buffalo. As Lilly and the old buffalo approached them, the laughter among the boys died down, and one by one they turned to look at her.

Lilly became nervous. She nodded at the boys and waved. They didn't wave back. Lilly knew, in the way that all children know, that she was in trouble.

Suddenly something wet and heavy landed against Lilly's face. One of the boys had thrown a fistful of river mud at her.

"*Adoah, adoah, adoah!*" the boys shouted. And more mud flew at Lilly. Mud hit her face, her arms, her neck, her chest. She didn't understand what they were shouting, but the hostility and glee in their voices needed no translation. The mud stung her eyes, and she couldn't stop the tears that followed. She covered her face with her arms, determined not to give the boys the satisfaction of hearing her cry out.

"Ow!" Lilly couldn't help herself. A rock hit her shoulder, followed by another against her thigh. She tumbled down from the back of the buffalo and tried to hide behind him by crouching down, but the boys only chanted louder and circled around the buffalo to continue tormenting her. She began to grab fistfuls of mud from around her and threw them back at the boys, blindly, angrily, desperately.

"*Kâu-gín-á, khòai-cháu, khòai-cháu!*" An old man's voice, full of authority, came to her. The rain of mud stopped. Lilly wiped the mud from her face with her sleeves and looked up. The boys were running away. The old man's voice yelled at them some more, and the boys picked up their speed, their water buffalo following them at a more leisurely pace.

Lilly stood up and looked around her old buffalo. An elderly Chinese man stood a few paces away, smiling kindly at her. Beside him stood another boy about Lilly's age. As Lilly watched, the boy threw a pebble after the rapidly diminishing figures of the fleeing boys. His throw was strong, and the pebble arched high into the air, landing just behind the last boy as he rounded a copse of trees and disappeared. The boy grinned at Lilly, revealing two rows of crooked teeth.

"Little miss," the old man said in accented but clear English. "Are you all right?"

Lilly stared at her rescuers, speechless.

"What were you doing with Ah Huang?" the boy asked. The old water buffalo gently walked over to him, and the boy reached up to pat him on the nose.

"I . . . uh . . . I was riding him." Lilly's throat felt dry. She swallowed. "I'm sorry."

"They are not bad kids," the old man said, "just a little rowdy and suspicious of strangers. As their teacher, it is my fault that I did not teach them better manners. Please accept my apology for them." He bowed to Lilly.

Lilly awkwardly bowed back. As she bent down, she saw that her shirt and pants were covered with mud, and she felt the throbbing in her shoulder and legs, where she had been hit with rocks. She was going to get an earful from Mom; that was for sure. She could just imagine what a sight she must have made, covered in mud from hair to toe.

Lilly had never felt so alone.

"Let me help you clean up a little," the old man offered. They walked to the bank of the river, and the old man used a handkerchief to wipe the mud from Lilly's face and rinsed it out in the clear river water. His touch was gentle.

"I'm Kan Chen-hua, and this is my grandson, Ch'en Chia-feng."

"You can call me Teddy," the boy added. The old man chuckled.

"It's nice to meet you," Lilly said. "I'm Lillian Dyer."

"So what do you teach?"

"Calligraphy. I teach the children how to write Chinese characters with a brush so that they don't frighten everyone, including their ancestors and wandering spirits, with their horrible chicken scratch."

Lilly laughed. Mr. Kan was not like any Chinese she had ever met. But her laugh did not last long. School was never far from her mind, and she knitted her brows as she thought about tomorrow.

Mr. Kan pretended not to notice. "But I also do some magic."

This piqued Lilly's interest. "What kind of magic?"

"I'm a literomancer."

"A *what?*"

"Grandpa tells people's fortunes based on the characters in their names and the characters they pick," Teddy explained.

Lilly felt as though she had walked into a wall of fog. She looked at Mr. Kan, not understanding.

"The Chinese invented writing as an aid to divination, so Chinese characters always had a deep magic to them. From characters, I can tell what's bothering people and what lies in their past and future. Here, I'll show you. Think of a word, any word."

Lilly looked around her. They were sitting on some rocks by the side of the river, and she could see that the leaves on the trees were starting to turn gold and red, and the rice stalks were heavy with grain, soon to be ready for the harvest.

"Autumn," she said.

Mr. Kan took a stick and wrote a character in the soft mud near their feet.

"You'll have to excuse the ugliness of writing with a stick in mud, but I don't have paper and brush with me. This is the character *ch'iu*, which means 'autumn' in Chinese."

"How do you tell my fortune from that?"

"Well, I have to take the character apart and put it back together. Chinese characters are put together from more Chinese characters, like building blocks. *Ch'iu* is composed of two other characters. The one on the left is the character *he*, which means 'millet' or 'rice' or any grain plant. Now, what you see there is stylized, but in ancient times, the character used to be written this way."

He drew on the mud.

"See how it looks like the drawing of a stalk bent over with the weight of a ripe head of grain on top?"

Lilly nodded, fascinated.

"Now, the right side of *ch'iu* is another character, *huo*, which means 'fire.' See how it looks like a burning flame, with sparks flying up?"

"In the northern part of China, where I'm from, we don't have rice. Instead, we grow millet, wheat, and sorghum. In autumn, after we've harvested and threshed out the grain, we pile the stalks in the fields and burn them so that the ashes will fertilize the fields for the coming year. Golden stalks and red flame, you put them together and you get *ch'iu*, autumn."

Lilly nodded, imagining the sight.

"But what does it tell me that you picked *ch'iu* as your character?" Mr. Kan paused in thought. He drew a few more strokes beneath *ch'iu*.

"Now, I've written the character for 'heart,' *hsin*, under *ch'iu*. It's a drawing of the shape of your heart. Together, they make a new character, *ch'ou*, and it means 'worry' and 'sorrow.'"

Lilly felt her heart squeeze, and suddenly everything looked blurry through her eyes. She held her breath.

"There's a lot of sorrow in your heart, Lilly, a lot of worry. Something is making you very, very sad."

Lilly looked up at his kind and wrinkled face, the neat white hair, and she walked over to him. Mr. Kan opened his arms and Lilly buried her face in his shoulders as he hugged her, lightly, gently.

As she cried, Lilly told Mr. Kan about her day at school, about the other girls and their chant, about the kitchen table empty of mail from friends.

"I'll teach you how to fight," Teddy said when Lilly had finished her story. "If you punch them hard enough, they won't bother you again."

Lilly shook her head. Boys were simple, and fists could do the talking for them. The magic of words between girls was much more complicated.

• • •

"There's a lot of magic in the word *gook*," Mr. Kan said after Lilly had wiped her tears and calmed down a little. Lilly looked up at him in surprise. She knew that the word was ugly and was afraid that he would be angry at hearing her say it, but Mr. Kan was not angry at all.

"Some people think that the word has a dark magic that can be used to slice into the hearts of the people of Asia and hurt them and those who would befriend them," Mr. Kan said. "But they do not understand its true magic. Do you know where the word comes from?"

"No."

"When American soldiers first went to Korea, they often heard the Korean soldiers say *miguk*. They thought the Koreans were saying 'me, gook.' But really they were talking about the Americans, and *miguk* means 'America.' The Korean word *guk* means 'country.' So when the American soldiers began calling the people of Asia 'gooks,' they didn't understand that they were in a way really just speaking about themselves."

"Oh," Lilly said. She wasn't sure how this information helped.

"I'll show you a bit of magic that you can use to protect yourself." Mr. Kan turned to Teddy. "Can I have that mirror that you use to tease the cats with?"

Teddy took out a small bit of glass from his pocket. It was broken from a larger mirror and the jagged edges had been wrapped in masking tape. Some Chinese characters had been written in ink on the masking tape.

"The Chinese have been using mirrors to ward off harm for millennia," Mr. Kan said. "Don't underestimate this little mirror. It has great magic in it. Next time, when the other girls tease you, bring out this mirror and shine it in their faces."

Lilly took the mirror. She didn't really believe what Mr. Kan was saying. He was kind and nice, but what he was saying sounded preposterous. Still, she needed a friend, and Mr. Kan and Teddy were the closest thing to friends she had on this side of the Pacific Ocean.

"Thank you," she said.

"Miss Lilly." Mr. Kan stood up and solemnly shook her hand. "When there is such a large gap of years between two friends, we Chinese call it *wang nien chih chiao*, a friendship that forgets the years. It's destiny that brings us together. I hope you will always think of me and Teddy as your friends."

Lilly explained her muddy appearance by blaming it all on Ah Huang, the "stubborn water buffalo" that she eventually subdued with her Texan cowgirl skills. Of course Mom was angry, seeing Lilly's ruined clothes. She gave Lilly a long lecture, and even Dad sighed and explained that her days of being a tomboy really needed to come to an end, now that she was a young lady. But on the whole, Lilly thought she had gotten off easy.

Lin Amah made Three-Cup Chicken, which was Dad's favorite. The sweet smell of sesame oil, rice wine, and soy sauce filled the kitchen and living room, and Lin Amah smiled and nodded as Mr. and Mrs. Dyer praised the food. She wrapped the leftovers into two rice balls and put them in the lunch box for Lilly. Lilly was apprehensive about bringing Three-Cup Chicken to lunch, but she fingered the mirror in her pocket and thanked Lin Amah.

"Good night," Lilly said to her parents, and went to her room.

In the hallway Lilly found a couple of sheets of paper lying on the floor. She picked them up and saw that they were filled with dense typescript:

> have successfully sabotaged numerous factories, railroads, bridges, and other infrastructure. Agents have also assassinated several local ChiCom cadres. We have captured dozens of ChiCom individuals on these raids, and their interrogation yielded valuable intelligence

concerning Red China's internal conditions. The covert program has been conducted with plausible deniability, and so far no elements of the US press have questioned our denials of ChiCom accusations of American involvement. (It should be noted that even if US involvement is revealed, we can legally justify our intervention under the Sino-American Mutual Defense Treaty as the ROC's sovereignty claims extend over all the territory of the PRC.)

Interrogations of ChiCom prisoners suggest that this program of harassment and terror, combined with the threat of an ROC invasion of the mainland, has pushed the ChiCom to further intensify internal repression and tighten domestic control. The ChiCom have increased military spending, and this likely has shifted scarce resources away from economic development and increased the suffering of the masses at a time when the PRC is experiencing great famines after the Great Leap Forward. As a result, there is a great deal of dissatisfaction with the regime.

President Kennedy has reoriented us toward a more confrontational stance with the ChiCom. I suggest that we weaken the PRC by all means short of all-out, general war. In addition to our continued support of ROC interdiction and harassment of PRC shipping and our support and direction of the insurgency in Tibet, we should increase our joint covert operations with the ROC in the PRC. I believe that by intensifying our covert operations against the ChiCom, we can force the ChiCom to curtail its support for North Viet Nam. In the best case, we may even provide the proverbial straw to break the camel's back, and successfully induce a domestic popular revolt to support a ChiNat invasion force from Taiwan and Burma. The Generalissimo is quite eager.

Should the PRC be provoked into a general war with us, it will be necessary to use atomic weapons to ensure the credibility of American resolve to our allies. The President should be prepared to manage popular perception in America and to induce our allies to accept atomic warfare as the means to victory.

At the same time, there is no question that the ChiCom would step up their efforts to infiltrate Taiwan and establish a network of agents and sympathizers within Taiwan. ChiCom propaganda and psywar techniques are not as sophisticated as ours, but appear to have been effective (at least in the past), especially among the native Taiwanese, by exploiting conflicts between the native-born penshengjen and the Nationalist waishengjen.

The maintenance of ChiNat morale is vital to our hold on Taiwan, the most vital link in the chain of islands that form the bulwark of American thalassocracy in the Western Pacific and the perimeter defense of the Free World. We must assist the ROC in counterespionage efforts on the island. Current ROC policy suppresses sensitive issues such as the so-called 228 Incident to avoid giving the ChiCom an opportunity to exploit penshengjen resentment, and we should give this policy our full support. We should also give all possible assistance to root out, suppress, and punish ChiCom agents, sympathizers, and other

They seemed to belong to Dad from work. Lilly stumbled over the many words that she didn't know, and finally stopped at "thalassocracy," whatever that meant. She quietly put the papers back down on the ground. Suzie Randling and tomorrow's lunch were far more pressing and worrisome to Lilly than whatever was typed on those sheets.

As expected, Suzie Randling and her gaggle of loyal lieutenants kept a watchful eye on Lilly as she sat at the other table with her back to the girls.

Lilly delayed taking out her lunch as long as she could, hoping that the girls would be distracted by their gossip and ignore her. She drank her juice and nibbled on the grapes that she brought for dessert, taking as long as she could, peeling the skin off each grape and carefully chewing on the sweet, juicy flesh inside.

But eventually, Lilly finished all the grapes. She willed her hands not to tremble as she took out the rice balls. She unwrapped the banana leaves from the first rice ball and bit into it. The sweet smell of sesame oil and chicken wafted across to the other table, and Suzie perked up right away.

"I smell Chinaman slops again," Suzie said. She sniffed the air exaggeratedly. The corners of her mouth turned up in a nasty grin. She loved the way Lilly seemed to shrink and cower at her voice. She took pleasure in it.

Suzie and the flock of girls around her took up the chant from yesterday again. Laughter was in their voices, the laughter of girls drunk on power. There was desire in their eyes, a lust for blood, a craving to see Lilly cry.

Well, it won't hurt to try, Lilly thought.

She turned around to face the girls, and in her raised right hand was the mirror that Mr. Kan had given her. She turned the mirror to Suzie.

"What's that in your hand?" Suzie laughed, thinking that Lilly was offering something as tribute, a peace offering. Silly girl. What could she offer besides her tears?

Suzie looked into the mirror.

Instead of her beautiful face, she saw a pair of bloodred lips, grinning like a clown, and instead of a tongue, an ugly, wormy mess of tentacles writhed inside the mouth. She saw a pair of blue eyes, opened wide as teacups, filled half with hatred and half with surprise. It was easily the most ugly and frightening sight she had ever seen. She saw a monster.

Suzie screamed and covered her mouth with her hands. The monster in the mirror lifted a pair of hairy paws in front of its bloody lips, and the long, daggerlike claws seemed to reach out of the mirror.

Suzie turned around and ran, and the chant stopped abruptly, replaced by the screams of the other girls as they, too, saw the monster inside the mirror.

Later, Mrs. Wyle had to send a hysterical Suzie home. Suzie had insisted that Mrs. Wyle take the mirror from Lilly, but after a minute of careful examination, Mrs. Wyle concluded that the mirror was perfectly ordinary and handed it back to Lilly. She sighed as she tried to pen a note to Suzie's parents. She suspected that Suzie had made up the whole episode as a way to get out of school, but the girl was a good actress.

Lilly fingered the mirror in her pocket and smiled to herself as she sat through the afternoon's lessons.

"You are really good at baseball," Lilly said from her perch on top of Ah Huang.

Teddy shrugged. He was walking ahead of Ah Huang, leading him by the nose and carrying a baseball bat over this shoulder. He walked slowly, so that Lilly's ride was smooth.

Teddy was quiet, and Lilly was getting used to that. At first Lilly thought it was because his English wasn't as good as Mr. Kan's. But then she found that he spoke just as little to the other Chinese children.

Teddy had introduced her to the other kids from the village, some of whom had thrown mud at Lilly the day before. The boys nodded at Lilly, but then looked away, embarrassed.

They played a game of baseball. Only Teddy and Lilly knew all the rules, but all the children were familiar with it from watching the American soldiers at the Base nearby. Lilly loved baseball, and one of the things she missed the most about home was playing baseball with Dad and watching games together on TV. But since they moved to Taiwan, there were no more games on TV, and he no longer seemed to be able to find the time.

When it was Lilly's turn to bat, the pitcher, one of the boys from yesterday, lobbed her a soft and slow pitch that Lilly turned into a gentle groundball that rolled into right field. The outfielders ran over and suddenly all of them seemed to have trouble locating the ball in the grass. Lilly easily circled the bases.

Lilly understood that that was the way the boys apologized. She smiled at them and bowed, showing that all was forgiven. The boys grinned back at her.

"Grandpa would say, 'pu ta pu hsiang shih.' It means that sometimes you can't become friends until you've fought each other."

Lilly thought that was a very good philosophy, but she doubted that it worked among girls.

Teddy was by far the best player among all the children. He was a good pitcher, but he was a great hitter. Every time he came up to bat, the opposing team fanned out, knowing that he would hit it way out.

"Someday, when I'm older, I'm going to move to America, and I'll play for the Red Sox," Teddy suddenly said, without looking back at Lilly on the water buffalo.

Lilly found the notion of a Chinese boy from Taiwan playing base-ball for the Red Sox pretty ridiculous, but she kept herself from laughing because Teddy didn't seem to be joking. She was partial to the Yankees because her mother's family was from New York. "Why Boston?"

"Grandpa went to school in Boston," Teddy said.

"Oh." *That must be how Mr. Kan learned English,* Lilly thought.

"I wish I were older. Then I could have gotten to play with Ted Williams. Now I will never get to see him play in person. He retired last year."

There was such sadness in his voice that neither spoke for a few minutes. Only Ah Huang's loud, even breathing accompanied their silent walk.

Lilly suddenly understood something. "Is that why you call yourself Teddy?"

Teddy didn't answer, but Lilly could see that his face was red. She tried to distract him from his embarrassment. "Maybe he'll come back to coach someday."

"Williams was the best hitter ever. He'll definitely show me how to improve my swing. But the guy they replaced him with, Carl Yaz, is really good too. Me and Yaz, someday we'll beat the Yankees and take the Sox to the World Series."

Well, it is called the World Series, Lilly thought. *Maybe a Chinese boy will really make it.*

"That's a really grand dream," Lilly said. "I hope it happens."

"Thanks," Teddy said. "When I'm successful in America, I'll buy the biggest house in Boston, and Grandpa and I will live there. And I'll marry an American girl, because American girls are the best and prettiest."

"What's she going to look like?"

"Blonde." Teddy looked back at Lilly, riding on Ah Huang, with her loose red curls and hazel eyes. "Or red-haired," he added quickly, and turned his face away, flushed.

Lilly smiled.

As they walked past the other houses in the village, Lilly noticed that many of the houses had slogans painted on their walls and doors. "What do those signs say?"

"That one says, 'Beware of Communist bandit spies. It is every-one's responsibility to keep secrets.' That one over there says, 'Even if we by mistake kill three thousand, we can't let a single Communist spy slip through our fingers.' And that one over there says, 'Study hard and work hard, we must rescue our mainland brothers from the Red bandits.'"

"That's frightening."

"The Communists are scary," Teddy agreed. "Hey, that's my house down there. You want to come in?"

"Am I going to meet your parents?"

Teddy suddenly slumped his shoulders. "It's just Grandpa and me. He's not my real grandpa, you know. My parents died when I was just a baby, and Grandpa took me in as an orphan."

Lilly didn't know what to say. "How . . . how did your parents die?"

Teddy looked around them to make sure that no one was nearby. "They tried to leave a wreath on an empty lot on February 28, 1952. My uncle and aunt had died there back in 1947." He seemed to think that was all that needed to be said.

Lilly had no idea what he was talking about, but she couldn't probe any further. They had arrived at Teddy's home.

The cottage was tiny. Teddy opened the door and showed Lilly in while he went to take care of Ah Huang. Lilly found herself standing in the kitchen. Through a doorway she could see a larger room—the only other room in the cottage, really—lined with tatami mats. That was evidently where Teddy and Mr. Kan slept.

Mr. Kan showed her to a seat by the small table in the kitchen and gave her a cup of tea. He was cooking something on the stove, and it smelled delicious.

"If you like," Mr. Kan said, "you are welcome to share some stew with us. Teddy likes it, and I think you would too. You'll have a hard time finding Mongolian-style mutton stewed in Shantung-style milk-fish soup anywhere else in the world, ha-ha."

Lilly nodded. Her stomach growled as she breathed in the wonderful cooking fumes. She was feeling relaxed and comfortable.

"Thank you for the mirror. It worked." Lilly took out the mirror and put it on the table. "What do the words on the tape mean?"

"It's a quote from the *Analects*. Jesus said something that means exactly the same thing: 'Do unto others as you would have them do unto you.'"

"Oh." Lilly was disappointed. She was hoping that the words were some secret magical chant.

Mr. Kan seemed to know what Lilly was thinking about. "Magic words are often misunderstood. When those girls and you all thought 'gook' was a magic word, it held a kind of power. But it was an empty magic based on ignorance. Other words also hold magic and power, but they require reflection and thought."

Lilly nodded, not sure she really understood.

"Can we do more literomancy?" she asked.

"Sure." Mr. Kan put the lid on the pot and wiped his hands. He retrieved some paper, ink, and a brush. "What word would you like?"

"It would be more impressive if you can do it in English," said Teddy as he came into the kitchen.

"Yes, can you do it in English?" Lilly clapped her hands.

"I can try." Mr. Kan laughed. "This will be a first." He handed the brush to Lilly.

Lilly slowly wrote out the first word that came into her head, a word she didn't understand: *thalassocracy*.

Mr. Kan was surprised. "Oh, I don't know that word. This is going to be difficult." He frowned.

Lilly held her breath. *Was the magic not going to work in English?*

Mr. Kan shrugged. "Well, I'll just have to give it a try. Let's see . . . in the middle of the word is another word: 'lass.' That means you." He tipped the end of the brush toward Lilly. "The lass has an *o*, a circle of rope, trailing after her, and that makes 'lasso.' Hmm, Lilly, do you want to grow up to be a cowgirl?"

Lilly nodded, smiling. "I was born in Texas. We are born knowing how to ride."

"And what letters do we have left after 'lasso'? We have 'tha'-space-'cracy.' Hmm, if you rearrange them, you can spell 'Cathay,' with a *c* and an *r* left over. *C* is just a way to say 'sea,' and Cathay is an old name for China. But what is *r*?

"Ah, I've got it! The way you've written the *r*, it looks like a bird flying. So, Lilly, this means that you are the lass with a lasso who was destined to fly across the sea and come to China. Ha-ha! It was fate that we should be friends!"

Lilly clapped and laughed with joy and amazement.

Mr. Kan ladled out mutton and fish stew into two bowls for Teddy and Lilly. The stew was good, but very different from anything Lin Amah made. It was savory, smooth, laced with the sharp fresh scent of scallions. Mr. Kan watched the children eat and happily sipped his tea.

"You've found out a lot about me, Mr. Kan, but I don't know much about you."

"True. Why don't you pick another word? We'll see what the characters want you to know."

Lilly thought about it. "How about the word for America? You lived there, didn't you?"

Mr. Kan nodded. "Good choice." He wrote with his brush.

"This is *mei*. It's the character for 'beauty,' and America, *Meikuo*, is the Beautiful Country. See how it's composed of two characters stacked on top of each other? The one on the top means 'sheep.' Can you see the horns of the ram sticking up? The one on the bottom means 'great,' and it's shaped like a person standing up, legs and arms spread out, feeling like a big man."

Mr. Kan stood up to demonstrate.

"The ancient Chinese were a simple people. If they had a great, big, fat sheep, that meant wealth, stability, comfort, and happiness. They thought that was a beautiful sight. And now, in my old age, I understand how they felt." Lilly thought about mutton busting, and she understood too.

Mr. Kan sat down and closed his eyes as he continued.

"I come from a family of salt merchants in Shantung. We were considered wealthy. When I was a boy, people praised me for being clever and good with words, and my father hoped that I would do something great to glorify the Kan name. When I was old enough, he borrowed a large sum of money to send me to study in America. I chose to study law because I liked words and their power."

Mr. Kan wrote another character on the paper. "Let's see what I can tell you with more characters formed from 'sheep.'"

"The first time I had this stew, I was a law student in Boston. My friend and I, we shared a room together. We had no money, and every meal we ate nothing but bread and water. But this one time, our landlord, the owner of a restaurant in Chinatown, took pity on us. He gave us some rotting fish and mutton scraps that he was going to throw away. I knew how to make a good fish stew, and my friend, who was from Manchuria, knew how to make good Mongolian mutton.

"I thought, since the character for 'savory' is made from 'fish' and 'lamb,' maybe if we put our dishes together, it would taste pretty good. And it worked! I don't think we'd ever been that happy. Literomancy is even useful for cooking." Mr. Kan chuckled like a kid.

Then his face turned more serious.

"Later, in 1931, Japan invaded Manchuria, and my friend left America to defend his home. I heard that he became a Communist guerrilla to fight the Japanese, and the Japanese killed him a year later."

Mr. Kan sipped his tea. His hands trembled.

"I was a coward. I had a job then and a comfortable life in America. I was safe, and I did not want to go to war. I made excuses, telling myself that I could do more to help if I waited for the war to be over.

"But Japan was not content with Manchuria. A few years later, it invaded the rest of China, and one day I woke up to find that my hometown had been captured, and I stopped getting any letters from my family. I waited and waited, trying to reassure myself that they had escaped south and that everything was all right. But eventually, a letter from my baby sister arrived, bringing with it the news that the Japanese army had killed everyone in our clan, including our parents, when the town fell. My sister was the only one who survived by playing dead. Because I dithered, I had let my parents die.

"I left for China. I asked to sign up for the army as soon as I stepped off the boat. The Nationalist officer couldn't care less that I had gone to school in America. What China needed were men who could shoot, not men who knew how to read and write and could interpret the laws. I was given a gun and ten bullets, and told that if I wanted more bullets, I had to get them from the dead bodies."

Mr. Kan wrote another character on the paper.

"Here's another character also built from 'sheep.' It looks a lot like *mei*. I just changed the 'great' on the bottom a bit. Do you recognize it?"

Lilly thought back to the drawings from a day earlier. "That's the character for 'fire.'"

Mr. Kan nodded. "You are a very smart girl."

"So this is a character for roasting mutton over fire?"

"Yes. But when 'fire' is on the bottom of a character, usually we change its shape to show that it's cooking at low heat. Like this."

"Originally, roasted lamb was an offering to the gods, and this character, *kao*, came to mean lamb in general."

"Like a sacrificial lamb?"

Mr. Kan nodded. "I guess so. We had no training and no support, and we lost more than we won. Behind you, officers with machine guns would shoot you if you tried to run. In front of you, the Japanese charged at you with bayonets. When you used up your bullets, you looked for more from your dead comrades. I wanted revenge for my dead family, but how could I get my revenge? I didn't even know which Japanese soldiers killed them.

"That was when I began to understand another kind of magic. Men spoke of the glory of *Japan* and the weakness of *China*, that *Japan* wants the best for Asia, and that *China* should accept what *Japan* wants and give up. But what do these words mean? How can '*Japan*' *want* something? '*Japan*' and '*China*' do not exist. They are just words, fiction. An individual Japanese may be glorious, and an individual Chinese may want something, but how can you speak of 'Japan' or 'China' *wanting, believing, accepting* anything? It is all just empty words, myths. But these myths have powerful magic, and they require sacrifices. They require the slaughter of men like sheep.

"When America finally entered the war, I was so happy. I knew that China was saved. Ah, see how powerful that magic is, that I can speak of these nonexistent things as though they are real. No matter. As soon as the war with Japan was over, I was told that we Nationalists now had to fight the Communists, who were our brothers-in-arms just days earlier against the Japanese. The Communists were evil and had to be stopped."

Mr. Kan wrote another character.

"This is the character *yi*, which used to mean 'righteousness,' and now also means '-ism,' as in Communism, Nationalism, Imperialism, Capitalism, Liberalism. It's formed from the character for 'sheep,' which you know, on top, and the character for 'I,' on the bottom. A man holds up a sheep for sacrifice, and he thinks he has truth, justice, and the magic that will save the world. It's funny, isn't it?

"But here's the thing. Even though the Communists had even worse equipment than we did, and less training, they kept on winning.

I couldn't understand it until one day, my unit was ambushed by the Communists, and I surrendered and joined them. You see, the Communists really were bandits. They would take the land from the landlords and distribute it to the landless peasants, and this made them very popular. They couldn't care less about the fiction of laws and property rights. Why should they? The rich and educated had made a mess of things, so why shouldn't the poor and illiterate have a chance at it? No one before the Communists had ever thought much of the lowly peasants, but when you have nothing, not even shoes for your feet, you are not afraid to die. The world had many more people who were poor and therefore fearless than people who were rich and afraid. I could see the logic of the Communists.

"But I was tired. I had been fighting for almost a decade of my life, and I was alone in the world. My family had been rich, and the Communists would have killed them, too. I did not want to fight for the Communists, even if I could understand them. I wanted to stop. A few friends and I slipped away in the middle of the night and stole a boat. We were going to try to get to Hong Kong and leave all this slaughter behind.

"But we did not know navigation, and the waves took us into the open sea. We ran out of water and food and waited to die. But a week later, we saw land on the horizon. We rowed with our last bits of strength until we came ashore, and we found ourselves in Taiwan.

"We swore each other to secrecy about our time with the Communists and our desertion. We each went about our own ways, determined to never have to fight again. Because I was good with the abacus and the brush, I was hired by a Taiwanese couple who owned a small general store, and I kept their books and ran the place for them.

"Most of Taiwan had been settled by immigrants from Fukien several centuries earlier, and after Japan took Taiwan from China in 1885, the Japanese tried to Japanize the island, much as they had done in Okinawa, and remake the *penshengjen* into loyal subjects of the Emperor. Many of the men fought in Japan's armies during the war. After Japan lost, Taiwan was to be given back to the Republic of China. The Nationalists came to Taiwan and brought a new wave of immigrants with them, the *waishengjen*. The *penshengjen* hated the Nationalist *waishengjen*, who took away the best jobs, and the Nationalist *waishengjen* hated the *penshengjen*, who had been traitors to their race during the war.

"I was working in the shop one day when a mob gathered in the streets. They shouted in Fukienese, and so I knew they were *penshengjen*. They stopped everyone they met, and if the person spoke Mandarin, they knew him to be a *waishengjen* and attacked him. There was no reasoning and no hesitation. They wanted blood. I was terrified and tried to hide under the counter."

"The character for 'mob' is formed from the character for 'nobility' on one side and the character for 'sheep' on the other. So that's what a mob is, a herd of sheep that turns into a pack of wolves because they believe themselves to be serving a noble cause.

"The *penshengjen* couple tried to protect me, saying that I was a good man. Someone in the mob shouted that they were traitors, and they attacked all of us and burned the shop down. I managed to crawl out of the fire, but the couple died."

"They were my uncle and aunt," Teddy said. Mr. Kan nodded and put a hand on his shoulder.

"The *penshengjen* rebellion began on February 28, 1947, and lasted for months. Because some of the rebels were led by Communists, the

Nationalists were especially brutal. It took the Nationalists a long time to finally put down the rebellion, and thousands were killed.

"In those killings a new kind of magic was born. Now, no one is allowed to talk about the 228 Massacre. The number 228 is taboo.

"I took Teddy in after his parents were executed for trying to commemorate that day. I came here, away from the city, so that I could live in a small cottage and drink my tea in peace. The villagers respect those who have read books, and they come to me to ask my advice on picking names for their children that will bring good fortune. Even after so many men died because of a few magic words, we continue to have faith in the power of words to do good.

"I have not heard from my baby sister for decades. I believe she is still alive on the mainland. Someday, before I die, I hope to see her again."

The three sat around the table, and no one said anything for a while. Mr. Kan wiped his eyes.

"I'm sorry to have told you such a sad story, Lilly. But the Chinese have not had happy stories to tell for a long time."

Lilly looked at the paper before Mr. Kan, filled with characters made from sheep. "Can you look into the future? Will there be good stories then?"

Mr. Kan's eyes brightened. "Good idea. What character should I write?"

"What about the character for China?"

Mr. Kan thought about this. "That's a difficult request, Lilly. 'China' may be a simple word in English, but it is not so easy in Chinese. We have many words for China and the people who call themselves Chinese. Most of these words are named after ancient dynasties, and the modern words are empty shells, devoid of real magic. What is the People's Republic? What is the Republic? These are not true words. Only more altars for sacrifices."

After thinking some more, he wrote another character.

華

"This is the character *hua*, and it is the only word for China and for the Chinese that has nothing to do with any Emperor, any Dynasty, anything that demands slaughter and sacrifice. Although both the People's Republic and the Republic put it in their names, it is far older than they and belongs to neither of them. *Hua* originally meant 'flowery' and 'magnificent,' and it is the shape of a bunch of wildflowers coming out of the ground. See?

"The ancient Chinese were called *huajen* by their neighbors because their dress was magnificent, made of silk and fine tulle. But I think that's not the only reason. The Chinese are like wildflowers, and they will survive and make joy wherever they go. A fire may burn away every living thing in a field, but after the rain the wildflowers will reappear as though by magic. Winter may come and kill everything with frost and snow, but when spring comes the wildflowers will blossom again, and they will be magnificent.

"For now, the red flames of revolution may be burning on the mainland, and the white frost of terror may have covered this island. But I know that a day will come when the steel wall of the Seventh Fleet will melt away, and the *penshengjen* and the *waishengjen* and all the other *huajen* back in my home will blossom together in magnificence."

"And I will be a *huajen* in America," Teddy added.

Mr. Kan nodded. "Wildflowers can bloom anywhere."

Lilly didn't have much of an appetite for dinner. She had had too much fish and mutton stew.

"Well, this Mr. Kan is no true friend of yours, if he's going to ruin your appetite with snacks," said Mom.

"It's all right," said Dad. "It's good for Lilly to make some native friends. You should invite them over for dinner sometime. Mom and I should get to know them if you are going to spend a lot of time with this family."

Lilly thought this a splendid idea. She couldn't wait to show Teddy her Nancy Drew books. She knew that he'd like the beautiful pictures on the covers.

"Dad, what does 'thalassocracy' mean?"

Dad paused. "Where did you hear that word?"

Lilly knew that she wasn't supposed to look at things from Dad's work. "I just read it somewhere."

Dad stared at Lilly, but then he relented. "It comes from the Greek word for sea, *thalassa*. It means 'rule by the sea.' You know, like 'Rule, Britannia! Rule the waves.'"

Lilly was disappointed at this. She thought Mr. Kan's explanation was much better, and said so.

"Why were you and Mr. Kan talking about thalassocracy?"

"No reason. I just wanted to see him do some magic."

"Lilly, there's no such thing as magic," Mom said.

Lilly wanted to argue but thought better of it.

"Dad, I don't understand why Taiwan is free if they can't talk about 228."

Dad put down his fork and knife. "What did you say?"

"Mr. Kan said that they can't talk about 228."

Dad pushed his plate away and turned to Lilly. "Now, from the beginning, tell me everything that you talked about with Mr. Kan today."

Lilly waited by the river. She was going to invite Teddy and Mr. Kan to come for dinner.

The village boys showed up, one after another, with their water buffalo. But none of them knew where Teddy was.

Lilly got into the river and joined the boys as they splashed water on each other. But she couldn't help feeling uneasy. Teddy always showed up at the river after school to wash Ah Huang. Where was he?

When the boys started to go back to the village, she went with them. *Maybe Teddy was sick and stayed home?*

Ah Huang was pacing in front of Mr. Kan's cottage, and he snorted at Lilly when he saw her, coming closer to nuzzle her as she petted his forehead.

"Teddy! Mr. Kan!" There was no answer.

Lilly knocked on the door. No one answered. The door was not locked, and Lilly pushed it open.

The cottage had been ransacked. The tatami mats were overturned and slashed apart. Tables and chairs were broken and the pieces scattered around the cottage. Pots, broken dishes, chopsticks littered the floor. There were papers and torn books everywhere. Teddy's baseball bat was carelessly lying on the ground.

Lilly looked down and saw that Mr. Kan's magic mirror had been shattered into a thousand little pieces scattered about her feet.

Did Communist bandits do this?

Lilly ran to the neighboring houses, frantically knocking on their doors and pointing at Mr. Kan's cottage. The neighbors either refused to answer the door or shook their heads, their faces full of fear.

Lilly ran home.

Lilly could not sleep.

Mom had refused to go to the police. Dad was working late, and Mom said if it wasn't just Lilly's imagination and there really were bandits about, then the best thing to do was to stay home and wait for Dad to come back. Eventually, Mom sent Lilly to bed because it was a school night, and she promised that she would tell Dad about Mr. Kan and Teddy. Dad would know what to do.

Lilly heard the front door open and close, and the sound of chairs sliding on the tile floor in the kitchen. Dad was home, and Mom was going to heat up some food for him.

She knelt up on her bed and opened the window. A cool, humid breeze carried the smell of decaying vegetation and night-blooming flowers into the room. Lilly crawled out the window.

Once she landed on the muddy ground, she quietly made her way around the house to the back, where the kitchen was. Inside, Lilly could see Mom and Dad sitting across from each other at the kitchen table. There was no food on the table. In front of Dad was a small glass, and he poured an amber liquid into it from a bottle. He drained the glass in one gulp and filled it again.

The bright, golden light inside the kitchen cast a trapezoid of illumination upon the ground outside the kitchen window. She stayed beyond its edge and crouched below the open window to listen.

Amid the sound of the fluttering wings of moths striking against the screened window, she listened to her father's voice

In the morning, David Cotton told me that the man I had referred to them had been arrested. If I wanted to, I could go help with the interrogation. I went over to the detention compound with two Chinese interrogators, Chen Pien and Li Hui.

"He's a tough nut to crack," Chen said. "We've tried a few things, but he's very resistant. We still have some heightened interrogation techniques we can try."

"The Communists are very good at psychological manipulation and resistance," I said. "It's not surprising. We need to get him to tell us who his accomplices are. I believe he came to Taiwan with a team of operatives."

We got to the holding cell, and I saw that they had worked him over pretty

good. Both of his shoulders had been dislocated, and his face was bloody. His right eye was swollen almost completely shut.

I asked that he be given some medical attention. I wanted to have him understand that I was the kind one, and that I could protect him if he trusted me. They fixed his shoulders and a nurse bandaged his face. I gave him some water.

"I'm not a spy," he said, in English.

"Tell me what your orders were," I said.

"I don't have any orders."

"Tell me who came to Taiwan with you," I said.

"I came to Taiwan alone."

"I know that's a lie."

He shrugged, wincing with the pain.

I nodded to Chen and Li, and they started pushing small, sharpened bamboo sticks under his fingernails. He tried to stay silent. Chen began to hit the base of the bamboo sticks with a small hammer, as though he were hammering nails into a wall. The man screamed like an animal. Eventually he passed out.

Chen hosed him down with cold water until he woke up. I asked him the same questions. He shook his head, refusing to talk.

"We just want to talk to your friends," I said. "If they are innocent, nothing will happen to them. They won't blame you."

He laughed.

"Let's try the Tiger Bench," Li said.

They brought over a narrow long bench and laid one end against a supporting column in the room. They sat him down on the bench so that his back was straight against the column. Bending his arms back and wrapping them around the column, they tied his hands together. Then they strapped his thighs and knees down to the top of the bench with thick leather straps. Finally, they tied his ankles together.

"We'll see if Communists have knees that can bend forward," Chen said to him.

They lifted his feet and placed a brick under his heels, then another one.

Because his thighs and knees were strapped tight to the bench, the bricks forced his feet and lower legs up and began to bend his knees at an impossible angle. Sweat dripped from his face and forehead, mixed with the blood from his wounds. He tried to squirm along the bench to relieve the stress on his knees but there was nowhere to go. He rubbed his arms, moving them up and down helplessly on the column until he broke the skin on his wrists and arms and blood streaked the whitewash on the column.

They put in another two bricks, and I could hear the bones in his knees crack. He began to moan and shout, but said nothing that we wanted to hear.

"I can't stop this if you won't talk," I said to him.

They brought in a long wooden wedge and pushed the thin end under the brick at the bottom. Then they took turns to strike a hammer against the thick end of the wedge. With each strike, the wedge moved in a little under the bricks and lifted his feet higher. He screamed and screamed. They forced a stick into his mouth so he wouldn't bite down on his tongue.

"Just nod if you are ready to talk."

He shook his head.

Suddenly, his knees broke at the next hammer strike, and his feet and lower legs jumped up, the broken bones sticking through the flesh and skin. He fainted again.

I was getting nauseous. If the Communists could train and prepare their agents to this degree, how could we possibly hope to win this war?

"This is not going to work," I said to the Chinese interrogators. "I have an idea. He has a grandson. Do we have him?" They nodded.

We brought the doctor in again to bandage his legs. The doctor gave him an injection so that he would stay awake.

"Kill me, please," he said to me. "Kill me."

We brought him out to the courtyard and sat him in a chair. Li brought in his grandson. He was a small boy, but seemed very bright. He was scared and tried to run to his grandfather. Li pulled him back, stood him against the wall and pointed a pistol at him.

"We are not going to kill you," I said. "But if you won't confess, we will execute your grandson as an accomplice."

"No, no," he begged. "Please. He doesn't know anything. We don't know anything. I'm not a spy. I swear."

Li stood back and held the pistol with both hands.

"You are making me do this," I said. "You have given me no choice. I don't want to kill your grandson, but you are going to make him die."

"I came here on a boat with four others," he said. He kept his eyes on the boy, and I could see that I was finally getting to him. "They are all good people. None of us are Communist spies."

"That's another lie," I said. "Tell me who they are."

Just then the boy jumped and grabbed Li's hands, and the boy tried to bite him. "Let my grandfather go," he yelled as he struggled with Li.

There were two gunshots, and the boy fell in a heap. Li dropped his gun and I rushed over. The boy had bitten his finger to the bone, and he was howling with pain. I picked up the gun.

I looked up and saw that the old man had fallen out of his chair. He was crawling to us, to the body of his grandson. He was crying, and I couldn't tell what language he was crying in.

Chen went to help Li while I watched the man crawl to the boy. He turned his body until he was sitting and lifted the boy's body into his lap, hugging the dead child to his chest. "Why, why?" he said to me. "He was just a boy. He didn't know anything. Kill me, please kill me."

I looked into his eyes: dark, glistening, like mirrors. In them I saw the reflections of my own face, and it was such a strange face, so full of crazed fury that I did not recognize myself.

Many things went through my head at that moment. I thought back to when I was a little boy in Maine, and the mornings when my grandfather would take me hunting. I thought about my sinology professor, and the stories he told of his boyhood in Shanghai and his Chinese friends and servants. I thought about yesterday morning, when David and I taught the class on counterintelligence to the Nationalist agents. I thought about Lilly, who is about the boy's age. What does she know about Communism and freedom? Somewhere, the world had gone horribly wrong.

"Please kill me, please kill me."

I pointed the pistol at the man and squeezed the trigger. I kept on squeezing the trigger, again and again, after the gun was empty.

"He was resisting," Chen said, later. "Trying to escape." It wasn't a question.

I nodded anyway.

"You had no choice," Mrs. Dyer said. "He forced you to do it. Freedom isn't without its price. You were trying to do the right thing."

He did not respond to this. After a while, he drained the glass again.

"You've told me how hardened these Communist agents are, and we've all heard the tales from Korea. But only now do I really understand. They must have really brainwashed him and made him without human feeling, without remorse. The blood of his grandson is on him. Just think what he could have done to Lilly."

He did not respond to this either. He looked across the table at her, and it seemed that there was a gulf between them, as wide as the Taiwan Strait.

"I don't know," he said finally. "I don't really know anything anymore."

Dad walked with Lilly next to the river, their feet sinking into the soft mud. Both stopped and took off their shoes, continuing barefoot. They did not speak to each other. Ah Huang followed behind them, and every once in a while Lilly stopped to pet him on the nose as he snorted into her palm.

"Lilly." Dad broke the silence. "Mom and I have decided to move back to Texas. I've gotten a transfer for work."

Lilly nodded without speaking. Autumn had settled over her heart. The trees along the river waved at their own reflections in the moving, rippling water, and Lilly wished she still had Mr. Kan's magic mirror.

"We have to find a new home for your water buffalo. We can't take him back to Texas."

Lilly stopped. She refused to look at him.

"It's too dry back there," Dad tried. "He won't be happy. He won't have a river to bathe in and rice paddies to wallow in. He won't be free."

Lilly wanted to tell him that she was no longer a little girl, and he did not need to speak to her that way. But instead she just stroked Ah Huang some more.

"Sometimes, Lilly, adults have to do things that they don't want to do, because it's the right thing to do. Sometimes we do things that seem wrong, but are really right."

Lilly thought about Mr. Kan's arms, and the way he held her the first time they met. She thought about the way his voice had sounded when he scared the boys away. She thought about the way the tip of his brush moved on paper, writing the character for "beautiful." She wished that she knew how to write his name. She wished she knew more about the magic of words and characters.

Even though it was a pleasant autumn afternoon, Lilly felt cold. She imagined the fields around her covered in white, a frost of terror that had come to freeze over the subtropical island.

The word "freeze" seemed to call for her attention. She closed her eyes and pictured the word in her head, examining it carefully the way she thought Mr. Kan would have. The letters jiggled and nudged against each other. The z took on the shape of a kneeling, supplicating man, the e the fetal curl of a dead child. And then the z and e disappeared, leaving *free* in its place.

It's okay, Lilly. Teddy and I are free now. Lilly tried to concentrate, to hold on to the fading smile and warm voice of Mr. Kan in her mind. *You are a very smart girl. You are destined to become a literomancer too, in America.*

Lilly squeezed her eyes tight so that no tears would fall out.

"Lilly, are you all right?" Dad's voice brought her back.

She nodded. She felt a little warmer.

They continued to walk, looking at the hunched-over figures of the women in the rice paddies harvesting the heavy grain with sickles.

"It's difficult to know how the future will turn out," Dad continued. "Things have a way of working themselves out to the surprise of everyone. Sometimes the most ugly things can turn out to be the cause for something wonderful. I know you haven't had a good time here, Lilly, and it's unfortunate. But this is a beautiful island. Formosa means 'most beautiful' in Latin."

Like America, Meikuo, *the Beautiful Country,* Lilly thought. *The wildflowers will bloom again when it is spring.*

In the distance, they could see the children from the village playing a game of baseball.

"Someday you'll see that our sacrifices here were worth it. This place will be free, and you'll see its beauty and remember your time here fondly. Anything is possible. Maybe one day we'll even see a boy from here playing baseball in America. Now wouldn't that be something, Lilly, a Chinese boy from Formosa playing at Yankee Stadium?"

Lilly focused on the scene in her head.

Teddy steps up to the plate in a Red Sox helmet, his calm eyes staring at the pitcher on the mound, the N *crossed with a* Y *on his cap. He swings at the first pitch, and there is a crisp, loud* thwack. *It's a hit. The ball floats high into the cold October air, into the dark sky and the bright lights, an arc that will end somewhere in the grandstands beyond right field. The crowd stands. Teddy begins to trot along the baselines, his face breaking into a wide grin, searching the crowd for Mr. Kan and Lilly. And the wild cheers shake the stadium as the pennant is clinched. The Red Sox are going to the World Series.*

"I've been thinking," Dad continued. "Maybe we should take a vacation before we go back to Clearwell. I was thinking that we can stop by New York to visit Grandma. The Yankees are playing the Reds in the World Series. I'll try to get tickets, and we can go see them and cheer them on."

Lilly shook her head and looked up at him. "I don't like the Yankees anymore."

•　•　•

AUTHOR'S NOTES: For a variety of reasons, this text does not use pinyin to romanize Chinese. Instead, Mandarin phrases and words are generally romanized using the Wade-Giles system, and Taiwanese Minnan (Fukienese) phrases and words are romanized using either the Pe̍h-ōe-jī system or English phonetic spelling.

An introductory account of the history of joint American-ROC covert operations against the PRC during the Cold War may be found in John W. Garver's *The Sino-American Alliance: Nationalist China and American Cold War Strategy in Asia*.

The art of literomancy is greatly simplified in this story. As well, the folk etymologies and decompositions used here are understood to have little relationship with academic conclusions.

SIMULACRUM

[A] photograph is not only an image (as a painting is an image), an interpretation of the real; it is also a trace, something directly stenciled off the real, like a footprint or a death mask.

—SUSAN SONTAG

PAUL LARIMORE:

You are already recording? I should start? Okay.

Anna was an accident. Both Erin and I were traveling a lot for work, and we didn't want to be tied down. But you can't plan for everything, and we were genuinely happy when we found out. We'll make it work somehow, we said. And we did.

When Anna was a baby, she wasn't a very good sleeper. She had to be carried and rocked as she gradually drifted to sleep, fighting against it the whole time. You couldn't be still. Erin had a bad back for months after the birth, and so it was me who walked around at night with the little girl's head against my shoulder after feedings. Although I know I must have been very tired and impatient, all I remember now is how close I felt to her as we moved back and forth for hours across the living room, lit only by moonlight, while I sang to her.

I wanted to feel that close to her, always.

I have no simulacra of her from back then. The prototype machines were very bulky, and the subject had to sit still for hours. That wasn't going to happen with a baby.

This is the first simulacrum I *do* have of her. She's about seven.

—Hello, sweetheart.
—*Dad!*
—Don't be shy. These men are here to make a documen-
tary movie about us. You don't have to talk to them. Just
pretend they're not here.
—*Can we go to the beach?*
—You know we can't. We can't leave the house. Besides,
it's too cold outside.
—*Will you play dolls with me?*
—Yes, of course. We'll play dolls as long as you want.

ANNA LARIMORE:

My father is a hard person for the world to dislike. He has made a great
deal of money in a way that seems like an American fairy tale: Lone
inventor comes up with an idea that brings joy to the world, and the
world rewards him deservedly. On top of it all, he donates generously
to worthy causes. The Larimore Foundation has cultivated my father's
name and image as carefully as the studios airbrush the celebrity sex
simulacra that they sell.

But I know the real Paul Larimore.

One day, when I was thirteen, I had to be sent home because of an
upset stomach. I came in the front door, and I heard noises from my parents' bedroom upstairs. They weren't supposed to be home. No one was.

A burglar? I thought. In the fearless and stupid way of teenagers, I
went up the stairs, and I opened the door.

My father was naked in bed, and there were four naked women
with him. He didn't hear me, and so they continued what they were
doing, there in the bed that my mother shared with him.

After a while, he turned around, and we looked into each other's eyes. He stopped, sat up, and reached out to turn off the projector on the nightstand. The women disappeared.

I threw up.

When my mother came home later that night, she explained to me that it had been going on for years. My father had a weakness for a certain kind of woman, she said. Throughout their marriage, he had trouble being faithful. She had suspected this was the case, but my father was very intelligent and careful, and she had no evidence.

When she finally caught him in the act, she was furious, and wanted to leave him. But he begged and pleaded. He said that there was something in his makeup that made real monogamy impossible for him. But, he said, he had a solution.

He had taken many simulacra of his conquests over the years, more and more lifelike as he improved the technology. If my mother would let him keep them and tolerate his use of them in private, he would try very hard to not stray again.

So this was the bargain that my mother made. He was a good father, she thought. She knew that he loved me. She did not want to make me an additional casualty of a broken promise that was only made to her.

And my father's proposal did seem like a reasonable solution. In her mind, his time with the simulacra was no different from the way other men used pornography. No touching was involved. They were not real. No marriage could survive if it did not contain some room for harmless fantasies.

But my mother did not look into my father's eyes the way I did when I walked in on him. It was more than a fantasy. It was a continuing betrayal that could not be forgiven.

•   •   •

PAUL LARIMORE:

The key to the simulacrum camera is *not* the physical imaging process, which, while not trivial, is ultimately not much more than the culmination of incremental improvements on technologies known since the days of the daguerreotype.

My contribution to the eternal quest of capturing reality is the oneiropagida, through which a snapshot of the subject's mental patterns—a representation of her personality—could be captured, digitized, and then used to reanimate the image during projection. The oneiropagida is at the heart of all simulacrum cameras, including those made by my competitors.

The earliest cameras were essentially modified medical devices, similar to those legacy tomography machines you still see at old hospitals. The subject had to have certain chemicals injected into her body and then lie still for a long time in the device's imaging tunnel until an adequate set of scans of her mental processes could be taken. These were then used to seed AI neural models, which then animated the projections constructed from detailed photographs of her body.

These early attempts were very crude, and the results were described variously as robotic, inhuman, or even comically insane. But even these earliest simulacra preserved something that could not be captured by mere videos or holography. Instead of replaying verbatim what was captured, the animated projection could interact with the viewer in the way that the subject would have.

The oldest simulacrum that still exists is one of myself, now preserved at the Smithsonian. In the first news reports, friends and acquaintances who interacted with it said that although they knew that the image was controlled by a computer, they elicited responses from it that seemed somehow "Paul": "That's something only Paul would say" or "That's a very Paul facial expression." It was then that I knew I had succeeded.

ANNA LARIMORE:

People find it strange that I, the daughter of the inventor of simulacra, write books about how the world would be better off without them, more authentic. Some have engaged in tiresome pop psychology, suggesting that I am jealous of my "sibling," the invention of my father that turned out to be his favorite child.

If only it were so simple.

My father proclaims that he works in the business of capturing reality, of stopping time and preserving memory. But the real attraction of such technology has never been about capturing reality. Photography, videography, holography . . . the progression of such "reality-capturing" technology has been a proliferation of ways to lie about reality, to shape and distort it, to manipulate and fantasize.

People shape and stage the experiences of their lives for the camera, go on vacations with one eye glued to the video camera. The desire to freeze reality is about avoiding reality.

The simulacra are the latest incarnation of this trend, and the worst.

PAUL LARIMORE:

Ever since that day, when she . . . well, I expect that you have already heard about it from her. I will not dispute her version of events.

We have never spoken about that day to each other. What she does not know is that after that afternoon, I destroyed all the simulacra of my old affairs. I kept no backups. I expect that knowing this will not make any difference to her. But I would be grateful if you can pass this knowledge on to her.

Conversations between us after that day were civil, careful performances that avoided straying anywhere near intimacy. We spoke about permission slips, the logistics of having her come to my office to solicit sponsors for walkathons, factors to consider in picking a college. We did not speak about her easy friendships, her difficult loves, her hopes for and disappointments with the world.

Anna stopped speaking to me completely when she went off to college. When I called, she would not pick up the phone. When she needed a disbursement from her trust to pay tuition, she would call my lawyer. She spent her vacations and summers with friends or working overseas. Some weekends she would invite Erin up to visit her in Palo Alto. We all understood that I was not invited.

—*Dad, why is the grass green?*
—It's because the green from the leaves on the trees
  drips down with the spring rain.
—*That's ridiculous.*
—All right, it's because the grass is on the other side of
  the fence. But if you were standing on the other side, it
  wouldn't look so green.
—*You are not funny.*
—Okay. It's because of chlorophyll in the grass. The
  chlorophyll has rings in it that absorb all colors of light
  except green.
—*You're not making this up, are you?*
—Would I ever make anything up, sweetheart?
—*It's very hard to tell with you sometimes.*

I began to play this simulacrum of her often when she was in high school, and over time it became a bit of a habit. Now I keep her on all the time, every day.

There were later simulacra when she was older, many of them with far better resolution. But this one is my favorite. It reminded me of better times, before the world changed irrevocably.

The day I took this, we finally managed to make an oneiropagida that was small enough to fit within a chassis that could be carried on your shoulder. That later became the prototype for the Carousel Mark I, our first successful home simulacrum camera. I brought it home and asked Anna to pose for it. She stood still next to the sun porch for two minutes while we chatted about her day.

She was perfect in the way that little daughters are always perfect in the eyes of their fathers. Her eyes lit up when she saw that I was home. She had just come back from day camp, and she was full of stories she wanted to tell me and questions she wanted to ask me. She wanted me to take her to the beach to fly her new kite, and I promised to help her with her sunprint kit. I was glad to have captured her at that moment.

That was a good day.

ANNA LARIMORE:

The last time my father and I saw each other was after my mother's accident. His lawyer called, knowing that I would not have answered my father.

My mother was conscious, but barely. The other driver was already dead, and she was going to follow soon after.

"Why can't you forgive him?" she said. "I have. A man's life is not defined by one thing. He loves me. And he loves you."

I said nothing. I only held her hand and squeezed it. He came in and we both spoke to her but not to each other, and after half an hour she went to sleep and did not wake up.

The truth was, I was ready to forgive him. He looked old—a quality that children are among the last to notice about their parents—and there was a kind of frailty about him that made me question myself. We walked silently out of the hospital together. He asked if I had a place to stay in the city, and I said no. He opened the passenger-side door, and after hesitating for only a second, I slipped into his car.

We got home, and it was exactly the way I remembered it, even though I hadn't been home in years. I sat at the dinner table while he prepared frozen dinners. We spoke carefully to each other, the way we used to when I was in high school.

I asked him for a simulacrum of my mother. I don't take simulacra or keep them, as a rule. I don't have the same rosy view of them as the general public. But at that moment, I thought I understood their appeal. I wanted a piece of my mother to be always with me, an aspect of her presence.

He handed me a disk, and I thanked him. He offered me the use of his projector, but I declined. I wanted to keep the memory of my mother by myself for a while before letting the computer's extrapolations confuse real memories with made-up ones.

(And as things turned out, I've never used that simulacrum. Here, you can take a look at it later, if you want to see what she looked like. Whatever I remember of my mother, it's all real.)

It was late by the time we finished dinner, and I excused myself.

I walked up to my room.

And I saw the seven-year-old me sitting on my bed. She had on this hideous dress that I must have blocked out of my memory—pink, flowery—and there was a bow in her hair.

—*Hello, I'm Anna. Pleased to meet you.*

So he had kept this thing around for years, this naive, helpless caricature of me. During the time I did not speak to him, did he turn to this frozen trace of me and contemplate this shadow of my lost faith and affection? Did he use this model of my childhood to fantasize about the conversations that he could not have with me? Did he even edit it, perhaps, to remove my petulance, to add in more saccharine devotion?

I felt violated. The little girl was undeniably me. She acted like me, spoke like me, laughed and moved and reacted like me. But she was not *me*.

I had grown and changed, and I'd come to face my father as an adult. But now I found a piece of myself had been taken and locked into this *thing*, a piece that allowed him to maintain a sense of connection with me that I did not want, that was not real.

The image of those naked women in his bed from years ago came rushing back. I finally understood why for so long they had haunted my dreams.

It is the way a simulacrum replicates the essence of the subject that makes it so compelling. When my father kept those simulacra of his women around, he maintained a connection to them, to the man he was when he had been with them, and thus committed a continuing emotional betrayal that was far worse than a momentary physical indiscretion. A pornographic image is a pure visual fantasy, but a simulacrum captures a state of mind, a dream. But *whose* dream? What I saw in his eyes that day was not sordid. It was too intimate.

By keeping and replaying this old simulacrum of my childhood, he was dreaming himself into reclaiming my respect and love, instead of facing the reality of what he had done and the real me.

Perhaps it is the dream of every parent to keep their child in that brief period between helpless dependence and separate selfhood, when the parent is seen as perfect, faultless. It is a dream of control and mastery disguised as love, the dream that Lear had about Cordelia.

I walked down the stairs and out of the house, and I have not spoken to him since.

PAUL LARIMORE:

A simulacrum lives in the eternal now. It remembers, but only hazily, since the oneiropagida does not have the resolution to discern and capture the subject's every specific memory. It learns, up to a fashion, but the further you stray from the moment the subject's mental life was captured, the less accurate the computer's extrapolations. Even the best cameras we offer can't project beyond a couple of hours.

But the oneiropagida is exquisite at capturing her mood, the emotional flavor of her thoughts, the quirky triggers for her smiles, the lilt of her speech, the precise, inarticulable quality of her turns of phrase.

And so, every two hours or so, Anna resets. She's again coming home from day camp, and again she's full of questions and stories for me. We talk, we have fun. We let our chat wander wherever it will. No conversation is ever the same. But she's forever the curious seven-year-old who worshipped her father, and who thought he could do no wrong.

—*Dad, will you tell me a story?*
—Yes, of course. What story would you like?
—*I want to hear your cyberpunk version of Pinocchio again.*
—I'm not sure if I can remember everything I said last time.
—*It's okay. Just start. I'll help you.*

I love her so much.

ERIN LARIMORE:

My baby, I don't know when you'll get this. Maybe it will only be after I'm gone. You can't skip over the next part. It's a recording. I want you to hear what I have to say.

Your father misses you.

He's not perfect, and he has committed his share of sins, the same as any man. But you have let that one moment, when he was at his weakest, overwhelm the entirety of your life together. You have compressed him, the whole of his life, into that one frozen afternoon, that sliver of him that was most flawed. In your mind, you traced that captured image again and again, until the person was erased by the stencil.

During all these years when you have locked him out, your father played an old simulacrum of you over and over, laughing, joking, pouring his heart out to you in a way that a seven-year-old would understand. I would ask you on the phone if you'd speak to him, and then I couldn't bear to watch as I hung up while he went back to play the simulacrum again.

See him for who he really is.

—Hello there. Have you seen my daughter Anna?

THE REGULAR

"This is Jasmine," she says.

"It's Robert."

The voice on the phone is the same as the one she had spoken to earlier in the afternoon.

"Glad you made it, sweetie." She looks out the window. He's standing at the corner, in front of the convenience store, as she asked. He looks clean and is dressed well, like he's going on a date. A good sign. He's also wearing a Red Sox cap pulled low over his brow, a rather amateurish attempt at anonymity. "I'm down the street from you, at 27 Moreland. It's the gray stone condo building converted from a church."

He turns to look. "You have a sense of humor."

They all make that joke, but she laughs, anyway. "I'm in unit twenty-four, on the second floor."

"Is it just you? I'm not going to see some linebacker type demanding that I pay him first?"

"I told you. I'm independent. Just have your donation ready, and you'll have a good time."

She hangs up and takes a quick look in the mirror to be sure she's ready. The black stockings and garter belt are new, and the lace bustier accentuates her thin waist and makes her breasts seem larger. She's done her makeup lightly, but the eye shadow is heavy to emphasize her eyes. Most of her customers like that. Exotic.

The sheets on the king-size bed are fresh, and there's a small wicker basket of condoms on the nightstand, next to a clock that says

5:58. The date is for two hours, and afterward she'll have enough time to clean up and shower and then sit in front of the TV to catch her favorite show. She thinks about calling her mom later that night to ask about how to cook porgy.

She opens the door before he can knock, and the look on his face tells her that she's done well. He slips in; she closes the door, leans against it, and smiles at him.

"You're even prettier than the picture in your ad," he says. He gazes into her eyes intently. "Especially the eyes."

"Thank you."

As she gets a good look at him in the hallway, she concentrates on her right eye and blinks rapidly twice. She doesn't think she'll ever need it, but a girl has to protect herself. If she ever stops doing this, she thinks she'll just have it taken out and thrown into the bottom of Boston Harbor, like the way she used to, as a little girl, write secrets down on bits of paper, wad them up, and flush them down the toilet.

He's good-looking in a nonmemorable way: over six feet, tanned skin, still has all his hair, and the body under that crisp shirt looks fit. The eyes are friendly and kind, and she's pretty sure he won't be too rough. She guesses that he's in his forties, and maybe works downtown in one of the law firms or financial services companies, where his long-sleeved shirt and dark pants make sense with the air-conditioning always turned high. He has that entitled arrogance that many mistake for masculine attractiveness. She notices that there's a paler patch of skin around his ring finger. Even better. A married man is usually safer. A married man who doesn't want her to know he's married is the safest of all: he values what he has and doesn't want to lose it.

She hopes he'll be a regular.

"I'm glad we're doing this." He holds out a plain white envelope.

She takes it and counts the bills inside. Then she puts it on top of the stack of mail on a small table by the entrance without saying anything. She takes him by the hand and leads him toward the bedroom. He pauses to look in the bathroom and then the other bedroom at the end of the hall.

"Looking for your linebacker?" she teases.

"Just making sure. I'm a nice guy."

He takes out a scanner and holds it up, concentrating on the screen.

"Geez, you *are* paranoid," she says. "The only camera in here is the one on my phone. And it's definitely off."

He puts the scanner away and smiles. "I know. But I just wanted to have a machine confirm it."

They enter the bedroom. She watches him take in the bed, the bottles of lubricants and lotions on the dresser, and the long mirrors covering the closet doors next to the bed.

"Nervous?" she asks.

"A little," he concedes. "I don't do this often. Or, at all."

She comes up to him and embraces him, letting him breathe in her perfume, which is floral and light, so that it won't linger on his skin. After a moment, he puts his arms around her, resting his hands against the naked skin on the small of her back.

"I've always believed that one should pay for experiences rather than things."

"A good philosophy," he whispers into her ear.

"What I give you is the girlfriend experience, old-fashioned and sweet. And you'll remember this and relive it in your head as often as you want."

"You'll do whatever I want?"

"Within reason," she says. Then she lifts her head to look up at him. "You have to wear a condom. Other than that, I won't say no to most things. But like I told you on the phone, for some you'll have to pay extra."

"I'm pretty old-fashioned myself. Do you mind if I take charge?"

He's made her relaxed enough that she doesn't jump to the worst conclusion. "If you're thinking of tying me down, that will cost you. And I won't do that until I know you better."

"Nothing like that. Maybe hold you down a little."

"That's fine."

He comes up to her, and they kiss. His tongue lingers in her mouth, and she moans. He backs up, puts his hands on her waist, turning her away from him. "Would you lie down with your face in the pillows?"

"Of course." She climbs onto the bed. "Legs up under me or spread out to the corners?"

"Spread out, please." His voice is commanding. And he hasn't stripped yet, not even taken off his Red Sox cap. She's a little disappointed. Some clients enjoy the obedience more than the sex. There's not much for her to do. She just hopes he won't be too rough and leave marks.

He climbs onto the bed behind her and knee-walks up between her legs. He leans down and grabs a pillow from next to her head. "Very lovely," he says. "I'm going to hold you down now."

She sighs into the bed, the way she knows he'll like.

He lays the pillow over the back of her head and pushes down firmly to hold her in place. He takes the gun out from where it's hidden against the small of his back, and in one swift motion, sticks the barrel—thick and long with the silencer—into the back of the bustier and squeezes off two quick shots into her heart. She dies instantly.

He removes the pillow, stores the gun away. Then he takes a small steel surgical kit out of his jacket pocket, along with a pair of latex gloves. He works efficiently and quickly, cutting with precision and grace. He relaxes when he's found what he's looking for; sometimes he picks the wrong girl—not often, but it has happened. He's careful to wipe off any sweat on his face with his sleeves as he works, and the hat helps to prevent any hair from falling on her. Soon, the task is done.

He climbs off the bed, takes off the bloody gloves, and leaves them and the surgical kit on the body. He puts on a fresh pair of gloves and moves through the apartment, methodically searching for places where she hid cash: inside the toilet tank, the back of the freezer, the nook above the door of the closet.

He goes into the kitchen and returns with a large plastic trash bag. He picks up the bloody gloves and the surgical kit and throws them into the bag. Picking up her phone, he presses the button for her voice mail. He deletes all the messages, including the one he had left when he first called her number. There's not much he can do about the call logs at the phone company, but he can take advantage of that by leaving his prepaid phone somewhere for the police to find.

He looks at her again. He's not sad, not exactly, but he does feel a sense of waste. The girl was pretty, and he would have liked to enjoy her first, but that would leave behind too many traces, even with a condom. And he can always pay for another, later. He likes paying for things. Power flows to *him* when he pays.

Reaching into the inner pocket of his jacket, he retrieves a sheet of paper, which he carefully unfolds and leaves by the girl's head.

He stuffs the trash bag and the money into a small gym bag he found in one of the closets. He leaves quietly, picking up the envelope of cash next to the entrance on the way out.

Because she's meticulous, Ruth Law runs through the numbers on the spreadsheet one last time, a summary culled from credit card and bank statements, and compares them against the numbers on the tax return. There's no doubt. The client's husband has been hiding money from the IRS, and more importantly, from the client.

Summers in Boston can be brutally hot. But Ruth keeps the air conditioner off in her tiny office above a butcher shop in Chinatown.

She's made a lot of people unhappy over the years, and there's no reason to make it any easier for them to sneak up on her with the extra noise.

She takes out her cell phone and starts to dial from memory. She never stores any numbers in the phone. She tells people it's for safety, but sometimes she wonders if it's a gesture, however small, of asserting her independence from machines.

She stops at the sound of someone coming up the stairs. The footfalls are crisp and dainty, probably a woman, probably one with sensible heels. The scanner in the stairway hasn't been set off by the presence of a weapon, but that doesn't mean anything—she can kill without a gun or knife, and so can many others.

Ruth deposits her phone noiselessly on the desk and reaches into her drawer to wrap the fingers of her right hand around the reassuring grip of the Glock 19. Only then does she turn slightly to the side to glance at the monitor showing the feed from the security camera mounted over the door.

She feels very calm. The Regulator is doing its job. There's no need to release any adrenaline yet.

The visitor, in her fifties, is in a blue short-sleeve cardigan and white pants. She's looking around the door for a button for the doorbell. Her hair is so black that it must be dyed. She looks Chinese, holding her thin, petite body in a tight, nervous posture.

Ruth relaxes and lets go of the gun to push the button to open the door. She stands up and holds out her hand. "What can I do for you?"

"Are you Ruth Law, the private investigator?" In the woman's accent, Ruth hears traces of Mandarin rather than Cantonese or Fukienese. Probably not well-connected in Chinatown, then.

"I am."

The woman looks surprised, as if Ruth isn't quite who she expected. "Sarah Ding. I thought you were Chinese."

As they shake hands, Ruth looks Sarah level in the eyes: They're about the same height, five foot four. Sarah looks well maintained, but her fingers feel cold and thin, like a bird's claw.

"I'm half-Chinese," Ruth says. "My father was Cantonese, second generation; my mother was white. My Cantonese is barely passable, and I never learned Mandarin."

Sarah sits down in the armchair across from Ruth's desk. "But you have an office here."

She shrugs. "I've made my enemies. A lot of non-Chinese are uncomfortable moving around in Chinatown. They stick out. So it's safer for me to have my office here. Besides, you can't beat the rent."

Sarah nods wearily. "I need your help with my daughter." She slides a collapsible file across the desk toward her.

Ruth sits down but doesn't reach for the file. "Tell me about her."

"Mona was working as an escort. A month ago she was shot and killed in her apartment. The police think it's a robbery, maybe gang related, and they have no leads."

"It's a dangerous profession," Ruth says. "Did you know she was doing it?"

"No. Mona had some difficulties after college, and we were never as close as . . . I would have liked. We thought she was doing better the last two years, and she told us she had a job in publishing. It's difficult to know your child when you can't be the kind of mother she wants or needs. This country has different rules."

Ruth nods. A familiar lament from immigrants. "I'm sorry for your loss. But it's unlikely I'll be able to do anything. Most of my cases now are about hidden assets, cheating spouses, insurance fraud, background checks—that sort of thing. Back when I was a member of the force, I did work in Homicide. I know the detectives are quite thorough in murder cases."

"They're not!" Fury and desperation strain and crack her voice. "They think she's just a Chinese whore and she died because she was stupid or got involved with a Chinese gang who wouldn't bother regular people. My husband is so ashamed that he won't even mention her name. But she's my daughter, and she's worth everything I have, and more."

Ruth looks at her. She can feel the Regulator suppressing her pity. Pity can lead to bad business decisions.

"I keep on thinking there was some sign I should have seen, some way to tell her that I loved her that I didn't know. If only I had been a little less busy, a little more willing to pry and dig and to be hurt by her. I can't stand the way the detectives talk to me, like I'm wasting their time but they don't want to show it."

Ruth refrains from explaining that the police detectives are all fitted with Regulators that should make the kind of prejudice she's implying impossible. The whole point of the Regulator is to make police work under pressure more regular, less dependent on hunches, emotional impulses, appeals to hidden prejudice. If the police are calling it a gang-related act of violence, there are likely good reasons for doing so.

She says nothing because the woman in front of her is in pain, and guilt and love are so mixed up in her that she thinks paying to find her daughter's killer will make her feel better about being the kind of mother whose daughter would take up prostitution.

Her angry, helpless posture reminds Ruth vaguely of something she tries to put out of her mind.

"Even if I find the killer," she says, "it won't make you feel better."

"I don't care." Sarah tries to shrug, but the American gesture looks awkward and uncertain on her. "My husband thinks I've gone crazy. I know how hopeless this is; you're not the first investigator I've spoken to. But a few suggested you because you're a woman and Chinese, so maybe you care just enough to see something they can't."

She reaches into her purse and retrieves a check, sliding it across the table to put on top of the file. "Here's eighty thousand dollars. I'll pay double your daily rate and all expenses. If you use it up, I can get you more."

Ruth stares at the check. She thinks about the sorry state of her finances. At forty-nine, how many more chances will she have to set aside some money for when she'll be too old to do this?

She still feels calm and completely rational, and she knows that the Regulator is doing its job. She's sure that she's making her decision based on costs and benefits and a realistic evaluation of the case, and not because of the hunched-over shoulders of Sarah Ding, looking like fragile twin dams holding back a flood of grief.

"Okay," she says. "Okay."

The man's name isn't Robert. It's not Paul or Matt or Barry, either. He never uses the name John, because jokes like that will only make the girls nervous. A long time ago, before he had been to prison, they had called him the Watcher, because he liked to observe and take in a scene, finding the best opportunities and escape routes. He still thinks of himself that way when he's alone.

In the room he's rented at the cheap motel along Route 128, he starts his day by taking a shower to wash off the night sweat.

This is the fifth motel he's stayed in during the last month. Any stay longer than a week tends to catch the attention of the people working at the motels. He watches; he does not get watched. Ideally, he supposes he should get away from Boston altogether, but he hasn't exhausted the city's possibilities. It doesn't feel right to leave before he's seen all he wants to see.

The Watcher got about sixty thousand dollars in cash from the girl's apartment, not bad for a day's work. The girls he picks are intensely aware of the brevity of their careers, and with no bad habits, they pack away money like squirrels preparing for the winter. Since they can't exactly put it into the bank without raising the suspicion of the IRS, they tuck the money away in stashes in their apartments, ready for him to come along and claim them like found treasure.

The money is a nice bonus, but not the main attraction.

He comes out of the shower, dries himself, and wrapped in a towel, sits down to work at the nut he's trying to crack. It's a small, silver half sphere, like half of a walnut. When he had first gotten it, it had been covered in blood and gore, and he had wiped it again and again with paper towels moistened under the motel sink until it gleamed.

He pries open an access port on the back of the device. Opening his laptop, he plugs one end of a cable into it and the other end into the half sphere. He starts a program he had paid a good sum of money for and lets it run. It would probably be more efficient for him to leave the program running all the time, but he likes to be there to see the moment the encryption is broken.

While the program runs, he browses the escort ads. Right now he's searching for pleasure, not business, so instead of looking for girls like Jasmine, he looks for girls he craves. They're expensive, but not too expensive, the kind that remind him of the girls he had wanted back in high school: loud, fun, curvaceous now but destined to put on too much weight in a few years, a careless beauty that was all the more desirable because it was fleeting.

The Watcher knows that only a poor man like he had been at seventeen would bother courting women, trying desperately to make them like him. A man with money, with power, like he is now, can buy what he wants. There's purity and cleanliness to his desire that he feels is nobler and less deceitful than the desire of poor men. They only wish they could have what he does.

The program beeps, and he switches back to it.

Success.

Images, videos, sound recordings are being downloaded onto the computer.

The Watcher browses through the pictures and video recordings. The pictures are face shots or shots of money being handed over—he immediately deletes the ones of him.

But the videos are the best. He settles back and watches the screen flicker, admiring Jasmine's camera work.

He separates the videos and images by client and puts them into folders. It's tedious work, but he enjoys it.

The first thing Ruth does with the money is to get some badly needed tune-ups. Going after a killer requires that she be in top condition.

She does not like to carry a gun when she's on the job. A man in a sport coat with a gun concealed under it can blend into almost any situation, but a woman wearing the kind of clothes that would hide a gun would often stick out like a sore thumb. Keeping a gun in a purse is a terrible idea. It creates a false sense of security, but a purse can be easily snatched away, and then she would be disarmed.

She's fit and strong for her age, but her opponents are almost always taller and heavier and stronger. She's learned to compensate for these disadvantages by being more alert and by striking earlier.

But it's still not enough.

She goes to her doctor. Not the one on her HMO card.

Doctor B had earned his degree in another country and then had to leave home forever because he pissed off the wrong people. Instead of doing a second residency and becoming licensed here, which would have made him easily traceable, he had decided to simply keep on practicing medicine on his own. He would do things doctors who cared about their licenses wouldn't do. He would take patients they wouldn't touch.

"It's been a while," Doctor B says.

"Check over everything," she tells him. "And replace what needs replacement."

"Rich uncle die?"

"I'm going on a hunt."

Doctor B nods and puts her under.

He checks the pneumatic pistons in her legs, the replacement composite tendons in her shoulders and arms, the power cells and artificial muscles in her arms, the reinforced finger bones. He recharges what needs to be recharged. He examines the results of the calcium-deposition treatments (a counter to the fragility of her bones, an unfortunate side effect of her Asian heritage), and makes adjustments to her Regulator so that she can keep it on for longer.

"Like new," he tells her. And she pays.

Next, Ruth looks through the file Sarah brought.

There are photographs: the prom, high school graduation, vacations with friends, college commencement. She notes the name of the school without surprise or sorrow, even though Jess had dreamed of going there as well. The Regulator, as always, keeps her equanimous, receptive to information, only useful information.

The last family photo Sarah selected was taken at Mona's twenty-fourth birthday earlier in the year. Ruth examines it carefully. In the picture, Mona is seated between Sarah and her husband, her arms around her parents in a gesture of careless joy. There's no hint of the secret she was keeping from them, and no sign, as far as Ruth can tell, of bruises, drugs, or other indications that life was slipping out of her control.

Sarah had chosen the photos with care. The pictures are designed to fill in Mona's life, to make people care for her. But she didn't need to do that. Ruth would have given it the same amount of effort, even if she knew nothing about the girl's life. She's a professional.

There's a copy of the police report and the autopsy results. The report mostly confirms what Ruth has already guessed: no sign of drugs in Mona's systems, no forced entry, no indication there was a struggle. There was pepper spray in the drawer of the nightstand, but it hadn't been used. Forensics had vacuumed the scene, and the hair and skin cells of dozens, maybe hundreds, of men had turned up, guaranteeing that no useful leads will result.

Mona had been killed with two shots through the heart, and then her body had been mutilated, with her eyes removed. She hadn't been sexually assaulted. The apartment had been ransacked of cash and valuables.

Ruth sits up. The method of killing is odd. If the killer had intended to mutilate her face, anyway, there was no reason not to shoot her in the back of the head, a cleaner, surer method of execution.

A note in Chinese was found at the scene, which declared that Mona had been punished for her sins. Ruth can't read Chinese, but she assumes the police translation is accurate. The police had also pulled Mona's phone records. There were a few numbers whose cell tower data showed their owners had been to Mona's place that day. The only one without an alibi was a prepaid phone without a registered owner. The police had tracked it down in Chinatown, hidden in a Dumpster. They hadn't been able to get any further.

A rather sloppy kill, Ruth thinks, *if the gangs did it.*

Sarah had also provided printouts of Mona's escort ads. Mona had used several aliases: Jasmine, Akiko, Sinn. Most of the pictures are of her in lingerie, a few in cocktail dresses. The shots are framed to emphasize her body: a side view of her breasts half-veiled in lace, a back view of her buttocks, lounging on the bed with her hand over her hip. Shots of her face have black bars over her eyes to provide some measure of anonymity.

Ruth boots up her computer and logs on to the sites to check out the other ads. She had never worked in vice, so she takes a while to familiarize herself with the lingo and acronyms. The Internet had apparently transformed the business, allowing women to get off the streets and become "independent providers" without pimps. The sites are organized to allow customers to pick out exactly what they want. They can sort and filter by price, age, services provided, ethnicity, hair and eye colors, time of availability, and customer ratings. The business is competitive, and there's a brutal efficiency to the sites that Ruth might have found depressing without the Regulator: You can measure, if you apply statistical software to it, how much a girl depreciates with each passing year; how much value men place on each pound, each inch of deviation from the ideal they're seeking; how much more a blonde really is worth than a brunette; and how much more a girl who can pass as Japanese can charge than one who cannot.

Some of the ad sites charge a membership fee to see pictures of the girls' faces. Sarah had also printed these "premium" photographs of Mona. For a brief moment, Ruth wonders what Sarah must have felt as she paid to unveil the seductive gaze of her daughter, the daughter who had seemed to have a trouble-free, promising future.

In these pictures, Mona's face was made up lightly, her lips curved in a promising or innocent smile. She was extraordinarily pretty, even compared to the other girls in her price range. She dictated incalls only, perhaps believing them to be safer, with her being more in control.

Compared to most of the other girls, Mona's ads can be described as "elegant." They're free of spelling errors and overtly crude language, hinting at the kind of sexual fantasies that men here harbor about Asian women while also promising an American wholesomeness, the contrast emphasizing the strategically placed bits of exoticism.

The anonymous customer reviews praised her attitude and willingness to "go the extra mile." Ruth supposes that Mona had earned good tips.

Ruth turns to the crime scene photos and the bloody, eyeless shots of Mona's face. Intellectually and dispassionately, she absorbs the details in Mona's room. She contemplates the contrast between them and the eroticism of the ad's photos. This was a young woman who had been vain about her education, who had believed that she could construct, through careful words and images, a kind of filter to attract the right kind of clients. It was naive and wise at the same time, and Ruth can almost feel, despite the Regulator, a kind of poignancy to her confident desperation.

Whatever caused her to go down this path, she had never hurt anyone, and now she was dead.

Ruth meets Luo in a room reached through long underground tunnels and many locked doors. It smells of mold and sweat and spicy foods rotting in trash bags.

Along the way she saw a few other locked rooms behind which she guessed were human cargo, people who indentured themselves to the snakeheads for a chance to be smuggled into this country so they could work for a dream of wealth. She says nothing about them. Her deal with Luo depends on her discretion, and Luo is kinder to his cargo than many others.

He pats her down perfunctorily. She offers to strip to show that she's not wired. He waves her off.

"Have you seen this woman?" she asks in Cantonese, holding up a picture of Mona.

Luo dangles the cigarette from his lips while he examines the picture closely. The dim light gives the tattoos on his bare shoulders and arms a greenish tint. After a moment, he hands it back. "I don't think so."

"She was a prostitute working out of Quincy. Someone killed her a month ago and left this behind." She brings out the photograph of the note left at the scene. "The police think the Chinese gangs did it."

Luo looks at the photo. He knits his brow in concentration and then barks out a dry laugh. "Yes, this is indeed a note left behind by a Chinese gang."

"Do you recognize the gang?"

"Sure." Luo looks at Ruth, a grin revealing the gaps in his teeth. "This note was left behind by the impetuous Tak-Kao, member of the Forever Peace Gang, after he killed the innocent Mai-Ying, the beautiful maid from the mainland, in a fit of jealousy. You can see the original in the third season of *My Hong Kong, Your Hong Kong*. You're lucky that I'm a fan."

"This is copied from a soap opera?"

"Yes. Your man either likes to make jokes or doesn't know Chinese well and got this from some Internet search. It might fool the police, but no, we wouldn't leave a note like that." He chuckles at the thought and then spits on the ground.

"Maybe it was just a fake to confuse the police." She chooses her words carefully. "Or maybe it was done by one gang to sic the police onto the others. The police also found a phone, probably used by the killer, in a Chinatown Dumpster. I know there are several Asian massage parlors in Quincy, so maybe this girl was too much competition. Are you sure you don't know anything about this?"

Luo flips through the other photographs of Mona. Ruth watches him, getting ready to react to any sudden movements. She thinks she can trust Luo, but one can't always predict the reaction of a man who often has to kill to make his living.

She concentrates on the Regulator, priming it to release adrenaline to quicken her movements if necessary. The pneumatics in her legs are charged, and she braces her back against the damp wall, in case she needs to kick out. The sudden release of pressure in the air canisters installed next to her tibia will straighten her legs in a fraction of a second, generating hundreds of pounds of force. If her feet connect with Luo's chest, she will almost certainly break a few ribs— though Ruth's back will ache for days afterward, as well.

"I like you, Ruth," Luo says, noting her sudden stillness out of the corner of his eyes. "You don't have to be afraid. I haven't forgotten how you found that bookie who tried to steal from me. I'll always tell you the truth or tell you I can't answer. We have nothing to do with this girl. She's not really competition. The men who go to massage parlors for sixty dollars an hour and a happy ending are not the kind who'd pay for a girl like this."

The Watcher drives to Somerville, just over the border from Cambridge, north of Boston. He parks in the back of a grocery store parking lot, where his Toyota Corolla, bought with cash off a lot, doesn't stick out.

Then he goes into a coffee shop and emerges with an iced coffee. Sipping it, he walks around the sunny streets, gazing from time to time at the little gizmo attached to his key chain. The gizmo tells him when he's in range of some unsecured home wireless network. Lots of students from Harvard and MIT live here, where the rent is high but not astronomical. Addicted to good wireless access, they often get powerful routers for tiny apartments and leak the network onto the streets without bothering to secure them (after all, they have friends coming over all the time who need to remain connected). And since it's summer, when the population of students is in flux, there's even less likelihood that he can be traced from using one of their networks.

It's probably overkill, but he likes to be safe.

He sits down on a bench by the side of the street, takes out his laptop, and connects to a network called "INFORMATION_WANTS_TO_BE_FREE." He enjoys disproving the network owner's theory. Information doesn't want to be free. It's valuable and wants to earn. And its existence doesn't free anyone; possessing it, however, can do the opposite.

The Watcher carefully selects a segment of video and watches it one last time.

Jasmine had done a good job, intentionally or not, with the

framing, and the man's sweaty grimace is featured prominently in the video. His movements—and as a result, Jasmine's—made the video jerky, and so he's had to apply software image stabilization. But now it looks quite professional.

The Watcher had tried to identify the man, who looks Chinese, by uploading a picture he got from Jasmine into a search engine. They are always making advancements in facial recognition software, and sometimes he gets hits this way. But it didn't seem to work this time. That's not a problem for the Watcher. He has other techniques.

The Watcher signs on to a forum where the expat Chinese congregate to reminisce and argue politics in their homeland. He posts the picture of the man in the video and writes below in English, "Anyone famous?" Then he sips his coffee and refreshes the screen from time to time to catch the new replies.

The Watcher doesn't read Chinese (or Russian, or Arabic, or Hindi, or any of the other languages where he plies his trade), but linguistic skills are hardly necessary for this task. Most of the expats speak English and can understand his question. He's just using these people as research tools, a human flesh-powered, crowdsourced search engine. It's almost funny how people are so willing to give perfect strangers over the Internet information, would even compete with each other to do it, to show how knowledgeable they are. He's pleased to make use of such petty vanities.

He simply needs a name and a measure of the prominence of the man, and for that, the crude translations offered by computers are sufficient.

From the almost-gibberish translations, he gathers that the man is a prominent official in the Chinese Transport Ministry, and like almost all Chinese officials, he's despised by his countrymen. The man is a bigger deal than the Watcher's usual targets, but that might make him a good demonstration.

The Watcher is thankful for Dagger, who had explained Chinese politics to him. One evening, after he had gotten out of jail the last time, the Watcher had hung back and watched a Chinese man rob a few Chinese tourists near San Francisco's Chinatown.

The tourists had managed to make a call to 911, and the robber had fled the scene on foot down an alley. But the Watcher had seen something in the man's direct, simple approach that he liked. He drove around the block, stopped by the other end of the alley, and when the man emerged, he swung open the passenger-side door and offered him a chance to escape in his car. The man thanked him and told him his name was Dagger.

Dagger was talkative and told the Watcher how angry and envious people in China were of the Party officials, who lived an extravagant life on the money squeezed from the common people, took bribes, and funneled public funds to their relatives. He targeted those tourists who he thought were the officials' wives and children and regarded himself as a modern-day Robin Hood.

Yet, the officials were not completely immune. All it took was a public scandal of some kind, usually involving young women who were not their wives. Talk of democracy didn't get people excited, but seeing an official rubbing their graft in their faces made them see red. And the Party apparatus would have no choice but to punish the disgraced officials, as the only thing the Party feared was public anger, which always threatened to boil out of control. If a revolution were to come to China, Dagger quipped, it would be triggered by mistresses, not speeches.

A light had gone on in the Watcher's head then. It was as if he could see the reins of power flowing from those who had secrets to those who knew secrets. He thanked Dagger and dropped him off, wishing him well.

The Watcher imagines what the official's visit to Boston had been like. He had probably come to learn about the city's experience with light rail, but it was likely in reality just another state-funded vacation, a chance to shop at the luxury stores on Newbury Street, to enjoy expensive foods without fear of poison or pollution, and to anonymously take delight in quality female companionship without the threat of recording devices in the hands of an interested populace.

He posts the video to the forum, and as an extra flourish, adds a link to the official's biography on the Transport Ministry's website. For a second, he regrets the forgone revenue, but it's been a while since he's done a demonstration, and these are necessary to keep the business going.

He packs up his laptop. Now, he has to wait.

Ruth doesn't think there's much value in viewing Mona's apartment, but she's learned over the years not to leave any stone unturned. She gets the key from Sarah Ding and makes her way to the apartment around six in the evening. Viewing the site at approximately the time of day when the murder occurred can sometimes be helpful.

She passes through the living room. There's a small TV facing a futon, the kind of furniture that a young woman keeps from her college days when she doesn't have a reason to upgrade. It's a living room that was never meant for visitors.

She moves into the room in which the murder happened. The forensics team has cleaned it out. The room—it wasn't Mona's real bedroom, which was a tiny cubby down the hall, with just a twin bed and plain walls—is stripped bare, most of the loose items having been collected as evidence. The mattress is naked, as are the nightstands. The carpet has been vacuumed. The place smells like a hotel room: stale air and faint perfume.

Ruth notices the line of mirrors along the side of the bed, hanging over the closet doors. Watching arouses people.

She imagines how lonely Mona must have felt living here, touched and kissed and fucked by a stream of men who kept as much of themselves hidden from her as possible. She imagines her sitting in front of the small TV to relax and dressing up to meet her parents so that she could lie some more.

Ruth imagines the way the murderer had shot Mona and then cut her after. Was there more than one of them so that Mona thought a struggle was useless? Did they shoot her right away, or did they ask her to tell them where she had hidden her money first? She can feel the Regulator starting up again, keeping her emotions in check. Evil has to be confronted dispassionately.

She decides she's seen all she needs to see. She leaves the apartment and pulls the door closed. As she heads for the stairs, she sees a man coming up, keys in hand. Their eyes briefly meet, and he turns to the door of the apartment across the hall.

Ruth is sure the police have interviewed the neighbor. But sometimes people will tell things to a nonthreatening woman that they are reluctant to tell the cops.

She walks over and introduces herself, explaining that she's a friend of Mona's family, here to tie up some loose ends. The man, whose name is Peter, is wary but shakes her hand.

"I didn't hear or see anything. We pretty much keep to ourselves in this building."

"I believe you. But it would be helpful if we can chat a bit, anyway. The family didn't know much about her life here."

He nods reluctantly and opens the door. He steps in and waves his arms up and around in a complex sequence as though he's conducting an orchestra. The lights come on.

"That's pretty fancy," Ruth says. "You have the whole place wired up like that?"

His voice, cautious and guarded until now, grows animated.

Talking about something other than the murder seems to relax him. "Yes. It's called EchoSense. They add an adapter to your wireless router, and a few antennas around the room, and then it uses the Doppler shifts generated by your body's movements in the radio waves to detect gestures."

"You mean it can see you move with just the signals from your Wi-Fi bouncing around the room?"

"Something like that."

Ruth remembers seeing an infomercial about this. She notes how small the apartment is and how little space separates it from Mona's. They sit down and chat about what Peter remembers about Mona.

"Pretty girl. Way out of my league, but she was always pleasant."

"Did she get a lot of visitors?"

"I don't pry into other people's business. But yeah, I remember lots of visitors, mostly men. I did think she might have been an escort. But that didn't bother me. The men always seemed clean, business types. Not dangerous."

"No one who looked like a gangster, for example?"

"I wouldn't know what gangsters look like. But no, I don't think so."

They chat on inconsequentially for another fifteen minutes, and Ruth decides that she's wasted enough time.

"Can I buy the router from you?" she asks. "And the EchoSense thing."

"You can just order your own set online."

"I hate shopping online. You can never return things. I know this one works; so I want it. I'll offer you two thousand, cash."

He considers this.

"I bet you can buy a new one and get another adapter yourself from EchoSense for less than a quarter of that."

He nods and retrieves the router, and she pays him. The act feels somehow illicit, not unlike how she imagines Mona's transactions were.

Ruth posts an ad to a local classifieds site, describing in vague terms what she's looking for. Boston is blessed with many good colleges and lots of young men and women who would relish a technical challenge even more than the money she offers. She looks through the résumés until she finds the one she feels has the right skills: jailbreaking phones, reverse-engineering proprietary protocols, a healthy disrespect for acronyms like DMCA and CFAA.

She meets the young man at her office and explains what she wants. Daniel—dark-skinned, lanky, and shy—slouches in the chair across from hers as he listens without interrupting.

"Can you do it?" she asks.

"Maybe," he says. "Companies like this one will usually send customer data back to the mothership anonymously to help improve their technology. Sometimes the data is cached locally for a while. It's possible I'll find logs on there a month old. If it's there, I'll get it for you. But I'll have to figure out how they're encoding the data and then make sense of it."

"Do you think my theory is plausible?"

"I'm impressed you even came up with it. Wireless signals can go through walls, so it's certainly possible that this adapter has captured the movements of people in neighboring apartments. It's a privacy nightmare, and I'm sure the company doesn't publicize that."

"How long will it take?"

"As little as a day or as much as a month. I won't know until I start. It will help if you can draw me a map of the apartments and what's inside."

Ruth does as he asked. Then she tells him, "I'll pay you three hundred dollars a day, with a five-thousand-dollar bonus if you succeed this week."

"Deal." He grins and picks up the router, getting ready to leave.

Because it never hurts to tell people what they're doing is

meaningful, she adds, "You're helping to catch the killer of a young woman who's not much older than you."

Then she goes home because she's run out of things to try.

The first hour after waking up is always the worst part of the day for Ruth.

As usual, she wakes from a nightmare. She lies still, disoriented, the images from her dream superimposed over the sight of the water stains on the ceiling. Her body is drenched in sweat.

The man holds Jessica in front of him with his left hand while the gun in his right hand is pointed at her head. She's terrified, but not of him. He ducks so that her body shields his, and he whispers something into her ear.

"Mom! Mom!" she screams. "Don't shoot. Please don't shoot!"

Ruth rolls over, nauseated. She sits up at the edge of the bed, hating the smell of the hot room, the dust that she never has time to clean filling the air pierced by bright rays coming in from the east-facing window. She shoves the sheets off her and stands up quickly, her breath coming too fast. She's fighting the rising panic without any help, alone, her Regulator off.

The clock on the nightstand says six o'clock.

She's crouching behind the opened driver's-side door of her car. Her hands shake as she struggles to keep the man's head, bobbing besides her daughter's, in the sight of her gun. If she turns on her Regulator, she thinks her hands may grow steady and give her a clear shot at him.

What are her chances of hitting him instead of her? Ninety-five percent? Ninety-nine?

"Mom! Mom! No!"

She gets up and stumbles into the kitchen to turn on the coffeemaker. She curses when she finds the can empty and throws it clattering into the sink. The noise shocks her, and she cringes.

Then she struggles into the shower, sluggishly, painfully, as though the muscles that she conditions daily through hard exercise were not there. She turns on the hot water, but it brings no warmth to her shivering body.

Grief descends on her like a heavy weight. She sits down in the shower, curling her body into itself. Water streams down her face so she does not know if there are tears as her body heaves.

She fights the impulse to turn on the Regulator. It's not time yet. She has to give her body the necessary rest.

The Regulator, a collection of chips and circuitry embedded at the top of her spine, is tied into the limbic system and the major blood vessels into the brain. Like its namesake from mechanical and electrical engineering, it maintains the levels of dopamine, noradrenaline, serotonin, and other chemicals in the brain and in her bloodstream. It filters out the chemicals when there's an excess and releases them when there's a deficit.

And it obeys her will.

The implant allows a person control over her basic emotions: fear, disgust, joy, excitement, love. It's mandatory for law enforcement officers, a way to minimize the effects of emotions on life-or-death decisions, a way to eliminate prejudice and irrationality.

"You have clearance to shoot," the voice in her headset tells her. It's the voice of her husband, Scott, the head of her department. His voice is completely calm. His Regulator is on.

She sees the head of the man bobbing up and down as he retreats with Jessica. He's heading for the van parked by the side of the road.

"He's got other hostages in there," her husband continues to speak in her ear. "If you don't shoot, you put the lives of those three other girls and who knows how many other people in danger. This is our best chance."

The sound of sirens, her backup, is still faint. Too far away.

After what seems an eternity, she manages to stand up in the shower and turn off the water. She towels herself dry and dresses slowly. She tries to think of something, anything, to take her mind off its current track. But nothing works.

She despises the raw state of her mind. Without the Regulator, she feels weak, confused, angry. Waves of despair wash over her, and everything appears in hopeless shades of gray. She wonders why she's still alive.

It will pass, she thinks. *Just a few more minutes.*

Back when she had been on the force, she had adhered to the regulation requirement not to leave the Regulator on for more than two hours at a time. There are physiological and psychological risks associated with prolonged use. Some of her fellow officers had also complained about the way the Regulator made them feel robotic, deadened. No excitement from seeing a pretty woman; no thrill at the potential for a car chase; no righteous anger when faced with an act of abuse. Everything had to be deliberate: You decided when to let the adrenaline flow, and just enough to get the job done and not too much to interfere with judgment. But sometimes, they argued, you needed emotions, instinct, intuition.

Her Regulator had been off when she came home that day and recognized the man hiding from the citywide manhunt.

Have I been working too much? she thinks. I don't know any of her friends. When did Jess meet him? Why didn't I ask her more questions when she was coming home late every night? Why did I stop for lunch instead of coming home half an hour earlier? There are a thousand things I could have done and should have done and would have done.

Fear and anger and regret are mixed up in her until she cannot tell which is which.

"Engage your Regulator," her husband's voice tells her. "You can make the shot."

Why do I care about the lives of the other girls? she thinks. All I care about is Jess. Even the smallest chance of hurting her is too much.

Can she trust a machine to save her daughter? Should she rely on a machine to steady her shaking hands, to clear her blurry vision, to make a shot without missing?

"Mom, he's going to let me go later. He won't hurt me. He just wants to get away from here. Put the gun down!"

Maybe Scott can make a calculus about lives saved and lives put at risk. She won't. She will not trust a machine.

"It's okay, baby," she croaks out. "It's all going to be okay."

She does not turn on the Regulator. She does not shoot.

Later, after she had identified the body of Jess—the bodies of all four of the girls had been badly burned when the bomb went off—after she had been disciplined and discharged, after Scott and she had split up, after she had found no solace in alcohol and pills, she did finally find the help she needed: she could leave the Regulator on all the time.

The Regulator deadened the pain, stifled grief, and numbed the ache of loss. It held down the regret, made it possible to pretend to forget. She craved the calmness it brought, the blameless, serene clarity.

She had been wrong to distrust it. That distrust had cost her Jess. She would not make the same mistake again.

Sometimes she thinks of the Regulator as a dependable lover, a comforting presence to lean on. Sometimes she thinks she's addicted. She does not probe deeply behind these thoughts.

She would have preferred to never have to turn off the Regulator, to never be in a position to repeat her mistake. But even Doctor B balked at that ("Your brain will turn into mush."). The illegal modifications he did agree to make allow the Regulator to remain on for a maximum of twenty-three hours at a stretch. Then she must take an hour-long break during which she must remain conscious.

And so there's always this hour in the morning, right as she wakes, when she's naked and alone with her memories, unshielded from the rush of red-hot hatred (for the man? for herself?) and white-cold rage, and the black, bottomless abyss that she endures as her punishment.

The alarm beeps. She concentrates like a monk in meditation and feels the hum of the Regulator starting up. Relief spreads out from the center of her mind to the very tips of her fingers, the soothing, numbing serenity of a regulated, disciplined mind. To be regulated is to be a regular person.

She stands up, limber, graceful, powerful, ready to hunt.

The Watcher has identified more of the men in the pictures. He's now in a new motel room, this one more expensive than usual because he feels like he deserves a treat after all he's been through. Hunching over all day to edit video is hard work.

He pans the cropping rectangle over the video to give it a sense of dynamism and movement. There's an artistry to this.

He's amazed how so few people seem to know about the eye implants. There's something about eyes—so vulnerable, so essential to the way people see the world and themselves—that makes people feel protective and reluctant to invade them. The laws regarding eye modifications are the most stringent, and after a while, people begin to mistake "not permitted" with "not possible."

They don't know what they don't want to know.

All his life, he's felt that he's missed some key piece of information, some secret that everyone else seemed to know. He's intelligent, diligent, but somehow things have not worked out.

He never knew his father, and when he was eleven, his mother had left him one day at home with twenty dollars and never came back. A string of foster homes had followed, and *nobody*, nobody could tell him what he was missing, why he was always at the mercy of judges and bureaucrats, why he had so little control over his life; not where he would sleep, not when he would eat, not who would have power over him next.

He made it his subject to study men, to watch and try to

understand what made them tick. Much of what he learned had disappointed him. Men were vain, proud, ignorant. They let their desires carry them away, ignored risks that were obvious. They did not think, did not plan. They did not know what they really wanted. They let the TV tell them what they should have and hoped that working at their pathetic jobs would make those wishes come true.

He craved control. He wanted to see them dance to his tune the way he had been made to dance to the tune of everyone else.

So he had honed himself to be pure and purposeful, like a sharp knife in a drawer full of ridiculous, ornate, fussy kitchen gadgets. He knew what he wanted, and he worked at getting it with singular purpose.

He adjusts the colors and the dynamic range to compensate for the dim light in the video. He wants there to be no mistake in identifying the man.

He stretches his tired arms and sore neck. For a moment, he wonders if he'll be better off if he pays to have parts of his body enhanced so he can work for longer, without pain and fatigue. But the momentary fancy passes.

Most people don't like medically unnecessary enhancements and would only accept them if they're required for a job. No such sentimental considerations for bodily integrity or "naturalness" constrain the Watcher. He does not like enhancements because he views reliance on them as a sign of weakness. He would defeat his enemies with his mind, and with the aid of planning and foresight. He does not need to depend on machines.

He had learned to steal, and then rob, and eventually how to kill for money. But the money was really secondary, just a means to an end. It was control that he desired. The only man he had killed was a lawyer, someone who lied for a living. Lying had brought him money, and that gave him power, made people bow down to him and smile at him and speak in respectful voices. The Watcher had loved that moment when the man begged him for mercy, when he would have done anything the Watcher wanted. The Watcher had taken what he wanted from the man rightfully, by superiority of intellect and strength. Yet, the Watcher had been caught and gone to jail for it. A system that rewarded liars and punished the Watcher could not in any sense be called just.

He presses "save." He's done with this video.

Knowledge of the truth gave him power, and he would make others acknowledge it.

Before Ruth is about to make her next move, Daniel calls, and they meet in her office again.

"I have what you wanted."

He takes out his laptop and shows her an animation, like a movie.

"They stored videos on the adapter?"

Daniel laughs. "No. The device can't really 'see,' and that would be far too much data. No, the adapter just stored readings, numbers. I made the animation so it's easier to understand."

She's impressed. The young man knows how to give a good presentation.

"The Wi-Fi echoes aren't captured with enough resolution to give you much detail. But you can get a rough sense of people's sizes and heights and their movements. This is what I got from the day and hour you specified."

They watch as a bigger, vaguely humanoid shape appears at Mona's apartment door, precisely at six, meeting a smaller, vaguely humanoid shape.

"Seems they had an appointment," Daniel says.

They watch as the smaller shape leads the bigger shape into the bedroom, and then the two embrace. They watch the smaller shape climb into space—presumably onto the bed. They watch the bigger shape climb up after it. They watch the shooting, and then the smaller shape collapses and disappears. They watch the bigger shape lean over, and the smaller shape flickers into existence as it's moved from time to time.

So there was only one killer, Ruth thinks. And he was a client.

"How tall is he?"

"There's a scale to the side."

Ruth watches the animation over and over. The man is six foot two or six foot three, maybe 180 to 200 pounds. She notices that he has a bit of a limp as he walks.

She's now convinced that Luo was telling the truth. Not many Chinese men are six foot two, and such a man would stick out too much to be a killer for a gang. Every witness would remember him. Mona's killer had been a client, maybe even a regular. It wasn't a random robbery but carefully planned.

The man is still out there, and killers that meticulous rarely kill only once.

"Thank you," she says. "You might be saving another young woman's life."

Ruth dials the number for the police department.

"Captain Brennan, please."

She gives her name, and her call is transferred, and then she hears the gruff, weary voice of her ex-husband. "What can I do for you?"

Once again, she's glad she has the Regulator. His voice dredges up memories of his raspy morning mumbles, his stentorian laughter, his tender whispers when they were alone, the soundtrack of twenty years of a life spent together, a life that they had both thought would last until one of them died.

"I need a favor."

He doesn't answer right away. She wonders if she's too abrupt—a side effect of leaving the Regulator on all the time. Maybe she should have started with "How've you been?"

Finally, he speaks. "What is it?" The voice is restrained, but laced with exhausted, desiccated pain.

"I'd like to use your NCIC access."

Another pause. "Why?"

"I'm working on the Mona Ding case. I think this is a man who's killed before and will kill again. He's got a method. I want to see if there are related cases in other cities."

"That's out of the question, Ruth. You know that. Besides, there's no point. We've run all the searches we can, and there's nothing similar. This was a Chinese gang protecting their business, simple as that. Until we have the resources in the Gang Unit to deal with it, I'm sorry, this will have to go cold for a while."

Ruth hears the unspoken. *The Chinese gangs have always preyed on their own. Until they bother the tourists, let's just leave them alone.* She'd heard similar sentiments often enough back when she was on the force. The Regulator could do nothing about certain kinds of prejudice. It's perfectly rational. And also perfectly wrong.

"I don't think so. I have an informant who says that the Chinese gangs have nothing to do with it."

Scott snorts. "Yes, of course you can trust the word of a Chinese snakehead. But there's also the note and the phone."

"The note is most likely a forgery. And do you really think this Chinese gang member would be smart enough to realize that the phone records would give him away and then decide that the best place to hide it was around his place of business?"

"Who knows? Criminals are stupid."

"The man is far too methodical for that. It's a red herring."

"You have no evidence."

"I have a good reconstruction of the crime and a description of the suspect. He's too tall to be the kind a Chinese gang would use."

This gets his attention. "From where?"

"A neighbor had a home motion-sensing system that captured wireless echoes into Mona's apartment. I paid someone to reconstruct it."

"Will that stand up in court?"

"I doubt it. It will take expert testimony, and you'll have to get the company to admit that they capture that information. They'll fight it tooth and nail."

"Then it's not much use to me."

"If you give me a chance to look in the database, maybe I can turn it into something you *can* use." She waits a second and presses on, hoping that he'll be sentimental. "I've never asked you for much."

"This is the first time you've ever asked me for something like this."

"I don't usually take on cases like this."

"What is it about this girl?"

Ruth considers the question. There are two ways to answer it. She can try to explain the fee she's being paid and why she feels she's adding value. Or she can give what she suspects is the real reason. Sometimes the Regulator makes it hard to tell what's true. "Sometimes people think the police don't look as hard when the victim is a sex worker. I know your resources are constrained, but maybe I can help."

"It's the mother, isn't it? You feel bad for her."

Ruth does not answer. She can feel the Regulator kicking in again. Without it, perhaps she would be enraged.

"She's not Jess, Ruth. Finding her killer won't make you feel better."

"I'm asking for a favor. You can just say no."

Scott does not sigh, and he does not mumble. He's simply quiet. Then, a few seconds later: "Come to the office around eight. You can use the terminal in my office."

•   •   •

The Watcher thinks of himself as a good client. He makes sure he gets his money's worth, but he leaves a generous tip. He likes the clarity of money, the way it makes the flow of power obvious. The girl he just left was certainly appreciative.

He drives faster. He feels he's been too self-indulgent the last few weeks, working too slowly. He needs to make sure the last round of targets have paid. If not, he needs to carry through. Action. Reaction. It's all very simple once you understand the rules.

He rubs the bandage around his ring finger, which allows him to maintain the pale patch of skin that girls like to see. The lingering, sickly sweet perfume from the last girl—Melody, Mandy, he's already forgetting her name—reminds him of Tara, who he will never forget.

Tara may have been the only girl he's really loved. She was blonde, petite, and very expensive. But she had liked him for some reason. Perhaps because they were both broken, and the jagged pieces happened to fit.

She had stopped charging him and told him her real name. He was a kind of boyfriend. Because he was curious, she explained her business to him. How certain words and turns of phrase and tones on the phone were warning signs. What she looked for in a desired regular. What signs on a man probably meant he was safe. He enjoyed learning about this. It seemed to require careful watching by the girl, and he respected those who looked and studied and made the information useful.

He had looked into her eyes as he fucked her and then said, "Is something wrong with your right eye?"

She had stopped moving. "What?"

"I wasn't sure at first. But yes, it's like you have something behind your eye."

She wriggled under him. He was annoyed and thought about holding her down. But he decided not to. She seemed about to tell him something important. He rolled off her.

"You're very observant."

"I try. What is it?"

She told him about the implant.

"You've been recording your clients having sex with you?"

"Yes."

"I want to see the ones you have of us."

She laughed. "I'll have to go under the knife for that. Not going to happen until I retire. Having your skull opened up once was enough."

She explained how the recordings made her feel safe, gave her a sense of power, like having bank accounts whose balances only she knew and kept growing. If she were ever threatened, she would be able to call on the powerful men she knew for aid. And after retirement, if things didn't work out and she got desperate, perhaps she could use them to get her regulars to help her out a little.

He had liked the way she thought. So devious. So like him.

He had been sorry when he killed her. Removing her head was more difficult and messy than he had imagined. Figuring out what to do with the little silver half sphere had taken months. He would learn to do better over time.

But Tara had been blind to the implications of what she had done. What she had wasn't just insurance, wasn't just a rainy-day fund. She had revealed to him that she had what it took to make his dream come true, and he had to take it from her.

He pulls into the parking lot of the hotel and finds himself seized by an unfamiliar sensation: sorrow. He misses Tara, like missing a mirror you've broken.

Ruth is working with the assumption that the man she's looking for targets independent prostitutes. There's an efficiency and a method to the way Mona was killed that suggests practice.

She begins by searching the NCIC database for prostitutes who had been killed by a suspect matching the EchoSense description. As she expects, she comes up with nothing that seems remotely similar. The man hadn't left obvious trails.

The focus on Mona's eyes may be a clue. Maybe the killer has a fetish for Asian women. Ruth changes her search to concentrate on body mutilations of Asian prostitutes similar to what Mona had suffered. Again, nothing.

Ruth sits back and thinks over the situation. It's common for serial killers to concentrate on victims of a specific ethnicity. But that may be a red herring here.

She expands her search to include all independent prostitutes who had been killed in the last year or so, and now there are too many hits. Dozens and dozens of killings of prostitutes of every description pop up. Most were sexually assaulted. Some were tortured. Many had their bodies mutilated. Almost all were robbed. Gangs were suspected in several cases. She sifts through them, looking for similarities. Nothing jumps out at her.

She needs more information.

She logs on to the escort sites in the various cities and looks up the ads of the murdered women. Not all of them remain online, as some sites deactivate ads when enough patrons complain about unavailability. She prints out what she can, laying them out side by side to compare.

Then she sees it. It's in the ads.

A subset of the ads triggers a sense of familiarity in Ruth's mind. They were all carefully written, free of spelling and grammar mistakes. They were frank but not explicit, seductive without verging on parody. The johns who posted reviews described them as "classy."

It's a signal, Ruth realizes. The ads are written to give off the air of being careful, selective, *discreet*. There is in them, for lack of a better word, a sense of *taste*.

All the women in these ads were extraordinarily beautiful, with smooth skin and thick, long, flowing hair. All of them were between twenty-two and thirty—not so young as to be careless or supporting themselves through school, and not old enough to lose the ability to pass for younger. All of them were independent, with no pimp or evidence of being on drugs.

Luo's words come back to her: *The men who go to massage parlors for sixty dollars an hour and a happy ending are not the kind who'd pay for a girl like this.*

There's a certain kind of client who would be attracted to the signs given out by these girls, Ruth thinks: men who care very much about the risk of discovery and who believe that they deserve something special, suitable for their distinguished tastes.

She prints out the NCIC entries for the women.

All the women she's identified were killed in their homes. No sign of struggle—possibly because they were meeting a client. One was strangled, the others shot in the heart through the back, like Mona. In all the cases except one—the woman who was strangled—the police had found record of a suspicious call on the day of the murder from a prepaid phone that was later found somewhere in the city. The killer had taken all the women's money.

Ruth knows she's on the right track. Now, she needs to examine the case reports in more detail to see if she can find more patterns to identify the killer.

The door to the office opens. It's Scott.

"Still here?" The scowl on his face shows that he does not have his Regulator on. "It's after midnight."

She notes, not for the first time, how the men in the department have often resisted the Regulator unless absolutely necessary, claiming that it dulled their instincts and hunches. But they had also asked her whether she had hers on whenever she dared to disagree with them. They would laugh when they asked.

"I think I'm onto something," she says calmly.

"You working with the goddamned feds now?"

"What are you talking about?"

"You haven't seen the news?"

"I've been here all evening."

He takes out his tablet, opens a bookmark, and hands it to her. It's an article in the international section of the *Globe*, which she rarely reads. "Scandal Unseats Chinese Transport Minister" says the headline.

She scans the article quickly. A video has surfaced on the Chinese microblogs showing an important official in the Transport Ministry having sex with a prostitute. Moreover, it seems that he had been paying her out of public funds. He's already been removed from his post due to the public outcry.

Accompanying the article is a grainy photo, a still capture from the video. Before the Regulator kicks in, Ruth feels her heart skip a beat. The image shows a man on top of a woman. Her head is turned to the side, directly facing the camera.

"That's your girl, isn't it?"

Ruth nods. She recognizes the bed and the nightstand with the clock and wicker basket from the crime scene photos.

"The Chinese are hopping mad. They think we had the man under surveillance when he was in Boston and released this video deliberately to mess with them. They're protesting through the back channels, threatening retaliation. The feds want us to look into it and see what we can find out about how the video was made. They don't know that she's already dead, but I recognized her as soon as I saw her. If you ask me, it's probably something the Chinese cooked up themselves to try to get rid of the guy in an internal purge. Maybe they even paid the girl to do it, and then they killed her. That, or our own spies decided to get rid of her after using her as bait, in which case I expect this investigation to be shut down pretty quickly. Either way, I'm not looking forward to this mess. And I advise you to back off as well."

Ruth feels a moment of resentment before the Regulator whisks it away. If Mona's death was part of a political plot, then Scott is right, she really is way out of her depth. The police had been wrong to conclude that it was a gang killing. But she's wrong too. Mona was an unfortunate pawn in some political game, and the trend she thought she had noticed was illusory, just a set of coincidences.

The rational thing to do is to let the police take over. She'll have to tell Sarah Ding that there's nothing she can do for her now.

"We'll have to sweep the apartment again for recording devices. And you better let me know the name of your informant. We'll need to question him thoroughly to see which gangs are involved. This could be a national security matter."

"You know I can't do that. I have no evidence he has anything to do with this."

"Ruth, we're picking this up now. If you want to find the girl's killer, help me."

"Feel free to round up all the usual suspects in Chinatown. It's what you want to do, anyway."

He stares at her, his face weary and angry, a look she's very familiar with. Then his face relaxes. He has decided to engage his Regulator, and he no longer wants to argue or talk about what couldn't be said between them.

Her Regulator kicks in automatically.

"Thank you for letting me use your office," she says placidly. "You have a good night."

The scandal had gone off exactly as the Watcher planned. He's pleased but not yet ready to celebrate. That was only the first step, a demonstration of his power. Next, he has to actually make sure it pays.

He goes through the recordings and pictures he's extracted from the dead girl and picks out a few more promising targets based on his research. Two are prominent Chinese businessmen connected with top Party bosses; one is the brother of an Indian diplomatic attaché; two more are sons of the House of Saud, studying in Boston. It's remarkable how similar the dynamics between the powerful and the people they ruled over are around the world. He also finds a prominent CEO and a justice of the Massachusetts Supreme Judicial Court, but these he sets aside. It's not that he's particularly patriotic, but he instinctively senses that if one of his victims decides to turn him in instead of paying up, he'll be in much less trouble if the victim isn't an American. Besides, American public figures also have a harder time moving money around anonymously, as evidenced by his experience with those two senators in DC, which almost unraveled his whole scheme. Finally, it never hurts to have a judge or someone famous that can be leaned on in case the Watcher is caught.

Patience, and an eye for details.

He sends off his e-mails. Each references the article about the Chinese Transport Minister ("See, this could be you!") and then includes two files. One is the full video of the minister and the girl (to show that he was the originator), and the second is a carefully curated video of the recipient coupling with her. Each e-mail contains a demand for payment and directions to make deposits to a numbered Swiss bank account or to transfer anonymous electronic crypto-currency.

He browses the escort sites again. He's narrowed down the girls he suspects to just a few. Now, he just has to look at them more closely to pick out the right one. He grows excited at the prospect.

He glances up at the people walking past him in the streets. All these foolish men and women moving around as if dreaming. They do not understand that the world is full of secrets, accessible only to those patient enough, observant enough to locate them and dig them out of their warm, bloody hiding places, like retrieving pearls from the soft flesh inside oysters. And then, armed with those secrets, you could make men half a world away tremble and dance.

He closes his laptop and gets up to leave. He thinks about packing up the mess in his motel room, setting out the surgical kit, the baseball cap, the gun, and a few other surprises he's learned to take with him when he's hunting.

Time to dig for more treasure.

Ruth wakes up. The old nightmares have been joined by new ones. She stays curled up in bed fighting waves of despair. She wants to lie here forever.

Days of work, and she has nothing to show for it.

She'll have to call Sarah Ding later, after she turns on the Regulator. She can tell her that Mona was probably not killed by a gang, but somehow had been caught up in events bigger than she could handle. How would that make Sarah feel better?

The image from yesterday's news will not leave her mind, no matter how hard she tries to push it away.

Ruth struggles up and pulls up the article. She can't explain it, but the image just *looks* wrong. Not having the Regulator on makes it hard to think.

She finds the crime scene photo of Mona's bedroom and compares it with the image from the article. She looks back and forth.

Isn't the basket of condoms on the wrong side of the bed?

The shot is taken from the left side of the bed. So the closet doors, with the mirrors on them, should be on the far side of the shot, behind the couple. But there's only a blank wall behind them in the shot. Ruth's heart is beating so fast that she feels faint.

The alarm beeps. Ruth glances up at the red numbers and turns the Regulator on.

The clock.

She looks back at the image. The alarm clock in the shot is tiny and fuzzy, but she can just make the numbers out. They're backward.

Ruth walks steadily over to her laptop and begins to search online for the video. She finds it without much trouble and presses play.

Despite the video stabilization and the careful cropping, she can see that Mona's eyes are always looking directly into the camera.

There's only one explanation: The camera was aimed at the mirrors, and it was located in Mona's eye.

The eyes.

She goes through the NCIC entries of the other women she printed out yesterday, and now the pattern that had proven elusive seems obvious.

There was a blonde in Los Angeles whose head had been removed after death and never found; there was a brunette, also in LA, whose skull had been cracked open and her brains mashed; there was a Mexican woman and a black woman in DC, whose faces had been subjected to postmortem trauma in more restrained ways, with the cheekbones crushed and broken. Then finally, there was Mona, whose eyes had been carefully removed.

The killer has been improving his technique.

The Regulator holds her excitement in check. She needs more data.

She looks through all of Mona's photographs again. Nothing out of place shows up in the earlier pictures, but in the photo from her birthday with her parents, a flash was used, and there's an odd glint in her left eye.

Most cameras can automatically compensate for red-eye, which is caused by the light from the flash reflecting off the blood-rich choroid in the back of the eye. But the glint in Mona's picture is not red; it's bluish.

Calmly, Ruth flips through the photographs of the other girls who have been killed. And in each, she finds the telltale glint. This must be how the killer identified his targets.

She picks up the phone and dials the number for her friend. She and Gail had gone to college together, and she's now working as a researcher for an advanced medical devices company.

"Hello?"

She hears the chatter of other people in the background. "Gail, it's Ruth. Can you talk?"

"Just a minute." She hears the background conversation grow muffled and then abruptly shut off. "You never call unless you're asking about another enhancement. We're not getting any younger, you know? You have to stop at some point."

Gail had been the one to suggest the various enhancements Ruth has obtained over the years. She had even found Doctor B for her because she didn't want Ruth to end up crippled. But she had done it reluctantly, conflicted about the idea of turning Ruth into a cyborg.

"This feels wrong," she would say. "You don't need these things done to you. They're not medically necessary."

"This can save my life the next time someone is trying to choke me," Ruth would say.

"It's not the same thing," she would say. And the conversations would always end with Gail giving in, but with stern warnings about no further enhancements.

Sometimes you help a friend even when you disapprove of their decisions. It's complicated.

Ruth answers Gail on the phone, "No. I'm just fine. But I want to know if you know about a new kind of enhancement. I'm sending you some pictures now. Hold on." She sends over the images of the girls where she can see the strange glint in their eyes. "Take a look. Can you see that flash in their eyes? Do you know anything like this?" She doesn't tell Gail her suspicion so that Gail's answer would not be affected.

Gail is silent for a while. "I see what you mean. These are not great pictures. But let me talk to some people and call you back."

"Don't send the full pictures around. I'm in the middle of an investigation. Just crop out the eyes if you can."

Ruth hangs up. The Regulator is working extra hard. Something about what she said—cropping out the girls' eyes—triggered a bodily response of disgust that the Regulator is suppressing. She's not sure why. With the Regulator, sometimes it's hard for her to see the connections between things.

While waiting for Gail to call her back, she looks through the active online ads in Boston once more. The killer has a pattern of killing a few girls in each city before moving on. He must be on the hunt for a second victim here. The best way to catch him is to find her before he does.

She clicks through ad after ad, the parade of flesh a meaningless blur, focusing only on the eyes. Finally, she sees what she's looking for. The girl uses the name Carrie, and she has dirty-blonde hair and green eyes. Her ad is clean, clear, well-written, like a tasteful sign amid the parade of flashing neon. The time stamp on the ad shows that she last modified it twelve hours ago. She's likely still alive.

Ruth calls the number listed.

"This is Carrie. Please leave a message."

As expected, Carrie screens her calls.

"Hello. My name is Ruth Law, and I saw your ad. I'd like to make an appointment with you." She hesitates, and then adds, "This is not a joke. I really want to see you." She leaves her number and hangs up.

The phone rings almost immediately. Ruth picks up. But it's Gail, not Carrie.

"I asked around, and people who ought to know tell me the girls are probably wearing a new kind of retinal implant. It's not FDA approved. But of course, you can go overseas and get them installed if you pay enough."

"What do they do?"

"They're hidden cameras."

"How do you get the pictures and videos out?"

"You don't. They have no wireless connections to the outside world. In fact, they're shielded to emit as little RF emissions as possible, so that they're undetectable to camera scanners, and a wireless connection would just mean another way to hack into them. All the storage is inside the device. To retrieve them, you have to have surgery again. Not the kind of thing most people would be interested in unless you're trying to record people who *really* don't want you to be recording them."

When you're so desperate for safety that you think this provides insurance, Ruth thinks. Some future leverage.

And there's no way to get the recordings out except to cut the girl open. "Thanks."

"I don't know what you're involved in, Ruth, but you really are getting too old for this. Are you still leaving the Regulator on all the time? It's not healthy."

"Don't I know it." She changes the subject to Gail's children. The Regulator allows her to have this conversation without pain. After a suitable amount of time, she says good-bye and hangs up.

The phone rings again.

"This is Carrie. You called me."

"Yes." Ruth makes her voice sound light, carefree.

Carrie's voice is flirtatious but cautious. "Is this for you and your boyfriend or husband?"

"No, just me."

She grips the phone, counting the seconds. She tries to will Carrie not to hang up.

"I found your website. You're a private detective?"

Ruth already knew that she would. "Yes, I am."

"I can't tell you anything about any of my clients. My business depends on discretion."

"I'm not going to ask you about your clients. I just want to see you." She thinks hard about how to gain her trust. The Regulator makes this difficult, as she has become unused to the emotive quality of judgments and impressions. She thinks the truth is too abrupt and strange to convince her. So she tries something else. "I'm interested in a new experience. I guess it's something I've always wanted to try and haven't."

"Are you working for the cops? I am stating now for the record that you're paying me only for companionship, and anything that happens beyond that is a decision between consenting adults."

"Look, the cops wouldn't use a woman to trap you. It's too suspicious."

The silence tells Ruth that Carrie is intrigued. "What time are you thinking of?"

"As soon as you're free. How about now?"

"It's not even noon yet. I don't start work until six."

Ruth doesn't want to push too hard and scare her off. "Then I'd like to have you all night."

She laughs. "Why don't we start with two hours for a first date?"

"That will be fine."

"You saw my prices?"

"Yes. Of course."

"Take a picture of yourself holding your ID and text it to me first so I know you're for real. If that checks out, you can go to the corner of Victory and Beech in Back Bay at six and call me again. Put the cash in a plain envelope."

"I will."

"See you, my dear." She hangs up.

Ruth looks into the girl's eyes. Now that she knows what to look for, she thinks she can see the barest hint of a glint in her left eye.

She hands her the cash and watches her count it. She's very pretty, and so young. The ways she leans against the wall reminds her of Jess. The Regulator kicks in.

She's in a lace nightie, black stockings, and garters. High-heeled fluffy bedroom slippers that seem more funny than erotic.

Carrie puts the money aside and smiles at her. "Do you want to take the lead or have me do it? I'm fine either way."

"I'd rather just talk for a bit first."

Carrie frowns. "I told you I can't talk about my clients."

"I know. But I want to show you something."

Carrie shrugs and leads her to the bedroom. It's a lot like Mona's room: king-size bed, cream-colored sheets, a glass bowl of condoms, a clock discreetly on the nightstand. The mirror is mounted on the ceiling.

They sit down on the bed. Ruth takes out a file and hands Carrie a stack of photographs.

"All of these girls have been killed in the last year. All of them have the same implants you do."

Carrie looks up, shocked. Her eyes blink twice, rapidly.

"I know what you have behind your eye. I know you think it makes you safer. Maybe you even think someday the information in there can be a second source of income, when you're too old to do this. But there's a man who wants to cut that out of you. He's been doing the same to the other girls."

She shows her the pictures of dead Mona, with the bloody, mutilated face.

Carrie drops the pictures. "Get out. I'm calling the police." She stands up and grabs her phone.

Ruth doesn't move. "You can. Ask to speak to Captain Scott Brennan. He knows who I am, and he'll confirm what I've told you. I think you're the next target."

She hesitates.

Ruth continues, "Or you can just look at these pictures. You know what to look for. They were all just like you."

Carrie sits down and examines the pictures. "Oh God. Oh God."

"I know you probably have a set of regulars. At your prices, you don't need and won't get many new clients. But have you taken on anyone new lately?"

"Just you and one other. He's coming at eight."

Ruth's Regulator kicks in.

"Do you know what he looks like?"

"No. But I asked him to call me when he gets to the street corner, just like you, so I can get a look at him first before having him come up."

Ruth takes out her phone. "I need to call the police."

"No! You'll get me arrested. Please!"

Ruth thinks about this. She's only guessing that this man might be the killer. If she involves the police now and he turns out to be just a customer, Carrie's life will be ruined.

"Then I'll need to see him myself, in case he's the one."

"Shouldn't I just call it off?"

Ruth hears the fear in the girl's voice, and it reminds her of Jess, too, when she used to ask her to stay in her bedroom after watching a scary movie. She can feel the Regulator kicking into action again. She cannot let her emotions get in the way. "That would probably be safer for you, but we'd lose the chance to catch him if he *is* the one. Please, I need you to go through with it so I can get a close look at him. This may be our best chance of stopping him from hurting others."

Carrie bites her bottom lip. "All right. Where will you hide?"

Ruth wishes she had thought to bring her gun, but she hadn't wanted to spook Carrie, and she didn't anticipate having to fight. She'll need to be close enough to stop the man if he turns out to be the killer, and yet not so close as to make it easy for him to discover her.

"I can't hide inside here at all. He'll look around before going into the bedroom with you." She walks into the living room, which faces the back of the building, away from the street, and lifts the window open. "I can hide out here, hanging from the ledge. If he turns out to be the killer, I have to wait till the last possible minute to come in to cut off his escape. If he's not the killer, I'll drop down and leave."

Carrie is clearly uncomfortable with this plan, but she nods, trying to be brave.

"Act as normal as you can. Don't make him think something is wrong."

Carrie's phone rings. She swallows and clicks the phone on. She walks over to the bedroom window. Ruth follows.

"This is Carrie."

Ruth looks out the window. The man standing at the corner appears to be the right height, but that's not enough to be sure. She has to catch him and interrogate him.

"I'm in the four-story building about a hundred feet behind you. Come up to apartment 303. I'm so glad you came, dear. We'll have a great time, I promise." She hangs up.

The man starts walking this way. Ruth thinks there's a limp to his walk, but again, she can't be sure.

"Is it him?" Carrie asks.

"I don't know. We have to let him in and see."

Ruth can feel the Regulator humming. She knows that the idea of using Carrie as bait frightens her, is repugnant, even. But it's the logical thing to do. She'll never get a chance like this again. She has to trust that she can protect the girl.

"I'm going outside the window. You're doing great. Just keep him talking and do what he wants. Get him relaxed and focused on you. I'll come in before he can hurt you. I promise."

Carrie smiles. "I'm good at acting."

Ruth goes to the living room window and deftly climbs out. She lets her body down, hanging on to the window ledge with her fingers so that she's invisible from inside the apartment. "Okay, close the window. Leave just a slit open, so I can hear what happens inside."

"How long can you hang like this?"

"Long enough."

Carrie closes the window. Ruth is glad for the artificial tendons and tensors in her shoulders and arms and the reinforced fingers holding her up. The idea had been to make her more effective in close combat, but they're coming in handy now, too.

She counts off the seconds. The man should be at the building. . . . He should now be coming up the stairs. . . . He should now be at the door.

She hears the door to the apartment open.

"You're even prettier than your pictures." The voice is rich, deep, satisfied.

"Thank you."

She hears more conversation, the exchange of money. Then the sound of more walking.

They're heading toward the bedroom. She can hear the man stopping to look into the other rooms. She almost can feel his gaze pass over the top of her head, out the window.

Ruth pulls herself up slowly, quietly, and looks in. She sees the man disappear into the hallway. There's a distinct limp.

She waits a few more seconds so that the man cannot rush back past her before she can reach the hallway to block it, and then she takes a deep breath and wills the Regulator to pump her blood full of adrenaline. The world seems to grow brighter, and time slows down as she flexes her arms and pulls herself onto the window ledge.

She squats down and pulls the window up in one swift motion. She knows that the grinding noise will alert the man, and she has only a few seconds to get to him. She ducks, rolls through the open window onto the floor inside. Then she continues to roll until her feet are under her and activates the pistons in her legs to leap toward the hallway.

She lands and rolls again to not give him a clear target, and jumps again from her crouch into the bedroom.

The man shoots, and the bullet strikes her left shoulder. She tackles him as her arms, held in front of her, slam into his midsection. He falls, and the gun clatters away.

Now the pain from the bullet hits. She wills the Regulator to pump up the adrenaline and the endorphins to numb the pain. She pants and concentrates on the fight for her life.

He tries to flip her over with his superior mass, to pin her down, but she clamps her hands around his neck and squeezes hard. Men have always underestimated her at the beginning of a fight, and she has to take advantage of it. She knows that her grip feels like iron clamps around him, with all the implanted energy cells in her arms and hands activated and on full power. He winces, grabs her hands to try to pry them off. After a few seconds, realizing the futility of it, he ceases to struggle.

He's trying to talk, but can't get any air into his lungs. Ruth lets up a little, and he chokes out, "You got me."

Ruth increases the pressure again, choking off his supply of air. She turns to Carrie, who's at the foot of the bed, frozen. "Call the police. Now."

She complies. As she continues to hold the phone against her ear as the 911 dispatcher has instructed her to do, she tells Ruth, "They're on their way."

The man goes limp with his eyes closed. Ruth lets go of his neck. She doesn't want to kill him, so she clamps her hands around his wrists while she sits on his legs, holding him still on the floor.

He revives and starts to moan. "You're breaking my fucking arms!"

Ruth lets up the pressure a bit to conserve her power. The man's nose is bleeding from the fall against the floor when she tackled him. He inhales loudly, swallows, and says, "I'm going to drown if you don't let me sit up."

Ruth considers this. She lets up the pressure further and pulls him into a sitting position.

She can feel the energy cells in her arms depleting. She won't have the physical upper hand much longer if she has to keep on restraining him this way.

She calls out to Carrie. "Come over here and tie his hands together."

Carrie puts down the phone and comes over gingerly. "What do I use?"

"Don't you have any rope? You know, for your clients?"

"I don't do that kind of thing."

Ruth thinks. "You can use stockings."

As Carrie ties the man's hands and feet together in front of him, he coughs. Some of the blood has gone down the wrong pipe. Ruth is unmoved and doesn't ease up on the pressure, and he winces. "Goddamn it. You're one psycho robo bitch."

Ruth ignores him. The stockings are too stretchy and won't hold him for long. But it should last long enough for her to get the gun and point it at him.

Carrie retreats to the other side of the room. Ruth lets the man go and backs away from him toward the gun on the floor a few yards away, keeping her eyes on him. If he makes any sudden movements, she'll be back on him in a flash.

He stays limp and unmoving as she steps backward. She begins to relax. The Regulator is trying to calm her down now, to filter the adrenaline out of her system.

When she's about halfway to the gun, the man suddenly reaches into his jacket with his hands still tied together. Ruth hesitates for only a second before pushing out with her legs to jump backward to the gun.

As she lands, the man locates something inside his jacket, and suddenly Ruth feels her legs and arms go limp, and she falls to the ground, stunned.

Carrie is screaming. "My eye! Oh God, I can't see out of my left eye!"

Ruth can't seem to feel her legs at all, and her arms feel like rubber. Worst of all, she's panicking. It seems she's never been this scared or in this much pain. She tries to feel the presence of the Regulator and there's nothing, just emptiness. She can smell the sweet, sickly smell of burned electronics in the air. The clock on the nightstand is dark.

She's the one who had underestimated *him*. Despair floods through her, and there's nothing to hold it back.

Ruth can hear the man stagger up off the floor. She wills herself to turn over, to move, to reach for the gun. She crawls. One foot, another foot. She seems to be moving through molasses because she's so weak. She can feel every one of her forty-nine years. She feels every sharp stab of pain in her shoulder.

She reaches the gun, grabs it, and sits up against the wall, pointing it back into the center of the room.

The man has gotten out of Carrie's ineffective knots. He's now holding Carrie, blind in one eye, shielding his body with hers. He holds a scalpel against her throat. He's already broken the skin, and a thin stream of blood flows down her neck.

He backs toward the bedroom door, dragging Carrie with him. Ruth knows that if he gets to the bedroom door and disappears around the corner, she'll never be able to catch him. Her legs are simply useless.

Carrie sees Ruth's gun and screams, "I don't want to die! Oh God. Oh God."

"I'll let her go once I'm safe," he says, keeping his head hidden behind hers.

Ruth's hands are shaking as she holds the gun. Through the waves of nausea and the pounding of her pulse in her ears, she struggles to think through what will happen next. The police are on their way and will probably be here in five minutes. Isn't it likely that he'll let her go as soon as possible to give himself some extra time to escape?

The man backs up another two steps; Carrie is no longer kicking or struggling but trying to find purchase on the smooth floor in her stockinged feet, trying to cooperate with him. But she can't stop crying.

Mom, don't shoot! Please don't shoot!

Or is it more likely that once the man has left the room, he will slit Carrie's throat and cut out her implant? He knows there's a recording of him inside, and he can't afford to leave that behind.

Ruth's hands are shaking too much. She wants to curse at herself. She cannot get a clear shot at the man with Carrie in front of him. She cannot.

Ruth wants to evaluate the chances rationally, to make a decision, but regret and grief and rage, hidden and held down by the Regulator until they could be endured, rise now all the sharper, kept fresh by the effort at forgetting. The universe has shrunken down to the wavering spot at the end of the barrel of the gun: a young woman, a killer, and time slipping irrevocably away.

She has nothing to turn to, to trust, to lean on but herself; her angry, frightened, trembling self. She is naked and alone, as she has always known she is, as we all are.

The man is almost at the door. Carrie's cries are now incoherent sobs.

It has always been the regular state of things. There is no clarity, no relief. At the end of all rationality, there is simply the need to decide and the faith to live through, to endure.

Ruth's first shot slams into Carrie's thigh. The bullet plunges through skin, muscle, and fat, and exits out the back, shattering the man's knee.

The man screams and drops the scalpel. Carrie falls, a spray of blood blossoming from her wounded leg.

Ruth's second shot catches the man in the chest. He collapses to the floor.

Mom, Mom!

She drops the gun and crawls over to Carrie, cradling her and tending to her wound. She's crying, but she'll be fine.

A deep pain floods through her like forgiveness, like hard rain after a long drought. She does not know if she will be granted relief, but she experiences this moment fully, and she's thankful.

"It's okay," she says, stroking Carrie as she lies in her lap. "It's okay."

•   •   •

AUTHOR'S NOTE: The EchoSense technology described in this story is a loose and liberal extrapolation of the principles behind the technology described in Qifan Pu et al, "Whole-Home Gesture Recognition Using Wireless Signals" (Nineteenth Annual International Conference on Mobile Computing and Networking, MobiCom 2013), available at wisee.cs.washington.edu/wisee_paper.pdf. There is no intent to suggest that the technology described in the paper resembles the fictional one portrayed here.

THE PAPER MENAGERIE

One of my earliest memories starts with me sobbing. I refused to be soothed no matter what Mom and Dad tried.

Dad gave up and left the bedroom, but Mom took me into the kitchen and sat me down at the breakfast table.

"Kan, kan," she said, as she pulled a sheet of wrapping paper from on top of the fridge. For years, Mom carefully sliced open the wrappings around Christmas gifts and saved them on top of the fridge in a thick stack.

She set the paper down, plain side facing up, and began to fold it. I stopped crying and watched her, curious.

She turned the paper over and folded it again. She pleated, packed, tucked, rolled, and twisted until the paper disappeared between her cupped hands. Then she lifted the folded-up paper packet to her mouth and blew into it, like a balloon.

"Kan," she said, *"laohu."* She put her hands down on the table and let go.

A little paper tiger stood on the table, the size of two fists placed together. The skin of the tiger was the pattern on the wrapping paper, white background with red candy canes and green Christmas trees.

I reached out to Mom's creation. Its tail twitched, and it pounced playfully at my finger. *"Rawrr-sa,"* it growled, the sound somewhere between a cat and rustling newspapers.

I laughed, startled, and stroked its back with an index finger. The paper tiger vibrated under my finger, purring.

"Zhe jiao zhezhi," Mom said. *This is called origami.*

I didn't know this at the time, but Mom's kind was special. She breathed into them so that they shared her breath, and thus moved with her life. This was her magic.

Dad had picked Mom out of a catalog.

One time, when I was in high school, I asked Dad about the details. He was trying to get me to speak to Mom again.

He had signed up for the introduction service back in the spring of 1973. Flipping through the pages steadily, he had spent no more than a few seconds on each page until he saw the picture of Mom.

I've never seen this picture. Dad described it: Mom was sitting in a chair, her side to the camera, wearing a tight green silk cheongsam. Her head was turned to the camera so that her long black hair was draped artfully over her chest and shoulder. She looked out at him with the eyes of a calm child.

"That was the last page of the catalog I saw," he said.

The catalog said she was eighteen, loved to dance, and spoke good English because she was from Hong Kong. None of these facts turned out to be true.

He wrote to her, and the company passed their messages back and forth. Finally, he flew to Hong Kong to meet her.

"The people at the company had been writing her responses. She didn't know any English other than 'hello' and 'good-bye.'"

What kind of woman puts herself into a catalog so that she can be bought? The high-school-me thought I knew so much about everything. Contempt felt good, like wine.

Instead of storming into the office to demand his money back, he paid a waitress at the hotel restaurant to translate for them.

"She would look at me, her eyes halfway between scared and hopeful, while I spoke. And when the girl began translating what I said, she'd start to smile slowly."

He flew back to Connecticut and began to apply for the papers for her to come to him. I was born a year later, in the Year of the Tiger.

At my request, Mom also made a goat, a deer, and a water buffalo out of wrapping paper. They would run around the living room while Laohu chased after them, growling. When he caught them he would press down until the air went out of them and they became just flat, folded-up pieces of paper. I would then have to blow into them to reinflate them so they could run around some more.

Sometimes, the animals got into trouble. Once, the water buffalo jumped into a dish of soy sauce on the table at dinner. (He wanted to wallow, like a real water buffalo.) I picked him out quickly but the capillary action had already pulled the dark liquid high up into his legs. The sauce-softened legs would not hold him up, and he collapsed onto the table. I dried him out in the sun, but his legs became crooked after that, and he ran around with a limp. Mom eventually wrapped his legs in Saran wrap so that he could wallow to his heart's content (just not in soy sauce).

Also, Laohu liked to pounce at sparrows when he and I played in the backyard. But one time, a cornered bird struck back in desperation and tore his ear. He whimpered and winced as I held him and Mom patched his ear together with tape. He avoided birds after that.

And then one day, I saw a TV documentary about sharks and asked Mom for one of my own. She made the shark, but he flapped about on the table unhappily. I filled the sink with water and put him in. He swam around and around happily. However, after a while he became soggy and translucent, and slowly sank to the bottom, the folds coming undone. I reached in to rescue him, and all I ended up with was a wet piece of paper.

Laohu put his front paws together at the edge of the sink and rested his head on them. Ears drooping, he made a low growl in his throat that made me feel guilty.

Mom made a new shark for me, this time out of tinfoil. The shark lived happily in a large goldfish bowl. Laohu and I liked to sit next to the bowl to watch the tinfoil shark chasing the goldfish, Laohu sticking his face up against the bowl on the other side so that I saw his eyes, magnified to the size of coffee cups, staring at me from across the bowl.

When I was ten, we moved to a new house across town. Two of the women neighbors came by to welcome us. Dad served them drinks and then apologized for having to run off to the utility company to straighten out the prior owner's bills. "Make yourselves at home. My wife doesn't speak much English, so don't think she's being rude for not talking to you."

While I read in the dining room, Mom unpacked in the kitchen. The neighbors conversed in the living room, not trying to be particularly quiet.

"He seems like a normal enough man. Why did he do that?"

"Something about the mixing never seems right. The child looks unfinished. Slanty eyes, white face. A little monster."

"Do you think *he* can speak English?"

The women hushed. After a while they came into the dining room.

"Hello there! What's your name?"

"Jack," I said.

"That doesn't sound very Chinesey."

Mom came into the dining room then. She smiled at the women. The three of them stood in a triangle around me, smiling and nodding at each other, with nothing to say, until Dad came back.

Mark, one of the neighborhood boys, came over with his Star Wars action figures. Obi-Wan Kenobi's lightsaber lit up and he could swing his arms and say, in a tinny voice, "Use the Force!" I didn't think the figure looked much like the real Obi-Wan at all.

Together, we watched him repeat this performance five times on the coffee table. "Can he do anything else?" I asked.

Mark was annoyed by my question. "Look at all the details," he said.

I looked at the details. I wasn't sure what I was supposed to say.

Mark was disappointed by my response. "Show me your toys."

I didn't have any toys except my paper menagerie. I brought Laohu out from my bedroom. By then he was very worn, patched all over with tape and glue, evidence of the years of repairs Mom and I had done on him. He was no longer as nimble and sure-footed as before. I sat him down on the coffee table. I could hear the skittering steps of the other animals behind in the hallway, timidly peeking into the living room.

"*Xiao laohu*," I said, and stopped. I switched to English. "This is Tiger." Cautiously, Laohu strode up and purred at Mark, sniffing his hands.

Mark examined the Christmas-wrap pattern of Laohu's skin. "That doesn't look like a tiger at all. Your mom makes toys for you from trash?"

I had never thought of Laohu as *trash*. But looking at him now, he was really just a piece of wrapping paper.

Mark pushed Obi-Wan's head again. The lightsaber flashed; he moved his arms up and down. "Use the Force!"

Laohu turned and pounced, knocking the plastic figure off the table. It hit the floor and broke, and Obi-Wan's head rolled under the couch. "*Rawwww,*" Laohu laughed. I joined him.

Mark punched me, hard. "This was very expensive! You can't even find it in the stores now. It probably cost more than what your dad paid for your mom!"

I stumbled and fell to the floor. Laohu growled and leapt at Mark's face.

Mark screamed, more out of fear and surprise than pain. Laohu was only made of paper, after all.

Mark grabbed Laohu and his snarl was choked off as Mark crumpled him in his hand and tore him in half. He balled up the two pieces of paper and threw them at me. "Here's your stupid cheap Chinese garbage."

After Mark left, I spent a long time trying, without success, to tape together the pieces, smooth out the paper, and follow the creases to refold Laohu. Slowly, the other animals came into the living room and gathered around us, me and the torn wrapping paper that used to be Laohu.

My fight with Mark didn't end there. Mark was popular at school. I never want to think again about the two weeks that followed.

I came home that Friday at the end of the two weeks. *"Xuexiao hao ma?"* Mom asked. I said nothing and went to the bathroom. I looked into the mirror. *I look nothing like her, nothing.*

At dinner I asked Dad, "Do I have a chink face?"

Dad put down his chopsticks. Even though I had never told him what happened in school, he seemed to understand. He closed his eyes and rubbed the bridge of his nose. "No, you don't."

Mom looked at Dad, not understanding. She looked back at me. *"Sha jiao* chink?"

"English," I said. "Speak English."

She tried. "What happen?"

I pushed the chopsticks and the bowl before me away: stir-fried green peppers with five-spice beef. "We should eat American food."

Dad tried to reason. "A lot of families cook Chinese sometimes."

"We are not other families." I looked at him. *Other families don't have moms who don't belong.*

He looked away. And then he put a hand on Mom's shoulder. "I'll get you a cookbook."

Mom turned to me. *"Bu haochi?"*

"English," I said, raising my voice. "Speak English."

Mom reached out to touch my forehead, feeling for my temperature. *"Fashao la?"*

I brushed her hand away. "I'm fine. Speak English!" I was shouting.

"Speak English to him," Dad said to Mom. "You knew this was going to happen someday. What did you expect?"

Mom dropped her hands to her side. She sat, looking from Dad to me, and back to Dad again. She tried to speak, stopped, and tried again, and stopped again.

"You have to," Dad said. "I've been too easy on you. Jack needs to fit in."

Mom looked at him. "If I say 'love,' I feel here." She pointed to her lips. "If I say *'ai,'* I feel here." She put her hand over her heart.

Dad shook his head. "You are in America."

Mom hunched down in her seat, looking like the water buffalo when Laohu used to pounce on him and squeeze the air of life out of him.

"And I want some real toys."

Dad bought me a full set of Star Wars action figures. I gave the Obi-Wan Kenobi to Mark.

I packed the paper menagerie in a large shoe box and put it under the bed.

The next morning, the animals had escaped and took over their old favorite spots in my room. I caught them all and put them back into the shoe box, taping the lid shut. But the animals made so much noise in the box that I finally shoved it into the corner of the attic as far away from my room as possible.

If Mom spoke to me in Chinese, I refused to answer her. After a while, she tried to use more English. But her accent and broken sentences embarrassed me. I tried to correct her. Eventually, she stopped speaking altogether if I was around.

Mom began to mime things if she needed to let me know something. She tried to hug me the way she saw American mothers did on TV. I thought her movements exaggerated, uncertain, ridiculous, graceless. She saw that I was annoyed, and stopped.

"You shouldn't treat your mother that way," Dad said. But he couldn't look me in the eyes as he said it. Deep in his heart, he must have realized that it was a mistake to have tried to take a Chinese peasant girl and expect her to fit in the suburbs of Connecticut.

Mom learned to cook American style. I played video games and studied French.

Every once in a while, I would see her at the kitchen table studying the plain side of a sheet of wrapping paper. Later a new paper animal would appear on my nightstand and try to cuddle up to me. I caught them, squeezed them until the air went out of them, and then stuffed them away in the box in the attic.

Mom finally stopped making the animals when I was in high school. By then her English was much better, but I was already at that age when I wasn't interested in what she had to say whatever language she used.

Sometimes, when I came home and saw her tiny body busily moving about in the kitchen, singing a song in Chinese to herself, it was hard for me to believe that she gave birth to me. We had nothing in common. She might as well be from the moon. I would hurry on to my room, where I could continue my all-American pursuit of happiness.

Dad and I stood, one on each side of Mom lying in her hospital bed. She was not yet even forty, but she looked much older.

For years she had refused to go to the doctor for the pain inside her that she said was no big deal. By the time an ambulance finally carried her in, the cancer had spread far beyond the limits of surgery.

My mind was not in the room. It was the middle of the on-campus recruiting season, and I was focused on résumés, transcripts, and strategically constructed interview schedules. I schemed about how to lie to the corporate recruiters most effectively so that they'd offer to buy me. I understood intellectually that it was terrible to think about this while your mother lay dying. But that understanding didn't mean I could change how I felt.

She was conscious. Dad held her left hand with both of his own. He leaned down to kiss her forehead. He seemed weak and old in a way that startled me. I realized that I knew almost as little about Dad as I did about Mom.

Mom smiled at him. "I'm fine."

She turned to me, still smiling. "I know you have to go back to school." Her voice was very weak, and it was difficult to hear her over the hum of the machines hooked up to her. "Go. Don't worry about me. This is not a big deal. Just do well in school."

I reached out to touch her hand, because I thought that was what I was supposed to do. I was relieved. I was already thinking about the flight back, and the bright California sunshine.

She whispered something to Dad. He nodded and left the room.

"Jack, if—" She was caught up in a fit of coughing, and could not speak for some time. "If I don't make it, don't be too sad and hurt your health. Focus on your life. Just keep that box you have in the attic with you, and every year, at *Qingming*, just take it out and think about me. I'll be with you always."

Qingming was the Chinese Festival for the Dead. When I was very young, Mom used to write a letter on *Qingming* to her dead parents back in China, telling them the good news about the past year of her life in America. She would read the letter out loud to me, and if I made a comment about something, she would write it down in the letter too. Then she would fold the letter into a paper crane and release it, facing west. We would then watch as the crane flapped its crisp wings on its long journey west, toward the Pacific, toward China, toward the graves of Mom's family.

It had been many years since I last did that with her.

"I don't know anything about the Chinese calendar," I said. "Just rest, Mom."

"Just keep the box with you and open it once in a while. Just open—" She began to cough again.

"It's okay, Mom." I stroked her arm awkwardly.

"*Haizi, mama ai ni*—" Her cough took over again. An image from years ago flashed into my memory: Mom saying *ai* and then putting her hand over her heart.

"All right, Mom. Stop talking."

Dad came back, and I said that I needed to get to the airport early because I didn't want to miss my flight.

She died when my plane was somewhere over Nevada.

Dad aged rapidly after Mom died. The house was too big for him and had to be sold. My girlfriend, Susan, and I went to help him pack and clean the place.

Susan found the shoe box in the attic. The paper menagerie, hidden in the uninsulated darkness of the attic for so long, had become brittle, and the bright wrapping paper patterns had faded.

"I've never seen origami like this," Susan said. "Your mom was an amazing artist."

The paper animals did not move. Perhaps whatever magic had animated them stopped when Mom died. Or perhaps I had only imagined that these paper constructions were once alive. The memory of children could not be trusted.

It was the first weekend in April, two years after Mom's death. Susan was out of town on one of her endless trips as a management consultant, and I was home, lazily flipping through the TV channels.

I paused at a documentary about sharks. Suddenly I saw, in my mind, Mom's hands, as they folded and refolded tinfoil to make a shark for me while Laohu and I watched.

A rustle. I looked up and saw that a ball of wrapping paper and torn tape was on the floor next to the bookshelf. I walked over to pick it up for the trash.

The ball of paper shifted, unfurled itself, and I saw that it was Laohu, who I hadn't thought about in a very long time. *"Rawrr-sa."* Mom must have put him back together after I had given up.

He was smaller than I remembered. Or maybe it was just that back then my fists were smaller.

Susan had put the paper animals around our apartment as decoration. She probably left Laohu in a pretty hidden corner because he looked so shabby.

I sat down on the floor and reached out a finger. Laohu's tail twitched, and he pounced playfully. I laughed, stroking his back. Laohu purred under my hand.

"How've you been, old buddy?"

Laohu stopped playing. He got up, jumped with feline grace into my lap, and proceeded to unfold himself.

In my lap was a square of creased wrapping paper, the plain side up. It was filled with dense Chinese characters. I had never learned to read Chinese, but I knew the characters for "son," and they were at the top, where you'd expect them in a letter addressed to you, written in Mom's awkward, childish handwriting.

I went to the computer to check the Internet. Today was *Qingming*.

I took the letter with me downtown, where I knew the Chinese tour buses stopped. I stopped every tourist, asking, *"Nin hui du zhongwen ma?"* Can you read Chinese? I hadn't spoken Chinese in so long that I wasn't sure if they understood.

A young woman agreed to help. We sat down on a bench together, and she read the letter to me aloud. The language that I had tried to forget for years came back, and I felt the words sinking into me, through my skin, through my bones, until they squeezed tight around my heart.

Son,

We haven't talked in a long time. You are so angry when I try to touch you that I'm afraid. And I think maybe this pain I feel all the time now is something serious.

So I decided to write to you. I'm going to write in the paper animals I made for you that you used to like so much.

The animals will stop moving when I stop breathing. But if I write to you with all my heart, I'll leave a little of myself behind on this paper, in these words. Then, if you think of me on Qingming, when the spirits of the departed are allowed to visit their families, you'll make the parts of myself I leave behind come alive too. The creatures I made for you will again leap and run and pounce, and maybe you'll get to see these words then.

Because I have to write with all my heart, I need to write to you in Chinese.

All this time I still haven't told you the story of my life. When you were little, I always thought I'd tell you the story when you were older, so you could understand. But somehow that chance never came up.

I was born in 1957, in Sigulu Village, Hebei Province. Your grandparents were both from very poor peasant families with few relatives. Only a few years after I was born, the Great Famines struck China, during which thirty million people died. The first memory I have was waking up to see my mother eating dirt so that she could fill her belly and leave the last bit of flour for me.

Things got better after that. Sigulu is famous for its zhezhi papercraft, and my mother taught me how to make paper animals and give them life. This was practical magic in the life of the village. We made paper birds to chase grasshoppers away from the fields, and paper tigers to keep away the mice. For Chinese New Year my friends and I made red paper dragons. I'll never forget the sight of all those little dragons zooming across the sky overhead, holding up strings of exploding firecrackers to scare away all the bad memories of the past year. You would have loved it.

Then came the Cultural Revolution in 1966. Neighbor turned on neighbor, and brother against brother. Someone remembered that my mother's brother, my uncle, had left for Hong Kong back in 1946 and became a merchant there. Having a relative in Hong Kong meant we were spies and enemies of the people, and we had to be struggled against in every way. Your poor grandmother— she couldn't take the abuse and threw herself down a well. Then some boys with hunting muskets dragged your grandfather away one day into the woods, and he never came back.

There I was, a ten-year-old orphan. The only relative I had in the world was my uncle in Hong Kong. I snuck away one night and climbed onto a freight train going south.

Down in Guangdong Province a few days later, some men caught me stealing food from a field. When they heard that I was trying to get to Hong Kong, they laughed. "It's your lucky day. Our trade is to bring girls to Hong Kong."

They hid me in the bottom of a truck along with other girls and smuggled us across the border.

We were taken to a basement and told to stand up and look healthy and intelligent for the buyers. Families paid the warehouse a fee and came by to look us over and select one of us to "adopt."

The Chin family picked me to take care of their two boys. I got up every morning at four to prepare breakfast. I fed and bathed the boys. I shopped for food. I did the laundry and swept the floors. I followed the boys around and did their bidding. At night I was locked into a cupboard in the kitchen to sleep. If I was slow or did anything wrong I was beaten. If the boys did anything wrong I was beaten. If I was caught trying to learn English I was beaten.

"Why do you want to learn English?" Mr. Chin asked. "You want to go to the police? We'll tell the police that you are a mainlander illegally in Hong Kong. They'd love to have you in their prison."

Six years I lived like this. One day, an old woman who sold fish to me in the morning market pulled me aside.

"I know girls like you. How old are you now, sixteen? One day, the man who owns you will get drunk, and he'll look at you and pull you to him and you can't stop him. The wife will find out, and then you will think you really have gone to hell. You have to get out of this life. I know someone who can help."

She told me about American men who wanted Asian wives. If I can cook, clean, and take care of my American husband, he'll give me a good life. It was the only hope I had. And that was how I got into the catalog with all those lies and met your father. It is not a very romantic story, but it is my story.

In the suburbs of Connecticut, I was lonely. Your father was kind and gentle with me, and I was very grateful to him. But no one understood me, and I understood nothing.

But then you were born! I was so happy when I looked into your face and saw shades of my mother, my father, and myself. I had lost my entire family, all of Sigulu, everything I ever knew and loved. But there you were, and your face was proof that they were real. I hadn't made them up.

Now I had someone to talk to. I would teach you my language, and we could together remake a small piece of everything that I loved and lost. When you said your first words to me, in Chinese that had the same accent as my mother and me, I cried for hours. When I made the first zhezhi animals for you, and you laughed, I felt there were no worries in the world.

You grew up a little, and now you could even help your father and I talk to each other. I was really at home now. I finally found a good life. I wished my parents could be here, so that I could cook for them and give them a good life too. But my parents were no longer around. You know what the Chinese think is the saddest feeling in the world? It's for a child to finally grow the desire to take care of his parents, only to realize that they were long gone.

Son, I know that you do not like your Chinese eyes, which are my eyes. I know that you do not like your Chinese hair, which is my hair. But can you understand how much joy your very existence brought to me? And can you understand how it felt when you stopped talking to me and won't let me talk to you in Chinese? I felt I was losing everything all over again.

Why won't you talk to me, son? The pain makes it hard to write.

The young woman handed the paper back to me. I could not bear to look into her face.

Without looking up, I asked for her help in tracing out the character for *ai* on the paper below Mom's letter. I wrote the character again and again on the paper, intertwining my pen strokes with her words.

The young woman reached out and put a hand on my shoulder. Then she got up and left, leaving me alone with my mother.

Following the creases, I refolded the paper back into Laohu. I cradled him in the crook of my arm, and as he purred, we began the walk home.

AN ADVANCED READERS'
PICTURE BOOK OF
COMPARATIVE COGNITION

My darling, my child, my connoisseur of sesquipedalian words and convoluted ideas and meandering sentences and baroque images, while the sun is asleep and the moon somnambulant, while the stars bathe us in their glow from eons ago and light-years away, while you are comfortably nestled in your blankets and I am hunched over in my chair by your bed, while we are warm and safe and still for the moment in this bubble of incandescent light cast by the pearl held up by the mermaid lamp, you and I, on this planet spinning and hurtling through the frigid darkness of space at dozens of miles per second, let's read.

The brains of Telosians record all the stimuli from their senses: every tingling along their hairy spine, every sound wave striking their membranous body, every image perceived by their simple-compound-refractive light-field eyes, every molecular gustatory and olfactory sensation captured by their waving stalk-feet, every ebb and flow in the magnetic field of their irregular, potato-shaped planet.

When they wish, they can recall every experience with absolute fidelity. They can freeze a scene and zoom in to focus on any detail; they can parse and reparse each conversation to extract every nuance. A joyful memory may be relived countless times, each replay introducing new discoveries. A painful memory may be replayed countless times as well, each time creating a fresh outrage. Eidetic reminiscence is a fact of existence.

Infinity pressing down upon the finite is clearly untenable.

The Telosian organ of cognition is housed inside a segmented body that buds and grows at one end while withering and shedding at the other. Every year, a fresh segment is added at the head to record the future; every year, an old segment is discarded from the tail, consigning the past to oblivion.

Thus, while the Telosians do not forget, they also do not remember. They are said to never die, but it is arguable whether they ever live.

It has been argued that thinking is a form of compression.

Remember the first time you tasted chocolate? It was a summer afternoon; your mother had just come back from shopping. She broke off a piece from a candy bar and put it in your mouth while you sat in the high chair.

As the stearate in the cocoa butter absorbed the heat from your mouth and melted over your tongue, complex alkaloids were released and seeped into your taste buds: twitchy caffeine, giddy phenethylamine, serotonic theobromine.

"Theobromine," your mother said, "means the food of the gods."

We laughed as we watched your eyes widen in surprise at the texture, your face scrunch up at the biting bitterness, and then your whole body relax as the sweetness overwhelmed your taste buds, aided by the dance of a thousand disparate organic compounds.

Then she broke the rest of the chocolate bar in halves and fed a piece to me and ate the other herself. "We have children because we can't remember our own first taste of ambrosia."

I can't remember the dress she wore or what she had bought; I can't remember what we did for the rest of that afternoon; I can't re-create the exact timbre of her voice or the precise shapes of her features, the lines at the corners of her mouth or the name of her perfume. I only remember the way sunlight through the kitchen window glinted from her forearm, an arc as lovely as her smile.

A lit forearm, laughter, food of the gods. Thus are our memories compressed, integrated into sparkling jewels to be embedded in the limited space of our minds. A scene is turned into a mnemonic, a conversation reduced to a single phrase, a day distilled to a fleeting feeling of joy.

Time's arrow is the loss of fidelity in compression. A sketch, not a photograph. A memory is a re-creation, precious because it is both more and less than the original.

Living in a warm, endless sea rich with light and clumps of organic molecules, the Esoptrons resemble magnified cells, some as large as our whales. Undulating their translucent bodies, they drift, rising and falling, tumbling and twisting, like phosphorescent jellyfish riding on the current.

The thoughts of Esoptrons are encoded as complex chains of proteins that fold upon themselves like serpents coiling in the snake charmer's basket, seeking the lowest energy level so that they may fit into the smallest space. Most of the time, they lie dormant.

When two Esoptrons encounter each other, they may merge temporarily, a tunnel forming between their membranes. This kissing union can last hours, days, or years, as their memories are awakened and exchanged with energy contributions from both members. The pleasurable ones are selectively duplicated in a process much like protein expression—the serpentine proteins unfold and dance mesmerizingly in the electric music of coding sequences as they're first read and then re-expressed—while the unpleasant ones are diluted by being spread among the two bodies. For the Esoptrons, a shared joy truly is doubled, while a shared sorrow is indeed halved.

By the time they part, they each have absorbed the experiences of the other. It is the truest form of empathy, for the very qualia of experience are shared and expressed without alteration. There is no translation, no medium of exchange. They come to know each other in a deeper sense than any other creatures in the universe.

But being the mirrors for each other's souls has a cost: by the time they part from each other, the individuals in the mating pair have become indistinguishable. Before their merger, they each yearned for the other; as they part, they part from the self. The very quality that attracted them to each other is also, inevitably, destroyed in their union.

Whether this is a blessing or a curse is much debated.

Your mother has never hidden her desire to leave.

We met on a summer night, in a campground high up in the Rockies. We were from opposite coasts, two random particles on separate trajectories: I was headed for a new job, driving across the country and camping to save money; she was returning to Boston after having moved a friend and her truckful of possessions to San Francisco, camping because she wanted to look at the stars.

We drank cheap wine and ate even cheaper grilled hot dogs. Then we walked together under the dark velvet dome studded with crystalline stars like the inside of a geode, brighter than I'd ever seen them, while she explained to me their beauty: each as unique as a diamond, with a different-colored light. I could not remember the last time I'd looked up at the stars.

"I'm going there," she said.

"You mean Mars?" That was the big news back then, the announcement of a mission to Mars. Everyone knew it was a propaganda effort to make America seem great again, a new space race to go along with the new nuclear arms race and the stockpiling of rare Earth elements and zero-day cyber vulnerabilities. The other side had already promised their own Martian base, and we had to mirror their move in this new Great Game.

She shook her head. "What's the point of jumping onto a reef just a few steps from shore? I mean out there."

It was not the kind of statement one questioned, so instead of why and how and what are you talking about, I asked her what she hoped to find out there among the stars.

> other Suns perhaps
> With thir attendant Moons thou wilt descrie
> Communicating Male and Femal Light,
> Which two great Sexes animate the World,
> Stor'd in each Orb perhaps with some that live.
> For such vast room in Nature unpossest
> By living Soule, desert and desolate,
> Onely to shine, yet scarce to contribute
> Each Orb a glimps of Light, conveyd so farr
> Down to this habitable, which returnes
> Light back to them, is obvious to dispute.

"What do they think about? How do they experience the world? I've been imagining such stories all my life, but the truth will be stranger and more wonderful than any fairy tale."

She spoke to me of gravitational lenses and nuclear pulse propulsion, of the Fermi Paradox and the Drake Equation, of Arecibo and Yevpatoria, of Blue Origin and SpaceX.

"Aren't you afraid?" I asked.

"I almost died before I could begin to remember."

She told me about her childhood. Her parents were avid sailors who had been lucky enough to retire early. They bought a boat and lived on it, and the boat was her first home. When she was three, her parents decided to sail across the Pacific. Halfway across the ocean, somewhere near the Marshall Islands, the boat sprung a leak. The family tried everything they could to save the vessel, but in the end had to activate the emergency beacon to call for help.

"That was my very first memory. I wobbled on this immense bridge between the sea and the sky, and as it sank into the water and we had to jump off, Mom had me say good-bye."

By the time they were rescued by a Coast Guard plane, they had been adrift in the water in life vests for almost a full day and night. Sunburned and sickened by the salt water she swallowed, she spent a month in the hospital afterward.

"A lot of people were angry at my parents, saying they were reckless and irresponsible to endanger a child like that. But I'm forever grateful to them. They gave me the greatest gift parents could give to a child: fearlessness. They worked and saved and bought another boat, and we went out to the sea again."

It was such an alien way of thinking that I didn't know what to say. She seemed to detect my unease, and, turning to me, smiled.

"I like to think we were carrying on the tradition of the Polynesians who set out across the endless Pacific in their canoes or the Vikings who sailed for America. We have always lived on a boat, you know? That's what Earth is, a boat in space."

For a moment, as I listened to her, I felt as if I could step through the distance between us and hear an echo of the world through her ears, see the stars through her eyes: an austere clarity that made my heart leap.

Cheap wine and burned hot dogs, other Suns perhaps, the diamonds in the sky seen from a boat adrift at sea, the fiery clarity of falling in love.

The Tick-Tocks are the only uranium-based life forms known in the universe.

The surface of their planet is an endless vista of bare rock. To human eyes it seems a wasteland, but etched into this surface are elaborate, colorful patterns at an immense scale, each as large as an airport or stadium: curlicues like calligraphy strokes; spirals like the tips of fiddlehead ferns; hyperbolas like the shadows of flashlights against a cave wall; dense, radiating clusters like glowing cities seen from space. From time to time, a plume of superheated steam erupts from the ground like the blow of a whale or the explosion of an ice volcano on Enceladus.

Where are the creatures who left these monumental sketches? These tributes to lives lived and lost, these recordings of joys and sorrows known and forgotten?

You dig beneath the surface. Tunneling into the sandstone deposits over granite bedrock, you find pockets of uranium steeped in water.

In the darkness, the nucleus of a uranium atom spontaneously breaks apart, releasing a few neutrons. The neutrons travel through the vast emptiness of internuclear space like ships bound for strange stars (this is not really an accurate picture, but it's a romantic image and easy to illustrate). The water molecules, nebula-like, slow down the neutrons until they touch down on another uranium nucleus, a new world.

But the addition of this new neutron makes the nucleus unstable. It oscillates like a ringing alarm clock, breaks apart into two new elemental nuclei and two or three neutrons, new starships bound for distant worlds, to begin the cycle again.

To have a self-sustaining nuclear chain reaction with uranium, you need enough concentration of the right kind of uranium, uranium-235, which breaks apart when it absorbs the free neutrons, and something to slow down the speeding neutrons so that they can be absorbed, and water works well enough. Creation has blessed the world of the Tick-Tocks with both.

The by-products of fission, those fragments split from the uranium atom, fall along a bimodal distribution. Cesium, iodine, xenon, zirconium, molybdenum, technetium . . . like new stars formed from the remnants of a supernova, some last a few hours, others millions of years.

The thoughts and memories of the Tick-Tocks are formed from these glowing jewels in the dark sea. The atoms take the place of neurons, and the neutrons act as neurotransmitters. The moderating medium and neutron poisons act as inhibitors and deflect the flight of neutrons, forming neural pathways through the void. The computation process emerges at the subatomic level, and is manifested in the flight paths of messenger neutrons; the topology, composition, and arrangement of atoms; and the brilliant flashes of fissile explosion and decay.

As the thoughts of the Tick-Tocks grow ever more lively, excited, the water in the pockets of uranium heats up. When the pressure is great enough, a stream of superheated water flows up a crack in the sandstone cap and explodes at the surface in a plume of steam. The grand, intricate, fractal patterns made by the varicolored salt deposits they leave on the surface resemble the ionization trails left by subatomic particles in a bubble chamber.

Eventually, enough of the water will have been boiled away that the fast neutrons can no longer be captured by the uranium atoms to sustain the reaction. The universe sinks into quiescence, and thoughts disappear from this galaxy of atoms. This is how the Tick-Tocks die: with the heat of their own vitality.

Gradually, water seeps back into the mines, trickling through seams in the sandstone and cracks in the granite. When enough water has filled the husk of the past, a random decaying atom will release the neutron that will start the chain reaction again, ushering forth a florescence of new ideas and new beliefs, a new generation of life lit from the embers of the old.

Some have disputed the notion that the Tick-Tocks can think.

How can they be said to be thinking, the skeptics ask, when the flight of neutrons are determined by the laws of physics with a soupçon of quantum randomness? Where is their free will? Where is their self-determination? Meanwhile, the electrochemical reactor piles in the skeptics' brains hum along, following the laws of physics with an indistinguishable rigor.

Like tides, the Tick-Tock nuclear reactions operate in pulses. Cycle after cycle, each generation discovers the world anew. The ancients leave no wisdom for the future, and the young do not look to the past. They live for one season and one season alone.

Yet, on the surface of the planet, in those etched, fantastic rock paintings, is a palimpsest of their rise and fall, the exhalations of empires. The chronicles of the Tick-Tocks are left for other intelligences in the cosmos to interpret.

As the Tick-Tocks flourish, they also deplete the concentration of uranium-235. Each generation consumes some of the nonrenewable resources of their universe, leaving less for future generations and beckoning closer the day when a sustained chain reaction will no longer be possible. Like a clock winding down inexorably, the world of the Tick-Tocks will then sink into an eternal, cold silence.

Your mother's excitement was palpable.

"Can you call a Realtor?" she asked. "I'll get started on liquidating our stocks. We don't need to save anymore. Your mother is going to go on that cruise she's always wanted."

"When did we win the lottery?" I asked.

She handed me a stack of paper. *LENS Program Orientation.*

I flipped through it. . . . *Your application essay is among the most extraordinary entries we've received . . . pending a physical examination and psychological evaluation . . . limited to the immediate family . . .*

"What is this?"

Her face fell as she realized that I truly did not understand.

Radio waves attenuated rapidly in the vastness of space, she explained. If anyone is shouting into the void in the orbs around those distant stars, they would not be heard except by their closest neighbors. A civilization would have to harness the energy of an entire star to broadcast a message that could traverse interstellar distances—and how often would that happen? Look at Earth: we'd barely managed to survive one Cold War before another started. Long before we get to the point of harnessing the energy of the Sun, our children will be either wading through a postapocalyptic flooded landscape or shivering in a nuclear winter, back in another Stone Age.

"But there is a way to cheat, a way for even a primitive civilization like ours to catch faint whispers from across the galaxy and perhaps even answer back."

The Sun's gravity bends the light and radio waves from distant stars around it. This is one of the most important results from general relativity.

Suppose some other world out there in our galaxy, not much more advanced than ours, sent out a message with the most powerful antenna they could construct. By the time those emissions reached us, the electromagnetic waves would be so faint as to be undetectable. We'd have to turn the entire Solar System into a parabolic dish to capture it.

But as those radio waves grazed the surface of the Sun, the gravity of the star would bend them slightly, much as a lens bends rays of light. Those slightly bent beams from around the rim of the sun would converge at some distance beyond.

"Just as rays of sunlight could be focused by a magnifying glass into a spot on the ground."

The gain of an antenna placed at the focal point of the sun's gravitational lens would be enormous, close to ten billion times in certain frequency ranges, and orders of magnitude more in others. Even a twelve-meter inflatable dish would be able to detect transmissions from the other end of the galaxy. And if others in the galaxy were also clever enough to harness the gravitational lenses of their own suns, we would be able to talk to them as well—though the exchange would more resemble monologues delivered across the lifetimes of stars than a conversation, messages set adrift in bottles bound for distant shores, from one long-dead generation to generations yet unborn.

This spot, as it turns out, is about 550 AU from the Sun, almost fourteen times the distance of Pluto. The Sun's light would take just over three days to reach it, but at our present level of technology, it would take more than a century for a spacecraft.

Why send people? Why now?

"Because by the time an automated probe reached the focal point, we don't know if anyone will still be here. Will the human race survive even another century? No, we must send people so that they can be there to listen, and perhaps talk back.

"I'm going, and I'd like you to come with me."

The Thereals live within the hulls of great starships.

Their species, sensing the catastrophe of a world-ending disaster, commissioned the construction of escape arks for a small percentage of their world's population. Almost all of the refugees were children, for the Thereals loved their young as much as any other species.

Years before their star went supernova, the arks were launched in various directions at possible new home worlds. The ships began to accelerate, and the children settled down to learning from machine tutors and the few adults on board, trying to carry on the traditions of a dying world.

Only when the last of the adults were about to die aboard each ship did they reveal the truth to the children: the ships were not equipped with means for deceleration. They would accelerate forever, asymptotically approaching the speed of light, until the ships ran out of fuel and coasted along at the final cruising speed, toward the end of the universe.

Within their frame of reference, time would pass normally. But outside the ship, the rest of the universe would be hurtling along to its ultimate doom against the tide of entropy. To an outside observer, time seemed to stop in the ships.

Plucked out of the stream of time, the children would grow a few years older, but not much more. They would die only when the universe ended. This was the only way to ensure their safety, the adults explained, an asymptotic approach to triumphing over death. They would never have their own children; they would never have to mourn; they would never have to fear, to plan, to make impossible choices in sacrifice. They would be the last Thereals alive and possibly the last intelligent beings in the universe.

All parents make choices for their children. Almost always they think it's for the best.

All along, I had thought I could change her. I had thought she would want to stay because of me, because of our child. I had loved her because she was different; I also thought she would transform out of love.

"Love has many forms," she said. "This is mine."

Many are the stories we tell ourselves of the inevitable parting of lovers when they're from different worlds: selkies, *gu huo niao*, *Hagoromo*, swan maidens . . . What they have in common is the belief by one half of a couple that the other half could be changed, when in fact it was the difference, the resistance to change, that formed the foundation of their love. And then the day would come when the old sealskin or feather cape would be found, and it would be time to return to the sea or the sky, the ethereal realm that was the beloved's true home.

The crew of *Focal Point* would spend part of the voyage in hibernation; but once they reached their first target point, 550 AU from the Sun, away from the galactic center, they would have to stay awake and listen for as long as they could. They would guide the ship along a helical path away from the Sun, sweeping out a larger slice of the galaxy from which they might detect signals. The farther they drifted from the Sun, the better the Sun's magnification effect would be due to the reduction of interference from the solar corona on the deflected radio waves. The crew was expected to last as long as a few centuries, growing up, growing old, having children to carry on their work, dying in the void, an outpost of austere hope.

"You can't make a choice like that for our daughter," I said.

"You're making a choice for her too. How do you know if she'll be safer or happier here? This is a chance for transcendence, the best gift we can give her."

And then came the lawyers and the reporters and the pundits armed with sound bites taking sides.

Then the night that you tell me you still remember. It was your birthday, and we were together again, just the three of us, for your sake because you said that was what you wished.

We had chocolate cake (you requested "teo-broom"). Then we went outside onto the deck to look up at the stars. Your mother and I were careful to make no mention of the fight in the courts or the approaching date for her departure.

"Is it true you grew up on a boat, Mommy?" you asked.

"Yes."

"Was it scary?"

"Not at all. We're all living on a boat, sweetheart. Earth is just a big raft in the sea of stars."

"Did you like living on a boat?"

"I loved that boat—well, I don't really remember. We don't remember much about what happened when we were really young; it's a quirk of being human. But I do remember being very sad when I had to say good-bye to it. I didn't want to. It was home."

"I don't want to say good-bye to my boat, either."

She cried. And so did I. So did you.

She gave you a kiss before she left. "There are many ways to say I love you."

The universe is full of echoes and shadows, the afterimages and last words of dead civilizations that have lost the struggle against entropy. Fading ripples in the cosmic background radiation, it is doubtful if most, or any, of these messages will ever be deciphered.

Likewise, most of our thoughts and memories are destined to fade, to disappear, to be consumed by the very act of choosing and living.

That is not a cause for sorrow, sweetheart. It is the fate of every species to disappear into the void that is the heat death of the universe. But long before then, the thoughts of any intelligent species worthy of the name will become as grand as the universe itself.

Your mother is asleep now on *Focal Point*. She will not wake up until you're a very old woman, possibly not even until after you're gone.

After she wakes up, she and her crewmates will begin to listen, and they'll also broadcast, hoping that somewhere else in the universe, another species is also harnessing the energy of their star to focus the faint rays across light-years and eons. They'll play a message designed to introduce us to strangers, written in a language based on mathematics and logic. I've always found it funny that we think the best way to communicate with extraterrestrials is to speak in a way that we never do in life.

But at the end, as a closing, there will be a recording of compressed memories that will not be very logical: the graceful arc of whales breaching, the flicker of campfire and wild dancing, the formulas of chemicals making up the smell of a thousand foods, including cheap wine and burned hot dogs, the laughter of a child eating the food of the gods for the first time. Glittering jewels whose meanings are not transparent, and for that reason, are alive.

And so we read this, my darling, this book she wrote for you before she left, its ornate words and elaborate illustrations telling fairy tales that will grow as you grow, an apologia, a bundle of letters home, and a map of the uncharted waters of our souls.

There are many ways to say I love you in this cold, dark, silent universe, as many as the twinkling stars.

•   •   •

AUTHOR'S NOTES: For more on consciousness as compression, see:

Maguire, Phil, et al. "Is Consciousness Computable? Quantifying Integrated Information Using Algorithmic Information Theory." *arXiv preprint arXiv:1405.0126* (2014) (available at arxiv.org/pdf/1405.0126).

For more on natural nuclear reactor piles, see:

Teper, Igor. "Inconstants of Nature," *Nautilus*, January 23, 2014 (available at nautil.us/issue/9/time/inconstants-of-nature).

Davis, E. D., C. R. Gould, and E. I. Sharapov. "Oklo reactors and implications for nuclear science." *International Journal of Modern Physics E* 23.04 (2014) (available at arxiv.org/pdf/1404.4948).

For more on SETI and the Sun's gravitational lens, see:

Maccone, Claudio. "Interstellar radio links enhanced by exploiting the Sun as a gravitational lens." *Acta Astronautica* 68.1 (2011): 76–84 (available at snolab.ca/public/JournalClub/alex1.pdf).

THE WAVES

Long ago, just after Heaven was separated from Earth, Nü Wa wandered along the bank of the Yellow River, savoring the feel of the rich loess against the bottom of her feet.

All around her, flowers bloomed in all the colors of the rainbow, as pretty as the eastern edge of the sky, where Nü Wa had to patch a leak made by petty warring gods with a paste made of melted gemstones. Deer and buffalo dashed across the plains, and golden carp and silvery crocodiles frolicked in the water.

But she was all alone. There was no one to converse with her, no one to share all this beauty.

She sat down next to the water, and scooping up a handful of mud, began to sculpt. Before long, she had created a miniature version of herself: a round head, a long torso, arms and legs and tiny hands and fingers that she carefully carved out with a sharp bamboo skewer.

She cupped the tiny, muddy figure in her hands, brought it up to her mouth, and breathed the breath of life into it. The figure gasped, wriggled in Nü Wa's hands, and began to babble.

Nü Wa laughed. Now she would be alone no longer. She sat the little figure down on the bank of the Yellow River, scooped up another handful of mud, and began to sculpt again.

Man was thus created from earth, and to earth he would return, always.

· · ·

"What happened next?" a sleepy voice asked.

"I'll tell you tomorrow night," Maggie Chao said. "It's time to sleep now."

She tucked in Bobby, five, and Lydia, six, turned off the bedroom light, and closed the door behind her.

She stood still for a moment, listening, as if she could hear the flow of photons streaming past the smooth, spinning hull of the ship.

The great solar sail strained silently in the vacuum of space as the *Sea Foam* spiraled away from the sun, accelerating year after year until the sun had shifted into a dull red, a perpetual, diminishing sunset.

There's something you should see, João, Maggie's husband and the first officer, whispered in her mind. They were able to speak to each other through a tiny optical-neural interface chip implanted in each of their brains. The chips stimulated genetically modified neurons in the language-processing regions of the cortex with pulses of light, activating them in the same way that actual speech would have.

Maggie sometimes thought of the implant as a kind of miniature solar sail, where photons strained to generate thought.

João thought of the technology in much less romantic terms. Even a decade after the operation, he still didn't like the way they could be in each other's heads. He understood the advantages of the communication system, which allowed them to stay constantly in touch, but it felt clumsy and alienating, as though they were slowly turning into cyborgs, machines. He never used it unless it was urgent.

I'll be there, Maggie said, and quickly made her way up to the research deck, closer to the center of the ship. Here, the gravity simulated by the spinning hull was lighter, and the colonists joked that the location of the labs helped people think better because more oxygenated blood flowed to the brain.

Maggie Chao had been chosen for the mission because she was an expert on self-contained ecosystems and also because she was young and fertile. With the ship traveling at a low fraction of the speed of light, it would take close to four hundred years (by the ship's frame of reference) to reach 61 Virginis, even taking into account the modest time-dilation effects. That required planning for children and grand-children so that, one day, the colonists' descendants might carry the memory of the three hundred original explorers onto the surface of an alien world.

She met João in the lab. He handed her a display pad without say-ing anything. He always gave her time to come to her own conclusions about something new without his editorial comment. That was one of the first things she liked about him when they started dating years ago.

"Extraordinary," she said as she glanced at the abstract. "First time Earth has tried to contact us in a decade."

Many on Earth had thought the *Sea Foam* a folly, a propaganda effort from a government unable to solve real problems. How could sending a centuries-long mission to the stars be justified when there were still people dying of hunger and diseases on Earth? After launch, communication with Earth had been kept to a minimum and then cut. The new administration did not want to keep paying for those expen-sive ground-based antennas. Perhaps they preferred to forget about this ship of fools.

But now, they had reached out across the emptiness of space to say something.

As she read the rest of the message, her expression gradually shifted from excitement to disbelief.

"They believe the gift of immortality should be shared by all of humanity," João said. "Even the farthest wanderers."

The transmission described a new medical procedure. A small, modified virus—a molecular nano-computer, for those who liked to think in those terms—replicated itself in somatic cells and roamed up and down the double helices of DNA strands, repairing damage, suppressing certain segments and overexpressing others, and the net effect was to halt cellular senescence and stop aging.

Humans would no longer have to die.

Maggie looked into João's eyes. "Can we replicate the procedure here?" *We will live to walk on another world, to breathe unrecycled air.*

"Yes," he said. "It will take some time, but I'm sure we can." Then he hesitated. "But the children . . ."

Bobby and Lydia were not the result of chance but the interplay of a set of careful algorithms involving population planning, embryo selection, genetic health, life expectancy, and rates of resource renewal and consumption.

Every gram of matter aboard the *Sea Foam* was accounted for. There was enough to support a stable population but little room for error. The children's births had to be timed so that they would have enough time to learn what they needed to learn from their parents, and then take their place as their elders died a peaceful death, cared for by the machines.

". . . would be the last children to be born until we land," Maggie finished João's thought. The *Sea Foam* had been designed for a precise population mix of adults and children. Supplies, energy, and thousands of other parameters were all tied to that mix. There was some margin of safety, but the ship could not support a population composed entirely of vigorous, immortal adults at the height of their caloric needs.

"We could either die and let our children grow," João said, "or we could live forever and keep them always as children."

Maggie imagined it: the virus could be used to stop the process of growth and maturation in the very young. The children would stay children for centuries, childless themselves.

Something finally clicked in Maggie's mind.

"That's why Earth is suddenly interested in us again," she said.

"Earth is just a very big ship. If no one is going to die, they'll run out of room eventually too. Now there is no other problem on Earth more pressing. They'll have to follow us and move into space."

You wonder why there are so many stories about how people came to be? It's because all true stories have many tellings.

Tonight, let me tell you another one.

There was a time when the world was ruled by the Titans, who lived on Mount Othrys. The greatest and bravest of the Titans was Cronus, who once led them in a rebellion against Uranus, his father and a tyrant. After Cronus killed Uranus, he became the king of the gods.

But as time went on, Cronus himself became a tyrant. Perhaps out of fear that what he had done to his own father would happen to him, Cronus swallowed all his children as soon as they were born.

Rhea, the wife of Cronus, gave birth to a new son, Zeus. To save the boy, she wrapped a stone in a blanket like a baby and fooled Cronus into swallowing that. The real baby Zeus she sent away to Crete, where he grew up drinking goat milk.

Don't make that face. I hear goat milk is quite tasty.

When Zeus was finally ready to face his father, Rhea fed Cronus a bitter wine that caused him to vomit up the children he had swallowed, Zeus's brothers and sisters. For ten years, Zeus led the Olympians, for that was the name by which Zeus and his siblings would come to be known, in a bloody war against his father and the Titans. In the end, the new gods won against the old, and Cronus and the Titans were cast into lightless Tartarus.

And the Olympians went on to have children of their own, for that was the way of the world. Zeus himself had many children, some mortal, some not. One of his favorites was Athena, the goddess who was born from his head, from his thoughts alone. There are many stories about them as well, which I will tell you another time.

But some of the Titans who did not fight by the side of Cronus were spared. One of these, Prometheus, molded a race of beings out of clay, and it is said that he then leaned down to whisper to them the words of wisdom that gave them life.

We don't know what he taught the new creatures, us. But this was a god who had lived to see sons rise up against fathers, each new generation replacing the old, remaking the world afresh each time. We can guess what he might have said.

Rebel. Change is the only constant.

"Death is the easy choice," Maggie said.

"It is the right choice," João said.

Maggie wanted to keep the argument in their heads, but João refused. He wanted to speak with lips, tongue, bursts of air, the old way.

Every gram of unnecessary mass had been shaved off the *Sea Foam*'s construction. The walls were thin and the rooms closely packed. Maggie and João's voices echoed through the decks and halls.

All over the ship, other families, who were having the same argument in their heads, stopped to listen.

"The old must die to make way for the new," João said. "You knew that we would not live to see the *Sea Foam* land when you signed up for this. Our children's children, generations down the line, are meant to inherit the new world."

"We can land on the new world ourselves. We don't have to leave all the hard work to our unborn descendants."

"We need to pass on a viable human culture for the new colony. We have no idea what the long-term consequences of this treatment will be on our mental health—"

"Then let's do the job we signed up for: exploration. Let's figure it out—"

"If we give in to this temptation, we'll land as a bunch of four-hundred-year-olds who were afraid to die and whose ideas were ossified from old Earth. How can we teach our children the value of sacrifice, the meaning of heroism, of beginning afresh? We'll barely be human."

"We stopped being human the moment we agreed to this mission!" Maggie paused to get her voice under control. "Face it, the birth allocation algorithms don't care about us, or our children. We're nothing more than vessels for the delivery of a planned, optimal mix of genes to our destination. Do you really want generations to grow and die in here, knowing nothing but this narrow metal tube? I worry about *their* mental health."

"Death is essential to the growth of our species." His voice was filled with faith, and she heard in it his hope that it was enough for both of them.

"It's a myth that we must die to retain our humanity." Maggie looked at her husband, her heart in pain. There was a divide between them, as inexorable as the dilation of time.

She spoke to him now inside his head. She imagined her thoughts, now transformed into photons, pushing against his brain, trying to illuminate the gap. *We stop being human at the moment we give in to death.*

João looked back at her. He said nothing, either in her mind or aloud, which was his way of saying all that he needed to say.

They stayed like that for a long time.

God first created mankind to be immortal, much like the angels.

Before Adam and Eve chose to eat from the Tree of the Knowledge of Good and Evil, they did not grow old and they never became sick. During the day, they cultivated the Garden, and at night, they enjoyed each other's company.

Yes, I suppose the Garden was a bit like the hydroponics deck.

Sometimes the angels visited them, and—according to Milton, who was born too late to get into the regular Bible—they conversed and speculated about everything: Did Earth revolve around the Sun or was it the other way around? Was there life on other planets? Did angels also have sex?

Oh no, I'm not joking. You can look it up in the computer.

So Adam and Eve were forever young and perpetually curious. They did not need death to give their life purpose, to be motivated to learn, to work, to love, to give existence meaning.

If that story is true, then we were never meant to die. And the knowledge of good and evil was really the knowledge of regret.

"You know some very strange stories, Gran-Gran," six-year-old Sara said.

"They're old stories," Maggie said. "When I was a little girl, my grandmother told me many stories, and I did a lot of reading."

"Do you want me to live forever like you, and not grow old and die someday like my mother?"

"I can't tell you what to do, sweetheart. You'll have to figure that out when you're older."

"Like the knowledge of good and evil?"

"Something like that."

She leaned down and kissed her great-great-great-great—she had long lost count—granddaughter as gently as she could. Like all children born in the low gravity of the *Sea Foam*, her bones were thin and delicate, like a bird's. Maggie turned off the night-light and left.

Though she would pass her four hundredth birthday in another month, Maggie didn't look a day older than thirty-five. The recipe for the fountain of youth, Earth's last gift to the colonists before they lost all communications, worked well.

She stopped and gasped. A small boy, about ten years in age, waited in front of the door to her room.

Bobby, she said. Except for the very young, who did not yet have the implants, all the colonists now conversed through thoughts rather than speech. It was faster and more private.

The boy looked at her, saying nothing and thinking nothing at her. She was struck by how like his father he was. He had the same expressions, the same mannerisms, even the same ways to speak by not speaking.

She sighed, opened the door, and walked in after him.

One more month, he said, sitting on the edge of the couch so that his feet didn't dangle.

Everybody on the ship was counting down the days. In one more month they'd be in orbit around the fourth planet of 61 Virginis, their destination, a new Earth.

*After we land, will you change your mind about—*she hesitated, but went on after a moment—*your appearance?*

Bobby shook his head, and a hint of boyish petulance crossed his face. *Mom, I've made my decision a long time ago. Let it go. I like the way I am.*

In the end, the men and women of the *Sea Foam* had decided to leave the choice of eternal youth to each individual.

The cold mathematics of the ship's enclosed ecosystem meant that when someone chose immortality, a child would have to remain a child until someone else on the ship decided to grow old and die, opening up a new slot for an adult.

João chose to age and die. Maggie chose to stay young. They sat together as a family, and it felt a bit like a divorce.

"One of you will get to grow up," João said.

"Which one?" Lydia asked.

"We think you should decide," João said, glancing at Maggie, who nodded reluctantly.

Maggie had thought it was unfair and cruel of her husband to put such a choice before their children. How could children decide if they wanted to grow up when they had no real idea what that meant?

"It's no more unfair than you and I deciding whether we want to be immortal," João had said. "We have no real idea what that means either. It is terrible to put such a choice before them, but to decide *for* them would be even more cruel." Maggie had to agree that he had a point.

It seemed like they were asking the children to take sides. But maybe that was the point.

Lydia and Bobby looked at each other, and they seemed to reach a silent understanding. Lydia got up, walked to João, and hugged him. At the same time, Bobby came and hugged Maggie.

"Dad," Lydia said, "when my time comes, I will choose the same as you." João tightened his arms around her and nodded.

Then Lydia and Bobby switched places and hugged their parents again, pretending that everything was fine.

For those who refused the treatment, life went on as planned. As João grew old, Lydia grew up: first an awkward teenager, then a beautiful young woman. She went into engineering, as predicted by her aptitude tests, and decided that she *did* like Catherine, the shy young doctor that the computers suggested would be a good mate for her.

"Will you grow old and die with me?" Lydia asked the blushing Catherine one day.

They married and had two daughters of their own—to replace them, when their time came.

"Do you ever regret choosing this path?" João asked her one time. He was very old and ill by then, and in another two weeks the computers would administer the drugs to allow him to fall asleep and not wake up.

"No," Lydia said, holding his hand with both of hers. "I'm not afraid to step out of the way when something new comes to take my place."

But who's to say that we aren't the "something new"? Maggie thought.

In a way, her side was winning the argument. Over the years, more and more colonists had decided to join the ranks of the immortals. But Lydia's descendants had always stubbornly refused. Sara was the last untreated child on the ship. Maggie knew Sara would miss the nightly story times when she grew up.

Bobby was frozen at the physical age of ten. He and the other perpetual children integrated only uneasily into the life of the colonists. They had decades—sometimes centuries—of experience, but retained juvenile bodies and brains. They possessed adult knowledge, but kept the emotional range and mental flexibility of children. They could be both old and young in the same moment.

There was a great deal of tension and conflict about what roles they should play on the ship, and occasionally, parents who once thought they wanted to live forever would give up their spots when their children demanded it of them.

But Bobby never asked to grow up.

My brain has the plasticity of a ten-year-old's. Why would I want to give that up? Bobby said.

Maggie had to admit that she always felt more comfortable with Lydia and her descendants. Even though they had all chosen to die, as João did, which could be seen as a kind of rebuke of her decision, she found herself better able to understand their lives and play a role in them.

With Bobby, on the other hand, she couldn't imagine what went on in his head. She sometimes found him a little creepy, which she agreed was a bit hypocritical, considering he only made the same choice she did.

But you won't experience what it's like to be grown, she said. *To love as a man and not a boy.*

He shrugged, unable to miss what he never had. *I can pick up new languages quickly. It's easy for me to absorb a new worldview. I'll always like new things.*

Bobby switched to speech, and his boyish voice rose as it filled with excitement and longing. "If we meet new life and new civilization down there, we'll need people like me, the forever children, to learn about them and understand them without fear."

It had been a long time since Maggie had really listened to her son. She was moved. She nodded, accepting his choice.

Bobby's face opened in a beautiful smile, the smile of a ten-year-old boy who had seen more than almost every human who had ever lived.

"Mom, I'll get that chance. I came to tell you that we've received the results of the first close-up scans of 61 Virginis e. It's inhabited."

Under the *Sea Foam*, the planet spun slowly. Its surface was covered by a grid of hexagonal and pentagonal patches, each a thousand miles across. About half of the patches were black as obsidian, while the rest were a grainy tan. 61 Virginis e reminded Maggie of a soccer ball.

Maggie stared at the three aliens standing in front of her in the shuttle bay, each about six feet tall. The metallic bodies, barrel-shaped and segmented, rested on four stick-thin, multijointed legs.

When the vehicles first approached the *Sea Foam*, the colonists had thought they were tiny scout ships until scans confirmed the absence of any organic matter. Then the colonists had thought they were autonomous probes until they came right up to the ship's camera, displayed their hands, and lightly tapped the lens.

Yes, *hands*. Midway up each of the metallic bodies, two long, sinuous arms emerged and terminated in soft, supple hands made of a fine alloy mesh. Maggie looked down at her own hands. The alien hands looked just like hers: four slender fingers, an opposable thumb, flexible joints.

On the whole, the aliens reminded Maggie of robotic centaurs.

At the very top of each alien body was a spherical protuberance studded with clusters of glass lenses, like compound eyes. Other than the eyes, this "head" was also covered by a dense array of pins attached to actuators that moved in synchrony like the tentacles of a sea anemone.

The pins shimmered as though a wave moved through them. Gradually, they took on the appearance of pixellated eyebrows, lips, eyelids—a face, a human face.

The alien began to speak. It sounded like English but Maggie couldn't make it out. The phonemes, like the shifting patterns of the pins, seemed elusive, just beyond coherence.

It is English, Bobby said to Maggie, *after centuries of pronunciation drift. He's saying, "Welcome back to humanity."*

The fine pins on the alien face shifted, unveiling a smile. Bobby continued to translate. *We left Earth long after your departure, but we were faster and passed you in transit centuries ago. We've been waiting for you.*

Maggie felt the world shift around her. She looked around, and many of the older colonists, the immortals, looked stunned.

But Bobby, the eternal child, stepped forward. "Thank you," he said aloud, and smiled back.

Let me tell you a story, Sara. We humans have always relied on stories to keep the fear of the unknown at bay.

I've told you how the Mayan gods created people out of maize, but did you know that before that, there were several other attempts at creation?

First came the animals: brave jaguar and beautiful macaw, flat fish and long serpent, the great whale and the lazy sloth, the iridescent iguana and the nimble bat. (We can look up pictures for all of these on the computer later.) But the animals only squawked and growled, and could not speak their creators' names.

So the gods kneaded a race of beings out of mud. But the mud men could not hold their shape. Their faces drooped, softened by water, yearning to rejoin the earth whence they were taken. They could not speak but only gurgled incoherently. They grew lopsided and were unable to procreate, to perpetuate their own existence.

The gods' next effort is the one of most interest to us. They created a race of wooden manikins, like dolls. The articulated joints allowed their limbs to move freely. The carved faces allowed their lips to flap and eyes to open. The stringless puppets lived in houses and villages, and went busily about their lives.

But the gods found that the wooden men had neither souls nor minds, and so they could not praise their makers properly. They sent a great flood to destroy the wooden men and asked the animals of the jungle to attack them. When the anger of the gods was over, the wooden men had become monkeys.

And only then did the gods turn to maize.

Many have wondered if the wooden men were really content to lose to the children of the maize. Perhaps they're still waiting in the shadows for an opportunity to come back, for creation to reverse its course.

The black hexagonal patches were solar panels, Atax, the leader of the three envoys from 61 Virginis e, explained. Together, they provided the power needed to support human habitation on the planet. The tan patches were cities, giant computing arrays where trillions of humans lived as virtual patterns of computation.

When Atax and the others colonists had first arrived, 61 Viriginis e was not particularly hospitable to life from Earth. It was too hot, the air was too poisonous, and the existing alien life, mostly primitive microbes, was quite deadly.

But Atax and the others who had stepped onto the surface were not human, not in the sense Maggie would have understood the term. They were composed of more metal than water, and they were no longer trapped by the limits of organic chemistry. The colonists quickly constructed forges and foundries, and their descendants soon spread out across the globe.

Most of the time they chose to merge into the Singularity, the overall World-Mind that was both artificial and organic, where eons passed in a second as thought was processed at the speed of quantum computation. In the world of bits and qubits, they lived as gods.

But sometimes, when they felt the ancestral longing for physicality, they could choose to become individuals and be embodied in machines, as Atax and his companions were. Here, they lived in the slow-time, the time of atoms and stars.

There was no more line between the ghost and the machine.

"This is what humanity looks like now," Atax said, spinning around slowly to display his metal body for the benefit of the colonists on the *Sea Foam*. "Our bodies are made of steel and titanium, and our brains graphene and silicon. We are practically indestructible. Look, we can even move through space without the need for ships, suits, layers of protection. We have left corruptible flesh behind."

Atax and the others gazed intently at the ancient humans around them. Maggie stared back into their dark lenses, trying to fathom how the machines felt. Curiosity? Nostalgia? Pity?

Maggie shuddered at the shifting, metallic faces, a crude imitation of flesh and blood. She looked over at Bobby, who appeared ecstatic.

"You may join us, if you wish, or continue as you are. It is of course difficult to decide when you have no experience of our mode of existence. Yet you must choose. We cannot choose for you."

Something new, Maggie thought.

Even eternal youth and eternal life did not appear so wonderful compared to the freedom of being a machine, a thinking machine endowed with the austere beauty of crystalline matrices instead of the messy imperfections of living cells.

At last, humanity has advanced beyond evolution into the realm of intelligent design.

"I'm not afraid," Sara said.

She had asked to stay behind for a few minutes with Maggie after all the others had left. Maggie gave her a long hug, and the little girl squeezed her back.

"Do you think Gran-Gran João would have been disappointed in me?" Sara asked. "I'm not making the choice he would have made."

"I know he would have wanted you to decide for yourself," Maggie said. "People change, as a species and as individuals. We don't know what he would have chosen if he had been offered your choice. But no matter what, never let the past pick your life for you."

She kissed Sara on the cheek and let go. A machine came to take Sara away by the hand so that she could be transformed.

She's the last of the untreated children, Maggie thought. *And now she'll be the first to become a machine.*

Though Maggie refused to watch the transformation of the others, at Bobby's request, she watched as her son was replaced piece by piece.

"You'll never have children," she said.

"On the contrary," he said, as he flexed his new metal hands, so much larger and stronger than his old hands, the hands of a child, "I will have countless children, born of my mind." His voice was a pleasant electronic hum, like a patient teaching program's. "They'll inherit from my thoughts as surely as I have inherited your genes. And someday, if they wish, I will construct bodies for them, as beautiful and functional as the ones I'm being fitted with."

He reached out to touch her arm, and the cold metal fingertips slid smoothly over her skin, gliding on nanostructures that flexed like living tissue. She gasped.

Bobby smiled as his face, a fine mesh of thousands of pins, rippled in amusement.

She recoiled from him involuntarily.

Bobby's rippling face turned serious, froze, and then showed no expression at all.

She understood the unspoken accusation. What right did she have to feel revulsion? She treated her body as a machine too, just a machine of lipids and proteins, of cells and muscles. Her mind was maintained in a shell too, a shell of flesh that had long outlasted its designed-for life. She was as "unnatural" as he.

Still, she cried as she watched her son disappear into a frame of animated metal.

He can't cry anymore, she kept on thinking, as if that was the only thing that divided her from him.

Bobby was right. Those who were frozen as children were quicker to decide to upload. Their minds were flexible, and to them, to change from flesh to metal was merely a hardware upgrade.

The older immortals, on the other hand, lingered, unwilling to leave their past behind, their last vestiges of humanity. But one by one, they succumbed as well.

For years, Maggie remained the only organic human on 61 Virginis e, and perhaps the entire universe. The machines built a special house for her, one insulated from the heat and poison and ceaseless noise of the planet, and Maggie occupied herself by browsing through the *Sea Foam*'s archives, the records of humanity's long, dead past. The machines left her pretty much alone.

One day, a small machine, about two feet tall, came into her house and approached her hesitantly. It reminded her of a puppy.

"Who are you?" Maggie asked.

"I'm your grandchild," the little machine said.

"So Bobby has finally decided to have a child," Maggie said. "It took him long enough."

"I'm the 5,032,322th child of my parent."

Maggie felt dizzy. Soon after his transformation into a machine, Bobby had decided to go all the way and join the Singularity. They had not spoken to each other for a long time.

"What's your name?"

"I don't have a name in the sense you think of it. But why don't you call me Athena?"

"Why?"

"It's a name from a story my parent used to tell me when I was little."

Maggie looked at the little machine, and her expression softened.

"How old are you?"

"That's a hard question to answer," Athena said. "We're born virtual and each second of our existence as part of the Singularity is composed of trillions of computation cycles. In that state, I have more thoughts in a second than you have had in your entire life."

Maggie looked at her granddaughter, a miniature mechanical centaur, freshly made and gleaming, and also a being much older and wiser than she by most measures.

"So why have you put on this disguise to make me think of you as a child?"

"Because I want to hear your stories," Athena said. "The ancient stories."

There are still young people, Maggie thought. *Still something new. Why can't the old become new again?*

And so Maggie decided to upload as well, to rejoin her family.

·　　·　　·

In the beginning, the world was a great void crisscrossed by icy rivers full of venom. The venom congealed, dripped, and formed into Ymir, the first giant, and Auðumbla, a great ice cow.

Ymir fed on Auðumbla's milk and grew strong.

Of course you have never seen a cow. Well, it is a creature that gives milk, which you would have drunk if you were still . . .

I suppose it is a bit like how you absorbed electricity, at first in trickles, when you were still young, and then in greater measure as you grew older, to give you strength.

Ymir grew and grew until finally, three gods, the brothers Vili, and Vé, and Odin, slew him. Out of his carcass the gods created the world: his blood became the warm, salty sea, his flesh the rich, fertile earth, his bones the hard, plow-breaking hills, and his hair, the swaying, dark forests. Out of his wide brows the gods carved Midgard, the realm in which humans lived.

After the death of Ymir, the three brother gods walked along a beach. At the end of the beach, they came upon two trees leaning against each other. The gods fashioned two human figures out of their wood. One of the brother gods breathed life into the wooden figures, another endowed them with intelligence, and the third gave them sense and speech. And this was how Ask and Embla, the first man and the first woman, came to be.

You are skeptical that men and women were once made from trees? But you're made of metal. Who's to say trees wouldn't do just as well?

Now let me tell you the story behind the names. "Ask" comes from "ash," a hard tree that is used to make a drill for fire. "Embla" comes from "vine," a softer sort of wood that is easy to set on fire. The motion of twirling a fire drill until the kindling is inflamed reminded the people who told this story of an analogy with sex, and that may be the real story they wanted to tell.

Once your ancestors would have been scandalized that I speak to you of sex so frankly. The word is still a mystery to you, but without the allure that it once held. Before we found how to live forever, sex and children were the closest we came to immortality.

Like a thriving hive, the Singularity began to send a constant stream of colonists away from 61 Virginis e.

One day, Athena came to Maggie and told her that she was ready to be embodied and lead her own colony.

At the thought of not seeing Athena again, Maggie felt an emptiness. *So it is possible to love again, even as a machine.*

Why don't I come with you? she asked. *It will be good for your children to have some connection with the past.*

And Athena's joy at her request was electric and contagious.

Sara came to say good-bye to her, but Bobby did not show up. He had never forgiven her for her rejection of him the moment he became a machine.

Even the immortals have regrets, she thought.

And so a million consciousnesses embodied themselves in metal shells shaped like robot centaurs, and like a swarm of bees leaving to found a new hive, they lifted into the air, tucked their limbs together so that they were shaped like graceful teardrops, and launched themselves straight up.

Up and up they went, through the acrid air, through the crimson sky, out of the gravity well of the heavy planet, and steering by the shifting flow of the solar wind and the dizzying spin of the galaxy, they set out across the sea of stars.

Light-year after light-year, they crossed the void between the stars. They passed the planets that had already been settled by earlier colonies, worlds now thriving with their own hexagonal arrays of solar panels and their own humming Singularities.

Onward they flew, searching for the perfect planet, the new world that would be their new home.

While they flew, they huddled together against the cold emptiness that was space. Intelligence, complexity, life, computation—everything seemed so small and insignificant against the great and eternal void. They felt the longing of distant black holes and the majestic glow of exploding novas. And they pulled closer to each other, seeking comfort in their common humanity.

As they flew on, half dreaming, half awake, Maggie told the colonists stories, weaving her radio waves among the constellation of colonists like strands of spider silk.

There are many stories of the Dreamtime, most secret and sacred. But a few have been told to outsiders, and this is one of them.

In the beginning there was the sky and the earth, and the earth was as flat and featureless as the gleaming titanium alloy surface of our bodies.

But under the earth, the spirits lived and dreamed.

And time began to flow, and the spirits woke from their slumber.

They broke through the surface, where they took on the forms of animals: Emu, Koala, Platypus, Dingo, Kangaroo, Shark . . . Some even took the shapes of humans. Their forms were not fixed but could be changed at will.

They roamed over the earth and shaped it, stamping out valleys and pushing up hills, scraping the ground to make deserts, digging through it to make rivers.

And they gave birth to children, children who could not change forms: animals, plants, humans. These children were born from the Dreamtime but not of it.

When the spirits were tired, they sank back into the earth whence they came. And the children were left behind with only vague memories of the Dreamtime, the time before there was time.

But who is to say that they will not return to that state, to a time when they could change form at will, to a time where time had no meaning?

And they woke from her words into another dream.

One moment, they were suspended in the void of space, still light-years from their destination. The next, they were surrounded by shimmering light.

No, not exactly *light*. Though the lenses mounted on their chassis could see far beyond the spectrum visible to primitive human eyes, this energy field around them vibrated at frequencies far above and below even their limits.

The energy field slowed down to match the subluminal flight of Maggie and the other colonists.

Not too far now.

The thought pushed against their consciousness like a wave, as though all their logic gates were vibrating in sympathy. The thought felt both alien and familiar.

Maggie looked at Athena, who was flying next to her.

Did you hear that? they said at the same time. Their thought strands tapped each other lightly, a caress with radio waves.

Maggie reached out into space with a thought strand, *You're human?*

A pause that lasted a billionth of a second, which seemed like an eternity at the speed they were moving.

We haven't thought of ourselves in that way in a long time.

And Maggie felt a wave of thoughts, images, feelings push into her from every direction. It was overwhelming.

In a nanosecond she experienced the joy of floating along the surface of a gas giant, part of a storm that could swallow Earth. She learned what it would be like to swim through the chromosphere of a star, riding white-hot plumes and flares that rose hundreds of thousands of miles. She felt the loneliness of making the entire universe your playground, yet having no home.

We came after you, and we passed you.

Welcome, ancient ones. Not too far now.

There was a time when we knew many stories of the creation of the world. Each continent was large and there were many peoples, each told their own story.

Then many peoples disappeared, and their stories forgotten.

This is one that survived. Twisted, mangled, retold to fit what strangers want to hear, there is nonetheless some truth left in it.

In the beginning the world was void and without light, and the spirits lived in the darkness.

The Sun woke up first, and he caused the water vapors to rise into the sky and baked the land dry. The other spirits—Man, Leopard, Crane, Lion, Zebra, Wildebeest, and even Hippopotamus—rose up next. They wandered across the plains, talking excitedly with each other.

But then the Sun set, and the animals and Man sat in darkness, too afraid to move. Only when morning came again did everyone start going again.

But Man was not content to wait every night. One night, Man invented fire to have his own sun, heat and light that obeyed his will, and that divided him from the animals that night and forever after.

So Man was always yearning for the light, the light that gives him life and the light to which he will return.

And at night, around the fire, they told each other the true stories, again and again.

Maggie chose to become part of the light.

She shed her chassis, her home and her body for such a long time.

Had it been centuries? Millennia? Eons? Such measures of time no longer had any meaning.

Patterns of energy now, Maggie and the others learned to coalesce, stretch, shimmer, and radiate. She learned how to suspend herself between stars, her consciousness a ribbon across both time and space.

She careened from one edge of the galaxy to the other.

One time, she passed right through the pattern that was now Athena. Maggie felt the child as a light tingling, like laughter.

Isn't this lovely, Gran-Gran? Come visit Sara and me sometime!

But it was too late for Maggie to respond. Athena was already too far away.

I miss my chassis.

That was Bobby, whom she met hovering next to a black hole.

For a few thousand years, they gazed at the black hole together from beyond the event horizon.

This is very lovely, he said. *But sometimes I think I prefer my old shell.*

You're getting old, she said. *Just like me.*

They pressed against each other, and that region of the universe lit up briefly like an ion storm laughing.

And they said good-bye to each other.

This is a nice planet, Maggie thought.

It was a small planet, rather rocky, mostly covered by water.

She landed on a large island near the mouth of a river.

The sun hovered overhead, warm enough that she could see steam rising from the muddy riverbanks. Lightly, she glided over the alluvial plains.

The mud was too tempting. She stopped, condensed herself until her energy patterns were strong enough. Churning the water, she scooped a mound of the rich, fertile mud onto the bank. Then she sculpted the mound until it resembled a man: arms akimbo, legs splayed, a round head with vague indentations and protrusions for eyes, nose, mouth.

She looked at the sculpture of João for a while, caressed it, and left it to dry in the sun.

Looking about herself, she saw blades of grass covered with bright silicon beads and black flowers that tried to absorb every bit of sunlight. She saw silver shapes darting through the brown water and golden shadows gliding through the indigo sky. She saw great scale-covered bodies lumbering and bellowing in the distance, and close by a great geyser erupted near the river, and rainbows appeared in the warm mist.

She was all alone. There was no one to converse with her, no one to share all this beauty.

She heard a nervous rustling and looked for the source of the sound. A little ways from the river, tiny creatures with eyes studded all over their heads like diamonds peered out of the dense forests, made of trees with triangular trunks and pentagonal leaves.

Closer and closer, she drifted to those creatures. Effortlessly, she reached inside them and took ahold of the long chains of a particular molecule, their instructions for the next generation. She made a small tweak, and then let go.

The creatures yelped, and skittered away at the strange sensation of having their insides adjusted.

She had done nothing drastic, just a small adjustment, a nudge in the right direction. The change would continue to mutate, and the mutations would accumulate long after she left. In another few hundred generations, the changes would be enough to cause a spark, a spark that would feed itself until the creatures would start to think of keeping a piece of the sun alive at night, of naming things, of telling stories to each other about how everything came to be. They would be able to choose.

Something new in the universe. Someone new to the family.

But for now, it was time to return to the stars.

Maggie began to rise from the island. Below her, the sea sent wave after wave to crash against the shore, each wave catching and surpassing the one before it, reaching a little farther up the beach. Bits of sea foam floated up and rode the wind to parts unknown.

MONO NO AWARE

The world is shaped like the kanji for "umbrella," only written so poorly, like my handwriting, that all the parts are out of proportion.

My father would be greatly ashamed at the childish way I still form my characters. Indeed, I can barely write many of them anymore. My formal schooling back in Japan ceased when I was only eight.

Yet for present purposes, this badly drawn character will do.

The canopy up there is the solar sail. Even that distorted kanji can only give you a hint of its vast size. A hundred times thinner than rice paper, the spinning disk fans out a thousand kilometers into space like a giant kite intent on catching every passing photon. It literally blocks out the sky.

Beneath it dangles a long cable of carbon nanotubes a hundred kilometers long: strong, light, and flexible. At the end of the cable hangs the heart of the *Hopeful*, the habitat module, a five-hundred-meter-tall cylinder into which all the 1,021 inhabitants of the world are packed.

The light from the sun pushes against the sail, propelling us on an ever widening, ever accelerating, spiraling orbit away from it. The acceleration pins all of us against the decks, gives everything weight.

Our trajectory takes us toward a star called 61 Virginis. You can't see it now because it is behind the canopy of the solar sail. The *Hopeful* will get there in about three hundred years, more or less. With luck, my great-great-great—I calculated how many "greats" I needed once, but I don't remember now—grandchildren will see it.

There are no windows in the habitat module, no casual view of the stars streaming past. Most people don't care, having grown bored of seeing the stars long ago. But I like looking through the cameras mounted on the bottom of the ship so that I can gaze at this view of the receding, reddish glow of our sun, our past.

"Hiroto," Dad said as he shook me awake. "Pack up your things. It's time."

My small suitcase was ready. I just had to put my Go set into it. Dad gave this to me when I was five, and the times we played were my favorite hours of the day.

The sun had not yet risen when Mom and Dad and I made our way outside. All the neighbors were standing outside their houses with their bags as well, and we greeted one another politely under the summer stars. As usual, I looked for the Hammer. It was easy. Ever since I could remember, the asteroid had been the brightest thing in the sky except for the moon, and every year it grew brighter.

A truck with loudspeakers mounted on top drove slowly down the middle of the street.

"Attention, citizens of Kurume! Please make your way in an orderly fashion to the bus stop. There will be plenty of buses to take you to the train station, where you can board the train for Kagoshima. Do not drive. You must leave the roads open for the evacuation buses and official vehicles!"

Every family walked slowly down the sidewalk.

"Mrs. Maeda," Dad said to our neighbor. "Why don't I carry your luggage for you?"

"I'm very grateful," the old woman said.

After ten minutes of walking, Mrs. Maeda stopped and leaned against a lamppost.

"It's just a little longer, Granny," I said. She nodded but was too out of breath to speak. I tried to cheer her. "Are you looking forward to seeing your grandson in Kagoshima? I miss Michi too. You will be able to sit with him and rest on the spaceships. They say there will be enough seats for everyone."

Mom smiled at me approvingly.

"How fortunate we are to be here," Dad said. He gestured at the orderly rows of people moving toward the bus stop, at the young men in clean shirts and shoes looking solemn, the middle-aged women helping their elderly parents, the clean, empty streets, and the quietness— despite the crowd, no one spoke above a whisper. The very air seemed to shimmer with the dense connections between all the people— families, neighbors, friends, colleagues—as invisible and strong as threads of silk.

I had seen on TV what was happening in other places around the world: looters screaming, dancing through the streets, soldiers and policemen shooting into the air and sometimes into crowds, burning buildings, teetering piles of dead bodies, generals shouting before frenzied crowds, vowing vengeance for ancient grievances even as the world was ending.

"Hiroto, I want you to remember this," Dad said. He looked around, overcome by emotion. "It is in the face of disasters that we show our strength as a people. Understand that we are not defined by our individual loneliness, but by the web of relationships in which we're enmeshed. A person must rise above his selfish needs so that all of us can live in harmony. The individual is small and powerless, but bound tightly together, as a whole, the Japanese nation is invincible."

· · ·

"Mr. Shimizu," eight-year-old Bobby says, "I don't like this game."

The school is located in the very center of the cylindrical habitat module, where it can have the benefit of the most shielding from radiation. In front of the classroom hangs a large American flag to which the children say their pledge every morning. To the sides of the American flag are two rows of smaller flags belonging to other nations with survivors on the *Hopeful*. At the very end of the left side is a child's rendition of the Hinomaru, the corners of the white paper now curled and the once bright red rising sun faded to the orange of sunset. I drew it the day I came aboard the *Hopeful*.

I pull up a chair next to the table where Bobby and his friend Eric are sitting. "Why don't you like it?"

Between the two boys is a nineteen-by-nineteen grid of straight lines. A handful of black and white stones have been placed on the intersections.

Once every two weeks, I have the day off from my regular duties monitoring the status of the solar sail and come here to teach the children a little bit about Japan. I feel silly doing it sometimes. How can I be their teacher when I have only a boy's hazy memories of Japan?

But there is no other choice. All the non-American technicians like me feel it is our duty to participate in the cultural-enrichment program at the school and pass on what we can.

"All the stones look the same," Bobby says, "and they don't move. They're boring."

"What game do you like?" I ask.

"*Asteroid Defender!*" Eric says. "Now *that* is a good game. You get to save the world."

"I mean a game you do not play on the computer."

Bobby shrugs. "Chess, I guess. I like the queen. She's powerful and different from everyone else. She's a hero."

"Chess is a game of skirmishes," I say. "The perspective of Go is bigger. It encompasses entire battles."

"There are no heroes in Go," Bobby says stubbornly.

I don't know how to answer him.

There was no place to stay in Kagoshima, so everyone slept outside along the road to the spaceport. On the horizon we could see the great silver escape ships gleaming in the sun.

Dad had explained to me that fragments that had broken off the Hammer were headed for Mars and the moon, so the ships would have to take us farther, into deep space, to be safe.

"I would like a window seat," I said, imagining the stars steaming by.

"You should yield the window seat to those younger than you," Dad said. "Remember, we must all make sacrifices to live together."

We piled our suitcases into walls and draped sheets over them to form shelters from the wind and the sun. Every day inspectors from the government came by to distribute supplies and to make sure everything was all right.

"Be patient!" the government inspectors said. "We know things are moving slowly, but we're doing everything we can. There will be seats for everyone."

We were patient. Some of the mothers organized lessons for the children during the day, and the fathers set up a priority system so that families with aged parents and babies could board first when the ships were finally ready.

After four days of waiting, the reassurances from the government inspectors did not sound quite as reassuring. Rumors spread through the crowd.

"It's the ships. Something's wrong with them."

"The builders lied to the government and said they were ready when they weren't, and now the prime minister is too embarrassed to admit the truth."

"I hear that there's only one ship, and only a few hundred of the most important people will have seats. The other ships are only hollow shells, for show."

"They're hoping that the Americans will change their mind and build more ships for allies like us."

Mom came to Dad and whispered in his ear.

Dad shook his head and stopped her. "Do not repeat such things."

"But for Hiroto's sake—"

"No!" I'd never heard Dad sound so angry. He paused, swallowed. "We must trust each other, trust the prime minister and the Self-Defense Forces."

Mom looked unhappy. I reached out and held her hand. "I'm not afraid," I said.

"That's right," Dad said, relief in his voice. "There's nothing to be afraid of."

He picked me up in his arms—I was slightly embarrassed, for he had not done such a thing since I was very little—and pointed at the densely packed crowd of thousands and thousands spread around us as far as the eye could see.

"Look at how many of us there are: grandmothers, young fathers, big sisters, little brothers. For anyone to panic and begin to spread rumors in such a crowd would be selfish and wrong, and many people could be hurt. We must keep to our places and always remember the bigger picture."

Mindy and I make love slowly. I like to breathe in the smell of her dark curly hair, lush, warm, tickling the nose like the sea, like fresh salt.

Afterward we lie next to each other, gazing up at my ceiling monitor.

I keep looping on it a view of the receding star field. Mindy works in navigation, and she records the high-resolution cockpit video feed for me.

I like to pretend that it's a big skylight, and we're lying under the stars. I know some others like to keep their monitors showing photographs and videos of old Earth, but that makes me too sad.

"How do you say 'star' in Japanese?" Mindy asks.

"Hoshi," I tell her.

"And how do you say 'guest'?"

"Okyakusan."

"So we are *hoshi okyakusan*? Star guests?"

"It doesn't work like that," I say. Mindy is a singer, and she likes the sound of languages other than English. "It's hard to hear the music behind the words when their meanings get in the way," she told me once.

Spanish is Mindy's first language, but she remembers even less of it than I do of Japanese. Often, she asks me for Japanese words and weaves them into her songs.

I try to phrase it poetically for her, but I'm not sure if I'm successful. *"Wareware ha, hoshi no aida ni kyaku ni kite."* We have come to be guests among the stars.

"There are a thousand ways of phrasing everything," Dad used to say, "each appropriate to an occasion." He taught me that our language is full of nuances and supple grace, each sentence a poem. The language folds in on itself, the unspoken words as meaningful as the spoken, context within context, layer upon layer, like the steel in samurai swords.

I wish Dad were around so that I could ask him: How do you say "I miss you" in a way that is appropriate to the occasion of your twenty-fifth birthday, as the last survivor of your race?

"My sister was really into Japanese picture books. Manga."

Like me, Mindy is an orphan. It's part of what draws us together.

"Do you remember much about her?"

"Not really. I was only five or so when I came on board the ship. Before that, I only remember a lot of guns firing and all of us hiding in the dark and running and crying and stealing food. She was always there to keep me quiet by reading from the manga books. And then . . ."

I had watched the video only once. From our high orbit, the blue-and-white marble that was Earth seemed to wobble for a moment as the asteroid struck, and then, the silent, roiling waves of spreading destruction that slowly engulfed the globe.

I pull her to me and kiss her forehead, lightly, a kiss of comfort. "Let us not speak of sad things."

She wraps her arms around me tightly, as though she will never let go.

"The manga, do you remember anything about them?" I ask.

"I remember they were full of giant robots. I thought: *Japan is so powerful.*"

I try to imagine it: heroic giant robots all over Japan, working desperately to save the people.

The prime minister's apology was broadcast through the loudspeakers. Some also watched it on their phones.

I remember very little of it except that his voice was thin and he looked very frail and old. He looked genuinely sorry. "I've let the people down."

The rumors turned out to be true. The shipbuilders had taken the money from the government but did not build ships that were strong enough or capable of what they promised. They kept up the charade until the very end. We found out the truth only when it was too late.

Japan was not the only nation that failed her people. The other nations of the world had squabbled over who should contribute how much to a joint evacuation effort when the Hammer was first discovered on its collision course with Earth. And then, when that plan had collapsed, most decided that it was better to gamble that the Hammer would miss and spend the money and lives on fighting with one another instead.

After the prime minister finished speaking, the crowd remained silent. A few angry voices shouted but soon quieted down as well. Gradually, in an orderly fashion, people began to pack up and leave the temporary campsites.

"The people just went home?" Mindy asks, incredulous.

"Yes."

"There was no looting, no panicked runs, no soldiers mutinying in the streets?"

"This was Japan," I tell her. And I can hear the pride in my voice, an echo of my father's.

"I guess the people were resigned," Mindy says. "They had given up. Maybe it's a culture thing."

"No!" I fight to keep the heat out of my voice. Her words irk me, like Bobby's remark about Go being boring. "That is not how it was."

"Who is Dad speaking to?" I asked.

"That is Dr. Hamilton," Mom said. "We—he and your father and I—went to college together in America."

I watched Dad speak English on the phone. He seemed like a completely different person: it wasn't just the cadences and pitch of his voice; his face was more animated, his hand gestured more wildly. He looked like a foreigner.

He shouted into the phone.

"What is Dad saying?"

Mom shushed me. She watched Dad intently, hanging on every word.

"No," Dad said into the phone. "No!" I did not need that translated.

Afterward Mom said, "He is trying to do the right thing, in his own way."

"He is as selfish as ever," Dad snapped.

"That's not fair," Mom said. "He did not call me in secret. He called you instead because he believed that if your positions were reversed, he would gladly give the woman he loved a chance to survive, even if it's with another man."

Dad looked at her. I had never heard my parents say "I love you" to each other, but some words did not need to be said to be true.

"I would never have said yes to him," Mom said, smiling. Then she went to the kitchen to make our lunch. Dad's gaze followed her.

"It's a fine day," Dad said to me. "Let us go on a walk."

We passed other neighbors walking along the sidewalks. We greeted one another, inquired after one another's health. Everything seemed normal. The Hammer glowed even brighter in the dusk overhead.

"You must be very frightened, Hiroto," he said.

"They won't try to build more escape ships?"

Dad did not answer. The late summer wind carried the sound of cicadas to us: *chirr, chirr, chirrrrrr.*

> *"Nothing in the cry*
> *Of cicadas suggests they*
> *Are about to die."*

"Dad?"

"That is a poem by Bashō. Do you understand it?"

I shook my head. I did not like poems much.

Dad sighed and smiled at me. He looked at the setting sun and spoke again:

"The fading sunlight holds infinite beauty
Though it is so close to the day's end."

I recited the lines to myself. Something in them moved me. I tried to put the feeling into words: "It is like a gentle kitten is licking the inside of my heart."

Instead of laughing at me, Dad nodded solemnly.

"That is a poem by the classical Tang poet Li Shangyin. Though he was Chinese, the sentiment is very much Japanese."

We walked on, and I stopped by the yellow flower of a dandelion. The angle at which the flower was tilted struck me as very beautiful. I got the kitten-tongue-tickling sensation in my heart again.

"The flower . . ." I hesitated. I could not find the right words.

Dad spoke,

"The drooping flower
As yellow as the moonbeam
So slender tonight."

I nodded. The image seemed to me at once so fleeting and so permanent, like the way I had experienced time as a young child. It made me a little sad and glad at the same time.

"Everything passes, Hiroto," Dad said. "That feeling in your heart: it's called *mono no aware*. It is a sense of the transience of all things in life. The sun, the dandelion, the cicada, the Hammer, and all of us: we are all subject to the equations of James Clerk Maxwell, and we are all ephemeral patterns destined to eventually fade, whether in a second or an eon."

I looked around at the clean streets, the slow-moving people, the grass, and the evening light, and I knew that everything had its place; everything was all right. Dad and I went on walking, our shadows touching.

Even though the Hammer hung right overhead, I was not afraid.

• • •

My job involves staring at the grid of indicator lights in front of me. It is a bit like a giant Go board.

It is very boring most of the time. The lights, indicating tension on various spots of the solar sail, course through the same pattern every few minutes as the sail gently flexes in the fading light of the distant sun. The cycling pattern of the lights is as familiar to me as Mindy's breathing when she's asleep.

We're already moving at a good fraction of the speed of light. Some years hence, when we're moving fast enough, we'll change our course for 61 Virginis and its pristine planets, and we'll leave the sun that gave birth to us behind like a forgotten memory.

But today, the pattern of the lights feels off. One of the lights in the southwest corner seems to be blinking a fraction of a second too fast.

"Navigation," I say into the microphone, "this is Sail Monitor Station Alpha, can you confirm that we're on course?"

A minute later Mindy's voice comes through my earpiece, tinged slightly with surprise. "I hadn't noticed, but there was a slight drift off course. What happened?"

"I'm not sure yet." I stare at the grid before me, at the one stubborn light that is out of sync, out of harmony.

Mom took me to Fukuoka without Dad. "We'll be shopping for Christmas," she said. "We want to surprise you." Dad smiled and shook his head.

We made our way through the busy streets. Since this might be the last Christmas on Earth, there was an extra sense of gaiety in the air.

On the subway I glanced at the newspaper held up by the man sitting next to us. USA STRIKES BACK! was the headline. The big photograph showed the American president smiling triumphantly. Below that was a series of other pictures, some I had seen before: the first experimental American evacuation ship from years ago exploding on its test flight; the leader of some rogue nation claiming responsibility on TV; American soldiers marching into a foreign capital.

Below the fold was a smaller article: AMERICAN SCIENTISTS SKEPTICAL OF DOOMSDAY SCENARIO. Dad had said that some people preferred to believe that a disaster was unreal rather than accept that nothing could be done.

I looked forward to picking out a present for Dad. But instead of going to the electronics district, where I had expected Mom to take me to buy him a gift, we went to a section of the city I had never been to before. Mom took out her phone and made a brief call, speaking in English. I looked up at her, surprised.

Then we were standing in front of a building with a great American flag flying over it. We went inside and sat down in an office. An American man came in. His face was sad, but he was working hard not to look sad.

"Rin." The man called my mother's name and stopped. In that one syllable I heard regret and longing and a complicated story.

"This is Dr. Hamilton," Mom said to me. I nodded and offered to shake his hand, as I had seen Americans do on TV.

Dr. Hamilton and Mom spoke for a while. She began to cry, and Dr. Hamilton stood awkwardly, as though he wanted to hug her but dared not.

"You'll be staying with Dr. Hamilton," Mom said to me.

"What?"

She held my shoulders, bent down, and looked into my eyes. "The Americans have a secret ship in orbit. It is the only ship they managed to launch into space before they got into this war. Dr. Hamilton designed the ship. He's my . . . old friend, and he can bring one person aboard with him. It's your only chance."

"No, I'm not leaving."

Eventually, Mom opened the door to leave. Dr. Hamilton held me tightly as I kicked and screamed.

We were all surprised to see Dad standing there.

Mom burst into tears.

Dad hugged her, which I'd never seen him do. It seemed a very American gesture.

"I'm sorry," Mom said. She kept saying "I'm sorry" as she cried.

"It's okay," Dad said. "I understand."

Dr. Hamilton let me go, and I ran up to my parents, holding on to both of them tightly.

Mom looked at Dad, and in that look she said nothing and everything.

Dad's face softened like a wax figure coming to life. He sighed and looked at me.

"You're not afraid, are you?" Dad asked.

I shook my head.

"Then it is okay for you to go," he said. He looked into Dr. Hamilton's eyes. "Thank you for taking care of my son."

Mom and I both looked at him, surprised.

> *"A dandelion*
>   *In late autumn's cooling breeze*
>   *Spreads seeds far and wide."*

I nodded, pretending to understand.

Dad hugged me, fiercely, quickly.

"Remember that you're Japanese."

And they were gone.

"Something has punctured the sail," Dr. Hamilton says.

The tiny room holds only the most senior command staff—plus

Mindy and me because we already know. There is no reason to cause a panic among the people.

"The hole is causing the ship to list to the side, veering off course. If the hole is not patched, the tear will grow bigger, the sail will soon collapse, and the *Hopeful* will be adrift in space."

"Is there any way to fix it?" the captain asks.

Dr. Hamilton, who has been like a father to me, shakes his headful of white hair. I have never seen him so despondent.

"The tear is several hundred kilometers from the hub of the sail. It will take many days to get someone out there because you can't move too fast along the surface of the sail—the risk of another tear is too great. And by the time we do get anyone out there, the tear will have grown too large to patch."

And so it goes. Everything passes.

I close my eyes and picture the sail. The film is so thin that if it is touched carelessly, it will be punctured. But the membrane is supported by a complex system of folds and struts that give the sail rigidity and tension. As a child, I had watched them unfold in space like one of my mother's origami creations.

I imagine hooking and unhooking a tether cable to the scaffolding of struts as I skim along the surface of the sail, like a dragonfly dipping across the surface of a pond.

"I can make it out there in seventy-two hours," I say. Everyone turns to look at me. I explain my idea. "I know the patterns of the struts well because I have monitored them from afar for most of my life. I can find the quickest path."

Dr. Hamilton is dubious. "Those struts were never designed for a maneuver like that. I never planned for this scenario."

"Then we'll improvise," Mindy says. "We're Americans, damn it. We never just give up."

Dr. Hamilton looks up. "Thank you, Mindy."

We plan, we debate, we shout at each other, we work throughout the night.

The climb up the cable from the habitat module to the solar sail is long and arduous. It takes me almost twelve hours.

Let me illustrate for you what I look like with the second character in my name:

It means "to soar." See that radical on the left? That's me, tethered to the cable with a pair of antennae coming out of my helmet. On my back are the wings—or, in this case, booster rockets and extra fuel tanks that push me up and up toward the great reflective dome that blocks out the whole sky, the gossamer mirror of the solar sail.

Mindy chats with me on the radio link. We tell each other jokes, share secrets, speak of things we want to do in the future. When we run out of things to say, she sings to me. The goal is to keep me awake.

"Wareware ha, hoshi no aida ni kyaku ni kite."

But the climb up is really the easy part. The journey across the sail along the network of struts to the point of puncture is far more difficult.

It has been thirty-six hours since I left the ship. Mindy's voice is now tired, flagging. She yawns.

"Sleep, baby," I whisper into the microphone. I'm so tired that I want to close my eyes just for a moment.

I'm walking along the road on a summer evening, my father next to me.

"We live in a land of volcanoes and earthquakes, typhoons and tsunamis, Hiroto. We have always faced a precarious existence, suspended in a thin strip on the surface of this planet between the fire underneath and the icy vacuum above."

And I'm back in my suit again, alone. My momentary loss of concentration causes me to bang my backpack against one of the beams of the sail, almost knocking one of the fuel tanks loose. I grab it just in time. The mass of my equipment has been lightened down to the last gram so that I can move fast, and there is no margin for error. I can't afford to lose anything.

I try to shake the dream and keep on moving.

"Yet it is this awareness of the closeness of death, of the beauty inherent in each moment, that allows us to endure. Mono no aware, my son, is an empathy with the universe. It is the soul of our nation. It has allowed us to endure Hiroshima, to endure the occupation, to endure deprivation and the prospect of annihilation without despair."

"Hiroto, wake up!" Mindy's voice is desperate, pleading. I jerk awake. I have not been able to sleep for how long now? Two days, three, four?

For the final fifty or so kilometers of the journey, I must let go of the sail struts and rely on my rockets alone to travel untethered, skimming over the surface of the sail while everything is moving at a fraction of the speed of light. The very idea is enough to make me dizzy.

And suddenly my father is next to me again, suspended in space below the sail. We're playing a game of Go.

"Look in the southwest corner. Do you see how your army has been divided in half? My white stones will soon surround and capture this entire group."

I look where he's pointing and I see the crisis. There is a gap that I missed. What I thought was my one army is in reality two separate groups with a hole in the middle. I have to plug the gap with my next stone.

I shake away the hallucination. I have to finish this, and then I can sleep.

There is a hole in the torn sail before me. At the speed we're traveling, even a tiny speck of dust that escaped the ion shields can cause havoc. The jagged edge of the hole flaps gently in space, propelled by solar wind and radiation pressure. While an individual photon is tiny, insignificant, without even mass, all of them together can propel a sail as big as the sky and push a thousand people along.

The universe is wondrous.

I lift a black stone and prepare to fill in the gap, to connect my armies into one.

The stone turns back into the patching kit from my backpack. I maneuver my thrusters until I'm hovering right over the gash in the sail. Through the hole I can see the stars beyond, the stars that no one on the ship has seen for many years. I look at them and imagine that around one of them, one day, the human race, fused into a new nation, will recover from near extinction, will start afresh and flourish again.

Carefully, I apply the bandage over the gash, and I turn on the heat torch. I run the torch over the gash, and I can feel the bandage melting to spread out and fuse with the hydrocarbon chains in the sail film. When that's done I'll vaporize and deposit silver atoms over it to form a shiny, reflective layer.

"It's working," I say into the microphone. And I hear the muffled sounds of celebration in the background.

"You're a hero," Mindy says.

I think of myself as a giant Japanese robot in a manga and smile.

The torch sputters and goes out.

"Look carefully," Dad says. "You want to play your next stone there to plug that hole. But is that what you really want?"

I shake the fuel tank attached to the torch. Nothing. This was the tank that I banged against one of the sail beams. The collision must have caused a leak and there isn't enough fuel left to finish the patch. The bandage flaps gently, only half attached to the gash.

"Come back now," Dr. Hamilton says. "We'll replenish your supplies and try again."

I'm exhausted. No matter how hard I push, I will not be able to make it back out here as fast. And by then who knows how big the gash will have grown? Dr. Hamilton knows this as well as I do. He just wants to get me back to the warm safety of the ship.

I still have fuel in my tank, the fuel that is meant for my return trip.

My father's face is expectant.

"I see," I speak slowly. "If I play my next stone in this hole, I will not have a chance to get back to the small group up in the northeast. You'll capture them."

"One stone cannot be in both places. You have to choose, son."

"Tell me what to do."

I look into my father's face for an answer.

"Look around you," Dad says. And I see Mom, Mrs. Maeda, the prime minister, all our neighbors from Kurume, and all the people who waited with us in Kagoshima, in Kyushu, in all the Four Islands, all over Earth, and on the *Hopeful*. They look expectantly at me, for me to do something.

Dad's voice is quiet:

"The stars shine and blink.
We are all guests passing through,
A smile and a name."

"I have a solution," I tell Dr. Hamilton over the radio.

"I knew you'd come up with something," Mindy says, her voice proud and happy.

Dr. Hamilton is silent for a while. He knows what I'm thinking. And then: "Hiroto, thank you."

I unhook the torch from its useless fuel tank and connect it to the tank on my back. I turn it on. The flame is bright, sharp, a blade of light. I marshal photons and atoms before me, transforming them into a web of strength and light.

The stars on the other side have been sealed away again. The mirrored surface of the sail is perfect.

"Correct your course," I speak into the microphone. "It's done."

"Acknowledged," Dr. Hamilton says. His voice is that of a sad man trying not to sound sad.

"You have to come back first," Mindy says. "If we correct course now, you'll have nowhere to tether yourself."

"It's okay, baby," I whisper into the microphone. "I'm not coming back. There's not enough fuel left."

"We'll come for you!"

"You can't navigate the struts as quickly as I did," I tell her gently. "No one knows their patterns as well as I do. By the time you get here, I will have run out of air."

I wait until she's quiet again. "Let us not speak of sad things. I love you."

Then I turn off the radio and push off into space so that they aren't tempted to mount a useless rescue mission. And I fall down, far, far below the canopy of the sail.

I watch as the sail turns away, unveiling the stars in their full glory. The sun, so faint now, is only one star among many, neither rising nor setting. I am cast adrift among them, alone and also at one with them.

A kitten's tongue tickles the inside of my heart.

I play the next stone in the gap.

Dad plays as I thought he would, and my stones in the northeast corner are gone, cast adrift.

But my main group is safe. They may even flourish in the future.

"Maybe there are heroes in Go," Bobby's voice says.

Mindy called me a hero. But I was simply a man in the right place at the right time. Dr. Hamilton is also a hero because he designed the *Hopeful*. Mindy is also a hero because she kept me awake. My mother is also a hero because she was willing to give me up so that I could survive. My father is also a hero because he showed me the right thing to do.

We are defined by the places we hold in the web of others' lives.

I pull my gaze back from the Go board until the stones fuse into larger patterns of shifting life and pulsing breath. "Individual stones are not heroes, but all the stones together are heroic."

"It is a beautiful day for a walk, isn't it?" Dad says.

And we walk together down the street, so that we can remember every passing blade of grass, every dewdrop, every fading ray of the dying sun, infinitely beautiful.

ALL THE FLAVORS
A Tale of Guan Yu, the Chinese God of War, in America

All life is an experiment.
—RALPH WALDO EMERSON

*For an American, one's entire life is spent as a game
of chance, a time of revolution, a day of battle.*
—ALEXIS DE TOCQUEVILLE

IDAHO CITY

The Missouri Boys snuck into Idaho City around four thirty a.m., when everything was still dark and Isabelle's Joy Club was the only house with a lit window.

Obee and Crick made straight for the Thirsty Fish. Earlier in the day, J. J. Kelly, the proprietor, had invited Obee and Crick out of his saloon with his Smith & Wesson revolver. With little effort and making no sound, Obee and Crick broke the latch on the door of the Thirsty Fish and quickly disappeared inside.

"I'll show that little Irishman some manners," Crick hissed. Through the alcoholic mist, his eyes could focus on only one image: the diminutive Kelly walking toward him, gun at the ready, and the jeering crowd behind him. *We might just bury you under the new outhouse next time you show yourselves in Idaho City.*

Though he was a little unsteady on his feet, he successfully tiptoed his way up the stairs to the family's living quarters, an iron crowbar in hand.

Obee, less drunk, set about rectifying that situation promptly by jumping behind the bar and helping himself to the supplies. Carelessly, he took down bottles of various sizes and colors from the shelves around him, and having taken a sip from each, smashed the bottles against the counters or dashed them to the ground. Alcohol flowed freely everywhere, soaking into the floors and the furniture.

A woman's scream tore out of the darkness upstairs. Obee jumped up and drew his revolver. Not sure whether to run upstairs to help his friend or out the door, down the street, and into the woods before he could be caught, he hesitated at the bottom of the stairs. Overhead came the sound of boots that no longer cared about silence, followed by the crash of something heavy and soft onto the floor. Obee cursed and jumped back, his big, dirty hands trying to rub out the coat of dust that just fell from the ceiling into his eyes. More muffled screams and cursing, and then, complete silence.

"Woo!" Crick appeared at the top of the stairs, the gleeful grin on his face limned by the light of the oil lamp he held aloft. "Grab some rags. Let's burn this dump down."

By the time the seven thousand people of Idaho City had tallied up the damage of the Great Fire of May 18, 1865, the Missouri Boys were miles away on the Wells Fargo trail, sleeping off the headache from hard drinking and fast riding. Idaho City lost a newspaper, two theaters, two photograph galleries, three express offices, four restaurants, four breweries, four drugstores, five groceries, six blacksmith shops, seven meat markets, seven bakeries, eight hotels, twelve doctor's offices, twenty-two law offices, twenty-four saloons, and thirty-six general merchandise stores.

This was why, when the band of weary and gaunt Chinamen showed up a few weeks later with their funny bamboo carrying poles over their shoulders and their pockets heavy with cold, hard cash sewn into the lining, the people of Idaho City almost held a welcome party for them. Everyone promptly set about the task of separating the Chinamen from their money.

Elsie Seaver, Lily's mother, complained to Lily's father about the Chinamen almost every evening.

"Thaddeus, will you please tell the heathens to keep their noise down? I can't hear myself think."

"For fourteen dollars a week in rent, Elsie, I think the Chinamen are entitled to a few hours of their own music."

The Seavers' store had been one of those burned down a few weeks earlier. Lily's father, Thad (though he preferred to be called Jack) Seaver, was still in the middle of rebuilding it. Elsie knew as well as her husband that they needed the Chinamen's rent. She sighed, stuffed some cotton balls in her ears, and took her sewing into the kitchen.

Lily rather liked the music of the Chinamen. It was indeed loud. The gongs, cymbals, wooden clappers, and drums made such a racket that her heart wanted to beat in time to their rhythm. The high-pitched fiddle with only two strings wailed so high and pure that Lily thought she could float on air just listening to it. And then in the fading light of the dusk, the big, red-faced Chinaman would pluck out a sad quiet tune on the three-stringed lute and sing his songs in the street, his companions squatting in a circle around him, quiet as they listened to him, and their faces by turns smiling and grave. He was more than six feet tall and had a dark, bushy beard that covered his chest. Lily thought his thin, long eyes looked like the eyes of a great eagle as he turned his head, looking at each of his companions. Once in a while they burst into loud guffaws, and they slapped the big, red-faced Chinaman on his back as he smiled and kept on singing.

"What do you think he's singing about?" Lily asked her mother from the porch.

"No doubt some unspeakably vile vice of their barbaric homeland. Opium dens and sing-song girls and such. Come back in here and close the door. Have you finished your sewing?"

Lily continued to watch them from her window, wishing she could understand what his songs were about. She was glad that the music made her mother unable to think. It meant that she couldn't think of more chores for Lily to do.

Lily's father was more intrigued by the Chinamen's cooking. Even their cooking was loud, the splattering and sizzling of hot oil and the *suh-suh-suh* beating of cleaver against chopping board making another kind of music. The cooking also smelled loud, the smoke drifting from the open door carrying the peppery smell of unknown spices and unknown vegetables across the street and making Lily's stomach growl.

"What in the world are they making over there? There's no way cucumbers can smell like that," Lily's father asked no one in particular. Lily saw him lick his lips.

"We could ask them," Lily suggested.

"Ha! Don't get any ideas. I'm sure the Chinamen would love to chop up a little Christian girl like you and fry you in those big saucepans of theirs. Stay away from them, you hear?"

Lily didn't believe that the Chinamen would eat her. They seemed friendly enough. And if they were going to supplement their diet with little girls, why would they bother spending all day working on that vegetable garden they'd planted behind their house?

There were many mysteries about the Chinamen, not the least of which was how they managed to all fit inside those tiny houses they had rented. The band of twenty-seven Chinamen rented five saltbox houses along Placer Street, two of them owned by Jack Seaver, and bought three others from Mr. Kenan, whose bank had been burned down and who was moving his family back East. The saltbox houses were simple, one-story affairs with a living room in the front that doubled as the kitchen, and a bedroom in the back. Twelve feet deep and thirty feet across, the small houses were made of thin planks of wood, and their front porches were squeezed so tightly together that they formed a covered sidewalk.

The white miners who had rented these houses from Jack Seaver in the past lived in them alone or at most shared a house with one roommate. The Chinamen, on the other hand, lived five or six to a house. This frugality rather disappointed some of the people in Idaho City, who had been hoping the Chinamen would be more free with their money. They broke down the tables and chairs left by the previous tenants of the houses and used the lumber to build bunks along the walls of the bedrooms and laid out mattresses on the floors of the living rooms. The previous occupants also left pictures of Lincoln and Lee on the walls. These the Chinamen left alone.

"Logan said he likes the pictures," Jack Seaver said at dinner.

"Who's Logan?"

"The big, red-faced Chinaman. He asked me who Lee was, and I told him he was a great general who picked the losing side but was still admired for his bravery and loyalty. He was impressed by that. Oh, and he also liked Lee's beard."

Lily had heard the conversation between her father and the Chinaman by hiding herself behind the piano. She didn't think the big Chinaman's name sounded anything like "Logan." She had listened to the other Chinamen calling out to him, and it sounded to her like they were saying "Lao Guan."

"Such a strange people, these Celestials," Elsie said. "That Logan scares me. The size of his hands! He has killed. I'm sure of it. I wish you could find some other tenants, Thaddeus."

No one except Lily's mother ever called her husband "Thaddeus." To everyone else he was either "Mr. Seaver" or "Jack." Lily was used to the fact that people had many names out here in the West. After all, everyone called the banker "Mr. Kenan" when they were at the bank, but when he wasn't around they called him "Shylock." And while Lily's mother always addressed her as "Liliane," Lily's father always called her "Nugget." And it seemed that the big Chinaman already got a new name in this house, "Logan."

"You are my nugget of gold, sweetie," Lily's father told her every morning, before he left for the store.

"You're going to puff her up full of vanity," Lily's mother said from the kitchen.

It was the height of the mining season, and the Chinamen began to head out to look for gold the moment they were settled in. They left as soon as it was light, dressed in their loose blouses and baggy trousers, their queues snaking out from under their big straw hats. A few of the older men stayed behind to work in the vegetable garden or to do the laundry and the cooking.

Lily was largely left alone during the day. While her mother went shopping or busied herself around the house, her father was away working at the site for the new store. Jack was thinking of setting aside a section in the new store for preserved duck eggs, pickled vegetables, dried tofu, spices, soy sauce, and bitter melons imported from San Francisco to sell to the Chinese miners.

"These Chinamen are going to be carting around a lot of gold dust soon, Elsie. I'll be ready to take it from them when they do."

Elsie didn't like this plan. The thought of the Chinamen's strange food making everything smell funny in her husband's store made her queasy. But she knew it was pointless to argue with Thad once he got a notion in his head. After all, he had packed up everything and dragged her and Lily all the way out here from Hartford, where he had been doing perfectly well as a tutor, just because he got it in his head that they'd be much happier on their own out West, where nobody knew them and they knew nobody.

Not even Elsie's father could persuade her husband to change his mind then. He had asked Thad to come to Boston and work for him in his law office. Business was good, he said, he could use his help. Elsie beamed at the thought of all the shops and the fashion of Beacon Hill.

"I appreciate the offer," Thad had said to her father. "But I don't think I'm cut out to be a lawyer."

Elsie had to placate her father for hours afterward with tea and a fresh batch of oatmeal cookies. And even then he refused to say good-bye to Thad the next day, when he left to go back to Boston. "Damned the day that I became friends with his father," he muttered, too loud for Elsie to pretend that she hadn't heard him.

"I'm sick of this," Thad said to her later. "We don't know anybody who's ever *done* anything. Everyone in Hartford just carries on what his father had started. Aren't we supposed to be a nation where every generation picks up and goes somewhere new? I think we should go and start our own life. You can even pick a new name for yourself. Wouldn't that be fun?"

Elsie was happy with her own name. But Thad wasn't. This was how he ended up as "Jack."

"I've always wanted to be a 'Jack,'" he told her, as if names were like shirts that you could just put on and take off. She refused to call him by his new name.

Once when Lily was alone with her mother she had told Lily that this was all because of the War.

"That Rebel bullet put him on his back in less than a day from when he got onto the field. This is what happens to a man when he has to lie on his back for eight months. He gets all sorts of strange notions into his head and not even an angelic manifestation can get those ideas out of him."

If the Rebels were responsible for getting her family out here to Idaho, Lily wasn't sure they were such evil people.

Lily had learned the hard way that if she stayed in the house her mother would always find something for her to do. Until school started again, the best thing for Lily was to get out of the house the first chance she had in the morning and not return until it was dinnertime.

Lily liked to be in the hills outside the town. The forest of Douglas firs, mountain maples, and ponderosa pines shaded her from the noon sun. She could take some bread and cheese with her for lunch, and there were plenty of streams to drink from. She spent some time picking out leaves that had been chewed by worms into shapes that reminded her of different animals. When she was bored with that she waded in a stream to cool off. Before she went into the water, she took the back hem of her dress, pulled it forward and up from between her legs, and tucked the hem into the sash at her waist. She was glad that her mother was not around to see her turning her skirt into pants. But it was much easier to wade in the mud and the water with her skirt out of the way.

Lily waded downstream along the shallow edge of the stream. The day was starting to get more hot than warm, and she splashed some water on her neck and forehead. Lily looked for bird nests in the trees and raccoon prints in the mud. She thought she could walk on like this forever, alone and not trying to get anything done in particular, her feet cool in the water, the sun warm on her back, and knowing that she had a good, filling lunch with her that she could have any time she wanted and would have an even better dinner waiting for her later.

Faint sounds of men singing came to her from around the bend in the river. Lily stopped. Maybe there was a camp of placer miners just downstream from where she was. That would be fun to watch.

She walked onto the bank of the river and into the woods. The singing became louder. Although she couldn't make out any of the words, the melody told her it wasn't any song that she recognized.

She carefully made her way among the trees. She was deep in the shadows now, and a light breeze quickly dried the sweat and water on her face. Her heart began to beat faster. She could hear the singing voices more clearly now. A lone deep, male voice sang in words that she could not make out, the strange shape of the melody reminding her of the way the Chinamen's music had sounded. Then a chorus of other male voices answered, the slow, steady rhythm letting her know that it was a working men's song, whose words and music came from the cycle of labored breath and heartbeat.

She came to the edge of the woods, and hiding herself behind the thick trunk of a maple, she peeked out at the singing men by the stream.

Except the stream was nowhere to be found.

After they found this bend to be a good placer spot, the Chinese miners had built a dam to divert the stream. Where the stream used to be, there were now five or six miners using picks and shovels to dig down to the bedrock. Others were digging out bits of gold-laden sand and gravel from between the crevices in areas where the digging had already been done. The men wore their straw hats to keep the sun off their heads. The solo singer, Lily now saw, was Logan. The red-faced Chinaman had wrapped a rolled-up handkerchief around his thick beard and tucked the ends of the handkerchief into his shirt to keep it out of his way as he worked. Every time he bellowed out another verse of the song, he stood still and leaned on his shovel, and his beard pouch moved with his singing like the neck of a rooster. Lily almost giggled out loud.

A loud bang cut through the noise and activity and echoed around the banks of the dry streambed. The singing stopped and all the miners stopped where they were. The mountain air suddenly became quiet and still, and only the sound of panicked birds taking flight into the air broke the silence.

Crick, slowly waving above his head the pistol that fired the shot, swaggered out of the woods across the streambed from where Lily was hiding. Obee came behind him, his shotgun's barrel shifting from pointing at one miner to the next with each step he took.

"Well, well, well," Crick said. "Lookee here. A singing circus of Chinee monkeys."

Logan stared at him. "What do you boys want?"

"*Boys?*" Crick let out a holler. "Obee, listen to this. The Chinaman just called us 'boys.'"

"He won't be saying much after I blow his head off," Obee said.

Logan began to walk toward them. The heavy shovel trailed from his large hand and long arm.

"Stop right where you are, you filthy yellow monkey." Crick pointed the pistol at him.

"What do you want?"

"Why, to collect what's ours, of course. We know you've been keeping our gold safe, and we've come to ask for it back."

"We don't have any of your gold."

"Jesus," Crick said, shaking his head. "I've always heard that Chinamen are thieves and liars, on account of them growing up eating rats and maggots, but I've always kept an open mind about the Celestials. But now I'm seeing it with my own eyes."

"Filthy liars," Obee affirmed.

"Obee and me, we found this spot last spring and claimed it. We've been a little busy lately, and so we thought we'd take pity on you and let you work the deposit and pay you a fair wage for your work. We thought we were doing our Christian duty."

"We were being nice," Obee added.

"Very generous of us," Crick agreed. "But look where that's gotten us? Being kind doesn't work with these heathens. On our way here I was still inclined to let you keep a little gold dust for your work these last few weeks, but now I think we are going to take it all."

"Ingrates," Obee said.

A young Chinaman, barely more than a boy, really, angrily shouted something in his own language at Logan. Logan waved his hand at the youth to keep him back, his gaze never leaving Crick's face.

"I don't think you have your facts straight," Logan said. Even though he didn't shout, his voice reverberated and echoed around the valley of the river and the woods in a way that made Lily tremble with its force and strength. "We found this deposit and we put the claim on it. You can go check at the courthouse."

"Are you deaf?" Crick asked. "What makes you think I need to check at the courthouse? I just told you the facts, and after conferring with the law"—he waved his pistol impatiently—"I'm told that the claim is indeed mine and you are the claim jumpers. By law I'm entitled to shoot you dead like so many rats right where you are. But as I am unwilling to shed blood needlessly, I'll let you hand over the gold and spare your worthless lives. I may even let you keep on working this deposit for me if you agree not to pull a stunt like this and deny us our gold in the future."

Without any warning that he was going to do it, Obee fired his gun. The shot shattered the rocks at the feet of the boy who had angrily shouted at Logan earlier. Obee and Crick doubled over in laughter as the boy jumped back and dropped his pickax, giving out a startled yelp. A piece of shattered rock had cut his hand, and he slowly sat down on the ground, staring incredulously as the blood from the wound in his palm quickly soaked the tan sleeves of his shirt. A few of the other Chinamen gathered around to tend to him. Lily barely managed to stifle her own scream. She wanted to turn around and run back into town, but her legs would not hold her up if she didn't hug tightly the tree she was hiding behind.

Logan turned his attention back to Crick. His face had turned an even darker shade of red, so that Lily was afraid that blood would pour from his eyes.

"Don't," he said.

"Hand over the gold," Crick said, "or I'll make him stop breathing instead of just getting him dancing."

Logan casually threw the shovel, which had been dangling from his hand until now, behind him. "Why don't you put down your gun, and we'll have a fair fight?"

Crick hesitated for a moment. If it came to that, he thought he could take care of himself in a fight, having survived enough brawls in New Orleans to know exactly how it felt to have your ribs stop a knife. But Logan was taller by about a foot and heavier by about fifty pounds, and though that beard made him look ancient, Crick wasn't sure whether Logan really was old enough to have his reflexes slow down. And in any case Crick was a little scared of the red-faced Chinaman: He looked angry enough to fight like a crazy man, and Crick knew enough about fights to know that you didn't come out of fights with crazy men without at least a few broken bones.

The plan was going all wrong! Crick and Obee knew all about Chinamen, having spent years in San Francisco. They had all been scrawny midgets, giving him and Obee barely more trouble than a bunch of women, which was not surprising considering all they did was women's work: cooking and laundry, and not one of them had ever put up a real fight. This band of Chinamen was supposed to fall down on their knees and beg for mercy as soon as he and Obee slowly walked out of the woods, and hand over all their gold. The red-faced giant was ruining their plan!

"I think we have a pretty fair fight right now," Crick said. He pointed his revolver at Logan. "Almighty God created men, but Colonel Colt made them equal."

Logan untied the handkerchief around his beard, unrolled it, and tied it around the top of his head like a bandanna. He took off his jacket and rolled up the sleeves of his shirt. The leathery, brown skin covering the wiry muscles on his arms was full of scars. He took a few steps toward Crick. Though his face was redder than ever, his walk was calm, like he was taking a stroll at night, singing his songs back in front of Lily's house back in Idaho City.

"Don't think I won't shoot," Crick said. "The Missouri Boys don't have a lot of patience."

Logan bent down and picked up a rock the size of an egg. He wrapped his fingers around it tightly. "Get out of here. We don't have any of your gold." He took another few calm steps toward Crick.

And in another moment he was running, his legs closing up the distance between him and the gunmen. He cocked his right arm back as he ran, looking steadily into Crick's face.

Obee fired. He didn't have the time to brace himself, and the force of the shot threw him on his back.

Logan's left shoulder exploded. A bright red shower of blood sprayed behind him. In the sunlight it looked to Lily like a rose was blossoming behind him.

None of the other Chinamen said anything. They looked on, stunned.

Lily's breath stopped. Time seemed frozen to her. The mist of blood hung in the air, refusing to fall or dissipate.

Then she sucked in a great gulp of air and screamed as loud as she could ever remember, louder even than the time she was stung on the lips by that wasp she hadn't seen hiding in her lemonade cup. Her scream echoed around the woods, startling more birds into the air. *Is that really me?* Lily thought. It didn't sound like her. It didn't even sound human.

Crick was looking into her eyes from across the river. His face was so filled with cold rage and hatred that Lily's heart stopped beating.

Oh God, please, please, I promise I'll pray every night from now on. I promise I won't disobey Mother ever again.

She tried to turn around and run, but her legs wouldn't listen to her. She stumbled back, tripped over an exposed root, and fell heavily to the ground. The fall knocked the air out of her and finally cut off her scream. She struggled to sit up, expecting to see Crick's gun pointed at her.

Logan was looking at her. Incredibly, he was still standing. Half of his body was soaked with blood. He was looking at her, and she thought he didn't look like someone who had just been shot, someone who was about to die. Though blood had splattered half of his face, the other half had lost its deep, crimson color. Still, Lily thought he looked calm, like he wasn't in any pain, though he was a little sad.

Lily felt a calmness come over her. She didn't know why, but she *knew* everything was going to be all right.

Logan turned away from her. He began to walk toward Crick again. His walk was slow, deliberate. His left arm was hanging limply at his side.

Crick aimed his pistol at Logan.

Logan stumbled. Then he stopped. The blood had soaked into his beard, and as the wind lifted it, droplets of blood flew into the air. He took a step back and let fly the rock in his hand. The rock made a graceful arc in the air. Crick stood frozen where he was. The rock smashed into his face, and the thud as the rock cracked open his skull was as loud as Obee's gunshot.

His body stayed up for a few seconds before collapsing into a lifeless heap on the ground. Obee scrambled to his feet, took a look at Crick's motionless body, and without looking back at the Chinamen began to run as fast as he could deep into the woods.

Logan fell to his knees. For a moment he swayed uncertainly in place as his left arm swung at his side, useless for stopping his fall. Then he toppled over. The other Chinamen ran to him.

It all seemed so unreal to Lily, like a play on a stage. She thought she should have been terrified. She should have been screaming, or maybe even fainted. That's what her mother would have done, she thought. But everything had slowed down in the last few seconds, and she felt safe, calm, like nothing could hurt her.

She came out from behind her tree and walked toward the crowd of Chinamen.

WHISKEY AND <u>WEI QI</u>

Lily wasn't sure if she would ever understand this game.

"I can't move the seeds at all? Ever?"

They were sitting in the vegetable garden behind Logan's house, where her mother wouldn't be able to see her if she happened to look out the living room window as she finished her needlework. They were both sitting with their legs folded under them, and Lily liked the way the cool, moist soil felt under her legs. ("This was how the Buddha sat," Logan had told her.) On the ground between them Logan had drawn a grid of nine horizontal lines intersected with nine vertical lines with the tip of his knife.

"No, you can't." Logan shifted his left arm to make it easier for Ah Yan, the young Chinaman who had been the target of Obee's first shot, to run the wet rag in his hand over the wound in Logan's shoulder. Lily gingerly touched the bandage on her leg. Her fall against the tree root had scraped off a large patch of skin on the back of her left calf. Ah Yan had cleaned it for her and wrapped it up in a plain cotton bandage that was coated in some black paste that smelled strongly of medicine and spices. The cool paste had stung at first against the wound, but Lily bit her lip and didn't cry out. Ah Yan's touch had been gentle, and Lily asked him if he was a doctor.

"No," the young Chinaman had said. Then he had smiled at her and given her a piece of dried plum coated in sugar for her to suck on. Lily thought it was the sweetest thing she had ever tasted.

Ah Yan rinsed the rag out in the basin next to Logan. The water was again bright red and this was already the third basin of hot water.

Logan paid no attention to Ah Yan's ministrations. "We'll play on a smaller board than usual since you are just learning. This game is called *wei qi*, which means 'the game of surrounding.' Think of laying down each seed as driving a post into the field as you build a fence to surround the land you are claiming. The posts don't move, do they?"

Lily was playing with lotus seeds while Logan's pieces were watermelon seeds. The white and black pieces made a pretty pattern on the grid between them.

"So it's kind of like the way they get land in Kansas," Lily said.

"Yes," Logan said. "I guess it's a little like that, though I've never been to Kansas. You want to surround the largest territory possible, and defend your land well so that my posts can't carve out another homestead in your land."

He took a long drink from the gourd in his hand. The gourd looked a little like a snowman, a small sphere on top of a larger one, with a piece of red silk tied around the narrow waist to provide a good grip. The golden surface of the gourd was shiny from constant use in Logan's rough, leathery palm. Logan had told her that the gourd grew on a vine. When the gourd was ripe it was cut down and the top sawn off so that the seeds inside could be taken out to make the shell into a good bottle for wine.

Logan smacked his lips and sighed. "Whiskey, it's almost as good as sorghum mead." He offered Lily a sip. Lily, shocked, shook her head. No wonder her mother thought these Chinamen barbaric. To drink whiskey out of a gourd was bad enough, but to offer a drink to a young Christian girl?

"There's no whiskey in China?"

Logan took another drink and wiped the whiskey from his beard. "When I was a boy I was taught that there were only five flavors in the world, and all the world's joys and sorrows came from different mixtures of the five. I've learned since then that's not true. Every place has a taste that's new to it, and whiskey is the taste of America."

"Lao Guan," Ah Yan called out. Logan turned toward him. Ah Yan spoke to him in Chinese, gesturing at the basin. After looking at the water in the basin, Logan nodded. Ah Yan got up with the basin and poured out the water in a far corner of the field before going into the house.

"He's gotten as much of the poisoned blood and dirt and torn rags out as possible," Logan explained. "Time to sew me up."

"My dad thinks your name is Logan," Lily said. "I knew he was wrong."

Logan laughed. His laugh was loud and careless, the same as the way he sang and told his stories. "All my friends call me *Lao Guan*, which just means 'Old Guan,' *Guan* being my family name. I guess it sounds like 'Logan' to your dad. I kind of like the ring of it. Maybe I'll just use it as my American name."

"He also picked out a new name for himself when we came here," Lily said. "Mother doesn't think he should do that."

"I don't know why she should be so against it. This is a country full of new names. Didn't she change her name when she married your father? Everyone gets a new name when they come here."

Lily thought about this. It was true. Her father didn't call her "Nugget" until they lived here.

Ah Yan came back with a needle and some thread. He proceeded to stitch up the wound on Logan's shoulder. Lily looked closely at Logan's face to see if he would wince with the pain.

"It's still your turn," Logan said. "And I'm going to capture all your seeds in that corner if you don't do something about it."

"Doesn't it hurt?"

"This?" The way he pointed at his shoulder by wagging his beard made Lily laugh. "This is nothing compared to the time I had to have my bones scraped."

"You had to have your bones scraped?"

"Once I was shot with a poisoned arrow, and the tip of the arrow was buried into the bones in my arm. I was going to die unless I got the poison out. Hua Tuo, the most skilled doctor in the world, came to help me. He had to cut into my arm, peel back the flesh and skin, and scrape off the poisoned bits of bone with his scalpel. Let me tell you, that hurt a lot more than this. It helped that Hua Tuo had me drink the strongest rice wine he could find, and I was playing *wei qi* against my first lieutenant, a very good player himself. It took my mind off the pain."

"Where was this? Back in China?"

"Yes, a long time ago back in China."

Ah Yan finished his sutures. Logan said something to him, and Ah Yan handed a small silk bundle to him. Lily was about to ask Ah Yan about the bundle, but he just smiled at her and held a finger to his lips. He pointed at Logan and mouthed "watch" at her.

Logan laid the bundle on the ground and unrolled the silk wrap. Inside was a set of long, silver needles. Logan picked up one of the needles in his right hand, and before Lily could even yell "Stop," he stuck the needle into his left shoulder, right above the wound.

"What did you do that for?" Lily squeaked. For some reason the sight of the long needle sticking out of Logan's shoulder made her more queasy than when Logan's shoulder had exploded with Obee's shot.

"It stops the pain," Logan said. He took another needle and stuck it into his shoulder about an inch above the other one. He twisted the end of the needle a little to make sure it settled in the right spot.

"I don't believe you."

Logan laughed. "There are many things little American girls don't understand, and many things old Chinamen don't understand. I can show you how it works. Does your leg still hurt?"

"Yes."

"Here, hold still." Logan leaned forward and held out his left palm low to the ground. "Put your foot in my hand."

"Hey, you can move your left arm again."

"Oh, this is nothing. The time I had to have my bones scraped, I was back on the battlefield within two hours."

Lily was sure that Logan was joking with her. "My father was shot in the leg and chest in the War, and it took him eight months before he could walk again. He still has a limp." She lifted her foot, wincing at the pain. Logan cupped her ankle with his palm.

His palm felt warm, hot actually, on Lily's ankle. Logan closed his eyes and began to breathe slowly and evenly. Lily felt the heat on her ankle increase. It felt nice, like having a very hot towel pressed around her injured calf. The pain gradually melted into the heat. Lily felt so relaxed and comfortable that she could fall asleep. She closed her eyes.

"Okay, you are all set."

Logan released her ankle and gently deposited her foot on the ground. Lily opened her eyes and saw a great silver needle sticking out from her leg just below her kneecap.

Lily was going to cry out in pain until she realized that she didn't feel any. There was a slight numbness around where the needle went into her skin, and heat continued to radiate from it, blocking any pain from her wound.

"That feels weird," Lily said. She experimentally flexed her leg a few times.

"As good as new."

"Mother is going to faint when she sees this."

"I'll take it out before you go home. Your skin won't heal for a few more days, but most of the poison in your blood should be gone with the medicine Ah Yan put on the bandage, and the acupuncture should have taken out the rest. Just get the bandage changed to a clean one tomorrow and you shouldn't even have a scar when this is over."

Lily wanted to thank him, but she suddenly felt shy. Talking with Logan was strange. He was unlike anyone she had ever met. One moment he was killing a man with his bare hands, and the next he was holding her ankle as gently as she would a kitten. One moment he was singing songs that seemed as old as the earth itself, and the next he was laughing with her over a game played with watermelon and lotus seeds. He was interesting but also more than a little scary.

"I like playing with the black seeds," Logan said as he placed another seed on the grid, capturing a block of Lily's seeds. He picked them up and popped the handful of lotus seeds into his mouth. "Lotus seeds are much better to eat."

Lily laughed. How could she be scared of an old man who talked with his mouth full?

"Logan, that story about the poisoned arrow and the doctor scraping your bones, that didn't really happen to you, did it?"

Logan tilted his head and looked at Lily thoughtfully. Slowly, he chewed the lotus seeds in his mouth, swallowed, and grinned. "That happened to Guan Yu, the Chinese God of War."

"I knew it! You're just like my father's friends, always telling me tall tales just because I'm a child."

Logan laughed his deep, booming laugh. "Not all stories are made up."

Lily had never heard of the Chinese God of War, and she was sure that her father hadn't either. It was now twilight, and the sounds and the smell of the loud and oily cooking of the Chinamen filled the garden.

"I should go home," Lily said, even though she desperately wanted to try some of the food that she was smelling and hear more about Guan Yu. "Can I come and visit you tomorrow, and you can tell me more stories about Guan Yu?"

Logan stroked his beard with his hand. His face was serious. "It would be an honor." Then his face broke into a smile. "Even though I'll have to eat all the seeds myself now."

The God of War

Before Guan Yu became a god, he was just a boy.

Actually, before that, he was almost just a ghost. His mother carried him in her belly for twelve months, and still he refused to be born. The midwife gave her some herbs and then told her husband to hold her down while she kicked and screamed. The baby finally came out and didn't breathe. Its face was bright red. *Either from choking or too much barbaric blood in the father,* the midwife thought.

"It would have been a huge baby," the midwife whispered to the father. The mother was asleep. "Too big to have a long life, anyway." She began to wrap up the body with what would have been his swaddling clothes. "Did you have a name picked out?"

"No."

"Just as well. You don't want to give the demons a name to hang on to on his way down below."

The baby let out an earsplitting cry. The midwife almost dropped him.

"He's too big to have a long life," the midwife insisted as she unwrapped the body, a little peeved that the baby dared to defy her authority on these matters. "And that face. So red!"

"Then I'll call him Chang Sheng, Long Life."

The dry summer sun and the dusty spring winds of Shanxi carved lines and sprinkled salt into the chapped, ruddy faces of the Chinese who tried to make a living here in the heart of northern China. When the barbarians climbed over the Great Wall and rode down from the north on their raids on the backs of their towering steeds, it was these men who took up their hoes and melted their plows to fight them to the death. It was these women who fought alongside the men with their kitchen knives, and, when they failed, ended up as the slaves and then the wives of the barbarians, learning their language and bearing their children, until the barbarians began to think of themselves as Chinese, and they, in turn, fought against the next wave of barbarians.

While weak men and delicate women who were afraid to die fled south so that they could row around on their flower boats and sing their drunken verses, those who stayed behind, matching the music of their lives to the rhythm of the howling rage of the desert, grew tall with the barbaric blood mixed into their veins and became full of pride at their life of toil.

"This is why," Chang Sheng's father said to him, "the Qin and Han Emperors all came out of the Great Northwest, our land. From us come the generals and the poets, the ministers and the scholars of the Empire. We are the only ones who value pride."

In addition to helping his father in the fields, it was Chang Sheng's job to gather the firewood and kindling for the kitchen. Chang Sheng's favorite time of the day was the hour or so before the sun set. That was when he took the rusty ax and the even rustier machete from behind the kitchen door and climbed the mountain behind the village.

Crack, the ax split the rotting trunk of a tree. *Zang*, the blade swung through the dry grass. It was hard work, but Chang Sheng pretended that he was a great hero cutting down his enemies like weeds.

Back home, dinner was stir-fried bitter melon and pickled cabbage to go with scallions dipped in soy sauce and wrapped in flat sorghum pancakes. Sometimes, when his father was in a particular good mood, Chang Sheng would even get a sip of plum wine, sweet on the tip of the tongue, burning hot down the throat. His face grew to an even darker shade of red.

"There you are, little one," his father said, smiling as Chang Sheng's eyes teared up from the alcohol burn while his hand reached out for another sip. "Sweet, sour, bitter, hot, and salty, all the flavors in balance."

Chang Sheng grew up to be a tall boy. His mother was forever sewing new robes for him as he outgrew the old ones. The drought that had already lasted five years showed no signs of letting up, and even though the men labored harder than ever in the fields, the harvest seemed to grew smaller year after year. There was no money to send him to school, so his father took up the task of teaching him.

History was his favorite subject, but there was always something sad in his father's eyes when they discussed history. Chang Sheng learned to not ask too many questions. Instead, he spent more time reading the history books. Then, when he was out gathering firewood, he acted out the great battles with his ax and machete against the endless hordes of the barbaric woods.

"You like to fight?" his father asked him one day.

He nodded.

"I'll teach you to play *wei qi*, then."

"Did Chang Sheng's father use lotus seeds and watermelon seeds too?"

"No, he used real stones."

"I prefer your way of playing wei qi. *Using seeds is more fun."*

"I think so too. And I like eating too much. Now, where was I?"

Within a day Chang Sheng was able to win one game out of three against his father. In a week he was losing only one out of five. In a month he was winning every game even when he gave his father the advantage of a five-stone handicap.

Wei qi was even better than plum wine. There was sweetness in the simplicity of the rules, bitterness in defeat, and burning-hot joy in victory. The patterns made by the stones were meant to be chewed over, savored.

While out walking, he got lost staring at the patterns made by black streaks of mud thrown up by passing oxcarts against the whitewashed house walls. Instead of chopping firewood, he carved the nineteen-by-nineteen playing grid into the floor of the kitchen with his ax. During dinner, Chang Sheng forgot to eat while he laid out formations on the table with grains of wild rice and black watermelon seeds. His mother wanted to scold him.

"Let him alone," his father said. "That boy has the makings of a great general."

"Maybe he does," his mother said. "But your family hasn't been in the Emperor's service for generations. What is he going to be a general of? A flock of geese?"

"He's still the son of queens and poets, generals and ministers," his father insisted.

"Playing a game is not going to put rice in the pot,

nor wood into the stove. We are going to need to borrow money again this year."

The neighboring villages sent their best players to challenge him. He defeated them all. Eventually, Hua Xiong, the son of the county's wealthiest man, heard about Chang Sheng, the *wei qi* prodigy.

Hua Xiong's family made its fortune by acquiring a coveted license to sell salt. There was a large lake in the county, its waters made salty by the blood of Chi Yu after he was defeated by the Yellow Emperor and his body chopped into pieces. The Han Emperors taxed the salt trade as their principal source of revenue, and the imperial salt monopoly was strictly enforced. Hua Xiong's grandfather placed some strategic bribes, and the family had been growing fat from the salt fortune ever since.

Hua Xiong was the same age as Chang Sheng. He was the sort of boy who tortured cats and delighted in galloping his horse through the fields of his father's tenants, trampling down the sorghum and wheat so that the tracks formed his name. That was how he showed up at the door of the Guan house when he came to play a game of *wei qi* with Chang Sheng, high on his horse, a swath of trampled sorghum behind him.

He brought his *wei qi* set with him: the board made from the pine trees of Mount Tai; the black stones were green jade while the white stones were polished pieces of coral. Chang Sheng made the game last as long as he could so he could finger the cool, smooth stones a little longer.

"The game is getting boring," Hua Xiong said. "I haven't lost to anyone in years."

Chang Sheng's father smiled as he thought, *Doesn't he know that people who have to borrow money from his father would make sure he wins the game?*

Hua Xiong was actually a pretty good *wei qi* player, but not as good as Chang Sheng.

"Very impressive," Hua Xiong said to Chang Sheng's father. "Brother Chang Sheng has a gift. I am ashamed to say that I am not his match."

Chang Sheng's father was surprised. He was too proud to ever tell his son to deliberately throw the game to Hua Xiong. He had expected Hau Xiong to throw a tantrum. But not this.

He's not so bad, he thought. *He's graceful in defeat. That's a quality that belongs to a phoenix among men.*

"What's so impressive about that? I never get mad when my father beats me at checkers. I know I just have to get better."

"Those are wise words. Not everyone sees a loss as an opportunity."

"So is this Hua Xiong really a good man?"

"If you don't interrupt me, you'll soon find out."

"I'll have more watermelon seeds. I won't be able to talk if my mouth is full."

The harvests grew even worse in the next five years. Locusts hit the province. A plague sealed off the next county. There were rumors of cannibalism. The Emperor raised the taxes.

Now eighteen years of age, Hua Xiong was the head of the family after his father choked to death on the leg bone of a pheasant cooked in rice wine. He took advantage of depressed property prices to buy up as much land as possible in the county. Chang Sheng's father went to see him on New Year's Eve.

"Don't worry, Master Guan," Hua Xiong said as they both signed the deed. "I have fond memories of the games Chang Sheng and I used to play as children. I will take care of you and your family."

In exchange for selling his land to Hua Xiong, Chang Sheng's father got enough money to pay off the family's mounting debt. He was then supposed to lease back the land from Hua Xiong and pay a share of the proceeds from the harvest each year as rent.

"He gave us a good deal," he told Chang Sheng's mother. "I always knew he would grow up to be a good man."

That year, they worked especially hard in the fields. The locusts came again to the county but missed their village. The sorghum stalks shot up tall and straight, bobbing in the dry winds of late summer. It was the best harvest they had had in years.

On New Year's Eve, Hua Xiong arrived with a retinue of burly servants.

"May the new year bring you good fortune, Master Guan." They bowed to each other at the door.

Chang Sheng's father invited him in for some tea and plum wine. They knelt down on the clean, new straw mats, across from each other, the small table with the pot of warm wine between them.

They toasted each other's health and had the customary three cups each. Hua Xiong gave a little awkward laugh. "Well, Master Guan, I came for the little matter of the rent."

"Of course," Chang Sheng's father said. He called for Chang Sheng to bring out the five taels of silver. "Here you are, Master Hua. Five percent of my year's proceeds."

Hua Xiong gave a little cough. "Of course I understand how things have been rather hard on you and your family for the last few years. If you'd like some time to prepare the rest of the payment, that is perfectly acceptable." He got up and bowed deeply.

"But I have all the money here. I can show you the books. I had a good year and took in ninety-three taels of silver at the market. Five percent of that is four taels and eight coins. But since you were generous to me in the original sale, I thought I would pay you five full taels to thank you."

Hua Xiong bowed even deeper. "Surely Master Guan is having a joke at lowly Hua Xiong's expense. Some evil persons have been saying that Master Guan is going to try to get out of paying the full amount of the rent this year, but lowly Hua Xiong did not believe them. Lowly Hua Xiong was sure that everything would be cleared up as soon as he came to see Master Guan in person."

"What are you talking about?"

Hua Xiong looked as if a spider were crawling up his spine. He spread out his hands helplessly. "Is Master Guan asking lowly Hua Xiong to produce the deed and the lease?"

Chang Sheng's father's face became an iron mask. "Show me."

Hua Xiong made a great show of searching for the documents. He patted down his sleeves and the breast pockets of his robe. He shouted at his burly servants to look in the wagon. Finally, one of them, a big man with gigantic, misshapen knuckles, came up to Hua Xiong and presented the rolled-up document to him, giving Chang Sheng's father a hard, long sneer.

"Whew." Hua Xiong wiped his forehead with his sleeve. "I thought we almost lost it. I had not thought it would be necessary."

They knelt down again, and Hua Xiong spread out the lease on the table between them. "The rent is to be eighty-five percent of the proceeds from the year's sale of crops," he read, pointing to the characters with his delicate, long fingers.

"Perhaps you could explain to me why the 'eighty' is written in such narrow characters as compared with the rest of the document," Chang Sheng's father said after examining the lease.

"The clerk who drafted the lease was indeed a poor writer," Hua Xiong said. He gave an ingratiating smile. "No doubt Master Guan is a much more cultivated calligrapher. But for a lease you will agree that it does not matter that his hand was poor?"

Chang Sheng's father stood up. Chang Sheng could see that the hem of his sleeves trembled. "Do you think I would have placed my seal on a lease like that? Eighty-five percent? I might as well go join a band of bandits if I want to live on that." He took a step toward Hua Xiong.

Hua Xiong backed up a few steps. Two of the big, burly men stepped up and formed a screen between him and the older man. "Please," Hua Xiong said, his face twisted in a show of regret. "Don't make me take this to the magistrate."

Chang Sheng looked at the ax leaning behind the door. He began to walk toward it.

"Oh no. Don't do it!"

"Go to the kitchen and see if your mother needs more wood," his father said.

Chang Sheng hesitated.

"Go!" his father said.

Chang Sheng walked away and the burly men relaxed.

"Sorry I interrupted."

"No, it's fine. You were trying to save Chang Sheng, like his father."

Later, after Hua Xiong left, the family ate the New Year's Eve dinner in silence.

"A phoenix among men indeed," his father finally said after the meal. He laughed long and hard. Chang Sheng stayed up the whole night with him, drinking the last of their plum wine.

The father wrote a long petition to the magistrate's court, detailing Hua Xiong's treachery.

"It is a sad thing that the bureaucrats must be involved," he said to Chang Sheng, "but sometimes we have no choice."

The soldiers showed up at their house a week later. They broke down the door and hauled Chang Sheng and his mother into the yard and proceeded to overturn every piece of furniture in the house and break every plate, cup, bowl, and dish.

"What is the charge against me?"

"Crafty peasant," the captain said as his soldiers locked the cangue around the neck and arms of Chang Sheng's father, "you are plotting to raise a band of bandits to join the Yellow Turbans. Now confess the names of your coconspirators."

Four soldiers had to hold Chang Sheng back, eventually wrestling him to the ground and sitting on him, as he struggled and cursed the soldiers.

"I think your son also has a rebellious spine," the captain said. "I think we'll bring him in too."

"Chang Sheng, stop fighting. This is not the time. I'll go see the magistrate. This will be cleared up."

His father did not come back the next day, or the day after that. Runners from the town came to the village to tell the family that he had been thrown into jail by the magistrate, pending his trial for treasonous rebellion. Horrified, mother and son made the trip into town to appeal to the magistrate at the *yamen*.

The magistrate refused to see them, or to let them see Chang Sheng's father.

"Crafty peasants, out, out!" The magistrate threw the scholar's rock that he used as a paperweight at Chang Sheng, missing him by a foot. Swinging their bamboo poles, the guards drove Chang Sheng and his mother out of the halls of the *yamen*.

Spring came but mother and son let the fields go fallow. Hua Xiong's henchmen came to cart away anything of value left in the house that hadn't been broken by the soldiers. His mother held him back as Chang Sheng clenched his teeth and ground them together until he felt the saltiness of blood on his tongue. His face grew redder and redder so that Hua Xiong's servants were frightened and left before they could take everything.

He took his ax and machete and spent the days in the mountains. He cleared out entire hillsides with his swinging blade. *Crack!* Boys playing in the mountains ran back to their mothers and spoke of how they had seen a great eagle swooping among the trees, breaking down the branches with its iron beak. *Zang!* Girls doing the washing by the river ran back to the village and told one another how they had heard an angry tiger crashing through the woods, tearing down saplings with its great paws.

The bundles of firewood and kindling were exchanged for sorghum meal and pickled vegetables from the neighbors. The son waited while the mother swallowed the food in silence, flavoring it with her tears. He seemed to survive on sorghum mead and plum wine alone. With each drink, his face grew darker and redder. The blood hue of sorghum and plum would not fade from his face.

The Meal

"Chila, chila!" Ah Yan called out, interrupting Logan's story.

"It's time for dinner," Logan said to Lily. He set down his bowl of watermelon seeds. "Will you join us? Ah Yan is making *Mala* Wife's Tofu and Duke of Wei's Meat, his best dishes."

Lily didn't want Logan to stop. She wanted Hua Xiong to get what he deserved. She wished she could see Chang Sheng angry in the forest, flying and dancing like an eagle or a tiger. But the Chinamen were bustling about, arranging empty crates and benches around the garden in a circle, talking loudly and laughing amongst themselves.

The smell emanating from the open kitchen door made Lily's stomach growl. She had been so absorbed in Logan's tale that she didn't even know she was hungry.

"I promise we'll finish the story some other time."

The miners were in high spirits. Logan had told her that the spot that they had been working on turned out to be a rich deposit, yielding gold by the panful. Ah Yan had checked on her leg as soon as he came back with the other Chinamen and pronounced himself satisfied with her healing process so long as she kept up with plenty of good food and exercise to keep up her strength.

"I have a good story for you," Ah Yan said.

During the day the Chinese miners were visited by the sheriff, Davey Gaskins. The territorial legislature had passed a Foreign Miner's Tax a few years earlier at the rate of five dollars per person per month, and he was there to collect it. The tax was meant to drive out the Chinamen, who were pouring into the territory like so many locusts. But the towns had a lot of trouble collecting it. Gaskins hated the monthly rounds to the Chinese mining camps. They made him feel like he was losing his mind.

First of all, the camps were so far apart that he could never hit all of them in a single day. And somehow they always knew when he was coming to collect the tax. There he would be, standing in a middle of a camp with enough picks, pans, and shovels strewn about for twenty or thirty men at least, and only five or six Chinamen would greet him, insisting that the extra tools were there because they worked so hard that the tools "wore out quickie quickie."

And even worse, they seemed to constantly move about.

"Howdy, Sheriff," Ah Yan greeted him that afternoon. "Good to see you again."

"What's your name again?" Gaskins could never tell the Chinamen apart.

"I'm Loh Yip," Ah Yan said. "You came for our taxes on Monday, remember?"

Gaskins was sure that he had not come to this camp on Monday. He was on the other side of the town, collecting the taxes from three claims that were each supposedly just being worked on by five men.

"I was over near Pioneerville on Monday."

"Sure, so were we. We just moved here yesterday."

Ah Yan showed the sheriff the tax receipts. Sure enough, there was the name "Loh Yip" and four others, followed by Gaskin's own signature.

"Sorry I didn't recognize you," Gaskins said. He felt for sure that he was being tricked, but he had no proof. There were the receipts, written out in his own hand.

"No problem," Ah Yan said, giving him a huge grin. "All Chinamen look alike. Easy mistake to make."

Lily laughed along with the miners as Ah Yan finished his story. She couldn't believe how silly Sheriff Gaskins was. How could he not recognize Ah Yan? It was absurd.

As they worked to set up the makeshift table and chairs in the vege-table garden, the Chinamen talked and joked with one another loudly and easily. Lily found it amusing to try to pick out the English words in their conversation. She was getting used to their accent, which she thought was like their music, brassy, percussive, and punctuated by a rhythm like the beating of a joyous heart.

I have to tell Dad about this later, she thought. *He always told me that the Irish accent of his uncles and aunts reminded him of his favorite drinking songs.*

Lily hadn't been able to go out to see the miners during the day while they were working. Her mother was adamant about keeping her inside the house after her "accident" yesterday.

"I just tripped, that's all. I promise to be more careful."

Her mother just told her to write out more verses in her copybook.

Lily knew that her mother suspected that there was more to the accident than she was telling. She had been dying to tell her dad about everything that happened to her yesterday, but her mother became so alarmed at the sight and smell of her bandaged leg that she insisted Lily wash off all the "Chinamen's poison" immediately. After that it was simply impossible to tell them the truth.

It was only after Jack Seaver got home that Lily managed to get out of the house.

"Elsie, she's a child, not a houseplant. You can't keep her in the house all day. She's got to get some skin scraped off now and then. Someday maybe you can put a corset on her and wrap her up for her husband, but not for a while. For now she needs to be out in the sun, running around."

Elsie Seaver was not happy with this, but she let Lily out. "Dinner is going to be late tonight," she said. "Your father and I need to talk."

Lily slipped out of the house before she could change her mind. The sun was low in the west, casting long shadows on the street, where a cool breeze carried the voices of the returning miners far among the houses of Idaho City. The two Chinamen at the door of the house across the street told her that Logan was in the vegetable garden. She had gone there directly, and, when Lily lost their *wei qi* game from yesterday, Logan began to tell her the story of Guan Yu, the God of War, to console her.

The results of Ah Yan's cooking were carried out of the kitchen into the garden on large plates and set on a makeshift table made out of overturned crates in the middle of the circle. The Chinamen, each holding a large bowl of steamed white rice, milled around the table to pile food on top of the rice. Ah Yan emerged from the crowd and handed Lily a small blue porcelain bowl decorated with pink birds and flowers. The rice in the bowl was covered with small cubes of tofu and pork coated in red sauce and dark pieces of roasted meat with scallions and slices of bitter melon. The smell from the unfamiliar hot spice made Lily's eyes and mouth water at the same time.

Ah Yan handed her a pair of chopsticks and headed back into the crowd to get his own food. He was so small and thin that he nimbly ducked under the shoulders and arms of the other men like a rabbit running under a hedgerow. Before long he ducked back out with his own large bowl of rice piled high with tofu and meat. He saw that Lily was watching him, anxious that he got his fair share. Lifting his bowl from his seat on a stool across the circle from Logan, he told Lily, "Eat, eat!"

Lily sort of got the hang of using chopsticks, after Logan showed her how. It amazed Lily to see his big clumsy hands manipulating his chopsticks so skillfully that he could pick up the delicate pieces of tofu and carry them to his mouth without crushing any of the pieces, causing them to fall, as Lily did the first few times she tried to eat the tofu.

Lily finally managed to get a piece of tofu into her mouth, and she gratefully bit down on it. Flavors until then unknown filled her mouth. Her whole tongue delighted in the richness of the taste: the saltiness, a hint of hot peppers, the almost-sweet base of the sauce, and something else that tickled her tongue. She tried to chew the tofu a little, to bring the flavor out so she could identify that new component more clearly. The taste of hot peppers became stronger, and the tickling grew into a tingling that covered her tongue from tip to base. She chewed yet a little more. . . .

"Awww!" Lily cried out. The tingling suddenly exploded into a thousand hot little needles all over her tongue. The back of her nose felt full of water and her vision became blurry with tears. The Chinamen, stunned into silence by her yelp, burst into laughter when they saw what caused it.

"Eat some white rice," Logan said to her. "Quick."

Lily gulped down several mouthfuls of rice as fast as she could, letting the soft grains massage her tongue and sooth the back of her throat. Her tongue felt numb, paralyzed, and the tingling, now subdued, continued to tickle the inside of her cheeks.

"Welcome to a new taste," Logan said to her, a mischievous joy in his eyes. "That was *mala*, the tingling hotness that made the Kingdom of Shu famous throughout China. You have to be careful with it, as the taste lures you in and then hits you like a mouthful of flame. But once you get used to it, it will make your tongue dance and nothing less will do."

Following Logan's suggestions, Lily tried a few pieces of bitter melon and scallions to rest her tongue a little between pieces of tofu. The bitterness of the melons contrasted nicely with the *mala* of the tofu.

"I bet you've never liked anything bitter before," Logan said.

Lily nodded. She couldn't think of a single dish her mother made that tasted bitter.

"It's all about the balance of the flavors. The Chinese know that you cannot avoid having things be sweet, sour, bitter, hot, salty, *mala*, and whiskey-smooth all at the same time—well, actually the Chinese don't know about whiskey, but you understand my point."

"Lily, it's time for dinner."

Lily looked up. Her father was standing beyond the edge of the vegetable garden, beckoning for her to come over.

"Jack," Logan called out. "Why don't you join us for some of Ah Yan's cooking?"

Taken aback by the suggestion, Jack Seaver nodded after a short pause. He could barely hide his grin as he strode between the rows of cucumbers and cabbages, coming up next to Logan.

"Thank you," he said. "I've been wanting to try this since the first time I smelled it back when you first moved in." He turned to the rest of the circle. "How's the mining been so far, boys?"

"Wonderful, Mr. Seaver." "The gold is everywhere." "Logan has the touch."

"That's just what I want to hear," Jack said. "I'm about to put in an order to San Francisco for my store. Tell me what you want from Chinatown, and I'll work on getting some of that gold out of your hands into mine."

While the circle laughed and shouted out suggestions, which Jack scribbled down on a piece of scrap paper, occasionally pausing so that one of the Chinamen could write down the suggestion in Chinese characters for his agent in San Francisco if the men didn't know the English name for something, Ah Yan ran back into the kitchen to retrieve a new bowl of rice for Jack.

Jack stared at the dishes in the middle of the circle, licking his lips appreciatively. "What are we having today?"

"*Mala* Wife's Tofu," Lily told him. "You have to be careful with it. It has a new taste. And Duke Wei's Meat."

"What kind of meat is it?"

"Dog meat roasted with scallions and bitter melon," Logan said.

Lily, who was about to eat a piece of the roasted meat, dropped her bowl. Rice and tofu and meat and red sauce spilled everywhere. She felt sick.

Jack picked her up and hugged her closely. "How can you do such a thing?" he demanded. "Whose dog did you kill? There's going to be trouble from this." His frown grew more pronounced. "Elsie is going to be hysterical if she hears about this."

"Nobody's. It was a wild dog running in the woods. It looked like a dog that's been abandoned out in the woods since it was a pup. I killed it when it tried to bite me," said Ah Yan, who had come out of the kitchen holding the new bowl of rice for Jack.

"But don't you have dogs as pets? Eating a dog is like . . . like eating a child," Jack said.

"We also have dogs as pets. We do not eat them if they are pets. But this dog was wild, and Ah Yan had to kill it to defend himself. Why would you let a wild dog's meat go to waste when it is delicious?" Logan said. The rest of the Chinamen had stopped eating, intent on the conversation.

"Whether it was wild or not, eating a dog is barbaric."

"You do not eat dogs because you like them too much." Logan thought about this. "I thought you also do not eat rats."

"Of course not! What a disgusting thought. Rats are dirty creatures full of disease." Jack's stomach turned at the very idea.

"We don't eat rats, as a rule," said Logan. "But if we are starving and there's no other meat, it could be cooked to be palatable."

Was there no end to the depravity of the Chinamen? "I can't imagine when I would willingly eat a rat."

"I see," said Logan. "You only eat animals you like a little, but not too much."

There really wasn't anything to say in response to that. Cradling Lily, who was trying hard not to throw up, Jack Seaver walked out of the vegetable garden back to his own house. Elsie had made a chicken pot pie, but neither he nor Lily was any longer in the mood for eating.

Feather, Long Clouds

The eastern sky was still as gray as the belly of a fish when Chang Sheng climbed over the wall. By the time he had finished, the rooster had yet to crow for the first time. The old house, its beams and walls hollowed out by termites and rats over the years, burned easily. By the time the villagers raised the alarm, he was already twenty *li* away.

The rising sun burned the clouds that were draped across the mountains on the eastern horizon in an unbroken chain to a hue red enough to match his face. *Bloodred long clouds,* he thought. *Even the Heavens are celebrating with me.* He laughed long and loud at the joy of vengeance. He felt light as a feather, like he could run forever toward the east, until he ran into the long clouds or into the ocean.

I will need a new name now, thought Chang Sheng. *I shall henceforth be known as* Guan Yu, *the Feather, also styled* Yun Chang, *Long Clouds.*

A month ago, the Autumn Assizes had taken place. Because the penalty for rebellion was death, the Circuit Intendant had overseen the trial himself. The Elder Guan had been hauled into the hall of the *yamen* in chains and made to kneel on the hard, stone floor while Chang Sheng and his mother watched from among the crowd that had gathered for the trial.

Hua Xiong, now fatter than ever and shaking like a leaf in the wind in front of the Intendant, a young scholar judge fresh out of Luo Yang and filled with the arrogance of the Emperor's favor, produced the lease for the Intendant's inspection. He recounted how he had tried to help out the Guan family during their time of need and was dumbfounded when the Elder Guan insisted on setting the lease at 85 percent.

"I asked him, 'How could you live on that?' And Your Reverence, he told me, 'Everyone is going to starve if that'—and here he disrespected the Son of Heaven's name—'is going to rule the country by the advice of his eunuchs and the flattering courtiers that pass for scholars these days. I might as well give all the harvest to you as to lose it all in taxes. It doesn't matter. I'll have a better chance joining the Yellow Turbans and living as a bandit." He bowed his head before the Intendant and continued to tremble.

The Intendant glanced at the kneeling figure of the Elder Guan below the dais of the *yamen*, the corners of his mouth turned down in displeasure. "Humph. 'Flattering courtiers that pass for scholars these days.' Indeed, peasant, is there no respect for the Emperor and the majesty of the law in your eyes? Have you lost all sense of piety? What do you have to say in answer to these accusations?"

The Elder Guan straightened his back as much as he could in his shackles. He looked up at the severe, young face of the Intendant. "It is true that I believe the Emperor has been misled by unscrupulous advisers who view the people as so much fish and meat to be squeezed for their last drop of wealth without regard for their suffering. But I have not forgotten my duty toward the Emperor or my family's many generations of service in the Imperial Army, and I would never raise my arm in rebellion to him. My accuser has fabricated these lies in order to impoverish my family and disgrace me, simply because my son had humiliated him in a game. The Emperor has entrusted you with the power of life and death no doubt because you have wisdom despite your youth, and I have no doubt that your wisdom will reveal the truth of my innocence to you."

Even though he was kneeling, the air that he spoke with made him seem to tower over everyone in the hall of the *yamen*. Even the Intendant seemed impressed.

Noting the change in the Intendant's mien, Hua Xiong fell to his knees and kowtowed three times in rapid succession. "Your Reverence, I should never have dared to accuse

Master Guan unless I had solid evidence, seeing as how his son and I have been childhood friends. I am merely a lowly merchant, while Master Guan is descended from a distinguished family of generals and scholars in the Emperor's service. But I was motivated by love and zeal for the Emperor, so much so that I dared to accuse such a man. It was my fear that he would use his family's glorious record as a shield to cover up all his impious vices. I pray that you would uphold justice." He kept on kowtowing after this speech.

"Stop that," the Intendant said impatiently. "You need not fear his family's history of glory. The Emperor's law is to be administered blindly and impartially. Even were he the son of a Duke or a Prince, if he plotted against the Emperor, you need not fear accusing him." He took another look at the Elder Guan, his face hardening. "I have known many evil men like him: puffed up with the honors heaped upon their families by the Emperor for their ancestors' loyal service, they think they are beyond the law. Well, I will be sure to punish them extra harshly. What other evidence do you have?"

Hua Xiong nodded toward three young girls cowering in the corner behind him. "These young women have seen and heard Master Guan practicing with his ax and machete in the woods. They saw him leaping about, pretending to . . . to . . ."

"To do what?"

"To be visiting those blows upon the Son of Heaven." Hua Xiong went back to his incessant kowtowing, drawing blood on his forehead.

"That is a lie," Chang Sheng cried out from the crowd.

He was livid at those young girls for agreeing to back up such a blatant falsehood. But then he saw that they were all from families who owed a great deal of money to Hua Xiong. He felt as if the veins in his neck would burst if he didn't speak. "I was the one—"

"Chang Sheng, whatever happens, do not speak," the Elder Guan shouted. "You must take care of your mother."

"Come," the Intendant called out to his soldiers, "drive that lawless child and his unchaste mother from the *yamen*. I will not have them make a spectacle of my court."

To keep himself from striking back, Chang Sheng bit down on his tongue until he drew blood. He tried to shield his mother from the blows of the soldiers as they stumbled away from the *yamen*.

The Elder Guan was sentenced to death that afternoon for plotting treason, and his head soon afterward was hung on the flagpole outside the *yamen*. That evening, Chang Sheng's mother put her head in a loop of rope tied to the beam in the middle of the kitchen and kicked the stool out from under herself.

Chang Sheng had left Hua Xiong alive until the end. After he had dispatched the rest of the Hua household (some twenty people), he woke Hua Xiong from his slumber (pausing first to slit the throats of the two concubines in bed with him with quick flicks of his wrist). In the dim light of the torch that Chang Sheng was carrying with him, Hua Xiong thought he looked like a red-faced demon, a soldier from hell coming for his soul.

"I'm sorry, I'm sorry," he blabbered, and lost control of his bowels.

Chang Sheng used his knife to cut the ligaments in Hua Xiong's shoulders and hips, completely paralyzing him. He laid the drooping, heavy body back down on the bed, cuddled between the lifeless bodies of the two concubines.

"I will not give you a clean death. You said my father was a bandit. I will now show you how a bandit deals with people like you."

He proceeded to set fire throughout the house. Soon the smoke was so heavy that Hua Xiong could no longer scream for help. His coughing grew spasmodic and panicked; he was choking on his own spit.

Guan Yu continued to run to the east, where the bloodred long clouds beckoned to him. His heart was light as a feather, and it seemed as if love of the fight and joy in vengeance would never leave him. He felt like a god.

IMPRESSIONS

There was a clearing in the middle of the woods on the side of the hill opposite the river from the Chinamen's mining camp. Now that it was late June, the syringa bushes were in full bloom in the rocky soil along the edge of the clearing, filling the air with their fresh, orangelike scent. The yellow of the blooming arrowleaf balsamroot carpeted the middle of the clearing, with a touch here and there of the purple-blue of the chicory to break the monotony.

Lily loved to sit in the shade of the trees at the edge of the clearing and stare at the colors in front of her. If she sat still long enough, the gentle breeze and the slanting rays of the sun would conspire to blend the individual flowers into an undulating field of light. The world seemed then made afresh to her, full of tomorrows and undiscovered delights. And singing seemed the only thing worth doing.

A plume of smoke rose at the edge of the clearing, breaking her reverie.

She walked across the clearing toward the smoke. The dark figure of a man crouched by it. He was cooking something that smelled delicious to Lily. But there was also a hint of something unpleasant in that smell, like burning hair.

Lily was close enough now to see that the man was large, even larger than Logan. Just as Lily realized that the man was roasting the whole carcass of a large dog whose hide was red as blood, he turned around and grinned at Lily, revealing a mouth full of sharp, daggerlike teeth.

It was Crick.

Lily screamed.

Jack told Elsie to go back to sleep.

"It's all right. I'll make some tea for her."

The sound of water boiling and the comforting warmth of her father's arms dissipated the last traces of the nightmare from Lily's mind. Sipping tea and whispering lest they be overheard by her mother, Lily told Jack what she had seen of the fight between Logan and Crick.

"What happened to Obee?"

"I don't know, he ran off."

"And what did they do with Crick's body?"

Lily wasn't sure about that either.

"And you definitely saw Obee shoot first? And the bullet hit Logan in the shoulder?"

Lily nodded vigorously. The image of Logan's shoulder exploding was carved indelibly into her brain. And she marveled again at how calm she felt when Logan looked at her, as if he had some power to pass his strength onto her, letting her know that she would be safe.

Jack pondered this. If Lily was right, the wound to Logan was serious, yet he had been back at work with his companions less than twelve hours later. Either the Chinaman was the toughest human being he had ever known, or Lily was exaggerating. But he knew his daughter. She was an imaginative child, but not one who lied.

Obee and Crick were notorious outlaws, and lots of people in town suspected that they were behind the fire that had ruined so many people in town and killed the Kellys. But there were no witnesses to the fire and the murders, and no charges had been brought. Now if Obee decided to accuse Logan of murder, he might indeed have a chance of getting Logan hanged since he and Lily and all the Chinamen actually saw it happen. The Chinamen weren't well liked by the whites, on account of their taking claims away from the white miners—never mind that most of these claims had been abandoned by the whites since they didn't have the Chinese rice farmers' skill and patience with water management or their willingness to survive on rice and vege-tables and to squeeze as many people as possible into the tiny saltbox houses in order to save money. There was no telling what a jury might do even if it sounded like Logan killed Crick to protect himself and the others.

"Dad, are you angry with me?"

Startled from his reverie, Jack collected himself. "No. Why should I be?"

"Because you said Logan looked like a killer and you told me to stay away from the Chinamen, and . . . and I almost ate a dog last week."

Jack laughed. "I can't be angry with you for that. The Chinamen's cooking smelled so good that I was interested in the dog myself—and still am, a little. You didn't do anything wrong. Although it was danger-ous for you to get mixed up in their fight, it wasn't by any means your fault. And I guess it turned out all right. You weren't hurt."

"I was, a little."

"Luckily, the Chinamen's medicine seemed to have fixed it. That Logan is quite a character."

"He tells good stories," Lily said. She wanted to tell him about the battles of Guan Yu, the God of War, or the songs of Jie You, the Princess Who Became a Barbarian. She wanted to describe to him how she felt, listening to Logan recite those stories in the rhythm of his clanging, whiskey-sharpened accent so that they sounded at the same time so fantastic and so familiar while the long, gnarled fingers of his large hands made the scene come alive with comic and solemn gestures. But it was all still so new and confusing, and she didn't think she knew the right words yet to paint a proper picture of those moments for her father.

"I'm sure he does. This is why we are out here, where the country belongs to nobody and everyone is a stranger with a tale of his own. The Celestials are filling up California and soon, Idaho Territory. Soon everyone here will know their stories."

Lily finished her tea. She was comfortable, but the lingering excitement from the nightmare kept her from being sleepy.

"Dad, will you sing me a song? I can't sleep now."

"Sure thing, Nugget. But let's go outside and take a walk, or else we'll wake your mother."

Lily and Jack threw jackets over their nightclothes and slipped outside the house. The summer evening was warm, and the sky, cloudless and moonless, glowed with the light of a million stars.

Some of the Chinamen were still up on the porch. They played a game with dice by the weak light of an oil lamp. Jack and Lily waved at them as the two of them strode down the street.

"Guess they can't sleep either," Jack said. "Don't blame them. Can't imagine how you'd sleep with five other guys packed in like sardines with you, all of them snoring and with smelly feet."

Before long they had left the weak light of the Chinamen's oil lamp behind them, and then they were beyond the edge of the town. Jack sat down on a rock by the side of the road into the hills and lifted Lily to sit beside him, his arm wrapped around her.

"What song would you like to hear?"

"How about the one that Mom would never let you sing, the one about the funeral?"

"That's a good one."

Jack took out his pipe and lit it to keep the insects away from them, and he began to sing:

> Tim Finnegan lived in Walkin' Street,
> A gentle Irishman mighty odd;
> He had a brogue both rich and sweet,
> And to rise in the world he carried a hod.
> Now Tim had a sort of a tipplin' way,
> With a love of the whiskey he was born,
> And to help him on with his work each day,
> He'd a drop of the craythur every morn.

Lily looked up into her father's face. Lit by the flame from the pipe, it took on a red glow that brought a sudden rush of love and comfort to her heart. Smiling at each other, father and daughter belted out the chorus:

> Whack fol the dah O, dance to your partner,
> Welt the floor, your trotters shake;
> Wasn't it the truth I told you,
> Lots of fun at Finnegan's wake!

Jack continued with the rest of the song:

One mornin' Tim was feelin' full,
His head was heavy which made him shake;
He fell from the ladder and broke his skull,
And they carried him home his corpse to wake.
They rolled him up in a nice clean sheet,
And laid him out upon the bed,
A gallon of whiskey at his feet,
And a barrel of porter at his head.

His friends assembled at the wake,
And Mrs. Finnegan called for lunch,
First they brought in tay and cake,
Then pipes, tobacco and whiskey punch.
Biddy O'Brien began to bawl,
"Such a nice clean corpse, did you ever see?
O Tim, mavourneen, why did you die?"
"Arragh, hold your gob," said Paddy McGhee!

Then Maggie O'Connor took up the job,
"O Biddy," says she. "You're wrong, I'm sure."
Biddy she gave her a belt in the gob,
And left her sprawlin' on the floor.
And then the war did soon engage,
'Twas woman to woman and man to man,
Shillelagh law was all the rage,
And a row and a ruction soon began.

Then Mickey Maloney ducked his head,
When a noggin of whiskey flew at him,
It missed, and falling on the bed,
The liquor scattered over Tim!

The corpse revives! See how he raises!
Timothy rising from the bed,
Says, "Whirl your whiskey around like blazes,
Thanum an Dhoul! Do you think I'm dead?"

"Feeling sleepy yet?"

"No."

"All right, we'll sing another one."

They stayed out under the stars for a long, long time.

The Apotheosis

It was whispered among the soldiers of all the Three Kingdoms that Guan Yu could not be killed. The generals of the deceitful Cao Cao and the arrogant Sun Quan tried to laugh at this rumor and executed those who spread it. All the same, when it came time to face Guan Yu on the battlefield, even the invincible Lü Bu hesitated.

But I have gotten ahead of myself. How did the Han Dynasty fall? How did the Three Kingdoms rise? Who were the heroes among whom Guan Yu made his way?

The Yellow Turbans ravaged the land, their rallying rebel cry that the Emperor was a child who had never set foot outside the Palace while his eunuchs preyed upon the blood and flesh of the peasants. Taking up arms against the rebels, the dreaded warlord Cao Cao made the Emperor a hostage in his own capital and ruled in his name from the plains and deserts of the North.

In the South, the rich rice fields and winding rivers propelled Sun Quan, the Little Tyrant, to hold sway over ships, and hunger for the title of Emperor.

Everywhere there was sickness and starvation, and armies marched over fields empty of cultivation.

Liu Bei, a man so full of charm that his earlobes reached his shoulders, was merely a peddler of straw shoes and straw mats when he met Zhang Fei, the butcher, and Guan Yu, the outlaw who was still running. Guan Yu now had the beginning of his famous beard, a bushy and vibrant beard that made him look old and young at the same time. It made a nice addition to a handsome face, whose smooth features looked like they were carved out of the red stone of the Crimson Cliffs of the Yangtze River.

"If I had men who could fight like tigers with me, I would restore the glory of the Han Dynasty," Liu Bei said to the two strangers who shared a bowl of sorghum mead with him in the peach orchard.

"And what good is that to me?" asked Zhang Fei, whose face was black as coal and whose arms daily wrestled oxen to the ground for the slaughter.

Liu Bei shrugged. "Maybe you do not care. But if I were Emperor, the magistrates would again mete out justice, the fields would be cultivated with industry and virtue, and the teahouses would again be filled with the songs and laughter of scholars and dancing women." His eyes lingered a moment longer on Guan Yu's face, which was familiar to him from the many posters putting a price on his head that he had seen around the city. "There are many men who are outlaws in this day and age, but many of them are outside the law only because the laws have not been administered with virtue. Were I Emperor, I would make them the judges, not the criminals."

"And what makes you think you will succeed?" asked

Guan Yu. His face darkened to the color of blood, but he stroked his beard carelessly, like a scholar stroking his brush as he was about to pen a poem about girls collecting flowers in May.

"I don't know I will succeed," Liu Bei said. "All life is an experiment. But when I die I will know that I once tried to fly as high as a dragon."

In the peach orchard then, they became sworn brothers.

"Though we were not born on the same day of the same month of the same year, we ask that Fate give us the satisfaction of dying on the same second of the same minute of the same hour."

They headed West, and there, in the mountainous Province of Shu, where Guan Yu first tasted *mala*, they founded the Kingdom of Shu Han.

All-Under-Heaven was thus split into the Three Kingdoms of Cao Cao, Sun Quan, and Liu Bei. Of the three, Cao Cao had the valor and wildness of the Northern Skies while Sun Quan had the wealth and resilience of the Southern Earth, but only Liu Bei had the virtue and love of the People.

Guan Yu was his greatest warrior. He had the strength of a thousand men and the love of even more.

"He is not made of flesh and blood." Cao Cao sighed when he heard the report of how Guan Yu slew six of his best generals and broke through five passes to rejoin Liu Bei on his Long March of a Thousand Li.

"He is a phoenix among swallows and sparrows." Sun Quan shook his head when he heard how Guan Yu laughed and played *wei qi* while his bones were scraped

free of poison. Guan Yu was back on his horse and swinging his sword the next day.

War raged between the Three Kingdoms for years,
neither one able to subdue the other two. Guan Yu's face
never lost its bloodred color, and his dark beard grew
longer and longer until he wore it in a silk pouch to keep
it clean and out of the way in battle.

Though Liu Bei was virtuous, the Mandate of Heaven
was not with him. His armies fought and lost, lost and
fought, in battle after battle. During a retreat on one of
their campaigns to the North, Guan Yu and Zhang Fei
were separated from the main army, and their detachment of one hundred scouts became surrounded by the
army of Cao Cao, numbering more than ten thousand.
Cao Cao asked for parley with the two.

"Surrender and swear fealty to me, and I shall make
you into Dukes who do not have to kneel even in the
presence of the Son of Heaven," Cao Cao said.

Guan Yu laughed. "You do not understand why men
like me fight. There is the joy of battle, of course, but
that is not all." He opened up his old, faded battle cape
to show Cao Cao the holes in the fabric, the frayed edges
and patches upon more patches. "This was given to me by
my sworn brother Liu Bei. Before I put on the cape, I was
nobody, a murderer running from the law. But after I put
on the cape, every swing of my sword was in the name of
virtue. What can you offer me better than that?"

Cao Cao turned around and rode back to his camp.
He ordered his army to begin attack immediately. The
generals gave the orders, but the soldiers, thousands upon
thousands of them lined up in rank after rank, refused to

advance against Guan Yu and Zhang Fei and their small circle of one hundred men.

Cao Cao ordered the soldiers standing in the back killed on the spot. The panicked soldiers pushed against their comrades in front. The tide of men surged slowly forward, closing in on Guan Yu and Zhang Fei.

The battle lasted from morning till night and then throughout the night till the next morning.

"Remember the Oath of the Peach Orchard," Guan Yu yelled to Zhang Fei. He was riding through Cao Cao's men on his war stallion, the great Red Hare, whose skin matched the hue of Guan Yu's face and who sweated blood as he trampled men beneath his giant hooves. "If Fate will have us succumb this day, then we will have at least fulfilled our oath."

"But then our brother Liu Bei will be late," replied Zhang Fei as he impaled two men at once on his iron-shafted spear.

"We will forgive him," Guan Yu said. The Brothers laughed and separated once again for the battle.

Wherever Guan Yu rode, swinging his moon-shaped sword, the soldiers of Cao Cao fell over one another to get away from the rider and his horse, parting before them like a flock of sheep before a tiger or a brood of chickens before an eagle. Guan Yu mowed them down mercilessly, and Red Hare frothed at the mouth, the bloodlust overcoming his exhaustion.

"When I am fighting next to you," Zhang Fei said, wiping streams of blood from his black face, "I do not know what fear is. My mind is harder, my heart keener, my spirit the greater as our might lessens."

The one hundred men with Guan Yu and Zhang Fei

gradually became fifty men, and then fifteen, and finally, only Guan Yu and Zhang Fei were left, charging back and forth through the sea of swords and spears that was Cao Cao's army.

It was evening again. Cao Cao called for a halt to the battle, pulling his troops back. Rivers of blood ran across the field, and hacked-off limbs and heads littered the ground like sea shells on the beach at low tide. The evening sun cast long, scarlet shadows over everything so that one could no longer be sure whether the redness was from the light or blood.

"Surrender," Cao Cao called out to them. "You have proven your courage and loyalty to Liu Bei. No god or man would ask more of you."

"I would," Guan Yu said.

Though Cao Cao was a man with a cold heart and a narrow mind, he was overwhelmed with admiration for Guan Yu.

"Will you drink with me," he said, "before you die?"

"Of course," said Guan Yu. "I never say no to sorghum mead."

"No sorghum mead here, I'm afraid. But I have some barrels of a new drink the barbarians of the West have given to me as tribute."

The drink was made from grapes, a new fruit brought over the desert by the barbarian emissaries of the West.

You mean wine?

Yes, but that was the first time Guan Yu had seen it.

Guan Yu and Cao Cao drank it in jade cups, whose cold stony surface complemented the warmth of the wine excellently. It was getting dark, but the jade from which the cups were made had an inner glow to them that lit up the faces of the two men. The pretty barbarian girls who were part of the tribute to Cao Cao played a mournful tune on their strange pear-shaped lutes, which they called *pi pa*.

Guan Yu listened to the music, lost in his own thoughts. Suddenly he stood up and began to sing to the tune of the barbarian lute:

> *Give me grape wine overflowing night-glowing cups,*
> *I would drink it all but the* pi pa *calls me to my horse.*
> *If I should fall down drunk on the battlefield, do not*
> *   laugh at me,*
> *For how many have ever returned from war, how many?*

He tossed the cup away. "Lord Cao Cao, I thank you for the wine, but I think it is now time to get back to what we have to do."

"So, that banjo-thing you were playing, that's a *pi pa*, isn't it?" The mournful song Logan had been singing was still in Lily's head. She wanted to ask Logan to teach it to her.

"Yes, it is." He shifted the *pi pa* around on his knees, cradling its pear-shaped body lovingly, like a baby. "This one is pretty old, and it sounds better with every year that passes."

"But it's not really Chinese, is it?"

Logan was thoughtful for a moment. "I don't know. I guess you'd say it's really not, not if you look back thousands of years. But I don't think that way. Lots of things start out not Chinese and end up that way."

"That's not what I would have expected to hear from a Celestial,"

Jack said. He was still trying to get used to the taste of the sorghum liquor that Logan assured him was what every Chinese boy drank along with mother's milk. Swallowing it was like swallowing a mouthful of razors. Lily saw his furrowed brows as he took another drink and laughed.

"Why not?"

"I thought you Celestials were supposed to be mighty jealous of your long history, Confucius being from before Christ and everything. I didn't think I'd hear one of you admit that you learned anything from the barbarians."

Logan laughed at this. "I myself have some blood of the northern barbarians flowing in my veins. What is Chinese? What is barbarian? These questions will not put rice into bellies or smiles onto the faces of my companions. I'd much rather sing about pretty girls with green eyes from west of the Gobi Desert and play my *pi pa*."

"If I didn't know better, Logan, I'd say you sound like a Chinese American."

Jack and Logan laughed at this. *"Gan bei, gan bei,"* they said, and tossed back cups of whiskey and sorghum liquor.

"I want to learn 'Finnegan's Wake' from you. Ever since I heard the two of you singing that night, I can't get it out of my head."

"You have to finish the story first!" Lily said.

"All right. But I have to warn you. I've told this story so many times, and each time I tell it, it's different. I'm not sure I know how the story ends anymore."

> How long did the battle last? Was it still against the treacherous Cao Cao or the deceitful Sun Quan? Guan Yu could not remember.
>
> He did remember telling Zhang Fei to leave and get back to Liu Bei.

"I am in charge of the men, and because of my carelessness, I have led them into death. I cannot show my face back in Cheng Du, where the wives and fathers of those men will ask me why I have returned when their husbands and sons have not. Fight your way out, Brother, and seek revenge for me."

Zhang Fei halted his horse and gave a long cry. At the piercing sound of that cry, full of sorrow and regret, the ten thousand men around them shook in their boots and stumbled back three steps each.

"Good-bye, Brother." Zhang Fei spurred his horse to the west, and the soldiers parted to make way for his spear and horse, fought with one another to get out of his path.

"On, on!" Cao Cao shouted angrily. "The man who captures Guan Yu shall be made a Duke."

Red Hare stumbled. He had lost too much blood. Guan Yu deftly leapt off the back of the war stallion just as he fell to the ground.

"I'm sorry, old friend. I wish I could have protected you." Blood and sweat dripped from his beard, and tears carved out clear channels through the dried blood and dirt on his face.

He threw down his sword and put his hands behind him, looking for all the world like a scholar-poet about to recite from the *Book of Poetry* in front of the Emperor at his court. He stared at the approaching soldiers with contempt.

"They cut off his head at the next sunrise," Logan said.

"Oh," said Lily. This wasn't the ending she had wanted to hear.

The three of them were silent for a bit, while the smoke from Ah Yan's cooking in the kitchen drifted into the clear sky. The sound of spatula on wok sounded like the din of sword on shield to Lily's ears.

"You are not going to ask me what happened next?" Logan said.

"What do you mean?" Jack and Lily said at the same time.

"What do you mean?" Cao Cao shouted, and stood up in a hurry, overturning the writing desk in the process. The ink stone and brushes flew everywhere. "What do you mean you can't find it?"

"Lord Cao Cao, I am telling you what I saw with my own eyes. One minute his head was rolling on the ground, and the next his head and body were simply nowhere to be found. He . . . he disappeared into thin air."

"What kind of fool do you take me for? Come!" Cao Cao gestured to the guards. "Tie him up and have him executed. We'll hang his head outside my tent since he lost Guan Yu's head."

"Of course he's not dead," the grizzled veteran said to the pink-faced new recruits. "I was there the day Lord Guan Yu was captured. Among the one hundred thousand men of the Army of Wei, he fought as if they were nothing more than motes of dust. A man like that, do you think he would succumb to an executioner's ax?"

"Of course he's not dead," Liu Bei said to Zhang Fei. They were both covered in the white armor of mourning, and they had raised an army of every last able-bodied man of the Kingdom of Shu for vengeance. "Our brother would not die when he still has the Oath of the Peach Orchard to fulfill."

"Of course he's not dead," Sun Quan said as he lay on

his deathbed. "Guan Yu had no fear of death, and my only regret is that I will not have his company where I am going. I had hoped we might one day be friends."

"Of course he's not dead," said Cao Cao to Liu Chan, Liu Bei's son, as he gave the order to break the Seal of the Kingdom of Shu, now that he had finally united the Three Kingdoms. "I have never thought much of your father or you, but if Guan Yu was willing to serve your father, then he must have seen something that I couldn't. As Lord Guan Yu may still be watching over you, I would show him that I am not without virtue. I will not harm you and you will always live in my house as an honored guest."

"Of course he's not dead," said the mother to the child. "Lord Guan Yu was the greatest man the Middle Kingdom has ever produced. If you have even one hundredth of his strength and courage, I will never need to fear thieves and bandits."

"Let us pray to Lord Guan Yu," said the scholar to his students. "He was a poet and a warrior, and he lived each day as a test of his honor."

"Let us pray to Lord Guan Yu," said the Emperor as he dedicated the Temple to the God of War. "May he grant us victory over the barbarians."

"Let us pray to Lord Guan Yu," said the player with the black stones. "All of us *wei qi* players wish we could play a game against him. If we play well today, perhaps he will deign to come and give us lessons."

"Let us pray to Lord Guan Yu," said the merchants as they prepared to set out across the ocean for the fabled ports of Ceylon and Singapore. "He will watch over us and subdue the pirates and typhoons."

"Let us pray to Lord Guan Yu," said the laborers as they boarded the sailing ships headed for the Sandalwood Mountains of Hawaii and the Old Gold Mountain of California. "He will help us endure the journey, and he will break apart mountains before us. He will keep us safe until we have made our fortune, and then he will guide us home."

THE CHINESE RESTAURANT

By late summer, the stream that fed the Chinamen's claim had dried to a trickle. Though Logan and his men were good at managing water, the onset of the dry season meant that it was no longer possible to mine the placer deposit effectively. They had to settle in and wait until next spring.

Though they had done well with the mining season during spring and summer, the Chinamen had by no means accumulated a large fortune. As they settled into the life of Idaho City and waited out the rest of the year, they tried to figure out other ways to make ends meet.

Ah Yan and some of the younger men looked for work around the town and talked amongst themselves. They noticed that there were plenty of single men in town who simply refused to or couldn't wash their own shirts, and there simply weren't enough laundresses taking in the washing for all the men.

"But that's women's work! Have these men no sense of decency?" Elsie was incredulous when Jack told her the Chinamen's plan.

"Well, what of it? Why do you seem to hate everything the Chinamen do?" Jack said, amusement and annoyance struggling in his voice.

"Thaddeus Seaver." Elsie looked sternly at her husband. She knew better than to expect that her husband would show any proper sense of shock at the antics of these outrageous Chinamen when Thad was the one who encouraged them to become bolder and bolder every day. But then she hit upon an argument that even Thad had to acknowledge.

"Why, think about it, Thad," she said. "I've seen the way these heathen Chinamen go about their work. When they set up their laundry shops, they'll work seven days a week, sixteen hours a day. They'll do it since their hearts are filled with greed for gold and pumped full of sinful opium so that they never stop for a moment to think about the Glory of God, not even on Sundays. And I've seen the way they eat. The Chinamen are like locusts: they survive on nothing but cheap rice and vegetables when honest Christian men and women need to eat meat to keep up their strength. And they do not spend money on honest wholesome entertainment and camaraderie that keep the town's shops and taverns afloat as our men do, but rather waste their evenings away wailing their cacophonous songs and telling their secretive stories. Finally, when night rolls around and every Christian family withdraws around the privacy of the familial hearth"—and here she paused to give Jack a meaningful stare—"the Chinamen squeeze as many bodies into as few beds as possible to save on rent."

"Why, Elsie," Jack laughed uproariously. "I've heard of faint praise before, but I do believe this is the first time I've ever heard of faint damnation. The way you go on, I'd think you are a lover of the Chinese if I didn't know better. You claim to be showing me their faults, but all you've said simply show that they are industrious, frugal, clever, happy with each other's company, and willing to bear hardships. If this is the worst you can say about the Chinamen, then it is all but certain that the Civilization of Confucius is going to triumph over the Civilization of Christ."

"You are not thinking," Elsie said coldly. "What do you think the inevitable result of the cheap labor of these Chinamen will be? These Chinamen are going to undercharge Mrs. O'Scannlain and Mrs. Day and all the other widows. These women have a hard enough time as it is, working day and night, their fingers all red and raw from the constant washing, and they barely make enough to feed themselves and their children. Naturally, the weak men of this town, uncertain of their Christian duty, will give their work to the Chinamen, who'll charge them less than the honest widows who must keep God and their virtue close to their hearts. What will you have these widows do when their work has been stolen from them by the Chinamen? Will you have them throwing themselves at the mercy of Madam Isabelle and her house of sin?"

For once, Jack Seaver didn't know what to say in reply to his wife.

"How about carpentry? Furniture finishing? I could hire you to come and work in my store as clerks," Jack said to Ah Yan.

"You can't afford me," Ah Yan said. "We charge twenty-five cents a shirt, and that means almost ten dollars a day from the bachelors alone. I'm not even counting the money from the blankets and sheets from the hotels. I've been told that we do a better job ironing than the women used to." Ah Yan gave a rueful smile and flexed out his wiry right arm to look at the distended thumb at the end. "Even my thumb is getting bigger from pushing that iron all day. My wife back home will be tickled pink to hear that I'm a master of the iron now."

To hear Ah Yan talk of his family was jarring to Jack, reminding him that Ah Yan, who looked so young to Jack's eyes, wasn't just some clever young man who knew how to cook and wash, but rather a husband and probably a father who was forced to learn how to do these things because his wife couldn't be with him.

Lily had told Jack a few days earlier that the Chinamen were coming up with some new ideas that they wanted to ask his advice on. Finally, this morning, he could leave the store for a few hours to come over with Lily, who ran into the backyard to be with Logan as soon as they arrived. Jack thoughtfully bit into the steamed bun that Ah Yan had given him for breakfast; the bun burst open in his mouth, filling his tongue with the juice and flavor of sweet pork and hot and salty vegetables.

"Wait." Jack swallowed quickly, regretting that he couldn't enjoy the taste as long as he would have liked. "I have an idea. Before tasting your cooking, I would never have believed that cabbage and beans could taste better than beef and sausage, or that bitterness that lingered could be something that you liked. But you've been able to prove me wrong. Why not show the other people in Idaho City? You and the others could open up a restaurant and make a lot more money."

Ah Yan shook his head. "Won't work, Mr. Seaver. My friends in Old Gold Mountain tried it. Most Americans aren't like you. They can't stand the taste of Chinese food. It makes them sick."

"I've heard of Chinese restaurants in San Francisco."

"Those aren't Chinese restaurants. Well, they are, but not the kind you are thinking of. They are owned by Chinese people, but all they serve is Western food: roast beef, chocolate cake, French toast. I don't know how to make any of that stuff, not even well enough to the point where I'd want to eat it myself."

"But I'm telling you, you are good, really good." Jack looked around and lowered his voice. "You cook a lot better than Elsie, and I know she cooks as well as most of the wives out here. If you open your restaurant and I pass the word to the men discreetly, you'll have filled tables every night."

"Mr. Seaver, you are too generous with your praise. I know that in the eyes of a husband, there's no way for anyone's cooking to best his wife's." He paused for a moment, as if his thoughts were momentarily somewhere far away. "Besides, we are not chefs. All the stuff I make is just homestyle cooking, the kind of thing the real chefs in Canton would not even feed to their dogs. There can't be a Chinese restaurant in America until there are enough Chinese people in America—and rich enough to want to eat at one."

"That just means more Chinese will have to become Americans," said Jack.

"Or lots more Americans will have to learn to be more Chinese," said Ah Yan.

A few of the other Chinamen had gathered around to listen to the conversation. One of them offered a comment in Chinese at this point, and the group exploded in laughter. Tears came out of Ah Yan's eyes.

"What did he say?" Although Jack was making an earnest effort to learn the language by singing drinking songs with Logan, he was nowhere good enough to follow a conversation yet, though Lily seemed to have picked it up much more easily and now often conversed with Logan half in Chinese and half in English.

Ah Yan wiped his eyes. "San Long said that we should name the restaurant 'Dog Won't Eat Here and You Won't Eat Dog.'"

"I don't get it."

"There's this really famous kind of steamed buns in China that's called 'Dog Won't Eat Here,' and you know how you Americans have this thing about eating dog meat"—Ah Yan gave up when he saw the expression on Jack's face. "Never mind. This humor is too Chinese for you."

San Long now picked up some twigs from the ground and mimed doing something with them and looked to Jack as if he were drunkenly throwing darts at some target a few inches in front of his face. Ah Yan and the others laughed even harder.

"He's saying that a Chinese restaurant will never work in America since every customer will have to learn to use chopsticks," Ah Yan explained to Jack.

"Yeah, yeah, very funny. Fine, no restaurant for you. And while we are on the subject of dogs and compliments that don't sound like compliments, you did manage to make me curious about eating a dog for the first time in my life that evening."

• • •

"Dad is worried about the laundresses who are now out of work," Lily told Logan.

They were walking down the middle of Chicory Lane together, side by side. Logan had a bamboo pole over his shoulder. At each end of the pole hung giant woven baskets filled with cucumbers, green onions, carrots, squash, tomatoes, string beans, and sugar beets.

"He's not sure what to do. He says Ah Yan and the others are charging too little for the washing and the ironing, but if the women don't charge less, the white men won't give them any work."

"Two dollars for a dozen cucumbers, a dollar for a dozen green onions!" Logan called out in his booming voice, which reverberated in all directions until the echoes disappeared into the alleyways between the tightly packed houses. "Fresh carrots, beans, and beets! Come and have a look for yourself. Girls, fresh vegetables make your skin soft and smooth. Boys, fresh vegetables get rid of sailor's lips!"

He called out his prices and offerings in a steady, rolling chant, not unlike the way he led the others in their work songs.

Doors opened on all sides of them. The curious wives and bachelors came out into the street to see what Logan was singing about.

"You should bring some of this up to Owyhee Creek, where Davey's crew is still working their claim on account of that spring the Indians helped them find," said one of the men. "I know they haven't had any greens for a week now, and they'd pay you five dollars for a dozen of those cucumbers."

"Thanks for the tip."

"Where did you get the produce?" one of the wives wanted to know. "It looks a lot fresher than what you find in Seaver's store, though I know he ships them in quick as he can."

"It's all grown right in our backyard, ma'am. Plucked those carrots from the ground myself this morning not even a hour ago."

"In your backyard? How do you manage it? I can't even get a bit of sage and rosemary to grow properly."

"Well," said Logan, "I started in China as a dirt-poor farmer. I guess I just have the knack for getting food to come out of dirt, one way or another."

"Sure wish I had these fresh green onions and cucumbers to eat back in the spring instead of having to chew on potatoes soaked in vinegar every other day," one of the older miners said, handling the giant cucumbers and tomatoes from Logan's basket lovingly. "You are right that scurvy is a terrible thing, and fresh vegetables are the only thing for it. Too bad none of the young men believe it till it's too late. I'll have a dozen of these."

"I don't think we are going to let you leave today without emptying out your baskets," another one of the younger wives said, to the sound of approval of the other women. "Did you save any for yourself and your friends?"

"Don't worry about us," Logan said. "I think we can get five or six harvests out of the garden this year. Buy as much as you want. I'll be back again in a few weeks."

Soon Logan sold all the vegetables he had with him. He counted out twenty dollars and handed the bills to Lily. "Give ten dollars to Mrs. O'Scannlain; I know she doesn't have much saved up, and she's got two growing boys to feed. Ask your father who should have the rest."

The old man and the young girl turned around and began the long, leisurely walk back to the Chinaman's house on the other side of the town. In the empty street bathed in the bright, shimmering sunlight of high noon, the loping gait of the tall Chinaman and the baskets swinging lazily at the end of the bamboo pole over his shoulder made him look like some graceful water strider gliding across the still surface of a sunlit pond.

And in a moment, the man and the girl disappeared around the street corner and all was still again in the street.

CHINESE NEW YEAR

It had been snowing nonstop for a whole week. The whole of Idaho City seemed asleep in the middle of February, resigned to wait for the spring that was still months away.

Well, almost the whole of Idaho City. The Chinamen were busy preparing for Chinese New Year.

For the whole week the Chinamen talked about nothing except the coming New Year celebration. Strings of bright red firecrackers shipped from San Francisco were unpacked and laid out on shelves so that they would be kept dry. A few of the more nimble-fingered were set to the task of folding and cutting the paper animals that would be offered along with bundles of incense to the ancestors. Everyone worked to wrap pieces of candy and dried lotus seeds in red paper to be handed out to the children as sweet beginnings to a new year. Two days before New Year's Eve, Ah Yan directed all the men in the preparation of the thousands of dumplings that would be consumed on New Year's Day. The living room was turned into an assembly line for a dumpling factory, with some men rolling out the dough at one end, others preparing the stuffing of diced pork and shrimp and chopped vegetables mixed with sesame oil, and the rest wrapping scoops of stuffing into dumplings shaped like closed clams. The finished dumplings were then packed into buckets covered with dried sheets of lotus leaves and left outside, frozen in the ice, until they could be cooked in boiling water on New Year's Eve.

Lily helped out wherever she could. She sorted the strings of firecrackers by size until her fingers smelled of gunpowder. She learned to cut pieces of colorful paper into the shapes of chickens and goats and sheep so that they could be burned in the presence of the gods and the ancestors and allow them to share in the feast of the people.

"Will Lord Guan Yu be there to appreciate the paper sheep?" Lily asked Logan.

Logan looked amused for a moment before his face, made even ruddier than usual because of the cold, turned serious. "I'm sure he will be there."

In the end, Lily proved most valuable as the final step in the dumpling assembly line. She was an expert at sculpting the edges of the dumplings with a fork to create the wavy scallop shell pattern that signified the unbroken line of prosperity.

"You are really good at that," Logan said. "If you didn't have red hair and green eyes, I'd think you were a Chinese girl."

"It's just like shaping a pie crust," Lily said. "Mom taught me."

"You'll have to show me how to make a proper pie crust after New Year's," Ah Yan said. "I've always wanted to learn that American trick."

The activity of the Chinamen stirred up all kinds of excitement in the rest of Idaho City.

"Everybody gets a red packet filled with money and sweets," the children whispered to one another. "All you have to do is to show up at their door and wish them to come into their fortune in the new year."

"Jack Seaver has been raving about the cooking of the Chinamen for months now," the women said to one another in the shops and streets. "Here's our only chance to try it out. They say the Chinamen will serve anyone who comes to their door with pork dumplings that combine all the flavors in the world."

"Are you going to be at the Chinamen's when they celebrate their New Year?" the men asked one another. "They say that the heathens will put on a parade to honor their ancestors, with lots of loud music and colorful costumes. At the end, they'll even serve up a feast such as never before seen in all of Boise Basin."

"What was Logan like back in China? Does he have a large family there?" Lily asked Ah Yan as she helped the young man carry large jars of sweet bamboo shoots into the house. She was tired from all the work she had done that day and couldn't wait until the feast tomorrow. Truth be told, she felt a little guilty. She was never this eager when her own mother asked her to help around the house. She resolved to do better after tomorrow.

"Don't know," Ah Yan said. "Logan wasn't from our village. He wasn't even a Southerner. He just showed up on the docks on the day we were supposed to ship out for San Francisco."

"So he was a stranger even in his own land."

"Yup. You should ask him to tell you the story of our trip here."

It is hardly the happy and the powerful who go into exile.
— *Alexis de Tocqueville*

When in America

On a good day the captain allowed a small number of his cargo to come up on deck from steerage for some air. The rest of the time each man made do with a six-foot bunk that was narrower than a coffin. In the complete darkness of the locked hold they tried to sleep away the hours, their dreams mixtures of unfounded hopes and cryptic dangers. Their constant companion was the smell of sixty men and their vomit and excrement and their food and unwashed bodies crammed into a space meant for bales of cotton and drums of rum. That, and the constant motion of the sailing ship as it made the six-week journey across the Pacific Ocean.

They asked for water. Sometimes that request was even granted. Other times they waited for it to rain and listened for leaks into the hold. They learned very quickly to cut salted fish out of their diet. It made them thirsty.

To keep the darkness from making them crazy, they told one another stories that they all knew by heart.

They took turns to recite the story of Lord Guan Yu, the God of War, and how he once made it through six forts and slew five of Treacherous Cao Cao's generals with the help of only Red Hare, his war steed, and Green Dragon Moon, his trusty sword.

"Lord Guan Yu would laugh at us as mere children if he heard us complaining about a little thirst and hunger and taking a trip in a boat," said the Chinaman whom the others called Lao Guan. He was so tall that he had to sleep with his knees curled up to his chest to fit into his bunk. "What are we afraid of? We are not going there to fight a war but to build a railroad. America is not a land of wolves and tigers. It is a land of men. Men who must work and eat, just as we do."

The others laughed in the darkness. They imagined the red face of Lord Guan Yu, fearless in any battle and full of witty stratagems to get himself out of any trap. What was a little hunger and thirst and darkness when Lord Guan Yu faced down dangers ten thousand times worse?

They sucked and nursed on the turnips and cabbages they had carried with them from the fields of their villages. The men held them up to their noses and inhaled deeply the smell of the soil that still clung to the roots. It would be the last time they would smell home for years.

Some of the men became sick and coughed all night, and the noise kept everyone awake for hours. Their foreheads felt like irons left for too long on the stove. The men had no medicine with them, no cubes of ice sugar or slices of goose pear. All they could do was to wait in the darkness silently.

"Let us sing the songs that our mothers sang to us as children," said Lao Guan. He was so tall he had to stoop as he felt his way around the dark hold, clasping the hand of each comrade, sick and healthy alike. "Since our families are not with us, we should do as Lord Guan Yu did with Lord Liu Bei and Lord Zhang Fei in the Peach Orchard. We must become as brothers to each other."

The men sang the nonsense songs of their childhood in the stifling air of the hold, and their voices washed over the bodies of the sick men like a cool breeze, lulling them to sleep.

In the morning the coughing did not resume. A few of the men were found in their coffin-wide bunks, their unmoving legs curled close to their still bodies like sleeping babies.

"Throw them overboard," said the captain. "The rest of you will now have to pay back the price of their tickets."

Lao Guan's face was redder than the fever-flushed faces of the sick. He stooped next to the bodies and cut off locks of hair from each of them, carefully sealing each lock into an envelope. "I'll bring these back to their ancestral villages so that their spirits will not wander the oceans without being able to return home."

Wrapped up in dirty sheets, the bodies were cast over the side of the ship.

At last they made it to San Francisco, the Old Gold Mountain. Although sixty men boarded the ship, only fifty walked down the planks onto the quays. The men squinted in the bright sunlight at the rows of small houses running up and down the steep, rolling hills. The streets, they found, were not paved with gold, and some of the white men on the quays looked as hungry and dirty as they felt.

They were taken by a Chinaman who was dressed like the white men to a dank basement in Chinatown. He didn't have a queue, and his hair was parted and slicked down with oil whose strange smell made the other Chinamen sneeze.

"Here are your employment contracts," the white Chinaman said. He gave them pieces of paper filled with characters smaller than flies' heads to sign.

"According to this," said Lao Guan, "we still owe you interest for the price of the passage from China. But the families of these men have already sold everything they could in order to raise money to buy the tickets that got us here."

"If you don't like it," said the white Chinaman, picking between his teeth with the long, manicured nail of his right pinkie, "you can try to find a way to go back on your own. What can I say? Shipping Chinamen is expensive."

"But it would take us three years of work to pay back the amount you say we owe you here, even longer since you have now made us responsible for the debts of the men who died on the sea."

"Then you should have taken care that they didn't get sick." The white Chinaman checked his pocket watch. "Hurry up and sign the contracts. I don't have all day."

The next day they were packed into wagons and taken inland. The camp in the mountains where they were finally dropped off was a city of tents. On one side of the camp the railroad stretched into the distance as far as they could see. On the other side was a mountain over which the Chinamen with spades and pickaxes swarmed like ants.

Night fell, and the Chinamen at the camp welcomed the new arrivals with a feast by the campfires.

"Eat, eat," they told the new arrivals. "Eat as much as you like." The Chinamen had trouble deciding which was sweeter: the food that went into their bellies, or the sound of those words in their ears.

They passed around bottles of a liquor that the old-timers said was called "whiskey." It was strong and there was enough for everyone to get drunk. When they ran out of drink the old-timers asked the new group whether they wanted to visit the large tent at the edge of the camp with them. A red silk scarf and a pair of women's shoes dangled from a pole outside the tent.

"You lucky bastards," grumbled one of the older man, whose name was San Long. "I gave all my money to Annie on Monday. I'll have to wait another week."

"She'll run a tab for you," said one of the others. "Though you might have to be with Sally instead of her tonight."

San Long cracked a huge smile and got up to join his companions.

"This must be heaven," said Ah Yan, who was barely more than a boy. "Look how free they are with money! They must be making so much that they paid off their debt early and can save up a fortune for their families while having all this fun."

Lao Guan shook his head and stroked his beard. He

sat next to the dying embers of the fire and smoked his pipe, staring at the big tent with the silk scarf and the pair of women's shoes. The light in that tent stayed lit until late into the night.

The work was hard. They had to carve a path through the mountain in front of them for the railroad. The mountain yielded to their pickaxes and chisels reluctantly, and only after repeated hammering that made the men's shoulders and arms sore down to the bones. There was so much mountain to move that it was like trying to gouge through the steel doors of the Emperor's palace with wooden spoons. All the while, the white foremen screamed at the Chinamen to move faster and set upon anyone who tried to sit down for a minute with whips and fists.

They were making so little progress day after day that the men were tired each morning before they had even begun their work. Their spirit sagged. One by one they laid down their tools. The mountain had defeated them. The white foremen jumped around, whipping at the Chinamen to get them to go back to work, but the Chinamen simply ducked away.

Lao Guan jumped onto a rock on the side of the mountain so that he was higher than everyone. "Tu-ne-mah!" he shouted, and spit at the mountain. "Tu-ne-mah!" He look at the white foremen and smiled at them.

The mountain pass was filled with the laughter of Chinamen. One by one they took up the chant. "Tu-ne-mah! Tu-ne-mah!" They smiled at the white foremen as they sang and gestured at them. The white foremen, not sure what was wanted, joined in the chanting. This seemed to make the Chinamen even happier. They picked up their tools and went back to hacking at the mountain with a fury and vengeance directed by the rhythm of their chant. They made more progress in that afternoon than they had all week.

"Goddamn these monkeys," said the site overseer. "But they certainly can work when they want to. What is that song they are singing?"

"Who knows?" The foremen shook their heads. "We can't ever make heads or tails of their pidgin. It sounds like a work song."

"Tell them that we'll name this pass Tunemah," said the overseer. "Maybe these monkeys will work even harder when they know that their song will be forever remembered every time a train passes this place."

The Chinamen continued their chant even after they were done with their work for the day. "Tu-ne-mah!" they shouted at the white foremen, their smiles as wide as they'd ever smiled. "Fuck your mother!"

At the end of the week the Chinamen were paid.

"This is not what I was promised," said Lao Guan to the clerk. "This is not even as much as half of what my wages should be."

"You are deducted for the food you eat and for your space in the tents. I'd show you the math if you could count that high." The clerk gestured for Lao Guan to move away from the table. "Next!"

"Have they always done this?" Lao Guan asked San Long.

"Oh, yeah. It's always been that way. The amount they charge for food and sleep has already gone up three times this year."

"But this means you'll never be able to pay back your debt and save up a fortune to take home with you."

"What else can you do?" San Long shrugged. "There's no place to buy food within fifty miles of here. We'll never be able to pay back the debt we owe them, anyway, since they just raise the interest whenever it seems like someone is about to pay it all back. All we can do is to take the money that we do get and drink and gamble and spend it all on Annie and the other girls. When you are drunk and asleep, you won't be thinking about it."

"They are playing a trick on us, then," said Lao Guan. "This is all a trap."

"Hey," said San Long, "it's too late to cry about that now. This is what you get for believing those stories told about the Old Gold Mountain. Serves us right."

Lao Guan went around and asked men to come and join him. He had a plan. They would run away into the mountains and go into hiding, and then make their way back to San Francisco.

"We'll need to learn English and understand the ways of this land if we want to make our fortune. Staying here will only make us into slaves with nothing to call our own excepting mounting debts in the white men's books." Lao Guan looked at each man in the eyes, and he was so tall and imposing that the other men avoided looking back.

"But we'll be breaking our contract and leaving our debts unpaid," said Ah Yan. "We will be burdening our families and ancestors with shame. It is not Chinese to break one's word."

"We've already paid back the debt we owe these

people twenty times and more. Why should we be faithful when they have not been honest with us? This is a land of trickery, and we must learn to become as tricky as the Americans."

The men were still not convinced. Lao Guan decided to tell them the story of of Jie You, the Han Princess whose name meant "Dissolver of Sorrows."

She was given away in marriage by the Martial Emperor to a barbarian king out in the Western Steppes, a thousand *li* from China, so that the barbarians would sell the Chinese the strong warhorses that the Chinese army needed to defend the Empire.

"I hear that you are homesick," wrote the Martial Emperor, "my precious daughter, and that you cannot swallow the rough uncooked meat of the foreigners, nor fall asleep on their beds made from the hairy hides of yaks and bears. I hear that the sandstorms have scarred your skin that was once as flawless as silk, and the deadly chill of the winters has darkened your eyes that were once bright as the moon. I hear that you call for home and cry yourself to sleep. If any of this is true, then write to me and I shall send the whole army to bring you home. I cannot bear to think that you are suffering, my child, for you are the light of my old age, the solace of my soul."

"Father and Emperor," wrote the Princess. "What you have heard is true. But I know my duty, and you know yours. The Empire needs horses for the defense of the frontier against the Xiong Nu raids. How can you let the unhappiness of your daughter cause you to risk the death and suffering of your people at the hands of the invading barbarian hordes? You have named me wisely, and I will dissolve my sorrow to learn the happiness of my new home. I will learn to mix the rough meat with milk, and I will learn to sleep with a nightshirt. I will learn to cover my face with a veil, and I will learn to keep warm by riding with my husband. Since I am in a foreign land, I will learn the foreigners' ways. By becoming one of the barbarians I will become truly Chinese. Though I will never return to China, I will bring glory to you."

"How can we be less wise or less manly than a young girl, even if she was a daughter of the Martial Emperor?" said Lao Guan. "If you truly want to bring glory to your ancestors and your families, then you must first become Americans."

"What will the gods think of this?" asked San Long. "We will become outlaws. Aren't we struggling against our fate? Some of us are not meant to have great fortunes, but only to work and starve—we are lucky to have what we have even now."

"Wasn't Lord Guan Yu once an outlaw? Didn't he teach us that the gods only smile upon those who take fate into their own hands? Why should we settle for having nothing for the rest of our lives when we know that we have enough strength in our arms to blast a path through mountains and enough wit in our heads to survive an ocean with only our stories and laughter?"

"But how do you know we'll find anything better if we run away?" asked Ah Yan. "What if we are caught? What if we are set upon by bandits? What if we find only more suffering and danger in the darkness out there, beyond the firelight of this camp?"

"I don't know what will happen to us out there," Lao Guan said. "All life is an experiment. But at the end of our lives we'd know that no man could do with our lives as he pleased except ourselves, and our triumphs and mistakes alike were our own."

He stretched out his arms and described the circle of the horizon around them. Long clouds piled low in the sky to the west. "Though the land here does not smell of home, the sky here is wider and higher than I have ever known. Every day I learn names for things I did not know existed and perform feats that I did not know that I could do. Why should we fear to rise as high as we can and make new names for ourselves?"

In the dim firelight Lao Guan looked to the others to be as tall as a tree, and his long, slim eyes glinted like jewels set in his flame-colored face. The hearts of the Chinamen were suddenly filled with resolve and a yearning for something that they did not yet know the name for.

"You feel it?" asked Lao Guan. "You feel that lift in your heart? That lightness in your head? That is the taste of whiskey, the essence of America. We have been wrong to be drunk and asleep. We should be drunk and fighting."

To exchange the pure and tranquil pleasures that the native country offers even to the poor for the sterile enjoyments that well-being provides under a foreign sky; to flee the paternal hearth and the fields where one's ancestors rest; to abandon the living and the dead to run after fortune—there is nothing that merits more praise in their eyes.
— Alexis de Tocqueville

Chicken Blood

The Idaho City Brass Band played "Finnegan's Wake" at the insistence of Logan.

"There's not enough noise," he told them. "In China we'd have all the children of the village setting off firecrackers and fireworks for the whole day to chase off the greedy evil spirits. Here we have only enough firecrackers to last a few hours. We'll need all the help you boys can give us to scare the evil sprits off."

The men of the brass band, their bellies now full of sweet sticky rice buns filled with bean paste and hot and spicy dumplings, set to their appointed task with gusto. They had not played with as much spirit even for Independence Day.

All the rumors about the Chinese New Year celebration were true. The children's pockets were filled with sweets and jangling coins, and the men and women were laughing as they enjoyed the feast that had been laid out before them. They had to shout to make one another heard amid the unending explosions of the firecrackers and the music blasting from the brass band.

Jack found Elsie among the other women in the vegetable garden. An open bonfire had been lit there so that the guests would be warm as they mingled and ate.

"I'm surprised at you," Jack said to her. "I'd swear that I saw you take three servings of the dumplings. I thought you said you'd never touch the food of the Chinamen."

"Thaddeus Seaver," Elsie said severely. "I don't know where you get such strange notions. It's positively unchristian to behave as you suggest when your neighbors have opened up their houses to you and invited you to break bread with them in their feast. If I didn't know better, I'd think you were the heathen here."

"That's my girl," said Jack. "Though isn't it time for you to start calling me Jack? Everyone else does now."

"I'll think about it after I've tried a piece of that sweet ginger," Elsie said. She laughed, and Jack realized how much he missed hearing that sound since they moved here to Idaho City. "Did you know that the first boy I liked was named Jack?"

The other women laughed, and Jack laughed along with them.

Abruptly the brass band stopped playing. One by one the men stopped talking and turned to the door of the house. There, in the door, stood Sheriff Gaskins, who was looking apologetic and a little ashamed.

"Sorry, folks," he said. "This isn't my idea."

He saw Ah Yan in the corner and waved to him. "Don't think I won't recognize you next time I come for your taxes."

"Time enough for that later, sheriff. This is a day of feasting and joy."

"You might want to wait on that. I'm here on official business."

Logan walked into the room, and the crowd parted before him. He was face-to-face with the sheriff before another man darted into view behind the sheriff and just as quickly skulked out of sight.

"Obee has accused you with murder," said the sheriff. "And I'm here to arrest you."

As a child growing up in Mock Turtle, Pennsylvania, the last thing Emmett Hayworth thought he would end up doing one day was to be a judge out in the middle of the Rocky Mountains.

Emmett was a big man, the same as his father, a banker who had retired from Philadelphia to live quietly out in the country. Before he was twenty, Emmett's greatest claim to fame was that he had won the all-county pie-eating contest three years in a row. It was assumed that Emmett would never amount to much, since he would have enough money to not have to work very hard, and not enough money to really get into much mischief. Everyone liked him, for he was always willing to buy you a drink if you called him "Sir."

And then came the War, and back then everyone still thought the Rebels would fold like a house of cards in three months. Emmett said to himself, "Why the heck not? This will probably be my only chance in life to see New Orleans." With his father's money he raised a regiment, and overnight he was Colonel Emmett Hayworth of the Union Army.

He took surprisingly well to being a soldier, and while his body slimmed down with riding and getting less than enough to eat, his good cheer never flagged. Somehow his regiment managed to stay out of the meat grinders that were the great battles that made newspaper headlines, and they lost fewer men than most. The men were grateful for Emmett's luck. "Oh, if I were a woman as I am a man," they sang, "Colonel Hayworth is the man I'd marry. His hands are steady, and his words are always merry. He'll bring us to New Orleans." Emmett laughed when he heard the song.

They did get to New Orleans eventually, but by then it wasn't much of a party town anymore. The War was over, and Emmett had scraped through with no bullet holes in him and no medals. "That's not so bad," he said to himself. "I can live with that."

But then he got the order that President Lincoln wanted to see him in DC.

Emmett did not remember much about the meeting, save that Lincoln was a lot taller than he had imagined. They shook hands, and Lincoln began to explain to him about the situation in Idaho Territory.

"The Confederate Democratic refugees from Missouri are filling up the mines of Idaho. I'll need men like you there, men who have proven their bravery, integrity, and dedication to the cause."

The only thing Emmett could think of was that they had the wrong man.

The trouble, as it turned out, had entirely been the fault of that song his men made up as a joke. It grew to be popular with the other regiments, and spread its way wherever the Union marched. New verses were added as it passed from man to man, and the soldiers, having no idea who Emmett Hayworth was, attributed great acts of courage and sacrifice to him. Colonel Hayworth became famous, almost as famous as John Brown.

Be that as it may, Emmett Hayworth packed up everything he owned and left for Boise, and only when he arrived did he find out that the Territorial Governor had just appointed him to be a district judge for the Idaho Territory.

Jack Seaver looked across the desk at the plump form of the Honorable Emmett Hayworth. The judge was still working on a plate of fried chicken that served as his lunch. Life out here in the booming territory of Idaho had been good to him, and he showed it in his barrel-like chest, his sacklike belly, his glistening forehead dripping with sweat from the effort of licking strips of juicy meat from the chicken bones.

The man was supposed to be some kind of war hero. Jack Seaver knew the type: a man accustomed to living off the money of his father who probably bought himself a cushy commission managing the supply lines and then puffed up his every accomplishment in the name of Union and Glory until he weaseled his way to a sinecure here while men like Jack Seaver dodged bullets in the mud and froze their toes off in winter. Jack clenched his teeth. This was neither the time nor the place to show his contempt. He did reflect upon the irony that despite what he had told Elsie's father back East, he now wished that he had studied to be a lawyer.

"What is this I hear about chicken blood?" Emmett asked.

"That's outrageous," said Obee. "I won't do it. Why are you even letting the Chinaman talk? This is not the way it works in California."

"You are going to have to," Judge Hayworth said to him. He hadn't been very enamored of the idea of the Chinamen's ceremony at first, but that Jack Seaver had been very persuasive. If he ever decided to become a lawyer, he'd eat the other guys in town for lunch. "Maybe in California they'll just take a white man's word for it since the Chinamen can't testify in court, but this isn't California. The accused has the right to a fair trial, and since he has agreed to swear with his hand on the Bible as is our custom, it's only fair that you agree to swear the way that his people have always sworn in witnesses."

"It's barbaric!"

"That may be. But if you won't do it, I'll have to direct the jury to acquit."

Obee swore under his breath.

"Fine," he said. He stared at Logan, who was across the courthouse from him. Obee's eyes were so filled with hate that he looked even more like a rat than usual.

Ah Yan was called for, and he came up to the witness box. In his left hand was a struggling hen dangling by her legs while in his right hand was a small bowl.

He set the bowl down in front of Obee. Taking a knife from his belt, he slit the hen's throat efficiently. The blood of the hen dripped into the bowl until the hen stopped kicking in Ah Yan's hands.

"Dip your hand into the blood and make sure it covers your whole hand," Ah Yan said. Obee reluctantly did as he was told. His hand shook so much that the bowl clattered against the wooden surface on which it was set.

"Now you have to clasp Logan's hand and look into his eyes, and swear that you'll tell the truth."

Logan was escorted over to the witness box by Sheriff Gaskins. Since his legs and arms were shackled together, this took some time.

Logan looked down at Obee, contempt written in every wrinkle in his bloodred face. He dipped both of his shackled hands into the bowl of chicken blood, soaking them thoroughly. Lifting his hands out of the bowl, he shook off the excess blood and stretched the open palm of his right hand toward Obee. The color of his hands now matched his face.

Obee hesitated.

"Well," Judge Hayworth said impatiently. "Get on with it. Shake the man's hand."

"Your honor." Obee turned toward him. "This is a trick. He's going to crush my hand if I give it to him."

Laughter shook the courtroom.

"No, he won't," said the judge, trying to control his smirk. "If he does, I'll personally thrash him."

Obee gingerly stretched his hand toward Logan's hand. He eyes were focused on the shrinking distance between their palms as if his life depended on it. He wasn't breathing, and his hand shook violently.

Logan stepped forward and made a grab for Obee's hand, and he gave a low growl from his throat.

Obee screamed as if he had been stabbed with a hot poker. He stumbled back frantically, pulling his hand out of Logan's grasp. A spreading, wet patch appeared at the crotch of his pants. A moment later the sheriff and the judge were hit with the unpleasant smell of excrement.

"I didn't even get to touch him," Logan said, holding up his hands. The pattern of chicken blood on his right palm was undisturbed with the print from Obee's hand.

"Order, order!" Judge Hayworth banged the gavel. Then he gave up and shook his head in disbelief. "Get him out of here and cleaned up," he said to Sheriff Gaskins, trying to keep himself from smiling. "Stop laughing. It's, uh, unbecoming for officers of the law. And hand me that chicken, will you? No sense in letting perfectly good poultry go to waste."

• • •

"All you have to do is to tell the truth," Lily said to Logan. "That's what Dad told me to do. It's easy."

"The law is a funny thing," said Logan. "You've heard my stories."

"It won't be like that here. I promise."

Earlier that day, she had told the jury what she saw on that day by the Chinamen's camp.

Mrs. O'Scannlain, who was in the front row of the courtroom, had smiled at her as she walked up to sit in the witness box next to the judge. It had made her feel very brave.

The faces of the men in the jury box were severe and expressionless, and she had been terrified. But then she told herself that it was just like telling a story, the way Logan told her his stories. The only thing was that it was all true so she didn't even have to make any of it up.

Afterward, she couldn't tell if they believed her. But Mrs. O'Scannlain and the others in the courtroom clapped after her testimony and that made her happy, even after the judge banged his gavel several times to get the crowd to settle down.

But now was not the time to tell Logan that. "Of course they will believe you," she said to Logan. "You have all these people who saw what happened."

"But except for you, they are all just worthless Chinamen."

"Why do you say that?" Lily became angry. "I'd rather be a Chinaman than someone who'd believe Obee's lies."

Logan laughed, but he was quickly serious again. "I'm sorry, Lily. Even men who have lived as long as I have sometimes get cynical."

They were silent for a while, each lost in their own thoughts.

Lily broke the silence after a while. "When you are freed, will you stay here instead of going back to China?"

"I'm going home."

"Oh," Lily said.

"Though I'd like to have my own house instead of always renting. Maybe your father will consider helping me build one?"

Lily looked at him, not understanding.

"This is home," Logan said, smiling at her. "This is where I have finally found all the flavors of the world, all the sweetness and bitterness, all the whiskey and sorghum mead, all the excitement and agitation of a wilderness of untamed, beautiful men and women, all the peace and solitude of a barely settled land—in a word, the exhilarating lift to the spirit that is the taste of America."

Lily wanted to shout for joy, but she didn't want to get her hopes up, not just yet. Logan had yet to tell his story to the jury tomorrow.

But meanwhile, there was a still a night of storytelling ahead.

"Will you tell me another story?" Lily asked.

"Sure, but I think from now on I won't tell you any more stories about my life as a Chinaman. I'll tell you the story of how I became an American."

When the band of weary and gaunt Chinamen showed up in Idaho City with their funny bamboo carrying poles over their shoulders . . .

EPILOGUE

The Chinese made up a large percentage of the population of Idaho Territory in the late 1800s.[1] They formed a vibrant community of miners, cooks, laundry operators, and gardeners that integrated well with the white communities of the mining towns. Almost all the Chinese were men seeking to make their fortune in America.[2]

By the time many of them decided to settle in America and

---

1. The Chinese were 28.5 percent of the population of Idaho in 1870.
2. For more on the history of the Chinese in gold-rush Idaho, see Zhu, Liping. *A Chinaman's Chance: The Chinese on the Rocky Mountain Mining Frontier.* Boulder: University Press of Colorado, 1997.

become Americans, anti-Chinese sentiment had swept the western half of the United States. Beginning with the passage of the Chinese Exclusion Act of 1882, a series of national laws, state laws, and court decisions forbade these men from bringing their wives into America from China and stemmed the flow of any more Chinese, men or women, from entering America. Intermarriage between whites and Chinese was not permitted by law. As a result, the bachelor communities of Chinese in the Idaho mining towns gradually dwindled until all the Chinese had died before the repeal of the Exclusion Acts during World War II.

To this day, some of the mining towns of Idaho still celebrate Chinese New Year in memory of the presence of the Chinese among them.

A BRIEF HISTORY OF THE
TRANS-PACIFIC TUNNEL

At the noodle shop, I wave the other waitress away, waiting for the American woman: skin pale and freckled as the moon; swelling breasts that fill the bodice of her dress; long chestnut curls spilling past her shoulders, held back with a flowery bandanna. Her eyes, green like fresh tea leaves, radiate a bold and fearless smile that is rarely seen among Asians. And I like the wrinkles around them, fitting for a woman in her thirties.

"*Hai.*" She finally stops at my table, her lips pursed impatiently. "*Hoka no okyakusan ga imasu yo. Nani wo chuumon shimasu ka?*" Her Japanese is quite good, the pronunciation maybe even better than mine—though she is not using the honorific. It is still rare to see Americans here in the Japanese half of Midpoint City, but things are changing now, in the thirty-sixth year of the Shōwa Era (she, being an American, would think of it as 1961).

"A large bowl of *tonkotsu* ramen," I say, mostly in English. Then I realize how loud and rude I sound. Old Diggers like me always forget that not everyone is practically deaf. "Please," I add, a whisper.

Her eyes widen as she finally recognizes me. I've cut my hair and put on a clean shirt, and that's not how I looked the past few times I've come here. I haven't paid much attention to my appearance in a decade. There hasn't been any need to. Almost all my time is spent alone and at home. But the sight of her has quickened my pulse in a way I haven't felt in years, and I wanted to make an effort.

"Always the same thing," she says, and smiles.

I like hearing her English. It sounds more like her natural voice, not so high-pitched.

"You don't really like the noodles," she says, when she brings me my ramen. It isn't a question.

I laugh, but I don't deny it. The ramen in this place is terrible. If the owner were any good he wouldn't have left Japan to set up shop here at Midpoint City, where the tourists stopping for a break on their way through the Trans-Pacific Tunnel don't know any better. But I keep on coming, just to see her.

"You are not Japanese."

"No," I say. "I'm Formosan. Please call me Charlie." Back when I coordinated work with the American crew during the construction of Midpoint City, they called me Charlie because they couldn't pronounce my Hokkien name correctly. And I liked the way it sounded, so I kept using it.

"Okay, Charlie. I'm Betty." She turns to leave.

"Wait," I say. I do not know from where I get this sudden burst of courage. It is the boldest thing I've done in a long time. "Can I see you when you are free?"

She considers this, biting her lip. "Come back in two hours."

From *The Novice Traveler's Guide to the Trans-Pacific Tunnel*, published by the TPT Transit Authority, 1963:

> *Welcome, traveler! This year marks the twenty-fifth anniversary of the completion of the Trans-Pacific Tunnel. We are excited to see that this is your first time through the Tunnel.*
>
> *The Trans-Pacific Tunnel follows a Great Circle path just below the seafloor to connect Asia to North America, with three surface terminus stations in Shanghai, Tokyo, and Seattle. The Tunnel takes the shortest path between the cities, arcing north*

to follow the Pacific Rim mountain ranges. Although this course increased the construction cost of the Tunnel due to the need for earthquake-proofing, it also allows the Tunnel to tap into geothermal vents and hot spots along the way, which generate the electrical power needed for the Tunnel and its support infrastructure, such as the air-compression stations, oxygen generators, and sub-seafloor maintenance posts.

The Tunnel is in principle a larger—gigantic—version of the pneumatic tubes or capsule lines familiar to all of us for delivering interoffice mail in modern buildings. Two parallel concrete-enclosed steel transportation tubes, one each for westbound and eastbound traffic, 60 feet in diameter, are installed in the Tunnel. The transportation tubes are divided into numerous shorter self-sealing sections, each with multiple air-compression stations. The cylindrical capsules, containing passengers and goods, are propelled through the tubes by a partial vacuum pulling in front and by compressed air pushing from behind. The capsules ride on a monorail for reduced friction. Current maximum speed is about a 120 miles per hour, and a trip from Shanghai to Seattle takes a little more than two full days. Plans are under way to eventually increase maximum speed to two hundred MPH.

The Tunnel's combination of capacity, speed, and safety makes it superior to zeppelins, aeroplanes, and surface shipping for almost all trans-Pacific transportation needs. It is immune to storms, icebergs, and typhoons, and very cheap to operate, as it is powered by the boundless heat of the Earth itself. Today, it is the chief means by which passengers and manufactured goods flow between Asia and America. More than 30% of global container shipping each year goes through the Tunnel.

We hope you enjoy your travel along the Trans-Pacific Tunnel, and wish you a safe journey to your final destination.

• • •

I was born in the second year of the Taishō Era (1913), in a small village in Shinchiku Prefecture, in Formosa. My family were simple peasants who never participated in any of the uprisings against Japan. The way my father saw it, whether the Manchus on the mainland or the Japanese were in charge didn't much matter, since they all left us alone except when it came time for taxes. The lot of the Hoklo peasant was to toil and suffer in silence.

Politics were for those who had too much to eat. Besides, I always liked the Japanese workers from the lumber company, who would hand me candy during their lunch break. The Japanese colonist families we saw were polite, well-dressed, and very lettered. My father once said, "If I got to choose, in my next life I'd come back as a Japanese."

During my boyhood, a new prime minister in Japan announced a change in policy: natives in the colonies should be turned into good subjects of the Emperor. The Japanese governor-general set up village schools that everyone had to attend. The more clever boys could even expect to attend high schools formerly reserved for the Japanese and then go on to study in Japan, where they would have bright futures.

I was not a good student, however, and never learned Japanese very well. I was content to know how to read a few characters and go back to the fields, the same as my father and his father before him.

All this changed in the year I turned seventeen (the fifth year of the Shōwa Era, or 1930), when a Japanese man in a Western suit came to our village, promising riches for the families of young men who knew how to work hard and didn't complain.

We stroll through Friendship Square, the heart of Midpoint City. A few pedestrians, both American and Japanese, stare and whisper as they see us walking together. But Betty does not care, and her carelessness is infectious.

347

Here, kilometers under the Pacific Ocean and the seafloor, it's late afternoon by the City's clock, and the arc lamps around us are turned up as bright as can be.

"I always feel like I'm at a night baseball game when I go through here," Betty says. "When my husband was alive, we went to many baseball games together as a family."

I nod. Betty usually keeps her reminiscences of her husband light. She mentioned once that he was a lawyer, and he had left their home in California to work in South Africa, where he died because some people didn't like who he was defending. "They called him a race traitor," she said. I didn't press for details.

Now that her children are old enough to be on their own, she's traveling the world for enlightenment and wisdom. Her capsule train to Japan had stopped at Midpoint Station for a standard one-hour break for passengers to get off and take some pictures, but she had wandered too far into the City and missed the train. She took it as a sign and stayed in the City, waiting to see what lessons the world had to teach her.

Only an American could lead such a life. Among Americans, there are many free spirits like hers.

We've been seeing each other for four weeks, usually on Betty's days off. We take walks around Midpoint City, and we talk. I prefer that we converse in English, mostly because I do not have to think much about how formal and polite to be.

As we pass by the bronze plaque in the middle of the Square, I point out to her my Japanese-style name on the plaque: Takumi Hayashi. The Japanese teacher in my village school had helped me pick the first name, and I had liked the characters: "open up, sea." The choice turned out to be prescient.

She is impressed. "That must have been something. You should tell me more about what it was like to work on the Tunnel."

There are not many of us old Diggers left now. The years of hard labor spent breathing hot and humid dust that stung our lungs had done invisible damage to our insides and joints. At forty-eight, I've said good-bye to all my friends as they succumbed to illnesses. I am the last keeper of what we had done together.

When we finally blasted through the thin rock wall dividing our side from the American side and completed the Tunnel in the thirteenth year of the Shōwa Era (1938), I had the honor of being one of the shift supervisors invited to attend the ceremony. I explain to Betty that the blast-through spot is in the main tunnel due north of where we are standing, just beyond Midpoint Station.

We arrive at my apartment building, on the edge of the section of the City where most Formosans live. I invite her to come up. She accepts.

My apartment is a single room eight mats in size, but there is a window. Back when I bought it, it was considered a very luxurious place for Midpoint City, where space was and is at a premium. I mortgaged most of my pension on it, since I had no desire ever to move. Most men made do with coffinlike one-mat rooms. But to her American eyes, it probably seems very cramped and shabby. Americans like things to be open and big.

I make her tea. It is very relaxing to talk to her. She does not care that I am not Japanese, and assumes nothing about me. She takes out a joint, as is the custom for Americans, and we share it.

Outside the window, the arc lights have been dimmed. It's evening in Midpoint City. Betty does not get up and say that she has to leave. We stop talking. The air feels tense, but in a good way, expectant. I reach out for her hand, and she lets me. The touch is electric.

From *Splendid America*, AP ed., 1995:

> In 1929, the fledging and weak Republic of China, in order
> to focus on the domestic Communist rebellion, appeased Japan

by signing the Sino-Japanese Mutual Cooperation Treaty. The treaty formally ceded all Chinese territories in Manchuria to Japan, which averted the prospect of all-out war between China and Japan and halted Soviet ambitions in Manchuria. This was the capstone on Japan's thirty-five-year drive for imperial expansion. Now, with Formosa, Korea, and Manchuria incorporated into the Empire and a collaborationist China within its orbit, Japan had access to vast reserves of natural resources, cheap labor, and a potential market of hundreds of millions for its manufactured goods.

Internationally, Japan announced that it would continue its rise as a Great Power henceforth by peaceful means. Western powers, however, led by Britain and the United States, were suspicious. They were especially alarmed by Japan's colonial ideology of a "Greater East Asia Co-Prosperity Sphere," which seemed to be a Japanese version of the Monroe Doctrine and suggested a desire to drive European and American influence from Asia.

Before the Western powers could decide on a plan to contain and encircle Japan's "Peaceful Ascent," however, the Great Depression struck. The brilliant Emperor Hirohito seized the opportunity and suggested to President Herbert Hoover his vision of the Trans-Pacific Tunnel as the solution to the worldwide economic crisis.

The work was hard and dangerous. Every day men were injured and sometimes killed. It was also very hot. In the finished sections, they installed machines to cool the air. But in the most forward parts of the Tunnel, where the actual digging happened, we were exposed to the heat of the Earth, and we worked in nothing but our undershorts, sweating nonstop. The work crews were segregated by race—there were Koreans, Formosans, Okinawans, Filipinos, Chinese (separated again by topolect)—but after a while we all looked the same, covered in sweat and dust and mud, only little white circles of skin showing around our eyes.

It didn't take me long to get used to living underground, to the constant noise of dynamite, hydraulic drills, the bellows cycling cooling air, and to the flickering faint yellow light of arc lamps. Even when you were sleeping, the next shift was already at it. Everyone grew hard of hearing after a while, and we stopped talking to each other. There was nothing to say, anyway; just more digging.

But the pay was good, and I saved up and sent money home. However, visiting home was out of the question. By the time I started, the head of the tunnel was already halfway between Shanghai and Tokyo. They charged you a month's wages to ride the steam train carrying the excavated waste back to Shanghai and up to the surface. I couldn't afford such luxuries. As we made progress, the trip back only grew longer and more expensive.

It was best not to think too much about what we were doing, about the miles of water over our heads, and the fact that we were digging a tunnel through the Earth's crust to get to America. Some men did go crazy under those conditions and had to be restrained before they could hurt themselves or others.

From *A Brief History of the Trans-Pacific Tunnel*, published by the TPT Transit Authority, 1960:

> *Osachi Hamaguchi, prime minister of Japan during the Great Depression, claimed that Emperor Hirohito was inspired by the American effort to build the Panama Canal to conceive of the Trans-Pacific Tunnel. "America has knit together two oceans," the Emperor supposedly said. "Now let us chain together two continents." President Hoover, trained as an engineer, enthusiastically*

promoted and backed the project as an antidote to the global economic contraction.

The Tunnel is, without a doubt, the greatest engineering project ever conceived by Man. Its sheer scale makes the Great Pyramids and the Great Wall of China seem like mere toys, and many critics at the time described it as hubristic lunacy, a modern Tower of Babel.

Although tubes and pressurized air have been used for passing around documents and small parcels since Victorian times, before the Tunnel, pneumatic tube transport of heavy goods and passengers had only been tried on a few intracity subway demonstration programs. The extraordinary engineering demands of the Tunnel thus drove many technological advances, often beyond the core technologies involved, such as fast-tunneling directed explosives. As one illustration, thousands of young women with abacuses and notepads were employed as computers for engineering calculations at the start of the project, but by the end of the project electronic computers had taken their place.

In all, construction of the 5,880-mile tunnel took ten years between 1929 and 1938. Some seven million men worked on it, with Japan and the United States providing the bulk of the workers. At its height, one in ten working men in the United States was employed in building the Tunnel. More than thirteen billion cubic yards of material were excavated, almost fifty times the amount removed during the construction of the Panama Canal, and the fill was used to extend the shorelines of China, the Japanese home islands, and Puget Sound.

Afterward we lie still on the futon, our limbs entwined. In the darkness I can hear her heart beating, and the smell of sex and our sweat, unfamiliar in this apartment, is comforting.

She tells me about her son, who is still going to school in America. She says that he is traveling with his friends in the southern states of America, riding the buses together.

"Some of the friends are Negroes," she says.

I know some Negroes. They have their own section in the American half of the City, where they mostly keep to themselves. Some Japanese families hire the women to cook Western meals.

"I hope he's having a good time," I say.

My reaction surprises Betty. She turns to stare at me and then laughs. "I forget that you cannot understand what this is about."

She sits up in bed. "In America, the Negroes and whites are separated: where they live, where they work, where they go to school."

I nod. That sounds familiar. Here in the Japanese half of the City, the races also keep to themselves. There are superior and inferior races. For example, there are many restaurants and clubs reserved only for the Japanese.

"The law says that whites and Negroes can ride the bus together, but the secret of America is that law is not followed by large swaths of the country. My son and his friends want to change that. They ride the buses together to make a statement, to make people pay attention to the secret. They ride in places where people do not want to see Negroes sitting in seats that belong only to whites. Things can become violent and dangerous when people get angry and form a mob."

This seems very foolish: to make statements that no one wants to hear, to speak when it is better to be quiet. What difference will a few boys riding a bus make?

"I don't know if it's going to make any difference, change anyone's mind. But it doesn't matter. It's good enough for me that he is speaking, that he is not silent. He's making the secret a little bit harder to keep, and that counts for something." Her voice is full of pride, and she is beautiful when she is proud.

I consider Betty's words. It is the obsession of Americans to speak, to express opinions on things that they are ignorant about. They believe in drawing attention to things that other people may prefer to keep quiet, to ignore and forget.

But I can't dismiss the image Betty has put into my head: a boy stands in darkness and silence. He speaks; his words float up like a bubble. It explodes, and the world is a little brighter, and a little less stiflingly silent.

I have read in the papers that back in Japan, they are debating about granting Formosans and Manchurians seats in the Imperial Diet. Britain is still fighting the native guerrillas in Africa and India, but may be forced soon to grant the colonies independence. The world is indeed changing.

"What's wrong?" Betty asks. She wipes the sweat from my forehead. She shifts to give me more of the flow from the air conditioner. I shiver. Outside, the great arc lights are still off, not yet dawn. "Another bad dream?"

We've been spending many of our nights together since that first time. Betty has upset my routine, but I don't mind at all. That was the routine of a man with one foot in the grave. Betty has made me feel alive after so many years under the ocean, alone in darkness and silence.

But being with Betty has also unblocked something within me, and memories are tumbling out.

If you really couldn't stand it, they provided comfort women from Korea for the men. But you had to pay a day's wages.

I tried it only once. We were both so dirty, and the girl stayed still like a dead fish. I never used the comfort women again.

A friend told me that some of the girls were not there willingly but had been sold to the Imperial Army, and maybe the one I had was like that. I didn't really feel sorry for her. I was too tired.

From *The Ignoramus's Guide to American History*, 1995:

> *So just when everyone was losing jobs and lining up for soup and bread, Japan came along and said, "Hey, America, let's build this big-ass tunnel and spend a whole lot of money and hire lots of workers and get the economy going again. Whaddya say?" And the idea basically worked, so everyone was like: "Dōmo arigatō, Japan!"*
>
> *Now, when you come up with a good idea like that, you get some chips you can cash in. So that's what Japan did the next year, in 1930. At the London Naval Conference, where the Big Bullies—oops, I meant "Great Powers"—figured out how many battleships and aircraft carriers each country got to build, Japan demanded to be allowed to build the same number of ships as the United States and Britain. And the US and Britain said fine.†*
>
> *This concession to Japan turned out to be a big deal. Remember Hamaguchi, the Japanese prime minister, and the way he kept on talking about how Japan was going to "ascend peacefully" from then on? This had really annoyed the militarists and nationalists in Japan because they thought Hamaguchi was selling out the country. But when Hamaguchi came home with such an impressive diplomatic victory, he was hailed as a hero, and people began to believe that his "Peaceful Ascent" policy was going to make Japan strong. People thought maybe he really*

---

† The Washington Naval Treaty of 1922 had set the ratio of capital ships among the US, Britain, and Japan at 5:5:3. This was the ratio Japan got adjusted in 1930.

*could get the Western powers to treat Japan as an equal with-
out turning Japan into a giant army camp. The militarists and
nationalists got less support after that.*

*At that fun party, the London Naval Conference, the Big Bullies
also scrapped all those humiliating provisions of the Treaty of
Versailles that made Germany toothless. Britain and Japan both
had their own reasons for supporting this: They each thought
Germany liked them better than the other and would join up
as an ally if a global brawl for Asian colonies broke out one day.
Everyone was wary about the Soviets, too, and wanted to set up
Germany as a guard dog of sorts for the polar bear.* [‡]

Things to Think About in the Shower

1. *Many economists describe the Tunnel as the first real Keynes-
   ian stimulus project, which shortened the Great Depression.*
2. *The Tunnel's biggest fan was probably President Hoover: He
   won an unprecedented four terms in office because of its success.*
3. *We now know that the Japanese military abused the rights of
   many of the workers during the Tunnel's construction, but it
   took decades for the facts to emerge. The bibliography points
   to some more books on this subject.*
4. *The Tunnel ended up taking a lot of business away from surface shipping, and many Pacific ports went bust. The most
   famous example of this occurred in 1949, when Britain sold*

---

‡ Allowing Germany to re-arm also let the German government heave a big sigh
of relief. The harsh Treaty of Versailles, especially those articles about neutering
Germany, made a lot of Germans very angry and some of them joined a group of
goose-stepping thugs called the German Nationalist Socialist Party, which scared
everyone, including the government. After those provisions of the treaty were
scrapped, the thugs got no electoral support at the next election in 1930, and
faded away. Heck, they are literally now a footnote of history, like this one.

Hong Kong to Japan because it didn't think the harbor city
was all that important anymore.
  5. *The Great War (1914–1918) turned out to be the last global*
"hot war" of the twentieth century (so far). Are we turning into
wimps? Who wants to start a new world war?

After the main work on the Tunnel was completed in the thirteenth year of the Shōwa Era (1938), I returned home for the first and only time since I left eight years earlier. I bought a window seat on the westbound capsule train from Midpoint Station, coach class. The ride was smooth and comfortable, the capsule quiet save for the low voices of my fellow passengers and a faint *whoosh* as we were pushed along by air. Young female attendants pushed carts of drinks and food up and down the aisles.

Some clever companies had bought advertising space along the inside of the tube and painted pictures at window height. As the capsule moved along, the pictures rushing by centimeters from the windows blurred together and became animated, like a silent film. My fellow passengers and I were mesmerized by the novel effect.

The elevator ride up to the surface in Shanghai filled me with trepidation, my ears popping with the changes in pressure. And then it was time to get on a boat bound for Formosa.

I hardly recognized my home. With the money I sent, my parents had built a new house and bought more land. My family was now rich, and my village a bustling town. I found it hard to speak to my siblings and my parents. I had been away so long that I did not understand much about their lives, and I could not explain to them how I felt. I did not realize how much I had been hardened and numbed by my experience, and there were things I had seen that I could not speak of. In some sense I felt that I had become like a turtle, with a shell around me that kept me from feeling anything.

My father had written to me to come home because it was long past time for me to find a wife. Since I had worked hard, stayed healthy, and kept my mouth shut—it also helped that as a Formosan I was considered superior to the other races except the Japanese and Koreans—I had been steadily promoted to crew chief and then to shift supervisor. I had money, and if I settled in my hometown, I would provide a good home.

But I could no longer imagine a life on the surface. It had been so long since I had seen the blinding light of the sun that I felt like a newborn when out in the open. Things were so quiet. Everyone was startled when I spoke because I was used to shouting. And the sky and tall buildings made me dizzy—I was so used to being underground, under the sea, in tight, confined spaces, that I had trouble breathing if I looked up.

I expressed my desire to stay underground and work in one of the station cities strung like pearls along the Tunnel. The faces of the fathers of all the girls tightened at this thought. I didn't blame them: Who would want their daughter to spend the rest of her life underground, never seeing the light of day? The fathers whispered to one another that I was deranged.

I said good-bye to my family for the last time, and I did not feel I was home until I was back at Midpoint Station, the warmth and the noise of the heart of the Earth around me, a safe shell. When I saw the soldiers on the platform at the station, I knew that the world was finally back to normal. More work still had to be done to complete the side tunnels that would be expanded into Midpoint City.

"Soldiers," Betty says, "why were there soldiers at Midpoint City?"

I stand in darkness and silence. I cannot hear or see. Words churn in my throat, like a rising flood waiting to burst the dam. I have been holding my tongue for a long, long time.

"They were there to keep the reporters from snooping around," I say.

I tell Betty about my secret, the secret of my nightmares, something I've never spoken of all these years.

As the economy recovered, labor costs rose. There were fewer and fewer young men desperate enough to take jobs as Diggers in the Tunnel. Progress on the American side had slowed for a few years, and Japan was not doing much better. Even China seemed to run out of poor peasants who wanted this work.

Hideki Tōjō, Army Minister, came up with a solution. The Imperial Army's pacification of the Communist rebellions supported by the Soviet Union in Manchuria and China resulted in many prisoners. They could be put to work, for free.

The prisoners were brought into the Tunnel to take the place of regular work crews. As shift supervisor, I managed them with the aid of a squad of soldiers. The prisoners were a sorry sight, chained together, naked, thin like scarecrows. They did not look like dangerous and crafty Communist bandits. I wondered sometimes how there could be so many prisoners, since the news always said that the pacification of the Communists was going well and the Communists were not much of a threat.

They usually didn't last long. When a prisoner was discovered to have expired from the work, his body was released from the shackles and a soldier would shoot it a few times. We would then report the death as the result of an escape attempt.

To hide the involvement of the slave laborers, we kept visiting reporters away from work on the main Tunnel. They were used mainly on the side excavations, for station cities or power stations, in places that were not well surveyed and more dangerous.

One time, while making a side tunnel for a power station, my crew blasted through to a pocket of undetected slush and water, and the side tunnel began to flood. We had to seal the breach quickly before the flood got into the main Tunnel. I woke up the crews of the two other shifts and sent a second chained crew into the side tunnel with sandbags to help with plugging up the break.

The corporal in charge of the squad of soldiers guarding the prisoners asked me, "What if they can't plug it?"

His meaning was obvious. We had to make sure that the water did not get into the main Tunnel, even if the repair crews we sent in failed. There was only one way to make sure, and as water was flowing back up the side tunnel, time was running out.

I directed the chained crew I'd kept behind as a reserve to begin placing dynamite around the side tunnel, behind the men we had sent in earlier. I did not much like this, but I told myself that these were hardened Communist terrorists, and they were probably sentenced to death already, anyway.

The prisoners hesitated. They understood what we were trying to do, and they did not want to do it. Some worked slowly. Others just stood.

The corporal ordered one of the prisoners shot. This motivated the remaining ones to hurry.

I set off the charges. The side tunnel collapsed, and the pile of debris and falling rocks filled most of the entrance, but there was still some space at the top. I directed the remaining prisoners to climb up and seal the opening. Even I climbed up to help them.

The sound of the explosion told the prisoners we sent in earlier what was happening. The chained men lumbered back, sloshing through the rising water and the darkness, trying to get to us. The corporal ordered the soldiers to shoot a few of the men, but the rest kept on coming, dragging the dead bodies with their chains, begging us to let them through. They climbed up the pile of debris toward us.

The man at the front of the chain was only a few meters from us, and in the remaining cone of light cast by the small opening that was left I could see his face, contorted with fright.

"Please," he said. "Please let me through. I just stole some money. I don't deserve to die."

He spoke to me in Hokkien, my mother tongue. This shocked me. Was he a common criminal from back home in Formosa, and not a Chinese Communist from Manchuria?

He reached the opening and began to push away the rocks, to enlarge the opening and climb through. The corporal shouted at me to stop him. The water level was rising. Behind the man, the other chained prisoners were climbing to help him.

I lifted a heavy rock near me and smashed it down on the hands of the man grabbing onto the opening. He howled and fell back, dragging the other prisoners down with him. I heard the splash of water.

"Faster, faster!" I ordered the prisoners on our side of the collapsed tunnel. We sealed the opening, then retreated to set up more dynamite and blast down more rocks to solidify the seal.

When the work was finally done, the corporal ordered all the remaining prisoners shot, and we buried their bodies under yet more blast debris.

There was a massive prisoner uprising. They attempted to sabotage the project, but failed and instead killed themselves.

This was the corporal's report of the incident, and I signed my name to it as well. Everyone understood that was the way to write up such reports.

I remember the face of the man begging me to stop very well. That was the face I saw in the dream last night.

The Square is deserted right before dawn. Overhead, neon advertising signs hang from the City's ceiling, a few hundred meters up. They take the place of long-forgotten constellations and the moon.

Betty keeps an eye out for unlikely pedestrians while I swing the hammer against the chisel. Bronze is a hard material, but I have not lost the old skills I learned as a Digger. Soon the characters of my name are gone from the plaque, leaving behind a smooth rectangle.

I switch to a smaller chisel and begin to carve. The design is simple: three ovals interlinked, a chain. These are the links that bound two continents and three great cities together, and these are the shackles that bound men whose voices were forever silenced, whose names were forgotten. There is beauty and wonder here, and also horror and death.

With each strike of the hammer, I feel as though I am chipping away the shell around me, the numbness, the silence.

Make the secret a bit harder to keep. That counts for something.

"Hurry," Betty says.

My eyes are blurry. And suddenly the lights around the Square come on. It is morning under the Pacific Ocean.

THE LITIGATION MASTER
AND THE MONKEY KING

The tiny cottage at the edge of Sanli Village—away from the villagers'
noisy houses and busy clan shrines and next to the cool pond filled
with lily pads, pink lotus flowers, and playful carp—would have made
an ideal romantic summer hideaway for some dissolute poet and his
silk-robed mistress from nearby bustling Yangzhou.

Indeed, having such a country lodge was the fashion among the
literati in the lower Yangtze region in this second decade of the glorious reign of the Qianlong Emperor. Everyone agreed—as they visited
one another in their vacation homes and sipped tea—that he was the
best Emperor of the Qing Dynasty: so wise, so vigorous, and so solicitous of his subjects! And as the Qing Dynasty, founded by Manchu
sages, was without a doubt the best dynasty ever to rule China, the
scholars competed to compose poems that best showed their gratitude for having the luck to bear witness to this golden age, gift of the
greatest Emperor who ever lived.

Alas, any scholar interested in *this* cottage must be disappointed,
for it was decrepit. The bamboo grove around it was wild and
unkempt; the wooden walls crooked, rotting, and full of holes; the
thatching over the roof uneven, with older layers peeking out through
holes in the newer layers—

—not unlike the owner and sole inhabitant of the cottage, actually. Tian Haoli was in his fifties but looked ten years older. He was
gaunt, sallow, his queue as thin as a pig's tail, and his breath often
smelled of the cheapest rice wine and even cheaper tea. An accident

in youth lamed his right leg, but he preferred to shuffle slowly rather than use a cane. His robe was patched all over, though his under-robe still showed through innumerable holes.

Unlike most in the village, Tian knew how to read and write, but as far as anyone knew, he never passed any level of the Imperial Examinations. From time to time, he would write a letter for some family or read an official notice in the teahouse in exchange for half a chicken or a bowl of dumplings.

But that was not how he really made his living.

The morning began like any other. As the sun rose lazily, the fog hanging over the pond dissipated like dissolving ink. Bit by bit, the pink lotus blossoms, the jade-green bamboo stalks, and the golden-yellow cottage roof emerged from the fog.

Knock, knock.

Tian stirred but did not wake up. The Monkey King was hosting a banquet, and Tian was going to eat his fill.

Ever since Tian was a little boy, he had been obsessed with the exploits of the Monkey King, the trickster demon who had seventy-two transformations and defeated hundreds of monsters, who had shaken the throne of the Jade Emperor with a troop of monkeys.

And Monkey liked good food and loved good wine, a must in a good host.

Knock, knock.

Tian ignored the knocking. He was about to bite into a piece of drunken chicken dipped in four different exquisite sauces—

You going to answer that? Monkey said.

As Tian grew older, Monkey would visit him in his dreams, or, if he was awake, speak to him in his head. While others prayed to the Goddess of Mercy or the Buddha, Tian enjoyed conversing with Monkey, who he felt was a demon after his own heart.

Whatever it is, it can wait, said Tian.

I think you have a client, said Monkey.

Knock-knock-knock—

The insistent knocking whisked away Tian's chicken and abruptly ended his dream. His stomach growled, and he cursed as he rubbed his eyes.

"Just a moment!" Tian fumbled out of bed and struggled to put on his robe, muttering to himself all the while. "Why can't they wait till I've woken up properly and pissed and eaten? These unlettered fools are getting more and more unreasonable. . . . I must demand a whole chicken this time. . . . It was such a nice dream. . . ."

I'll save some plum wine for you, said Monkey.

You better.

Tian opened the door. Li Xiaoyi, a woman so timid that she apologized even when some rambunctious child ran into *her*, stood there in a dark green dress, her hair pinned up in the manner prescribed for widows. Her fist was lifted and almost smashed into Tian's nose.

"Aiya!" Tian said. "You owe me the best drunk chicken in Yangzhou!" But Li's expression, a combination of desperation and fright, altered his tone. "Come on in."

He closed the door behind the woman and poured a cup of tea for her.

Men and women came to Tian as a last resort, for he helped them when they had nowhere else to turn, when they ran into trouble with the law.

The Qianlong Emperor might be all-wise and all-seeing, but he still needed the thousands of *yamen* courts to actually govern. Presided over by a magistrate, a judge-administrator who held the power of life and death over the local citizens in his charge, a *yamen* court was a mysterious, opaque place full of terror for the average man and woman.

Who knew the secrets of the Great Qing Code? Who understood

how to plead and prove and defend and argue? When the magistrate spent his evenings at parties hosted by the local gentry, who could predict how a case brought by the poor against the rich would fare? Who could intuit the right clerk to bribe to avoid torture? Who could fathom the correct excuse to give to procure a prison visit?

No, one did not go near the *yamen* courts unless one had no other choice. When you sought justice, you gambled everything.

And you needed the help of a man like Tian Haoli.

Calmed by the warmth of the tea, Li Xiaoyi told Tian her story in halting sentences.

She had been struggling to feed herself and her two daughters on the produce from a tiny plot of land. To survive a bad harvest, she had mortgaged her land to Jie, a wealthy distant cousin of her dead husband, who promised that she could redeem her land at any time, interest free. As Li could not read, she had gratefully inked her thumbprint to the contract her cousin handed her.

"He said it was just to make it official for the tax collector," Li said.

Ah, a familiar story, said the Monkey King.

Tian sighed and nodded.

"I paid him back at the beginning of this year, but yesterday Jie came to my door with two bailiffs from the *yamen*. He said that my daughters and I had to leave our house immediately because we had not been making the payments on the loan. I was shocked, but he took out the contract and said that I had promised to pay him back double the amount loaned in one year or else the land would become his forever. 'It's all here in black characters on white paper,' he said, and waved the contract in my face. The bailiffs said that if I don't leave by tomorrow, they'll arrest me and sell me and my daughters to a blue house to satisfy the debt." She clenched her fists. "I don't know what to do!"

Tian refilled her teacup and said, "We'll have to go to court and defeat him."

You sure about this? said the Monkey King. *You haven't even seen the contract.*

You worry about the banquets, and I'll worry about the law.

"How?" Li asked. "Maybe the contract does say what he said."

"I'm sure it does. But don't worry, I'll think of something."

To those who came to Tian for help, he was a *songshi*, a litigation master. But to the *yamen* magistrate and the local gentry, to the men who wielded money and power, Tian was a *songgun*, a "litigating hooligan."

The scholars who sipped tea and the merchants who caressed their silver taels despised Tian for daring to help the illiterate peasants draft complaints, devise legal strategies, and prepare for testimony and interrogation. After all, according to Confucius, neighbors should not sue neighbors. A conflict was nothing more than a misunderstanding that needed to be harmonized by a learned Confucian gentleman. But men like Tian Haoli dared to make the crafty peasants think that they could haul their superiors into court and could violate the proper hierarchies of respect! The Great Qing Code made it clear that champerty, maintenance, barratry, pettifoggery—whatever name you used to describe what Tian did—were crimes.

But Tian understood the *yamen* courts were parts of a complex machine. Like the watermills that dotted the Yangtze River, complicated machines had patterns, gears, and levers. They could be nudged and pushed to do things, provided you were clever. As much as the scholars and merchants hated Tian, sometimes they also sought his help and paid him handsomely for it too.

"I can't pay you much."

Tian chuckled. "The rich pay my fee when they use my services but hate me for it. In your case, it's payment enough to see this moneyed cousin of yours foiled."

•   •   •

Tian accompanied Li to the *yamen* court. Along the way, they passed
the town square, where a few soldiers were putting up posters of
wanted men.

Li glanced at the posters and slowed down. "Wait, I think I may
know—"

"Shush!" Tian pulled her along. "Are you crazy? Those aren't the
magistrate's bailiffs, but real Imperial soldiers. How can you possibly
recognize a man wanted by the Emperor?"

"But—"

"I'm sure you're mistaken. If one of them hears you, even the
greatest litigation master in China won't be able to help you. You have
trouble enough. When it comes to politics, it's best to see no evil, hear
no evil, speak no evil."

That's a philosophy a lot of my monkeys used to share, said the Monkey
King. *But I disagree with it.*

You would, you perpetual rebel, thought Tian Haoli. *But you can grow a
new head when it's cut off, a luxury most of us don't share.*

Outside the *yamen* court, Tian picked up the drumstick and began to
beat the Drum of Justice, petitioning the court to hear his complaint.

Half an hour later, an angry Magistrate Yi stared at the two people
kneeling on the paved-stone floor below the dais: the widow trembling in fear, and that troublemaker, Tian, his back straight with a false
look of respect on his face. Magistrate Yi had hoped to take the day off
to enjoy the company of a pretty girl at one of the blue houses, but
here he was, forced to work. He had a good mind to order both of
them flogged right away, but he had to at least keep up the appearance
of being a caring magistrate lest one of his disloyal underlings make a
report to the judicial inspector.

"What is your complaint, guileful peasant?" asked the magistrate,
gritting his teeth.

Tian shuffled forward on his knees and kowtowed. "Oh, Most Honored Magistrate," he began—Magistrate Yi wondered how Tian managed to make the phrase sound almost like an insult—"Widow Li cries out for justice, justice, justice!"

"And why are *you* here?"

"I'm Li Xiaoyi's cousin, here to help her speak, for she is distraught over how she's been treated."

Magistrate Yi fumed. This Tian Haoli always claimed to be related to the litigant to justify his presence in court and avoid the charge of being a litigating hooligan. He slammed his hardwood ruler, the symbol of his authority, against the table. "You lie! How many cousins can you possibly have?"

"I lie not."

"I warn you, if you can't prove this relation in the records of the Li clan shrine, I'll have you given forty strokes of the cane." Magistrate Yi was pleased with himself, thinking that he had finally come up with a way to best the crafty litigation master. He gave a meaningful look to the bailiffs standing to the sides of the court, and they pounded their staffs against the ground rhythmically, emphasizing the threat.

But Tian seemed not worried at all. "Most Sagacious Magistrate, it was Confucius who said that 'Within the Four Seas, all men are brothers.' If all men were brothers at the time of Confucius, then it stands to reason that being descended from them, Li Xiaoyi and I are related. With all due respect, surely, Your Honor isn't suggesting that the genealogical records of the Li family are more authoritative than the words of the Great Sage?"

Magistrate Yi's face turned red, but he could not think of an answer. Oh, how he wished he could find some excuse to punish this sharp-tongued *songgun*, who always seemed to turn black into white and right into wrong. The Emperor needed better laws to deal with men like him.

"Let's move on." The magistrate took a deep breath to calm himself. "What is this injustice she claims? Her cousin Jie read me the contract. It's perfectly clear what happened."

"I'm afraid there's been a mistake," Tian said. "I ask that the contract be brought so it can be examined again."

Magistrate Yi sent one of the bailiffs to bring back the wealthy cousin with the contract. Everyone in court, including Widow Li, looked at Tian in puzzlement, unsure what he planned. But Tian simply stroked his beard, appearing to be without a care in the world.

You do have a plan, yes? said the Monkey King.

Not really. I'm just playing for time.

Well, said Monkey, *I always like to turn my enemies' weapons against them. Did I tell you about the time I burned Nezha with his own fire-wheels?*

Tian dipped his hand inside his robe, where he kept his writing kit.

The bailiff brought back a confused, sweating Jie, who had been interrupted during a luxurious meal of swallow-nest soup. His face was still greasy as he hadn't even gotten a chance to wipe himself. Jie knelt before the magistrate next to Tian and Li and lifted the contract above his head for the bailiff.

"Show it to Tian," the magistrate ordered.

Tian accepted the contract and began to read it. He nodded his head from time to time, as though the contract was the most fascinating poetry.

Though the legalese was long and intricate, the key phrase was only eight characters long:

上賣莊稼，下賣田地

The mortgage was structured as a sale with a right of redemption, and this part provided that the widow sold her cousin "the crops above, and the field below."

"Interesting, most interesting," said Tian as he held the contract and continued to move his head about rhythmically.

Magistrate Yi knew he was being baited, yet he couldn't help but ask, "*What* is so interesting?"

"Oh Great, Glorious Magistrate, you who reflect the truth like a perfect mirror, you must read the contract yourself."

Confused, Magistrate Yi had the bailiff bring him the contract. After a few moments, his eyes bulged out. Right there, in clear black characters, was the key phrase describing the sale:

上賣莊稼，不賣田地

"The crops above, but *not* the field," muttered the magistrate.

Well, the case was clear. The contract did not say what Jie claimed. All that Jie had a right to were the crops, but not the field itself. Magistrate Yi had no idea how this could have happened, but his embarrassed fury needed an outlet. The sweaty, greasy-faced Jie was the first thing he laid his eyes on.

"How dare you lie to me?" Yi shouted, slamming his ruler down on the table. "Are you trying to make me look like a fool?"

It was now Jie's turn to shake like a leaf in the wind, unable to speak.

"Oh, now you have nothing to say? You're convicted of obstruction of justice, lying to an Imperial official, and attempting to defraud another of her property. I sentence you to a hundred and twenty strokes of the cane and confiscation of half of your property."

"Mercy, mercy! I don't know what happened—" The piteous cries of Jie faded as the bailiffs dragged him out of the *yamen* to jail.

Litigation Master Tian's face was impassive, but inside he smiled and thanked Monkey. Discreetly, he rubbed the tip of his finger against his robe to eliminate the evidence of his trick.

A week later, Tian Haoli was awakened from another banquet-dream with the Monkey King by persistent knocking. He opened the door to find Li Xiaoyi standing there, her pale face drained of blood.

"What's the matter? Is your cousin again—"

"Master Tian, I need your help." Her voice was barely more than a whisper. "It's my brother."

"Is it a gambling debt? A fight with a rich man? Did he make a bad deal? Was he—"

"Please! You have to come with me!"

Tian Haoli was going to say no because a clever *songshi* never got involved in cases he didn't understand—a quick way to end a career. But the look on Li's face softened his resolve. "All right. Lead the way."

Tian made sure that there was no one watching before he slipped inside Li Xiaoyi's hut. Though he didn't have much of a reputation to worry about, Xiaoyi didn't need the village gossips wagging their tongues.

Inside, a long, crimson streak could be seen across the packed-earth floor, leading from the doorway to the bed against the far wall. A man lay asleep on the bed, bloody bandages around his legs and left shoulder. Xiaoyi's two children, both girls, huddled in a shadowy corner of the hut, their mistrustful eyes peeking out at Tian.

One glance at the man's face told Tian all he needed to know: It was the same face on those posters the soldiers were putting up.

Tian Haoli sighed. "Xiaoyi, what kind of trouble have you brought me now?"

Gently, Xiaoyi shook her brother, Xiaojing, awake. He became alert almost immediately, a man used to light sleep and danger on the road.

"Xiaoyi tells me that you can help me," the man said, gazing at Tian intently.

Tian rubbed his chin as he appraised Xiaojing. "I don't know."

"I can pay." Xiaojing struggled to turn on the bed and lifted a corner of a cloth bundle. Tian could see the glint of silver underneath.

"I make no promises. Not every disease has a cure, and not every fugitive can find a loophole. It depends on who's after you and why." Tian walked closer and bent down to examine the promised payment, but the tattoos on Xiaojing's scarred face, signs that he was a convicted criminal, caught his attention. "You were sentenced to exile."

"Yes, ten years ago, right after Xiaoyi's marriage."

"If you have enough money, there are doctors that can do something about those tattoos, though you won't look very handsome afterward."

"I'm not very worried about looks right now."

"What was it for?"

Xiaojing laughed and nodded at the table next to the window, upon which a thin book lay open. The wind fluttered its pages. "If you're as good as my sister says, you can probably figure it out."

Tian glanced at the book and then turned back to Xiaojing.

"You were exiled to the border near Vietnam," Tian said to himself as he deciphered the tattoos. "Eleven years ago . . . the breeze fluttering the pages . . . ah, you must have been a servant of Xu Jun, the Hanlin Academy scholar."

Eleven years ago, during the reign of the Yongzheng Emperor, someone had whispered in the Emperor's ear that the great scholar Xu Jun was plotting rebellion against the Manchu rulers. But when the Imperial guards seized Xu's house and ransacked it, they could find nothing incriminating.

However, the Emperor could never be wrong, and so his legal advisers had to devise a way to convict Xu. Their solution was to point at one of Xu's seemingly innocuous lyric poems:

清風不識字，何故亂翻書
Breeze, you know not how to read,
So why do you mess with my book?

The first character in the word for "breeze," *qing*, was the same as the name of the dynasty. The clever legalists serving the Emperor— and Tian did have a begrudging professional admiration for their skill—construed it as a treasonous composition mocking the Manchu rulers as uncultured and illiterate. Xu and his family were sentenced to death, his servants exiled.

"Xu's crime was great, but it has been more than ten years." Tian paced beside the bed. "If you simply broke the terms of your exile, it might not be too difficult to bribe the right officials and commanders to look the other way."

"The men after me cannot be bribed."

"Oh?" Tian looked at the bandaged wounds covering the man's body. "You mean . . . the Blood Drops."

Xiaojing nodded.

The Blood Drops were the Emperor's eyes and talons. They moved through the dark alleys of cities like ghosts and melted into the streaming caravans on roads and canals, hunting for signs of treason. They were the reason that teahouses posted signs for patrons to avoid talk of politics and neighbors looked around and whispered when they complained about taxes. They listened, watched, and sometimes came to people's doors in the middle of the night, and those they visited were never seen again.

Tian waved his arms impatiently. "You and Xiaoyi are wasting my time. If the Blood Drops are after you, I can do nothing. Not if I want to keep my head attached to my neck." Tian headed for the door of the hut.

"I'm not asking you to save me," said Xiaojing.

Tian paused.

"Eleven years ago, when they came to arrest Master Xu, he gave me a book and told me it was more important than his life, than his family. I kept the book hidden and took it into exile with me.

"A month ago, two men came to my house, asking me to turn over everything I had from my dead master. Their accents told me they were from Beijing, and I saw in their eyes the cold stare of the Emperor's falcons. I let them in and told them to look around, but while they were distracted with my chests and drawers, I escaped with the book.

"I've been on the run ever since, and a few times they almost caught me, leaving me with these wounds. The book they're after is over there on the table. *That's* what I want you to save."

Tian hesitated by the door. He was used to bribing *yamen* clerks and prison guards and debating Magistrate Yi. He liked playing games with words and drinking cheap wine and bitter tea. What business did a lowly *songgun* have with the Emperor and the intrigue of the Court?

I was once happy in Fruit-and-Flower Mountain, spending all day in play with my fellow monkeys, said the Monkey King. *Sometimes I wish I hadn't been so curious about what lay in the wider world.*

But Tian was curious, and he walked over to the table and picked up the book. *An Account of Ten Days at Yangzhou*, it said, by Wang Xiuchu.

A hundred years earlier, in 1645, after claiming the Ming Chinese capital of Beijing, the Manchu Army was intent on completing its conquest of China.

Prince Dodo and his forces came to Yangzhou, a wealthy city of salt merchants and painted pavilions, at the meeting point of the Yangtze River and the Grand Canal. The Chinese commander, Grand Secretary Shi Kefa, vowed to resist to the utmost. He rallied the city's residents to reinforce the walls and tried to unite the remaining Ming warlords and militias.

His efforts came to naught on May 20, 1645, when the Manchu forces broke through the city walls after a seven-day siege. Shi Kefa was executed after refusing to surrender. To punish the residents of Yangzhou and to teach the rest of China a lesson about the price of resisting the Manchu Army, Prince Dodo gave the order to slaughter the entire population of the city.

One of the residents, Wang Xiuchu, survived by moving from hiding place to hiding place and bribing the soldiers with whatever he had. He also recorded what he saw:

One Manchu soldier with a sword was in the lead, another with a lance was in the back, and a third roamed in the middle to prevent the captives from escaping. The three of them herded dozens of captives like dogs and sheep. If any captive walked too slow, they would beat him immediately or else kill him on the spot.

The women were strung together with ropes, like a strand of pearls. They stumbled as they walked through the mud, and filth covered their bodies and clothes. Babies were everywhere on the ground, and as horses and people trampled over them, their brains and organs mixed into the earth, and the howling of the dying filled the air.

Every gutter or pond we passed was filled with corpses, their arms and legs entangled. The blood mixing with the green water turned into a painter's palette. So many bodies filled the canal that it turned into flat ground.

The mass massacre, raping, pillaging, and burning of the city lasted six days.

On the second day of the lunar month, the new government ordered all the temples to cremate the bodies. The temples had sheltered many women, though many had also died from hunger and fright. The final records of the cremations included hundreds of thousands of bodies, though this figure does not include all those who had committed suicide by jumping into wells or canals or through self-immolation and hanging to avoid a worse fate. . . .

On the fourth day of the lunar month, the weather finally turned sunny. The bodies piled by the roadside, having soaked in rainwater, had inflated and the skin on them was a bluish black and stretched taut like the surface of a drum. The flesh inside rotted and the stench was overwhelming. As the sun baked the bodies, the smell grew worse. Everywhere in Yangzhou, the survivors

were cremating bodies. The smoke permeated inside all the houses and formed a
miasma. The smell of rotting bodies could be detected a hundred li *away.*

Tian's hands trembled as he turned over the last page.

"Now you see why the Blood Drops are after me," said Xiaojing,
his voice weary. "The Manchus have insisted that the Yangzhou Massacre is a myth, and anyone speaking of it is guilty of treason. But here
is an eyewitness account that will reveal their throne as built on a
foundation of blood and skulls."

Tian closed his eyes and thought about Yangzhou, with its
teahouses full of indolent scholars arguing with singing girls about
rhyme schemes, with its palatial mansions full of richly robed merchants celebrating another good trading season, with its hundreds of
thousands of inhabitants happily praying for the Manchu Emperor's
health. Did they know that each day, as they went to the markets and
laughed and sang and praised this golden age they lived in, they were
treading on the bones of the dead, they were mocking the dying cries
of the departed, they were denying the memories of ghosts? He himself had not even believed the stories whispered in his childhood about
Yangzhou's past, and he was quite sure that most young men in Yangzhou now had never even heard of them.

Now that he knew the truth, could he allow the ghosts to continue to be silenced?

But then he also thought about the special prisons the Blood
Drops maintained, the devious tortures designed to prolong the journey from life to death, the ways that the Manchu Emperors always
got what they wanted in the end. The Emperor's noble Banners had
succeeded in forcing all the Chinese to shave their heads and wear
queues to show submission to the Manchus, and to abandon their
hanfu for Manchu clothing on pain of death. They had cut the Chinese
off from their past, made them a people adrift without the anchor of

their memories. They were more powerful than the Jade Emperor and ten thousand heavenly soldiers.

It would be so easy for them to erase this book, to erase him, a lowly *songgun*, from the world, like a momentary ripple across a placid pond.

Let others have their fill of daring deeds; he was a survivor.

"I'm sorry," Tian said to Xiaojing, his voice low and hoarse. "I can't help you."

Tian Haoli sat down at his table to eat a bowl of noodles. He had flavored it with fresh lotus seeds and bamboo shoots, and the fragrance was usually refreshing, perfect for a late lunch.

The Monkey King appeared in the seat opposite him: fierce eyes, wide mouth, a purple cape that declared him to be the Sage Equal to Heaven, rebel against the Jade Emperor.

This didn't happen often. Usually Monkey spoke to Tian only in his mind.

"You think you're not a hero," the Monkey King said.

"That's right," replied Tian. He tried to keep the defensiveness out of his voice. "I'm just an ordinary man making a living by scrounging for crumbs in the cracks of the law, happy to have enough to eat and a few coppers left for drink. I just want to live."

"I'm not a hero either," the Monkey King said. "I just did my job when needed."

"Ha!" said Tian. "I know what you're trying to do, but it's not going to work. Your job was to protect the holiest monk on a perilous journey, and your qualifications consisted of peerless strength and boundless magic. You could call on the aid of the Buddha and Guanyin, the Goddess of Mercy, whenever you needed to. Don't you compare yourself to me."

"Fine. Do you know of *any* heroes?"

Tian slurped some noodles and pondered the question. What he had read that morning was fresh in his mind. "I guess Grand Secretary Shi Kefa was a hero."

"How? He promised the people of Yangzhou that as long as he lived, he would not let harm come to them, and yet when the city fell, he tried to escape on his own. He seems to me more a coward than a hero."

Tian put down his bowl. "That's not fair. He held the city when he had no reinforcements or aid. He pacified the warlords harassing the people in Yangzhou and rallied them to their defense. In the end, despite a moment of weakness, he willingly gave his life for the city, and you can't ask for more than that."

The Monkey King snorted contemptuously. "Of course you can. He should have seen that fighting was futile. If he hadn't resisted the Manchu invaders and instead surrendered the city, maybe not so many would have died. If he hadn't refused to bow down to the Manchus, maybe he wouldn't have been killed." The Monkey King smirked. "Maybe he wasn't very smart and didn't know how to survive."

Blood rushed to Tian's face. He stood up and pointed a finger at the Monkey King. "Don't you talk about him that way. Who's to say that had he surrendered, the Manchus wouldn't have slaughtered the city, anyway? You think lying down before a conquering army bent on rape and pillage is the right thing to do? To turn your argument around, the heavy resistance in Yangzhou slowed the Manchu Army and might have allowed many people to escape to safety in the south, and the city's defiance might have made the Manchus willing to give better terms to those who did surrender later. Grand Secretary Shi was a real hero!"

The Monkey King laughed. "Listen to you, arguing like you are in Magistrate Yi's *yamen*. You're awfully worked up about a man dead for a hundred years."

"I won't let you denigrate his memory that way, even if you're the Sage Equal to Heaven."

The Monkey King's face turned serious. "You speak of memory. What do you think about Wang Xiuchu, who wrote the book you read?"

"He was just an ordinary man like me, surviving by bribes and hiding from danger."

"Yet he recorded what he saw, so that a hundred years later the men and women who died in those ten days can be remembered. Writing that book was a brave thing to do—look at how the Manchus are hunting down someone today just for *reading* it. I think he was a hero too."

After a moment, Tian nodded. "I hadn't thought about it that way, but you're right."

"There are no heroes, Tian Haoli. Grand Secretary Shi was both courageous and cowardly, capable and foolish. Wang Xiuchu was both an opportunistic survivor and a man of greatness of spirit. I'm mostly selfish and vain, but sometimes even I surprise myself. We're all just ordinary men—well, I'm an ordinary demon—faced with extraordinary choices. In those moments, sometimes heroic ideals demand that we become their avatars."

Tian sat down and closed his eyes. "I'm just an old and frightened man, Monkey. I don't know what to do."

"Sure you do. You just have to accept it."

"Why me? What if I don't want to?"

The Monkey King's face turned somber, and his voice grew faint. "Those men and women of Yangzhou died a hundred years ago, Tian Haoli, and nothing can be done to change that. But the past lives on in the form of memories, and those in power are always going to want to erase and silence the past, to bury the ghosts. Now that you know about that past, you're no longer an innocent bystander. If you do not act, you're complicit with the Emperor and his Blood Drops in this new act of violence, this deed of erasure. Like Wang Xiuchu, you're now a witness. Like him, you must choose what to do. You must decide if, on the day you die, you will regret your choice."

The figure of the Monkey King faded away, and Tian was left alone in his hut, remembering.

"I have written a letter to an old friend in Ningbo," said Tian. "Bring it with you to the address on the envelope. He's a good surgeon and will erase these tattoos from your face as a favor to me."

"Thank you," said Li Xiaojing. "I will destroy the letter as soon as I can, knowing how much danger this brings you. Please accept this as payment." He turned to his bundle and retrieved five taels of silver.

Tian held up a hand. "No, you'll need all the money you can get." He handed over a small bundle. "It's not much, but it's all I have saved."

Li Xiaojing and Li Xiaoyi both looked at the litigation master, not understanding.

Tian continued. "Xiaoyi and the children can't stay here in Sanli because someone will surely report that she harbored a fugitive when the Blood Drops start asking questions. No, all of you must leave immediately and go to Ningbo, where you will hire a ship to take you to Japan. Since the Manchus have sealed the coast, you will need to pay a great deal to a smuggler."

"To Japan!?"

"So long as that book is with you, there is nowhere in China where you'll be safe. Of all the states around, only Japan would dare to defy the Manchu Emperor. Only there will you and the book be safe."

Xiaojing and Xiaoyi nodded. "You will come with us, then?"

Tian gestured at his lame leg and laughed. "Having me along will only slow you down. No, I'll stay here and take my chances."

"The Blood Drops will not let you go if they suspect you helped us."

Tian smiled. "I'll come up with something. I always do."

. . .

A few days later, when Tian Haoli was just about to sit down and have his lunch, soldiers from the town garrison came to his door. They arrested him without explanation and brought him to the *yamen*.

Tian saw that Magistrate Yi wasn't the only one sitting behind the judging table on the dais this time. With him was another official, whose hat indicated that he came directly from Beijing. His cold eyes and lean build reminded Tian of a falcon.

May my wits defend me again, Tian whispered to the Monkey King in his mind.

Magistrate Yi slammed his ruler on the table. "Deceitful Tian Haoli, you're hereby accused of aiding the escape of dangerous fugitives and of plotting acts of treason against the Great Qing. Confess your crimes immediately so that you may die quickly."

Tian nodded as the magistrate finished his speech. "Most Merciful and Farsighted Magistrate, I have absolutely no idea what you're talking about."

"You presumptuous fool! Your usual tricks will not work this time. I have ironclad proof that you gave comfort and aid to the traitor Li Xiaojing and read a forbidden, treasonous, false text."

"I have indeed read a book recently, but there was nothing treasonous in it."

"What?"

"It was a book about sheepherding and pearl stringing. Plus some discussions about filling ponds and starting fires."

The other man behind the table narrowed his eyes, but Tian went on as if he had nothing to hide. "It was very technical and very boring."

"You lie!" The veins on Magistrate Yi's neck seemed about to burst.

"Most Brilliant and Perspicacious Magistrate, how can you say that I lie? Can you tell me the contents of this forbidden book, so that I may verify if I have read it?"

"You . . . you . . ." The magistrate's mouth opened and closed like the lips of a fish.

Of course Magistrate Yi wouldn't have been told what was in the book—that was the point of it being forbidden—but Tian was also counting on the fact that the man from the Blood Drops wouldn't be able to say anything either. To accuse Tian of lying about the contents of the book was to admit that the accuser had read the book, and Tian knew that no member of the Blood Drops would admit such a crime to the suspicious Manchu Emperor.

"There has been a misunderstanding," said Tian. "The book I read contained nothing that was false, which means that it can't possibly be the book that has been banned. Certainly, Your Honor can see the plain and simple logic." He smiled. Surely, he had found the loophole that would allow him to escape.

"Enough of this charade." The man from the Blood Drops spoke for the first time. "There's no need to bother with the law with traitors like you. On the Emperor's authority, I hereby declare you guilty without appeal and sentence you to death. If you do not wish to suffer much longer, immediately confess the whereabouts of the book and the fugitives."

Tian felt his legs go rubbery and, for a moment, he saw only darkness and heard only an echo of the Blood Drop's pronouncement: *sentence you to death.*

I guess I've finally run out of tricks, he thought.

You've already made your choice, said the Monkey King. *Now you just have to accept it.*

Besides being great spies and assassins, the Blood Drops were experts at the art of torture.

Tian screamed as they doused his limbs in boiling water.

Tell me a story, said Tian to the Monkey King. *Distract me so I don't give in.*

Let me tell you about the time they cooked me in the alchemical furnace of the Jade Emperor, said the Monkey King. *I survived by hiding among smoke and ashes.*

And Tian told his torturers a tale about how he had helped Li Xiaojing burn his useless book and saw it turn into smoke and ashes. But he had forgotten where the fire was set. Perhaps the Blood Drops could search the nearby hills thoroughly?

They burned him with iron pokers heated until they glowed white.

Tell me a story, Tian screamed as he breathed in the smell of charred flesh.

Let me tell you about the time I fought the Iron Fan Princess in the Fire Mountains, said the Monkey King. *I tricked her by pretending to run away in fear.*

And Tian told his torturers a tale about how he had told Li Xiaojing to escape to Suzhou, famed for its many alleys and canals, as well as refined lacquer fans.

They cut his fingers off one by one.

Tell me a story, Tian croaked. He was weak from loss of blood.

Let me tell you about the time they put that magical headband on me, said the Monkey King. *I almost passed out from the pain but still I wouldn't stop cursing.*

And Tian spat in the faces of his torturers.

Tian woke up in the dim cell. It smelled of mildew and shit and piss. Rats squeaked in the corners.

He was finally going to be put to death tomorrow, as his torturers had given up. It would be death by a thousand cuts. A skilled executioner could make the victim suffer for hours before taking his final breath.

I didn't give in, did I? he asked the Monkey King. *I can't remember everything I told them.*

You told them many tales, none true.

Tian thought he should be content. Death would be a release. But he worried that he hadn't done enough. What if Li Xiaojing didn't make it to Japan? What if the book was destroyed at sea? If only there were some way to save the book so that it could *not* be lost.

Have I told you about the time I fought Lord Erlang and confused him by transforming my shape? I turned into a sparrow, a fish, a snake, and finally a temple. My mouth was the door, my eyes the windows, my tongue the buddha, and my tail a flagpole. Ha, that was fun. None of Lord Erlang's demons could see through my disguises.

I am clever with words, thought Tian. *I am, after all, a* songgun.

The voices of children singing outside the jail cell came to him faintly. He struggled and crawled to the wall with the tiny barred window at the top and called out, "Hey, can you hear me?"

The singing stopped abruptly. After a while, a timid voice said, "We're not supposed to talk to condemned criminals. My mother says that you're dangerous and crazy."

Tian laughed. "I *am* crazy. But I know some good songs. Would you like to learn them? They're about sheep and pearls and all sorts of other fun things."

The children conferred among themselves, and one of them said, "Why not? A crazy man must have some good songs."

Tian Haoli mustered up every last bit of his strength and concentration. He thought about the words from the book:

The three of them herded dozens of captives like dogs and sheep. If any captive walked too slow, they would beat him immediately, or else kill him on the spot. The women were strung together with ropes, like a strand of pearls.

He thought about disguises. He thought about the way the tones differed between Mandarin and the local topolect, the way he could make puns and approximations and rhymes and shift the words and transform them until they were no longer recognizable. And he began to sing:

The Tree of Dem herded dozens of Cap Tea
Like dogs and sheep.
If any Cap Tea walked too slow, the Wood Beet
Hmm'd immediately.
Or else a quill, slim on the dot.
The Why-Men were strong to gather wits & loupes
Like a strand of pearls.

And the children, delighted by the nonsense, picked up the songs quickly.

They tied him to the pole on the execution platform and stripped him naked.

Tian watched the crowd. In the eyes of some, he saw pity, in others, he saw fear, and in still others, like Li Xiaoyi's cousin Jie, he saw delight at seeing the hooligan *songgun* meet this fate. But most were expectant. This execution, this horror, was entertainment.

"One last chance," the Blood Drop said. "If you confess the truth now, we will slit your throat cleanly. Otherwise, you can enjoy the next few hours."

Whispers passed through the crowd. Some tittered. Tian gazed at the bloodlust in some of the men. *You have become a slavish people,* he thought. *You have forgotten the past and become docile captives of the Emperor. You have learned to take delight in his barbarity, to believe that you live in a golden age, never bothering to look beneath the gilded surface of the Empire at its rotten, bloody foundation. You desecrate the very memory of those who died to keep you free.*

His heart was filled with despair. *Have I endured all this and thrown away my life for nothing?*

Some children in the crowd began to sing:

The Tree of Dem herded dozens of Cap Tea
Like dogs and sheep.
If any Cap Tea walked too slow, the Wood Beet
Hmm'd immediately.
Or else a quill, slim on the dot.
The Why-Men were strong to gather wits & loupes
Like a strand of pearls.

The Blood Drop's expression did not change. He heard nothing but the nonsense of children. True, this way, the children would not be endangered by knowing the song. But Tian also wondered if anyone would ever see through the nonsense. Had he hidden the truth too deep?

"Stubborn till the last, eh?" The Blood Drop turned to the executioner, who was sharpening his knives on the grindstone. "Make it last as long as possible."

What have I done? thought Tian. *They're laughing at the way I'm dying, the way I've been a fool. I've accomplished nothing except fighting for a hopeless cause.*

Not at all, said the Monkey King. *Li Xiaojing is safe in Japan, and the children's songs will be passed on until the whole county, the whole province, the whole country fills with their voices. Someday, perhaps not now, perhaps not in another hundred years, but someday the book will come back from Japan, or a clever scholar will finally see through the disguise in your songs as Lord Erlang finally saw through mine. And then the spark of truth will set this country aflame, and this people will awaken from their torpor. You have preserved the memories of the men and women of Yangzhou.*

The executioner began with a long, slow cut across Tian's thighs, removing chunks of flesh. Tian's scream was like that of an animal's, raw, pitiful, incoherent.

Not much of a hero, am I? thought Tian. *I wish I were truly brave.*

You're an ordinary man who was given an extraordinary choice, said the Monkey King. *Do you regret your choice?*

No, thought Tian. And as the pain made him delirious and reason began to desert him, he shook his head firmly. *Not at all.*

You can't ask for more than that, said the Monkey King. And he bowed before Tian Haoli, not the way you kowtowed to an Emperor, but the way you would bow to a great hero.

•   •   •

AUTHOR'S NOTES: For more about the historical profession of *song-shi* (or *songgun*), please contact the author for an unpublished paper. Some of Tian Haoli's exploits are based on folktales about the great Litigation Master Xie Fangzun collected by the anthologist Ping Heng in *Zhongguo da zhuangshi* ("Great Plaintmasters of China"), published in 1922.

For more than 250 years, *An Account of Ten Days at Yangzhou* was suppressed in China by the Manchu emperors, and the Yangzhou Massacre, along with numerous other atrocities during the Manchu Conquest, was forgotten. It wasn't until the decade before the Revolution of 1911 that copies of the book were brought back from Japan and republished in China. The text played a small, but important, role in the fall of the Qing and the end of Imperial rule in China. I translated the excerpts used in this story.

Due to the long suppression, which continues to some degree to this day, the true number of victims who died in Yangzhou may never be known. This story is dedicated to their memory.

THE MAN WHO ENDED
HISTORY: A DOCUMENTARY

Akemi Kirino, Chief Scientist, Feynman Laboratories:

[*Dr. Kirino is in her early forties. She has the kind of beauty that doesn't require much makeup. If you look closely, you can see bits of white in her otherwise black hair.*]

Every night, when you stand outside and gaze upon the stars, you are bathing in time as well as light.

For example, when you look at this star in the constellation Libra called Gliese 581, you are really seeing it as it was just over two decades ago because it's about twenty light-years from us. And conversely, if someone around Gliese 581 had a powerful enough telescope pointed to around *here* right now, they'd be able to see Evan and me walking around Harvard Yard, back when we were graduate students.

[*She points to Massachusetts on the globe on her desk, as the camera pans to zoom in on it. She pauses, thinking over her words. The camera pulls back, moving us farther and farther away from the globe, as though we are flying away from it.*]

The best telescopes we have today can see as far back as about thirteen billion years ago. If you strap one of those to a rocket moving away from the Earth at a speed that's faster than light—a detail that I'll get to in a minute—and point the telescope back at the Earth, you'll see the history of humanity unfold before you in reverse. The view of everything that has happened on Earth leaves here in an ever-expanding sphere of light. And you only have to control how far away you travel in space to determine how far back you'll go in time.

[*The camera keeps on pulling back, through the door of her office, down the hall, as the globe and Dr. Kirino become smaller and smaller in our view. The long hallway we are backing down is dark, and in that sea of darkness, the open door of the office becomes a rectangle of bright light framing the globe and the woman.*]

Somewhere about here you'll witness Prince Charles's sad face as Hong Kong is finally returned to China. Somewhere about here you'll see Japan's surrender aboard the USS *Missouri*. Somewhere about here you'll see Hideyoshi's troops set foot on the soil of Korea for the first time. And somewhere about here you'll see Lady Murasaki completing the first chapter of the *Tale of Genji*. If you keep on going, you can go back to the beginning of civilization and beyond.

But the past is consumed even as it is seen. The photons enter the lens, and from there they strike an imaging surface, be it your retina or a sheet of film or a digital sensor, and then they are gone, stopped dead in their paths. If you look but don't pay attention and miss a moment, you cannot travel farther out to catch it again. That moment is erased from the universe, forever.

[*From the shadows next to the door to the office an arm reaches out to slam the door shut. Darkness swallows Dr. Kirino, the globe, and the bright rectangle of light. The screen stays black for a few seconds before the opening credits roll.*]

> *Remembrance Films HK Ltd.*
> *in association with*
> *Yurushi Studios*
> *presents*
> *a Heraclitus Twice Production*

THE MAN WHO ENDED HISTORY
This film has been banned by the Ministry of Culture of the
People's Republic of China and is released under strong protest
from the government of Japan

Akemi Kirino:

[*We are back in the warm glow of her office.*]

Because we have not yet solved the problem of how to travel faster than light, there is no real way for us to actually get a telescope out there to see the past. But we've found a way to cheat.

Theorists long suspected that at each moment, the world around us is literally exploding with newly created subatomic particles of a certain type, now known as Bohm-Kirino particles. My modest contribution to physics was to confirm their existence and to discover that these particles always come in pairs. One member of the pair shoots away from the Earth, riding the photon that gave it birth and traveling at the speed of light. The other remains behind, oscillating in the vicinity of its creation.

The pairs of Bohm-Kirino particles are under quantum entanglement. This means that they are bound together in such a way that no matter how far apart they are from each other physically, their properties are linked together as though they are but aspects of a single system. If you take a measurement on one member of the pair, thereby collapsing the wave function, you would immediately know the state of the other member of the pair, even if it is light-years away.

Since the energy levels of Bohm-Kirino particles decay at a known rate, by tuning the sensitivity of the detection field, we can attempt to capture and measure Bohm-Kirino particles of a precise age created in a specific place.

When a measurement is taken on the local Bohm-Kirino particle in an entangled pair, it is equivalent to taking a measurement on that particle's entangled twin, which, along with its host photon, may be trillions of miles away, and thus, decades in the past. Through some complex but standard mathematics, the measurement allows us to calculate and infer the state of the host photon. But, like any measurement performed on entangled pairs, the measurement can be taken only once, and the information is then gone forever.

In other words, it is as though we have found a way to place a telescope as far away from the Earth, and as far back in time, as we like. If you want, you can look back on the day you were married, your first kiss, the moment you were born. But for each moment in the past, we get only one chance to look.

Archival Footage: September 18, 20XX. Courtesy of APAC
Broadcasting Corporation

[*The camera shows an idle factory on the outskirts of the city of Harbin, Heilongjiang Province, China. It looks just like any other factory in the industrial heartland of China in the grip of another downturn in the country's merciless boom-and-bust cycles: ramshackle, silent, dusty, the windows and doors shuttered and boarded up. Samantha Paine, the correspondent, wears a wool cap and scarf. Her cheeks are bright red with the cold, and her eyes are tired. As she speaks in her calm voice, the condensation from her breath curls and lingers before her face.*]

Samantha:

On this day, back in 1931, the first shots in the Second Sino-Japanese War were fired near Shenyang, here in Manchuria. For the Chinese, that was the beginning of World War Two, more than a decade before the United Stat es would be involved.

We are in Pingfang District, on the outskirts of Harbin. Although the name "Pingfang" means nothing to most people in the West, some have called Pingfang the Asian Auschwitz. Here, Unit 731 of the Japanese Imperial Army performed gruesome experiments on thousands of Chinese and Allied prisoners throughout the war as part of Japan's effort to develop biological weapons and to conduct research into the limits of human endurance.

On these premises, Japanese army doctors directly killed thousands of Chinese and Allied prisoners through medical and weapons experiments, vivisections, amputations, and other systematic methods of torture. At the end of the War, the retreating Japanese army killed all remaining prisoners and burned the complex to the ground, leaving behind only the shell of the administrative building and some pits used to breed disease-carrying rats. There were no survivors.

Historians estimate that between two hundred thousand and half a million Chinese persons, almost all civilians, were killed by the biological and chemical weapons researched and developed in this place and other satellite labs: anthrax, cholera, the bubonic plague. At the end of the War, General MacArthur, supreme commander of the Allied forces, granted all members of Unit 731 immunity from war crimes prosecution in order to get the data from their experiments and to keep the data away from the Soviet Union.

Today, except for a small museum nearby with few visitors, little evidence of those atrocities is visible. Over there, at the edge of an empty field, a pile of rubble stands where the incinerator for destroying the bodies of the victims used to be. This factory behind me is built on the foundation of a storage depot used by Unit 731 for germ-breeding supplies. Until the recent economic downturn, which shuttered its doors, the factory built moped engines for a Sino-Japanese joint venture in Harbin. And in a gruesome echo of the past, several pharmaceutical companies have quietly settled in around the site of Unit 731's former headquarters.

Perhaps the Chinese are content to leave behind this part of their past and move on. And if they do, the rest of the world will probably move on as well.

But not if Evan Wei has anything to say about it.

[*Samantha speaks over a montage of images of Evan Wei lecturing in front of a classroom and posing before complex machinery with Dr. Kirino. In the photographs they look to be in their twenties.*]

Dr. Evan Wei, a Chinese-American historian specializing in Classical Japan, is determined to make the world focus on the suffering of the victims of Unit 731. He and his wife, Dr. Akemi Kirino, a noted Japanese-American experimental physicist, have developed a controversial technique that they claim will allow people to travel back in time and experience history as it occurred. Today, he will publicly demonstrate his technique by traveling back to the year 1940, at the height of Unit 731's activities, and personally bear witness to the atrocities of Unit 731.

The Japanese government claims that China is engaged in a propaganda stunt, and it has filed a strongly worded protest with Beijing for allowing this demonstration. Citing principles of international law, Japan argues that China does not have the right to sponsor an expedition into World War Two—era Harbin because Harbin was then under the control of Manchukuo, a puppet regime of the Japanese Empire. China has rejected the Japanese claim, and responded by declaring Dr. Wei's demonstration an "excavation of national heritage" and now claims ownership rights over any visual or audio record of Dr. Wei's proposed journey to the past under Chinese antiquities-export laws.

Dr. Wei has insisted that he and his wife are conducting this experiment in their capacities as individual American citizens, with no connection to any government. They have asked the American Consul General in nearby Shenyang, as well as representatives of the United

Nations, to intervene and protect their effort from any governmental interference. It's unclear how this legal mess will be resolved.

Meanwhile, numerous groups from China and overseas, some in support of Dr. Wei, some against, have gathered to hold protests. China has mobilized thousands of riot police to keep these demonstrators from approaching Pingfang.

Stay tuned, and we will bring you up-to-date reports on this historic occasion. This is Samantha Paine, for APAC.

Akemi Kirino:

To truly travel back in time, we still had to jump over one more hurdle.

The Bohm-Kirino particles allow us to reconstruct, in detail, all types of information about the moment of their creation: sight, sound, microwaves, ultrasound, the smell of antiseptic and blood, and the sting of cordite and gunpowder in the back of the nose.

But this is a staggering amount of information, even for a single second. We had no realistic way to store it, let alone process it in real time. The amount of data gathered for a few minutes would have overwhelmed all the storage servers at Harvard. We could open up a door to the past, but would see nothing in the tsunami of bits that flooded forth.

[Behind Dr. Kirino is a machine that looks like a large clinical MRI scanner. She steps to the side so that the camera can zoom slowly inside the tube of the scanner where the volunteer's body would go during the process. As the camera moves through the tube, continuing toward the light at the end of the tunnel, her voice continues off camera.]

Perhaps given enough time, we could have come up with a solution that would have allowed the data to be recorded. But Evan believed that we could not afford to wait. The surviving relatives of the victims were aging, dying, and the War was about to fade out of living memory. There was a duty, he felt, to offer the surviving relatives whatever answers we could get.

So I came up with the idea of using the human brain to process the information gathered by the Bohm-Kirino detectors. The brain's massively parallel processing capabilities, the bedrock of consciousness, proved quite effective at filtering and making sense of the torrent of data from the detectors. The brain could be given the raw electrical signals, throw 99.999 percent of it away, and turn the rest into sight, sound, smell, and make sense of it all and record them as memories.

This really shouldn't surprise us. After all, this is what our brains do, every second of our lives. The raw signals from our eyes, ears, skin, and tongue would overwhelm any supercomputer, but from second to second, our brain manages to construct the consciousness of our existence from all that noise.

"For our volunteer subjects, the process creates the illusion of experiencing the past, as though they were in that place, at that time," I wrote in *Nature*.

How I regret using the word "illusion" now. So much weight ended up being placed on my poor word choice. History is like that: The truly important decisions never seemed important at the time.

Yes, the brain takes the signals and makes a story out of them, but there's nothing illusory about it, whether in the past or now.

Archibald Ezary, Radhabinod Pal Professor of Law, Codirector
of East Asian Studies, Harvard Law School:

[*Ezary has a placid face that is belied by the intensity of his gaze. He enjoys giving lectures, not because he likes hearing himself talk, but because he thinks he will learn something new each time he tries to explain.*]

The legal debate between China and Japan about Wei's work, almost twenty years ago, was not really new. Who should have control over the past is a question that has troubled all of us, in various forms, for many years. But the invention of the Kirino Process made this struggle to control the past a literal, rather than merely a metaphorical, issue.

A state has a temporal dimension as well as a spatial one. It grows and shrinks over time, subjugating new peoples and sometimes freeing their descendants. Japan today may be thought of as just the home islands, but back in 1942, at its height, the Japanese Empire ruled Korea, most of China, Taiwan, Sakhalin, the Philippines, Vietnam, Thailand, Laos, Burma, Malaysia, and large parts of Indonesia, as well as large swaths of the islands in the Pacific. The legacy of that time shapes Asia to this day.

One of the most vexing problems created by the violent and unstable process by which states expand and contract over time is this: As control over a territory shifts between sovereigns over time, which sovereign should have jurisdiction over that territory's past?

Before Evan Wei's demonstration, the most that the issue of jurisdiction over the past intruded on real life was an argument over whether Spain or America would have the right to the sovereign's share of treasure from sunken sixteenth-century Spanish galleons recovered in contemporary American waters, or whether Greece or England should keep the Elgin Marbles. But now the stakes are much higher.

So, is Harbin during the years between 1931 and 1945 Japanese territory, as the Japanese government contends? Or is it Chinese, as the People's Republic argues? Or perhaps we should treat the past as something held in trust for all of humanity by the United Nations?

The Chinese view would have had the support of most of the Western world—the Japanese position is akin to Germany arguing that attempts to travel to Auschwitz-Birkenau between 1939 and

1945 should be subject to its approval—but for the fact that it is the People's Republic of China, a Western pariah, which is now making the claim. And so you see how the present and the past will strangle each other to death.

Moreover, behind both the Japanese and the Chinese positions is the unquestioned assumption that if we can resolve whether *China* or *Japan* has sovereignty over World War Two–era Harbin, then either the People's Republic or the present Japanese government would be the right authority to exercise that sovereignty. But this is far from clear. Both sides have problems making the legal case.

First, Japan has always argued, when it comes to Chinese claims for compensation for wartime atrocities, that the present Japan, founded on the Constitution drafted by America, cannot be the responsible party. Japan believes that those claims are against its predecessor government, the Empire of Japan, and all such claims have been resolved by the Treaty of San Francisco and other bilateral treaties. But if that is so, for Japan now to assert sovereignty over that era in Manchuria, when it has previously disavowed all responsibility for it, is more than a little inconsistent.

But the People's Republic is not home free either. At the time Japanese forces took control of Manchuria in 1932, it was only nominally under the control of the Republic of China, the entity that we think of as the "official" China during the Second World War, and the People's Republic of China did not even exist. It is true that during the War, armed resistance in Manchuria to the Japanese occupation came almost entirely from the Han Chinese, Manchu, and Korean guerrillas led by Chinese and Korean Communists. But these guerrillas were not under the real direction of the Chinese Communist Party led by Mao Zedong and so had little to do with the eventual founding of the People's Republic.

So why should we think that either the present government of

Japan or China has any claim to Harbin during that era? Wouldn't the Republic of China, which now resides in Taipei and calls itself Taiwan, have a more legitimate claim? Or perhaps we should conjure up a "Provisional Historical Manchurian Authority" to assume jurisdiction over it?

Our doctrines concerning the succession of states, developed under the Westphalian framework, simply cannot deal with these questions raised by Dr. Wei's experiments.

If these debates have a clinical and evasive air to them, that is intentional. "Sovereignty," "jurisdiction," and similar words have always been mere conveniences to allow people to evade responsibility or to sever inconvenient bonds. "Independence" is declared, and suddenly the past is forgotten; a "revolution" occurs, and suddenly memories and blood debts are wiped clean; a treaty is signed, and suddenly the past is buried and gone. Real life does not work like that.

However you want to parse the robber's logic that we dignify under the name "international law," the fact remains that the people who call themselves Japanese today are connected to those who called themselves Japanese in Manchuria in 1937, and the people who call themselves Chinese today are connected to those who called themselves Chinese there and then. These are the messy realities, and we make do with what we are given.

All along, we have made international law work only by assuming that the past would remain silent. But Dr. Wei has given the past a voice and made dead memories come alive. What role, if any, we wish to give the voices of the past in the present is up to us.

Akemi Kirino:

Evan always called me *Tóngyě Míngměi*, or just *Míngměi*, which are the Mandarin readings for the kanji that are used to write my name (桐野明美). Although this is the customary way to pronounce

Japanese names in Chinese, he's the only Chinese I've ever permitted that liberty.

Saying my name like that, he told me, allowed him to picture it in those old characters that are the common heritage of China and Japan, and thus keep in mind their meaning. The way he saw it, "the sound of a name doesn't tell you anything about the person, only the characters do."

My name was the first thing he loved about me.

"A paulownia tree alone in the field, bright and beautiful," he said to me, the first time we met at a Graduate School of Arts and Sciences mixer.

That was also how my grandfather explained my name to me, years earlier, when he taught me how to write the characters in my name as a little girl. A paulownia is a pretty, deciduous tree, and in old Japan it was the custom to plant one when a baby girl was born and make a dresser out of the wood for her trousseau when she got married. I remember the first time my grandfather showed me the paulownia that he had planted for me the day I was born, and I told him that I didn't think it looked very special.

"But a paulownia is the only tree on which a phoenix would land and rest," my grandfather then said, stroking my hair in that slow, gentle way that he had that I loved. I nodded, and I was glad that I had such a special tree for my name.

Until Evan spoke to me, I hadn't thought about that day with my grandfather in years.

"Have you found your phoenix yet?" Evan asked, and then he asked me out.

Evan wasn't shy, not like most Chinese men I knew. I felt at ease listening to him. And he seemed genuinely happy about his life, which was rare among the grad students and made it fun to be around him.

In a way it was natural that we would be drawn to each other. We had both come to America as young children and knew something about the meaning of growing up as outsiders trying hard to become Americans.

It made it easy for us to appreciate each other's foibles, the little corners of our personalities that remained defiantly fresh-off-the-boat.

He wasn't intimidated by the fact that I had a much better sense about numbers, statistics, the "hard" qualities in life. Some of my old boyfriends used to tell me that my focus on the quantifiable and the logic of mathematics made me seem cold and unfeminine. It didn't help that I knew my way around power tools better than most of them—a necessary skill for a lab physicist. Evan was the only man I knew who was perfectly happy to defer to me when I told him that I could do something requiring mechanical skills better than he could.

Memories of our courtship have grown hazy with time and are now coated with the smooth, golden glow of sentiment—but they are all that I have left. If ever I am allowed to run my machine again, I would like to go back to those times.

I liked driving with him to bed-and-breakfasts up in New Hampshire in the fall to pick apples. I liked making simple dishes from a book of recipes and seeing that silly grin on his face. I liked waking up next to him in the mornings and feeling happy that I was a woman. I liked that he could argue passionately with me and hold his ground when he was right and back down gracefully when he was wrong. I liked that he always took my side whenever I was in an argument with others and backed me up to the hilt, even when he thought I was wrong.

But the best part was when he talked to me about the history of Japan.

Actually, he gave me an interest in Japan that I never had. Growing up, whenever people found out that I was Japanese, they assumed that I would be interested in anime, love karaoke, and giggle into my cupped hands, and the boys, in particular, thought I would act out their Oriental sex fantasies. It was tiring. As a teenager, I rebelled by refusing to do anything that seemed "Japanese," including speaking Japanese at home. Just imagine how my poor parents felt.

Evan told the history of Japan to me not as a recitation of dates or myths, but as an illustration of scientific principles embedded in humanity. He showed me that the history of Japan is not a story about emperors and generals, poets and monks. Rather, the history of Japan is a model demonstrating the way all human societies grow and adapt to the natural world as the environment, in turn, adapts to their presence.

As hunter-gatherers, the ancient Jōmon Japanese were the top predators in their environment; as self-sufficient agriculturalists, the Japanese of the Nara and Heian periods began to shape and cultivate the ecology of Japan into a human-centric symbiotic biota, a process that wasn't completed until the intensive agriculture and population growth that came with feudal Japan; finally, as industrialists and entrepreneurs, the people of Imperial Japan began to exploit not merely the living biota, but also the dead biota of the past: the drive for reliable sources of fossil fuels would dominate the history of modern Japan, as it has the rest of the modern world. We are all now exploiters of the dead.

Clearing away the superficial structure of the reigns of emperors and the dates of battles, there was the deeper rhythm of history's ebb and flow not as the deeds of great men, but as lives lived by ordinary men and women wading through the currents of the natural world around them: its geology, its seasons, its climate and ecology, the abundance and scarcity of the raw material for life. It was the kind of history that a physicist could love.

Japan was at once universal and unique. Evan made me aware of the connection between me and the people who have called themselves Japanese for millennia.

Yet, history was not merely deep patterns and the long now. There was also a time and a place where individuals could leave an extraordinary impact. Evan's specialty was the Heian Period, he told me, because that was when Japan first became *Japan*. A courtly elite of at most a few thousand people transformed continental influences into a uniquely native, Japanese aesthetic ideal that would reverberate throughout the centuries and define what it meant to be Japanese until the present day. Unique among the world's ancient cultures, the high culture of Heian Japan was made as much by women as by men. It was a golden age as lovely as it was implausible, unrepeatable. That was the kind of surprise that made Evan love history.

Inspired, I took a Japanese history class and asked my father to teach me calligraphy. I took a new interest in advanced Japanese language classes, and I learned to write *tanka*, the clean, minimalist Japanese poems that follow strict, mathematical metrical requirements. When I was finally satisfied with my first attempt, I was so happy, and I'm certain that I did, for a moment, feel what Murasaki Shikibu felt when she completed her first *tanka*. More than a millennium in time and more than ten thousand miles in space separated us, but there, in that moment, we would surely have understood each other.

Evan made me proud to be Japanese, and so he made me love myself. That was how I knew I was really in love with him.

Li Jianjian, Manager, Tianjin Sony Store:

The War has been over for a long time, and at some point you have to move on. What is the point of digging up memories like this now? Japanese investment in China has been very important for jobs, and all the young people in China like Japanese culture. I don't like it that Japan does not want to apologize, but what can we do? If we dwell on it, then only we will be angry and sad.

Song Yuanwu, waitress:

I read about it in the newspapers. That Dr. Wei is not Chinese; he's an American. The Chinese all know about Unit 731, so it's not news to us.

I don't want to think about it much. Some stupid young people shout about how we should boycott Japanese goods, but then they can't wait to buy the next issue of manga. Why should I listen to them? This just upsets people without accomplishing anything.

Name withheld, executive:

Truth be told, the people who were killed there in Harbin were mostly peasants, and they died like weeds during that time all over China. Bad things happen in wars, that's all.

What I'm going to say will make everyone hate me, but many people also died during the Three Years of Natural Disasters under the Chairman and then during the Cultural Revolution. The War is sad, but it is just one sadness among many for the Chinese. The bulk of China's sorrow lies unmourned. That Dr. Wei is a stupid troublemaker. You can't eat, drink, or wear memories.

Nie Liang and Fang Rui, college students:

Nie: I'm glad that Wei did his work. Japan has never faced up to its history. Every Chinese knows that these things happened, but Westerners don't, and they don't care. Maybe now that they know the truth they'll put pressure on Japan to apologize.

Fang: Be careful, Nie. When Westerners see this, they are going to call you a *fenqing* and a brainwashed nationalist. They like Japan in the West. China, not so much. The Westerners don't want to understand China. Maybe they just can't. We have nothing to say to these journalists. They won't believe us, anyway.

Sun Maying, office worker:

I don't know who Wei is, and I don't care.

Akemi Kirino:

Evan and I wanted to go see a movie that night. The romantic comedy we wanted was sold out, and so we chose the movie with the next earliest start time. It was called *Philosophy of a Knife*. Neither of us had heard of it. We just wanted to spend some time together.

Our lives are ruled by these small, seemingly ordinary moments that turn out to have improbably large effects. Such randomness is much more common in human affairs than in nature, and there was no way that I, as a physicist, could have foreseen what happened next.

Scenes from Andrey Iskanov's Philosophy of a Knife *are shown as Dr. Kirino speaks.*

The movie was a graphical portrayal of the activities of Unit 731, with many of the experiments reenacted. "God created heaven, men created hell" was the tagline.

Neither of us could get up at the end of it. "I didn't know," Evan murmured to me. "I'm sorry. I didn't know."

He was not apologizing for taking me to the movie. Instead, he was consumed by guilt because he had not known about the horrors committed by Unit 731. He had never encountered it in his classes or in his research. Because his grandparents had taken refuge in Shanghai during the War, no one in his family was directly affected.

But due to their employment with the puppet government in Japanese-occupied Shanghai, his grandparents were later labeled collaborationists after the War, and their harsh treatment at the hands of the government of the People's Republic eventually caused his family to flee for the United States. And so the War shaped Evan's life, as it has shaped the lives of all Chinese, even if he was not aware of all its ramifications.

For Evan, ignorance of history, a history that determined who he was in many ways, was a sin in itself.

"It's just a film," our friends told him. "Fiction."

But in that moment, history as he understood it ended for Evan. The distance he had once maintained, the abstractions of history at a grand scale, which had so delighted him before, lost meaning to him in the bloody scenes on the screen.

He began to dig into the truth behind the film, and it soon consumed all his waking moments. He became obsessed with the activities of Unit 731. It became his waking life and his nightmare. For him, his ignorance of those horrors was simultaneously a rebuke and a call to arms. He could not let the victims' suffering be forgotten. He would not allow their torturers to get away.

That was when I explained to him the possibilities presented by Bohm-Kirino particles.

Evan believed that time travel would make people care.

When Darfur was merely a name on a distant continent, it was possible to ignore the deaths and atrocities. But what if your neighbors came to you and told you of what they had seen in their travels to Darfur? What if the victims' relatives showed up at the door to recount their memories in that land? Could you still ignore it?

Evan believed that something similar would happen with time travel. If people could see and hear the past, then it would no longer be possible to remain apathetic.

Excerpts from the televised hearing before the Subcommittee
on Asia, the Pacific, and the Global Environment of the
Committee on Foreign Affairs, House of Representatives, 11Xth
Congress, courtesy of C-SPAN

Testimony of Lillian C. Chang-Wyeth, witness:
Mr. Chairman and Members of the Subcommittee, thank you for giving me the opportunity to testify here today. I would also like to

thank Dr. Wei and Dr. Kirino, whose work has made my presence here today possible.

I was born on January 5, 1962, in Hong Kong. My father, Jaiyi "Jimmy" Chang, had come to Hong Kong from mainland China after World War Two. There, he became a successful merchant of men's shirts and married my mother. Each year we celebrated my birthday one day early. When I asked my mother why we did this, she said that it had something to do with the War.

As a little girl, I didn't know much about my father's life before I was born. I knew that he had grown up in Japanese-occupied Manchuria, that his whole family was killed by the Japanese, and that he was rescued by Communist guerrillas. But he did not tell me any details.

Only once did Father talk to me directly about his life during the War. It was the summer before I went to college, in 1980. A traditionalist, he held a *jìjīlì* ceremony for me where I would pick my *biǎozì*, or courtesy name. That is the name young Chinese people traditionally chose for themselves when they came of age and by which they would be known by their peers. It wasn't something that most Chinese, even the Hong Kong Chinese, did anymore.

We prayed together, bowing before the shrine to our ancestors, and I lit my joss sticks and placed them in the bronze incense brazier in the courtyard. For the first time in my life, instead of me pouring tea for him, my father poured tea for *me*. We lifted our cups and drank tea together, and my father told me how proud he was of me.

I put down the teacup and asked him which of my older female relatives he most admired so that I might choose a name that would honor her memory. That was when he showed me the only photograph he had of his family. I have brought it here today and would like to enter it into the record.

This picture was taken in 1940 on the occasion of my father's tenth birthday. The family lived in Sanjiajiao, a village about twenty kilometers from Harbin, where they went to take this portrait in a studio. In this picture you can see my grandparents sitting together in the center. My father is standing next to my grandfather, and here, next to my grandmother, is my aunt, Changyi (暢怡). Her name means "smooth happiness." Until my father showed me this picture, I did not know that I had an aunt.

My aunt was not a pretty girl. You can see that she was born with a large, dark birthmark shaped like a bat on her face that disfigured her. Like most girls in her village, she never went to school and was illiterate. But she was very gentle and kind and clever, and she did all of the cooking and cleaning in the house starting at the age of eight. My grandparents worked in the fields all day, and as the big sister, Changyi was like a mother to my father. She bathed him, fed him, changed his swaddling clothes, played with him, and protected him from the other kids in the village. At the time this picture was taken, she was sixteen.

What happened to her? I asked my father.

She was taken, he said. The Japanese came to our village on January 5, 1941, because they wanted to make an example of it so that other villages would not dare to support the guerrillas. I was eleven at the time and Changyi was seventeen. My parents told me to hide in the hole under the granary. After the soldiers bayoneted our parents, I saw them drag Changyi to a truck and drive her away.

Where was she taken?

They said they were taking her to a place called Pingfang, south of Harbin.

What kind of place was it?

Nobody knew. At the time the Japanese said the place was a lumber mill. But trains passing by there had to pull down their curtains, and the Japanese evicted all the villages nearby and patrolled the area heavily. The guerrillas who saved me thought it was probably a weapons depot or a headquarters building for important Japanese generals. I think maybe she was taken there to serve as a sex slave for the Japanese soldiers. I do not know if she survived.

And so I picked my *biǎozì* to be Changyi (長憶) to honor my aunt, who was like a mother to my father. My name sounds like hers but it is written with different characters, and instead of "smooth happiness," it means "long remembrance." We prayed that she had survived the War and was still alive in Manchuria.

The next year, in 1981, the Japanese author Morimura Seiichi published *The Devil's Gluttony*, which was the first Japanese publication ever to talk about the history of Unit 731. I read the Chinese translation of the book, and the name Pingfang suddenly took on a different meaning. For years, I had nightmares about what happened to my aunt.

My father died in 2002. Before his death, he asked that if I ever found out for sure what happened to my aunt, I should let him know when I made my annual visit to his grave. I promised him that I would.

This is why, a decade later, I volunteered to undertake the journey when Dr. Wei offered this opportunity. I wanted to know what happened to my aunt. I hoped against hope that she had survived and escaped, even though I knew there were no Unit 731 survivors.

Chung-Nian Shih, Director, Department of Archaeology, National Independent University of Taiwan:

I was one of the first to question Evan's decision to prioritize sending volunteers who are relatives of the victims of Unit 731 rather than professional historians or journalists. I understand that he wanted to bring peace to the victims' families, but it also meant large segments of history were consumed in private grief and are now lost forever to the world. His technique, as you know, is destructive. Once he has sent an observer to a particular place at a particular time, the

Bohm-Kirino particles are gone, and no one can ever go back there again.

There are moral arguments for and against his choice: is the suffering of the victims above all a private pain? Or should it primarily be seen as a part of our shared history?

It's one of the central paradoxes of archaeology that in order to excavate a site so as to study it, we must consume it and destroy it in that process. Within the profession we are always debating over whether it's better to excavate a site now or to preserve it *in situ* until less destructive techniques could be developed. But without such destructive excavations, how can new techniques be developed?

Perhaps Evan should also have waited until they developed a way to record the past without erasing it in the process. But by then it may have been too late for the families of the victims, who would benefit from those memories the most. Evan was forever struggling with the competing claims between the past and the present.

Lillian C. Chang-Wyeth:

I took my first trip five years ago, just as Dr. Wei first began to send people back.

I went to January 6, 1941, the day after my aunt was captured.

I arrived on a field surrounded by a complex of brick buildings. It was very cold. I don't know exactly how cold, but Harbin in January usually stayed far below zero degrees Fahrenheit. Dr. Wei had taught me how to move with my mind only, but it was still shocking to suddenly find yourself in a place with no physical presence while feeling everything, a ghost. I was still getting used to moving around when I heard a loud *whack, whack* sound behind me.

I turned around and saw a line of Chinese prisoners standing in the field. They were chained together by their legs and wore just a thin layer of rags. But what struck me was that their arms were left bare, and they held them out in the freezing wind.

A Japanese officer walked in front of them, striking their frozen arms with a short stick. *Whack, whack.*

Interview with Shiro Yamagata, former member of Unit 731, courtesy of Nippon Broadcasting Co.

[*Yamagata and his wife sit on chairs behind a long folding table. He is in his nineties. His hands are folded in front of him on the table, as are his wife's. He keeps his face placid and does not engage in any histrionics. His voice is frail but clear underneath that of the translator's.*]

We marched the prisoners outside with bare arms so that the arms would freeze solid quicker in the Manchurian air. It was very cold, and I did not like the times when it was my duty to march them out.

We sprayed the prisoners with water to create frostbite quicker. To make sure that the arms have been frozen solid, we would hit them with a short stick. If we heard a crisp *whack*, it meant that the arms were frozen all the way through and ready for the experiments. It sounded like whacking against a piece of wood.

I thought that was why we called the prisoners *maruta*, wood logs. *Hey, how many logs did you saw today?* We'd joke with each other. *Not many, just three small logs.*

We performed those experiments to study the effects of frostbite and extreme temperatures on the human body. They were valuable. We learned that the best way to treat frostbite is to immerse the limb in warm water, not rubbing it. It probably saved many Japanese soldiers' lives. We also observed the effects of gangrene and disease as the frozen limbs died on the prisoners.

I heard that there were experiments where we increased the pressure in an airtight room until the person inside exploded, but I did not personally witness them.

I was one of a group of medical assistants who arrived in January 1941. In order to practice our surgery techniques, we performed amputations and other surgery on the prisoners. We used both healthy prisoners and prisoners from the frostbite experiments. When all the limbs had been amputated, the survivors were used to test biological weapons.

Once, two of my friends amputated a man's arms and reattached them to opposite sides of his body. I watched but did not participate. I did not think it was a useful experiment.

Lillian C. Chang-Wyeth:

I followed the line of prisoners into the compound. I walked around to see if I could find my aunt.

I was very lucky, and after only about half an hour, I found where the women prisoners were kept. But when I looked through all the cells, I did not see a woman that looked like my aunt. I then continued walking around aimlessly, looking into all the rooms. I saw many specimen jars with preserved body parts. I remember that in one of the rooms I saw a very tall jar in which one half of a person's body, cleaved vertically in half, was floating.

Eventually, I came to an operating room filled with young Japanese doctors. I heard a woman scream, and I went in. One doctor was raping a Chinese woman on the operating table. There were several other Chinese women in the room, all of them naked and they were holding the woman on the table down so that the Japanese doctor could focus on the rape.

The other doctors looked on and spoke in a friendly manner with each other. One of them said something, and everybody laughed, including the doctor who was raping the woman on the table. I looked at the women who were holding her down and saw that one of them had a bat-shaped birthmark that covered half of her face. She was talking to the woman on the table, trying to comfort her.

What truly shocked me wasn't the fact that she was naked, or what was happening. It was the fact that she looked so young. Seventeen, she was a year younger than I was when I left for college. Except for the birthmark, she looked just like me from back then, and just like my daughter.

[*She stops*]

Representative Kotler: Ms. Chang, would you like to take a break? I'm sure the Subcommittee would understand—

Lillian C. Chang-Wyeth: No, thank you. I'm sorry. Please let me continue.

After the first doctor was done, the woman on the table was brought away. The group of doctors laughed and joked amongst themselves. In a few minutes two soldiers returned with a naked Chinese man walking between them. The first doctor pointed to my aunt, and the other women pushed her onto the table without speaking. She did not resist.

The doctor then pointed to the Chinese man and gestured toward my aunt. The man did not at first understand what was wanted of him. The doctor said something, and the two soldiers prodded the man with their bayonets, making him jump. My aunt looked up at him.

They want you to fuck me, she said.

Shiro Yamagata:

Sometimes we took turns raping the women and girls. Many of us had not ever been with a woman or seen a live woman's organs. It was a kind of sex education.

One of the problems the army faced was venereal disease. The military doctors examined the comfort women weekly and gave them shots, but the soldiers would rape the Russian and Chinese women and got infected all the time. We needed to understand better the development of syphilis, in particular, and to devise treatments.

In order to do so, we would inject some prisoners with syphilis and make the prisoners have sex with each other so that they could be infected the regular way. Of course we would not then touch these infected women. We could then study the effects of the disease on body organs. It was all research that had not been done before.

Lillian C. Chang-Wyeth:

The second time I went back was a year later, and this time I went back to June 8, 1941, about five months after my aunt's capture. I thought that if I picked a date much later my aunt might have already been killed. Dr. Wei was facing a lot of opposition, and he was concerned that taking too many trips to the era would destroy too much of the evidence. He explained that it would have to be my last trip.

I found my aunt in a cell by herself. She was very thin, and I saw that her palms were covered with a rash, and there were bumps around her neck from inflamed lymph nodes. I could also tell that she was pregnant. She must have been very sick because she was lying on the floor, her eyes open and making a light moan—*"aiya, aiya"*—the whole time I was with her.

I stayed with her all day, watching her. I kept on trying to comfort her, but of course she couldn't hear me or feel my touch. The words were for my benefit, not hers. I sang a song for her, a song that my father used to sing to me when I was little:

萬里長城萬里長，長城外面是故鄉
高粱肥，大豆香，遍地黃金少災殃。

The Great Wall is ten thousand li *long, on the other side is my*
hometown
Rich sorghum, sweet soybeans, happiness spreads like gold on
the ground.

I was getting to know her and saying good-bye to her at the same time.

Shiro Yamagata:

To study the progress of syphilis and other venereal diseases, we would vivisect the women at various intervals after they were infected. It was important to understand the effects of the disease on living organs, and vivisection also provided valuable surgical practice. The vivisection was sometimes done with chloroform, sometimes not. We usually vivisected the subjects for the anthrax and cholera experiments without use of anesthesia since anesthesia might have affected the results, and it was felt that the same would be true with the women with syphilis.

I do not remember how many women I vivisected.

Some of the women were very brave, and would lie down on the table without being forced. I learned to say, "*bútòng, bútòng*" or "it won't hurt" in Chinese to calm them down. We would then tie them to the table.

Usually the first incision, from thorax to stomach, would cause the women to scream horribly. Some of them would keep on screaming for a long while during the vivisection. We used gags later because the screaming interfered with discussion during the vivisections. Generally the women stayed alive until we cut open the heart, and so we saved that for last.

I remember once vivisecting a woman who was pregnant. We did not use chloroform initially, but then she begged us, "Please kill me, but do not kill my child." We then used chloroform to put her under before finishing her.

None of us had seen a pregnant woman's insides before, and it was very informative. I thought about keeping the fetus for some experiment, but it was too weak and died soon after being removed.

We tried to guess whether the fetus was from the seed of a Japanese doctor or one of the Chinese prisoners, and I think most of us agreed in the end that it was probably one of the prisoners due to the ugliness of the fetus.

I believed that the work we did on the women was very valuable and gained us many insights.

I did not think that the work we did at Unit 731 was particularly strange. After 1941, I was assigned to northern China, first in Hebei Province and then in Shanxi Province. In army hospitals, we military doctors regularly scheduled surgery practice sessions with live Chinese subjects. The army would provide the subjects on the announced days. We practiced amputations, cutting out sections of intestines and suturing together the remaining sections, and removing various internal organs.

Often the practice surgeries were done without anesthesia to simulate battlefield conditions. Sometimes a doctor would shoot a prisoner in the stomach to simulate war wounds for us to practice on. After the surgeries, one of the officers would behead the Chinese subject or strangle him. Sometimes vivisections were also used as anatomy lessons for the younger trainees and to give them a thrill. It was important for the army to produce good surgeons quickly, so that we could help the soldiers.

"John," last name withheld, high school teacher, Perth, Australia:
You know old people are very lonely, so when they want attention, they'll say anything. They would confess to these ridiculous made-up stories about what they did. It's really sad. I'm sure I can find some old Australian soldier who'll confess to cutting up some abo woman if you put out an ad asking about it. The people who tell these stories just want attention, like those Korean prostitutes who claim to have been kidnapped by the Japanese Army during the War.

Patty Ashby, homemaker, Milwaukee, Wisconsin:

I think it's hard to judge someone if you weren't there. It was during the War, and bad things happen during wars. The Christian thing to do is to forget and forgive. Dragging up things like this is uncharitable. And it's wrong to mess with time like that. Nothing good can come of it.

Sharon, actress, New York, New York:

You know, the thing is that the Chinese have been very cruel to dogs, and they even eat dogs. They have also been very mean to the Tibetans. So it makes you think, was it karma?

Shiro Yamagata:

On August 15, 1945, we heard that the Emperor had surrendered to America. Like many other Japanese in China at that time, my unit decided that it was easier to surrender to the Chinese Nationalists. My unit was then reformed and drafted into a unit of the Nationalist Army under Chiang Kai-Shek, and I continued to work as an army doctor assisting the Nationalists against the Communists in the Chinese Civil War. As the Chinese had almost no qualified surgeons, my work was very much needed, and I was treated well.

The Nationalists were no match for the Communists, however, and in January, 1949, the Communists captured the army field hospital I was staffed in and took me prisoner. For the first month, we were not allowed to leave our cells. I tried to make friends with the guards. The Communists soldiers were very young and thin, but they seemed to be in much better spirits than their Nationalist counterparts.

After a month, we, along with the guards, were given daily lessons on Marxism and Maoism.

The War was not my fault and I was not to be blamed, I was told. I was just a soldier, deceived by the Shōwa Emperor and Hideki Tōjō into fighting a war of invasion and oppression against the Chinese. Through studying Marxism, I was told, I would come to understand that all poor men, the Chinese and Japanese alike, were brothers. We were expected to reflect on what we did to the Chinese people and to write confessions about the crimes we committed during the War. Our punishment would be lessened, we were told, if our confessions showed sincere hearts. I wrote confessions, but they were always rejected for not being sincere enough.

Still, because I was a doctor, I was allowed to work at the provincial hospital to treat patients. I was the most senior surgeon at the hospital and had my own staff.

We heard rumors that a new war was about to start between the United States and China in Korea. *How could China win against the United States?* I thought. *Even the mighty Japanese Army could not stand against America. Perhaps I will be captured by the Americans next.* I suppose I was never very good at predicting the outcomes of wars.

Food became scarce after the Korean War began. The guards ate rice with scallions and wild weeds, while prisoners like me were given rice and fish.

Why is this? I asked.

You are prisoners, my guard, who was only sixteen, said. You are from Japan. Japan is a wealthy country, and you must be treated in a manner that matched as closely as possible the conditions in your home country.

I offered the guard my fish, and he refused.

You do not want to touch the food that had been touched by a Japanese Devil? I joked with him. I was also teaching him how to read, and he would sneak me cigarettes.

I was a very good surgeon, and I was proud of my work. Sometimes I felt that despite the War, I was doing China a great deal of good, and I helped many patients with my skills.

One day, a woman came to see me in the hospital. She had broken her leg, and because she lived far from the hospital, by the time her family brought her to me, gangrene had set in, and the leg had to be amputated.

She was on the table, and I was getting ready to administer anesthesia. I looked into her eyes, trying to calm her. *"Bútòng, bútòng."*

Her eyes became very wide, and she screamed. She screamed and screamed, and scrambled off the table, dragging her dead leg with her until she was as far away from me as possible.

I recognized her then. She had been one of the Chinese girl prisoners that we had trained to help us as nurses at the army hospital during the War with China. She had helped me with some of the practice surgery sessions. I had slept with her a few times. I didn't know her name. She was just "#4" to me, and some of the younger doctors had joked about cutting her open if Japan lost and we had to retreat.

[Interviewer (off-camera): Mr. Yamagata, you cannot cry. You know that. We cannot show you being emotional on film. We have to stop if you cannot control yourself.]

I was filled with unspeakable grief. It was only then that I understood what kind of a life and career I had. Because I wanted to be a successful doctor, I did things that no human being should do. I wrote my confession then, and when my guard read my confession, he would not speak to me.

I served my sentence and was released and allowed to return to Japan in 1956.

I felt lost. Everyone was working so hard in Japan. But I didn't know what to do.

"You should not have confessed to anything," one of my friends, who was in the same unit with me, told me. "I didn't, and they released me years ago. I have a good job now. My son is going to be a doctor. Don't say anything about what happened during the War."

I moved here to Hokkaido to be a farmer, as far away from the heart of Japan as possible. For all these years I stayed silent to protect my friend. And I believed that I would die before him and so take my secret to the grave.

But my friend is now dead, and so, even though I have not said anything about what I did all these years, I will not stop speaking now.

Lillian C. Chang-Wyeth:

I am speaking only for myself, and perhaps for my aunt. I am the last connection between her and the living world. And I am turning into an old woman myself.

I don't know much about politics, and don't care much for it. I have told you what I saw, and I will remember the way my aunt cried in that cell until the day I die.

You ask me what I want. I don't know how to answer that.

Some have said that I should demand that the surviving members of Unit 731 be brought to justice. But what does that mean? I am no longer a child. I do not want to see trials, parades, spectacles. The law does not give you real justice.

What I really want is for what I saw to never have happened. But no one can give me that. And so I resort to wanting to have my aunt's story remembered, to have the guilt of her killers and torturers laid bare to the gaze of the world, the way that they laid her bare to their needle and scalpel.

I do not know how to describe those acts other than as crimes against humanity. They were denials against the very idea of life itself.

The Japanese government has never acknowledged the actions of Unit 731, and it has never apologized for them. Over the years, more and more evidence of the atrocities committed during those years have come to life, but always the answer is the same: there is not enough evidence to know what happened.

Well, now there is. I have seen what happened with my own eyes. And I will speak about what happened, speak out against the denialists. I will tell my story as often as I can.

The men and women of Unit 731 committed those acts in the name of Japan and the Japanese people. I demand that the government of Japan acknowledge these crimes against humanity, that it apologize for them, and that it commit to preserving the memory of the victims and condemning the guilt of those criminals so long as the word *justice* still has meaning.

I am also sorry to say, Mr. Chairman and Members of the Subcommittee, that the government of the United States has also never acknowledged or apologized for its role in shielding these criminals from justice after the War or in making use of the information bought at the expense of torture, rape, and death. I demand that the government of the United States acknowledge and apologize for these acts.

That is all.

Representative Hogart:

I would like to again remind members of the public that they must maintain order and decorum during this hearing or risk being forcibly removed from this room.

Ms. Chang-Wyeth, I am sorry for whatever it is you think you have experienced. I have no doubt that it has deeply affected you. I thank the other witnesses as well for sharing their stories.

Mr. Chairman, and Members of the Subcommittee, I must again note for the record my objection to this hearing and to the resolution that has been proposed by my colleague, Representative Kotler.

The Second World War was an extraordinary time during which the ordinary rules of human conduct did not apply, and there is no doubt that terrible events occurred and terrible suffering resulted. But whatever happened—and we have no definitive proof of anything other than the results of some sensational high-energy physics that no one present, other than Dr. Kirino herself, understands—it would be a mistake for us to become slaves to history, and to subject the present to the control of the past.

The Japan of today is the most important ally of the United States in the Pacific, if not the world, while the People's Republic of China takes daily steps to challenge our interests in the region. Japan is vital in our efforts to contain and confront the Chinese threat.

It is ill-advised at best, and counterproductive at worst, for Representative Kotler to introduce his resolution at this time. The resolution will no doubt embarrass and dishearten our ally and give encouragement and comfort to our challengers at a time when we cannot afford to indulge in theatrical sentiments, premised upon stories told by emotional witnesses who may have been experiencing "illusions," and I am quoting the words of Dr. Kirino, the creator of the technology involved.

Again, I must call upon the Subcommittee to stop this destructive, useless process.

Representative Kotler:

Mr. Chairman, and Members of the Subcommittee, thank you for giving me the chance to respond to Representative Hogart.

It's easy to hide behind intransitive verbal formulations like "terrible events occurred" and "suffering resulted." And I am sorry to hear my honored colleague, a member of the United States Congress, engage in the same shameful tactics of denial and evasion employed by those who denied that the Holocaust was real.

Every successive Japanese government, with the encouragement and complicity of the successive administrations in this country, has refused to even acknowledge, let alone apologize for, the activities of Unit 731. In fact, for many years, the Unit's very existence was unacknowledged. These denials and refusals to face Japanese atrocities committed during the Second World War form a pattern of playing-down and denial of the war record, whether we are talking about the so-called "comfort women," The Nanjing Massacre, or the forced slave laborers of Korea and China. This pattern has harmed the relationship of Japan with its Asian neighbors.

The issue of Unit 731 presents its unique challenges. Here, the United States is not an uninterested third party. As an ally and close friend of Japan, it is the duty of the United States to point out where our friend has erred. But more than that, the United States played an active role in helping the perpetrators of the crimes of Unit 731 escape justice. General MacArthur granted the men of Unit 731 immunity to get their experimental data. We are in part responsible for the denials and the cover-ups because we valued the tainted fruits of those atrocities more than we valued our own integrity. We have sinned as well.

What I want to emphasize is that Representative Hogart has misunderstood the resolution. What the witnesses and I are asking for, Mr. Chairman, is not some admission of guilt by the present government of Japan or its people. What we are asking for is a declaration from this body that it is the belief of the United States Congress that the victims of Unit 731 should be honored and remembered, and that the perpetrators of these heinous crimes be condemned. There is no bill of attainder here, no corruption of blood. We are not calling on Japan to pay compensation. All we are asking for is a commitment to truth, a commitment to remember.

Like memorials to the Holocaust, the value of such a declaration is simply a public affirmation of our common bond of humanity with the victims and our unity in standing against the ideology of evil and barbarity of the Unit 731 butchers and the Japanese militarist society that permitted and ordered such evil.

Now, I want to make it clear that "Japan" is not a monolithic thing, and it is not just the Japanese government. Individual Japanese citizens have done heroic work in bringing these atrocities to light throughout the years, almost always against government resistance and against the public's wish to forget and move on. And I offer them my heartfelt thanks.

The truth cannot be brushed away, and the families of the victims and the people of China should not be told that justice is not possible, that because their present government is repugnant to the government of the United States, that a great injustice should be covered up and hidden from the judgment of the world. Is there any doubt that this *nonbinding* resolution, or even much more stringent versions of it, would have passed without trouble if the victims were a people whose government has the favor of the United States? If we, for "strategic" reasons, sacrifice the truth in the name of gaining something of value for short-term advantage, then we will have simply repeated the errors of our forefathers at the end of the War.

It is not who we are. Dr. Wei has offered us a way to speak the truth about the past, and we must ask the government of Japan and our government to stand up and take up our collective responsibility to history.

Li Ruming, Director of the Department of History, Zhejiang University, the People's Republic of China:

When I was finishing my doctorate in Boston, Evan and Akemi often had my wife and me over to their place. They were very friendly and helpful and made us feel the enthusiasm and warmth that America is rightly famous for. Unlike many Chinese Americans I met, Evan did not give off a sense that he felt he was superior to the Chinese from the mainland. It was wonderful to have him and Akemi as lifelong friends and not have every interaction between us filtered through the lens of the politics between our two countries, as is so often the case between Chinese and American scholars.

Because I am his friend and I am also Chinese, it is difficult for me to speak about Evan's work with objectivity, but I will try my best.

When Evan first announced his intention to go to Harbin and try to travel to the past, the Chinese government was cautiously support-ive. As none of it had been tried before, the full implications of Evan's destructive process for time travel were not yet clear. Due to destruc-tion of evidence at the end of the War and continuing stonewalling by the Japanese government, we do not have access to large archives of documentary evidence and artifacts from Unit 731, and it was felt that Evan's work would help fill in the gap by providing firsthand accounts of what happened. The Chinese government granted Evan and Akemi visas under the assumption that their work would help promote West-ern understanding of China's historical disputes with Japan.

But they wanted to monitor his work. The War is deeply emo-tional for my compatriots, its unhealed wounds exacerbated by years of postwar disputes with Japan, and as such, it was not politically feasi-ble for the government to not be involved. World War Two was not the distant past, involving ancient peoples, and China could not permit two foreigners to go traipsing through that recent history like adven-turers through ancient tombs.

But from Evan's point of view—and I think he was justified in his belief—any support, monitoring, or affiliation with the Chinese govern-ment would have destroyed all credibility for his work in Western eyes.

He thus rejected all offers of Chinese involvement and even called for intervention by American diplomats. This angered many Chinese and alienated him from them. Later, when the Chinese government finally shut down his work after the storm of negative publicity, very few Chinese would speak up for him because they felt that he and Akemi had—perhaps even intentionally—done more damage to China's history and her people. The accusations were unfair, and I'm sorry to say that I do not feel that I did enough to defend his reputation.

Evan's focus throughout his project was both more universal and more atomistic than the people of China. On the one hand, he had an American devotion to the idea of the individual, and his commitment was first and foremost to the individual voice and memory of each victim. On the other hand, he was also trying to transcend nations, to make people all over the world empathize with these victims, condemn their torturers, and affirm the common humanity of us all.

But in that process, he was forced to distance his effort from the Chinese people in order to preserve the political credibility of his project in the West. He sacrificed their goodwill in a bid to make the West care. Evan tried to appease the West and Western prejudices against China. Was it cowardly? Should he have challenged them more? I do not know.

History is not merely a private matter. Even the family members of the victims understand that there is a communitarian aspect to history. The War of Resistance Against the Japanese Invasion is the founding story of modern China, much as the Holocaust is the founding story of Israel and the Revolution and the Civil War are the founding stories of America. Perhaps this is difficult to understand for a Westerner, but to many Chinese, Evan, because he feared and rejected their involvement, was *stealing* and erasing their history. He sacrificed the history of the Chinese people, without their consent, for a Western ideal. I understand why he did it, but I cannot agree that his choice was right.

As a Chinese, I do not share Evan's utter devotion to the idea of a personalized sense of history. Telling the individual stories of all the victims, as Evan sought to do, is not possible and in any event would not solve all problems.

Because of our limited capacity for empathy for mass suffering, I think there's a risk that his approach would result in sentimentality and only selective memory. More than sixteen million civilians died in

China from the Japanese invasion. The great bulk of this suffering did not occur in death factories like Pingfang or killing fields like Nanjing, which grab headlines and shout for our attention; rather, it occurred in the countless quiet villages, towns, remote outposts, where men and women were slaughtered and raped and slaughtered again, their screams fading with the chill wind, until even their names became blanks and forgotten. But they also deserve to be remembered.

It is not possible that every atrocity would find a spokesperson as eloquent as Anne Frank, and I do not believe that we should seek to reduce all of history to a collection of such narratives.

But Evan always told me that an American would rather work on the problem that he could solve rather than wring his hands over the vast realm of problems that he could not.

It was not an easy choice that he made, and I would not have chosen the same way. But Evan was always true to his American ideals.

Bill Pacer, Professor of Modern Chinese Language and Culture, University of Hawaii at Manoa:

It has often been said that since everybody in China knew about Unit 731, Dr. Wei had nothing useful to teach the Chinese and was only an activist campaigning against Japan. That's not quite right. One of the more tragic aspects of the dispute between China and Japan over history is how much their responses have mirrored each other. Wei's goal was to rescue history from both.

In the early days of the People's Republic, between 1945 and 1956, the Communists' overall ideological approach was to treat the Japanese invasion as just another historical stage in mankind's unstoppable march toward socialism. While Japanese militarism was condemned and the Resistance celebrated, the Communists also sought to forgive the Japanese individually if they showed contrition—a surprisingly Christian/Confucian approach for an atheistic regime. In this atmosphere of revolutionary zeal, the Japanese prisoners were treated, for the most part, humanely. They were given Marxist classes and told to write confessions of their crimes. (These classes became the basis for the Japanese public's belief that any man who would confess to horrible crimes during the War must have been brainwashed by the Communists.) Once they were deemed sufficiently reformed through "re-education," They were released back to Japan. Memories of the War were then suppressed in China as the country feverishly moved to build a socialist utopia, with well-known disastrous consequences.

Yet, this generosity toward the Japanese was matched by Stalinist harsh treatment of landowners, capitalists, intellectuals, and the Chinese who collaborated with the Japanese. Hundreds of thousands of people were killed, often on little evidence and with no effort given to observe legal forms.

Later, during the 1990s, the government of the People's Republic began to invoke memories of the War in the context of patriotism to legitimize itself in the wake of the collapse of Communism. Ironically, this obvious ploy prevented large segments of the populace from being able to come to terms with the War—distrust of the government infected everything it touched.

And so the People's Republic's approach to historical memory created a series of connected problems. First, the leniency they showed the prisoners became the ground for denialists to later question the veracity of confessions by Japanese soldiers. Second, yoking patriotism to the memory of the War invited charges that any effort to remember was politically motivated. And lastly, individual victims of the atrocities became symbols, anonymized to serve the needs of the state.

However, it has rarely been acknowledged that behind Japan's postwar silence regarding wartime atrocities lay the same impulses that drove the Chinese responses. On the left, the peace movement attributed all suffering during the War to the concept of war itself and advocated universal forgiveness and peace among all nations without a sense of blame. In the center, focus was placed on material development as a bandage to cover the wounds of the War. On the right, the question of wartime guilt became inextricably yoked to patriotism. In contrast to Germany, which could rely on Nazism—distinct from the nation itself—to absorb the blame, it was impossible to acknowledge the atrocities committed by the Japanese during the War without implicating a sense that Japan itself was under attack.

And so, across a narrow sea, China and Japan unwittingly converged on the same set of responses to the barbarities of World War Two: forgetting in the name of universal ideals like "peace" and "socialism"; welding memories of the War to patriotism; abstracting victims and perpetrators alike into symbols to serve the state. Seen in this light, the abstract, incomplete, fragmentary memories in China and the silence in Japan are flip sides of the same coin.

The core of Wei's belief is that without real memory, there can be no real reconciliation. Without real memory, the individual persons of each nation have not been able to empathize with and remember and experience the suffering of the victims. An individualized story that each of us can tell ourselves about what happened is required before we can move beyond the trap of history. That, all along, was what Wei's project was about.

Crosstalk, January 21, 20XX, courtesy of FXNN

Amy Rowe: Thank you, Ambassador Yoshida and Dr. Wei, for agreeing to come on to *Cross-Talk* tonight. Our viewers want to have their questions answered, and I want to see some fireworks!

Ambassador Yoshida, let's start with you. Why won't Japan apologize?

Yoshida: Amy, Japan has apologized. This is the whole point. Japan has apologized many many times for World War Two. Every few years we have to go through this spectacle where it's said that Japan needs to apologize for its actions during World War Two. But Japan has done so, repeatedly. Let me read you a few quotes.

This is from a statement by Prime Minister Tomiichi Murayama, on August 31, 1994. "Japan's actions in a certain period of the past not only claimed numerous victims here in Japan but also left the peoples of neighboring Asia and elsewhere with scars that are painful even today. I am thus taking this opportunity to state my belief, based on my profound remorse for these acts of aggression, colonial rule, and the like caused such unbearable suffering and sorrow for so many people, that Japan's future path should be one of making every effort to build world peace in line with my no-war commitment. It is imperative for us Japanese to look squarely to our history with the peoples of neighboring Asia and elsewhere."

And again, from a statement by the Diet, on June 9, 1995: "On the occasion of the 50th anniversary of the end of World War II, this House offers its sincere condolences to those who fell in action and victims of wars and similar actions all over the world. Solemnly reflecting upon many instances of colonial rule and acts of aggression in the modern history of the world, and recognizing that Japan carried out those acts in the past, inflicting pain and suffering upon the peoples of other countries, especially in Asia, the Members of this House express a sense of deep remorse."

I can go on and read you dozens of other quotes like this. Japan *has* apologized, Amy.

Yet, every few years, the propaganda organs of certain regimes hostile to a free and prosperous Japan try to dredge up settled historical events to manufacture controversy. When is this going to end? And some men of otherwise good intellect have allowed themselves to become the tools of propaganda. I wish they would wake up and see how they are being used.

Rowe: Dr. Wei, I have to say, those do sound like apologies to me.

Wei: Amy, it is not my aim or goal to humiliate Japan. My commitment is to the victims and their memory, not theater. What I'm asking for is for Japan to acknowledge the truth of what happened at Pingfang. I want to focus on specifics, and acknowledgment of specifics, not empty platitudes.

But since Ambassador Yoshida has decided to bring up the issue of apologies, let's look closer at them, shall we?

The statements quoted by the ambassador are grand and abstract, and they refer to vague and unspecified sufferings. They are apologies only in the most watered-down sense. What the ambassador is not telling you is the Japanese government's continuing refusal to admit many specific war crimes and to honor and remember the real victims.

Moreover, every time one of these statements quoted by the ambassador is made, it is matched soon after by another statement from a prominent Japanese politician purporting to cast doubt upon what happened in World War Two. Year after year, we are treated to this show of the Japanese government as a Janus speaking with two faces.

Yoshida: It's not that unusual to have differences of opinion when it comes to matters of history, Dr. Wei. In a democracy it's what you would expect.

Wei: Actually, Ambassador, Unit 731 *has* been consistently handled by the Japanese government: For more than fifty years the official position was absolute silence regarding Unit 731, despite the steady accumulation of physical evidence, including human remains, from Unit 731's activities. Even the Unit's existence was not admitted until the 1990s, and the government consistently denied that it had researched or used biological weapons during the War.

It wasn't until 2005, in response to a lawsuit by some relatives of Unit 731's victims for compensation, that the Tokyo High Court finally acknowledged Japan's use of biological weapons during the War. This was the first time that an official voice of the Japanese government admitted to that fact. Amy, you'll notice that this was a decade after those lofty statements read by Ambassador Yoshida. The Court denied compensation.

Since then the Japanese government has consistently stated that there is insufficient evidence to confirm exactly what experiments were carried out by Unit 731 or the details of their conduct. Official denial and silence continue despite the dedicated efforts of some Japanese scholars to bring the truth to light.

But numerous former members of Unit 731 have come forward since the 1980s to testify and confess to the grisly acts they committed. And we have confirmed and expanded upon those accounts with new eyewitness accounts by volunteers who have traveled to Pingfang. Everyday, we are finding out more about Unit 731's crimes. We will tell the world all the victims' stories.

Yoshida: I am not sure that "telling stories" is what historians should be doing. If you want to make fiction, go ahead, but do not tell people that it is history. Extraordinary claims require extraordinary proof. And there is insufficient proof for the accusations currently being directed against Japan.

Wei: Ambassador Yoshida, is your position really that nothing happened at Pingfang? Are you saying that these reports by the American occupational authority from immediately after the War are lies? Are you saying that these contemporaneous diary entries by the officers of Unit 731 are lies? Are you really denying all of this?

There is a simple solution to all this. Will you take a trip to Pingfang in 1941? Will you believe your own eyes?

Yoshida: I'm—I am not—I'm making a distinction—It was a time of war, Dr. Wei, and perhaps it is possible that some unfortunate things happened. But "stories" are not evidence.

Wei: Will you take a trip, Ambassador?

Yoshida: I will not. I see no reason to subject myself to your process. I see no reason to undergo your "time travel" hallucinations.

Rowe: Now we are seeing some fireworks!

Wei: Ambassador Yoshida, let me make this clear. The deniers are committing a fresh crime against the victims of those atrocities: Not only would they stand with the torturers and the killers, but they are also engaged in the practice of erasing and silencing the victims from history, to kill them afresh.

In the past, their task was easy. Unless the denials were actively resisted, eventually memories would dim with old age and death, and the voices of the past would fade away, and the denialists would win. The people of the present would then become exploiters of the dead, and that has always been the way history was written.

But we have now come to the end of history. What my wife and I have done is to take narrative away, and to give us all a chance to see the past with our own eyes. In place of memory, we now have incontrovertible evidence. Instead of exploiting the dead, we must look into the face of the dying. *I have seen these crimes with my own eyes.* You cannot deny that.

Archival footage of Dr. Evan Wei delivering the keynote for the Fifth International War Crimes Studies Conference in San Francisco, on November 20, 20XX. Courtesy of the Stanford University Archives

History is a narrative enterprise, and the telling of stories that are true, that affirm and explain our existence, is the fundamental task of the historian. But truth is delicate, and it has many enemies. Perhaps that is why, although we academics are supposedly in the business of pursuing the truth, the word "truth" is rarely uttered without hedges, adornments, and qualifications.

Every time we tell a story about a great atrocity, like the Holocaust or Pingfang, the forces of denial are always ready to pounce, to erase, to silence, to forget. History has always been difficult because of the delicacy of the truth, and denialists have always been able to resort to labeling the truth as fiction.

One has to be careful, whenever one tells a story about a great injustice. We are a species that loves narrative, but we have also been taught not to trust an individual speaker.

Yes, it is true that no nation, and no historian, can tell a story that completely encompasses every aspect of the truth. But it is not true that just because all narratives are constructed, that they are equally far from the truth. The Earth is neither a perfect sphere nor a flat disk, but the model of the sphere is much closer to the truth. Similarly, there are some narratives that are closer to the truth than others, and we must always try to tell a story that comes as close to the truth as is humanly possible.

The fact that we can never have complete, perfect knowledge does not absolve us of the moral duty to judge and to take a stand against evil.

Victor P. Lowenson, Professor of East Asian History, Director of the Institute of East Asian Studies, UC Berkeley:

I have been called a denialist, and I have been called worse. But I am not a Japanese right-winger who believes that Unit 731 is a myth. I do not say that nothing happened there. What I am saying is that, unfortunately, we do not have enough evidence to be able to describe with certainty all that happened there.

I have enormous respect for Wei, and he remains and will remain one of my best students. But in my view, he has abdicated the responsibility of the historian to ensure that the truth is not ensnared in doubt. He has crossed the line that divides a historian from an activist.

As I see it, the fight here isn't ideological, but methodological. What we are fighting over is what constitutes *proof*. Historians trained in Western and Asian traditions have always relied on the documentary record, but Dr. Wei is now raising the primacy of eyewitness accounts, and not even contemporaneous eyewitness accounts, mind you, but accounts by witnesses out of the stream of time.

There are many problems with his approach. We have a great deal of experience from psychology and the law to doubt the reliability of eyewitness accounts. We also have serious concerns with the single-use nature of the Kirino Process, which seems to destroy the very thing it is studying, and erases history even as it purports to allow it to be witnessed. You literally cannot ever go back to a moment of time that has already been experienced—and thus consumed—by another witness. When each eyewitness account is impossible to verify independently of *that* account, how can we rely on such a process to establish the truth of what happened?

I understand that from the perspective of supporters of Dr. Wei, the raw experience of actually seeing history unfold before your eyes makes it impossible to doubt the evidence indelibly etched in your mind. But that is simply not good enough for the rest of us. The Kirino Process requires a leap of faith: Those who have witnessed the ineffable have no doubt of its existence, but that clarity is incapable of being replicated for anyone else. And so we are stuck here, in the present, trying to make sense of the past.

Dr. Wei has ended the process of rational historical inquiry and transformed it into a form of personal religion. What one witness has seen, no one else can ever see. This is madness.

Naoki, last name withheld, clerk:

I have seen the videos of the old soldiers who supposedly confessed to these horrible things. I do not believe them. They cry and act so emotional, as though they are insane. The Communists were great brainwashers, and it is undoubtedly a result of their plot.

I remember one of those old men describing the kindness of his Communist guards. *Kind* Communist guards! If that is not evidence of brainwashing, what is?

Kazue Sato, housewife:

The Chinese are great manufacturers of lies. They have produced fake food, fake Olympics, and fake statistics. Their history is also faked. This Wei is an American, but he is also Chinese, and so we cannot trust anything he does.

Hiroshi Abe, retired soldier:

The soldiers who "confessed" have brought great shame upon their country.

Interviewer: Because of what they did?

Because of what they said.

Ienaga Ito, Professor of Oriental History, Kyoto University:

We live in an age that prizes authenticity and personalized narratives, as embodied in the form of the memoir. Eyewitness accounts have an immediacy and reality that compels belief, and we think they can convey a truth greater than any fiction. Yet, perhaps paradoxically, we are also eager to seize upon any factual deviation and inconsistency in such narratives and declare the entirety to be *mere* fiction. There's an all-or-nothing bleakness to this dynamic. But we should have conceded from the start that narratives are irreducibly subjective, though that does not mean that they do not also convey the truth.

Evan was a greater radical than most people realized. He sought to free the past from the present so that history could not be ignored, put out of our minds, or made to serve the needs of the present. The possibility of witnessing actual history and experiencing that past by all of us means that the past is not past, but alive at this very moment.

What Evan did was to transform historical investigation itself into a form of memoir writing. That kind of emotional experience is important in the way we think about history and make decisions. Culture is not merely a product of reason but also of real, visceral empathy. And I am afraid that it is primarily empathy that has been missing from the postwar Japanese responses to history.

Evan tried to introduce more empathy and emotion into historical inquiry. For this he was crucified by the academic establishment. But adding empathy and the irreducibly subjective dimension of the personal narrative to history does not detract from the truth. It enhances the truth. That we accept our own frailties and subjectivity does not free us to abdicate the moral responsibility to tell the truth, even if, and especially if, "truth" is not singular but a set of shared experiences and shared understandings that together make up our humanity.

Of course, drawing attention to the importance and primacy of eyewitness accounts unleashed a new danger. With a little money and the right equipment, anyone can eliminate the Bohm-Kirino particles from a desired era, in a specified place, and so erase those events from direct experience. Unwittingly, Evan had also invented the technology to end history forever, by denying us and future generations of that emotional experience of the past that he so cherished.

Akemi Kirino:

It was difficult during the years immediately after the Comprehensive Time Travel Moratorium was signed. Evan was denied tenure in a close vote, and that editorial in the *Wall Street Journal* by his old friend and teacher, Victor Lowenson, calling him a "tool of propaganda," deeply hurt him. Then, there were the death threats and harassing phone calls, every day.

But I think it was what they did to me that really got to him. At the height of the attacks from the denialists, the IT division of the Institute asked me if I would mind being delisted from the public faculty directory. Whenever they listed me on the website, the site would be hacked within hours, and the denialists would replace my bio page with pictures where these men, so brave and eloquent, displayed their courage and intellect by illustrating what they would do to me if they had me in their power. And you probably remember the news reports about that night when I walked home alone from work.

I don't really want to dwell on that time, if that's all right with you.

We moved away to Boise, where we tried to hide from the worst of it. We kept a low profile, got an unlisted number, and basically stayed out of sight. Evan went on medication for his depression. On the weekends we went hiking in the Sawtooth Mountains, and Evan took up charting abandoned mining sites and ghost towns from during the gold rush. That was a happy time for us, and I thought he was feeling better. The sojourn in Idaho reminded him that sometimes the world is a kind place, and all is not darkness and denial.

But he was feeling lost. He felt that he was hiding from the truth. I knew that he was feeling torn between his sense of duty to the past and his sense of loyalty to the present, to me.

I could not bear to see him being torn apart, and so I asked if he wanted to return to the fight.

We flew back to Boston, and things had grown even worse. He had sought to end history as mere *history* and to give the past living voices to speak to the present. But it did not work out the way he had intended. The past did come to life, but when faced with it, the present decided to recast history as religion.

The more Evan did, the more he felt he had to do. He would not come to bed, and fell asleep at his desk. He was writing, writing, constantly writing. He believed that he had to single-handedly refute all the lies and take on all his enemies. It was never enough, never enough for him. I stood by, helpless.

"I have to speak for them, because they have no one else," he would tell me.

By then perhaps he was living more in the past than in the present. Even though he no longer had access to our machine, in his mind he relived those trips he took, over and over again. He believed that he had let the victims down.

A great responsibility had been thrust upon him, and he had failed them. He was trying to uncover to the world a great injustice, and yet in the process he seemed to have only stirred up the forces of denial, hate, and silence.

Excerpts from the Economist, *November 26, 20XX*

[*A woman's voice, flat, calm, reads out loud the article text as the camera swoops over the ocean, the beaches, and then the forests and hills of Manchuria. From the shadow of a small plane racing along the ground beneath us we can tell that the camera is shooting from the open door of the airplane. An arm, the hand clenched tight into a fist, moves into the foreground from off-frame. The fingers open. Dark ashes are scattered into the air beneath the airplane.*]

We will soon come upon the ninetieth anniversary of the Mukden Incident, the start of the Japanese invasion of China. To this day, that war remains the alpha and omega of the relationship between the two countries.

. . .

439

[*A series of photographs of the leaders of Unit 731 are shown. The reader's voice fades out and then fades back in.*]

. . .

The men of Unit 731 then moved on to prominent careers in postwar Japan. Three of them founded the Japan Blood Bank (which later became the Green Cross, Japan's largest pharmaceutical company) and used their knowledge of methods for freezing and drying blood derived from human experiments during the War to produce dried-blood products for sale to the United States Army at great profit. General Shiro Ishii, the commander of Unit 731, may have spent some time after the War working in Maryland, researching biological weapons. Papers were published using data obtained from human subjects, including babies (sometimes the word "monkey" was substituted as a cover-up)—and it is possible that medical papers published today still contain citations traceable to these results, making all of us the unwitting beneficiaries of these atrocities.

. . .

[*The reading voice fades out as the sound of the airplane's engine cuts in. The camera shifts to images of clashing protestors waving Japanese flags and Chinese flags, some of the flags on fire.*

Then the voice fades in again.]

. . .

Many inside and outside Japan objected to the testimonies by the surviving members of Unit 731: The men are old, they point out, with failing memories; they may be seeking attention; they may be mentally ill; they may have been brainwashed by the Chinese Communists. Reliance on oral testimony alone is an unwise way to construct a solid historical case. To the Chinese this sounded like more of the same excuses issued by the deniers of the Nanjing Massacre and other Japanese atrocities.

Year after year, history grew as a wall between the two peoples.

[*The camera switches to a montage of pictures of Evan Wei and Akemi Kirino throughout their lives. In the first pictures, they smile for the camera. In later pictures, Kirino's face is tired, withdrawn, impassive. Wei's face is defiant, angry, and then full of despair.*]

Evan Wei, a young Chinese-American specialist on Heian Japan, and Akemi Kirino, a Japanese-American experimental physicist, did not seem like the kind of revolutionary figures who would bring the world to the brink of war. But history has a way of mocking our expectations.

If lack of evidence was the issue, they had a way to provide irrefutable evidence: You could watch history as it occurred, like a play.

The governments of the world went into a frenzy. While Wei sent relatives of the victims of Unit 731 into the past to bear witness to the horrors committed in the operating rooms and prison cells of Pingfang, China and Japan waged a bitter war in courts and in front of cameras, staking out their rival claims to the past. The United States was reluctantly drawn into the fight, and, citing national security reasons, finally shut down Wei's machine when he unveiled plans to investigate the truth of America's alleged use of biological weapons (possibly derived from Unit 731's research) during the Korean War.

Armenians, Jews, Tibetans, Native Americans, Indians, the Kikuyu, the descendants of slaves in the New World—victim groups around the world lined up and demanded use of the machine, some out of fear that their history might be erased by the groups in power, others wishing to use their history for present political gain. As well, the countries who initially advocated access to the machine hesitated when the implications became clear: Did the French wish to relive the depravity of their own people under Vichy France? Did the Chinese want to re-experience the self-inflicted horrors of the Cultural Revolution? Did the British want to see the genocides that lay behind their Empire?

With remarkable alacrity, democracies and dictatorships around the world signed the Comprehensive Time Travel Moratorium while they wrangled over the minutiae of the rules for how to divide up jurisdiction of the past. Everyone, it seemed, preferred not to have to deal with the past just yet.

Wei wrote, "All written history shares one goal: to bring a coherent narrative to a set of historical facts. For far too long we have been mired in controversy over facts. Time travel will make truth as accessible as looking outside the window."

But Wei did not help his case by sending large numbers of Chinese relatives of Unit 731 victims, rather than professional historians, through his machine. (Though it is also fair to ask if things really would have turned out differently had he sent more professional historians. Perhaps accusations would still have been made that the visions were mere fabrications of the machine or historians partisan to his cause.) In any event, the relatives, being untrained observers, did not make great witnesses. They failed to correctly answer observational questions posed by skeptics. ("Did the Japanese doctors wear uniforms with breast pockets?" "How many prisoners in total were in the compound at that time?") They did not understand the Japanese they heard on their trips. Their rhetoric had the unfortunate habit of echoing that of their distrusted government. Their accounts contained minor discrepancies between one retelling and the next. Moreover, as they broke down on camera, their emotional testimonies simply added to the skeptics' charge that Wei was more interested in emotional catharsis rather than historical inquiry.

The criticisms outraged Wei. A great atrocity had occurred in

Pingfang, and it was being willfully forgotten by the world through a cover-up. Because China's government was despised, the world was countenancing Japan's denial. Debates over whether the doctors vivisected all or only some of the victims without use of anesthesia, whether most of the victims were political prisoners, innocent villagers caught on raids, or common criminals, whether the use of babies and infants in experiments was known to Ishii, and so forth, seemed to him beside the point. That the questioners would focus on inconsequential details of the uniform of the Japanese doctors as a way to discredit his witnesses did not seem to him to deserve a response.

As he continued the trips to the past, other historians who saw the promise of the technology objected. History, as it turned out, was a limited resource, and each of Wei's trips took out a chunk of the past that could never be replaced. He was riddling the past with holes like Swiss cheese. Like early archaeologists who destroyed entire sites as they sought a few precious artifacts, thereby consigning valuable information about the past to oblivion, Wei was destroying the very history that he was trying to save.

When Wei jumped onto the tracks in front of a Boston subway train last Friday, he was undoubtedly haunted by the past. Perhaps he was also despondent over the unintended boost his work had given to the forces of denial. Seeking to end controversy in history, he succeeded only in causing more of it. Seeking to give voice to the victims of a great injustice, he succeeded only in silencing some of them forever.

[*Dr. Kirino speaks to us from in front of Evan Wei's grave. In the bright May sunlight of New England, the dark shadows beneath her eyes make her seem older, more frail.*]

Akemi Kirino:

I've kept only one secret from Evan. Well, actually two.

The first is my grandfather. He died before Evan and I met. I never took Evan to visit his grave, which is in California. I just told him that it wasn't something I wanted to share with him, and I never told Evan his name.

The second is a trip I took to the past, the only one I've ever taken personally. We were in Pingfang at the time, and I went to July 9, 1941. I knew the layout of the place pretty well from the descriptions and the maps, and I avoided the prison cells and the laboratories. I went to the building that housed the command center.

I looked around until I found the office for the Director of Pathology Studies. The Director was inside. He was a very handsome man: tall, slim, and he held his back very straight. He was writing a letter. I knew he was thirty-two, which was the same age as mine at that time.

I looked over his shoulder at the letter he was writing. He had beautiful calligraphy.

> I have now finally settled into my work routine, and things are going well. Manchukuo is a very beautiful place. The sorghum fields spread out as far as the eye can see, like an ocean. The street vendors here make wonderful tofu from fresh soybeans, which smells delicious. Not quite as good as the Japanese tofu, but very good nonetheless.
>
> You will like Harbin. Now that the Russians are gone, the streets of Harbin are a harmonious patchwork of the five races: the Chinese, Manchus, Mongolians, and Koreans bow as our beloved Japanese soldiers and colonists pass by, grateful for the liberation and wealth we have brought to this beautiful land. It has taken a decade to pacify this place and eliminate the Communist

bandits, who are but an occasional and minor nuisance now. Most of the Chinese are very docile and safe.

But all that I really can think about these days when I am not working are you and Naoko. It is for her sake that you and I are apart. It is for her sake and the sake of her generation that we make our sacrifices. I am sad that I will miss her first birthday, but it gladdens my heart to see the Greater East Asia Co-Prosperity Sphere blossom in this remote but rich hinterland. Here, you truly feel that our Japan is the light of Asia, her salvation.

Take heart, my dear, and smile. All our sacrifices today will mean that one day, Naoko and her children will see Asia take its rightful place in the world, freed from the yoke of the European killers and robbers who now trample over her and desecrate her beauty. We will celebrate together when we finally chase the British out of Hong Kong and Singapore.

Red sea of sorghum
Fragrant bowls of crushed soybeans
I see only you
And her, our treasure
Now, if only you were here.

This was not the first time I had read this letter. I had seen it once before, as a little girl. It was one of my mother's treasured possessions, and I remember asking her to explain all the faded characters to me.

"He was very proud of his literary learning," my mother had said. "He always closed his letters with a *tanka*."

By then Grandfather was well into his long slide into dementia. Often he would confuse me with my mother and call me by her name.

He would also teach me how to make origami animals. His fingers were very dextrous—the legacy of being a good surgeon.

I watched my grandfather finish his letter and fold it. I followed him out of the office to his lab. He was getting ready for an experiment, his notebook and instruments laid out neatly along the workbench.

He called to one of the medical assistants. He asked the assistant to bring him something for the experiment. The assistants returned about ten minutes later, holding a bloody mess on a tray, like a dish of steaming tofu. It was a human brain, still so warm from the body from which it was taken that I could see the heat rising from it.

"Very good," my grandfather said, nodding. "Very fresh. This will do."

Akemi Kirino:

There have been times when I wished Evan weren't Chinese, just as there have been times when I wished I weren't Japanese. But these are moments of passing weakness. I don't mean them. We are born into strong currents of history, and it is our lot to swim or sink, not to complain about our luck.

Ever since I became an American, people have told me that America is about leaving your past behind. I've never understood that. You can no more leave behind your past than you can leave behind your skin.

The compulsion to delve into the past, to speak for the dead, to recover their stories: that's part of who Evan was, and why I loved him. Just the same, my grandfather is part of who I am, and what he did, he did in the name of my mother and me and my children. I am responsible for his sins, in the same way that I take pride in inheriting the tradition of a great people, a people who, in my grandfather's time, committed great evil.

In an extraordinary time, he faced extraordinary choices, and maybe some would say this means that we cannot judge him. But how can we really judge anyone except in the most extraordinary of circumstances?

It's easy to be civilized and display a patina of orderliness in calm times, but your true character only emerges in darkness and under great pressure: is it a diamond or merely a lump of the blackest coal?

Yet, my grandfather was not a monster. He was simply a man of ordinary moral courage whose capacity for great evil was revealed to his and my lasting shame. Labeling someone a monster implies that he is from another world, one which has nothing to do with us. It cuts off the bonds of affection and fear, assures us of our own superiority, but there's nothing learned, nothing gained. It's simple, but it's cowardly. I know now that only by empathizing with a man like my grandfather can we understand the depth of the suffering he caused. There are no monsters. The monster is us.

Why didn't I tell Evan about my grandfather? I don't know. I suppose I was a coward. I was afraid that he might feel that something in me would be tainted, a corruption of blood. Because I could not then find a way to empathize with my grandfather, I was afraid that Evan could not empathize with me. I kept my grandfather's story to myself, and so I locked away a part of myself from my husband. There were times when I thought I would go to the grave with my secret and so erase forever my grandfather's story.

I regret it, now that Evan is dead. He deserved to know his wife whole, complete, and I should have trusted him rather than silenced my grandfather's story, which is also my story. Evan died believing that by unearthing more stories, he caused people to doubt their truth. But he was wrong. The truth is not delicate and it does not suffer from denial—the truth only dies when true stories are untold.

This urge to speak, to tell the story, I share with the aging and dying former members of Unit 731, with the descendants of the victims, with all the untold horrors of history. The silence of the victims of the past imposes a duty on the present to recover their voices, and we are most free when we willingly take up that duty.

[*Dr. Kirino's voice comes to us off-camera, as the camera pans to the star-studded sky.*]

It has been a decade since Evan's death, and the Comprehensive Time Travel Moratorium remains in place. We still do not know quite what to do with a past that is transparently accessible, a past that will not be silenced or forgotten. For now, we hesitate.

Evan died thinking that he had sacrificed the memory of the Unit 731 victims and permanently erased the traces that their truth left in our world, all for nought, but he was wrong. He was forgetting that even with the Bohm-Kirino particles gone, the actual photons forming the images of those moments of unbearable suffering and quiet heroism are still out there, traveling as a sphere of light into the void of space.

Look up at the stars, and we are bombarded by light generated on the day the last victim at Pingfang died, the day the last train arrived at Auschwitz, the day the last Cherokee walked out of Georgia. And we know that the inhabitants of those distant worlds, if they are watching, will see those moments, in time, as they stream from here to there at the speed of light. It is not possible to capture all of those photons, to erase all of those images. They are our permanent record, the testimony of our existence, the story that we tell the future. Every moment, as we walk on this earth, we are watched and judged by the eyes of the universe.

For far too long, historians, and all of us, have acted as exploiters of the dead. But the past is not dead. It is with us. Everywhere we walk, we are bombarded by fields of Bohm-Kirino particles that will let us see the past like looking through a window. The agony of the dead is with us, and we hear their screams and walk among their ghosts. We cannot avert our eyes or plug up our ears. We must bear witness and speak for those who cannot speak. We have only one chance to get it right.

• • •

AUTHOR'S NOTES: This story is dedicated to the memory of Iris Chang and all the victims of Unit 731.

I first got the idea for writing a story in the form of a documentary after reading Ted Chiang's "Liking What You See: a Documentary."

The following sources were consulted during the research for this story. Their help is hereby gratefully acknowledged, though any errors in relating their facts and insights are entirely my own.

For the phrase "exploiters of the dead" and the history of Heian and premodern Japan:

Totman, Conrad. *A History of Japan, Second Edition.* Malden, MA: Blackwell Publishing, 2005.

For the history of Unit 731 and the experiments performed by Unit 731 personnel:

Gold, Hal. *Unit 731 Testimony*, Tokyo: Tuttle Publishing, 1996.

Harris, Sheldon H. *Factories of Death: Japanese Biological Warfare 1932–45 and the American Cover-Up*, New York: Routledge, 1994.

(Numerous other newspaper and journal articles, interviews, and analyses were also consulted. Their authors include, among others, Keiichi Tsuneishi, Doug Struck, Christopher Reed, Richard Lloyd Parry, Christopher Hudson, Mark Simkin, Frederick Dickinson, John Dower, Tawara Yoshifumi, Yuki Tanaka, Takashi Tsuchiya, Tien-wei Wu, Shane Green, Friedrich Frischknecht, Nicholas Kristof, Jun Hongo, Richard James Havis, Edward Cody, and Judith Miller. I thank these authors and regret that the sources are not listed here individually for space reasons.)

For descriptions of the vivisections and practice surgery sessions with live Chinese victims conducted by Japanese doctors, their treatment as prisoners after the War, and Japan's postwar responses to memories of the War:

Noda, Masaaki. "Japanese Atrocities in the Pacific War: One Army Surgeon's Account of Vivisection on Human Subjects in China," *East Asia: An International Quarterly*, 18:3 (2000) 49–91.

Note that based on testimonies and other documentation, the Japanese doctors of Unit 731 typically infected their victims while wearing protective suits to avoid the possibility that resisting prisoners would infect the doctors by struggling.

Aspects of Shiro Yamagata's post-Unit 731 recollections are modeled on the experiences of Ken Yuasa (a Japanese military doctor who was *not* a member of Unit 731), described in the Noda article.

The obituary for Evan Wei is modeled upon the *Economist*'s November 25, 2004 obituary for Iris Chang.

The hearing of the Subcommittee on Asia, the Pacific, and the Global Environment is modeled upon the February 15, 2007, hearing before that same Subcommittee on House Resolution 121, concerning Japan's wartime enslavement of women for sexual purposes (known as "comfort women").

Austin Yoder provided pictures from modern-day Pingfang, Harbin, and the Unit 731 War Crimes Museum.

The various denialist statements attributed to "men in the street" are modeled on Internet forum comments, postings, and direct communication to the author from individuals who hold such views.

KEN LIU

THE
PAPER
MENAGERIE

AND

OTHER STORIES

Introduction

Bestselling author Ken Liu selects his multiple award-winning stories for a groundbreaking collection—including a brand-new piece exclusive to this volume.

This mesmerizing collection features many of Ken's award-winning and award-finalist short fiction, including: "The Man Who Ended History: A Documentary" (Finalist for the Hugo, Nebula, and Theodore Sturgeon Awards), "Mono no aware" (Hugo Award winner), "The Waves" (Nebula Award finalist), "The Bookmaking Habits of Select Species" (Nebula and Sturgeon Awards finalist), "All the Flavors" (Nebula Award finalist), "The Litigation Master and the Monkey King" (Nebula Award finalist), and the most awarded story in the genre's history, "The Paper Menagerie" (The only story to win the Hugo, Nebula, and World Fantasy awards).

Insightful and stunning stories that plumb the struggle against history and betrayal of relationships in pivotal moments, this collection showcases one of our greatest and most original voices.

Topics and Questions for Discussion

1. In the preface, on page vii, Liu writes "Every act of communication is a miracle of translation." Is this true for two people speaking the same language or does it mean that no one is ever speaking the same language? Discuss how this idea relates to the collection as a whole.

2. In making this collection, Liu carefully selected these works from more than seventy pieces of his own short fiction. Why do you think Liu chose these stories in this order? The stories cover a variety of topics, genres, and themes and contain distinct structures and characters—is there one story, arc, or idea they come together to illuminate? Are there any works you would rearrange?

3. Discuss the significance of the Allatian method in "The Bookmaking Habit of Select Species." Why do you think the rest of the story is structured as reference-like sections? Talk about storytelling as a universal constant throughout this piece and this collection as a whole.

4. Talk about how Liu handles historical events in "All the Flavors: A Tale of Guan Yu, the Chinese God of War, in America," "A Brief History of the Trans-Pacific Tunnel," and "The Man Who Ended History: A Documentary." How does he as the author, and you as the reader, distinguish fact from fiction?

5. Within the collection, we see people—and aliens—communicate through a variety of ways: scratches on a surface, oral histories, paper figures, life experiences, written words. Is there a time when something appears to be mistranslated? How well does each method work to communicate straightforward ideas and hidden meanings?

6. "The Paper Menagerie" made history as the first work of fiction to win a Hugo, Nebula, and World Fantasy Award—why do you think it has resonated across so many audiences? Why was this chosen to be the collection's titular story?

7. In "Good Hunting" Liang and Yan adapt to a world that has completely changed their way of life. In "The Paper Menagerie," Jack separates himself from his cultural identity in order to fit in. Though they share some themes, the stories are tonally disparate. Discuss why. What are the differences between Liang, Yan, and Jack's modes of integration? Talk about the distinctions between adaptation, assimilation, and cultural abandonment.

8. When does convenience outweigh independence? "The Perfect Match" shows a future in which people allow their "smart" devices to make their decisions. Discuss your image of the future. How do you think technology will change the human mentality?

9. "Mono no aware" flips the trope of a future "monoculture" to show a character infused with Japanese ideals. Discuss the significance and meaning of the phrase "mono no aware" and how it influences Hiroto's fate.

10. On a surface level, "The Regular" is one of the stories that is most dissimilar to others within the collection. Amid stories of storytelling and translation, memory and identity, how does the sci-fi noir fit into the collection?

11. "Wildflowers can bloom anywhere" is one of Mr. Kan's messages to Lily. Talk about how his statement relates to the collection. Discuss the structure of Chinese characters as ideograms. Think about the moments Liu chose to use Chinese characters: Why those moments in the text? What does it add to that moment and to the larger narrative?

12. "The Man Who Ended History: A Documentary" shows a future in which history can only be experienced once by one person. What does that say about who history belongs to? History and heritage are themes throughout the collection, so what does it mean that the final story is about "ending history"?

13. Talk about the structure and style of "The Man Who Ended

History: A Documentary." Why did Liu decide to include editing notes and directions? How did it affect your experience as a reader?

14. The collection ends with "We must bear witness and speak for those who cannot speak. We have only one chance to get it right." Discuss what you think Liu means. Why did he decide to end the collection with these words? What do you think this means to Liu?

15. The stories of *The Paper Menagerie and Other Stories* cross genre lines. Within the collection are works of science fiction, alternate history, magical realism, fantasy, and noir. Discuss how these stories affect the boundary between science and history with fantasy and spirituality.

Enhance Your Book Club

1. Rina's soul in "State Change" manifests as ice. Before meeting, ask all members to write three random objects on slips of paper. Combine all of the papers and have each member draw from a hat. Each person's random object is the physical representation of their soul. Discuss how your objectified soul would change your everyday life. How does this speak to privilege and the circumstances of birth?

2. Immigration is one of the most significant issues of the 21st century and a recurring theme in the collection. Discuss some current events as they relate to the immigrant experience shown within this novel.

3. Before meeting, think of some of your own cultural or familial traditions. Which of those have faded away and which have stayed constant? Why do you think some last longer than others?

THOMAS MERTON

The Seven Storey
Mountain

"For I tell you that God is able of these stones
to raise up children to Abraham."

IMAGE BOOKS
A Division of Doubleday & Company, Inc.
Garden City, New York

Image Books edition 1970
by special arrangement with Harcourt, Brace & World
Image Books edition published September 1970

Ex parte Ordinis:
Nihil obstat: FR. M. GABRIEL O'CONNELL, O.C.S.O.
FR. M. ANTHONY CHASSAGNE, O.C.S.O.
Imprimi potest: FR. M. FREDERIC DUNNE, O.C.S.O.
Abbot of Our Lady of Gethsemani
Nihil obstat: JOHN M. A. FEARNS, S.T.D.,
Censor librorum
Imprimatur: ✠ FRANCIS CARDINAL SPELLMAN,
Archbishop of New York

CHRISTO
VERO
REGI

Contents

Part One

1

Prisoner's Base

On the last day of January 1915, under the sign of the Water Bearer, in a year of a great war, and down in the shadow of some French mountains on the borders of Spain, I came into the world. Free by nature, in the image of God, I was nevertheless the prisoner of my own violence and my own selfishness, in the image of the world into which I was born. That world was the picture of Hell, full of men like myself, loving God and yet hating Him; born to love Him, living instead in fear and hopeless self-contradictory hungers.

Not many hundreds of miles away from the house where I was born, they were picking up the men who rotted in the rainy ditches among the dead horses and the ruined seventy-fives, in a forest of trees without branches along the river Marne.

My father and mother were captives in that world, knowing they did not belong with it or in it, and yet unable to get away from it. They were in the world and not of it—not because they were saints, but in a different way: because they were artists. The integrity of an artist lifts a man above the level of the world without delivering him from it.

My father painted like Cézanne and understood the southern French landscape the way Cézanne did. His vision of the world was sane, full of balance, full of veneration for structure, for the relations of masses and for all the circumstances that impress an individual identity on each created thing. His vision was religious and clean, and therefore his paintings were without decoration or superfluous comment, since a religious man respects the power of God's creation to bear witness for itself. My father was a very good artist.

Neither of my parents suffered from the little spooky prejudices that devour the people who know nothing but automobiles and movies and what's in the ice-box and what's in the papers and which neighbors are getting a divorce.

I inherited from my father his way of looking at things and some of his integrity and from my mother some of her dissatisfaction with the mess the world is in, and some of her versatility. From both I got capacities for work and vision and enjoyment and expression that ought to have made me some kind of a King, if the standards the world lives by were the real ones. Not that we ever had any money: but any fool knows that you don't need money to get enjoyment out of life.

If what most people take for granted were really true—if all you needed to be happy was to grab everything and see everything and investigate every experience and then talk about it, I should have been a very happy person, a spiritual millionaire, from the cradle even until now.

If happiness were merely a matter of natural gifts, I would never have entered a Trappist monastery when I came to the age of a man.

ii

My father and mother came from the ends of the earth, to Prades, and though they came to stay, they stayed there barely long enough for me to be born and get on my small feet, and then they left again. And they continued and I began a somewhat long journey: for all three of us, one way and another, it is now ended.

And though my father came from the other side of the earth, beyond many oceans, all the pictures of Christchurch, New Zealand, where he was born, look like the suburbs of London, but perhaps a little cleaner. There is more sunlight in New Zealand, and I think the people are healthier.

My father's name was Owen Merton. Owen because his mother's family had lived for a generation or two in Wales, though I believe they were originally Lowland Scotch. And my father's father was a music master, and a pious man, who taught at Christ's College, Christchurch, on the South Island.

My father had a lot of energy and independence. He told me how it was in the hill country and in the mountains of the South Island, out on the sheep farms and in the forests where he had been, and once, when one of the Antarctic expeditions came that way, my father nearly joined it, to go to the South Pole. He would have been frozen to death along with all the others, for that was the one from which no one returned.

When he wanted to study art, there were many difficulties in his way, and it was not easy for him to convince his people that that was really his vocation. But eventually he went to London, and then to Paris, and in Paris he met my mother, and married her, and never went back to New Zealand.

My mother was an American. I have seen a picture of her as a rather slight, thin, sober little person with a serious and somewhat anxious and very sensitive face. And this corresponds with my memory of her—worried, precise, quick, critical of me, her son. Yet in the family she has always been spoken of as gay and very light-hearted. My grandmother kept great locks of Mother's red hair, after she died, and Mother's happy laughter as a boarding-school girl was what never ceased to echo in my grandmother's memory.

It seems to me, now, that Mother must have been a person full of insatiable dreams and of great ambition after perfection: perfection in art, in interior decoration, in dancing, in housekeeping, in raising children. Maybe that is why I remember her mostly as worried: since the imperfection of myself, her first son, had been a great deception. If this book does not prove anything else, it will certainly show that I was nobody's dream-child. I have seen a diary Mother was keeping, in the time of my infancy and first childhood, and it reflects some astonishment at the stubborn and seemingly spontaneous development of completely unpredictable features in my character, things she had never bargained for: for example, a deep and serious urge to adore the gas-light in the kitchen, with no little ritualistic veneration, when I was about four. Churches and formal religion were things to which Mother attached not too much importance in the training of a modern child, and my guess is that she thought, if I were left to myself, I would grow up into a nice, quiet Deist of some sort, and never be perverted by superstition.

My baptism, at Prades, was almost certainly Father's idea, because he had grown up with a deep and well-developed faith, according to the doctrines of the Church of England. But I don't think there was much power, in the waters of the baptism I got in Prades, to untwist the warping of my essential freedom, or loose me from the devils that hung like vampires on my soul.

My father came to the Pyrenees because of a dream of his own: more single, more concrete and more practical than Mother's numerous and haunting ideals of perfection. Father wanted to get some place where he could settle in France, and raise a family, and paint, and live on practically nothing, because we had practically nothing to live on.

Father and Mother had many friends at Prades, and when they had moved there, and had their furniture in their flat, and the canvasses piled up in the corner, and the whole place smelling of fresh oil-paints and water-color and cheap pipe tobacco and cooking, more friends came down from Paris. And Mother would paint in the hills, under a large canvass parasol, and Father would paint in the sun, and the friends would drink red wine and gaze out over the valley at Canigou, and at the monastery on the slopes of the mountain.

There were many ruined monasteries in those mountains. My mind goes back with great reverence to the thought of those clean, ancient stone cloisters, those low and mighty rounded arches hewn and set in place by monks who have perhaps prayed me where I now am. St. Martin and St. Michael the Archangel, the great patron of monks, had churches in those mountains. Saint Martin-du-Canigou; Saint Michel-de-Cuxa. Is it any wonder I should have a friendly feeling about those places?

One of them, stone by stone, followed me across the Atlantic a score of years later, and got itself set up within convenient reach of me when I most needed to see what a cloister looked like, and what kind of place a man might live in, to live according to his rational nature, and not like a stray dog. St. Michel-de-Cuxa is all fixed up in a special and considerably tidy little museum in an uptown park, in New York, overlooking the Hudson River, in such a way that you don't recall what kind of a city you are in. It is called The Cloisters. Synthetic as it is, it still preserves enough of its own reality to be a reproach to everything else around it, except the trees and the Palisades.

But when the friends of my father and mother came to Prades, they brought the newspapers, rolled up in their coat pockets, and they had many postcards carrying patriotic cartoons, representing the Allies overcoming the Germans. My grandparents—that is, my mother's father and mother in America—were worried about her being in a land at war, and it was evident that we could not stay much longer at Prades.

I was barely a year old. I remember nothing about the journey, as we went to Bordeaux, to take the boat that had a gun mounted on the foredeck. I remember nothing about the crossing of the sea, nothing of the anxiety about U-boats, or the arrival in New York, and in the land where there was no war. But I can easily reconstruct the first encounter between my American grandparents and their new son-in-law and their grandson.

For Pop, as my American grandfather was called in the family, was a buoyant and excitable man who, on docks, boats, trains, in stations, in elevators, on busses, in hotels, in restaurants, used to get keyed up and start ordering everybody around, and making new arrangements, and changing them on the spur of the moment. My grandmother, whom we called Bonnemaman, was just the opposite, and her natural deliberateness and hesitancy and hatred of activity always seemed to increase in proportion to Pop's excesses in the opposite direction. The more active Pop became and the more he shouted and gave directions, the more hesitant and doubtful and finally inert was my grandmother. But perhaps this obscure and innocent and wholly subconscious conflict had not yet developed, in 1916, to the full pitch of complications which it was to attain some fifteen years later.

I have no doubt that there was a certain amount of conflict between the two generations when Father and Mother determined that they were going to find their own kind of a house and live in it. It was a small house, very old and rickety, standing under two or three high pine trees, in Flushing, Long Island, which was then a country town. We were out in the fields in the direction of Kiljordan and Jamaica and the old Truant School. The house had four rooms, two downstairs and two upstairs, and two of the rooms were barely larger than closets. It must have been very cheap.

Our landlord, Mr. Duggan, ran a nearby saloon. He got in trouble with Father for helping himself to the rhubarb which we were growing in the garden. I remember the grey summer dusk in which this happened. We were at the supper table, when the bended Mr. Duggan was observed, like some whale in the sea of green rhubarb, plucking up the red stalks. Father rose to his feet and hastened out into the garden. I could hear indignant words. We sat at the supper table, silent, not eating, and when Father returned I began to question him, and to endeavor to work out the morality of the situation. And I still remember it as having struck me as a difficult case, with much to be said on both sides. In fact, I had assumed that if the landlord felt like it, he could simply come and harvest all our vegetables, and there was nothing we could do about it. I mention this with the full consciousness that someone will use it against me, and say that the real reason I became a monk in later years was that I had the mentality of a medieval serf when I was barely out of the cradle.

Father did as much painting as he could. He filled several sketch books and finished some water-colors along the waterfront in New York, and eventually even had an exhibition in a place in Flushing which was maintained by some artists there. Two doors away from us, up the road, in a white house with pointed gables, surrounded by a wide sweep of sloping lawn, and with a stable that had been turned into a studio, lived Bryson Burroughs, who painted pale, classical pictures something like Puvis de Chavannes and who, with some of the gentleness you could see in his work, was very kind to us.

Father could not support us by painting. During the war years we lived on his work as a landscape gardener: which was mostly plain manual labor, for he not only laid out the gardens of some rich people in the neighborhood, but did most of the work planting and caring for them: and that was how we lived. Father did not get this money under false pretenses. He was a very good gardener, understood flowers, and knew how to make things grow. What is more, he liked this kind of work almost as much as painting.

Then in November 1918, about a week before the Armistice of that particular World War, my younger brother was born. He was a child with a much serener nature than mine, with not so many obscure drives and impulses. I remember that everyone was impressed by his constant and unruffled happiness. In the long evenings, when he was put to bed before the sun went down, instead of protesting and fighting, as I did when I had to go to bed, he would lie upstairs in his crib, and we would hear him singing a little tune. Every evening it was the same tune, very simple, very primitive; a nice little tune, very suitable for the time of day and for the season. Downstairs, we would all fall more or less silent, lulled by the singing of the child in the crib, and we would see the sunrays slanting across the fields and through the windows as the day ended.

I had an imaginary friend, called Jack, who had an imaginary dog, called Doolittle. The chief reason why I had an imaginary friend was that there were no other children to play with, and my brother John Paul was still a baby. When I tried to seek diversion watching the gentlemen who played pool at Mr. Duggan's saloon, I got into much trouble. On the other hand, I could go and play at Burroughs' place, in their garden and in the room full of old lumber over the studio. Betty Burroughs knew how to join in games in a way that did not imply patronage, though she was practically grown up. But for friends of my own age, I had to fall back on my imagination, and it was perhaps not a good thing.

Mother did not mind the company I kept in my imagination, at least to begin with, but once I went shopping with

17

her, and refused to cross Main Street, Flushing, for fear that the imaginary dog, Doolittle, might get run over by real cars. This I later learned from her record of the affair in her diary.

By 1920 I could read and write and draw. I drew a picture of the house, and everybody sitting under the pine trees, on a blanket, on the grass, and sent it to Pop in the mail. He lived at Douglaston, which was about five miles away. But most of the time I drew pictures of boats. Ocean liners with many funnels and hundreds of portholes, and waves all around as jagged as a saw, and the air full of "v's" for the sea-gulls.

Things were stimulated by the momentous arrival of my New Zealand grandmother, who had come from the Antipodes to visit her scattered children in England and America, as soon as the war had ended. I think she brought one of my aunts along with her, but I was most of all impressed by Granny. She must have talked to me a great deal, and asked me many questions and told me a great number of things, and though there are few precise details I remember about that visit, the general impression she left was one of veneration and awe—and love. She was very good and kind, and there was nothing effusive and overwhelming about her affection. I have no precise memory of what she looked like, except that she wore dark clothes, grey and dark brown, and had glasses and grey hair and spoke quietly and earnestly. She had been a teacher, like her husband, my New Zealand grandfather.

The clearest thing I remember about her was the way she put salt on her oatmeal at breakfast. Of this I am certain: it made a very profound impression on me. Of one other thing I am less certain, but it is in itself much more important: she taught me the Lord's Prayer. Perhaps I had been taught to say the "Our Father" before, by my earthly father. I never used to say it. But evidently Granny asked me one night if I had said my prayers, and it turned out that I did not know the "Our Father," so she taught it to me. After that I did not forget it, even though I went for years without saying it at all.

It seems strange that Father and Mother, who were concerned almost to the point of scrupulosity about keeping the minds of their sons uncontaminated by error and mediocrity and ugliness and sham, had not bothered to give us any formal religious training. The only explanation I have is the guess that Mother must have had strong views on the subject. Possibly she considered any organized religion below the standard of intellectual perfection she demanded of any child of hers. We never went to church in Flushing.

In fact, I remember having an intense desire to go to church one day, but we did not go. It was Sunday. Perhaps it was an Easter Sunday, probably in 1920. From across the fields, and beyond the red farmhouse of our neighbor, I could see the spire of St. George's church, above the trees. The sound of the churchbells came to us across the bright fields. I was playing in front of the house, and stopped to listen. Suddenly, all the birds began to sing in the trees above my head, and the sound of birds singing and churchbells ringing lifted up my heart with joy. I cried out to my father:

"Father, all the birds are in their church."

And then I said: "Why don't we go to church?"

My father looked up and said: "We will."

"Now?" said I.

"No, it is too late. But we will go some other Sunday."

And yet Mother did go somewhere, sometimes, on Sunday mornings, to worship God. I doubt that Father went with her; he probably stayed at home to take care of me and John Paul, for we never went. But anyway, Mother went to the Quakers, and sat with them in their ancient meeting house. This was the only kind of religion for which she had any use, and I suppose it was taken for granted that, when we grew older, we might be allowed to tend in that direction too. Probably no influence would have been brought to bear on us to do so. We would have been left to work it out more or less for ourselves.

Meanwhile, at home, my education was progressing along the lines laid down by some progressive method that Mother had read about in one of those magazines. She answered an advertisement that carried an oval portrait of some bearded scholar with a pince-nez, and received from Baltimore a set of books and some charts and even a small desk and black-board. The idea was that the smart modern child was to be turned loose amid this apparatus, and allowed to develop spontaneously into a midget university before reaching the age of ten.

The ghost of John Stuart Mill must have glided up and down the room with a sigh of gratification as I opened the desk and began. I forget what came of it all, except that one night I was sent to bed early for stubbornly spelling "which" without the first "h": "w-i-c-h." I remember brooding about this as an injustice. "What do they think I am, anyway?" After all, I was still only five years old.

Still, I retain no grudge against the fancy method or the desk that went with it. Maybe that was where my geography book came from—the favorite book of my childhood. I was so fond of playing prisoner's base all over those maps that I wanted to become a sailor. I was only too eager for the kind of foot-loose and unstable life I was soon to get into.

My second best book confirmed me in this desire. This was a collection of stories called the *Greek Heroes*. It was more than I could do to read the Victorian version of these Greek myths for myself, but Father read them aloud, and I learned of Theseus and the Minotaur, of the Medusa, of Perseus and Andromeda. Jason sailed to a far land, after the Golden Fleece. Theseus returned victorious, but forgot to change the black sails, and the King of Athens threw himself down from the rock, believing that his son was dead. In those days I learned the name Hesperides, and it was from these things that I unconsciously built up the vague fragments of a religion and of a philosophy, which remained hidden and implicit in my acts, and which, in due time, were to assert themselves in a deep and all-embracing attachment to my own judgement and my own will and a constant turning away from subjection, towards the freedom of my own ever-changing horizons.

In a sense, this was intended as the fruit of my early train-ing. Mother wanted me to be independent, and not to run with the herd. I was to be original, individual, I was to have a definite character and ideals of my own. I was not to be an article thrown together, on the common bourgeois pattern, on everybody else's assembly line.

If we had continued as we had begun, and if John Paul and I had grown up in that house, probably this Victorian-Greek complex would have built itself up gradually, and we would have turned into good-mannered and earnest sceptics, polite, intelligent, and perhaps even in some sense useful. We might have become successful authors, or editors of magazines, professors at small and progressive colleges. The way would have been all smooth and perhaps I would never have ended up as a monk.

But it is not yet the time to talk about that happy consummation, the thing for which I most thank and praise God, and which is of all things the ultimate paradoxical fulfilment of my mother's ideas for me—the last thing she would ever have dreamed of: the boomerang of all her solicitude for an individual development.

But oh, how many possibilities there were ahead of me and my brother in that day! A brand-new conscience was just coming into existence as an actual, operating function of a soul. My choices were just about to become responsible. My mind was clean and unformed enough to receive any set of standards, and work with the most perfect of them, and work with grace itself, and God's own values, if I had ever had the chance.

Here was a will, neutral, undirected, a force waiting to be applied, ready to generate tremendous immanent powers of light or darkness, peace or conflict, order or confusion, love or sin. The bias which my will was to acquire from the circumstances of all its acts would eventually be the direction of my whole being towards happiness or misery, life or death, heaven or hell.

More than that: since no man ever can, or could, live by himself and for himself alone, the destinies of thousands of other people were bound to be affected, some remotely, but some very directly and near-at-hand, by my own choices and decisions and desires, as my own life would also be formed and modified according to theirs. I was entering into a moral

21

universe in which I would be related to every other rational being, and in which whole masses of us, as thick as swarming bees, would drag one another along towards some common end of good or evil, peace or war.

I think it must have been after Mother went to the hospital that, one Sunday, I went to the Quaker meeting house with Father. He had explained to me that the people came and sat there, silent, doing nothing, saying nothing, until the Holy Spirit moved someone to speak. He also told me that a famous old gentleman, who was one of the founders of the Boy Scouts of America, would be there. That was Dan Beard. Consequently I sat among the Quakers with three more or less equal preoccupations running through my mind. Where was Dan Beard? Would he not only be called beard, but have one on his chin? And what was the Holy Spirit going to move all these people to do or say?

I forget how the third question was answered. But after the man sitting in the high wooden rostrum, presiding over the Quakers, gave the signal that the meeting was ended, I saw Dan Beard among the people under the low sunny porch, outside the meeting-house door. He had a beard.

It was almost certainly in the last year or so of Mother's life, 1921, that Father got a job as organist at the Episcopal church in Douglaston. It was not a job that made him very happy or enthusiastic. He did not get along very well with the minister. But I began to go to the church on Sundays, which makes me think that Mother was in the hospital, because I must have been living with Pop and Bonnemaman in Douglaston.

The old Zion church was a white wooden building, with a squat, square little belfry, standing on a hill, surrounded by high trees and a large graveyard, and in a crypt underneath it were buried the original Douglas family, who had settled there on the shore of the Sound some hundred years before. It was pleasant enough on Sundays. I remember the procession that came out of the sacristy, a choir of men and women, dressed in black, with white surplices, and led by a Cross. There were stained glass windows up behind the altar, one had an anchor on it, for its design, which interested me because I wanted to go to sea, and travel all over the world. Strange interpretation of a religious symbol ordinarily taken to signify stability in Hope: the theological virtue of Hope, dependence on God. To me it suggested just the opposite. Travel, adventure, the wide sea, and unlimited possibilities of human heroism, with myself as the hero.

Then there was a lectern, shaped like an eagle with outspread wings, on which rested a huge Bible. Nearby was an American flag, and above that was one of those little boards they have in Protestant churches, on which the numbers of the hymns to be sung are indicated by black and white cards. I was impressed by the lighting of candles on the altar, by the taking up of the collection, and by the singing of hymns, while Father, hidden behind the choir somewhere, played the organ.

One came out of the church with a kind of comfortable and satisfied feeling that something had been done that needed to be done, and that was all I knew about it. And now, as I consider it after many years, I see that it was very good that I should have got at least that much of religion in my childhood. It is a law of man's nature, written into his very essence, and just as much a part of him as the desire to build houses and cultivate the land and marry and have children and read books and sing songs, that he should want to stand together with other men in order to acknowledge their common dependence on God, their Father and Creator. In fact, this desire is much more fundamental than any purely physical necessity.

At this same time my father played the piano every evening in a small movie theater which had been opened in the next town, Bayside. We certainly needed money.

iii

And probably the chief reason why we needed money was that Mother had cancer of the stomach.

That was another thing that was never explained to me.

23

Everything about sickness and death was more or less kept hidden from me, because consideration of these things might make a child morbid. And since I was destined to grow up with a nice, clear, optimistic and well-balanced outlook on life, I was never even taken to the hospital to see Mother, after she went there. And this was entirely her own idea.

How long she had been ill and suffering, still keeping house for us, not without poverty and hardship, without our knowing anything of what it was, I cannot say. But her sickness probably accounts for my memory of her as thin and pale and rather severe.

With a selfishness unusual even in a child, I was glad to move from Flushing to my grandparents' house at Douglaston. There I was allowed to do more or less as I pleased, there was plenty of food, and we had two dogs and several cats to play with. I did not miss Mother very much, and did not weep when I was not allowed to go and see her. I was content to run in the woods with the dogs, or climb trees, or pester the chickens, or play around in the clean little studio where Bonnemaman sometimes painted china, and fired it in a small kiln.

Then one day Father gave me a note to read. I was very surprised. It was for me personally, and it was in my mother's handwriting. I don't think she had ever written to me before—there had never been any occasion for it. Then I understood what was happening, although, as I remember, the language of the letter was confusing to me. Nevertheless, one thing was quite evident. My mother was informing me, by mail, that she was about to die, and would never see me again.

I took the note out under the maple tree in the back yard, and worked over it, until I had made it all out, and had gathered what it really meant. And a tremendous weight of sadness and depression settled on me. It was not the grief of a child, with pangs of sorrow and many tears. It had something of the heavy perplexity and gloom of adult grief, and was therefore all the more of a burden because it was, to that extent, unnatural. I suppose one reason for this was that I had more or less had to arrive at the truth by induction.

Prayer? No, prayer did not even occur to me. How fantastic that will seem to a Catholic—that a six-year-old child should find out that his mother is dying, and not know enough to pray for her! It was not until I became a Catholic, twenty years later, that it finally occurred to me to pray for my mother.

My grandparents did not have a car, but they hired one to go in to the hospital, when the end finally came. I went with them in the car, but was not allowed to enter the hospital. Perhaps it was just as well. What would have been the good of my being plunged into a lot of naked suffering and emotional crisis without any prayer, any Sacrament to stabilize and order it, and make some kind of meaning out of it? In that sense, Mother was right. Death, under those circumstances, was nothing but ugliness, and if it could not possibly have any ultimate meaning, why burden a child's mind with the sight of it?

I sat outside, in the car, with the hired driver. Again, I knew nothing definite about what was going on. But I think there was also by this time no little subconscious rejection of everything that might have given me any certainty that Mother was really dying: for if I had wanted to find out, I would not have had much trouble.

It seemed like a very long time.

The car was parked in a yard entirely enclosed by black brick buildings, thick with soot. On one side was a long, low shed, and rain dripped from the eaves, as we sat in silence, and listened to the drops falling on the roof of the car. The sky was heavy with mist and smoke, and the sweet sick smell of hospital and gas-house mingled with the stuffy smell of the automobile.

But when Father and Pop and Bonnemaman and my Uncle Harold came out of the hospital door, I did not need to ask any questions. They were all shattered by sorrow.

When we got home to Douglaston, Father went into a room alone, and I followed him and found him weeping, over by the window.

He must have thought of the days before the war, when he

had first met Mother in Paris, when she had been so happy, and gay, and had danced, and had been full of ideas and plans and ambitions for herself and for him and for their children. It had not turned out as they had planned. And now it was all over. And Bonnemaman was folding away the big heavy locks of red hair that had fallen from the shears when my mother was a girl, folding them away now in tissue paper, in the spare room, and weeping bitterly.

They hired the same car again a day or so later, for another journey, and this time I am definitely glad I stayed in the car.

Mother, for some reason, had always wanted to be cremated. I suppose that fits in with the whole structure of her philosophy of life: a dead body was simply something to be put out of the way as quickly as possible. I remember how she was, in the house at Flushing, with a rag tied tightly around her head to keep the dust out of her hair, cleaning and sweeping and dusting the rooms with the greatest energy and intensity of purpose: and it helps one to understand her impatience with useless and decaying flesh. That was something to be done away with, without delay. When life was finished, let the whole thing be finished, definitely, for ever.

Once again, the rain fell, the sky was dark. I cannot remember if Cousin Ethel (my mother's cousin, called Mrs. McGovern, who was a nurse) remained in the car to keep me from getting too gloomy. Nevertheless I was very sad. But I was not nearly so unhappy as I would have been if I had gone up to that mournful and appalling place and stood behind a big pane of glass to watch my mother's coffin glide slowly between the steel doors that led to the furnace.

iv

Mother's death had made one thing evident: Father now did not have to do anything but paint. He was not tied down to any one place. He could go wherever he needed to go, to find subjects and get ideas, and I was old enough to go with him.

And so, after I had been a few months in the local school

at Douglaston, and had already been moved up to the second grade, in the evil-smelling grey annex on top of the hill, Father came back to New York and announced that he and I were going somewhere new.

It was with a kind of feeling of triumph that I watched the East River widen into Long Island Sound, and waited for the moment when the Fall River boat, in all her pride, would go sweeping past the mouth of Bayside Bay and I would view Douglaston, as I thought, from the superiority of the open water and pass it by, heading for a new horizon called Fall River and Cape Cod and Provincetown.

We could not afford a cabin, but slept down below decks in the crowded steerage, if you could call it that, among the loud Italian families and the colored boys who spent the night shooting craps under the dim light, while the waters spoke loudly to us, above our heads, proclaiming that we were well below the waterline.

And in the morning we got off the boat at Fall River, and walked up the street beside the textile mills, and found a lunch wagon crowded with men getting something to eat on the way to work; and we sat at the counter and ate ham and eggs.

All day long after that we were in a train. Just before we crossed the great black drawbridge over the Cape Cod Canal, Father got off at a station and went to a store across the street and bought me a bar of Baker's chocolate, with a blue wrapper and a picture of a lady in an old-fashioned cap and apron, serving cups of chocolate. I was almost completely overwhelmed with surprise and awe at the fact of such tremendous largesse. Candy had always been strictly rationed.

Then came the long, long journey through the sand dunes, stopping at every station, while I sat, weary and entranced, with the taste of chocolate thick and stale in my mouth, turning over and over in my mind the names of places where we were going: Sandwich, Falmouth, Truro, Provincetown. The name Truro especially fascinated me. I could not get it out of my mind: Truro. Truro. It was a name as lonely as the edge of the sea.

That summer was full of low sand dunes, and coarse grasses as sharp as wires, growing from the white sand. And the wind blew across the sand. And I saw the breakers of the grey sea come marching in towards the land, and I looked out at the ocean. Geography had begun to become a reality.

The whole town of Provincetown smelled of dead fish, and there were countless fishing boats, of all sizes, tied up along the wharves; and you could run all day on the decks of the schooners, and no one would prevent you, or chase you away. I began to know the smell of ropes and of pitch and of the salt, white wood of decks, and the curious smell of seaweed, under the docks.

When I got the mumps, Father read to me out of a book by John Masefield, which was full of pictures of sailing ships, and the only punishment I remember getting that summer was a mild reproof for refusing to eat an orange.

By the time we returned to Douglaston, and Father left me with my grandparents, where John Paul had been all the time, I had learned how to draw pictures of schooners and barks and clippers and brigs, and knew far more about all these distinctions than I do now.

Perhaps I went back to the rickety grey annex of the Public School for a couple of weeks—not for longer. Because Father had found a new place where he wanted to go and paint pictures, and having found it, came back to get his drawing boards and me, and there we went together. It was Bermuda.

Bermuda in those days had no big hotels and no golf-courses to speak of. It was not famous for anything. It was simply a curious island, two or three days out of New York, in the Gulf Stream, where the British had a small naval base and where there were no automobiles and not much of anything else either.

We took a small boat called the *Fort Victoria*, with a red and black funnel, and surprisingly soon after we had left New York harbor, the flying fishes began to leap out of the foam before her bows and skid along over the surface of the warm waves. And although I was very eager for my first sight of the island, it came upon us suddenly before I was aware, and stood up before us in the purple waters, green and white. You could already see the small white houses, made of coral, cleaner than sugar, shining in the sun, and all around us the waters paled over the shallows and became the color of emeralds, where there was sand, or lavender where there were rocks below the surface. We threaded our way in a zig-zag between the buoys that marked the path through the labyrinthine reefs.

The *H.M.S. Calcutta* lay at anchor off Ireland Island dockyard, and Father pointed to Somerset where, among the dark green cedars, was the place where we would live. Yet it was evening before we finally got there. How quiet and empty it was, in Somerset, in the gathering dusk! Our feet padded softly in the creamy dust of the deserted road. No wind stirred the paper leaves of the banana trees, or in the oleanders. Our voices seemed loud, as we spoke. Nevertheless it was a very friendly island. Those who occasionally came by saluted us as if we were old acquaintances.

The boarding house had a green verandah and many rocking chairs. The dark green paint needed renewing. The British officers, or whatever they were who lived in the place, sat and smoked their pipes, and talked, if they talked at all, about matters extremely profane. And here Father put down our bags. They were expecting us. In the shadows, we sat down to dinner. I quickly adjusted myself to the thought that this was home.

It is almost impossible to make much sense out of the continual rearrangement of our lives and our plans from month to month in my childhood. Yet every new development came to me as a reasonable and worthy change. Sometimes I had to go to school, sometimes I did not. Sometimes Father and I were living together, sometimes I was with strangers and only saw him from time to time. People came into our lives and went out of our lives. We had now one set of friends, now another. Things were always changing. I accepted it all. Why should it ever have occurred to me that nobody else lived like that? To me, it seemed as natural as the variations of

29

the weather and the seasons. And one thing I knew: for days on end I could run where I pleased, and do whatever I liked, and life was very pleasant.

When Father left the boarding house, I remained there, and continued to live in it, because it was near the school. He was living in some other part of Somerset, with some people he had met, and he spent his days at work, painting landscapes. In fact, after that winter in Bermuda he had finished enough work to have an exhibition, and this made him enough money to go back to Europe. But meanwhile, I was going to the local school for white children, which was next to a large public cricket field, and I was constantly being punished for my complete inability to grasp the principles of multiplication and division.

It must have been very difficult for Father to try to make all these decisions. He wanted me to go to school, and he wanted me to be with him. When both these things ceased to be possible at the same time, he first decided in favor of the school: but then, after considering at length the nature of the place where I had to live, and the kind of talk I heard there, all day long, with my wide-open and impassive understanding, he took me out of the school, and brought me to live where he was. And I was very glad, because I was relieved of the burden of learning multiplication and long division.

The only worry was that my former teacher passed along that road on her bicycle on her way home, and if I was playing by the road, I had to get out of sight for fear that she would send the truant officer around and make me come back to school. One evening I did not see her coming, and I was a little late in diving into the bushes that filled a deserted quarry and, as I peeked out between the branches, I could see her looking back over her shoulder as she slowly pedalled up the white hill.

Day after day the sun shone on the blue waters of the sea, and on the islands in the bay, and on the white sand at the head of the bay, and on the little white houses strung along the hillside. I remember one day looking up into the sky, and taking it into my head to worship one of the clouds,

30

which was shaped at one end like the head of Minerva with a helmet—like the head of the armed lady on the big British pennies.

Father left me in Bermuda with his friends, who were literary people and artists, and went to New York and had an exhibition. It got a good press and he sold many pictures. His style had developed, since Mother's death had delivered him from landscape gardening. It was becoming at the same time more abstract, more original, and simpler, and more definite in what it had to say. I think that the people in New York did not yet see the full force of his painting, or the direction in which he was going, because the Brooklyn Museum, for instance, bought the kind of pictures of Bermuda that might be thought remotely to resemble Winslow Homer, rather than the things that indicated Father's true originality. And anyway, there was not much in common between him and Winslow Homer, except the bare fact of having painted water-colors of sub-tropical scenes. As a water-colorist, he was more like John Marin, without any of Marin's superficiality.

After the exhibition was over, and the pictures were sold, and Father had the money in his pocket, I returned from Bermuda, and found out that Father was going to sail for France, with his friends, and leave me in America.

v

Pop's office always seemed to me a fine place. The smell of typewriters and glue and office stationery had something clean and stimulating about it. The whole atmosphere was bright and active, and everybody was especially friendly, because Pop was very well liked. The term "live-wire" was singularly appropriate for him. He was always bristling with nervous energy, and most people were happy when he came shouting through their departments, snapping his fingers and whacking all the desks with a rolled-up copy of the *Evening Telegram*.

Pop worked for Grosset and Dunlap, publishers who specialized in cheap reprints of popular novels, and in children's books of an adventurous cast. They were the ones who gave the world Tom Swift and all his electrical contrivances, together with the Rover Boys and Jerry Todd and all the rest. And there were several big showrooms full of these books, where I could go and curl up in a leather armchair and read all day without being disturbed until Pop came along to take me down to Childs and eat chicken à la king.

This was nineteen-twenty-three and Grosset and Dunlap were at a peak of prosperity. As a matter of fact, it was just about this time that Pop had carried off the one great stroke of his career. He had sold his employers the notion of printing the books of popular movies illustrated with stills from the film, to be sold in connection with the publicity given to the picture itself. This idea took on very quickly and remained popular all through the twenties, and made a lot of money for the company, and it was to be the cornerstone of Pop's own economic stability and, in fact, of the whole family's for fifteen years to come.

And so, *Black Oxen* and the *Ten Commandments* and the *Eternal City* and I forget what else went forth into all the drugstores and bookstores in all the small towns from Boston to San Francisco, full of pictures of Pola Negri and other stars of the time.

In those days movies were still occasionally made on Long Island, and more than once, my brother and I and all our friends in the neighborhood would hear they were taking some scene or other down at Alley Pond. Once, under the trees, we witnessed what was supposed to be a gypsy wedding between Gloria Swanson and some forgotten hero. The idea was that the two of them allowed their wrists to be slashed, and bound together, so that their blood would mingle: that was the gypsy wedding, according to the ideas of whoever was producing this immortal masterpiece. Frankly, however, we were not very much interested in all this. As children, we had enough sense to find the whole concept extremely heavy. We were much more excited when W. C. Fields came to Alley Pond to make part of a short comedy. First they set up the cameras in front of an old tumbledown house. I don't

32

remember whether our hero was supposed to be drunk or scared, but the door of the house would fly open, and W. C. Fields would come hurtling out and go careering down the steps in a way that made you wonder how he got to the bottom of them without breaking both legs and all of his ribs. After he had done this over and over again innumerable times, with a singular patience and philosophical tenacity, the men moved their cameras up on top of a big pile of old lumber that was standing by, and filmed what was evidently part of the same sequence. There was a steep wooded slope, full of trees and bushes, ending in a sheer drop of about six feet. At the bottom of this, they planted a couple of extremely tame cows. Then W. C. Fields came blundering through the bushes, in his same hysterical, stumbling flight from some unseen menace. Looking behind him, he failed to see the drop, and went plunging over, landing on top of the two tame cows, which were supposed to run madly away with him on their backs. However, they just let Fields land on top of them with a heavy thud, and then stood there, chewing on the grass, and looking bored, until he fell off, and climbed stoically back up the hill to start all over again.

I mention all this because, as a matter of fact, the movies were really the family religion at Douglaston.

That summer, 1923, Pop and Bonnemaman had taken John Paul with them, and had gone to California, and had visited Hollywood, with the status of something more than simple tourists, since Pop knew a lot of movie people in a business way. The trip had something of the nature of a pilgrimage, however, and we never heard the end of what Jackie Coogan had personally said to them and how he had acted personally in their presence, in a real actual personal face-to-face-meeting-with-Jackie-Coogan.

Pop and Bonnemaman's other heroes were Doug and Mary. I admit, that what with *Robin Hood* and the *Thief of Baghdad* we all paid Douglas Fairbanks a somewhat corrupt form of hyperdulia, although neither I nor John Paul could get excited over Mary Pickford. But to Pop and Bonnemaman, Doug and Mary seemed to sum up every possible

33

human ideal: in them was all perfection of beauty and wit, majesty, grace and decorum, bravery and love, gaiety and tenderness, all virtues and every admirable moral sentiment, truth, justice, honor, piety, loyalty, zeal, trust, citizenship, valor and, above all, marital fidelity. Day after day these two gods were extolled for the perfection of their mutual love, their glorious, simple, sincere, pious, faithful conjugal devotion to one another. Everything that good, plain, trusting middle-class optimism could devise, was gathered up into one big sentimental holocaust of praise, by my innocent and tender-hearted grandparents, and laid at the feet of Doug and Mary. It was a sad day in our family when Doug and Mary were divorced.

My grandfather's favorite place of worship was the Capitol theatre, in New York. When the Roxy theatre was built, he transferred his allegiance to that huge pile of solidified caramel, and later on there was no shrine that so stirred his devotion as the Music Hall.

There is no need to go into details of the trouble and confusion my brother and I often managed to create in the Douglaston household. When guests came whom we did not like, we would hide under the tables, or run upstairs and throw hard and soft objects down into the hall and into the living room.

One thing I would say about my brother John Paul. My most vivid memories of him, in our childhood, all fill me with poignant compunction at the thought of my own pride and hard-heartedness, and his natural humility and love.

I suppose it is usual for elder brothers, when they are still children, to feel themselves demeaned by the company of a brother four or five years younger, whom they regard as a baby and whom they tend to patronise and look down upon. So when Russ and I and Bill made huts in the woods out of boards and tar-paper which we collected around the foundations of the many cheap houses which the speculators were now putting up, as fast as they could, all over Douglaston, we severely prohibited John Paul and Russ's little brother Tommy and their friends from coming anywhere near us.

And if they did try to come and get into our hut, or even to look at it, we would chase them away with stones.

When I think now of that part of my childhood, the picture I get of my brother John Paul is this: standing in a field, about a hundred yards away from the clump of sumachs where we have built our hut, is this little perplexed five-year-old kid in short pants and a kind of a leather jacket, standing quite still, with his arms hanging down at his sides, and gazing in our direction, afraid to come any nearer on account of the stones, as insulted as he is saddened, and his eyes full of indignation and sorrow. And yet he does not go away. We shout at him to get out of there, to beat it, and go home, and wing a couple of more rocks in that direction, and he does not go away. We tell him to play in some other place. He does not move.

And there he stands, not sobbing, not crying, but angry and unhappy and offended and tremendously sad. And yet he is fascinated by what we are doing, nailing shingles all over our new hut. And his tremendous desire to be with us and to do what we are doing will not permit him to go away. The law written in his nature says that he must be with his elder brother, and do what he is doing: and he cannot understand why this law of love is being so wildly and unjustly violated in his case.

Many times it was like that. And in a sense, this terrible situation is the pattern and prototype of all sin: the deliberate and formal will to reject disinterested love for us for the purely arbitrary reason that we simply do not want it. We will to separate ourselves from that love. We reject it entirely and absolutely, and will not acknowledge it, simply because it does not please us to be loved. Perhaps the inner motive is that the fact of being loved disinterestedly reminds us that we all need love from others, and depend upon the charity of others to carry on our own lives. And we refuse love, and reject society, in so far as it seems, in our own perverse imagination, to imply some obscure kind of humiliation.

There was a time when I and my magnificent friends, in our great hut, having formed a "gang," thought we were sufficiently powerful to antagonize the extremely tough Polish kids who had formed a real gang in Little Neck, a mile away. We used to go over in their neighborhood, and stand, facing in the general direction of the billboards, behind which they had their headquarters, and, from a very safe distance, we would shout defiance and challenge them to come out and fight.

Nobody came out. Perhaps there was nobody at home.

But then, one cold and rainy afternoon, we observed that numbers of large and small figures, varying in age from ten to sixteen, most of them very brawny, with caps pulled down over their eyes in a business-like way, were filtering in, by the various streets, and gathering in the vacant lot outside our house. And there they stood, with their hands in their pockets. They did not make any noise, or yell, or shout any challenges, they just stood around, looking at the house.

There were twenty or twenty-five of them. There were four of us. The climax of the situation came when Frieda, our German maid, told us that she was very busy with house-cleaning, and that we must all get out of the house immediately. Without listening to our extremely nervous protests, she chased us out the back way. We made a dash through several back yards and went down the other block, and ended up safely in the house where Bill lived, which was at the other end of the vacant lot, and from which we viewed the silent and pugnacious group from Little Neck, still standing around, and with the evident determination of staying there for quite a while.

And then an extraordinary thing happened.

The front door of our house, at the other end of the lot, opened. My little brother John Paul came walking down the steps, with a certain amount of dignity and calm. He crossed the street, and started across the lot. He walked towards the Little Neck gang. They all turned towards him. He kept on walking, and walked right into the middle of them. One or two of them took their hands out of their pockets. John Paul just looked at them, turning his head on one side, then on

36

the other. And he walked right through the middle of them, and nobody even touched him.

And so he came to the house where we were. We did not chase him away.

My grandparents were like most other Americans. They were Protestants, but you could never find out precisely what kind of Protestants they were. I, their own grandson, was never able to ascertain. They put money in the little envelopes that came to them from Zion church, but they never went near the place itself. And they also contributed to the Salvation Army and a lot of other things: so you could not tell what they were by the places which they helped to support. Of course, they had sent my uncle in his boyhood to the choir school of the Cathedral of St. John the Divine, on the rock above Harlem, which was then a peaceful bourgeois neighborhood. And they sent John Paul there too, in due course. Indeed, there was even some talk of sending me there. Yet that did not make them Episcopalians. It was not the religion that they patronised, but the school and the atmosphere. In practice, Bonnemaman used to read the little black books of Mary Baker Eddy, and I suppose that was the closest she got to religion.

On the whole, the general attitude around that house was the more or less inarticulate assumption that all religions were more or less praiseworthy on purely natural or social grounds. In any decent suburb of a big city you would expect to run across some kind of a church, once in a while. It was part of the scenery, like the High School and the Y.M.C.A. and the big whale-back roof and water-tank of the movie theater.

The only exceptions to this general acceptability of religions were the Jews and Catholics. Who would want to be a Jew? But then, that was a matter of race more than of religion. The Jews were Jews, but they could not very well help it. But as for the Catholics—it seemed, in Pop's mind, that there was a certain sinister note of malice connected with the

37

profession of anything like the Catholic faith. The Catholic Church was the only one against which I ever heard him speak with any definite bitterness or animosity.

The chief reason was that he himself belonged to some kind of a Masonic organization, called, oddly enough, the Knights Templars. Where they picked up that name, I do not know: but the original Knights Templars were a military religious Order in the Catholic Church, who had an intimate connection with the Cistercians, of which the Trappists are a reform.

Being Knights, the Knights Templars had a sword. Pop kept his sword first in the closet in his den, and then, for a while, it was in the coat closet by the front door, mixed up with the canes and umbrellas, and with the huge policeman's club which Pop evidently believed would be useful if a burglar came around.

I suppose that at the meetings of the Knights Templars to which Pop went less and less frequently, he heard how wicked the Catholic Church was. He had probably heard that from his childhood up. This is what some children hear at home, and it becomes part of their religious training.

If there was another reason why he feared the Church of Rome, it was because of the accident that some of the most corrupt politicians that ever passed a bribe in a New York election were known to be Catholics. To Pop, the word "Catholic" and "Tammany" meant just about the same thing. And since this fitted in very well with what many children have been told about the duplicity and hypocrisy of Catholics, Catholicism had become associated, in his mind, with everything dishonest and crooked and immoral.

This was an impression that probably remained with him to the end of his days, but it ceased to be explicit when a Catholic lady came to live with us as a sort of companion to Bonnemaman, and a general nurse and housekeeper to the whole family. This was no temporary addition to the household. I think we were all very fond of Elsie from the beginning, and Bonnemaman got to depending on her so much that she stayed around and became more and more a part of

38

the family, until she finally entered it altogether by marrying my uncle. With her arrival, Pop no longer let loose any of his tirades against Rome unless some bitter word happened to slip out without deliberation.

This was one of the few things I got from Pop that really took root in my mind, and became part of my mental attitude: this hatred and suspicion of Catholics. There was nothing overt about it. It was simply the deep, almost subconscious aversion from the vague and evil thing, which I called Catholicism, which lived back in the dark corners of my mentality with the other spooks, like death and so on. I did not know precisely what the word meant. It only conveyed a kind of a cold and unpleasant feeling.

The devil is no fool. He can get people feeling about heaven the way they ought to feel about hell. He can make them fear the means of grace the way they do not fear sin. And he does so, not by light but by obscurity, not by realities but by shadows; not by clarity and substance, but by dreams and the creatures of psychosis. And men are so poor in intellect that a few cold chills down their spine will be enough to keep them from ever finding out the truth about anything.

As a matter of fact, by this time I was becoming more and more positively averse to the thought of any religion, although I was only nine. The reason was that once or twice I had to go to Sunday School, and found it such a bore that from then on I went to play in the woods instead. I don't think the family was very grieved.

All this time, Father was abroad. He had gone first to the South of France, to the Roussillon, where I was born. He was living first at Banyuls, then at Collioure, painting landscapes along the Mediterranean shore, and in the red mountains, all the way down to Port Vendres and the borders of Catalonia. Then, after a while, he and the people he was with crossed over into Africa and went inland in Algeria, to a place on the edge of the desert, and there he painted some more.

Letters came from Africa. He sent me a package containing a small burnous, which I could wear, and a stuffed lizard of some sort. At that time I had gathered a small natural history museum of pieces of junk that are to be found around Long Island, like arrowheads and funny-looking stones.

During those years, he was painting some of the best pictures he had ever painted in his life. But then something happened, and we got a letter from one of his friends, telling us that he was seriously ill. He was, in fact, dying.

When Bonnemaman told me this news, I was old enough to understand what it meant, and I was profoundly affected, filled with sorrow and with fear. Was I never to see my father again? This could not happen. I don't know whether or not it occurred to me to pray, but I think by this time it must have, at least once or twice, although I certainly had very little of anything that could be called faith. If I did pray for my father it was probably only one of those blind, semi-instinctive movements of nature that will come to anyone, even an atheist in a time of crisis, and which do not prove the existence of God, exactly, but which certainly show that the need to worship and acknowledge Him is something deeply ingrained in our dependent natures, and simply inseparable from our essence.

It seems that for days Father lay in delirium. Nobody appeared to know what was the matter with him. He was expected to die from moment to moment. But he did not die.

Finally he got past the crisis of this strange sickness, and recovered his consciousness, and began to improve and get well. And when he was on his feet again, he was able to finish some more pictures, and get his things together, and go to London, where he held his most successful exhibition, at the Leicester Galleries, early in 1925.

When he returned to New York, in the early summer of that year, he came in a kind of triumph. He was beginning to be a successful artist. Long ago he had been elected to one of those more or less meaningless British societies, so that he could write F.R.B.A. after his name—which he never did—and I think he was already in *Who's Who*, although that was the kind of thing for which he had supreme contempt.

But now, what was far more useful to an artist, he had

gained the attention and respect of such an important and venerable critic as Roger Fry, and the admiration of people who not only knew what a good painting was, but had some money with which to buy one.

As he landed in New York, he was a very different person —more different than I realized—from the man who had taken me to Bermuda two years before. All I noticed, at the moment, was the fact that he had a beard, to which I strenuously objected, being filled with the provincial snobbery so strong in children and adolescents.

"Are you going to shave it off now, or later?" I inquired, when we got to the house in Douglaston.

"I am not going to shave it off at all," said my father.

"That's crazy," I said. But he was not disturbed. He did shave it off, a couple of years later, by which time I had got used to it.

However, he had something to tell me that upset my complacency far more than the beard. For by now, having become more or less acclimatised in Douglaston, after the unusual experience of remaining some two years in the same place, I was glad to be there, and liked my friends, and liked to go swimming in the bay. I had been given a small camera with which I took pictures, which my uncle caused to be developed for me at the Pennsylvania Drug Store, in the city. I possessed a baseball bat with the word "Spalding" burnt on it in large letters. I thought maybe I would like to become a Boy Scout and, indeed, I had seen a great competition of Boy Scouts in the Flushing Armory, just next door to the Quaker meeting house where I had once got a glimpse of Dan Beard, with his beard.

My father said: "We are going to France."

"France!" I said, in astonishment. Why should anybody want to go to France? I thought: which shows that I was a very stupid and ignorant child. But he persuaded me that he meant what he said. And when all my objections were useless, I burst into tears. Father was not at all unsympathetic about it. He kindly told me that I would be glad to be in France, when I got there, and gave me many reasons why it

41

was a good idea. And finally he admitted that we would not start right away.

With this compromise I was temporarily comforted, thinking perhaps the plan would be dropped after a while. But fortunately it was not. And on August the twenty-fifth of that year the game of Prisoner's Base began again, and we sailed for France. Although I did not know it, and it would not have interested me then, it was the Feast of St. Louis of France.

2

Our Lady of the Museums

How did it ever happen that, when the dregs of the world had collected in western Europe, when Goth and Frank and Norman and Lombard had mingled with the rot of old Rome to form a patchwork of hybrid races, all of them notable for ferocity, hatred, stupidity, craftiness, lust and brutality—how did it happen that, from all this, there should come Gregorian chant, monasteries and cathedrals, the poems of Prudentius, the commentaries and histories of Bede, the *Moralia* of Gregory the Great, St. Augustine's *City of God*, and his *Trinity*, the writings of St. Anselm, St. Bernard's sermons on the Canticles, the poetry of Caedmon and Cynewulf and Langland and Dante, St. Thomas' *Summa*, and the *Oxoniense* of Duns Scotus?

How does it happen that even today a couple of ordinary French stonemasons, or a carpenter and his apprentice, can put up a dovecote or a barn that has more architectural perfection than the piles of eclectic stupidity that grow up at the cost of hundreds of thousands of dollars on the campuses of American universities?

When I went to France, in 1925, returning to the land of my birth, I was also returning to the fountains of the intellectual and spiritual life of the world to which I belonged. I was returning to the spring of natural waters, if you will, but waters purified and cleaned by grace with such powerful effect that even the corruption and decadence of the French society of our day has never been able to poison them entirely, or reduce them once again to their original and barbarian corruption.

And yet it was France that grew the finest flowers of delicacy and grace and intelligence and wit and understanding and proportion and taste. Even the countryside, even the landscape of France, whether in the low hills and lush mead-

43

ows and apple orchards of Normandy or in the sharp and arid and vivid outline of the mountains of Provence, or in the vast, rolling red vineyards of Languedoc, seems to have been made full of a special perfection, as a setting for the best of the cathedrals, the most interesting towns, the most fervent monasteries, and the greatest universities.

But the wonderful thing about France is how all her perfections harmonize so fully together. She has possessed all the skills, from cooking to logic and theology, from bridge-building to contemplation, from vine-growing to sculpture, from cattle-breeding to prayer: and possessed them more perfectly, separately and together, than any other nation.

Why is it that the songs of the little French children are more graceful, their speech more intelligent and sober, their eyes calmer and more profound than those of the children of other nations? Who can explain these things?

France, I am glad I was born in your land, and I am glad God brought me back to you, for a time, before it was too late.

I did not know all these things about France the rainy September evening when we landed at Calais, coming from England through which we had passed on our way.

Nor did I share or understand the enthusiastic satisfaction with which Father got off the boat and walked into the noise of the French station, filled with the cries of porters and with the steam of the French trains.

I was tired, and fell asleep long before we got to Paris. I woke up long enough to be impressed by the welter of lights in the wet streets, and the dark sweep of the Seine, as we crossed one of the countless bridges, while far away the fires on the Eiffel tower spelled "C-I-T-R-O-Ë-N."

The words Montparnasse, Rue des Saints Pères, Gare d'Orléans filled my mind with their unmeaning, and spelled me no certitude concerning the tall grey houses, and the wide shady awnings of the cafés, and the trees, and the people, and the churches, and the flying taxis, and the green and white busses full of noise.

I did not have time, at the age of ten, to make anything

out of this city, but already I knew I was going to like France: and then, once more, we were on a train.

That day, on that express, going into the south, into the Midi, I discovered France. I discovered that land which is really, as far as I can tell, the one to which I do belong, if I belong to any at all, by no documentary title but by geographical birth.

We flew over the brown Loire, by a long, long bridge at Orléans, and from then on I was home, although I had never seen it before, and shall never see it again. It was there, too, that Father told me about Joan of Arc, and I suppose the thought of her was with me, at least in the back of my mind, all the day long. Maybe the thought of her, acting as a kind of implicit prayer by the veneration and love it kindled in me, won me her intercession in heaven, so that through her I was able to get some sort of actual grace out of the sacrament of her land, and to contemplate God without realizing it in all the poplars along those streams, in all the low-roofed houses gathered about the village churches, in the woods and the farms and the bridged rivers. We passed a place called Châteaudun. When the land became rockier, we came to Limoges, with a labyrinth of tunnels, ending in a burst of light and a high bridge and a panorama of the city crowding up the side of a steep hill to the feet of the plain-towered cathedral. And all the time we were getting deeper and deeper into Aquitaine: towards the old provinces of Quercy and Rouergue, where, although we were not sure yet of our destination, I was to live and drink from the fountains of the Middle Ages.

In the evening we came to a station called Brive. Brive-la-Gaillarde. The dusk was gathering. The country was hilly, and full of trees, yet rocky, and you knew that the uplands were bare and wild. In the valleys were castles. It was too dark for us to see Cahors.

And then: Montauban.

What a dead town! What darkness and silence, after the train. We came out of the station into an empty, dusty square, full of shadows, and a dim light, here and there. The hoofs of

45

a cab-horse clopped away along the empty street, taking some of the other people who had descended from the express off into the mysterious town. We picked up our bags and crossed the square to a hotel that was there, one of those low, undefined, grey little hotels, with a dim bulb burning in a downstairs window, illuminating a small café, with a lot of iron tables and a few calendars covered with flyspecks and the big volumes of the Bottin crowding the rickety desk of the sour-faced lady in black who presided over the four customers.

And yet, instead of being dreary, it was pleasant. And although I had no conscious memory of anything like this, it was familiar, and I felt at home. Father threw open the wooden shutters of the room, and looked out into the quiet night, without stars, and said:

"Do you smell the woodsmoke in the air? That is the smell of the Midi."

ii

When we woke up in the morning, and looked out into the bright sunlit air, and saw the low tiled roofs, we realized that we had come upon a scene different from the last kind of landscape we had seen by the light of the previous evening in the train.

We were at the borders of Languedoc. Everything was red. The town was built of brick. It stood on a kind of low bluff, over the clay-colored eddies of the river Tarn. We might almost have been in a part of Spain. But oh! It was dead, that town!

Why were we there? It was not only that Father wanted to continue painting in the south of France. He had come back to us that year with more than a beard. Whether it was his sickness or what, I do not know, but something had made him certain that he could not leave the training and care of his sons to other people, and that he had a responsibility to make some kind of a home, somewhere, where he could at the same time carry on his work and have us living with him, growing up under his supervision. And, what is more, he had become

46

definitely aware of certain religious obligations for us as well as for himself.

I am sure he had never ceased to be a religious man: but now—a thing which I did not remember from my earlier years —he told me to pray, to ask God to help us, to help him paint, to help him have a successful exhibition, to find us a place to live.

When we were settled then, perhaps after a year or two, he would bring John Paul over to France too. Then we would have a home. So far, of course, everything was indefinite. But the reason why he had come to Montauban was that he had been advised that there was a very good school there.

The school in question was called the Institut Jean Calvin, and the recommendation had come from some prominent French Protestants whom Father knew.

I remember we went and visited the place. It was a big, clean, white building overlooking the river. There were some sunny cloisters, full of greenery, and all the rooms were empty, because it was still the time of summer vacation. However, there was something about it that Father did not like, and I was, thank God, never sent there. As a matter of fact it was not so much a school as a kind of Protestant residence where a lot of youths (who belonged, mostly, to fairly well-to-do families) boarded and received religious instruction and supervision and, for the rest, attended the classes of the local Lycée.

And so I obscurely began to realize that, although Father was anxious for me to get some kind of religious training, he was by no means in love with French Protestantism. As a matter of fact, I learned later from some of his friends, that at that time there had been not a little likelihood that he might become a Catholic. He seems to have been much attracted to the Church, but in the end he resisted the attraction because of the rest of us. I think he felt that his first duty was to take the ordinary means at his disposal to get me and John Paul to practice whatever religion was nearest at hand to us, for if he became a Catholic there might have been immense complications with the rest of the family, and we would perhaps have remained without any religion at all.

He would have felt far less hesitant if he had only had some Catholic friends of his own intellectual level—someone who would be able to talk to him intelligently about the faith. But as far as I know, he had none. He had a tremendous respect for the good Catholic people we met, but they were too inarticulate about the Church to be able to tell him anything about it that he could understand—and also, they were generally far too shy.

Then, too, after the first day, it became clear that Montauban was no place for us. There was really nothing there worth painting. It was a good enough town, but it was dull. The only thing that interested Father was the Musée Ingres, filled with meticulous drawings by that painter, who had been born in Montauban: and that collection of cold and careful sketches was not enough to keep anyone at a high pitch of inspiration for much more than fifteen minutes. More characteristic of the town was a nightmarish bronze monument by Bourdelle, outside the museum, which seemed to represent a group of cliff-dwellers battling in a mass of molten chocolate.

However, when we happened to inquire at the Syndicat d'Initiative about places to live, we saw photographs of some little towns which, as we were told, were in a valley of a river called the Aveyron not very far away to the northeast of the city.

The afternoon we took the peculiar, antiquated train out of Montauban into the country, we felt something like the three Magi after leaving Herod and Jerusalem when they caught sight once again of their star.

The locomotive had big wheels and a low, squat boiler, and an inordinately high smoke-stack, so that it seemed to have escaped from the museum, except that it was very sturdy and did its work well. And the three or four little coaches sped us quickly into a territory that was certainly sacramental.

The last town that had a brick campanile to its church, after the manner of all Languedoc, was Montricoux. Then the

48

train entered the Aveyron valley. After that, we were more or less in Rouergue. And then we began to see something.

I did not realize what we were getting into until the train swept around a big curve of the shallow river, and came to stop under the sunny plane trees along the platform of a tiny station, and we looked out the window, and saw that we had just passed along the bottom of a sheer cliff one or two hundred feet high, with a thirteenth-century castle on the top of it. That was Bruniquel. All around us, the steep hills were thick with woods, small gnarled oaks, clinging to the rock. Along the river, the slender poplars rippled with the light of late afternoon, and green waters danced on the stones. The people who got on and off the train were peasants with black smocks, and on the roads we saw men walking beside teams of oxen, drawing their two-wheeled carts: and they guided the placid beasts with their long sticks. Father told me that the people were all talking, not French, but the old patois, langue d'oc.

The next place was Penne. At the meeting of two valleys, a thin escarpment of rock soared up boldly over the river, bent and sharply rising, like an open wing. On the top were the ruins of another castle. Further down, straggling along the ridge, went the houses of the village and somewhere among them the small square tower of a church, an open iron belfry on top, with a visible bell.

The valley seemed to get narrower and deeper as the train followed its narrow single track between the river and the rocks. Sometimes there was enough space between us and the river to contain a small hayfield. Occasionally a deserted dirt road or cattle track would cross our way, and there would be a house and a crossing-gate and one of furious French bells, throwing the sudden scare of its clangor through the windows of the carriage as we passed by.

The valley widened a little to contain the village of Cazals, hanging on to the foot of the hill across the river, and then we were back in the gorge. If you went to the window and looked up, you could see the grey and yellow cliffs towering up so high they almost blocked out the sky. And now we could

49

begin to distinguish caves high up on the rock. Later I would climb up there and visit some of them. Passing through tunnel after tunnel, and over many bridges, through bursts of light and greenery followed by deep shadow, we came at last to the town of our destination.

It was an old, old town. Its history went back to the Roman days—which were the times of the martyred saint, its patron. Antoninus had brought Christianity to the Roman colony in this valley, and later he had been martyred in another place, Pamiers, down in the foothills of the Pyrenees, near Prades, where I was born.

Even in 1925, St. Antonin preserved the shape of a round, walled *bourg:* only the walls themselves were gone, and were replaced on three sides by a wide circular street lined with trees and spacious enough to be called a Boulevard, although you hardly ever saw anything on it but ox-carts and chickens. The town itself was a labyrinth of narrow streets, lined by old thirteenth-century houses, mostly falling into ruins. Nevertheless, the medieval town was there, but for the fact that the streets were no longer crowded and busy, and the houses and shops were no longer occupied by prosperous merchants and artisans, and there was nothing left of the color and gaiety and noise of the Middle Ages. Nevertheless, to walk through those streets was to be in the Middle Ages: for nothing had been touched by man, only by ruin and by the passage of time.

It seems that one of the busiest guilds of the town had been that of the tanners and the old tanneries were still there, along a narrow foul-smelling sewer of a stream that ran through a certain section of the town. But in those old days the whole place had been filled with the activity of all the work belonging to a free and prosperous commune.

And as I say, the center of it all was the church.

Unfortunately, the very importance of the ancient shrine of St. Antonin had drawn down violence upon it in the days of the religious wars. The church that now stood on the ruins was entirely modern, and we could not judge what the old one had been like, or see, reflected in its work and construction, the attitude of the citizens who had built it. Even now, however, the church dominated the town, and each noon and evening sent forth the Angelus bells over the brown, ancient tiled roofs reminding people of the Mother of God who watched over them.

And even now, although I never thought of it and was, indeed, incapable of doing so, since I had no understanding of the concept of Mass, even now, several times each morning, under those high arches, on the altar over the relics of the martyr, took place that tremendous, secret and obvious immolation, so secret that it will never be thoroughly understood by a created intellect, and yet so obvious that its very obviousness blinds us by excess of clarity: the unbloody Sacrifice of God under the species of bread and wine.

Here, in this amazing, ancient town, the very pattern of the place, of the houses and streets and of nature itself, the circling hills, the cliffs and trees, all focussed my attention upon the one, important central fact of the church and what it contained. Here, everywhere I went, I was forced, by the disposition of everything around me, to be always at least virtually conscious of the church. Every street pointed more or less inward to the center of the town, to the church. Every view of the town, from the exterior hills, centered upon the long grey building with its high spire.

The church had been fitted into the landscape in such a way as to become the keystone of its intelligibility. Its presence imparted a special form, a particular significance to everything else that the eye beheld, to the hills, the forests, the fields, the white cliff of the Rocher d'Anglars and to the red bastion of the Roc Rouge, to the winding river, and the green valley of the Bonnette, the town and the bridge, and even to the white stucco villas of the modern bourgeois that dotted the fields and orchards outside the precinct of the vanished ramparts: and the significance that was thus imparted was a supernatural one.

The whole landscape, unified by the church and its heavenward spire, seemed to say: this is the meaning of all created things: we have been made for no other purpose than that men may use us in raising themselves to God, and in proclaiming the glory of God. We have been fashioned, in all our perfection, each according to his own nature, and all our natures ordered and harmonized together, that man's reason and his love might fit in this one last element, this God-given key to the meaning of the whole.

Oh, what a thing it is, to live in a place that is so constructed that you are forced, in spite of yourself, to be at least a virtual contemplative! Where all day long your eyes must turn, again and again, to the House that hides the Sacramental Christ!

I did not even know who Christ was, that He was God. I had not the faintest idea that there existed such a thing as the Blessed Sacrament. I thought churches were simply places where people got together and sang a few hymns. And yet now I tell you, you who are now what I once was, unbelievers, it is that Sacrament, and that alone, the Christ living in our midst, and sacrificed by us, and for us and with us, in the clean and perpetual Sacrifice, it is He alone Who holds our world together, and keeps us all from being poured headlong and immediately into the pit of our eternal destruction. And I tell you there is a power that goes forth from that Sacrament, a power of light and truth, even into the hearts of those who have heard nothing of Him and seem to be incapable of belief.

iii

We soon rented an apartment in a three-story house at the edge of the town, on the Place de la Condamine, where they held the cattle market. But Father planned to build a house of his own, and soon he bought some land nearby on the lower slopes of the big hill that closed off the western arm of the valley of the Bonnette. On top of the hill was a little chapel, now abandoned, called Le Calvaire, and indeed up the rocky path through the vineyards behind our land there had once been a series of shrines, making the fourteen Stations of the Cross between the town and the top of the hill.

But that kind of piety had died away in the nineteenth century: there were not enough good Catholics left to keep it alive.

And then when Father began to make plans for building his house, we travelled all over the countryside looking at places, and also visiting villages where there might be good subjects for pictures.

Thus I was constantly in and out of old churches, and stumbled upon the ruins of ancient chapels and monasteries. We saw wonderful hill towns like Najac and Cordes. Cordes was even more perfectly preserved than St. Antonin, but it did not have the form of our town built around its shrine, although Cordes was, of course, centered upon its church too. But Cordes had been built as a sort of fortified summer resort for the Counts of Languedoc, and its chief attraction were the more or less fancy houses of the court officials who came out there for the hunting with their lord.

Then, too, we went down into the plains to the south, and came to Albi, with the red cathedral of St. Cecilia frowning over the Tarn like a fortress, and from the top of that tower we looked out over the plains of Languedoc, where all the churches were forts. This land was long wild with heresy, and with the fake mysticism that tore men away from the Church and from the Sacraments, and sent them into hiding to fight their way to some strange, suicidal nirvana.

There was a factory in St. Antonin—the only factory in the place—employing the only proletarians, three or four men, one of whom was also the only Communist. The factory made some kind of a machine for raising hay effortlessly from the surface of a field on to the top of a wagon. The man who owned it was called Rodolausse, the town capitalist. He had two sons who ran his plant for him. One of them was a tall, lanky, solemn, dark-haired man with horn-rimmed spectacles.

One evening we were sitting in one of the cafés of the town, a deserted place run by a very old man. Rodolausse got to talking with Father, and I remember his polite enquiry as to whether we were Russians. He got that idea from the beard.

When he found out we had come there to live, he immediately offered to sell us his house, and invited us out there to dinner, that we might see it. The House of Simon de Montfort, as it was called, was a big farm a mile or two out of town on the road to Caylus. It stood up the slope of a hill overlooking the valley of the Bonnette and was itself in the mouth of a deep circular valley full of woods where, as we found, a small stream full of watercress rose from a clear spring. The house itself was an ancient place, and looked as if De Montfort might indeed have lived in it. But it also looked as if he might still be haunting it. It was very dark and gloomy: and, being dark, was no place for a painter. Besides, it was too expensive for us. And Father preferred to build a house of his own.

It was not long after I had started to go to the local elementary school, where I sat with great embarrassment among the very smallest children, and tried to pick up French as we went along, that Father had already drawn up plans for the house we would build on the land he had now bought at the foot of Calvary. It would have one big room, which would be a studio and dining room and living room, and then upstairs there would be a couple of bedrooms. That was all.

We traced out the foundations and Father and a workman began to dig. Then a water diviner came in and found us water and we had a well dug. Near the well Father planted two poplar trees—one for me, one for John Paul—and to the east of the house he laid out a large garden when the following spring came around.

Meanwhile, we had made a lot of friends. I do not know whether it was through the capitalist, Rodolausse, or through the radical-socialist teamster Pierrot, that we got in contact with the local rugby football club, or they with us: but one of the first things that happened after our arrival was that a delegation from the club, the "Avant-Garde de Saint-Antonin," presented themselves to Father and asked him to become president of the club. He was English, and therefore he was an expert, they assumed, in every type of sport. As a matter of fact, he had played rugby for his school in New Zealand. So he became president of the club, and occasionally

54

refereed their wild games, at the risk of his life. It was not only that the rules had changed, since his time, but there was a special interpretation of the rules in St. Antonin which no one could discover without a private revelation or the gift of the discernment of souls. However, he lived through the season.

I used to accompany him and the team to all the games they played away from home, going as far as Figeac to the northeast, deep in the hill country of Rouergue; or Gaillac, on the plains of Languedoc, to the south, a town with one of those fortress-churches and a real stadium for its rugby team. St. Antonin was not, of course, called in to play the Gaillac first-fifteen, but only to play an opener, while the crowds were coming in for the principal game.

In those days the whole south of France was infected with a furious and violent passion for rugby football, and played it with a blood-thirsty energy that sometimes ended in mortal injuries. In the really important games, the referee usually had to be escorted from the grounds afterwards by a special bodyguard, and not infrequently had to make his escape over the fence and through the fields. The only sport that raised a more universal and more intense excitement than rugby, was long-distance bicycle racing. St. Antonin was off the circuit of the big road races, but occasionally there would be a race that came through our hills, and we would stand at the end of the long climb to the top of Rocher d'Anglars, and watch them coming slowly up the hill, with their noses almost scraping the front wheels of their bikes as they bent far down and toiled, with all their muscles clenched into tremendous knots. And the veins stood out on their foreheads.

One of the members of the rugby team was a small, rabbit-like man, the son of the local hay and feed dealer, who owned a car and drove most of the team back and forth from the games. One night he nearly killed himself and about six of us when a rabbit got into the lights on the road ahead of us and kept running in front of the car. Immediately, this wild Frenchman jammed his foot down on the gas and started after the rabbit. The white tail bobbed up and down in the light, always just a few feet ahead of the wheels, and whipping from one side of the road to the other, to throw the auto off his scent: only the auto didn't hunt that way. It just kept roaring after the rabbit, zig-zagging from one side of the road to the other and nearly spilling us all into the ditch.

Those of us who were piled up in the back seat began to get a little nervous, especially when we observed that we were coming to the top of the long steep hill that went winding down into the valley where St. Antonin was. If we kept after that rabbit, we would surely go over the bank, and then we wouldn't stop turning over until we landed in the river, a couple of hundred feet below.

Somebody growled a modest complaint:

"*C'est assez, hein? Tu ne l'attraperas pas!*"

The son of the hay and feed dealer said nothing. He bent over the wheel with his eyes popping at the road, and the white tail in front of us kept darting away from the wheels of the car, zig-zagging from the high bank on one side to the ditch on the other.

And then we came over the hill. The darkness and emptiness of the valley was before us. The road began to descend.

The complaints in the back seat increased, became a chorus. But the driver stepped on the gas even harder. The car careened wildly across the road; we had nearly caught the rabbit. But not quite. He was out there ahead of us again.

"We'll get him on the hill," exclaimed the driver. "Rabbits can't run down-hill, their hind legs are too long."

The rabbit ahead of us was doing a fine job of running down-hill, just about five feet ahead of our front wheels.

Then somebody began to yell: "Look out, look out!"

We were coming to a fork in the road. The main road went on to the left, and an older road sloped off at a steeper incline to the right. In between them was a wall. And the rabbit headed straight for the wall.

"Stop! Stop!" we implored. Nobody could tell which way the rabbit was going to go: and the wall was flying straight at us.

"Hold on!" somebody shouted.

56

The car gave a wild lurch, and if there had been any room in the back we would all have fallen on the floor. But we were not dead. The car was still on the main road, roaring down into the valley and, to our immense relief, there was no rabbit, out there in the lights.

"Did you catch him?" I asked hopefully. "Maybe you caught him back there?"

"Oh, no," replied the driver sadly, "he took the other road."

Our friend the teamster Pierrot was a huge, powerful man, but he did not play on the football team. He was too lazy and too dignified, although he would have been a decorative addition to the outfit. There were three or four others like him, big men with huge black moustaches and bristling eyebrows, as wild as the traditional representations of Gog and Magog. One of them used to play whole games wearing a grey, peaked street-cap. I suppose if we had ever played on a really hot day he would have come out on the field with a straw hat on. Anyway, this element of the team would have made a fine subject for Douanier-Rousseau, and Pierrot would have fitted in admirably. Only his sport was sitting at the table of a café imbibing cognac. Sometimes, too, he made excursions to Toulouse, and once, while we were standing on the bridge, he gave me a bloodcurdling description of a fight he had had with an Arab, with a knife, in the big city.

It was Pierrot who took us to a wedding feast at a farm up by Caylus. I went to several of these feasts, during the time when I was at St. Antonin, and I never saw anything so Gargantuan: and yet it was never wild or disordered. The peasants and the foresters and the others who were there certainly ate and drank tremendously: but they never lost their dignity as human beings. They sang and danced and played tricks on one another, and the language was often fairly coarse, but in a manner which was more or less according to custom, and on the whole the atmosphere was good and healthy, and all this pleasure was sanctified by a Sacramental occasion.

On this occasion Pierrot put on his good black suit and his clean cap and hitched up a gig, and we drove to Caylus. It was the farm of his uncle or cousin. The place was crowded with carts and carriages, and the feast was a more or less communal affair. Everybody had provided something towards it, and Father brought a bottle of strong, black Greek wine which nearly pulverized the host.

There were too many guests to be contained in the big dining room and kitchen of the farm, with its blood-sausages and strings of onions hanging from the beams. One of the barns had been cleaned out and tables had been set up in there, and about one o'clock in the afternoon everybody sat down and began to eat. After the soups, the women began to bring in the main courses from the kitchen: and there were plates and plates of every kind of meat. Rabbit, veal, mutton, lamb, beef, stews and steaks, and fowl, fried, boiled, braised, roasted, sautéed, fricasseed, dished this way and that way, with wine sauces and all other kinds of sauces, with practically nothing else to go with it except an occasional piece of potato or carrot or onion in the garnishing.

"All the year round they live on bread and vegetables and bits of sausage," Father explained, "so now they don't want anything but meat." And I suppose he had the right explanation. But before the meal was half over, I got up from the table and staggered out into the air, and leaned against the wall of the barn, and watched the huge, belligerent geese parading up and down the barn-yard, dragging their tremendous overstuffed livers in the dirt, those livers which would soon be turned into the kind of pâté de foie gras which even now made me sick.

The feast lasted until late in the afternoon, and even when night fell some were still at it there in the barn. But meanwhile the owner of the farm and Pierrot and Father and I had gone out to see an old abandoned chapel that stood on the property. I wonder what it had been: a shrine, a hermitage perhaps? But now, in any case, it was in ruins. And it had a beautiful thirteenth- or fourteenth-century window, empty of course of its glass. Father bought the whole thing, with some of the money he had saved up from his last exhibition, and we eventually used the stones and the window and the door-arches and so on in building our house at St. Antonin.

By the time the summer of 1926 came around, we were well established in St. Antonin, although work on the house had not yet really begun. By this time I had learned French, or all the French that a boy of eleven was expected to use in the ordinary course of his existence, and I remember how I had spent hours that winter reading books about all the other wonderful places there were in France.

Pop had sent us money, at Christmas, and we used some of it to buy a big expensive three volume set of books, full of pictures, called *Le Pays de France*. And I shall never forget the fascination with which I studied it, and filled my mind with those cathedrals and ancient abbeys and those castles and towns and monuments of the culture that had so captivated my heart.

I remember how I looked at the ruins of Jumièges and Cluny, and wondered how those immense basilicas had looked in the days of their glory. Then there was Chartres, with its two unequal spires; the long vast nave of Bourges; the soaring choir of Beauvais; the strange fat romanesque cathedral of Angouleme, and the white byzantine domes of Perigueux. And I gazed upon the huddled buildings of the ancient Grande Chartreuse, crowded together in their solitary valley, with the high mountains loaded with firs, soaring up to their rocky summits on either side. What kind of men had lived in those cells? I cannot say that I wondered much about that, as I looked at the pictures. I had no curiosity about monastic vocations or religious rules, but I know my heart was filled with a kind of longing to breathe the air of that lonely valley and to listen to its silence. I wanted to be in all these places, which the pictures of *Le Pays de France* showed me: indeed, it was a kind of a problem to me and an unconscious source of obscure and half-realized woe, that I could not be in all of them at once.

iv

That summer, 1926, much to Father's distress—because he wanted to stay at St. Antonin and work on the house and at his painting—Pop gathered up a great mountain of baggage in

59

New York, stirred Bonnemaman into action, dressed up my brother John Paul in a new suit and, armed with passports and a whole sheaf of tickets from Thomas Cook and Son, boarded the liner *Leviathan* and started for Europe.

News of this invasion had been disturbing Father for some time. Pop was not content to come and spend a month or two in St. Antonin with us. In fact, he was not particularly anxious to come to this small, forgotten town at all. He wanted to keep on the move and, since he had two months at his disposal, he saw no reason why he could not cover the whole of Europe from Russia to Spain and from Scotland to Constantinople. However, being dissuaded from this Napoleonic ambition, he consented to restrict his appetite for sightseeing to England, Switzerland and France.

In May or June the information reached us that Pop had descended in force upon London, had scoured the Shakespeare country and other parts of England—and was now preparing to cross the channel and occupy the north of France.

We were instructed to get ourselves together and to move northward, join forces with him in Paris, after which we would proceed together to the conquest of Switzerland.

Meanwhile at St. Antonin we had peaceful visitors, two gentle old ladies, friends of the family in New Zealand, and with them we started out, with no haste, on our northward journey. We all wanted to see Rocamadour.

Rocamadour is a shrine to the Mother of God, where an image of Our Lady is venerated in a cave-chapel halfway up a cliff, against the side of which a monastery was built in the Middle Ages. The legend says that the place was first settled by the publican Zacchaeus, the man who climbed the sycamore tree to see Christ as He came by, and whom Christ told to climb down again, and entertain Him in his own house.

At the moment when we were leaving Rocamadour, after a short visit that filled my mind with memory of a long summer evening, with swallows flying around the wall of the old monastery up against the cliff, and around the tower of the new shrine on top of it, Pop was riding around all the châteaux of the Loire in a bus full of Americans. And as they went whizzing through Chenonceaux and Blois and Tours, Pop, who had his pockets crammed full of two- and five-sou pieces, and even francs and two-franc pieces, would dig in and scatter handfuls of coins into the streets whenever they passed a group of playing children. And the dusty wake of the bus would ring with his burst of laughter as all the kids plunged after the coins in a wild scramble.

It was that way all through the valley of the Loire.

When we got to Paris, having left the two old ladies from New Zealand in an obscure town called Saint Céré down in the south, we found Pop and Bonnemaman entrenched in the most expensive hotel they could find. The *Continental* was far beyond their means, but it was 1926 and the franc was so low that Pop's head was completely turned by it, and he had lost all sense of values.

The first five minutes in that hotel room in Paris told us all we needed to know about the way it was going to be for the next two weeks, in the whirlwind tour of Switzerland that was just about to begin.

The room was crammed to the doors with so much useless luggage that you could hardly move around in it. And Bonnemaman and John Paul let it be known that they had sunk into a state of more or less silent opposition and passive resistance to all of Pop's enthusiastic displays of optimism and pep.

When Pop told us about the Loire campaign and the largesse with which he had showered every village from Orléans to Nantes, we realized from the mute pain in Bonnemaman's expression, as she turned an eloquent and pleading look to my father, just how the rest of the family felt about all this. And, seeing what we were in for, we more or less instinctively took sides with the oppressed. It was clear that every move, from now on, was going to be rich in public and private humiliation for the more or less delicate sensibilities of the rest of us, from Bonnemaman who was extremely touchy by nature, to John Paul and myself who were quick to see or imagine that others were laughing at Pop and felt ourselves included in the derision by implication.

And thus we started out for the Swiss frontier, travelling in easy stages seven or eight hours a day in the train and stopping overnight. There was the constant embarkation and debarkation from trains and taxis and hotel busses and each time every one of the sixteen pieces of luggage had to be accounted for, and the voice of my grandfather would be heard echoing along the walls of the greatest railway stations in Europe. "Martha, where the dickens did you leave that pigskin bag?"

On every piece of luggage, by way of identification, Pop had pasted a pink American two-cent stamp, a device which had aroused sharp and instantaneous criticism from myself and John Paul. "What are you trying to do, Pop," we asked with sarcasm. "Are you going to send that stuff through the mail?"

The first day was not so bad for me and Father, because we were still in France. We saw a little of Dijon, and the train passed through Besançon on the way to Basle. But as soon as we got into Switzerland, things were different.

For some reason, we found Switzerland extremely tedious. It was not Father's kind of landscape, and anyway he had no time to sketch or paint anything, even if he had wanted to. In every city we hunted, first thing of all, for the museum. But the museums were never satisfactory. They were filled mostly with huge canvasses by some modern Swiss national artist, paintings representing monstrous great executioners trying to chop the heads off Swiss patriots. Besides, it was always hard for us to find the museum in the first place, because we did not know German, and we couldn't make any sense out of the answers people gave us. Then when we finally did get there, instead of the comfort of a few decent pictures, we would immediately be confronted by another immense red and yellow cartoon by this Swiss jingo whose name I have forgotten.

Finally we took to making fun of everything in the museums, and playing around, and putting our hats on the statues, which was all right because the place was always totally deserted anyway. But once or twice we nearly got in trouble with the stuffy Swiss custodians, who came around the corner by surprise and found us mocking the hatted masterworks, kidding the busts of Beethoven and the rest.

As a matter of fact, the only pleasure Father got out of the whole expedition was a jazz concert he heard in Paris, given by a big American Negro orchestra—I cannot imagine who it was. I think it was too far back for Louis Armstrong: but Father was very happy with that. I did not go. Pop did not approve of jazz. But when we got to Lucerne, there was an orchestra in the hotel, and our table in the dining room was so close to it that I could reach out and touch the drum. And the drummer was a Negro with whom I immediately made friends, although he was rather shy. Meals were very interesting with all this business-like drumming going on right in my ear, and I was more fascinated by the activities of the drummer than I was by the melons and meats that were set before us. This was the only pleasure I got out of Switzerland and then, almost immediately, Pop got our table changed.

The rest of the time was one long fight. We fought on pleasure steamers, we fought on funicular railways, we fought on the tops of mountains and at the foot of mountains and by the shores of lakes and under the heavy branches of the evergreens.

In the hotel at Lucerne, John Paul and I nearly came to blows (Bonnemaman being on John Paul's side) over the question as to whether the English had stolen the tune of *God Save the King* from *My Country 'Tis of Thee* or whether the Americans had cribbed *My Country 'Tis of Thee* from *God Save the King*. By this time, since I was on Father's British passport, I considered myself English.

Perhaps the worst day of all was the day we climbed the Jungfrau—in a train. All the way up I was arguing with Pop, who thought we were being cheated, for he contended that the Jungfrau was not nearly so high as all the other mountains around us, and he had embarked on this excursion on the more or less tacit assumption that the Jungfrau was the highest mountain around these parts: and now look, the Eiger and the Monch were much higher! I was vehement in explaining that the Jungfrau looked lower because it was further away, but Pop did not believe in my theory of perspective.

By the time we got to the Jungfrau *joch*, everybody was ready to fall down from nervous exhaustion, and the height made Bonnemaman faint, and Pop began to feel sick, and I had a big crisis of tears in the dining room, and then when Father and I and John Paul walked out into the blinding white-snow field without dark glasses we all got headaches; and so the day, as a whole, was completely horrible.

Then, in Interlaken, although Pop and Bonnemaman had the intense consolation of being able to occupy the same rooms that had been used only a few months before by Douglas Fairbanks and Mary Pickford, John Paul humiliated the whole family by falling fully dressed into a pond full of gold-fish and running through the hotel dripping with water and green-weeds. Finally, we were all scared out of our wits when one of the maids, exhausted by the strain of waiting on so many hundreds of English and American tourists, fainted, while carrying a loaded tray, and crashed to the floor in a tornado of dishes right behind my chair.

We were glad to get out of Switzerland, and back into France, but by the time we reached Avignon, I had developed such a disgust for sightseeing that I would not leave the hotel to go and see the Palace of the Popes. I remained in the room and read *Tarzan of the Apes*, finishing the whole book before Father and John Paul returned from what was probably the only really interesting thing we had struck in the whole miserable journey.

v

Pop had come very unwillingly to St. Antonin, and as soon as he got there he tried to leave again. The streets were too dirty. They disgusted him. But Bonnemaman refused to move until the full month, or whatever time they had planned to stay, had passed.

However, one of the official family acts that took place during this time was an excursion to Montauban, and the inspection of the Lycée to which I was to be sent in the fall.

I suppose those brick cloisters looked innocent enough in the afternoon sun of late August, when they were empty of the fiends in black smocks who were to fill them in late September. I was to get my fill of bitterness in those buildings, in due time.

Pop and Bonnemaman and John Paul and all the luggage left on the express for Paris as August came to an end. Then, in the first week of September, came the patronal feast of Saint Antonin, with torchlight processions, and everybody dancing the polka and the schottische under the Japanese lanterns on the esplanade. There were many other attractions and excitements, including a certain fanciful novelty in shooting galleries. At one end of town, there was a pigeon tied by the leg to the top of a tree, and everybody blasted at it with a shotgun until it was dead. At the other end of town, by the river bank, men were shooting at a chicken which was tied to a floating box, moored out in the center of the stream.

For my own part, I entered a great competition with most of the boys and youths of the town, in which we all jumped into the river and swam after a duck that was thrown off the bridge. It was finally caught by a respectable fellow called Georges who was studying to be a school-teacher at the normal school in Montauban.

At this time, too, being eleven and a half years old, I fell in love with a mousy little girl with blonde locks called Henriette. It was a rather desultory affair. She went home and told her parents that the son of the Englishman was in love with her, and her mother clapped her hands and their household rang with alleluias on that day. The next time I saw her she was very friendly, and during one of the dances, with a kind of official artfulness, she allowed me to chase her 'round and 'round a tree.

Then the artificiality of the business dawned on me and I went home. Father said to me: "What's this I hear about you chasing after girls at your age?" After that life became very serious, and a few weeks later I put on my new blue uniform and went off to the Lycée.

Although by this time I knew French quite well, the first day in the big, gravelled yard, when I was surrounded by those fierce, cat-like little faces, dark and morose, and looked into those score of pairs of glittering and hostile eyes, I forgot every word, and could hardly answer the furious questions that were put to me. And my stupidity only irritated them all the more. They began to kick me, and to pull and twist my ears, and push me around, and shout various kinds of insults. I learned a great deal of obscenity and blasphemy in the first few days, simply by being the direct or indirect object of so much of it.

After this everybody accepted me and became quite friendly and pleasant, once they were used to my pale, blue-eyed and seemingly stupid English face. Nevertheless, when I lay awake at night in the huge dark dormitory and listened to the snoring of the little animals all around me, and heard through the darkness and the emptiness of the night the far screaming of the trains, or the mad iron cry of a bugle in a distant *caserne* of Senegalese troops, I knew for the first time in my life the pangs of desolation and emptiness and abandonment.

At first I used to go home nearly every Sunday taking the early train from Montauban-Villenouvelle, at about five-thirty in the morning. And I would plead with Father to let me out of that miserable school, but it was in vain. After about two months I got used to it and ceased to be so unhappy. The wound was no longer so raw: but I was never happy or at peace in the violent and unpleasant atmosphere of those brick cloisters.

The children I had associated with at St. Antonin had not been by any means angels, but there had at least been a certain simplicity and affability about them. Of course, the boys who went to the Lycée were of the same breed and the same stamp: there was no specific difference, except that they came from families that were better off. All my friends at St. Antonin had been the children of workmen and peasants, with whom I sat in the elementary school. But when a couple of hundred of these southern French boys were thrown together in the prison of that Lycée, a subtle change was operated in their spirit and mentality. In fact, I noticed that when you were with them separately, outside the school, they were mild and peaceable and humane enough. But when they were all together there seemed to be some diabolical spirit of cruelty and viciousness and obscenity and blasphemy and envy and hatred that banded them together against all goodness and against one another in mockery and fierce cruelty and in vociferous, uninhibited filthiness. Contact with that wolf-pack felt very patently like contact with the mystical body of the devil: and, especially in the first few days, the members of that body did not spare themselves in kicking me around without mercy.

The students were divided into two strictly segregated groups, and I was among "les petits," those in "quatrième," the fourth class, and below it. The oldest among us were fifteen and sixteen, and among these were five or six big morose bullies with thick black hair growing out of their foreheads almost down to the eyebrows. They were physically stronger than anybody else and, though less intelligent, they were craftier in the works of evil, louder in obscenity and completely unrestrained in their brutality, when the mood was on them. Of course, they were not always unpleasant and hostile: but in a sense their friendship was more dangerous than their enmity and, in fact, it was this that did the most harm: because the good children who came to the school quickly got into the habit of tolerating all the unpleasantness of these individuals, in order not to get their heads knocked off for failing to applaud. And so the whole school, or at least our part of it, was dominated by their influence.

When I think of the Catholic parents who sent their children to a school like that, I begin to wonder what was wrong with their heads. Down by the river, in a big clean white building, was a college run by the Marist Fathers. I had never been inside it: indeed, it was so clean that it frightened me. But I knew a couple of boys who went to it. They were sons of the little lady who ran the pastry shop opposite the church at St. Antonin and I remember them as exceptionally nice fellows, very pleasant and good. It never occurred to anyone to despise them for being pious. And how unlike the products of the Lycée they were!

When I reflect on all this, I am overwhelmed at the thought of the tremendous weight of moral responsibility that Catholic parents accumulate upon their shoulders by not sending their children to Catholic schools. Those who are not of the Church have no understanding of this. They cannot be expected to. As far as they can see, all this insistence on Catholic schools is only a moneymaking device by which the Church is trying to increase its domination over the minds of men, and its own temporal prosperity. And of course most non-Catholics imagine that the Church is immensely rich, and that all Catholic institutions make money hand over fist, and that all the money is stored away somewhere to buy gold and silver dishes for the Pope and cigars for the College of Cardinals.

Is it any wonder that there can be no peace in a world where everything possible is done to guarantee that the youth of every nation will grow up absolutely without moral and religious discipline, and without the shadow of an interior life, or of that spirituality and charity and faith which alone can safeguard the treaties and agreements made by governments?

And Catholics, thousands of Catholics everywhere, have the consummate audacity to weep and complain because God does not hear their prayers for peace, when they have neglected not only His will, but the ordinary dictates of natural reason and prudence, and let their children grow up according to the standards of a civilization of hyenas.

The experience of living with the kind of people I found in the Lycée was something new to me, but in degree, rather than in kind. There was the same animality and toughness and insensitivity and lack of conscience that existed to some extent in my own character, and which I had found more or less everywhere.

But these French children seemed to be so much tougher and more cynical and more precocious than anyone else I had ever seen. How, then, could I fit them in with the ideal of France which my father had, and which even I had then in an obscure and inchoate form? I suppose the only answer is *corruptio optimi pessima*. Since evil is the defect of good, the lack of a good that ought to be there, and nothing positive in itself, it follows that the greatest evil is found where the highest good has been corrupted. And I suppose the most shocking thing about France is the corruption of French spirituality into flippancy and cynicism; of French intelligence into sophistry; of French dignity and refinement into petty vanity and theatrical self-display; of French charity into a disgusting fleshly concupiscence, and of French faith into sentimentality or puerile atheism. There was all of this in the Lycée Ingres, at Montauban.

However, as I say, I adjusted myself to the situation, and got into a group of more or less peaceful friends who had more wit than obscenity about them and were, in fact, the more intelligent children in the three lower classes. I say intelligent; I mean, also, precocious.

But they had ideals and ambitions and, as a matter of fact, by the middle of my first year, I remember we were all furiously writing novels. On the days when we went out for walks, two by two into the country in a long line which broke up into groups at the edge of town, my friends and I would get together, walking in a superior way, with our caps on the backs of our heads and our hands in our pockets, like the great intellectuals that we were, discussing our novels. The discussion was not merely confined to telling the plot of what we were writing: a certain amount of criticism was passed back and forth.

For instance—I was engaged in a great adventure story, the scene of which was laid in India, and the style of which was somewhat influenced by Pierre Loti. It was written in French. At one point in the story I had the hero, who was in financial difficulties, accept a loan of some money from the heroine. This concept evoked loud cries of protest from my confrères, who found that it offended all the most delicate standards required in a romantic hero. What do you mean, accept money from the heroine! *Allons donc, mon vieux, c'est impossible, ça! C'est tout à fait inouï!* I had not thought of that at all, but I made the change.

That particular novel was never finished, as I remember. But I know I finished at least one other, and probably two, besides one which I wrote at St. Antonin before coming to the Lycée. They were all scribbled in exercise books, profusely illustrated in pen and ink—and the ink was generally bright blue.

One of the chief of these works, I remember, was inspired by Kingsley's *Westward Ho!* and by *Lorna Doone,* and it was about a man living in Devonshire in the sixteenth century. The villains were all Catholics, in league with Spain, and the book ended in a tremendous naval battle off the coast of Wales, which I illustrated with great care. At one point in the book a priest, one of the villains, set fire to the house of the heroine. I did not tell my friends this. I think they would have been offended. They were at least nominal Catholics, and were among the students who lined up two by two to go to Mass at the Cathedral on Sunday mornings.

On the other hand, I do not think they can have been very well instructed Catholics, for one day, as we were emerging from the Lycée, on the way out to one of those walks, we passed two religious in black soutanes, with black bushy beards, standing in the square before the school, and one of my friends hissed in my ear: "Jesuits!" For some reason or other he was scared of Jesuits. And, as a matter of fact, now that I know more about religious Orders, I realize that they were not Jesuits but Passionist missionaries, with the white insignia of the Passionists on their breasts.

At first, on the Sundays when I remained at the Lycée, I stayed in *Permanence* with the others who did not go to Mass at the Cathedral. That is, I sat in the study hall reading the novels of Jules Verne or Rudyard Kipling (I was very much affected by a French translation of *The Light That Failed*). But later on, Father arranged for me to receive instructions, with a handful of others, from a little fat Protestant minister who came to the Lycée to evangelize us.

On Sunday mornings we gathered around the stove in the bleak, octagonal edifice which had been erected in one of the courts as a Protestant "temple" for the students. The minister was a serious little man, and he explained the parables of the Good Samaritan and the Pharisee and the Publican and so on. I don't remember that there was any particularly deep spirituality about it, but there was nothing to prevent him from showing us the obvious moral lessons.

I am grateful that I got at least that much of religion, at an age when I badly needed it: it was years since I had even been inside a church for any other purpose than to look at the stained glass windows or the Gothic vaulting. However, it was practically useless. What is the good of religion without personal spiritual direction? Without Sacraments, without any means of grace except a desultory prayer now and then, at intervals, and an occasional vague sermon?

There was also a Catholic chapel in the Lycée, but it was falling into ruins and the glass was out of most of the windows. Nobody ever saw the inside of it, because it was locked up tight. I suppose back in the days when the Lycée was built the Catholics had managed, at the cost of several years of patient effort, to get this concession out of the government people who were erecting the school: but in the long run it did not do them much good.

The only really valuable religious and moral training I ever got as a child came to me from my father, not systematically, but here and there and more or less spontaneously, in the course of ordinary conversations. Father never applied himself, of set purpose, to teach me religion. But if something spiritual was on his mind, it came out more or less naturally. And this is the kind of religious teaching, or any other kind of teaching, that has the most effect. "A good man out of the good treasure of his heart, bringeth forth good fruit; and an evil man out of the evil treasure bringeth forth that which is evil. For out of the abundance of the heart the mouth speaketh."

71

And it is precisely this speech "out of the abundance of the heart" that makes an impression and produces an effect in other people. We give ear and pay at least a partially respectful attention to anyone who is really sincerely convinced of what he is saying, no matter what it is, even if it is opposed to our own ideas.

I have not the slightest idea what the little *pasteur* told us about the Pharisee and the Publican, but I shall never forget a casual remark Father happened to make, in which he told me of St. Peter's betrayal of Christ, and how, hearing the cock crow, Peter went out and wept bitterly. I forget how it came up, and what the context was that suggested it: we were just talking casually, standing in the hall of the flat we had taken on the Place de la Condamine.

I have never lost the vivid picture I got, at that moment, of Peter going out and weeping bitterly. I wonder how I ever managed to forget, for so many years, the understanding I acquired at that moment of how St. Peter felt, and of what his betrayal meant to him.

Father was not afraid to express his ideas about truth and morality to anybody that seemed to need them—that is, if a real occasion arose. He did not, of course, go around interfering with everybody else's business. But once his indignation got the better of him, and he gave a piece of his mind to a shrew of a French-woman, one of those spiteful sharp-tongued *bourgeoises*, who was giving free expression to her hatred of one of her neighbors who very much resembled herself.

He asked her why she thought Christ had told people to love their enemies. Did she suppose God commanded this for His benefit? Did He get anything out of it that He really needed from us? Or was it not rather for our own good that he had given us this commandment? He told her that if she had any sense, she would love other people if only for the sake of the good and health and peace of her own soul, instead of tearing herself to pieces with her own envy and spitefulness. It was St. Augustine's argument, that envy and hatred try to pierce our neighbor with a sword, when the blade cannot reach him unless it first passes through our own body. I suppose Father had never read any of St. Augustine, but he would have liked him.

This incident with the shrew reminds one a little of Léon Bloy. Father had not read him either, but he would have liked him too. They had much in common, but Father shared none of Bloy's fury. If he had been a Catholic, his vocation as a lay-contemplative would certainly have developed along the same lines. For I am sure he had that kind of a vocation. But unfortunately it never really developed, because he never got to the Sacraments. However, there were in him the latent germs of the same spiritual poverty and all of Bloy's hatred of materialism and of false spiritualities and of worldly values in people who called themselves Christians.

In the winter of 1926 Father went to Murat. Murat is in the Cantal, the old Province of Auvergne, a Catholic province. It is in the mountains of central France, green mountains, old volcanoes. The valleys are full of rich pastures and the mountains are heavy with fir trees or raise their green domes into the sky, bare of woods, covered with grass. The people of this land are Celts, mostly. The Auvergnats have been more or less laughed at, in French tradition, for their simplicity and rusticity. They are very stolid people, but very good people.

At Murat, Father boarded with a family who had a little house, a sort of a small farm, on the slope of one of the steep hills outside the town, and I went up there to spend the Christmas holidays, that year.

Murat was a wonderful place. It was deep in snow, and the houses with their snow-covered roofs relieved the grey and blue and slate-dark pattern of the buildings crowded together on the sides of three hills. The town huddled at the foot of a rock crowned by a colossal statue of the Immaculate Conception, which seemed to me, at the time, to be too big, and to bespeak too much religious enthusiasm. By now I realize that it did not indicate any religious excess at all. These people wanted to say in a very obvious way that they loved Our Lady, who should indeed be loved and revered, as a Queen of great power and a Lady of immense goodness and mercy, mighty in her intercession for us before the throne of God, tremen-

73

dous in the glory of her sanctity and her fullness of grace as Mother of God. For she loves the children of God, who are born into the world with the image of God in their souls, and her powerful love is forgotten, and it is not understood, in the blindness and foolishness of the world.

However, I did not bring up the subject of Murat in order to talk about this statue, but about M. and Mme. Privat. They were the people with whom we boarded, and long before we got to Murat, when the train was climbing up the snowy valley, from Aurillac, on the other side of the Puy du Cantal, Father was telling me: "Wait until you see the Privats."

In a way, they were to be among the most remarkable people I ever knew.

The Auvergnats are, as a rule, not tall. The Privats were both of them not much taller than I was, being then twelve, but tall for my age. I suppose M. Privat was about five foot three or four, but not more. But he was tremendously broad, a man of great strength. He seemed to have no neck, but his head rose from his shoulders in a solid column of muscle and bone, and for the rest, his shadow was almost completely square. He wore a black broad-brimmed hat, like most of the peasants of the region, and it gave his face an added solemnity when his sober and judicious eyes looked out at you peacefully from under the regular brows and that regular brim above them. These two decks, two levels of regularity, added much to the impression of solidity and immobility and impassiveness which he carried with him everywhere, whether at work or at rest.

His little wife was more like a bird, thin, serious, earnest, quick, but also full of that peacefulness and impassiveness which, as I now know, came from living close to God. She wore a funny little headdress which I find it almost impossible to describe, except to say that it looked like a little sugar-loaf perched on top of her head, and garnished with a bit of black lace. The women of Auvergne still wear that headdress.

It is a great pleasure for me to remember such good and kind people and to talk about them, although I no longer possess any details about them. I just remember their kindness and goodness to me, and their peacefulness and their utter simplicity. They inspired real reverence, and I think, in a way, they were certainly saints. And they were saints in that most effective and telling way: sanctified by leading ordinary lives in a completely supernatural manner, sanctified by obscurity, by usual skills, by common tasks, by routine, but skills, tasks, routine which received a supernatural form from grace within, and from the habitual union of their souls with God in deep faith and charity.

Their farm, their family, and their Church were all that occupied these good souls; and their lives were full.

Father, who thought more and more of my physical and moral health, realized what a treasure he had found in these two, and consequently Murat was more and more in his mind as a place where I should go and get healthy.

That winter, at the Lycée, I had spent several weeks in the infirmary with various fevers, and the following summer, when Father had to go to Paris, he took the opportunity to send me once again to Murat, to spend a few weeks living with the Privats, who would feed me plenty of butter and milk and would take care of me in every possible way.

Those were weeks that I shall never forget, and the more I think of them, the more I realize that I must certainly owe the Privats for more than butter and milk and good nourishing food for my body. I am indebted to them for much more than the kindness and care they showed me, the goodness and the delicate solicitude with which they treated me as their own child, yet without any assertive or natural familiarity. As a child, and since then too, I have always tended to resist any kind of a possessive affection on the part of any other human being—there has always been this profound instinct to keep clear, to keep free. And only with truly supernatural people have I ever felt really at my ease, really at peace.

That was why I was glad of the love the Privats showed me, and was ready to love them in return. It did not burn you, it did not hold you, it did not try to imprison you in

75

demonstrations, or trap your feet in the snares of its interest.

I used to run in the woods, and climb the mountains. I went up the Plomb du Cantal, which is nothing more than a huge hill, with a boy who was, I think, the Privats' nephew. He went to a Catholic school taught, I suppose, by priests. It had not occurred to me that every boy did not talk like the brats I knew at the Lycée. Without thinking, I let out some sort of a remark of the kind you heard all day long at Montauban, and he was offended and asked where I had picked up that kind of talk. And yet, while being ashamed of myself, I was impressed by the charitableness of his reaction. He dismissed it at once, and seemed to have forgotten all about it, and left me with the impression that he excused me on the grounds that I was English and had used the expression without quite knowing what it meant.

After all, this going to Murat was a great grace. Did I realize it? I did not know what a grace was. And though I was impressed with the goodness of the Privats, I could not fail to realize what was its root and its foundation. And yet it never occurred to me at the time to think of being like them, of profiting in any way by their example.

I think I only talked to them once about religion. We were all sitting on the narrow balcony looking out over the valley, at the hills turning dark blue and purple in the September dusk. Somehow, something came up about Catholics and Protestants and immediately I had the sense of all the solidity and rectitude of the Privats turned against me, accusing me like the face of an impregnable fortification.

So I began to justify Protestantism, as best I could. I think they had probably said that they could not see how I managed to go on living without the faith: for there was only one Faith, one Church. So I gave them the argument that every religion was good: they all led to God, only in different ways, and every man should go according to his own conscience, and settle things according to his own private way of looking at things.

They did not answer me with any argument. They simply looked at one another and shrugged and Monsieur Privat said quietly and sadly: *"Mais c'est impossible."*

It was a terrible, a frightening, a very humiliating thing to feel all their silence and peacefulness and strength turned against me, accusing me of being estranged from them, isolated from their security, cut off from their protection and from the strength of their inner life by my own fault, by my own wilfulness, by my own ignorance, and my uninstructed Protestant pride.

One of the humiliating things about it was that I wanted them to argue, and they despised argument. It was as if they realized, as I did not, that my attitude and my desire of argument and religious discussion implied a fundamental and utter lack of faith, and a dependence on my own lights, and attachment to my own opinion.

What is more, they seemed to realize that I did not believe in anything, and that anything I might say I believed would be only empty talk. Yet they did not give me the feeling that this was some slight matter, something to be indulged in a child, something that could be left to work itself out in time, of its own accord. I had never met people to whom belief was a matter of such moment. And yet there was nothing they could do for me directly. But what they could do, I am sure they did, and I am glad they did it. And I thank God from the bottom of my heart that they were concerned, and so deeply and vitally concerned, at my lack of faith.

Who knows how much I owe to those two wonderful people? Anything I say about it is only a matter of guessing but, knowing their charity, it is to me a matter of moral certitude that I owe many graces to their prayers, and perhaps ultimately the grace of my conversion and even of my religious vocation. Who shall say? But one day I shall know, and it is good to be able to be confident that I will see them again and be able to thank them.

vi

Father had gone to Paris to be best man at the wedding of one of his friends from the old days in New Zealand. Capt. John Chrystal had made himself a career in the British army

77

and was an officer in the hussars. Later on he became Governor of a prison: but he was not as dreary as that might imply. After the wedding, the Captain and his wife went off on their honeymoon, and the mother of the new Mrs. Chrystal came down to St. Antonin with Father.

Mrs. Stratton was an impressive kind of a person. She was a musician, and a singer, but I forget whether she had been on the stage: in any case, she was not a very theatrical character, rather the opposite, although she had a certain amount of dash about her.

She was not what you would call elderly, by any means, and besides she was a woman of great vitality and strength of character, with rich intelligence and talent, and strong and precise ideas about things. Her convictions commanded respect, as did her many talents, and above all her overwhelming personal dignity. You felt that she ought to have been called Lady Stratton, or the Countess of something.

At first I was secretly resentful of the great influence she at once began to exercise over our lives, and thought she was bossing our affairs too much, but even I was able to realize that her views and advice and guidance were very valuable things. But so strong was her influence that I think it was due to her more than to anyone else that we gave up the idea of living permanently in St. Antonin.

The house was almost finished and ready for occupation, and it was a beautiful little house too, simple and solid. It looked good to live in, with that one big room with the medieval window and a huge medieval fireplace. Father had even managed to procure a winding stone stair and it was by that that you went up to the bedroom. The garden around the house, where Father had done much work, would have been fine.

On the other hand, Father was travelling too much for the house to be really useful. In the winter of 1927 he was some months at Marseilles and the rest of the time at Cette, another Mediterranean port. Soon he would have to go to England, for by this time he was ready for another exhibition. All this time I was at the Lycée, becoming more and more hard-boiled in my precocity, and getting accustomed to the idea of growing up as a Frenchman.

Then Father went to London for the exhibition.

It was the spring of 1928. The school year would soon be over. I was not thinking much about the future. All I knew was that Father would be back from England in a few days.

It was a bright, sunny morning in May when he arrived at the Lycée, and the first thing he told me was to get my things packed: we were going to England.

I looked around me like a man that has had chains struck from his hands. How the light sang on the brick walls of the prison whose gates had just burst open before me, sprung by some invisible and beneficent power: my escape from the Lycée was, I believe, providential.

In the last moments in which I had an opportunity to do so, I tasted the ferocious delights of exultant gloating over the companions I was about to leave. They stood around me in the sun, with their hands hanging at their sides, wearing their black smocks and their berets, and laughing and sharing my excitement, not without envy.

And then I was riding down the quiet street in a carriage, with my luggage beside me, and Father talking about what we were going to do. How lightly the cab-horse's hoofs rang out in the hard, white dirt of the street! How gaily they echoed along the pale smug walls of the dusty houses! "Liberty!" they said, "liberty, liberty, liberty, liberty," all down the street.

We passed the big polygonal barn of a post-office, covered with the tatters of ancient posters, and entered under the dappled shadow of the plane trees. I looked ahead, up the long street to Villenouvelle station, where I had taken the train so many times in the small hours of the morning, on my way home to spend the Sunday in St. Antonin.

When we got on the little train, and travelled the way we had first come to the Aveyron valley, I did indeed feel my heart tighten at the loss of my thirteenth century: but oh, it had long ceased to belong to us. We had not been able to hold on, for very long, to the St. Antonin of the first year:

and the bitter lye of the Lycée had burned all its goodness out of me again, and I was cauterized against it, and had become somewhat insensitive to it: not so much so, however, that I did not feel a little sad at leaving it for ever.

It is sad, too, that we never lived in the house that Father built. But never mind! The grace of those days has not been altogether lost, by any means.

Before I was really able to believe that I was out of the Lycée for good, we were racing through Picardy on the Nord railway. Pretty soon the atmosphere would take on that dim pearlish grey that would tell us we were nearing the Channel, and all along the line we would read the big billboards saying, in English: "Visit Egypt!"

Then, after that, the channel steamer, Folkestone cliffs, white as cream in the sunny haze, the jetty, the grey-green downs and the line of prim hotels along the top of the rock: these things all made me happy. And the cockney cries of the porters and the smell of strong tea in the station refreshment room spelled out all the associations of what had, up to now, always been a holiday country for me, a land heavy with awe-inspiring proprieties, but laden with all kinds of comforts, and in which every impact of experience seemed to reach the soul through seven or eight layers of insulation.

England meant all this for me, in those days, and continued to do so for a year or two more, because going to England meant going to Aunt Maud's house in Ealing.

The red brick house at 18 Carlton Road, with the little lawn that was also a bowling green and the windows looking out on the enclosed patch of grass which was the Durston House cricket field, was a fortress of nineteenth-century security. Here in Ealing, where all the Victorian standards stood entrenched in row upon row of identical houses, Aunt Maud and Uncle Ben lived in the very heart and the center of the citadel, and indeed Uncle Ben was one of the commanders.

The retired headmaster of Durston House Preparatory School for Boys, on Castlebar Road, looked like almost all the great, tearful, solemn war-lords of Victorian society. He was a stoop-shouldered man with a huge, white waterfall moustache, a pince-nez, ill-fitting tweeds. He walked slowly and with a limp, because of his infirmities, and required much attention from everybody, especially Aunt Maud. When he spoke, although he spoke quietly and distinctly, you knew he had a booming voice if he wanted to use it, and sometimes when he had a particularly dramatic statement to make, his eyes would widen, and he would stare you in the face, and shake his finger at you, and intone the words like the ghost in Hamlet: then, if that had been the point of some story, he would sit back in his chair, and laugh quietly, displaying his great teeth, and gazing from face to face of those who sat at his feet.

As for Aunt Maud, I think I have met very few people in my life so like an angel. Of course, she was well on in years, and her clothes, especially her hats, were of a conservatism most extreme. I believe she had not forsaken a detail of the patterns that were popular at the time of the Diamond Jubilee. She was a sprightly and charming person, a tall, thin, quiet, meek old lady who still, after all the years, had something about her of the sensible and sensitive Victorian girl. Nice, in the strict sense, and in the broad colloquial sense, was a word made for her: she was a very nice person. In a way, her pointed nose and her thin smiling lips even suggested the expression of one who had just finished pronouncing that word. "How nice!"

Now that I was going to go to school in England, I would be more and more under her wing. In fact, I had barely landed, when she took me on one of those shopping expeditions in Oxford Street that was the immediate prelude to Ripley Court—a school in Surrey which was now in the hands of her sister-in-law, Mrs. Pearce, the wife of Uncle Ben's late brother, Robert. He had been killed in a cycling accident when, coming to the bottom of a hill, he had failed to turn the corner and had run straight into a brick wall. His brakes had gone back on him halfway down.

It was on one of those mornings in Oxford Street, perhaps not the very first one, that Aunt Maud and I had a great conversation about my future. We had just bought me several pairs of grey flannel trousers and a sweater and some shoes and some grey flannel shirts and one of those floppy flannel hats that English children have to wear, and now, having emerged from D. H. Evans, were riding down Oxford Street on the top of an open bus, right up in the front, where one could see simply everything.

"I wonder if Tom has thought at all about his future," Aunt Maud said and looked at me, winking and blinking with both eyes as a sign of encouragement. I was Tom. She sometimes addressed you in the third person, like that, perhaps as a sign of some delicate, inward diffidence about bringing the matter up at all.

I admitted that I had thought a little about the future, and what I wanted to be. But I rather hesitated to tell her that I wanted to be a novelist.

"Do you think writing would be a good profession for anyone?" I said tentatively.

"Yes indeed, writing is a very fine profession! But what kind of writing would you like to do?"

"I have been thinking that I might write stories," I said.

"I imagine you would probably do quite well at that, some day," said Aunt Maud, kindly, but added: "Of course, you know that writers sometimes find it very difficult to make their way in the world."

"Yes, I realize that," I said reflectively.

"Perhaps if you had some other occupation, as a means of making a living, you might find time to write in your spare moments. Novelists sometimes get their start that way, you know."

"I might be a journalist," I suggested, "and write for the newspapers."

"Perhaps that is a good idea," she said. "A knowledge of languages would be very valuable in that field, too. You could work your way up to the position of a foreign correspondent."

"And I could write books in my spare time."

"Yes, I suppose you probably could manage it that way."

I think we rode all the way out to Ealing, talking in this somewhat abstract and utopian strain, and finally we got off, and crossed Haven Green to Castlebar Road where we had to stop in at Durston House for something or other.

It was not the first time I had met Mrs. Pearce, the head-mistress of Ripley Court. She was a bulky and rather belligerent-looking woman with great pouches under her eyes. She was standing in a room in which were hung several of my father's paintings. She had probably been looking at them, and considering the error and instability of an artist's way of life when Aunt Maud mentioned the fact that we had been talking about my own future.

"Does he want to be a dilettante like his father?" said Mrs. Pearce roughly, surveying me with a rather outraged expression through the lenses of her spectacles.

"We were thinking that perhaps he might become a journalist," said Aunt Maud gently.

"Nonsense," said Mrs. Pearce, "let him go into business and make a decent living for himself. There's no use in his wasting his time and deceiving himself. He might as well get some sensible ideas into his head from the very start, and prepare himself for something solid and reliable and not go out into the world with his head full of dreams." And then, turning to me, she cried out: "Boy! Don't become a dilettante, do you hear?"

I was received at Ripley Court, although the summer term was almost over, more or less as if I were an orphan or some kind of a stray that required at once pity and a special, not unsuspicious kind of attention. I was the son of an artist, and had just come from two years in a French school, and the combination of artist and France added up to practically everything that Mrs. Pearce and her friends suspected and disliked. Besides, to crown it all, I did not know any Latin. What was to be made of a boy who was already in the middle of his fourteenth year and could not decline *mensa*—had never even opened a Latin grammar?

So I had the humiliation of once again descending to the lowest place and sitting with the smallest boys in the school and beginning at the beginning.

But Ripley was a pleasant and happy place after the prison

of the Lycée. The huge, dark green sweep of the cricket field, and the deep shadows of the elm trees where one sat waiting for his innings, and the dining room where we crammed ourselves with bread and butter and jam at tea-time and listened to Mr. Onslow reading aloud from the works of Sir Arthur Conan Doyle, all this was immense luxury and peace after Montauban.

And the mentality of the red-faced, innocent English boys was a change. They seemed to be much pleasanter and much happier—and indeed they had every reason to be so, since they all came from the shelter of comfortable and secure homes and were so far protected from the world by a thick wall of ignorance—a wall which was to prove no real protection against anything as soon as they passed on to their various Public Schools, but which, for the time being, kept them children.

On Sundays, we all dressed up in the ludicrous clothes that the English conceive to be appropriate to the young, and went marching off to the village church, where a whole transept was reserved for us. There we all sat in rows, in our black Eton jackets and our snow-white Eton collars choking us up to the chin, and bent our well-brushed and combed heads over the pages of our hymnals. And at last I was really going to Church.

On Sunday evenings, after the long walk in the country, through the lush Surrey fields, we gathered again in the wooden drill-room of the school, and sat on benches, and sang hymns, and listened to Mr. Onslow reading aloud from *Pilgrim's Progress*.

Thus, just about the time when I most needed it, I did acquire a little natural faith, and found many occasions of praying and lifting up my mind to God. It was the first time I had ever seen people kneel publicly by their beds before getting into them, and the first time I had ever sat down to meals after a grace.

And for about the next two years I think I was almost sincerely religious. Therefore, I was also, to some extent, happy and at peace. I do not think there was anything very supernatural about it, although I am sure grace was working in all our souls in some obscure and uncertain way. But at least we were fulfilling our natural duties to God—and therefore satisfying a natural need: for our duties and our needs, in all the fundamental things for which we were created, come down in practice to the same thing.

Later on, like practically everyone else in our stupid and godless society, I was to consider these two years as "my religious phase." I am glad that that now seems very funny. But it is sad that it is funny in so few cases. Because I think that practically everybody does go through such a phase, and for the majority of them, that is all that it is, a phase and nothing more. If that is so, it is their own fault: for life on this earth is not simply a series of "phases" which we more or less passively undergo. If the impulse to worship God and to adore Him in truth by the goodness and order of our own lives is nothing more than a transitory and emotional thing, that is our own fault. It is so only because we make it so, and because we take what is substantially a deep and powerful and lasting moral impetus, supernatural in its origin and in its direction, and reduce it to the level of our own weak and unstable and futile fancies and desires.

Prayer is attractive enough when it is considered in a context of good food, and sunny joyous country churches, and the green English countryside. And, as a matter of fact, the Church of England means all this. As a religion, it is the cult of a special society and group, not even of a whole nation, but of the ruling minority in a nation. That is the principal basis for its rather strong coherence up to now. There is certainly not much doctrinal unity, much less a mystical bond between people many of whom have even ceased to believe in grace or Sacraments. The thing that holds them together is the powerful attraction of their own social tradition, and the stubborn tenacity with which they cling to certain social standards and customs, more or less for their own sake. The Church of England depends, for its existence, almost entirely on the solidarity and conservatism of the English ruling class. Its strength is not in anything supernatural, but in the strong social and racial instincts which bind the members of this caste together; and the English cling to their Church the way they cling to their King and to their old schools: because of a big, vague, sweet complex of subjective dispositions regarding the English countryside, old castles and cottages, games of cricket in the long summer afternoons, tea-parties on the Thames, croquet, roast-beef, pipe-smoking, the Christmas panto, *Punch* and the London *Times* and all those other things the mere thought of which produces a kind of a warm and inexpressible ache in the English heart.

I got mixed up in all this as soon as I entered Ripley Court, and it was strong enough in me to blur and naturalize all that might have been supernatural in my attraction to pray and to love God. And consequently the grace that was given me was stifled, not at once, but gradually. As long as I lived in this peaceful hothouse atmosphere of cricket and Eton collars and synthetic childhood, I was pious, perhaps sincerely. But as soon as the frail walls of this illusion broke down again—that is, as soon as I went to a Public School and saw that, underneath their sentimentality, the English were just as brutal as the French—I made no further effort to keep up what seemed to me to be a more or less manifest pretense.

At the time, of course, I was not capable of reasoning about all this. Even if my mind had been sufficiently developed to do so, I would never have found the perspective for it. Besides, all this was going on in my emotions and feelings, rather than in my mind and will—thanks to the vagueness and total unsubstantiality of Anglican doctrine as it gets preached, in practice, from most pulpits.

It is a terrible thing to think of the grace that is wasted in this world, and of the people that are lost. Perhaps one explanation of the sterility and inefficacy of Anglicanism in the moral order is, besides its lack of vital contact with the Mystical Body of the True Church, the social injustice and the class oppression on which it is based: for, since it is mostly a class religion, it contracts the guilt of the class from which it is inseparable. But this is a guess which I am not prepared to argue out.

I was already nearly too old for Ripley Court, being by now fourteen, but I had to pick up enough Latin to be able to make at least a presentable showing in a scholarship examination for some Public School. As to the school where I should go, Uncle Ben made a more or less expert choice, in his capacity as retired headmaster of a prep school. Since Father was poor, and an artist, there would be no thinking of one of the big schools like Harrow or Winchester—though Winchester was the one for which Uncle Ben had the greatest respect, having achieved his ambition of sending many of his pupils there with scholarships. The reason was twofold: not merely that Father could not be considered able to pay the bills (although, in fact, Pop was to pay them, from America) but the scholarship examinations would be altogether too hard for me.

The final choice was regarded by everyone as very suitable. It was an obscure but decent little school in the Midlands, an old foundation, with a kind of a little tradition of its own. It had recently gone up slightly in its rating because of the work of its greatest headmaster, who was just about to retire—all of this was the kind of thing Uncle Ben knew and told me, and Aunt Maud confirmed it, saying:

"I am sure you will find Oakham a very nice school."

3

The Harrowing of Hell

In the autumn of 1929 I went to Oakham. There was something very pleasant and peaceful about the atmosphere of this
little market town, with its school and its old fourteenth-
century church with the grey spire, rising in the middle of a
wide Midland vale.

Obscure it certainly was. Oakham's only claim to fame was
the fact that it was the county town, and in fact the only real
town in the smallest county in England. And there were not
even any main roads or main railway lines running through
Rutland, except for the Great North Road which skirted the
Lincolnshire border.

In this quiet back-water, under the trees full of rooks, I
was to spend three and a half years getting ready for a career.
Three and a half years were a short time: but when they were
over, I was a very different person from the embarrassed and
clumsy and more or less well-meaning, but interiorly unhappy
fourteen-year-old who came there with a suitcase and a brown
felt hat and a trunk and a plain wooden tuck-box.

Meanwhile, before I entered Oakham, and took up my
abode in the ratty, gaslit corner of Hodge Wing that was
called the "Nursery," things had happened to complicate and
sadden my life still further.

In the Easter vacation of 1929 I had been with Father at
Canterbury, where he was working, painting pictures mostly
in the big, quiet Cathedral close. I had spent most of my days
walking in the country around Canterbury, and the time went
quietly except for the momentous occasion of a big Charlie
Chaplin movie which came, late indeed, to Canterbury. It
was *The Gold Rush*.

When the holidays were over and I went back to Ripley
Court, Father crossed over to France. The last I heard about
him was that he was at Rouen. Then, one day, towards the

end of the summer term, when the school cricket eleven went in to Ealing to play Durston House, I was surprised to find myself appointed to go along as scorer. There was, of course, no likelihood of my ever going as a member of the team, since I was a hopeless cricketer from the start. On the way into town, on the bus or somewhere, I learned that my father was in Ealing, at Aunt Maud's, and that he was ill. This was why they had sent me along, I suppose: during the tea-interval I would have a chance to run in to the house which overlooked the cricket field and see Father.

The bus unloaded us in the lane that led to the field. In the tiny pavilion, the other scorer and I opened our large, green-ruled books, and wrote down the names of one another's team in the boxes down the side of the big rectangular page. Then, with our pencils all sharpened we waited, as the first pair went in to bat, striding heavily in their big white pads.

The dim June sun shone down on the field. Over yonder, where the poplars swayed slightly in the haze, was Aunt Maud's house, and I could see the window in the brick gable where Father probably was.

So the match began.

I could not believe that Father was very ill. If he were, I supposed that they would have made more fuss about it. During the tea interval, I went over, and passed through the green wooden door in the wall to Aunt Maud's garden and entered the house and went upstairs. Father was in bed. You could not tell from his appearance how ill he was: but I managed to gather it from the way he talked and from his actions. He seemed to move with difficulty and pain, and he did not have much to say. When I asked him what was the matter, he said nobody seemed to know.

I went back to the cricket pavilion a little saddened and unquiet. I told myself that he would probably get better in a week or two. And I thought this guess had proved to be right when, at the end of term, he wrote to me that we would be spending the summer in Scotland, where an old friend of his, who had a place in Aberdeenshire, had invited him to come and rest and get well.

We took one of those night trains from King's Cross. Father seemed well enough, although by the time we got to Aberdeen the following noon, after stopping at a lot of grey and dreary Scotch stations, he was weary and silent.

We had a long wait at Aberdeen, and we thought of going out and taking a look at the city. We stepped out of the station into a wide, deserted cobbled street. In the distance there was a harbor. We saw gulls, and the masts and funnel of what appeared to be a couple of trawlers. But the place seemed to have been struck by a plague. There was no one in sight. Now that I think of it, it must have been Sunday, for dead as Aberdeen is, it surely could not have been so completely deserted on a week day. The whole place was as grey as a tomb, and the forbidding aspect of all that hostile and untenanted granite depressed us both so much that we immediately returned to the station, and sat down in the refreshment room, and ordered some hotch-potch, which did little or nothing to lighten our spirits.

It was late afternoon by the time we got to Insch. The sun came out, and slanted a long ray at the far hills of heather which constituted our host's grouse-moor. The air was clear and silent as we drove out of the forsaken town that seemed to us more of a settlement than a town, and headed into the wilderness.

For the first few days Father kept to his room, coming down for meals. Once or twice he went out into the garden. Soon he could not even come down for meals. The doctor paid frequent visits, and soon I understood that Father was not getting better at all.

Finally, one day he called me up to the room.

"I have to go back to London," he said.

"London?"

"I must go to a hospital, son."

"Are you worse?"

"I don't get any better."

"Have they still not found out what it is that is the matter with you, Father?"

He shook his head. But he said: "Pray God to make me

well. I think I ought to be all right in due course. Don't be unhappy."

But I was unhappy.

"You like it here, don't you?" he asked me.

"Oh, it's all right, I suppose."

"You'll stay here. They are very nice. They will take care of you, and it will do you good. Do you like the horses?"

I admitted without any undue excitement or enthusiasm that the ponies were all right. There were two of them. The two nieces of the family and I spent part of the day grooming them and cleaning out their stalls, and part of the day riding them. But, as far as I was concerned, it was too much work. The nieces, divining this unsportsmanlike attitude of mine, tended to be a little hostile and to boss me around in a patronising sort of a way. They were sixteen or seventeen, and seemed to have nothing whatever on their minds except horses, and they did not even look like their normal selves when they were not in riding breeches.

And so Father said good-bye, and we put him on the train, and he went to London to the Middlesex Hospital.

The summer days dragged on, cold days full of mist, some days bright with sun. I became less and less interested in the stable and the ponies, and before August was half done, the nieces had given me up in disgust and I was allowed to drop away into my own unhappy isolation, my world without horses, without hunting and shooting, without tartans and without the Braemar gathering and all those other noble institutions.

Instead, I sat in the branches of a tree reading the novels of Alexandre Dumas, volume after volume, in French, and later, in rebellion against the world of horses, I would borrow a bicycle that happened to be around the place, and go off into the country and look at the huge ancient stone circles where the druids had once congregated to offer human sacrifice to the rising sun—when there *was* a rising sun.

One day I was in the deserted house all by myself with Athos, Porthos, Aramis and D'Artagnan (Athos being my favorite and, in a sense, the one into whom I tended to project myself). The telephone rang. I thought for a while of letting it ring and not answering it, but eventually I did. It turned out to be a telegram for me.

At first I could not make out the words, as the Scotch lady in the telegraph office was pronouncing them. Then, when I did make them out, I did not believe them.

The message ran: "Entering New York harbor. All well." And it came from Father, in the hospital, in London. I tried to argue the woman at the other end of the wire into telling me that it came from my Uncle Harold, who had been travelling in Europe that year. But she would not be argued into anything but what she saw right in front of her nose. The telegram was signed Father, and it came from London.

I hung up the receiver and the bottom dropped out of my stomach. I walked up and down in the silent and empty house. I sat down in one of the big leather chairs in the smoking room. There was nobody there. There was nobody in the whole huge house.

I sat there in the dark, unhappy room, unable to think, unable to move, with all the innumerable elements of my isolation crowding in upon me from every side: without a home, without a family, without a country, without a father, apparently without any friends, without any interior peace or confidence or light or understanding of my own—without God, too, without God, without heaven, without grace, without anything. And what was happening to Father, there in London? I was unable to think of it.

The first thing that Uncle Ben did when I entered the house at Ealing was to tell me the news with all the dramatic overtones he gave to his most important announcements.

His eyes widened and he stared at me and bared his great teeth, pronouncing every syllable with tremendous distinctness and emphasis, saying: "Your father has a malignant tumor on the brain."

Father lay in a dark ward in the hospital. He did not have much to say. But it was not as bad as I had feared, from the telegram he had sent me. Everything he said was lucid and intelligible and I was comforted, in the sense that a clearly apparent physiological cause seemed to me to exclude the thought of insanity in the strict sense. Father was not out of his mind. But you could already see the evil, swelling lump on his forehead.

He told me, weakly, that they were going to try and operate on him, but they were afraid they could not do very much. Again he told me to pray.

I did not say anything about the telegram.

Leaving the hospital, I knew what was going to happen. He would lie there like that for another year, perhaps two or three years. And then he would die—unless they first killed him on an operating table.

Since those days, doctors have found out that you can cut away whole sections of the brain, in these operations, and save lives and minds and all. In 1929 they evidently did not yet know this. It was Father's lot to die slowly and painfully in the years when the doctors were just reaching the point of the discovery.

ii

Oakham, Oakham! The grey murk of the winter evenings in that garret where seven or eight of us moiled around in the gaslight, among the tuck-boxes, noisy, greedy, foul-mouthed, fighting and shouting! There was one who had a ukulele which he did not know how to play. And Pop used to send me the brown rotogravure sections of the New York Sunday papers, and we would cut out the pictures of the actresses and paste them up on the walls.

And I toiled with Greek verbs. And we drank raisin wine and ate potato chips until we fell silent and sat apart, stupefied and nauseated. And under the gaslight I would write letters to Father in the hospital, letters on cream-colored notepaper, stamped with the school crest in blue.

After three months it was better. I was moved up into the Upper Fifth, and changed to a new study downstairs, with more light, though just as crowded and just as much of a mess. And we had Cicero and European history—all about the nineteenth century, with a certain amount of cold scorn poured on Pio Nono. In the English class we read *The Tempest* and the *Nun's Priest's Tale* and the *Pardoner's Tale* and Buggy Jerwood, the school chaplain, tried to teach us trigonometry. With me, he failed. Sometimes he would try to teach us something about religion. But in this he also failed.

In any case, his religious teaching consisted mostly in more or less vague ethical remarks, an obscure mixture of ideals of English gentlemanliness and his favorite notions of personal hygiene. Everybody knew that his class was liable to degenerate into a demonstration of some practical points about rowing, with Buggy sitting on the table and showing us how to pull an oar.

There was no rowing at Oakham, since there was no water. But the chaplain had been a rowing "blue" at Cambridge, in his time. He was a tall, powerful, handsome man, with hair greying at the temples, and a big English chin, and a broad, uncreased brow, with sentences like "I stand for fair-play and good sportsmanship" written all over it.

His greatest sermon was on the thirteenth chapter of First Corinthians—and a wonderful chapter indeed. But his exegesis was a bit strange. However, it was typical of him and, in a way, of his whole church. "Buggy's" interpretation of the word "charity" in this passage (and in the whole Bible) was that it simply stood for "all that we mean when we call a chap a 'gentleman.' " In other words, charity meant good-sportsmanship, cricket, the decent thing, wearing the right kind of clothes, using the proper spoon, not being a cad or a bounder.

There he stood, in the plain pulpit, and raised his chin above the heads of all the rows of boys in black coats, and said: "One might go through this chapter of St. Paul and simply substitute the word 'gentleman' for 'charity' wherever it occurs. 'If I talk with the tongues of men and of angels, and be not a gentleman, I am become as sounding brass, or a tinkling cymbal . . . A gentleman is patient, is kind; a gentle-

94

man envieth not, dealeth not perversely; is not puffed up.
. . . A gentleman never falleth away.' . . ."

And so it went. I will not accuse him of finishing the chapter with "Now there remain faith, hope and gentlemanliness, and the greatest of these is gentlemanliness . . ." although it was the logical term of his reasoning.

The boys listened tolerantly to these thoughts. But I think St. Peter and the other Apostles would have been rather surprised at the concept that Christ had been scourged and beaten by soldiers, cursed and crowned with thorns and subjected to unutterable contempt and finally nailed to the Cross and left to bleed to death in order that we might all become gentlemen.

As time went on, I was to get into fierce arguments with the football captain on this subject, but that day was yet to come. As long as I was among the fourteen- and fifteen-year-olds in Hodge Wing, I had to mind my behaviour with the lords of the school, or at least in their presence. We were disciplined by the constant fear of one of those pompous and ceremonious sessions of bullying, arranged with ritualistic formality, when a dozen or so culprits were summoned into one of the hollows around Brooke hill, or up the Braunston road, and beaten with sticks, and made to sing foolish songs and to hear themselves upbraided for their moral and social defects.

When I got into the sixth form, which I did after a year, I came more directly under the influence and guidance of the new Headmaster, F. C. Doherty. He was a young man for a Headmaster, about forty, tall, with a great head of black hair, a tremendous smoker of cigarettes and a lover of Plato. Because of the cigarettes, he used to like to give his class in his own study, when he decently could, for there he could smoke one after another, while in the classrooms he could not smoke at all.

He was a broad-minded man, and I never realized how much I owed to him until I left Oakham. If it had not been for him, I would probably have spent years in the fifth form trying to pass the School Certificate in mathematics. He saw that I could far easier pass the Higher Certificate, specializing in French and Latin where, although the examination in these subjects would be very hard, there would be no maths. And the Higher Certificate meant far more than the other. It was he who began, from the start, to prepare me for the university, getting me to aim at a Cambridge scholarship. And it was he who let me follow the bent of my own mind, for Modern Languages and Literature, although that meant that I spent much of my time studying alone in the library, since there was no real "Modern" course at Oakham at the time.

This was all the more generous of him for the fact that he really was very much attached to the Classics, and especially Plato, and he would have liked all of us to catch some of that infection. And yet this infection—which, in my eyes, was nothing short of deadly—was something I resisted with all my will. I do not exactly know why I hated Plato: but after the first ten pages of *The Republic* I decided that I could not stand Socrates and his friends, and I don't think I ever recovered from that repugnance. There can hardly have been any serious intellectual reason for my dislike of these philosophers, although I do have a kind of congenital distaste for philosophic idealism. But we were reading *The Republic* in Greek, which meant that we never got far enough into it to be able to grasp the ideas very well. Most of the time I was too helpless with the grammar and syntax to have time for any deeper difficulties.

Nevertheless, after a couple of months of it, I got to a state where phrases like "the Good, the True, and the Beautiful" filled me with a kind of suppressed indignation, because they stood for the big sin of Platonism: the reduction of all reality to the level of pure abstraction, as if concrete, individual substances had no essential reality of their own, but were only shadows of some remote, universal, ideal essence filed away in a big card-index somewhere in heaven, while the demiurges milled around the Logos piping their excitement in high, fluted, English intellectual tones. Platonism entered very much into the Headmaster's ideas of religion, which were deeply spiritual and intellectual. Also he was slightly more High-Church than most of the people at Oakham. However, it was no easier to find out, concretely, what he believed than it was to find out what anybody else believed in that place.

I had several different Masters in the one hour a week devoted to religious instruction (outside of the daily chapel). The first one just plodded through the third Book of Kings. The second, a tough little Yorkshireman, who had the virtue of being very definite and outspoken in everything he said, once exposed to us Descartes' proof of his own and God's existence. He told us that as far as he was concerned, that was the foundation of what religion meant to him. I accepted the *Cogito ergo sum* with less reserve than I should have, although I might have had enough sense to realize that any proof of what is self-evident must necessarily be illusory. If there are no self-evident first principles, as a foundation for reasoning to conclusions that are not immediately apparent, how can you construct any kind of a philosophy? If you have to prove even the basic axioms of your metaphysics, you will never have a metaphysics, because you will never have any strict proof of anything, for your first proof will involve you in an infinite regress, proving that you are proving what you are proving and so on, into the exterior darkness where there is wailing and gnashing of teeth. If Descartes thought it was necessary to prove his own existence, by the fact that he was thinking, and that his thought therefore existed in some subject, how did he prove that he was thinking in the first place? But as to the second step, that God must exist because Descartes had a clear idea of him—that never convinced me, then or at any other time, or now either. There are much better proofs for the existence of God than that one.

As for the Headmaster, when he gave us religious instruction, as he did in my last year or so at Oakham, he talked Plato, and told me to read A. E. Taylor, which I did, but under compulsion, and taking no trouble to try and understand what I was reading.

In 1930, after I had turned fifteen, and before most of

97

these things happened, the way began to be prepared for my various intellectual rebellions by a sudden and very definite sense of independence, a realization of my own individuality which, while being natural at that age, took an unhealthy egotistic turn. And everything seemed to conspire to encourage me to cut myself off from everybody else and go my own way. For a moment, in the storms and confusion of adolescence, I had been humbled by my own interior sufferings, and having a certain amount of faith and religion, I had subjected myself more or less willingly and even gladly to the authority of others, and to the ways and customs of those around me.

But in Scotland I had begun to bare my teeth and fight back against the humiliation of giving in to other people, and now I was rapidly building up a hard core of resistance against everything that displeased me: whether it was the opinions or desires of others, or their commands, or their very persons. I would think what I wanted and do what I wanted, and go my own way. If those who tried to prevent me had authority to prevent me, I would have to be at least externally polite in my resistance: but my resistance would be no less determined, and I would do my own will, have my own way.

When Pop and Bonnemaman came to Europe again in 1930, they practically threw the doors of the world wide open to me and gave me my independence. The economic crisis of 1929 had not altogether ruined Pop: he did not have all his substance invested in companies that crashed, but the indirect effect on him was just as serious as it was on every other ordinary business man.

In June 1930, they all came down to Oakham—Pop, Bonnemaman and John Paul. It was a quiet visit. They no longer took towns by storm. The depression had changed all that. Besides, they were used to travelling in Europe by now. The fear and trepidation that had been so strong an element in their excitement in the old days were somewhat allayed. Their voyages were comparatively—but only comparatively—serene.

They had a couple of big rooms in the labyrinthine "Crown Inn" at Oakham, and one of the first things Pop did was to take me apart into one of them and talk to me in a way that amounted to an emancipation.

I think it was the first time in my life I had ever been treated as if I were completely grown up and able to take care of myself in everything, and to hold my own in a business conversation. In reality, I have never been able to talk intelligently about business. But I listened to Pop exposing our financial affairs as if I understood every word about it, and when it was over I had, indeed, grasped all the essentials.

No one knew what was going to happen in the world in the next ten or twenty years. Grosset and Dunlap was still in business, and so was Pop: but one could never tell when the business itself might fold up, or if he himself would be turned out. But in order to make sure that John Paul and I would be able to finish school, and even go on to the university, and have something to keep us from starving while we were looking for a job afterwards, Pop had taken the money he had planned to leave us in his will, and had put it away for us where it would be as safe as possible, in some kind of insurance policy which would pay us so much a year. He worked it out on a piece of paper and showed me all the figures and I nodded wisely. I didn't grasp the details but I understood that I ought to be able to get along all right until about 1940. And in any case, before a couple of years had gone by, Pop discovered that the big magic insurance policy did not work as neatly as he had expected, so he had to change his plans again, with a loss of a little money somewhere.

When it was all done, Pop gave me the piece of paper with all the figures on it, and sat up straight in his chair, and looked out the window, running his hand over the top of his bald head and said: "So now it's all settled. No matter what happens to me, you will both be taken care of. You've got nothing to worry about for a few years, anyway."

I was a bit dazed by the momentousness of it, and by Pop's own great generosity. Because, after all, he really meant it that way. What he was trying to do was to arrange everything so that even if he were ruined, we would be able to take care of ourselves. Fortunately, he was never ruined.

That day at Oakham, Pop crowned his generosity and his recognition of my maturity by an altogether astounding concession. He not only told me he was in favor of my smoking, but even bought me a pipe. I was fifteen, mind you, and Pop had always hated smoking anyway. Besides, it was forbidden by the rules of the school—rules which I had been systematically breaking all that year, more for the sake of asserting my independence than for the pleasure of lighting and relighting those cold, biting pipefuls of Rhodesian cut-plug.

When the holidays came there was another big change. It was decided that I would no longer spend my holidays with Aunt Maud or other relatives in the suburbs or outside of London. My godfather, an old friend of Father's from New Zealand, who was by now a Harley Street specialist, offered to let me stay at his place in town when I was in London: and that meant that most of the day and night I was more or less free to do what I liked.

Tom—my godfather—was to be the person I most respected and admired and consequently the one who had the greatest influence on me at this time in my life. He too gave me credit for being more intelligent and mature than I was, and this of course pleased me very much. He was later to find out that his trust in me was misplaced.

Life in the flat where Tom and his wife lived was very well-ordered and amusing. You got breakfast in bed, served by a French maid, on a small tray: coffee or chocolate in a tiny pot, toast or rolls, and, for me, fried eggs. After breakfast, which came in at about nine, I knew I would have to wait a little to get a bath, so I would stay in bed for an hour or so more reading a novel by Evelyn Waugh or somebody like that. Then I would get up and take my bath and get dressed and go out and look for some amusement—walk in the park, or go to a museum, or go to some gramophone shop and listen to a lot of hot records—and then buy one, to pay for the privilege of listening to all the rest. I used to go to Levy's, on the top floor of one of those big buildings in the crescent of Regent Street, because they imported all the latest Victors and Brunswicks and Okeh's from America, and I would lock myself up in one of those little glass-doored booths, and play all the Duke Ellingtons and Louis Armstrongs and the old King Olivers and all the other things I have forgotten. Basin Street Blues, Beale Street Blues, Saint James Infirmary, and all the other places that had blues written about them: all these I suddenly began to know much of by indirection and woeful hearsay, and I guess I lived vicariously in all the slums in all the cities of the South: Memphis and New Orleans and Birmingham, places which I have never yet seen. I don't know where those streets were, but I certainly knew something true about them, which I found out on that top floor in Regent Street and in my study at Oakham.

Then I would go back to my godfather's place, and we would have lunch in the dining room, sitting at the little table that always seemed to me so small and delicate that I was afraid to move for fear the whole thing would collapse and the pretty French dishes would smash on the floor and scatter the French food on the waxed floorboards. Everything in that flat was small and delicate. It harmonised with my godfather and his wife. Not that he was delicate, but he was a little man who walked quietly and quickly on small feet, or stood at the fireplace with a cigarette between his fingers, neat and precise as a decent doctor ought to be. And he had something of the pursed lips of medical men—the contraction of the lips that they somehow acquire leaning over wide-open bodies.

Tom's wife was delicate. In fact, she looked almost brittle. She was French, and the daughter of a great Protestant patriarch with a long white beard who dominated French Calvinism from the Rue des Saints-Pères.

Everything in their flat was in proportion to their own stature and delicacy and precision and neatness and wit. Yet I do not say it looked like a doctor's place—still less like an English doctor's place. English doctors always seem to go in for very heavy and depressing kinds of furniture. But Tom was not the kind of specialist that always wears a frock coat and a wing-collar. His flat was bright and full of objects I was afraid to break and, on the whole, I was scared to walk too heavily for fear I might suddenly go through the floor.

What I most admired about Tom and Iris, from the start, was that they knew everything and had everything in its proper place. From the first moment when I discovered that one was not only allowed to make fun of English middle-class notions and ideals but encouraged to do so in that little bright drawing-room, where we balanced coffee-cups on our knees, I was very happy. I soon developed a habit of wholesale and glib detraction of all the people with whom I did not agree or whose taste and ideas offended me.

They, in turn, lent me all the novels and told me about the various plays, and listened with amusement to Duke Ellington, and played me their records of La Argentina. It was from them that I was to discover all the names that people most talked about in modern writing: Hemingway, Joyce, D. H. Lawrence, Evelyn Waugh, Céline with his *Voyage au Bout de la Nuit*, Gide and all the rest, except that they did not bother much with poets. I heard about T. S. Eliot from the English Master at Oakham who had just come down from Cambridge and read me aloud "The Hollow Men."

It was Tom who, once when we were in Paris, took me to see a lot of pictures by Chagall and several others like him, although he did not like Braque and the Cubists and never developed any of my enthusiasm for Picasso. It was he who showed me that there was some merit in Russian movies and in René Clair: but he never understood the Marx Brothers. It was from him that I discovered the difference between the Café Royal and the Café Anglais, and many other things of the same nature. And he also could tell you what members of the English nobility were thought to take dope.

Really, all these things implied a rather strict standard of values: but values that were entirely worldly and cosmopolitan. Values they were, however, and one kept to them with a most remarkably nice fidelity. I only discovered much later on that all this implied not only esthetic but a certain worldly moral standard, the moral and artistic values being fused inseparably in the single order of taste. It was an unwritten law, and you had to be very smart and keenly attuned to their psychology to get it: but there it was, a strict moral law, which never expressed any open hatred of evil, or even any direct and explicit condemnation of any other sins than bourgeois pharisaism and middle-class hypocrisy, which they attacked without truce. Nevertheless their code disposed of other deordinations with quiet and pointed mockery. The big difficulty with me and my failure was that I did not see, for instance, that their interest in D. H. Lawrence as art was, in some subtle way, disconnected from any endorsement of his ideas about how a man ought to live. Or rather, the distinction was more subtle still: and it was between their interest in and amusement at those ideas, and the fact, which they took for granted, that it was rather vulgar to practice them the way Lawrence did. This was a distinction which I did not grasp until it was too late.

Until the time I went to Cambridge, I developed rapidly under their influence, and in many ways the development was valuable and good: and of course, there must be no question of the kindness and sincerity of the interest which they took in me, or their generosity in devoting themselves so whole-heartedly to my care and to my training, in their informal and unofficial way.

It was Tom who definitely assured me that I should prepare for the English diplomatic or at least consular service, and did not spare any effort to see that I advanced steadily, in every possible way, towards that end. He was able to foresee an infinity of little details that would have to be taken care of long before they arose—the value, for instance, of "reading for the bar" which simply meant eating a certain number of dinners at one of the Inns of Court, so as to fulfil the minimum residence requirements of a London Law student, and the payment of a fee for a minor distinction which would be useful in the diplomatic service. As it happened, I never got around to eating those dinners, and I dare to hope I shall be no lower in heaven for my failure to do so.

It was the summer of 1930, before most of these things had happened. I mean, the summer when Pop had made over to me the portion of my inheritance and threw open the door for me to run away and be a prodigal, or be a prodigal without running away from any earthly home, for that matter. I could very well eat the husks of swine without the inconvenience of going into a far country to look for them.

Most of that summer we were all together in London. The reason was, that we could be near the hospital and visit Father. I remember the first of those visits.

It was several months since I had been in London, and then only in passing, so I had really hardly seen Father at all since he had entered the hospital the autumn before.

So all of us went to the hospital. Father was in a ward. We had arrived much too early, and had to wait. We were in a new wing of the big hospital. The floor was shiny and clean. Vaguely depressed by the smell of sickness and disinfectant and the general medical smell that all hospitals have, we sat in a corridor downstairs for upwards of half an hour. I had just bought Hugo's *Italian Self-Taught*, and began to teach myself some verbs, sitting there in the hall, with John Paul restive on the bench beside me. And the time dragged.

Finally the clock we had been watching got around to the appropriate hour; we went up in an elevator. They all knew where the ward was—it was a different ward. I think they had changed his ward two or three times. And he had had more than one operation. But none of them had been successful.

We went into the ward. Father was in bed, to the left, just as you went in the door.

And when I saw him, I knew at once there was no hope of his living much longer. His face was swollen. His eyes were not clear but, above all, the tumor had raised a tremendous swelling on his forehead.

I said: "How are you, Father?"

He looked at me and put forth his hand, in a confused and unhappy way, and I realized that he could no longer even speak. But at the same time, you could see that he knew us, and knew what was going on, and that his mind was clear, and that he understood everything.

But the sorrow of his great helplessness suddenly fell upon me like a mountain. I was crushed by it. The tears sprang to my eyes. Nobody said anything more.

I hid my face in the blanket and cried. And poor Father wept, too. The others stood by. It was excruciatingly sad. We were completely helpless. There was nothing anyone could do.

When I finally looked up and dried my tears, I noticed that the attendants had put screens all around the bed. I was too miserable to feel ashamed of my un-English demonstration of sorrow and affection. And so we went away.

What could I make of so much suffering? There was no way for me, or for anyone else in the family, to get anything out of it. It was a raw wound for which there was no adequate relief. You had to take it, like an animal. We were in the condition of most of the world, the condition of men without faith in the presence of war, disease, pain, starvation, suffering, plague, bombardment, death. You just had to take it, like a dumb animal. Try to avoid it, if you could. But you must eventually reach the point where you can't avoid it any more. Take it. Try to stupefy yourself, if you like, so that it won't hurt so much. But you will always have to take some of it. And it will all devour you in the end.

Indeed, the truth that many people never understand, until it is too late, is that the more you try to avoid suffering, the more you suffer, because smaller and more insignificant things begin to torture you, in proportion to your fear of being hurt. The one who does most to avoid suffering is, in the end, the one who suffers most: and his suffering comes to him from things so little and so trivial that one can say that it is no longer objective at all. It is his own existence, his own being, that is at once the subject and the source of his pain, and his very existence and consciousness is his greatest torture. This is another of the great perversions by which the devil uses our philosophies to turn our whole nature inside out, and eviscerate all our capacities for good, turning them against ourselves.

All summer we went regularly and faithfully to the hospital once or twice a week. There was nothing we could do but sit there, and look at Father and tell him things which he could not answer. But he understood what we said.

In fact, if he could not talk, there were other things he could still do. One day I found his bed covered with little sheets of blue notepaper on which he had been drawing. And the drawings were real drawings. But they were unlike anything he had ever done before—pictures of little, irate Byzantine-looking saints with beards and great halos.

Of us all, Father was the only one who really had any kind of a faith. And I do not doubt that he had very much of it, and that behind the walls of his isolation, his intelligence and his will, unimpaired, and not hampered in any essential way by the partial obstruction of some of his senses, were turned to God, and communed with God Who was with him and in him, and Who gave him, as I believe, light to understand and to make use of his suffering for his own good, and to perfect his soul. It was a great soul, large, full of natural charity. He was a man of exceptional intellectual honesty and sincerity and purity of understanding. And this affliction, this terrible and frightening illness which was relentlessly pressing him down even into the jaws of the tomb, was not destroying him after all.

Souls are like athletes, that need opponents worthy of them, if they are to be tried and extended and pushed to the full use of their powers, and rewarded according to their capacity. And my father was in a fight with this tumor, and none of us understood the battle. We thought he was done for, but it was making him great. And I think God was already weighing out to him the weight of reality that was to be his reward, for he certainly believed far more than any theologian would require of a man to hold explicitly as "necessity of means," and so he was eligible for this reward, and

106

his struggle was authentic, and not wasted or lost or thrown away.

In the Christmas holidays I only saw him once or twice. Things were about the same. I spent most of the holidays in Strasbourg, where Tom had arranged for me to go for the sake of the languages: German and French. I stayed in a big Protestant *pension* in the Rue Finkmatt, and was under the unofficial tutelage of a professor at the University, a friend of Tom's family and of the Protestant patriarch.

Professor Hering was a kind and pleasant man with a red beard, and one of the few Protestants I have ever met who struck one as being at all holy: that is, he possessed a certain profound interior peace, which he probably got from his contact with the Fathers of the Church, for he was a teacher of theology. We did not talk much about religion, however. Once when some students were visiting him, one of them explained to me the essentials of Unitarianism, and when I asked the professor about it afterwards, he said it was all right, in a way which indicated that he approved, in a sort of academic and eclectic way, of all these different forms of belief: or rather that he was interested in them as objectively intriguing manifestations of a fundamental human instinct, regarding them more or less through the eyes of a sociologist. As a matter of fact, sometimes Protestant theology does, in certain circumstances, amount to little more than a combination of sociology and religious history, but I will not accuse him of teaching it altogether in that sense, for I really have no idea how he taught it.

Under the inspiration of the environment, I went to a Lutheran church and sat through a long sermon in German which I did not understand. But I think that was all the worship of God I did in Strasbourg. I was more interested in Josephine Baker, a big skinny colored girl from some American city like St. Louis, who came to one of the theaters and sang *J'ai deux amours, mon pays et Paris*.

So I went back to school, after seeing Father for a moment on the way through London. I had been back for barely a week when I was summoned, one morning, to the Headmaster's study, and he gave me a telegram which said that Father was dead.

The sorry business was all over. And my mind made nothing of it. There was nothing I seemed to be able to grasp. Here was a man with a wonderful mind and a great talent and a great heart: and, what was more, he was the man who had brought me into the world, and had nourished me and cared for me and had shaped my soul and to whom I was bound by every possible kind of bond of affection and attachment and admiration and reverence: killed by a growth on his brain.

Tom got an obituary printed in the *Times*, and he saw to it that the funeral went off more or less decently: but it was still another one of those cremations. This time it was at Golders Green. The only difference was that the minister said more prayers, and the chapel looked a little more like a chapel, and Tom had got them to hide the coffin under a very beautiful shroud of silk from the Orient somewhere, China or Bali or India.

But in the end they took the shroud off and rolled the coffin through one of those sliding doors and then, in the sinister secrecy of the big, intricate crematory, out of our sight, the body was burned, and we went away.

Nevertheless, all that is of no importance, and it can be forgotten. For I hope that, in the living Christ, I shall one day see my father again: that is, I believe that Christ, Who is the Son of God, and Who is God, has power to raise up all those who have died in His grace, to the glory of His own Resurrection, and to share, body and soul, in the glory of His Divine inheritance, at the last day.

The death of my father left me sad and depressed for a couple of months. But that eventually wore away. And when it did, I found myself completely stripped of everything that impeded the movement of my own will to do as it pleased. I imagined that I was free. And it would take me five or six years to discover what a frightful captivity I had got myself into. It was in this year, too, that the hard crust of my dry soul finally squeezed out all the last traces of religion that had ever been in it. There was no room for any God in that empty temple full of dust and rubbish which I was now so jealously to guard against all intruders, in order to devote it to the worship of my own stupid will.

And so I became the complete twentieth-century man. I now belonged to the world in which I lived. I became a true citizen of my own disgusting century: the century of poison gas and atomic bombs. A man living on the doorsill of the Apocalypse, a man with veins full of poison, living in death. Baudelaire could truly address me, then, reader: *Hypocrite lecteur, mon semblable, mon frère . . .*

iv

Meanwhile there was one discovery of mine, one poet who was a poet indeed, and a Romantic poet, but vastly different from those contemporaries, with whom he had so little to do. I think my love for William Blake had something in it of God's grace. It is a love that has never died, and which has entered very deeply into the development of my life.

Father had always liked Blake, and had tried to explain to me what was good about him when I was a child of ten. The funny thing about Blake is that although the *Songs of Innocence* look like children's poems, and almost seem to have been written for children, they are, to most children, incomprehensible. Or at least, they were so to me. Perhaps if I had read them when I was four or five, it would have been different. But when I was ten, I knew too much. I knew that tigers did not burn in the forests of the night. That was very silly, I thought. Children are very literal-minded.

I was less literal when I was sixteen. I could accept Blake's metaphors and they already began, a little, to astound and to move me, although I had no real grasp of their depth and power. And I liked Blake immensely. I read him with more patience and attention than any other poet. I thought about him more. And I could not figure him out. I do not mean, I could not figure out the Prophetic Books—nobody can do that! But I could not place him in any kind of a context, and I did not know how to make his ideas fit together.

One grey Sunday in the spring, I walked alone out the Brooke Road and up Brooke Hill, where the rifle range was. It was a long, bare hog-back of a hill, with a few lone trees along the top, and it commanded a big sweeping view of the Vale of Catmos, with the town of Oakham lying in the midst of it, gathered around the grey, sharp church spire. I sat on a stile on the hill top, and contemplated the wide vale, from the north, where the kennels of the Cottesmore hounds were, to Lax Hill and Manton in the south. Straight across was Burley House, on top of its hill, massed with woods. At my feet, a few red brick houses straggled out from the town to the bottom of the slope.

And all the time I reflected, that afternoon, upon Blake. I remember how I concentrated and applied myself to it. It was rare that I ever really thought about such a thing of my own accord. But I was trying to establish what manner of man he was. Where did he stand? What did he believe? What did he preach?

On one hand he spoke of the "priests in black gowns who were going their rounds binding with briars my joys and desires." And yet on the other hand he detested Voltaire and Rousseau and everybody like them and everything that they stood for, and he abominated all materialistic deism, and all the polite, abstract natural religions of the eighteenth century, the agnosticism of the nineteenth, and, in fact, most of the common attitudes of our day.

> The atoms of Democritus
> And Newton's particles of light
> Are sands upon the Red-Sea shore
> Where Israel's tents do shine so bright. . .

I was absolutely incapable of reconciling, in my mind, two things that seemed so contrary. Blake was a revolutionary, and yet he detested the greatest and most typical revolutionaries of his time, and declared himself opposed without compromise to people who, as I thought, seemed to exemplify some of his own most characteristic ideals.

How incapable I was of understanding anything like the ideals of a William Blake! How could I possibly realize that his rebellion, for all its strange heterodoxies, was fundamentally the rebellion of the saints. It was the rebellion of the lover of the living God, the rebellion of one whose desire of God was so intense and irresistible that it condemned, with all its might, all the hypocrisy and petty sensuality and skepticism and materialism which cold and trivial minds set up as unpassable barriers between God and the souls of men.

The priests that he saw going their rounds in black gowns —he knew no Catholics at the time, and had probably never even seen a Catholic priest—were symbols, in his mind, of the weak, compromising, pharisaic piety of those whose god was nothing but an objectification of their own narrow and conventional desires and hypocritical fears.

He did not distinguish any particular religion or sect as the objects of his disdain: he simply could not stand false piety and religiosity, in which the love of God was stamped out of the souls of men by formalism and conventions, without any charity, without the light and life of a faith that brings man face to face with God. If on one page of Blake these priests in black gowns were frightening and hostile figures, on another, the "Grey Monk of Charlemaine" was a saint and a hero of charity and of faith, fighting for the peace of the true God with all the ardent love that was the only reality Blake lived for. Towards the end of his life, Blake told his friend Samuel Palmer that the Catholic Church was the only one that taught the love of God.

I am not, of course, recommending the study of William Blake to all minds as a perfect way to faith and to God. Blake is really extraordinarily difficult and obscure and there is, in him, some of the confusion of almost all the heterodox and heretical mystical systems that ever flourished in the west— and that is saying a lot. And yet, by the grace of God, at least in my opinion, he was kept very much uncontaminated by all his crazy symbols precisely because he was such a good and holy man, and because his faith was so real and his love for God so mighty and so sincere.

The Providence of God was eventually to use Blake to awaken something of faith and love in my own soul—in spite of all the misleading notions, and all the almost infinite possibilities of error that underlie his weird and violent figures. I do not, therefore, want to seem to canonize him. But I have to acknowledge my own debt to him, and the truth which may appear curious to some, although it is really not so: that through Blake I would one day come, in a round-about way, to the only true Church, and to the One Living God, through His Son, Jesus Christ.

v

In three months, the summer of 1931, I suddenly matured like a weed.

I cannot tell which is the more humiliating: the memory of the half-baked adolescent I was in June or the glib and hard-boiled specimen I was in October when I came back to Oakham full of a thorough and deep-rooted sophistication of which I was both conscious and proud.

The beginning was like this: Pop wrote to me to come to America. I got a brand-new suit made. I said to myself, "On the boat I am going to meet a beautiful girl, and I am going to fall in love."

So I got on the boat. The first day I sat in a deck chair and read the correspondence of Goethe and Schiller which had been imposed on me as a duty, in preparation for the scholarship examinations at the university. What is worse, I not only tolerated this imposition but actually convinced myself that it was interesting.

The second day I had more or less found out who was on the boat. The third day I was no longer interested in Goethe and Schiller. The fourth day I was up to my neck in the trouble that I was looking for.

It was a ten-day boat.

I would rather spend two years in a hospital than go

through that anguish again! That devouring, emotional, passionate love of adolescence that sinks its claws into you and consumes you day and night and eats into the vitals of your soul! All the self-tortures of doubt and anxiety and imagination and hope and despair that you go through when you are a child, trying to break out of your shell, only to find yourself in the middle of a legion of full-armed emotions against which you have no defense! It is like being flayed alive. No one can go through it twice. This kind of a love affair can really happen only once in a man's life. After that he is calloused. He is no longer capable of so many torments. He can suffer, but not from so many matters of no account. After one such crisis he has experience and the possibility of a second time no longer exists, because the secret of the anguish was his own utter guilelessness. He is no longer capable of such complete and absurd surprises. No matter how simple a man may be, the obvious cannot go on astonishing him for ever.

I was introduced to this particular girl by a Catholic priest who came from Cleveland and played shuffleboard in his shirt sleeves without a Roman collar on. He knew everybody on the boat in the first day, and as for me, two days had gone by before I even realized that she was on board. She was travelling with a couple of aunts and the three of them did not mix in with the other passengers very much. They kept to themselves in their three deck chairs and had nothing to do with the gentlemen in tweed caps and glasses who went breezing around and around the promenade deck.

When I first met her I got the impression she was no older than I was. As a matter of fact she was about twice my age: but you could be twice sixteen without being old, as I now realize, sixteen years after the event. She was small and delicate and looked as if she were made out of porcelain. But she had big wide-open California eyes and was not afraid to talk in a voice that was at once ingenuous and independent and had some suggestion of weariness about it as if she habitually stayed up too late at night.

To my dazzled eyes she immediately became the heroine of

every novel and I all but flung myself face down on the deck at her feet. She could have put a collar on my neck and led me around from that time forth on the end of a chain. Instead of that I spent my days telling her and her aunts all about my ideals and my ambitions and she in her turn attempted to teach me how to play bridge. And that is the surest proof of her conquest, for I never allowed anyone else to try such a thing as that on me, never! But even she could not succeed in such an enterprise.

We talked. The insatiable wound inside me bled and grew, and I was doing everything I could to make it bleed more. Her perfume and the peculiar smell of the denicotinized cigarettes she smoked followed me everywhere and tortured me in my cabin.

She told me how once she was in a famous night club in a famous city when a famous person, a prince of the royal blood, had stared very intently at her for a long time and had finally got up and started to lurch in the direction of her table when his friends had made him sit down and behave himself.

I could see that all the counts and dukes who liked to marry people like Constance Bennett would want also to marry her. But the counts and dukes were not here on board this glorified cargo boat that was carrying us all peacefully across the mild dark waves of the North Atlantic. The thing that crushed me was that I had never learned to dance.

We made Nantucket Light on Sunday afternoon and had to anchor in quarantine that night. So the ship rode in the Narrows on the silent waters, and the lights of Brooklyn glittered in the harbor like jewels. The boat was astir with music and with a warm glowing life that pulsated within the dark hull and poured out into the July night through every porthole. There were parties in all the cabins. Everywhere you went, especially on deck where it was quiet, you were placed in the middle of movie scenery—the setting for the last reel of the picture.

I made a declaration of my undying love. I would not, could not, ever love anyone else but her. It was impossible, unthinkable. If she went to the ends of the earth, destiny would bring us together again. The stars in their courses from the beginning of the world had plotted this meeting which was the central fact in the whole history of the universe. Love like this was immortal. It conquered time and outlasted the futility of human history. And so forth.

She talked to me, in her turn, gently and sweetly. What it sounded like was: "You do not know what you are saying. This can never be. We shall never meet again." What it meant was: "You are a nice kid. But for heaven's sake grow up before someone makes a fool of you." I went to my cabin and sobbed over my diary for a while and then, against all the laws of romance, went peacefully to sleep.

However, I could not sleep for long. At five o'clock I was up again, and walking restlessly around the deck. It was hot. A grey mist lay on the Narrows. But when it became light, other anchored ships began to appear as shapes in the mist. One of them was a Red Star liner on which, as I learned from the papers when I got on shore, a passenger was at that precise moment engaged in hanging himself.

At the last minute before landing I took a snapshot of her which, to my intense sorrow, came out blurred. I was so avid for a picture of her that I got too close with the camera and it was out of focus. It was a piece of poetic justice that filled me with woe for months.

Of course the whole family was there on the dock. But the change was devastating. With my heart ready to explode with immature emotions I suddenly found myself surrounded by all the cheerful and peaceful and comfortable solicitudes of home. Everybody wanted to talk. Their voices were full of questions and information. They took me for a drive on Long Island and showed me where Mrs. Hearst lived and everything. But I only hung my head out of the window of the car and watched the green trees go swirling by, and wished that I were dead.

I would not tell anybody what was the matter with me, and this reticence was the beginning of a kind of estrangement between us. From that time on no one could be sure what I was doing or thinking. I would go to New York and I would not come home for meals and I would not tell anyone where I had been.

Most of the time I had not been anywhere special; I would go to the movies, and then wander around the streets and look at the crowds of people and eat hot dogs and drink orange juice at Nedicks. Once with great excitement I got inside a speak-easy. And when I found out that the place was raided a few days later I grew so much in my own estimation that I began to act as if I had shot my way out of the wildest joints in town.

Bonnemaman was the one who suffered most from my reticence. For years she had been sitting at home wondering what Pop was doing in the city all day, and now that I was developing the same wandering habits it was quite natural for her to imagine strange things about me, too.

But the only wickedness I was up to was that I roamed around the city smoking cigarettes and hugging my own sweet sense of independence.

I found out that Grosset and Dunlap published more than the Rover Boys. They brought out reprints of writers like Hemingway and Aldous Huxley and D. H. Lawrence and I devoured them all, on the cool sleeping porch of the house at Douglaston, while the moths of the summer darkness came batting and throbbing against the screens, attracted by my light that burned until all hours.

Most of the time I was running into my uncle's room to borrow his dictionary, and when he found out what words I was looking up he arched his eyebrows and said: "What are you reading, anyway?"

At the end of the summer I started back for England on the same boat on which I had come. This time the passenger list included some girls from Bryn Mawr and some from Vassar and some from somewhere else, all of whom were going to a finishing school in France. It seems as if all the rest of the people on board were detectives. Some of them were professional detectives. Others were amateurs; all of them made me and the Bryn Mawr girls the object of their untiring investigations. But in any case the ship was divided into these two groups: on the one hand the young people, on the other the elders. We sat in the smoking room all the rainy days playing Duke Ellington records on the portable vic that belonged to one of the girls. When we got tired of that we wandered all over the ship looking for funny things to do. The hold was full of cattle, and there was also a pack of fox-hounds down there. We used to go down and play with the dogs. At Le Havre, when the cattle were unloaded, one of the cows broke loose and ran all over the dock in a frenzy. One night three of us got up in the crow's nest on the fore-mast, where we certainly did not belong. Another time we had a party with the radio operators and I got into a big argument about Communism.

That was another thing that had happened that summer: I had begun to get the idea that I was a Communist, although I wasn't quite sure what Communism was. There are a lot of people like that. They do no little harm by virtue of their sheer, stupid inertia, lost in between all camps, in the no-man's-land of their own confusion. They are fair game for anybody. They can be turned into fascists just as quickly as they can be pulled into line with those who are really Reds.

The other group was made up of the middle-aged people. At their core were the red-faced, hard-boiled cops who spent their time drinking and gambling and fighting among themselves and spreading scandal all over the boat about the young ones who were so disreputable and wild.

The truth is that we did have quite a big bar bill, the Bryn Mawr girls and myself, but we were never drunk, because we drank slowly and spent the whole time stuffing ourselves with sardines on toast and all the other dainties which are the stock in trade of English liners.

In any case, I set foot once more on the soil of England dressed up in a gangster suit which Pop had bought me at Wallach's, complete with padded shoulders. And I had a new, pale grey hat over my eye and walked into England pleased with the consciousness that I had easily acquired a very lurid reputation for myself with scarcely any trouble at all.

The separation of the two generations on board the ship

117

had pleased me. It had flattered me right down to the soles of my feet. It was just what I wanted. It completed my self-confidence, guaranteed my self-assertion. Anyone older than myself symbolized authority. And the vulgarity of the detectives and the stupidity of the other middle-aged people who had believed all their stories about us fed me with a pleasantly justifiable sense of contempt for their whole generation. Therefore I concluded that I was now free of all authority, and that nobody could give me any advice that I had to listen to. Because advice was only the cloak of hypocrisy or weakness or vulgarity or fear. Authority was constituted by the old and weak, and had its roots in their envy for the joys and pleasures of the young and strong. . . .

Finally, when I arrived at Oakham several days after the beginning of the term I was convinced that I was the only one in the whole place who knew anything about life, from the Headmaster on down.

I was now a house prefect in Hodge Wing with a great big study and a lot of slightly lop-sided wicker armchairs full of cushions. On the walls I hung Medici prints of Manet and some other impressionists and photographs of various Greco-Roman Venuses from museums in Rome. And my bookshelf was full of a wide variety of strange bright-colored novels and pamphlets, all of which were so inflammatory that there would never be any special need for the Church to put them on the *Index*, for they would all be damned *ipso jure*—most of them by the natural law itself. I will not name the ones I remember, because some fool might immediately go and read them all: but I might mention that one of the pamphlets was Marx's Communist Manifesto—not because I was seriously exercised about the injustices done to the working class, which were and are very real, but were too serious for my empty-headed vanity—but simply because I thought it fitted in nicely with the décor in which I now moved in all my imaginings.

For it had become evident to me that I was a great rebel. I fancied that I had suddenly risen above all the errors and stupidities and mistakes of modern society—there are enough of them to rise above, I admit—and that I had taken my place in the ranks of those who held up their heads and squared their shoulders and marched into the future. In the modern world, people are always holding up their heads and marching into the future, although they haven't the slightest idea what they think the "future" is or could possibly mean. The only future we seem to walk into, in actual fact, is full of bigger and more terrible wars, wars well calculated to knock our upraised heads off those squared shoulders.

Here in this study I edited the school magazine which had fallen into my hands that autumn, and read T. S. Eliot, and even tried to write a poem myself about Elpenor, in Homer, getting drunk and falling off the roof of a palace. And his soul fled into the shades of hell. And the rest of the time I played Duke Ellington's records or got into arguments about politics and religion.

All those vain and absurd arguments! My advice to an ordinary religious man, supposing anyone were to desire my advice on this point, would be to avoid all arguments about religion, and especially about the existence of God. However, to those who know some philosophy I would recommend the study of Duns Scotus' proofs for the actual existence of an Infinite Being, which are given in the Second Distinction of the First Book of the *Opus Oxoniense*—in Latin that is hard enough to give you many headaches. It is getting to be rather generally admitted that, for accuracy and depth and scope, this is the most perfect and complete and thorough proof for the existence of God that has ever been worked out by any man.

I doubt if it would have done much good to bring these considerations before me in those days, when I was just turning seventeen, and thought I knew all about philosophy without ever having learned any. However, I did have a desire to learn. I was attracted to philosophy. It was an attraction the Headmaster had worked hard to implant in our souls: but there was, and could be, no course in philosophy at Oakham. I was left to my own devices.

I remember once mentioning all this to Tom, my guardian.

We were walking out of his front door, into Harley Street, and I told him of my desire to study philosophy, and to know the philosophers.

He, being a doctor, told me to leave philosophy alone: there were few things, he told me, that were a greater waste of time.

Fortunately, this was one of the matters in which I decided to ignore his advice. Anyway, I went ahead and tried to read some philosophy. I never got very far with it. It was too difficult for me to master all by myself. People who are immersed in sensual appetites and desires are not very well prepared to handle abstract ideas. Even in the purely natural order, a certain amount of purity of heart is required before an intellect can get sufficiently detached and clear to work out the problems of metaphysics. I say a certain amount, however, because I am sure that no one needs to be a saint to be a clever metaphysician. I dare say there are plenty of metaphysicians in hell.

However, the philosophers to whom I was attracted were not the best. For the most part, I used to take their books out of libraries, and return them without ever having opened them. It was just as well. Nevertheless during the Easter vacation, when I was seventeen, I earnestly and zealously set about trying to figure out Spinoza.

I had gone to Germany, by myself as usual, for the vacation. In Cologne I had bought a big rucksack and slung it over my shoulders and started up the Rhine valley on foot, in a blue jersey and an old pair of flannel bags, so that people in the inns along the road asked me if I was a Dutch sailor off one of the river barges. In the rucksack, which was already heavy enough, I had a couple of immoral novels and the Everyman Library edition of Spinoza. Spinoza and the Rhine valley! I certainly had a fine sense of appropriateness. The two go very well together. However I was about eighty years too late. And the only thing that was lacking was that I was not an English or American student at Heidelberg: then the mixture would have been perfect in all its mid-nineteenth-century ingredients.

I picked up more, on this journey, than a few intellectual errors, half understood. Before I got to Koblenz, I had trouble in one foot. Some kind of an infection seemed to be developing under one of the toenails. But it was not especially painful, and I ignored it. However, it made walking unpleasant, and so, after going on as far as St. Goar, I gave up in disgust. Besides, the weather had turned bad, and I had got lost in the forest, trying to follow the imaginary hiker's trail called the Rheinhöhenweg.

I went back to Koblenz, and sat in a room over a big beer hall called the Neuer Franziskaner and continued my desultory study of Spinoza and my modern novelists. Since I understood the latter much better than the philosopher, I soon gave him up and concentrated on the novels.

After a few days, I returned to England, passing through Paris, where Pop and Bonnemaman were. There I picked up some more and even worse books, and went back to school.

I had not been back for more than a few days when I began to feel ill. At first, I thought I was only out of sorts because of the sore foot and a bad toothache, which had suddenly begun to afflict me.

They sent me down to the school dentist, Dr. McTaggart, who lived in a big brick building like a barracks, on the way to the station. Dr. McTaggart was a lively little fellow. He knew me well, for I was always having trouble with my teeth. He had a theory that you should kill the nerves of teeth, and he had already done so to half a dozen of mine. For the rest, he would trot gaily around and around the big chair in which I sat, mute and half frozen with terror. And he would sing, as he quickly switched his drills: "It won't be a stylish marriage— We can't afford a carriage— But you'll look sweet— Upon the seat— Of a bicycle built for two." Then he would start wrecking my teeth once again, with renewed gusto.

This time he tapped at the tooth, and looked serious.

"It will have to come out," he said.

I was not sorry. The thing was hurting me, and I wanted to get rid of it as soon as possible.

But Dr. McTaggart said: "I can't give you anything to deaden the pain, you know."

"Why not?"

"There is a great deal of infection, and the matter has spread far beyond the roots of the tooth."

I accepted his reasoning on trust and said: "Well, go ahead."

And I sat back in the chair, mute with misgivings, while he happily trotted over to his tool-box singing "It won't be a stylish marriage" and pulled out an ugly-looking forceps.

"All ready?" he said, jacking back the chair, and brandishing the instrument of torture. I nodded, feeling as if I had gone pale to the roots of my hair.

But the tooth came out fast, in one big, vivid flash of pain and left me spitting a lot of green and red business into the little blue whispering whirlpool by the side of the dentist's chair.

"Oh, goodness," said Dr. McTaggart, "I don't like that very much, I must say."

I walked wearily back to school, reflecting that it was not really so terrible after all to have a tooth pulled out without novocain. However, instead of getting better, I got worse. By evening, I was really ill, and that night—that sleepless night— was spent in a fog of sick confusedness and general pain. The next morning they took my temperature and put me to bed in the sick-room, where I eventually got to sleep.

That did not make me any better. And I soon gathered in a vague way that our matron, Miss Harrison, was worried about me, and communicated her worries to the Headmaster, in whose own house this particular sick-room was.

Then the school doctor came around. And he went away again, returning with Dr. McTaggart who, this time, did not sing.

And I heard them agreeing that I was getting to be too full of gangrene for my own good. They decided to lance a big hole in my gum, and see if they could not drain the pocket of infection there and so, having given me a little ether, they

122

went ahead. I awoke with my mouth full of filth, both doctors urging me to hurry up and get rid of it.

When they had gone, I lay back in bed and closed my eyes and thought: "I have blood-poisoning."

And then my mind went back to the sore foot I had developed in Germany. Well, I would tell them about it when they came back the next time.

Sick, weary, half asleep, I felt the throbbing of the wound in my mouth. Blood-poisoning.

The room was very quiet. It was rather dark, too. And as I lay in bed, in my weariness and pain and disgust, I felt for a moment the shadow of another visitor pass into the room.

It was death, that came to stand by my bed.

I kept my eyes closed, more out of apathy than anything else. But anyway, there was no need to open one's eyes to see the visitor, to see death. Death is someone you see very clearly with eyes in the center of your heart: eyes that see not by reacting to light, but by reacting to a kind of a chill from within the marrow of your own life.

And, with those eyes, those interior eyes, open upon that coldness, I lay half asleep and looked at the visitor, death.

What did I think? All I remember was that I was filled with a deep and tremendous apathy. I felt so sick and disgusted that I did not very much care whether I died or lived. Perhaps death did not come very close to me, or give me a good look at the nearness of his coldness and darkness, or I would have been more afraid.

But at any rate, I lay there in a kind of torpor and said: "Come on, I don't care." And then I fell asleep.

What a tremendous mercy it was that death did not take me at my word, that day, when I was still only seventeen years old. What a thing it would have been if the trapdoors that were prepared for me had yawned and opened their blackness and swallowed me down in the middle of that sleep! Oh, I tell you, it is a blessing beyond calculation that I woke up again, that day, or the following night, or in the week or two that came after.

And I lay there with nothing in my heart but apathy—there

123

was a kind of pride and spite in it: as if it was life's fault that I had to suffer a little discomfort, and for that I would show my scorn and hatred of life, and die, as if that were a revenge of some sort. Revenge upon what? What was life? Something existing apart from me, and separate from myself? Don't worry, I did not enter into any speculations. I only thought: "If I have to die—what of it. What do I care? Let me die, then, and I'm finished."

Religious people, those who have faith and love God and realize what life is and what death means, and know what it is to have an immortal soul, do not understand how it is with the ones who have no faith, and who have already thrown away their souls. They find it hard to conceive that anyone could enter into the presence of death without some kind of compunction. But they should realize that millions of men die the way I was then prepared to die, the way I then might have died.

They might say to me: "Surely you thought of God, and you wanted to pray to Him for mercy."

No. As far as I remember, the thought of God, the thought of prayer did not even enter my mind, either that day, or all the rest of the time that I was ill, or that whole year, for that matter. Or if the thought did come to me, it was only as an occasion for its denial and rejection. I remember that in that year, when we stood in the chapel and recited the Apostles' Creed, I used to keep my lips tight shut, with full deliberation and of set purpose, by way of declaring my own creed which was: "I believe in nothing." Or at least I thought I believed in nothing. Actually, I had only exchanged a certain faith, faith in God, Who is Truth, for a vague uncertain faith in the opinions and authority of men and pamphlets and newspapers—wavering and varying and contradictory opinions which I did not even clearly understand.

I wish I could give those who believe in God some kind of an idea of the state of a soul like mine was in then. But it is impossible to do it in sober, straight, measured, prose terms. And, in a sense, image and analogy would be even more misleading, by the very fact that they would have life in them,

124

and convey the notion of some real entity, some kind of energy, some sort of activity. But my soul was simply dead. It was a blank, a nothingness. It was empty, it was a kind of a spiritual vacuum, as far as the supernatural order was concerned. Even its natural faculties were shrivelled husks of what they ought to have been.

A soul is an immaterial thing. It is a principle of activity, it is an "act," a "form," an energizing principle. It is the life of the body, and it must also have a life of its own. But the life of the soul does not inhere in any physical, material subject. So to compare a soul without grace to a corpse without life is only a metaphor. But it is very true.

St. Theresa had a vision of hell. She saw herself confined in a narrow hole in a burning wall. The vision terrified her above all with the sense of the appalling stress of this confinement and heat. All this is symbolic, of course. But a poetic grasp of the meaning of the symbol should convey something of the experience of a soul which is reduced to an almost infinite limit of helplessness and frustration by the fact of dying in sin, and thus being eternally separated from the principle of all vital activity which, for the soul in its own proper order, means intellection and love.

But I now lay on this bed, full of gangrene, and my soul was rotten with the corruption of my sins. And I did not even care whether I died or lived.

The worst thing that can happen to anyone in this life is to lose all sense of these realities. The worst thing that had ever happened to me was this consummation of my sins in abominable coldness and indifference, even in the presence of death.

What is more, there was nothing I could do for myself. There was absolutely no means, no natural means within reach, for getting out of that state. Only God could help me. Who prayed for me? One day I shall know. But in the economy of God's love, it is through the prayers of other men that these graces are given. It was through the prayers of someone who loved God that I was, one day, to be delivered out of that hell where I was already confined without knowing it.

The big gift God gave me was that I got well. They bundled me up and put me on a stretcher with blankets all up around my face and nothing sticking out but my nose, and carried me across the stone quadrangle where my friends were playing "quad-cricket" with a sawed-off bat and a grey tennis ball. They stood aside in awe as I passed on the way to the school sanatorium.

I had explained to the doctor about my foot, and they came and cut off the toenail and found the toe full of gangrene. But they gave me some anti-toxin and did not have to cut off the toe. Dr. McTaggart came around every day or two to treat the infected place in my mouth, and gradually I began to get better, and to eat, and sit up, and read my filthy novels again. Nobody thought of prohibiting them, because nobody else had heard of the authors.

It was while I was in the sanatorium that I wrote a long essay on the modern novel—Gide, Hemingway, Dos Passos, Jules Romains, Dreiser, and so on, for the Bailey English Prize, and won a lot of books bound in tree-calf for my efforts.

Two attempts were made to convert me to less shocking tastes. The music master lent me a set of records of Bach's B Minor Mass, which I liked, and sometimes played on my portable gramophone, which I had with me in the big airy room looking out on the Headmaster's garden. But most of the time I played the hottest and loudest records, turning the vic towards the classroom building, eighty yards away across the flowerbeds, hoping that my companions, grinding out the syntax of Virgil's *Georgics*, would be very envious of me.

The other loan was that of a book. The Headmaster came along, one day, and gave me a little blue book of poems. I looked at the name on the back. "Gerard Manley Hopkins." I had never heard of him. But I opened the book, and read the "Starlight Night" and the Harvest poem and the most lavish and elaborate early poems. I noticed that the man was a Catholic and a priest and, what is more, a Jesuit.

I could not make up my mind whether I liked his verse or not.

It was elaborate and tricky and in places it was a little lush and overdone, I thought. Yet it was original and had a lot of vitality and music and depth. In fact the later poems were all far too deep for me, and I could not make anything out of them at all.

Nevertheless, I accepted the poet, with reservations. I gave the book back to the Head, and thanked him, and never altogether forgot Hopkins, though I was not to read him again for several years.

I got out of the sanatorium in a month or six weeks. With the end of June, came our big examination—the higher certificate, which I took in French and German and Latin. Then we went away for the vacation, and I settled down to wait until September for the results of the exam. Pop and Bonnemaman and John Paul were once again in Europe for the summer, and we all spent a couple of months in a big, dreary hotel in Bournemouth, standing on top of a cliff and facing the sea with a battery of white iron balconies, painted silver, so that they gleamed in the pale, English summer sun and in the morning mists. I will not go into the emotions of that summer, in which I and a girl I met there kept going through storms of sentiment alternating with adolescent quarrels, during which I used to escape from Bournemouth into the Dorset downs and wander around for the whole day in the country trying to recover my equilibrium.

But at the end of the summer, when she went back to London, and my family also took the boat at Southampton and went home, I packed up my rucksack and went into the New Forest, with a pup tent, and sat down under some pine trees at the edge of a common a couple of miles from Brockenhurst. Oh, the tremendous loneliness of that first night in the forest! The frogs sang in the brackish stream, and the fireflies played in the gorse, and occasionally a lone car would pass along the distant road, exaggerating the silence by the sound that died in the wake of its passing. And I sat in the door of my tent, uneasily trying to digest the eggs and bacon I had fried and the bottle of cider I had brought out from the village.

She had said she would write me a letter, addressed to the Post-office at Brockenhurst, as soon as she got home, but I thought this camp site at the edge of the common was too dreary. Besides, the water of the stream tasted funny and I thought maybe I might get poisoned, so I moved on down toward Beaulieu, where I did not have to eat my own cooking, but ate in an inn. And I spent the afternoon lying in the grass in front of the old Cistercian abbey, copiously pitying myself for my boredom and for the loneliness of immature love. At the same time, however, I was debating in my mind whether to go to a "Gymkhana," that is a sort of a polite amateur horse-show, and mingle with all the gentry of the county, perhaps meeting someone even more beautiful than the girl for whom I thought I was, at the moment, pining away even unto death. However, I wisely decided to avoid the tents of such a dull affair.

As for the Cistercian abbey, which was the scene of these meditations, I did not think much about it at all. I had wandered through the ruins of the old buildings, and had stood in the parish church that had taken over the old refectory of the monks, and I had tasted a little of the silence and peacefulness of the greensward under the trees, where the cloister used to be. But it was all in the usual picnic spirit with which the average modern Englishman visits one of his old abbeys. If he does happen to wonder what kind of men once lived in such places, or why they ever did so, he does not ask himself if people still try to do the same thing today. That would seem to him a kind of impertinence. But by this time I had practically lost all interest in such speculations. What did I care about monks and monasteries? The world was going to open out before me, with all its entertainments, and everything would be mine and with my intelligence and my five sharp senses I would rob all its treasures and rifle its coffers and empty them all. And I would take what pleased me, and the rest I would throw away. And if I merely felt like spoiling the luxuries I did not want to use, I would spoil them and misuse them, to suit myself, because I was master of everything. It did not matter that I would not have much money: I would have enough, and my wits would do the rest. And I was aware that the best pleasures can be had without very much money—or with none at all.

I was at the house of one of my friends from school when the results of the higher certificate came out in September, and I could not decently indulge all my vanity at my success, because he had failed. However, he and I were to go up to Cambridge together for the scholarship examinations that December.

Andrew was the son of a country parson in the Isle of Wight and he had been cricket captain at Oakham. He wore horn-rimmed spectacles and had a great chin that he held up in the air, and a lock of black hair fell down over his forehead, and he was one of the school intellectuals. He and I used to work, or rather sit, in the library at Oakham, with many books open before us, but talking about impertinent matters and drinking a foul purple concoction called Vimto out of bottles which we concealed under the table or behind the volumes of the Dictionary of National Biography.

He had discovered a black book called, as I think, *The Outline of Modern Knowledge,* which was something that had just come to the library and was full of information about psychoanalysis. Indeed, it went into some details of psychoanalytical fortune-telling by the inspection of faeces which I never ran into anywhere else, and which I still preserved enough sense to laugh at, at that time. But later, at Cambridge, psychoanalysis was to provide me with a kind of philosophy of life and even a sort of pseudo-religion which was nearly the end of me altogether. By that time, Andrew himself had lost interest in it.

When we went up to the university, to sit for the scholarship exam, in the dank heavy-hanging mists of December, I spent most of the time between papers devouring D. H. Lawrence's *Fantasia of the Unconscious* which, even as psychoanalysis, is completely irresponsible and, just as it says, a fantasia. Lawrence picked up a lot of terms like "lumbar ganglion" and threw them all together and stewed them up with his own worship of the sex-instinct to produce the weird mixture which I read as reverently as if it were some kind of sacred revelation, sitting in the rooms of an undergraduate who liked Picasso, but who had gone down for the Christmas vacation. Andrew, for his part, was at St. Catherine's, terrified of a tutor who had a reputation for being a very ferocious person. All that week I sat under the high, silent rafters of the Hall, at Trinity College, and covered long sheets of foolscap with my opinions concerning Molière and Racine and Balzac and Victor Hugo and Goethe and Schiller and all the rest, and a few days after it was all over, we looked in the *Times* and this time both Andrew and I had succeeded. We were exhibitioners, he at St. Catherine's and I at Clare, while his study-mate, Dickens, who was the only other person at Oakham besides myself who liked hot records, had another exhibition at St. John's.

My satisfaction was very great. I was finished with Oakham —not that I disliked the school, but I was glad of my liberty. Now, at last, I imagined that I really was grown up and independent, and I could stretch out my hands and take all the things I wanted.

So during the Christmas holidays I ate and drank so much and went to so many parties that I made myself sick.

But I picked myself up, and dusted myself off, and on January 31st of the New Year, my eighteenth birthday, Tom took me to the Café Anglais and treated me to champagne and the next day I was off on the way to Italy.

vi

Already at Avignon I foresaw that I was going to run out of money before I got to Genoa. I had a letter of credit on a bank there. So from Avignon I wrote back to Tom asking for money. From Marseilles I started out on foot along the coast, walking on the white mountain road, overlooking the bright blue water, having on my hip a flask of rum and in the rucksack some more of the same novels. At Cassis all the restaurants were crammed with people who had come out from Marseilles for the day, since it was Sunday, and I had to wait long for my *bouillabaisse*. It was dark by the time I arrived at the grim little port of La Ciotat, under its sugar-loaf rock. Tired, I sat on the jetty and contemplated the moon.

At Hyères I had to wait a couple of days before the money arrived, and when it did, the letter that went with it was filled with sharp reproofs. Tom, my guardian, took occasion of my impracticality to call attention to most of my other faults as well, and I was very humiliated. So after a month of my precious liberty, I received my first indication that my desires could never be absolute: they must necessarily be conditioned and modified by contacts and conflicts with the desires and interests of others. This was something that it would take me a long time to find out, and indeed in the natural order alone I would never really get to understand it. I believed in the beautiful myth about having a good time so long as it does not hurt anybody else. You cannot live for your own pleasure and your own convenience without inevitably hurting and injuring the feelings and the interests of practically everybody you meet. But, as a matter of fact, in the natural order no matter what ideals may be theoretically possible, most people more or less live for themselves and for their own interests and pleasures or for those of their own family or group, and therefore they are constantly interfering with one another's aims, and hurting one another and injuring one another, whether they mean it or not.

I started out from Hyères again, this time more weary and depressed, walking among the pines, under the hot sun, looking at the rocks and the yellow mimosas and the little pink villas and the light blazing on the sea. That night I came down a long hill in the dusk to a hamlet called Cavalaire, and slept in a boarding house full of sombre retired accountants who drank vin-rosé with their wives under the dim light of weak electric bulbs, and I went to bed and dreamt that I was in jail.

At Saint Tropez I had a letter of introduction to a friend of Tom's, a man with t.b., living in a sunny house on top of a hill, and there I met a couple of Americans who had rented a villa in the hills behind Cannes and they invited me there, when I came that way.

On the way to Cannes, I got caught by a storm, towards evening, in the mountains of the Esterel, and was picked up by a chauffeur driving a big fancy Delage. I slung my rucksack off my shoulder and threw it in the back seat and settled down, with the warmth of the motor seeping up through the boards and into my wet, tired feet. The chauffeur was an Englishman who had an auto-hiring business in Nice and said he had just picked up the Lindbergh family off the liner at Villefranche and had taken them somewhere down the road here. At Cannes he took me to a very dull place, a club for English chauffeurs and sailors off the yachts of the rich people who were wintering on the Riviera. There I ate ham and eggs and watched the chauffeurs politely playing billiards, and grew depressed at the smell of London that lingered in the room—the smell of English cigarettes and English beer. It reminded me of the fogs I thought I had escaped.

Then I found the villa of the people I had met at Saint Tropez, and stayed there a couple of days, and finally, fed up with walking, and seeing that I would probably be bored with the rest of the road along the coast, I got on the train and went to Genoa.

Perhaps the boredom that I felt had its roots in some physical cause, because the first morning I woke up in Genoa, with a bunch of Italian housepainters working on the roof outside my window, I was out of sorts and had a great boil on my elbow, which I clumsily tried to heal by my own private treatments, which did not work.

So I cashed my letter of credit and got on another train and went to Florence, where I had another letter of introduction to a man who was a sculptor. Florence was freezing. I took a trolley out across the Arno, and found the steep road up the hill where my man lived, and climbed it in the icy silence of a Tuscan winter evening. At first I thought nobody was going to answer my knock on the big hollow-sounding door, but presently an old Italian cook came out, and led me in to the studio where I made myself known and explained that I had a boil on my elbow. So the cook got some hot water and I sat in the dry dust of plaster and among the stone chips around the base of some half-finished work, and talked to the sculptor while his cook fixed up a poultice for my boil.

The artist was the brother of the former Headmaster of Oakham, the one who had preceded Doherty. I had seen some of his bas-reliefs which decorated the front of the school chapel. He was not as old as his brother, the ex-head. But he was a kind, stoop-shouldered person with greying hair, and had most of the old head's geniality. He said to me: "I was thinking of going down and seeing the Greta Garbo film in town this evening. Do you like Greta Garbo?"

I admitted that I did. "Very well, then," he said, "we will go."

But Florence was too cold, and I thought the boil was getting better. So the next day I left, on the way to Rome. I was tired of passing through places. I wanted to get to the term of my journey, where there was some psychological possibility that I would stop in one place and remain.

The train ambled slowly through the mountains of Umbria. The blue sky glared down upon the rocks. The compartment was empty save for myself, and nobody got in until one of the last stations before Rome. All day I stared out at the bare hills, at the wild, ascetic landscape. Somewhere out there, on one of those mountains, St. Francis had been praying and the seraph with the fiery, blood-red wings had appeared before him with the Christ in the midst of those wings: and from the wounds, other wounds had been nailed in Francis's hands and feet and side. If I had thought of that, that day, it would have been all I needed to complete the discouragement of my pagan soul, for it turned out that the boil was no better after all, and that I had another toothache. For that matter, my head felt as if I had a fever as well, and I wondered if the old business of blood-poisoning was starting once again.

So there I was, with all the liberty that I had been promising myself for so long. The world was mine. How did I like it? I was doing just what I pleased, and instead of being filled with happiness and well-being, I was miserable. The love of pleasure is destined by its very nature to defeat itself and end in frustration. But I was one of the last men in the world who would have been convinced by the wisdom of a St. John of the Cross in those strange days.

But now I was entering a city which bears living testimony to these truths, to those who can see it, to those who know where to look for it—to those who know how to compare the Rome of the Caesars with the Rome of the martyrs.

I was entering the city that had been thus transformed by the Cross. Square white apartment houses were beginning to appear in thick clusters at the foot of the bare, grey-green hills, with clumps of cypress here and there, and presently over the roofs of the buildings, I saw, rising up in the dusk, the mighty substance of St. Peter's dome. The realization that it was not a photograph filled me with great awe.

My first preoccupation in Rome was to find a dentist. The people in the hotel sent me to one nearby. There were a couple of nuns in the waiting room. After they left, I entered. The dentist had a brown beard. I did not trust my Italian for so important a matter as a toothache. I spoke to him in French. He knew a little French. And he looked at the tooth.

He knew what he thought was wrong with it, but he did not know the technical word in French.

"Ah," he said, "vous avez un *colpo d'aria*."

I figured it out easily enough to mean that I had caught a chill in my tooth—according to this man with the brown beard. But still, cowardice closed my mouth, and I was content not to argue that I thought it was by no means a chill, but an abscess.

"I shall treat it with ultra-violet rays," said the dentist. With a mixture of relief and scepticism, I underwent this painless and futile process. It did nothing whatever to relieve the toothache. But I left with warm assurances from the dentist that it would all disappear during the night.

Far from disappearing during the night, the toothache did what all toothaches do during the night: kept me awake, in great misery, cursing my fate.

The next morning I got up and staggered back to my friend *colpo d'aria* next door. I met him coming down the stairs with his beard all brushed and a black hat on his head, with gloves and spats and everything. Only then did I realize that it was Sunday. However, he consented to give a look at the chilled tooth.

In a mixture of French and Italian he asked me if I could stand ether. I said yes, I could. He draped a clean handkerchief over my nose and mouth and dropped a couple of drops of ether on it. I breathed deeply, and the sweet sick knives of the smell reached in to my consciousness and the drumming of the heavy dynamos began. I hoped that he wasn't breathing too deeply himself, or that his hand wouldn't slip, and spill the whole bottle of it in my face.

However, a minute or two later I woke up again and he was waving the red, abscessed roots of the tooth in my face and exclaiming: "C'est fini!"

I moved out of my hotel and found a *pensione* with windows that looked down on the sunny Triton fountain in the middle of the Piazza Barberini and the Bristol Hotel and the Barberini Cinema and the Barberini Palace, and the maid brought me some hot water to treat the boil on my arm. I went to bed and tried to read a novel by Maxim Gorki which very quickly put me to sleep.

I had been in Rome before, on an Easter vacation from school, for about a week. I had seen the Forum and the Colosseum and the Vatican museum and St. Peter's. But I had not really seen Rome.

This time, I started out again, with the misconception common to Anglo-Saxons, that the real Rome is the Rome of the ugly ruins, the Rome of all those grey cariated temples wedged in between the hills and the slums of the city. I tried to reconstruct the ancient city, in my mind—a dream which did not work very well, because of the insistent shouting of the sellers of postcards who beset me on every side. After a few days of trying the same thing, it suddenly struck me that it was not worth the trouble. It was so evident, merely from the masses of stone and brick that still represented the palaces and temples and baths, that imperial Rome must have been one of the most revolting and ugly and depressing cities the world has ever seen. In fact, the ruins with cedars and cypresses and umbrella pines scattered about among them were far more pleasant than the reality must have been.

However, I still roamed about the museums, especially the one in the Baths of Diocletian, which had also been, at one time, a Carthusian monastery—probably not a very successful one—and I studied Rome in a big learned book that I had bought, together with an old second-hand Baedeker in French.

And after spending the day in museums and libraries and bookstores and among the ruins, I would come home again and read my novels. In fact, I was also beginning to write one of my own, although I did not get very far with it as long as I was at Rome.

I had a lot of books with me—a strange mixture: Dryden, the poems of D. H. Lawrence, some Tauchnitz novels, and James Joyce's *Ulysses* in a fancy India-paper edition, slick and expensive, which I lent to someone, later on, and never got back.

Things were going on as they usually did with me. But after about a week—I don't know how it began—I found myself looking into churches rather than into ruined temples. Perhaps it was the frescoes on the wall of an old chapel— ruined too—at the foot of the Palatine, at the edge of the Forum, that first aroused my interest in another and a far different Rome. From there it was an easy step to Sts. Cosmas and Damian, across the Forum, with a great mosaic, in the apse, of Christ coming in judgement in a dark blue sky, with a suggestion of fire in the small clouds beneath His feet. The effect of this discovery was tremendous. After all the vapid, boring, semi-pornographic statuary of the Empire, what a thing it was to come upon the genius of an art full of spiritual vitality and earnestness and power—an art that was tremendously serious and alive and eloquent and urgent in all that it had to say. And it was without pretentiousness, without fakery, and had nothing theatrical about it. Its solemnity was made all the more astounding by its simplicity—and by the obscurity of the places where it lay hid, and by its subservience to higher ends, architectural, liturgical and spiritual ends which I could not even begin to understand, but which I could not avoid guessing, since the nature of the mosaics themselves and their position and everything about them proclaimed it aloud.

I was fascinated by these Byzantine mosaics. I began to haunt the churches where they were to be found, and, as an indirect consequence, all the other churches that were more or less of the same period. And thus without knowing anything about it I became a pilgrim. I was unconsciously and unintentionally visiting all the great shrines of Rome, and seeking out their sanctuaries with some of the eagerness and avidity and desire of a true pilgrim, though not quite for the right reason. And yet it was not for a wrong reason either. For these mosaics and frescoes and all the ancient altars and thrones and sanctuaries were designed and built for the instruction of people who were not capable of immediately understanding anything higher.

I never knew what relics and what wonderful and holy things were hidden in the churches whose doors and aisles and arches had become the refuge of my mind. Christ's cradle and the pillar of the Flagellation and the True Cross and St. Peter's chains, and the tombs of the great martyrs, the tomb of the child St. Agnes and the martyr St. Cecilia and of Pope St. Clement and of the great deacon St. Lawrence who was burned on a gridiron. . . . These things did not speak to me, or at least I did not know they spoke to me. But the churches that enshrined them did, and so did the art on their walls.

And now for the first time in my life I began to find out something of Who this Person was that men called Christ. It was obscure, but it was a true knowledge of Him, in some sense, truer than I knew and truer than I would admit. But it was in Rome that my conception of Christ was formed. It was there I first saw Him, Whom I now serve as my God and my King, and Who owns and rules my life.

It is the Christ of the Apocalypse, the Christ of the Martyrs, the Christ of the Fathers. It is the Christ of St.

John, and of St. Paul, and of St. Augustine and St. Jerome and all the Fathers—and of the Desert Fathers. It is Christ God, Christ King, *"for in Him dwelleth the fulness of the Godhead corporeally, and you are filled in Him, Who is the Head of all principality and power . . . For in Him were all things created in heaven and on earth, visible and invisible, whether thrones or dominations or principalities or powers, all things were created by Him and in Him. And He is before all, and by Him all things consist . . . because in Him it hath well pleased the Father that all fulness should dwell . . . Who is the image of the invisible God, the first-born of every creature . . .*[1]*" "The first-begotten of the dead, and the prince of the kings of the earth, Who hath loved us, and washed us from our sins in His own Blood, and hath made us a kingdom and priests to God His Father."*[2]

The saints of those forgotten days had left upon the walls of their churches words which by the peculiar grace of God I was able in some measure to apprehend, although I could not decode them all. But above all, the realest and most immediate source of this grace was Christ Himself, present in those churches, in all His power, and in His Humanity, in His Human Flesh and His material, physical, corporeal Presence. How often I was left entirely alone in these churches with the tremendous God, and knew nothing of it—except I had to know something of it, as I say, obscurely. And it was He Who was teaching me Who He was, more directly than I was capable of realising.

These mosaics told me more than I had ever known of the doctrine of a God of infinite power, wisdom and love Who had yet become Man, and revealed in His Manhood the infinity of power, wisdom and love that was His Godhead. Of course I could not grasp and believe these things explicitly. But since they were implicit in every line of the pictures I contemplated with such admiration and love, surely I grasped them implicitly—I had to, in so far as the mind of the artist

[1] Col. I and II.
[2] Apoc. I.

reached my own mind, and spoke to it his conception and his thought. And so I could not help but catch something of the ancient craftsman's love of Christ, the Redeemer and Judge of the World.

It was more or less natural that I should want to discover something of the meaning of the mosaics I saw—of the Lamb standing as though slain, and of the four-and-twenty elders casting down their crowns. And I had bought a Vulgate text, and was reading the New Testament. I had forgotten all about the poems of D. H. Lawrence except for the fact that he had four poems about the Four Evangelists, based on the traditional symbols from Ezechiel and the Apocalypse of the four mystical creatures. One evening, when I was reading these poems, I became so disgusted with their falseness and futility that I threw down the book and began to ask myself why I was wasting my time with a man of such unimportance as this. For it was evident that he had more or less completely failed to grasp the true meaning of the New Testament, which he had perverted in the interests of a personal and home-made religion of his own which was not only fanciful, but full of unearthly seeds, all ready to break forth into hideous plants like those that were germinating in Germany's unweeded garden, in the dank weather of Nazism.

So for once I put my favorite aside. And I read more and more of the Gospels, and my love for the old churches and their mosaics grew from day to day. Soon I was no longer visiting them merely for the art. There was something else that attracted me: a kind of interior peace. I loved to be in these holy places. I had a kind of deep and strong conviction that I belonged there: that my rational nature was filled with profound desires and needs that could only find satisfaction in churches of God. I remember that one of my favorite shrines was that of St. Peter in Chains, and I did not love it for any work of art that was there, since the big attraction, the big "number," the big "feature" in that place is Michelangelo's Moses. But I had always been extremely bored by that horned and pop-eyed frown and by the crack in the knee.

I'm glad the thing couldn't speak, for it would probably have given out some very heavy statements.

Perhaps what was attracting me to that Church was the Apostle himself to whom it is dedicated. And I do not doubt that he was praying earnestly to get me out of my own chains: chains far heavier and more terrible than ever were his.

Where else did I like to go? St. Pudenziana, St. Praxed's, above all St. Mary Major and the Lateran, although as soon as the atmosphere got heavy with baroque melodrama I would get frightened, and the peace and the obscure, tenuous sense of devotion I had acquired would leave me.

So far, however, there had been no deep movement of my will, nothing that amounted to a conversion, nothing to shake the iron tyranny of moral corruption that held my whole nature in fetters. But that also was to come. It came in a strange way, suddenly, a way that I will not attempt to explain.

I was in my room. It was night. The light was on. Suddenly it seemed to me that Father, who had now been dead more than a year, was there with me. The sense of his presence was as vivid and as real and as startling as if he had touched my arm or spoken to me. The whole thing passed in a flash, but in that flash, instantly, I was overwhelmed with a sudden and profound insight into the misery and corruption of my own soul, and I was pierced deeply with a light that made me realize something of the condition I was in, and I was filled with horror at what I saw, and my whole being rose up in revolt against what was within me, and my soul desired escape and liberation and freedom from all this with an intensity and an urgency unlike anything I had ever known before. And now I think for the first time in my whole life I really began to pray—praying not with my lips and with my intellect and my imagination, but praying out of the very roots of my life and of my being, and praying to the God I had never known, to reach down towards me out of His darkness and to help me to get free of the thousand terrible things that held my will in their slavery.

There were a lot of tears connected with this, and they did

me good, and all the while, although I had lost that first vivid, agonizing sense of the presence of my father in the room, I had him in my mind, and I was talking to him as well as to God, as though he were a sort of intermediary. I do not mean this in any way that might be interpreted that I thought he was among the saints. I did not really know what that might mean then, and now that I do know I would hesitate to say that I thought he was in Heaven. Judging by my memory of the experience I should say it was "as if" he had been sent to me out of Purgatory. For after all, there is no reason why the souls in Purgatory should not help those on earth by their prayers and influence, just like those in Heaven: although usually they need our help more than we need theirs. But in this case, assuming my guess has some truth in it, things were the other way 'round.

However, this is not a thing on which I would place any great stress. And I do not offer any definite explanation of it. How do I know it was not merely my own imagination, or something that could be traced to a purely natural, psychological cause—I mean the part about my father? It is impossible to say. I do not offer any explanation. And I have always had a great antipathy for everything that smells of necromancy—table-turning and communications with the dead, and I would never deliberately try to enter in to any such thing. But whether it was imagination or nerves or whatever else it may have been, I can say truly that I did feel, most vividly, as if my father were present there, and the consequences that I have described followed from this, as though he had communicated to me without words an interior light from God, about the condition of my own soul—although I wasn't even sure I had a soul.

The one thing that seems to me morally certain is that this was really a grace, and a great grace. If I had only followed it through, my life might have been very different and much less miserable for the years that were to come.

Before now I had never prayed in the churches I had visited. But I remember the morning that followed this experience. I remember how I climbed the deserted Aventine, in the spring sun, with my soul broken up with contrition, but broken and clean, painful but sanitary like a lanced abscess, like a bone broken and re-set. And it was true contrition, too, for I don't think I was capable of mere attrition, since I did not believe in hell. I went to the Dominicans' Church, Santa Sabina. And it was a very definite experience, something that amounted to a capitulation, a surrender, a conversion, not without struggle, even now, to walk deliberately into the church with no other purpose than to kneel down and pray to God. Ordinarily, I never knelt in these churches, and never paid any formal or official attention to Whose house it was. But now I took holy water at the door and went straight up to the altar rail and knelt down and said, slowly, with all the belief I had in me, the Our Father.

It seems almost unbelievable to me that I did no more than this, for the memory remains in me as that of such an experience that it would seem to have implied at least a half hour of impassioned prayer and tears. The thing to remember is that I had not prayed at all for some years.

Another thing which Catholics do not realize about converts is the tremendous, agonizing embarrassment and self-consciousness which they feel about praying publicly in a Catholic Church. The effort it takes to overcome all the strange imaginary fears that everyone is looking at you, and that they all think you are crazy or ridiculous, is something that costs a tremendous effort. And that day in Santa Sabina, although the church was almost entirely empty, I walked across the stone floor mortally afraid that a poor devout old Italian woman was following me with suspicious eyes. As I knelt to pray, I wondered if she would run out and accuse me at once to the priests, with scandalous horror, for coming and praying in their church—as if Catholics were perfectly content to have a lot of heretic tourists walking about their churches with complete indifference and irreverence, and would get angry if one of them so far acknowledged God's presence there as to go on his knees for a few seconds and say a prayer!

However, I prayed, then I looked about the church, and

went into a room where there was a picture by Sassoferrato, and stuck my face out a door into a tiny, simple cloister, where the sun shone down on an orange tree. After that I walked out into the open feeling as if I had been reborn, and crossed the street, and strolled through the suburban fields to another deserted church where I did not pray, being scared by some carpenters and scaffolding. I sat outside, in the sun, on a wall and tasted the joy of my own inner peace, and turned over in my mind how my life was now going to change, and how I would become better.

vii

It was a wan hope, however. But the last week or ten days that I was in Rome were very happy and full of joy, and on one of those afternoons I took the trolley out to San Paolo, and after that got on a small rickety bus which went up a country road into a shallow saucer of a valley in the low hills south of the Tiber, to the Trappist monastery of Tre Fontane. I went in to the dark, austere old church, and liked it. But I was scared to visit the monastery. I thought the monks were too busy sitting in their graves beating themselves with disciplines. So I walked up and down in the silent afternoon, under the eucalyptus trees, and the thought grew on me: "I should like to become a Trappist monk."

There was very little danger of my doing so, then. The thought was only a daydream—and I suppose it is a dream that comes to many men, even men who don't believe in anything. Is there any man who has ever gone through a whole lifetime without dressing himself up, in his fancy, in the habit of a monk and enclosing himself in a cell where he sits magnificent in heroic austerity and solitude, while all the young ladies who hitherto were cool to his affections in the world come and beat on the gates of the monastery crying, "Come out, come out!"

Ultimately, I suppose, that is what my dream that day amounted to. I had no idea what Trappist monks were, or what they did, except that they kept silence. In fact, I also thought they lived in cells like the Carthusians, all alone.

In the bus, going back to San Paolo, I ran into a student from the American Academy whom I knew. He was riding with his mother, and introduced me to her, and we talked about the monastery, and I said I wished I were a monk. The student's mother looked at me with a horror and astonishment so extreme that I was really a little shocked by it.

The days went by. Letters came from America, telling me to take the boat and come there. Finally I bade farewell to the Italian typewriter salesman and the other inhabitants of the *pensione*, including the lady who ran the place and whose mother had been overwhelmed with thoughts of death when I played *St. Louis Blues* on the piano, sending in the maid to ask me to desist.

With sorrow in my heart I saw the last of the Piazza Barberini and the big curved boulevard that ran into it; and the last of the Pincio gardens, and St. Peter's dome in the distance and the Piazza di Spagna; but above all, I had sorrow and emptiness in my heart at leaving my beloved churches —San Pietro in Vincoli, Santa Maria Maggiore, San Giovanni in Laterano, Santa Pudenziana, Santa Prassede, Santa Sabina, Santa Maria sopra Minerva, Santa Maria in Cosmedin, Santa Maria in Trastevere, Santa Agnese, San Clemente, Santa Cecilia . . .

The train crossed the Tiber. The little pyramid and the cypresses of the English cemetery where Keats was buried disappeared. I remembered some allusion in Plautus to a big hill of rubbish and potsherds that had once stood in this part of the city. Then we came out into the bare plain between Rome and the sea. In this distance were San Paolo, and the low hills that concealed the Trappist monastery of Tre Fontane. "O Rome," I said in my heart, "will I ever see you again?"

The first two months after I landed in New York, and went to the house in Douglaston, I continued to read the Bible surreptitiously—I was afraid someone might make fun of me. And since I slept on the sleeping porch, which opened on the upstairs hall through glass doors and which, in any case, I shared with my uncle, I no longer dared to pray on my knees before going to sleep, though I am sure everybody would have been pleased and edified. The real reason for this was that I did not have the humility to care nothing about what people thought or said. I was afraid of their remarks, even kind ones, even approving ones. Indeed, it is a kind of quintessence of pride to hate and fear even the kind and legitimate approval of those who love us! I mean, to resent it as a humiliating patronage.

There is no point in telling all the details of how this real but temporary religious fervor of mine cooled down and disappeared. At Easter we went to the church where my father had once been organist, Zion Church, with the white spire standing among the locust trees on the hill between us and the station. And there I was very irritated by the services, and my own pride increased the irritation and complicated it. And I used to walk about the house or sit at the dinner table telling everybody what a terrible place Zion Church was, and condemning everything that it stood for.

One Sunday I went to the Quaker meeting house in Flushing, where Mother had once sat and meditated with the Friends. I sat down there too, in a deep pew in the back, near a window. The place was about half full. The people were mostly middle-aged or old, and there was nothing that distinguished them in any evident way from the congregation in a Methodist or a Baptist or an Episcopalian or any other Protestant church, except that they sat silent, waiting for the inspiration of the Holy Ghost. I liked that. I liked the silence. It was peaceful. In it, my shyness began to die down, and I ceased to look about and criticize the people, and entered, somewhat superficially, into my own soul, and some nebulous good resolutions began to take shape there.

But it did not get very far, for presently one of the middle-aged ladies thought the Holy Ghost was after her to get up and talk. I secretly suspected that she had come to the meeting all prepared to make a speech anyway, for she

145

reached into her handbag, as she stood up, and cried out in a loud earnest voice:

"When I was in Switzerland I took this snapshot of the famous Lion of Lucerne. . . ." With that she pulled out a picture. Sure enough, it was the famous Lion of Lucerne. She held it up and tried to show it around to the Friends, at the same time explaining that she thought it was a splendid exemplification of Swiss courage and manliness and patience and all the other virtues of the watchmaking Swiss which she mentioned and which I have now forgotten.

The Friends accepted it in patience, without enthusiasm or resentment. But I went out of the meeting house saying to myself: "They are like all the rest. In other churches it is the minister who hands out the commonplaces, and here it is liable to be just anybody."

Still, I think I had enough sense to know that it would be madness to look for a group of people, a society, a religion, a church from which all mediocrity would absolutely be excluded. But when I read the works of William Penn and found them to be about as supernatural as a Montgomery Ward catalogue I lost interest in the Quakers. If I had run across something by Evelyn Underhill it might have been different.

I think that one could find much earnest and pure and humble worship of God and much sincere charity among the Quakers. Indeed, you are bound to find a little of this in every religion. But I have never seen any evidence of its rising above the natural order. They are full of natural virtues and some of them are contemplatives in a natural sense of the word. Nor are they excluded from God's graces if He wills. For He loves them, and He will not withhold His light from good people anywhere. Yet I cannot see that they will ever be anything more than what they claim to be—a "Society of Friends."

That summer, when I went on a slow and dirty train in a roundabout way to Chicago to see the World's Fair, I picked up two pamphlets on the Mormons in the Hall of Religion, but the story of the holy books discovered through revelation on a hill in upper New York State did not convince me and I was not converted. The thin red and yellow walls of the palaces of the Fair, scattered between the lake and the slums and freight-yards, amused me with their noise, and for the first time I walked in the wide-open air of the flat and endless Middle West.

Out of sheer bravado I got myself a job for a few days as a barker in front of a side-show in a part of the Fair called the Streets of Paris, the nature of which is sufficiently evident from that name. The ease with which I got the job astounded and flattered me, and it gave me a sense of power and importance to be so suddenly transported from the order of those who were fleeced of their money to the level of those who did the fleecing. However, in a couple of days I also discovered that perhaps I had not risen above the ranks of the "suckers" after all, since the boss of the side-show was more ready to pay me in promises and fancy words than in dollars, for my services. Besides, it was very tiring to stand in the heat and dust from noon to midnight shouting at the sea of straw-hatted heads and shoulders dressed in duck and seersucker or in open-necked shirts and dresses soaked with healthy Middle-Western sweat. The absolutely open and undisguised and noncommittal frankness of the paganism of Chicago and of this Fair and of this particular part of the Fair and, apparently, of the whole country which it represented, amazed me after the complicated reticences of England and the ornate pornography of France.

When I got back to New York I had lost most of my temporary interest in religion. My friends in that city had a religion of their own: a cult of New York itself, and of the peculiar manner in which Manhattan expressed the bigness and gaudiness and noisiness and frank animality and vulgarity of this American paganism.

I used to go to the Burlesque and hang around Fourteenth Street with Reg Marsh, who was an old friend of my father's, and who is famous for painting all these things in his pictures. Reginald Marsh was (and I suppose still is) a thick-set man of short stature who gave the impression that he was a retired light-weight prize-fighter. He had a way of talking out of the corner of his mouth, and yet at the same time his face had something babyish and cherubic about it, as he looked out at the world through the simple and disinterested and uncritical eyes of the artist, taking everything as he found it, and considering everything as possible subject matter for one of his Hogarthian compositions, provided only it was alive.

We got along very well together, because of the harmony of our views, I worshipping life as such, and he worshipping it especially in the loud, wild bedlam of the crowded, crazy city that he loved. His favorite places of devotion were Union Square and the Irving Place Burlesque, stinking of sweat and cheap cigars and ready to burn down or collapse at any minute. But I guess his cathedral was Coney Island. Everybody who has ever seen his pictures, knows that much about Reg Marsh.

All that summer I hung around his Fourteenth Street studio, and went with him to many of the parties to which he was invited, and got to know my way around New York.

But when September came I sailed for England once more. This time I made the crossing on the *Manhattan,* a garish and turbulent cabin class steamer full of Nazi spies working as stewards and detesting the Jewish passengers. The voyage was a violent one. One night I looked down one of the deep stair-wells and saw six or seven half-drunk passengers having a general fight on the swaying linoleum floor of E deck. And one afternoon in the middle of one of those paralyzing synthetic amusements that are fixed up for the passengers on Atlantic liners—I think it must have been the "horse race"— an American dentist stood up with a loud roar and challenged a French tailor to come out and fight him on the promenade deck. The challenge was not taken up, but all the business men and tourists savored the delicious scandal, for there was no one on board who was not aware that behind it all stood the six-foot daughter of someone prominent in Washington, D. C.

At Plymouth they put those of us who were bound for

London on to a fat launch in the middle of the harbor, and once again I looked upon the pale green downs of England. I landed with one of the worst colds I ever had in my life.

And so on the tide of all these circumstances of confusion I swept into the dark, sinister atmosphere of Cambridge and began my university career.

viii

Perhaps to you the atmosphere of Cambridge is neither dark nor sinister. Perhaps you were never there except in May. You never saw anything but the thin Spring sun half veiled in the mists and blossoms of the gardens along the Backs, smiling on the lavender bricks and stones of Trinity and St. John's, or my own college, Clare.

I am even willing to admit that some people might live there for three years, or even a lifetime, so protected that they never sense the sweet stench of corruption that is all around them—the keen, thin scent of decay that pervades everything and accuses with a terrible accusation the superficial youthfulness, the abounding undergraduate noise that fills those ancient buildings. But for me, with my blind appetites, it was impossible that I should not rush in and take a huge bite of this rotten fruit. The bitter taste is still with me after not a few years.

My freshman year went by very fast. It was a dizzy business that began in the dark, brief afternoons of the English autumn and ended after a short series of long summer evenings on the river. All those days and nights were without romance, horrible. They could not help being everything that I did not want them to be.

I was breaking my neck trying to get everything out of life that you think you can get out of it when you are eighteen. And I ran with a pack of hearties who wore multicolored scarves around their necks and who would have barked all night long in the echoing shadows of the Petty Cury if they had not been forced to go home to bed at a certain time.

At first it was confusing. It took me a month or two to find my level in this cloudy semi-liquid medium in whose dregs I was ultimately destined to settle. There were my friends from Oakham. At first we clung together for protection, and used to spend much time in one another's rooms, although Andrew's digs were far away in the wilds beyond Addenbrooke's hospital. To get there I cycled through a mysterious world of new buildings dedicated to chemistry, and at the end of the journey drank tea and played *St. Louis Blues* on the piano. Dickens was much nearer. He was around the corner from my lodgings. You travelled through two or three courts of St. John's College and crossed the river. He was in the so-called New Building. His room directly overlooked the river and he and I and Andrew would eat breakfast there and throw bits of toast to the ducks while he told us all about Pavlov and conditioned reflexes.

As the year went on I drifted apart from them, especially from Andrew who ended up as the leading man in the Footlights show that year. He was something of a singer. My crowd had no interest in singing and a certain amount of contempt, indeed, for the Footlights and all that it represented. I remember that I almost made friends with one or two serious and somewhat complicated young men who were reading modern languages with me and belonged to my own college, but their reticences bored me. And they, in their turn, were rather shocked by the two-handed heartiness with which I was grabbing at life.

In the room underneath mine, in my lodgings, was a round red-faced Yorkshireman who was a pacifist. He too was full of reticences. But on Armistice Day he got into some kind of a demonstration and all the rugger players and oarsmen threw eggs at him. I knew nothing about it until I saw the pictures in the evening paper.

I would not have been interested in making friends with him either—he was too tame and shy. But in any case the landlord took to coming into my room and calumniating the poor man while I listened patiently, knowing of no way to shut him up. Before the end of the year the landlord was much more disgusted with me than with any lodger he had ever had before or, probably, since.

I think it was after Armistice Day, when I had finally become acquainted with some two hundred different people, that I drifted into the crowd that had been gravitating around the nether pole of Cambridge life.

We were the ones who made all the noise when there was a "bump supper." We lived in the Lion Inn. We fought our way in and out of the "Red Cow."

In that year most of my friends were gated at one time or another, and by the end of it not a few of us were sent down. I cannot even clearly remember who most of them were—except for Julian. He stands out vividly enough. He wore horn-rimmed spectacles and looked, I will not say like an American, but like a Frenchman trying to look like an American. He could tell long complicated stories in an American accent too nasal to be true. He was the grandson or the great-grandson of a Victorian poet and lived in the old man's house on the Isle of Wight. He roomed in a big rabbit warren of a place on Market Hill which was going to be torn down at the end of the year to make room for a new building, belonging to Caius College. Before the wreckers came in, Julian's friends had already begun the ruin of the house by attempting to destroy the precarious section of it where he himself lived. I seem to remember some trouble when somebody threw a teapot out of the window of these rooms and nearly brained the Dean of Kings who was passing by in the street below.

Then there was a laconic, sallow-faced fellow who came from Oundle and drove a racing car. He sat still and quiet most of the time with the strange, fevered mysticism of the racing driver in his veins while the rest of us talked and yelled. But when he got under the wheel of his car—which he was not allowed to drive as a freshman—he was transformed into a strange sort of half-spiritual being, possessed by a weird life belonging to another frightening world. The prohibition on driving could not, of course, hold him. Once in a while he would disappear. Then he would come back relatively happy, and sit down and play poker with anybody who would take him on. I think he was finally sent down altogether for the wildest of his expeditions which ended with him trying to drive his car down one of the zig-zag cliff paths at Bournemouth.

But why dig up all this old scenery and reconstruct the stews of my own mental Pompeii after enough years have covered them up? Is it even worth the obvious comment that in all this I was stamping the last remains of spiritual vitality out of my own soul, and trying with all my might to crush and obliterate the image of the divine liberty that had been implanted in me by God? With every nerve and fibre of my being I was laboring to enslave myself in the bonds of my own intolerable disgust. There is nothing new or strange about the process. But what people do not realize is that this is the crucifixion of Christ: in which He dies again and again in the individuals who were made to share the joy and the freedom of His grace, and who deny Him.

Aunt Maud died that November. I found my way to London and to Ealing, and was at the funeral.

It was a grey afternoon, and rainy, almost as dark as night. Everywhere the lights were on. It was one of those short, dark, foggy days of the early English winter.

Uncle Ben sat in a wheel-chair, broken and thin, with a black skull-cap on his head, and this time he really did look like a ghost. He seemed to have lost the power of speech, and looked about him with blank uncomprehension, as if all this story of a funeral were a gratuitous insult to his intelligence. Why were they trying to tell him that Maud was dead?

They committed the thin body of my poor Victorian angel to the clay of Ealing, and buried my childhood with her. In an obscure, half-conscious way I realized this and was appalled. She it was who had presided in a certain sense over my most innocent days. And now I saw those days buried with her in the ground.

Indeed the England I had seen through the clear eyes of her own simplicity, that too had died for me here. I could no longer believe in the pretty country churches, the quiet villages, the elm-trees along the common where the cricketers wait in white while the bowler pensively paces out a run for himself behind the wicket. The huge white clouds that sail over Sussex, the bell-charmed spires of the ancient county towns, the cathedral closes full of trees, the deaneries that ring with rooks—none of this any longer belonged to me, for I had lost it all. Its fragile web of charmed associations had been broken and blown away and I had fallen through the surface of old England into the hell, the vacuum and the horror that London was nursing in her avaricious heart.

It was the last time that I saw any of my family in England.

I took the last train back to Cambridge and was so exhausted that I fell asleep and woke up at Ely, and had to turn back, so that I got in long after midnight. And I felt offended at being gated for what was not, as I thought, my fault. It was the first of the two times I was gated that year.

Shall I follow the circle of the season down into the nadir of winter darkness, and wake up the dirty ghosts under the trees of the Backs, and out beyond the Clare New Building and in some rooms down on the Chesterton Road? When it began to be spring, I was trying to row in the Clare fourth boat, although it nearly killed me. But at least, since we were supposed to be in training, I got up early for a few weeks and went to the College for breakfast, and went to bed without being too dizzy in the nighttime.

In these days I seem to remember there was a little sunlight. It fell through the ancient windows of Professor Bullough's room in Caius. It was a large, pleasant room, lined with books, and with windows opening on the grass of two courts. It was below the level of those lawns and you had to go down a couple of steps to get into his sitting room. In fact I think his sitting room itself was on two levels, and in the corner he had a high medieval lectern. There he stood, a tall, thin, grey, somewhat ascetic scholar, placidly translating Dante to us, while ten or a dozen students, men and women, sat about in the chairs and followed in our Italian texts.

In the winter term we had begun with the *Inferno*, and had progressed slowly, taking each day part of a Canto. And now Dante and Virgil had come through the icy heart of hell, where the three-headed devil chewed the greatest traitors, and had climbed out to the peaceful sea at the foot of the seven-circled mountain of Purgatory. And now, in the Christian Lent, which I was observing without merit and without reason, for the sake of a sport which I had grown to detest because I was so unsuccessful in it, we were climbing from circle to circle of Purgatory.

I think the one great benefit I got out of Cambridge was this acquaintance with the lucid and powerful genius of the greatest Catholic poet—greatest in stature, though not in perfection or sanctity. Because of his genius, I was ready to accept all that he said about such things as Purgatory and Hell at least provisionally, as long as I had the book under my eyes, in his own terms. That was already much. I suppose it would have been too much to expect some kind of an application of his ideas to myself, in the moral order, just because I happened to have a sort of esthetic sensitiveness to them. No, it seems to me that I was armored and locked in within my own defectible and blinded self by seven layers of imperviousness, the capital sins which only the fires of Purgatory or of Divine Love (they are about the same) can burn away. But now I was free to keep away from the attack of those flames merely by averting my will from them: and it was by now permanently and habitually turned away and immunized. I had done all that I could to make my heart untouchable by charity and had fortified it, as I hoped, impregnably in my own impenetrable selfishness.

At the same time, I could listen, and listen with gladness and a certain intentness, to the slow and majestic progress of the myths and symbols in which Dante was building up a whole poetic synthesis of scholastic philosophy and theology. And although not one of his ideas took firm root in my mind, which was both too coarse and too lazy to absorb anything so clean, nevertheless, there remained in me a kind of armed neutrality in the presence of all these dogmas, which I tended to tolerate in a vague and general way, in bulk, in so far as that was necessary to an understanding of the poem.

This, as I see it, was also a kind of a grace: the greatest grace in the positive order that I got out of Cambridge.

All the rest were negative. They were only graces in the sense that God in His mercy was permitting me to fly as far as I could from His love but at the same time preparing to confront me, at the end of it all, and in the bottom of the abyss, when I thought I had gone farthest away from Him. *Si ascendero in coelum, tu illic es. Si descendero in infernum, ades.* For in my greatest misery He would shed, into my soul, enough light to see how miserable I was, and to admit that it was my own fault and my own work. And always I was to be punished for my sins by my sins themselves, and to realize, at least obscurely, that I was being so punished and burn in the flames of my own hell, and rot in the hell of my own corrupt will until I was forced at last, by my own intense misery, to give up my own will.

I had tasted something of this before: but that was nothing compared to the bitterness that soon began to fill me in that year at Cambridge.

The mere realization of one's own unhappiness is not salvation: it may be the occasion of salvation, or it may be the door to a deeper pit in Hell, and I had much deeper to go than I realized. But now, at least, I realized where I was, and I was beginning to try to get out.

Some people may think that Providence was very funny and very cruel to allow me to choose the means I now chose to save my soul. But Providence, that is the love of God, is very wise in turning away from the self-will of men, and in having nothing to do with them, and leaving them to their own devices, as long as they are intent on governing themselves, to show them to what depths of futility and sorrow their own helplessness is capable of dragging them.

And all the irony and cruelty of this situation came, not from Providence, but from the devil, who thought he was cheating God of my stupid and uninteresting little soul.

So it was, then, that I began to get all the books of Freud and Jung and Adler out of the big redecorated library of the Union and to study, with all the patience and application which my hangovers allowed me, the mysteries of sex-repression and complexes and introversion and extroversion and all the rest. I, whose chief trouble was that my soul and all its faculties were going to seed because there was nothing to control my appetites—and they were pouring themselves out in an incoherent riot of undirected passion—came to the conclusion that the cause of all my unhappiness was sex-repression! And, to make the thing more subtly intolerable, I came to the conclusion that one of the biggest crimes in this world was introversion, and, in my efforts to be an extro-vert, I entered upon a course of reflections and constant self-examinations, studying all my responses and analyzing the quality of all my emotions and reactions in such a way that I could not help becoming just what I did not want to be: an introvert.

Day after day I read Freud, thinking myself to be very enlightened and scientific when, as a matter of fact, I was about as scientific as an old woman secretly poring over books about occultism, trying to tell her own fortune, and learning how to dope out the future from the lines in the palm of her hand. I don't know if I ever got very close to needing a padded cell: but if I ever had gone crazy, I think psychoanalysis would have been the one thing chiefly responsible for it.

Meanwhile, I had received several letters from my guardian. They were sharp, and got sharper as they went on, and finally, in March or April, I got a curt summons to come to London.

I had to wait a long time, a long, long time in the waiting-room, where I turned over the pages of all the copies of *Punch* for two years back. I suppose this was part of a de-liberate plan to sap my morale, this leaving me alone in a dismal, foggy room, with all those copies of that dreary mag-azine.

Finally, after about an hour and a half, I was summoned to climb the narrow stairs to the consulting room immedi-ately above. The floor was waxed, and once again I got this sense of precariousness in my footing, and was glad to get across the room to the chair by the desk without falling down and breaking a hip.

With polished and devastating coolness, which carried with it a faint suggestion of contempt, Tom offered me a cigarette. The implication was that I was going to need it. Therefore, obviously, I refused it.

Nevertheless, the fifteen or twenty minutes that followed were among the most painful and distressing I have ever lived through: not because of anything that he said to me, for he was not angry or even unkind. In fact I do not even remember exactly what he did say. The thing that made me suffer was that he asked me very bluntly and coldly for an explanation of my conduct and left me to writhe. For as soon as I was placed in the position of having to give some kind of positive explanation or defence of so much stupidity and unpleasantness, as if to justify myself by making it seem possible for a rational creature to live that way, the whole bitterness and emptiness of it became very evident to me, and my tongue would hardly function. And the words I murmured about my "making mistakes" and "not wanting to hurt others" sounded extremely silly and cheap.

So I was very glad to get out of there, and as soon as I was in the street I smoked plenty of cigarettes.

Months went by, and things did not change at all. After the Easter vacation, I was called in to my tutor to explain why I was not attending most of my lectures, and a few other things besides. This time I was not so uncomfortable. As to the exams that were soon to come—I was to take the first part of the Modern Language Tripos in French and Italian—I thought I would be able to pass them, which as a matter of fact I did, getting a second in both. The results were wired to me by one of my friends when I was already on the boat for America—one of those ten-day boats out of London. We were going through the Straits of Dover, and the sun was on the white cliffs, and my lungs were filling with the fresh air.

I was planning to come back the next year, and had already arranged for a room in the Old Court of Clare, right over the gate that led out to Clare bridge. I would have looked out over the President's garden. But certainly, considering the kind of undergraduate I was, that was the worst possible place for me to have wanted to room: for I was right in between the President and the Senior Tutor. However, I never went up to Cambridge again as a member of the University.

That summer Tom sent me a letter in New York suggesting that I had better give up the idea of ever entering the British Diplomatic service, and that Cambridge was, henceforth, useless. To return would be to waste my time and money. He thought it would be very sensible if I stayed in America.

It did not take me five minutes to come around to agreeing with him. I do not know whether it was entirely subjective, but it seemed to me that there was some kind of a subtle poison in Europe, something that corrupted me, something the very thought and scent of which sickened me, repelled me.

What was it? Some kind of a moral fungus, the spores of which floated in that damp air, in that foggy and half-lighted darkness?

The thought that I was no longer obliged to go back into those damp and fetid mists filled me with an immense relief —a relief that far overbalanced the pain of my injured pride, the shame of comparative failure. I say I was no longer obliged to return: I would have to go back long enough to get on the quota and enter America permanently, for now I was only in the country on a temporary visa. But that did not matter so much. The feeling that I did not have to stay was another liberation.

Once again, I ask myself if it was not mostly subjective—perhaps it was. For I do not accuse the whole of England of the corruption that I had discovered in only a part of it. Nor do I blame England for this as a nation, as if it alone were infected with the sweet and nasty disease of the soul that seemed to be rotting the whole of Europe, in high places above all.

It was something I had not known or seen, in the England of those first days when I had been a child, and walked in the innocent countryside, and looked at the old village churches and read the novels of Dickens and wandered by the streams on picnics with my aunt and cousins.

What was wrong with this place, with all these people? Why was everything so empty?

Above all, why did the very boisterousness of the soccer blues, the rugger players, the cricketers, the oarsmen, the huntsmen and drinkers in the Lion and the clumsy dancers in the Rendezvous—why was all their noise so oafish and hollow and ridiculous? It seemed to me that Cambridge and, to some extent, the whole of England was pretending, with an elaborate and intent and conscious, and perhaps in some cases a courageous effort, to act as if it were alive. And it took a lot of acting. It was a vast and complicated charade, with expensive and detailed costuming and scenery and a lot of inappropriate songs: and yet the whole thing was so intolerably dull, because most of the people were already morally dead, asphyxiated by the steam of their own strong yellow tea, or by the smell of their own pubs and breweries, or by the fungus on the walls of Oxford and Cambridge.

I speak of what I remember: perhaps the war that grew out of all this did something to cure it or to change it.

For those who had nothing but this emptiness in the middle of them, no doubt the things they had to do and to suffer during the war filled that emptiness with something stronger and more resilient than their pride—either that or it destroyed them utterly. But when I had been away from Cambridge about a year, I heard what had happened to one of them, a friend of mine.

Mike was a beefy and red-faced and noisy youth who came from somewhere in Wales, and was part of the crowd in which I milled around in the daytime and the nighttime during that year at Cambridge. He was full of loud laughter and a lot of well-meaning exclamations, and in his quieter moments he got into long and complicated sentences about life. But what was more characteristic of him was that he liked to put his fist through windows. He was the noisy and hearty type; he was altogether jolly. A great eater and drinker, he chased after girls with an astounding heaviness of passion and emotion. He managed to get into a lot of trouble. That was the way it was when I left Cambridge. The next year I heard how he ended up. The porter, or somebody, went down into the showers, under the buildings of the Old Court at Clare, and found Mike hanging by his neck from a rope slung over one of the pipes, with his big hearty face black with the agony of strangulation. He had hanged himself.

The Europe I finally left for good, in the late November of 1934, was a sad and unquiet continent, full of forebodings.

Of course, there were plenty of people who said: "There will not be a war . . ." But Hitler had now held power in Germany for some time, and that summer all the New York evening papers had been suddenly filled with the news of Dollfuss' murder in Austria, and the massing of Italian troops on the Austrian borders. It was one of the nights when I was down at Coney Island, with Reginald Marsh, and I walked in the whirl of lights and noise and drank glasses of thin, icy beer, and ate hot dogs full of mustard, and wondered if I would soon be in some army or other, or perhaps dead.

It was the first time I had felt the cold steel of the war-scare in my vitals. There was a lot more to come. It was only 1934.

And now, in November, when I was leaving England forever—the ship sailed quietly out of Southampton water by night—the land I left behind me seemed silent with the silence before a storm. It was a land all shut up and muffled in layers of fog and darkness, and all the people were in the rooms behind the thick walls of their houses, waiting for the first growl of thunder as the Nazis began to warm up the motors of a hundred thousand planes.

Perhaps they did not know they were waiting for all this. Perhaps they thought they had nothing better to occupy their minds than the wedding of Prince George and Princess Marina which had taken place the day before. Even I myself was more concerned with the thought of some people I was leaving than with the political atmosphere at that precise moment. And yet that atmosphere was something that would not allow itself to be altogether ignored.

I had seen enough of the things, the acts and appetites, that were to justify and to bring down upon the world the tons of bombs that would someday begin to fall in millions. Did I know that my own sins were enough to have destroyed the whole of England and Germany? There has never yet been a bomb invented that is half so powerful as one mortal sin—and yet there is no positive power in sin, only negation, only annihilation: and perhaps that is why it is so destructive, it is a nothingness, and where it is, there is nothing left—a blank, a moral vacuum.

It is only the infinite mercy and love of God that has prevented us from tearing ourselves to pieces and destroying His entire creation long ago. People seem to think that it is in some way a proof that no merciful God exists, if we have so many wars. On the contrary, consider how in spite of centuries of sin and greed and lust and cruelty and hatred and avarice and oppression and injustice, spawned and bred by the free wills of men, the human race can still recover, each time, and can still produce men and women who overcome evil with good, hatred with love, greed with charity, lust and cruelty with sanctity. How could all this be possible without the merciful love of God, pouring out His grace upon us? Can there be any doubt where wars come from and where peace comes from, when the children of this world, excluding God from their peace conferences, only manage to bring about greater and greater wars the more they talk about peace?

We have only to open our eyes and look about us to see what our sins are doing to the world, and have done. But we cannot see. We are the ones to whom it is said by the prophets of God: "Hearing hear, and understand not; and see the vision, and know it not."

There is not a flower that opens, not a seed that falls into the ground, and not an ear of wheat that nods on the end of its stalk in the wind that does not preach and proclaim the greatness and the mercy of God to the whole world.

161

There is not an act of kindness or generosity, not an act of sacrifice done, or a word of peace and gentleness spoken, not a child's prayer uttered, that does not sing hymns to God before His throne, and in the eyes of men, and before their faces.

How does it happen that in the thousands of generations of murderers since Cain, our dark bloodthirsty ancestor, that some of us can still be saints? The quietness and hiddenness and placidity of the truly good people in the world all proclaim the glory of God.

All these things, all creatures, every graceful movement, every ordered act of the human will, all are sent to us as prophets from God. But because of our stubbornness they come to us only to blind us further.

"Blind the heart of this people and make their ears heavy, and shut their eyes: lest they see with their eyes, and hear with their ears and understand with their heart and be converted, and I heal them."

We refuse to hear the million different voices through which God speaks to us, and every refusal hardens us more and more against His grace—and yet He continues to speak to us: and we say He is without mercy!

"But the Lord dealeth patiently for your sake, not willing that any should perish, but that all should return to penance."

Mother of God, how often in the last centuries have you not come down to us, speaking to us in our mountains and groves and hills, and telling us what was to come upon us, and we have not heard you. How long shall we continue to be deaf to your voice, and run our heads into the jaws of the hell that abhors us?

Lady, when on that night I left the Island that was once your England, your love went with me, although I could not know it, and could not make myself aware of it. And it was your love, your intercession for me, before God, that was preparing the seas before my ship, laying open the way for me to another country.

I was not sure where I was going, and I could not see what

I would do when I got to New York. But you saw further and clearer than I, and you opened the seas before my ship, whose track led me across the waters to a place I had never dreamed of, and which you were even then preparing for me to be my rescue and my shelter and my home. And when I thought there was no God and no love and no mercy, you were leading me all the while into the midst of His love and His mercy, and taking me, without my knowing anything about it, to the house that would hide me in the secret of His Face.

Glorious Mother of God, shall I ever again distrust you, or your God, before Whose throne you are irresistible in your intercession? Shall I ever turn my eyes from your hands and from your face and from your eyes? Shall I ever look anywhere else but in the face of your love, to find out true counsel, and to know my way, in all the days and all the moments of my life?

As you have dealt with me, Lady, deal also with all my millions of brothers who live in the same misery that I knew then: lead them in spite of themselves and guide them by your tremendous influence, O Holy Queen of souls and refuge of sinners, and bring them to your Christ the way you brought me. *Illos tuos misericordes oculos ad nos converte, et Jesum, benedictum fructum ventris tui, nobis ostende.* Show us your Christ, Lady, after this our exile, yes: but show Him to us also now, show Him to us here, while we are still wanderers.

4

The Children in the Market Place

I had a long way to go. I had more to cross than the Atlantic. Perhaps the Styx, being only a river, does not seem so terribly wide. It is not its width that makes it difficult to cross, especially when you are trying to get out of hell, and not in. And so, this time, even though I got out of Europe, I still remained in hell. But it was not for want of trying.

It was a stormy crossing. When it was possible, I walked on the wide, empty decks that streamed with spray. Or I would get up forward where I could see the bows blast their way headfirst into the mountains of water that bore down upon us. And I would hang on to the rail while the ship reeled and soared into the wet sky, riding the sea that swept under us while every stanchion and bulkhead groaned and complained.

When we got on to the Grand Banks, the seas calmed and there was a fall of snow, and the snow lay on the quiet decks, and made them white in the darkness of the evening. And because of the peacefulness of the snow, I imagined that my new ideas were breeding within me an interior peace.

The truth is, I was in the thick of a conversion. It was not the right conversion, but it was a conversion. Perhaps it was a lesser evil. I do not doubt much that it was. But it was not, for all that, much of a good. I was becoming a Communist.

Stated like that, it sounds pretty much the same as if I said: "I was growing a moustache." As a matter of fact, I was still unable to grow a moustache. Or I did not dare to try. And, I suppose, my Communism was about as mature as my face—as the sour, perplexed, English face in the photo on my quota card. However, as far as I know, this was about as sincere and complete a step to moral conversion as I was then able to make with my own lights and desires, such as they then were.

A lot of things had happened to me since I had left the

relative seclusion of Oakham, and had been free to indulge all my appetites in the world, and the time had come for a big readjustment in my values. I could not evade that truth. I was too miserable, and it was evident that there was too much wrong with my strange, vague, selfish hedonism.

It did not take very much reflection on the year I had spent at Cambridge to show me that all my dreams of fantastic pleasures and delights were crazy and absurd, and that everything I had reached out for had turned to ashes in my hands, and that I myself, into the bargain, had turned out to be an extremely unpleasant sort of a person—vain, self-centered, dissolute, weak, irresolute, undisciplined, sensual, obscene and proud. I was a mess. Even the sight of my own face in a mirror was enough to disgust me.

When I came to ask myself the reasons for all this, the ground was well prepared. My mind was already facing what seemed to be an open door out of my spiritual jail. It was some four years since I had first read the Communist Manifesto, and I had never entirely forgotten about it. One of those Christmas vacations at Strasbourg I had read some books about Soviet Russia, how all the factories were working overtime, and all the ex-moujiks wore great big smiles on their faces, welcoming Russian aviators on their return from Polar flights, bearing the boughs of trees in their hands. Then I often went to Russian movies, which were pretty good from the technical point of view, although probably not so good as I thought they were, in my great anxiety to approve of them.

Finally, I had in my mind the myth that Soviet Russia was the friend of all the arts, and the only place where true art could find a refuge in a world of bourgeois ugliness. Where I ever got that idea is hard to find out, and how I managed to cling to it for so long is harder still, when you consider all the photographs there were, for everyone to see, showing the Red Square with gigantic pictures of Stalin hanging on the walls of the world's ugliest buildings—not to mention the views of the projected monster monument to Lenin, like a huge mountain of soap-sculpture, and the Little Father of Communism standing on top of it, and sticking out one of his hands. Then, when I went to New York in the summer, I found the *New Masses* lying around the studios of my friends and, as a matter of fact, a lot of the people I met were either party members or close to being so.

So now, when the time came for me to take spiritual stock of myself, it was natural that I should do so by projecting my whole spiritual condition into the sphere of economic history and the class-struggle. In other words, the conclusion I came to was that it was not so much I myself that was to blame for my unhappiness, but the society in which I lived.

I considered the person that I now was, the person that I had been at Cambridge, and that I had made of myself, and I saw clearly enough that I was the product of my times, my society and my class. I was something that had been spawned by the selfishness and irresponsibility of the materialistic century in which I lived. However, what I did not see was that my own age and class only had an accidental part to play in this. They gave my egoism and pride and my other sins a peculiar character of weak and supercilious flippancy proper to this particular century: but that was only on the surface. Underneath, it was the same old story of greed and lust and self-love, of the three concupiscences bred in the rich, rotted undergrowth of what is technically called "the world," in every age, in every class.

"If any man love the world, the charity of the Father is not in him. For all that is in the world is the concupiscence of the flesh and the concupiscence of the eyes and the pride of life." That is to say, all men who live only according to their five senses, and seek nothing beyond the gratification of their natural appetites for pleasure and reputation and power, cut themselves off from that charity which is the principle of all spiritual vitality and happiness because it alone saves us from the barren wilderness of our own abominable selfishness.

It is true that the materialistic society, the so-called culture that has evolved under the tender mercies of capitalism, has produced what seems to be the ultimate limit of this worldliness. And nowhere, except perhaps in the analogous society of pagan Rome, has there ever been such a flowering of cheap and petty and disgusting lusts and vanities as in the world of capitalism, where there is no evil that is not fostered and encouraged for the sake of making money. We live in a society whose whole policy is to excite every nerve in the human body and keep it at the highest pitch of artificial tension, to strain every human desire to the limit and to create as many new desires and synthetic passions as possible, in order to cater to them with the products of our factories and printing presses and movie studios and all the rest.

Being the son of an artist, I was born the sworn enemy of everything that could obviously be called "bourgeois," and now I only had to dress up that aversion in economic terms and extend it to cover more ground than it had covered before—namely, to include anything that could be classified as semi-fascist, like D. H. Lawrence and many of the artists who thought they were rebels without really being so—and I had my new religion all ready for immediate use.

It was an easy and handy religion—too easy in fact. It told me that all the evils in the world were the product of capitalism. Therefore, all that had to be done to get rid of the evils of the world was to get rid of capitalism. This would not be very hard, for capitalism contained the seeds of its own decay (and that indeed is a very obvious truth which nobody would trouble to deny, even some of the most stupid defenders of the system now in force: for our wars are altogether too eloquent in what they have to say on the subject). An active and enlightened minority—and this minority was understood to be made up of the most intelligent and vital elements of society, was to have the two-fold task of making the oppressed class, the proletariat, conscious of their own power and destiny as future owners of all the means of production, and to "bore from within" in order to gain control of power by every possible means. Some violence, no doubt, would probably be necessary, but only because of the inevitable reaction of capitalism by the use of fascist methods to keep the proletariat in subjection.

It was capitalism that was to blame for everything unpleasant, even the violence of the revolution itself. Now, of course, the revolution had already taken the first successful step in Russia. The Dictatorship of the Proletariat was already set up there. It would have to spread through the rest of the world before it could be said that the revolution had really been a success. But once it had, once capitalism had been completely overthrown, the semi-state, or Dictatorship of the Proletariat, would itself only be a temporary matter. It would be a kind of guardian of the revolution, a tutor of the new classless society, during its minority. But as soon as the citizens of the new, classless world had had all the greed educated out of them by enlightened methods, the last vestiges of the "state" would wither away, and there would be a new world, a new golden age, in which all property would be held in common, at least all capital goods, all the land, means of production and so on, and nobody would desire to seize them for himself: and so there would be no more poverty, no more wars, no more misery, no more starvation, no more violence. Everybody would be happy. Nobody would be overworked. They would all amicably exchange wives whenever they felt like it, and their offspring would be brought up in big shiny incubators, not by the state because there wouldn't be any state, but by that great, beautiful surd, the lovely, delicious unknown quantity of the new "Classless Society."

I don't think that even I was gullible enough to swallow all the business about the ultimate bliss that would follow the withering away of the state—a legend far more naive and far more oversimplified than the happy hunting ground of the most primitive Indian. But I simply assumed that things would be worked out by the right men at the right time. For the moment, what was needed was to get rid of capitalism.

The thing that made Communism seem so plausible to me was my own lack of logic which failed to distinguish between the reality of the *evils* which Communism was trying to overcome and the validity of its diagnosis and the chosen cure.

For there can be no doubt that modern society is in a terrible condition, and that its wars and depressions and its slums and all its other evils are principally the fruits of an unjust social system, a system that must be reformed and purified or else replaced. However, if you are wrong, does that make me right? If you are bad, does that prove that I am good? The chief weakness of Communism is that it is, itself, only another breed of the same materialism which is the source and root of all the evils which it so clearly sees, and it is evidently nothing but another product of the breakdown of the capitalist system. Indeed, it seems to be pieced together out of the ruins of the same ideology that once went into the vast, amorphous, intellectual structure underlying capitalism in the nineteenth century.

I don't know how anybody who pretends to know anything about history can be so naive as to suppose that after all these centuries of corrupt and imperfect social systems, there is eventually to evolve something perfect and pure out of them— the good out of the evil, the unchanging and stable and eternal out of the variable and mutable, the just out of the unjust. But perhaps revolution is a contradiction of evolution, and therefore means the replacement of the unjust by the just, of the evil by the good. And yet it is still just as naive to suppose that members of the same human species, without having changed anything but their minds, should suddenly turn around and produce a perfect society, when they have never been able, in the past, to produce anything but imperfection and, at best, the barest shadow of justice.

However, as I say, perhaps the hopefulness that suddenly began to swell in my breast as I stood on the deck of this ten-day liner going to New York, via Halifax, was largely subjective and imaginary. The chance association, in my mind, with fresh air and the sea and a healthy feeling and a lot of good resolutions, coinciding with a few superficial notions of Marxism, had made me—like so many others—a Communist in my own fancy, and I would become one of the hundreds of thousands of people living in America who are willing to buy an occasional Communist pamphlet and listen without rancor to a Communist orator, and to express open dislike of those who attack Communism, just because they are aware that there is a lot of injustice and suffering in the world, and somewhere got the idea that the Communists were the ones who were most sincerely trying to do something about it.

Added to this was my own personal conviction, the result of the uncertain and misdirected striving for moral reform, that I must now devote myself to the good of society, and apply my mind, at least to some extent, to the tremendous problems of my time.

I don't know how much good there was in this: but I think there was some. It was, I suppose, my acknowledgment of my selfishness, and my desire to make reparation for it by developing some kind of social and political consciousness. And at the time, in my first fervor, I felt myself willing to make sacrifices for this end. I wanted to devote myself to the causes of peace and justice in the world. I wanted to do something positive to interrupt and divert the gathering momentum that was dragging the whole world into another war—and I felt there was something I could do, not alone, but as the member of an active and vocal group.

It was a bright, icy-cold afternoon when, having passed Nantucket Light, we first saw the long, low, yellow shoreline of Long Island shining palely in the December sun. But when we entered New York harbor the lights were already coming on, glittering like jewels in the hard, clear buildings. The great, debonair city that was both young and old, and wise and innocent, shouted in the winter night as we passed the Battery and started up the North River. And I was glad, very glad to be an immigrant once again.

I came down on to the dock with a great feeling of confidence and possessiveness. "New York, you are mine! I love you!" It is the glad embrace she gives her lovers, the big, wild city: but I guess ultimately it is for their ruin. It certainly did not prove to be any good for me.

With my mind in the ferment in which it was, I thought for a moment of registering for courses at the New School for Social Research, in the shiny, black building on Twelfth Street, but I was easily persuaded that I had better finish out a regular university course and get a degree. And therefore I entered upon all the complicated preambles to admission to Columbia.

I came out of the subway at 116th Street. All around the campus were piles of dirty snow, and I smelled the wet, faintly exhilarating air of Morningside Heights in the winter time. The big, ugly buildings faced the world with a kind of unpretentious purposefulness, and people hurried in and out the glass doors with none of the fancy garments of the Cambridge undergraduate—no multicolored ties and blazers and scarfs, no tweeds and riding breeches, no affectations of any kind, but only the plain, drab overcoats of city masses. You got the impression that all these people were at once more earnest and more humble, poorer, smarter perhaps, certainly more diligent than those I had known at Cambridge.

Columbia was, for the most part, stripped of fancy academic ritual. The caps and gowns were reserved for occasions which, as a matter of fact, nobody really had to attend. I only got mixed up in one of them purely by accident, several months after I had acquired my degree, rolled up in a cardboard container, through one of the windows of the post-office-like registration bureau in University Hall.

Compared with Cambridge, this big sooty factory was full of light and fresh air. There was a kind of genuine intellectual vitality in the air—at least relatively speaking. Perhaps the reason was that most of the students had to work hard to pay for every classroom hour. Therefore they appreciated what they got, even when there was not much in it to appreciate. Then there was the big, bright, shiny, new library, with a complicated system of tickets and lights, at the main loan desk: and there I soon came out with a great armful of things, books which excited me more than I now can understand. I think it was not the books themselves but my own sense of energy and resolve that made me think everything was more interesting than it was.

What, for instance, did I find to enthrall me in a book about esthetics by a man called Yrjö Hirn? I cannot remember. And even in spite of my almost congenital dislike for Platonism, I was happy with the *Enneads* of Plotinus, in

Marsilio Ficino's Latin translation. The truth is that there is a considerable difference between Plato and Plotinus, but I am not enough of a philosopher to know what it is. Thank God I shall never again have to try and find out, either. But anyway, I dragged this huge volume into the subway and out on the Long Island Railroad to the house in Douglaston, where I had a room with a big glass-enclosed bookcase full of Communist pamphlets and books on psychoanalysis, in which the little Vulgate I had once bought in Rome lay neglected and out of place . . .

For some reason I became intensely interested in Daniel Defoe, and read his whole life and dipped into most of the strange journalistic jobs of writing which he did besides *Robinson Crusoe*. I made a hero for myself out of Jonathan Swift, because of his writing. Towards May of that year I remember going in to the Columbia Bookstore and selling them a copy of T. S. Eliot's essays and a lot of other things which I was getting rid of in a conscious reaction against artiness—as if all that were too bourgeois for my serious and practical new-self.

Then, because of the wide general curriculum of an American university, which, instead of trying to teach you any one thing completely, strives to give its students a superficial knowledge of everything, I found myself mildly interested in things like geology and economics, and interiorly cursing a big, vague course in current events called "Contemporary Civilization," which was imposed on all the sophomores whether they liked it or not.

Soon I was full of all the economic and pseudo-scientific jargon appropriate to a good Columbia man, and was acclimated to the new atmosphere which I found so congenial. That was true. Columbia, compared with Cambridge, was a friendly place. When you had to go and see a professor or an advisor or a dean about something, he would tell you, more or less simply, what you needed to know. The only trouble was that you usually had to wait around for about half an hour before you got a chance to see anybody. But once you did, there were no weird evasions and none of the pompous beating about the bush, mixed up with subtle academic allusions and a few dull witticisms which was what you were liable to get out of almost anybody at Cambridge, where everybody cultivated some special manner of his own, and had his own individual and peculiar style. I suppose it is something that you have to expect around a university, this artificiality. For a man to be absolutely sincere with generation after generation of students requires either supernatural simplicity or, in the natural order, a kind of heroic humility.

There was—and still is—one man at Columbia, or rather one among several, who was most remarkable for this kind of heroism. I mean Mark Van Doren.

The first semester I was at Columbia, just after my twentieth birthday, in the winter of 1935, Mark was giving part of the "English sequence" in one of those rooms in Hamilton Hall with windows looking out between the big columns on to the wired-in track on South Field. There were twelve or fifteen people with more or less unbrushed hair, most of them with glasses, lounging around. One of them was my friend Robert Gibney.

It was a class in English literature, and it had no special bias of any kind. It was simply about what it was supposed to be about: the English literature of the eighteenth century. And in it literature was treated, not as history, not as sociology, not as economics, not as a series of case-histories in psychoanalysis but, *mirabile dictu*, simply as literature.

I thought to myself, who is this excellent man Van Doren who being employed to teach literature, teaches just that: talks about writing and about books and poems and plays: does not get off on a tangent about the biographies of the poets or novelists: does not read into their poems a lot of subjective messages which were never there? Who is this man who does not have to fake and cover up a big gulf of ignorance by teaching a lot of opinions and conjectures and useless facts that belong to some other subject? Who is this who really loves what he has to teach, and does not secretly detest all literature, and abhor poetry, while pretending to be a professor of it?

That Columbia should have in it men like this who, instead

of subtly destroying all literature by burying and concealing it under a mass of irrelevancies, really purified and educated the perceptions of their students by teaching them how to read a book and how to tell a good book from a bad, genuine writing from falsity and pastiche: all this gave me a deep respect for my new university.

Mark would come into the room and, without any fuss, would start talking about whatever was to be talked about. Most of the time he asked questions. His questions were very good, and if you tried to answer them intelligently, you found yourself saying excellent things that you did not know you knew, and that you had not, in fact, known before. He had "educed" them from you by his question. His classes were literally "education"—they brought things out of you, they made your mind produce its own explicit ideas. Do not think that Mark was simply priming his students with thoughts of his own, and then making the thought stick to their minds by getting them to give it back to him as their own. Far from it. What he did have was the gift of communicating to them something of his own vital interest in things, something of his manner of approach: but the results were sometimes quite unexpected—and by that I mean good in a way that he had not anticipated, casting lights that he had not himself foreseen.

Now a man who can go for year after year—although Mark was young then and is young now—without having any time to waste in flattering and cajoling his students with any kind of a fancy act, or with jokes, or with storms of temperament, or periodic tirades—whole classes spent in threats and imprecations, to disguise the fact that the professor himself has come in unprepared—one who can do without all these non-essentials both honors his vocation and makes it fruitful. Not only that, but his vocation, in return, perfects and ennobles him. And that is the way it should be, even in the natural order: how much more so in the order of grace!

Mark, I know, is no stranger to the order of grace: but considering his work as teacher merely as a mission on the natural level—I can see that Providence was using him as an instrument more directly than he realized. As far as I can see, the influence of Mark's sober and sincere intellect, and his manner of dealing with his subject with perfect honesty and objectivity and without evasions, was remotely preparing my mind to receive the good seed of scholastic philosophy. And there is nothing strange in this, for Mark himself was familiar at least with some of the modern scholastics, like Maritain and Gilson, and he was a friend of the American neo-Thomists, Mortimer Adler and Richard McKeon, who had started out at Columbia but had had to move to Chicago, because Columbia was not ripe enough to know what to make of them.

The truth is that Mark's temper was profoundly scholastic in the sense that his clear mind looked directly for the quiddities of things, and sought being and substance under the covering of accident and appearances. And for him poetry was, indeed, a virtue of the practical intellect, and not simply a vague spilling of the emotions, wasting the soul and perfecting none of our essential powers.

It was because of this virtual scholasticism of Mark's that he would never permit himself to fall into the naive errors of those who try to read some favorite private doctrine into every poet they like of every nation or every age. And Mark abhorred the smug assurance with which second-rate left-wing critics find adumbrations of dialectical materialism in everyone who ever wrote from Homer and Shakespeare to whomever they happen to like in recent times. If the poet is to their fancy, then he is clearly seen to be preaching the class struggle. If they do not like him, then they are able to show that he was really a forefather of fascism. And all their literary heroes are revolutionary leaders, and all their favorite villains are capitalists and Nazis.

It was a very good thing for me that I ran into someone like Mark Van Doren at that particular time, because in my new reverence for Communism, I was in danger of docilely accepting any kind of stupidity, provided I thought it was something that paved the way to the Elysian fields of classless society.

175

There was a legend in New York, fostered by the Hearst papers, that Columbia University was a hotbed of Communists. All the professors and students were supposed to be Reds, except perhaps the president of the university, Nicholas Murray Butler, living in solitary misery in his big brick house on Morningside Drive. I have no doubt that the poor old man's misery was real, and that his isolation from most of the university was very real. But the statement that everybody in the university was a Communist was far from true.

I know that, as far as the faculty was concerned, Columbia University was built up in concentric rings, about a solid core of well-meaning, unenlightened stuffiness, the veterans, the beloved of the trustees and the alumni, and Butler's intellectual guard of honor. Then there was an inner circle of sociologists and economists and lawyers, whose world was a mystery to me, and who exercised a powerful influence in Washington under the New Deal. About all of them and their satellites I never knew anything, except that they were certainly not Communists. Then there was the little galaxy of pragmatists in the school of philosophy, and all the thousands of their pale spiritual offspring in the jungles of Teachers College and New College. They were not Communists either. They cast a mighty influence over the whole American Middle West, and were to a great extent conditioned by the very people whom they were trying to condition, so that Teachers College always stood for colorlessness and mediocrity and plain, hapless behaviorism. These three groups were then the real Columbia. I suppose they all prided themselves on their liberalism, but that is precisely what they were: "liberals," not Communists, and they brought down upon their heads all the scorn the Communists could pour upon them for their position of habitual compromise.

I do not understand much about politics. Besides, it would be outside the scope of my present vocation if I tried to make any political analysis of anything. But I can say that there were, at that time, quite a few Communists or Communist sympathizers among the undergraduates, and especially in Columbia College where most of the smartest students were Reds.

The Communists had control of the college paper and were strong on some of the other publications and on the Student Board. But this campus Communism was more a matter of noise than anything else, at least as far as the rank and file were concerned.

The Spectator was always starting some kind of a fight and calling for mass-meetings and strikes and demonstrations. Then the fraternity boys, who elected to play "Fascist" in this children's game, would get up in the classroom buildings and turn the firehoses on the people who were standing around the Communist speaker. Then the whole thing would come out in the New York *Journal* that evening and all the alumni would choke on their mock turtle soup down at the Columbia Club.

By the time I arrived at Columbia, the Communists had taken to holding their meetings at the sundial on 116th Street, in the middle of the wide-open space between the old domed library and South Field. This was well out of the range of the firehoses in the Journalism building and Hamilton Hall. The first meeting I went to, there, was very tame. It was against Italian Fascism. There were one or two speeches—by students practicing the art. Those who stood around were mostly members of the National Students' League, who were there out of a sense of duty or partisanship. A few curious passers-by stopped awhile on their way to the subway. There was not much excitement. A girl with a mop of black hair stood by, wearing a placard pronouncing some kind of a judgement on Fascism. Someone sold me a pamphlet.

Presently I picked out the quiet, earnest, stocky little man in the grey overcoat, a hatless, black-haired Communist from downtown, who was running the affair. He was not a student. He was the real article. This was his assignment: forming and training the material that offered itself to him at Columbia. He had an assistant, a younger man, and the two of them were kept pretty busy. I went up to him and started to talk. When he actually listened to me, and paid attention to my ideas, and seemed to approve of my interest, I was very flattered. He got my name and address and told me to come to the meetings of the N.S.L.

Soon I was walking up and down in front of the Casa Italiana wearing two placards, front and back, accusing Italy of injustice in the invasion of Ethiopia that had either just begun or was just about to begin. Since the accusation was manifestly true, I felt a certain satisfaction in thus silently proclaiming it as a picket. There were two or three of us. For an hour and a half or two hours we walked up and down the pavement of Amsterdam Avenue, in the grey afternoon, bearing our dire accusations, while the warm sense of justification in our hearts burned high, even in spite of the external boredom.

For during that whole time no one even came near the Casa Italiana, and I even began to wonder if there were anyone at all inside it. The only person who approached us was a young Italian who looked as if he might be a Freshman football player, and tried to get into an argument. But he was too dumb. He went away mumbling that the Hearst papers were very excellent because of the great prizes which they offered, in open competition, to their many readers.

I forget how the picketing ended: whether we waited for someone else to come and take over, or whether we just decided we had done enough and took off our signs and went away. But anyway I had the feeling that I had done something that was good, if only as a gesture: for it certainly did not seem to have accomplished anything. But at least I had made a kind of public confession of faith. I had said that I was against war—against all war. That I believed wars to be unjust. That I thought they could only ruin and destroy the world. . . . Someone will ask where I managed to get all that out of the placard I was carrying. But as far as I remember, that was the party line that year—at least it was the line that was handed out to the public.

I can still hear the tired, determined chanting of students at campus demonstrations: "Books, not Battleships!" "No More WAR!" There was no distinction made. It was war as such that we hated and said we wanted no more of. We wanted books, not battleships, we said. We were all burned up with the thirst for knowledge, for intellectual and spiritual improvement. And here the wicked capitalists were forcing the government to enrich them by buying armaments and building battleships and planes and tanks, when the money ought to be spent on volumes of lovely cultural books for us students. Here we were on the threshold of life, we cried: our hands were reaching out for education and culture. Was the government going to put a gun in them, and send us off on another imperialistic war? And the line of reasoning behind all this definitely held, in 1935, that all war was imperialistic war. War, according to the party line in 1935, was an exclusively capitalist amusement. It was purely and simply a device to enrich the armament manufacturers and the international bankers, coining fortunes for them with the blood of the workers and students.

One of the big political events of that spring was a "Peace Strike." I was never quite able to understand by virtue of what principle a student could manage to consider himself on strike by cutting a class. Theoretically, I suppose, it amounted to a kind of defiance of authority: but it was a defiance that did not cost anybody anything except perhaps the student himself. And besides, I was quite used to cutting classes whenever I felt like it, and it seemed to me rather bombastic to dress it up with the name of "strike." However, on another of those grey days, we went on "strike," and this time there were several hundred people in the gymnasium, and even one or two members of the faculty got up on the platform and said something.

They were not all Communists, but all the speeches had more or less the same burden: that it was absurd to even think of such a thing as a just war in our time. Nobody wanted war: there was no justification for any war of any kind on the part of anybody, and consequently, if a war did start, it would

179

certainly be the result of a capitalist plot, and should be firmly resisted by everybody with any kind of a conscience.

That was just the kind of a position that attracted me, that appealed to my mind at that time. It seemed to cut across all complexities by its sweeping and uncompromising simplicity. All war was simply unjust, and that was that. The thing to do was to fold your arms and refuse to fight. If everybody did that, there would be no more wars.

That cannot seriously have been the Communist position, but at least I thought it was. And anyway, the theme of this particular meeting was the "Oxford Pledge." The words of that pledge were written out in huge letters on a great big placard that hung limply in the air over the speakers' platform, and all the speakers waved their arms at it and praised it, and repeated it, and urged it upon us, and in the end we all took it, and acclaimed it, and solemnly pledged ourselves to it.

Perhaps everybody has, by now, forgotten what the Oxford Pledge was. It was a resolution that had been passed by the Oxford Union, which said that they, these particular Oxford undergraduates, simply would refuse to fight for King and Country in any war whatever. The fact that a majority of those who happened to be at a meeting of a university debating society, one evening, voted that way certainly did not commit the whole university, or even any one of the voters, to what the resolution said, and it was only other student groups, all over the world, that had transformed it into a "pledge." And this "pledge" was then taken by hundreds of thousands of students in all kinds of schools and colleges and universities with some of the solemnity that might make it look as if they intended to bind themselves by it—the way we were doing at Columbia that day. All this was usually inspired by the Reds, who were very fond of the Oxford Pledge that year. . . .

However, the next year the Spanish Civil War broke out. The first thing I heard about that war was that one of the chief speakers at the 1935 Peace Strike, and one who had been so enthusiastic about this glorious pledge that we would never fight in any war, was now fighting for the Red Army against Franco, and all the N.S.L. and the Young Communists were going around picketing everybody who seemed to think that the war in Spain was not holy and sacrosanct and a crusade for the workers against Fascism.

The thing that perplexes me is: what did all the people in the gymnasium at Columbia, including myself, think we were doing when we took that pledge? What did a pledge mean to us? What was, in our minds, the basis of such an obligation? How could we be obliged? Communists don't believe in any such thing as a natural law, or the law of conscience, although they seem to. They are always crying out against the injustice of capitalism and yet, as a matter of fact, they very often say in the same breath that the very concept of justice is simply a myth devised by the ruling classes to beguile and deceive the proletariat.

As far as I can remember, it seems that what most of us thought we were doing, when we took that pledge, was simply making a public statement, and doing so in sufficient numbers, as we hoped, to influence politicians. There was no intention of binding ourselves under any obligation. The notion never even occurred to us. Most of us probably secretly thought we were gods anyway, and therefore the only law we had to obey was our own ineffable little wills. It was sufficient to say that we did not intend to go to war for anybody: and that was enough. And if, afterwards, we changed our minds— well, were we not our own gods?

It's a nice, complex universe, the Communist universe: it gravitates towards stability and harmony and peace and order on the poles of an opportunism that is completely irresponsible and erratic. Its only law is, it will do whatever seems to be profitable to itself at the moment. However, that seems to have become the rule of all modern political parties. I have nothing to say about it. I do not profess to be either amazed or broken-hearted that such a thing should be possible. Let the dead bury their dead: they have certainly got enough to bury. It is the fruit of their philosophy that they should: and that is all that they need to be reminded of. But you cannot make them believe it.

I had formed a kind of an ideal picture of Communism in my mind, and now I found that the reality was a disappointment. I suppose my daydreams were theirs also. But neither dream is true.

I had thought that Communists were calm, strong, definite people, with very clear ideas as to what was wrong with everything. Men who knew the solution, and were ready to pay any price to apply the remedy. And their remedy was simple and just and clean, and it would definitely solve all the problems of society, and make men happy, and bring the world peace.

It turned out that some of them indeed were calm, and strong, and had a kind of peace of mind that came from definite convictions and from a real devotion to their cause, out of motives of a kind of vague natural charity and sense of justice. But the trouble with their convictions was that they were mostly strange, stubborn prejudices, hammered into their minds by the incantation of statistics, and without any solid intellectual foundation. And having decided that God is an invention of the ruling classes, and having excluded Him, and all moral order with Him, they were trying to establish some kind of a moral system by abolishing all morality in its very source. Indeed, the very word morality was something repugnant to them. They wanted to make everything right, and they denied all the criteria given us for distinguishing between right and wrong.

And so it is an indication of the intellectual instability of Communism, and the weakness of its philosophical foundations, that most Communists are, in actual fact, noisy and shallow and violent people, torn to pieces by petty jealousies and factional hatreds and envies and strife. They shout and show off and generally give the impression that they cordially detest one another even when they are supposed to belong to the same sect. And as for the inter-sectional hatred prevailing between all the different branches of radicalism, it is far bitterer and more virulent than the more or less sweeping and abstract hatred of the big general enemy, capitalism. All this is something of a clue to such things as the wholesale executions of Communists who have moved their chairs to too prominent a position in the ante-chamber of Utopia which the Soviet Union is supposed to be.

iii

My active part in the world revolution was not very momentous. It lasted, in all, about three months. I picketed the Casa Italiana, I went to the Peace Strike, and I think I made some kind of a speech in the big classroom on the second floor of the Business School, where the N.S.L. had their meetings. Maybe it was a speech on Communism in England —a topic about which I knew absolutely nothing; in that case, I was loyally living up to the tradition of Red oratory. I sold some pamphlets and magazines. I don't know what was in them, but I could gather their contents from the big black cartoons of capitalists drinking the blood of workers.

Finally, the Reds had a party. And, of all places, in a Park Avenue apartment. This irony was the only amusing thing about it. And after all it was not so ironical. It was the home of some Barnard girl who belonged to the Young Communist League and her parents had gone away for the week-end. I could get a fair picture of them from the way the furniture looked, and from the volumes of Nietzsche and Schopenhauer and Oscar Wilde and Ibsen that filled the bookcases. And there was a big grand piano on which someone played Beethoven while the Reds sat around on the floor. Later we had a sort of Boy Scout campfire group in the living room, singing heavy Communist songs, including that delicate anti-religious classic, "There'll be pie in the sky when you die."

One little fellow with buck teeth and horn-rimmed glasses pointed to two windows in a corner of one of the rooms. They commanded a whole sweep of Park Avenue in one direction and the cross-town street in another. "What a place for a machine-gun nest," he observed. The statement came from a middle-class adolescent. It was made in a Park Avenue apartment. He had evidently never even seen a machine-gun, except in the movies. If there had been a revolution going on at

183

the time, he would have probably been among the first to get his head knocked off by the revolutionists. And in any case he, like all the rest of us, had just finished making the famous Oxford Pledge that he would not fight in any war whatever . . .

One reason why I found the party so dull was that nobody was very enthusiastic about getting something to drink except me. Finally one of the girls encouraged me, in a businesslike sort of a way, to go out and buy bottles of rye at a liquor store around the corner on Third Avenue, and when I had drunk some of the contents she invited me into a room and signed me up as a member of the Young Communist League. I took the party name of Frank Swift. When I looked up from the paper the girl had vanished like a not too inspiring dream, and I went home on the Long Island Railroad with the secret of a name which I have been too ashamed to reveal to anyone until this moment when I am beyond humiliation.

I only went to one meeting of the Young Communist League, in the apartment of one of the students. It was a long discussion as to why Comrade So-and-so did not come to any of the meetings. The answer was that his father was too bourgeois to allow it. So after that, I walked out into the empty street, and let the meeting end however it would.

It was good to be in the fresh air. My footsteps rang out on the dark stones. At the end of the street, the pale amber light of a bar-room beckoned lovingly to me from under the steel girders of the elevated. The place was empty. I got a glass of beer and lit a cigarette and tasted the first sweet moment of silence and relief.

And that was the end of my days as a great revolutionary. I decided that it would be wiser if I just remained a "fellow-traveller." The truth is that my inspiration to do something for the good of mankind had been pretty feeble and abstract from the start. I was still interested in doing good for only one person in the world—myself.

May came, and all the trees on Long Island were green, and when the train from the city got past Bayside and started across the meadows to Douglaston, you could see the pale, soft haze of summer beginning to hang over the bay, and count the boats that had been set afloat again after the winter, and were riding jauntily at their moorings off the end of the little dock. And now in the lengthening evenings the dining room was still light with the rays of the sun when Pop came home for dinner, slamming the front door and whooping at the dog and smacking the surface of the hall table with the evening paper to let everybody know that he had arrived.

Soon John Paul was home from his school in Pennsylvania, and my exams were over, and we had nothing to do but go swimming and hang around the house playing hot records. And in the evening we would wander off to some appalling movie where we nearly died of boredom. We did not have a car, and my uncle would not let us touch the family Buick. It would not have done me any good anyway, because I never learned to drive. So most of the time, we would get a ride to Great Neck and then walk back the two or three miles along the wide road when the show was over.

Why did we ever go to all those movies? That is another mystery. But I think John Paul and I and our various friends must have seen all the movies that were produced, without exception, from 1934 to 1937. And most of them were simply awful. What is more, they got worse from week to week and from month to month, and day after day we hated them more. My ears are ringing with the false, gay music that used to announce the Fox movietone and the Paramount newsreels with the turning camera that slowly veered its aim right at your face. My mind still echoes with the tones of Pete Smith and Fitzpatrick of the Travel-talks saying, "And now farewell to beautiful New South Wales."

And yet I confess a secret loyalty to the memory of my great heroes: Chaplin, W. C. Fields, Harpo Marx, and many others whose names I have forgotten. But their pictures were rare, and for the rest, we found ourselves perversely admiring the villains and detesting the heroes. The truth is that the villains were almost always the better actors. We were delighted with everything they did. We were almost always in danger of being thrown out of the theater for our uproarious laughter at scenes that were supposed to be most affecting, tender and appealing to the finer elements in the human soul—the tears of Jackie Cooper, the brave smile of Alice Faye behind the bars of a jail.

The movies soon turned into a kind of hell for me and my brother and indeed for all my closest friends. We could not keep away from them. We were hypnotised by those yellow flickering lights and the big posters of Don Ameche. Yet as soon as we got inside, the suffering of having to sit and look at such colossal stupidities became so acute that we sometimes actually felt physically sick. In the end, it got so that I could hardly sit through a show. It was like lighting cigarettes and taking a few puffs and throwing them away, appalled by the vile taste in one's mouth.

In 1935 and 1936, without my realizing it, life was slowly, once more, becoming almost intolerable.

In the fall of 1935, John Paul went to Cornell, and I went back to Columbia, full of all kinds of collegiate enthusiasms, so that in a moment of madness I even gave my name for the Varsity lightweight crew. After a couple of days on the Harlem River and then on the Hudson, when we tried to row to Yonkers and back in what seemed to me to be a small hurricane, I decided that I did not wish to die so young, and after that carefully avoided the Boat-House all the rest of the time I was in college.

However, October is a fine and dangerous season in America. It is dry and cool and the land is wild with red and gold and crimson, and all the lassitudes of August have seeped out of your blood, and you are full of ambition. It is a wonderful time to begin anything at all. You go to college, and every course in the catalogue looks wonderful. The names of the subjects all seem to lay open the way to a new world. Your arms are full of new, clean notebooks, waiting to be filled. You pass through the doors of the library, and the smell of thousands of well-kept books makes your head swim with a clean and subtle pleasure. You have a new hat, a new sweater perhaps, or a whole new suit. Even the nickels and the quarters in your pocket feel new, and the buildings shine in the glorious sun.

In this season of resolutions and ambitions, in 1935, I signed up for courses in Spanish and German and Geology and Constitutional Law and French Renaissance Literature and I forget what else besides. And I started to work for *The Spectator* and the yearbook and *The Review* and I continued to work for *Jester* as I had already done the spring before. And I found myself pledging one of the fraternities.

It was a big, gloomy house behind the new library. On the ground floor there was a pool-room as dark as a morgue, a dining room, and some stairs led up to a big dark wainscotted living room where they held dances and beer-parties. Above that were two floors of bedrooms where telephones were constantly ringing and all day long somebody or other was singing in the showerbath. And there was somewhere in the building a secret room which I must not reveal to you, reader, at any price, even at the cost of life itself. And there I was eventually initiated. The initiation with its various tortures lasted about a week, and I cheerfully accepted penances which, if they were imposed in a monastery, for a supernatural motive, and for some real reason, instead of for no reason at all, would cause such an uproar that all religious houses would be closed and the Catholic Church would probably have a hard time staying in the country.

When that was over I had a gold and enamel pin on my shirt. My name was engraved on the back of it, and I was quite proud of it for about a year, and then it went to the laundry on a shirt and never came back.

I suppose there were two reasons why I thought I ought to join a fraternity. One was the false one, that I thought it would help me to "make connections" as the saying goes, and get a marvelous job on leaving college. The other, truer one was that I imagined that I would thus find a multitude of occasions for parties and diversions, and that I would meet many very interesting young ladies at the dances that would be held in that mausoleum. Both these hopes turned out to be illusory. As a matter of fact, I think the only real explanation was that I was feeling the effects of October.

Anyway, when John Paul went to Cornell the whole family, except me, drove up to Ithaca in the Buick and came back with words and concepts that filled the house with a kind of collegiate tension for a couple of weeks to come. Everybody was talking about football and courses and fraternities.

As a matter of fact, John Paul's first year at Cornell turned out to be sad in the same way as my first year at Cambridge— a thing that was not long in becoming apparent, when the bills he could not pay began to show up at home. But it was even more obvious to me when I saw him again.

He was naturally a happy and optimistic sort of a person and he did not easily get depressed. And he had a clear, quick intelligence and a character as sensitive as it was well-balanced. Now his intelligence seemed a little fogged with some kind of an obscure, interior confusion, and his happiness was perverted by a sad, lost restlessness. Although he maintained all his interests and increased them, the increase was in extent, not in depth, and the result was a kind of scattering of powers, a dissipation of the mind and will in a variety of futile aims.

He stood for some time, with great uncertainty, on the threshold of a fraternity house at Cornell, and even let them put a pledge pin on him, and then after a couple of weeks he took it off again and ran away. And with three friends he rented a house on one of those steep, shady Ithaca streets, and after that the year was a long and sordid riot, from which he derived no satisfaction. They called the place Grand Hotel, and had stationery printed with that title, on which desultory and fragmentary letters would come to Douglaston, and fill everyone with unquiet. When he came back from Cornell, John Paul looked tired and disgusted.

I suppose it is true, at least theoretically, the brothers watch over one another and help one another along in the fraternity house. In my fraternity house at Columbia, I know that the wiser members used to get together and shake their heads a little when somebody was carrying his debauchery too far.

And when there was any real trouble, the concern of the brothers was sincere and dramatic, but it was useless. And there is always trouble in a fraternity house. The trouble, which came in the year after I was initiated, was the disappearance of one of the brothers, whom we shall call Fred.

Fred was a tall, stoop-shouldered, melancholy individual, with dark hair growing low on his brows. He never had much to say, and he liked to go apart and drink in mournful solitude. The only vivid thing I remember about him was that he stood over me, during one of the peculiar ceremonies of the initiation, when all the pledges had to stuff themselves with bread and milk for a special reason. And while I tried with despairing efforts to get the huge mouthfuls swallowed down, this Fred was standing over me with woeful cries of: "EAT, EAT, EAT!" It must have been sometime after Christmas that he disappeared.

I came into the house one night, and they were sitting around in the leather chairs talking earnestly. "Where's Fred?" was the burden of the discussion. He had not been seen anywhere for a couple of days. Would his family be upset if someone called up his home to see if he was there? Evidently, but it had to be done: he had not gone home either. One of the brothers had long since visited all his usual haunts. People tried to reconstruct the situation in which he had last been seen. With what dispositions had he last walked out of the front door. The usual ones, of course: silence, melancholy, the probable intention of getting drunk. A week passed and Fred was not found. The earnest concern of the brothers was fruitless. The subject of Fred was more or less dropped and, after a month, most of us had forgotten it. After two months, the whole thing was finally settled.

"They found Fred," somebody told me.

"Yes? Where?"

"In Brooklyn."

"Is he all right?"

"No, he's dead. They found him in the Gowanus Canal."

"What did he do, jump in?"

"Nobody knows what he did. He'd been there a long time."

"How long?"

"I don't know, a couple of months. They figured out who it was from the fillings in his teeth."

It was a picture that was not altogether vague to me. Our famous course in Contemporary Civilization had involved me, one winter afternoon, in a visit to the Bellevue Morgue, where I had seen rows and rows of iceboxes containing the blue, swollen corpses of drowned men along with all the other human refuse of the big, evil city: The dead that had been picked up in the streets, ruined by raw alcohol. The dead that had been found starved and frozen lying where they had tried to sleep in a pile of old newspapers. The pauper dead from Randalls Island. The dope-fiend dead. The murdered dead. The run-over. The suicides. The dead Negroes and Chinese. The dead of venereal disease. The dead from unknown causes. The killed by gangsters. They would all be shipped for burial up the East River in a barge to one of those islands where they also burned garbage.

Contemporary Civilization! One of the last things we saw on the way out of the morgue was the hand of a man pickled in a jar, brown and vile. They were not sure whether he was a criminal or not, and they wanted to have some part of him, after they had sent the rest of him up to the ghats. In the autopsy room a man on the table with his trunk wide open pointed his sharp, dead nose at the ceiling. The doctors held his liver and kidneys in their hands and sprayed them over with a trickle of water from a little rubber hose. I have never forgotten the awful, clammy silence of the city morgue at Bellevue, where they collect the bodies of those who died of contemporary civilization, like Fred.

Nevertheless, during that year I was so busy and so immersed in activities and occupations that I had no time to think for very long on these things. The energy of that golden October and the stimulation of the cold, bright winter days when the wind swept down as sharp as knives from the shining Palisades kept driving me through the year in what seemed to be fine condition. I had never done so many different things at the same time or with such apparent success. I had discovered in myself something of a capacity for work and for activity and for enjoyment that I had never dreamed of. And everything began to come easy, as the saying goes.

It was not that I was really studying hard or working hard: but all of a sudden I had fallen into a kind of a mysterious knack of keeping a hundred different interests going in the air at the same time. It was a kind of a stupendous juggling act, a tour-de-force, and what surprised me most was that I managed to keep it up without collapsing. In the first place, I was carrying about eighteen points in my courses—the average amount. I had found out the simplest way of fulfilling the minimum requirements for each one.

Then there was the "Fourth Floor." The fourth floor of John Jay Hall was the place where all the offices of the student publications and the Glee Club and the Student Board and all the rest were to be found. It was the noisiest and most agitated part of the campus. It was not gay, exactly. And I hardly ever saw, anywhere, antipathies and contentions and jealousies at once so petty, so open and so sharp. The whole floor was constantly seething with the exchange of insults from office to office. Constantly, all day long, from morning to night, people were writing articles and drawing cartoons calling each other Fascists. Or else they were calling one another up on the phone and assuring one another in the coarsest terms of their undying hatred. It was all intellectual and verbal, as vicious as it could be, but it never became concrete, never descended into physical rage. For this reason, I think that it was all more or less of a game which everybody played for purposes that were remotely esthetic.

The campus was supposed to be, in that year, in a state of "intellectual ferment." Everybody felt and even said that there were an unusual number of brilliant and original minds in the college. I think that it was to some extent true. Ad Reinhardt was certainly the best artist that had ever drawn for *Jester*, perhaps for any other college magazine. His issues of *Jester* were real magazines. I think that in cover designs and layouts he could have given lessons to some of the art-editors downtown. Everything he put out was original, and it was also funny, because for the first time in years *Jester* had some real writers contributing to it, and was not just an anthology of the same stale and obscene jokes that have been circulating through the sluggish system of American college magazines for two generations. By now Reinhardt had graduated, and so had the editor of the 1935 *Spectator*, Jim Wechsler.

My first approach to the Fourth Floor had been rather circumspect, after the manner of Cambridge. I went to my adviser, Prof. McKee, and asked him how to go about it, and he gave me a letter of introduction to Leonard Robinson who was editor of *The Columbia Review*, the literary magazine. I don't know what Robinson would have made of a letter of introduction. Anyway, I never got to meeting him after all. When I went to the *Review* office I gave the note to Bob Giroux, an associate editor, and he looked at it and scratched his head some bit and told me to write something if I got an idea.

By 1936 Leonard Robinson had vanished. I always heard a lot about Robinson, and it all adds up to nothing very clear, so that I have always had the impression that he somehow lives in the trees. I pray that he may go to heaven.

As for *Review*, Robert Paul Smith and Robert Giroux were both editing it together, and it was good. I don't know whether you would use the term "ferment" in their case, but Smith and Giroux were both good writers. Also, Giroux was a Catholic and a person strangely placid for the Fourth Floor. He had no part in its feuds and, as a matter of fact, you did not see him around there very much. John Berryman was more or less the star on *Review* that year. He was the most earnest-looking man on the campus.

There was not an office on that floor where I did not have something to do, except the Glee Club and Student Board and the big place where all the football coaches had their desks. I was writing stories for *Spectator*, and columns that were supposed to be funny; I was writing things for the yearbook and trying to sell copies of it—a thankless task. The yearbook was the one thing nobody wanted: it was expensive and dull. Of this I eventually became editor, without any evident benefit to myself or to the book or to Columbia or to the world.

I was never particularly drawn to the Varsity show: but they had a piano in their room, and the room was almost always empty, so I used to go in there and play furious jazz, after the manner I had taught myself—a manner which offended every ear but my own. It was a way of letting off steam —a form of athletics if you like. I have ruined more than one piano by this method.

The place where I was busiest was the *Jester* office. Nobody really worked there, they just congregated about noontime and beat violently with the palms of their hands on the big empty filing cabinets, making a thunderous sound that echoed up and down the corridor, and was sometimes answered from the *Review* office across the hall. There I usually came and drew forth from the bulging leather bag of books that I carried, copy and drawings which I put into the editor's hand. The editor that year was Herb Jacobson, and he printed all my worst cartoons very large in the most prominent parts of the magazine.

I thought I had something to be proud of when I became art-editor of *Jester* at the end of that year. Robert Lax was to be editor and Ralph Toledano managing editor, and we got along well together. The next year *Jester* was well put together because of Toledano and well written because of Lax and sometimes popular with the masses because of me. When it was really funny, it was not popular at all. The only really funny issues were mostly the work of Lax and Bob Gibney, the fruit of ideas that came to them at four o'clock in the morning in their room on the top floor of Furnald Hall.

The chief advantage of *Jester* was that it paid most of our bills for tuition. We were happy about it all, and wandered around the campus with little golden crowns dangling on our watch chains. Indeed, that was the only reason why I had a watch chain. I did not have a watch.

I have barely begun the list of all the things that occupied me in those days. For example, I gave my name to Miss Wegener at the appointments office. Miss Wegener was—and I hope she still is—a kind of a genius. She sat all day long behind her desk in that small, neat office in the Alumni house. No matter how many people she had talked to, she always looked unruffled and at peace. Every time you went to see her, one or two phone calls would come in, and she would make a note on a little pad of paper. In summer she never seemed to be worried by the hot weather. And she always smiled at you with a smile that was at the same time efficient and kind, pleasant and yet a little impersonal. She was another one who had a vocation and was living up to it!

One of the best jobs she ever got for me was that of guide and interpreter on the observation roof of the R.C.A. building, Rockefeller Center. It was an easy job. So easy in fact that it was boring. You simply had to stand there and talk to the people who came pouring out of the elevator with all their questions. And for this you got twenty-seven and a half dollars a week, which was very good pay in 1936. I also worked in another office in Radio City, for some people who handled publicity for all the manufacturers of Paper Cups and Containers. For them I did cartoons that said you would surely get trench mouth if you ever drank out of an ordinary glass. For each cartoon I was paid six dollars. It made me feel like an executive, to go walking in and out of the doors of the R.C.A. building with my pockets full of money. Miss Wegener would also send me off on the subway with little slips of paper with the addresses of apartments where I would interview rich Jewish ladies about tutoring their children in Latin, which meant that I got two or two and a half dollars an hour for sitting with them and doing their homework.

I also handed in my name for the Cross Country team. The fact that the coach was not sorry to get me is sufficient indication of one reason why we were the worst college Cross Country team in the East that year. And so, in my afternoons, I would run around and around South Field on the cinder path. And when winter came, I would go round and round the board track until I had blisters all over the soles of my feet and was so lame I could hardly walk. Occasionally I would go up to Van Cortlandt Park and run along the sandy and rocky paths through the woods. When we raced any other college, I was never absolutely the last one home—there were always two or three other Columbia men behind me. I was one of those who never came in until the crowd had lost interest and had begun to disperse. Perhaps I would have been more of a success as a long-distance runner if I had gone into training, and given up smoking and drinking, and kept regular hours.

But no. Three or four nights a week my fraternity brothers and I would go flying down in the black and roaring subway to 52nd Street, where we would crawl around the tiny, noisy and expensive nightclubs that had flowered on the sites of the old speakeasies in the cellars of those dirty brownstone houses. There we would sit, for hours, packed in those dark rooms, shoulder to shoulder with a lot of surly strangers and their girls, while the whole place rocked and surged with storms of jazz. There was no room to dance. We just huddled there between the blue walls, shoulder to shoulder and elbow to elbow, crouching and deafened and taciturn. If you moved your arm to get your drink you nearly knocked the next man off his stool. And the waiters fought their way back and forth through the sea of unfriendly heads, taking away the money of all the people.

It was not that we got drunk. No, it was this strange business of sitting in a room full of people and drinking without much speech, and letting yourself be deafened by the jazz that throbbed through the whole sea of bodies binding them all together in a kind of fluid medium. It was a strange, animal travesty of mysticism, sitting in those booming rooms, with the noise pouring through you, and the rhythm jumping and throbbing in the marrow of your bones. You couldn't call any of that, *per se*, a mortal sin. We just sat there, that was all. If we got hangovers the next day, it was more because of the smoking and nervous exhaustion than anything else.

How often, after a night of this, I missed all the trains home to Long Island and went and slept on a couch somewhere, at the Fraternity House, or in the apartment of somebody I knew around town. What was worst of all was going home on the subway, on the chance that one might catch a bus at Flushing! There is nothing so dismal as the Flushing bus station, in the grey, silent hour just before the coming of dawn. There were always at least one or two of those same characters whose prototypes I had seen dead in the morgue. And perhaps there would be a pair of drunken soldiers trying to get back to Fort Totten. Among all these I stood, weary and ready to fall, lighting the fortieth or fiftieth cigarette of the day—the one that took the last shreds of lining off my throat.

The thing that depressed me most of all was the shame and despair that invaded my whole nature when the sun came up, and all the laborers were going to work: men healthy and awake and quiet, with their eyes clear, and some rational purpose before them. This humiliation and sense of my own misery and of the fruitlessness of what I had done was the nearest I could get to contrition. It was the reaction of nature. It proved nothing except that I was still, at least, morally alive: or rather that I had still some faint capacity for moral life in me. The term "morally alive" might obscure the fact that I was spiritually dead. I had been that long since!

iv

In the fall of 1936 Pop died. The manner of his death was this. I had been on a geology field trip in Pennsylvania, and had come back, late one Sunday night after a long cold ride through New Jersey, back from the coal mines and the slate quarries, in an open Ford. The icy wind of the Delaware Water Gap was still in my flesh. I went to bed without seeing anybody. They were all in their rooms by the time I got home.

The next morning I looked in Pop's room, and he was sitting up in bed looking strangely unhappy and confused.

"How do you feel?" I said.

"Rotten," he answered. There was nothing surprising about that. He was always getting ill. I supposed he had caught another cold. I said:

"Take some more sleep, then."

"Yes," he said, "I guess I will."

I went back into the bathroom, and hastened to dress and drink my coffee and run for the train.

That afternoon I was on the track, in the pale November sun, taking an easy work-out. I came down the shady side of the field, in front of the library. There was one of the juniors who worked for the Yearbook standing behind the high wire fence, at the corner nearest John Jay, where the bushes and poplar trees were. As I came down to the bend he called out to me and I went over to the fence.

"Your aunt was on the phone just now," he told me. "She said your grandfather is dead."

There was nothing I could say.

I trotted back along the field and went down and took a quick shower and got into my clothes and went home. There was no train but one of those slow ones, that ambled out on to the Island half empty, with long stops at every station. But I knew there was no particular hurry. I could not bring him back to life.

Poor old Pop. I was not surprised that he was dead, or that he had died that way. I supposed his heart had failed. It was typical of him, that kind of death: he was always in a hurry, always ahead of time. And now, after a whole long lifetime of impatience, waiting for Bonnemaman to get ready to go to the theater, or to come to dinner, or to come down and open the Christmas presents, after all that, he had brooked no delay about dying. He had slipped out on us, in his sleep, without premeditation, on the spur of the moment.

I would miss Pop. In the last year or two we had drawn rather close together. He often got me to come to lunch with him downtown and there he would tell me all his troubles, and talk over the prospects for my future—I had returned to the old idea of becoming a newspaper man. There was a great deal of simplicity about Pop. It was a simplicity, an ingenuousness that belonged to his nature: and it was something peculiarly American. Or at least, it belonged to the Americans of his generation, this kind and warm-hearted and vast and universal optimism.

When I got to the house, I knew where I would find his

body. I went up to his bed-room and opened the door. The only shock was to find that the windows were all open and the room was full of the cold November air. Pop, who in his life had feared all draughts and had lived in overheated houses, now lay under a sheet in this icy cold death-chamber. It was the first death that had been in the house that he had built for his family twenty-five years before.

Now a strange thing happened. Without my having thought about it, or debating about it in my mind, I closed the door and got on my knees by the bed and prayed. I suppose it was just the spontaneous response of my love for poor Pop—the obvious way to do something for him, to acknowledge all his goodness to me. And yet, I had seen other deaths without praying or being even drawn to pray. Two or three summers before an old relative of mine had died, and the only thing that had occurred to me was the observation that her lifeless corpse was no more than a piece of furniture. I did not feel that there was anybody there, only a *thing*. This did not teach me what it taught Aristotle, about the existence of the soul . . .

But now I only wanted to pray.

Unfortunately, I knew that Bonnemaman was going to come in and tell me to look at the body, and soon I heard her steps in the hall. I got off my knees before she opened the door.

"Aren't you going to look at him?" she said to me.

I said nothing. She raised the corner of the sheet, and I looked at Pop's dead face. It was pale, and it was dead. She let the sheet fall back, and together we walked out of the room, and I sat and talked to her for an hour or so, while the sun was going down.

Everybody knew that now this would be the end of Bonnemaman too. Although our family had been one of those curious modern households in which everybody was continually arguing and fighting, and in which there had been for years an obscure and complicated network of contentions and suppressed jealousies, Bonnemaman had been tremendously attached to her husband. She soon began to languish, but it was months before she finally died.

First, she fell down and broke her arm. It mended slowly and painfully. But as it did, she turned into a bent and silent old woman, with a rather haggard face. When the summer came, she could no longer get out of bed. Then came the alarms at night when we thought she was dying, and stood for hours by her bed, listening to the harsh gasp in her throat. And then too I was praying, looking into the mute, helpless face she turned towards my face. This time I was more conscious of what I was doing, and I prayed for her to live, although in some sense it was obviously better that she should die.

I was saying, within myself: "You Who made her, let her go on living." The reason I said this was that life was the only good I was certain of. And if life was the one big value, the one chief reality, its continuance depended on the will (otherwise why pray?) of the supreme Principle of all life, the ultimate Reality, He Who is Pure Being. He Who is Life Itself. He Who, simply, is. By praying, I was implicitly acknowledging all this. And now twice I had prayed, although I continued to think I believed in nothing.

Bonnemaman lived. I hope it had something to do with grace, with something that was given to Bonnemaman from God, in those last weeks that she continued to live, speechless and helpless on her bed, to save her soul. Finally, in August, she died, and they took her away and made an end of her body like all the rest. That was the summer of 1937.

Pop had died in November 1936. Already, in that fall, I had begun to feel ill. Still I kept on trying to do all the things I was doing—following my courses, editing the Yearbook, working, and running on the Cross Country Team without going into training. . . .

One day we raced Army and Princeton. I was not last, but as usual I was about twenty-third or -fourth out of thirty or so. When I got to the end of the course, I simply fell down and lay on the ground, waiting for my stomach to turn inside out within me. I felt so bad that I did not even mind what the people thought. I did not try to look brave, or to make any jokes about myself, or to hide the way I felt. I lay there until I felt better, then I got up and went away, and never came back to the locker rooms again. The coach did not bother to come looking for me. Nobody tried to persuade me to go back on the team. We were all equally satisfied: I was through. However, it did not help much to get rid of this burden.

One day I was coming into town on the Long Island train. I had a bagful of work that was already late, and had to be handed in that day. After that, I had a date with someone with whom I liked very much to have a date. While the train was going through the freight yards in Long Island City my head suddenly began to swim. It was not that I was afraid of vomiting, but it was as if some center of balance within me had been unexpectedly removed, and as if I were about to plunge into a blind abyss of emptiness without end. I got up and stood in the gap between the cars to get some air, but my knees were shaking so much that I was afraid I would slip through the chains between the cars and end up under the wheels, so I got back and propped myself against the wall and held on. This strange vertigo came and went, while the train dived into the tunnel under the river, and everything around me went dark and began to roar. I think the business had passed over by the time we got to the station.

I was scared. And the first thing that occurred to me was to go and find the house physician in the Pennsylvania Hotel. He examined me and listened to my heart and took my blood pressure, and gave me something to drink and told me I was over-stimulated. What did I do for a living, he asked me. I told him I went to college and did quite a few other things besides. He told me to give some of them up. And then he suggested that I ought to go to bed and get some sleep, and then go home when I felt better.

So next I found myself in a room in the Pennsylvania Hotel, lying on a bed, trying to go to sleep. But I could not.

It was a small, narrow room, rather dark, even though the window seemed to occupy most of the wall that was in front of me. You could hear the noise of the traffic coming up from far below, on 32nd Street. But the room itself was quiet, with a quietness that was strange, ominous.

I lay on the bed and listened to the blood pounding rapidly inside my head. I could hardly keep my eyes closed. Yet I did not want to open them, either. I was afraid that if I even looked at the window, the strange spinning inside my head would begin again.

That window! It was huge. It seemed to go right down to the floor. Maybe the force of gravity would draw the whole bed, with me on it, to the edge of that abyss, and spill me headlong into the emptiness.

And far, far away in my mind was a little, dry, mocking voice that said: "What if you threw yourself out of that window. . . ."

I turned over on the bed, and tried to go to sleep. But the blood drummed and drummed in my head. I could not sleep.

I thought to myself: "I wonder if I am having a nervous breakdown."

Then, again, I saw that window. The mere sight of it made my head spin. The mere thought that I was high above the ground almost knocked me out again.

The doctor came in and saw me lying there wide awake and said:

"I thought I told you to go to sleep."

"I couldn't sleep," I said. He gave me a bottle of medicine, and went away again. All I wanted was to get out of that room.

When he was gone, I got up and went downstairs and paid for the room and took a train home. I did not feel bad in the train going home. The house was empty. I lay down on a thing in the living room that they called the chaise-longue, and went to sleep.

When Else came home, she said: "I thought you were going to stay up town for dinner."

But I said: "I felt bad, so I came home."

What was the matter with me? I never found out. I suppose it was a sort of a nervous breakdown. In connection with it, I developed gastritis, and thought I was beginning to get a stomach ulcer.

The doctors gave me a diet and some medicine. The effect of both was more psychological than anything else. Every time

I went to eat anything, I studied what was there, and only chose certain things and ate them with a sort of conscious scrupulosity. I remember one of the things that I was told to eat: it was ice-cream. I had no objection to eating ice-cream, especially in summer. How delightful not only to enjoy this dish, but also to feed my imagination with thoughts of its healthfulness and wholesomeness. I could almost see it kindly and blandly and mercifully covering the incipient ulcer with its cool, health-giving substance.

The whole result of this diet was to teach me this trivial amusement, this cult of foods that I imagined to be bland and healthful. It made me think about myself. It was a game, a hobby, something like psychoanalysis had been. I even sometimes fell into the discussion of foods and their values and qualities in relation to health, as if I were an authority on the subject. And for the rest, I went around with my mind in my stomach and ate quarts and quarts of ice-cream.

Now my life was dominated by something I had never really known before: fear. Was it really something altogether new? No, for fear is inseparable from pride and lust. They may hide it for a time: but it is the reverse of the coin. The coin had turned over and I was looking at the other side: the eagle that was to eat out my insides for a year or so, cheap Prometheus that I had become! It was humiliating, this strange wariness that accompanied all my actions, this self-conscious watchfulness. It was a humiliation I had deserved more than I knew. There was more justice in it than I could understand.

I had refused to pay any attention to the moral laws upon which all our vitality and sanity depend: and so now I was reduced to the condition of a silly old woman, worrying about a lot of imaginary rules of health, standards of food-value, and a thousand minute details of conduct that were in themselves completely ridiculous and stupid, and yet which haunted me with vague and terrific sanctions. If I eat this, I may go out of my mind. If I do not eat that, I may die in the night.

I had at last become a true child of the modern world,

completely tangled up in petty and useless concerns with myself, and almost incapable of even considering or understanding anything that was really important to my own true interests.

Here I was, scarcely four years after I had left Oakham and walked out into the world that I thought I was going to ransack and rob of all its pleasures and satisfactions. I had done what I intended, and now I found that it was I who was emptied and robbed and gutted. What a strange thing! In filling myself, I had emptied myself. In grasping things, I had lost everything. In devouring pleasures and joys, I had found distress and anguish and fear. And now, finally, as a piece of poetic justice, when I was reduced to this extremity of misery and humiliation, I fell into a love affair in which I was at last treated in the way I had treated not a few people in these last years.

This girl lived on my own street, and I had the privilege of seeing her drive off with my rivals ten minutes after she had flatly refused to go out with me, asserting that she was tired and wanted to stay home. She did not even bother to conceal the fact that she found me amusing when there was nothing better to occupy her mind. She used to regale me with descriptions of what she considered to be a good time, and of the kind of people she admired and liked—they were precisely the shallow and superficial ones that gave me gooseflesh when I saw them sitting around in the Stork Club. And it was the will of God that for my just punishment I should take all this in the most abject meekness, and sit and beg like some kind of a pet dog until I finally got a pat on the head or some small sign of affection.

This could not last long, and it did not. But I came out of it chastened and abject, though not nearly as abject as I ought to have been, and returned to the almost equal humiliation of my quarts of ice-cream.

Such was the death of the hero, the great man I had wanted to be. Externally (I thought) I was a big success. Everybody knew who I was at Columbia. Those who had not yet found out, soon did when the Yearbook came out, full of pictures of myself. It was enough to tell them more about me than I intended, I suppose. They did not have to be very acute to see through the dumb self-satisfied expression in all those portraits. The only thing that surprises me is that no one openly reproached or mocked me for such ignominious vanity. No one threw any eggs at me, nobody said a word. And yet I know how capable they were of saying many words, not tastefully chosen, perhaps, but deadly enough.

The wounds within me were, I suppose, enough. I was bleeding to death.

If my nature had been more stubborn in clinging to the pleasures that disgusted me: if I had refused to admit that I was beaten by this futile search for satisfaction where it could not be found, and if my moral and nervous constitution had not caved in under the weight of my own emptiness, who can tell what would eventually have happened to me? Who could tell where I would have ended?

I had come very far, to find myself in this blind-alley: but the very anguish and helplessness of my position was something to which I rapidly succumbed. And it was my defeat that was to be the occasion of my rescue.

Part Two

With a Great Price

There is a paradox that lies in the very heart of human existence. It must be apprehended before any lasting happiness is possible in the soul of a man. The paradox is this: man's nature, by itself, can do little or nothing to settle his most important problems. If we follow nothing but our natures, our own philosophies, our own level of ethics, we will end up in hell.

This would be a depressing thought, if it were not purely abstract. Because in the concrete order of things God gave man a nature that was ordered to a supernatural life. He created man with a soul that was made not to bring itself to perfection in its own order, but to be perfected by Him in an order infinitely beyond the reach of human powers. We were never destined to lead purely natural lives, and therefore we were never destined in God's plan for a purely natural beatitude. Our nature, which is a free gift of God, was given to us to be perfected and enhanced by another free gift that is not due it.

This free gift is "sanctifying grace." It perfects our nature with the gift of a life, an intellection, a love, a mode of existence infinitely above its own level. If a man were to arrive even at the abstract pinnacle of natural perfection, God's work would not even be half done: it would be only about to begin, for the real work is the work of grace and the infused virtues and the gifts of the Holy Ghost.

What is "grace"? It is God's own life, shared by us. God's life is Love. *Deus caritas est.* By grace we are able to share in the infinitely self-less love of Him Who is such pure actuality that He needs nothing and therefore cannot conceivably exploit anything for selfish ends. Indeed, outside of Him there is nothing, and whatever exists exists by His free gift of its being, so that one of the notions that is absolutely contradictory to the perfection of God is selfishness. It is meta-physically impossible for God to be selfish, because the existence of everything that is depends upon His gift, depends upon His unselfishness.

When a ray of light strikes a crystal, it gives a new quality to the crystal. And when God's infinitely disinterested love plays upon a human soul, the same kind of thing takes place. And that is the life called sanctifying grace.

The soul of man, left to its own natural level, is a potentially lucid crystal left in darkness. It is perfect in its own nature, but it lacks something that it can only receive from outside and above itself. But when the light shines in it, it becomes in a manner transformed into light and seems to lose its nature in the splendor of a higher nature, the nature of the light that is in it.

So the natural goodness of man, his capacity for love which must always be in some sense selfish if it remains in the natural order, becomes transfigured and transformed when the Love of God shines in it. What happens when a man loses himself completely in the Divine Life within him? This perfection is only for those who are called the saints—for those rather who *are* the saints and who live in the light of God alone. For the ones who are called saints by human opinion on earth may very well be devils, and their light may very well be darkness. For as far as the light of God is concerned, we are owls. It blinds us and as soon as it strikes us we are in darkness. People who look like saints to us are very often not so, and those who do not look like saints very often are. And the greatest saints are sometimes the most obscure —Our Lady, St. Joseph.

Christ established His Church, among other reasons, in order that men might lead one another to Him and in the process sanctify themselves and one another. For in this work it is Christ Who draws us to Himself through the action of our fellow men.

We must check the inspirations that come to us in the depths of our own conscience against the revelation that is given to us with divinely certain guarantees by those who

have inherited in our midst the place of Christ's Apostles—
by those who speak to us in the Name of Christ and as it
were in His own Person. *Qui vos audit me audit; qui vos
spernit, me spernit.*

When it comes to accepting God's own authority about
things that cannot possibly be known in any other way except
as revealed by His authority, people consider it insanity to
incline their ears and listen. Things that cannot be known
in any other way, they will not accept from this source. And
yet they will meekly and passively accept the most appalling
lies from newspapers when they scarcely need to crane their
necks to see the truth in front of them, over the top of the
sheet they are holding in their hands.

For example, the very thought of an *imprimatur* on the
front of a book—the approbation of a bishop, allowing the
book to be printed on the grounds that it contains safe
doctrine—is something that drives some people almost out of
their minds with indignation.

One day, in the month of February 1937, I happened to
have five or ten loose dollars burning a hole in my pocket. I
was on Fifth Avenue, for some reason or other, and was attracted by the window of Scribner's bookstore, all full of
bright new books.

That year I had signed up for a course in French Medieval
Literature. My mind was turning back, in a way, to the things
I remembered from the old days in Saint Antonin. The deep,
naive, rich simplicity of the twelfth and thirteenth centuries
was beginning to speak to me again. I had written a paper on
a legend of a "Jongleur de Notre Dame," compared with a
story from the Fathers of the Desert, in Migne's *Latin Patrol-
ogy*. I was being drawn back into the Catholic atmosphere,
and I could feel the health of it, even in the merely natural
order, working already within me.

Now, in Scribner's window, I saw a book called *The Spirit
of Medieval Philosophy*. I went inside, and took it off the
shelf, and looked at the table of contents and at the title page
which was deceptive, because it said the book was made up
of a series of lectures that had been given at the University

of Aberdeen. That was no recommendation, to me especially. But it threw me off the track as to the possible identity and character of Etienne Gilson, who wrote the book.

I bought it, then, together with one other book that I have completely forgotten, and on my way home in the Long Island train, I unwrapped the package to gloat over my acquisitions. It was only then that I saw, on the first page of *The Spirit of Medieval Philosophy*, the small print which said: "Nihil Obstat . . . Imprimatur."

The feeling of disgust and deception struck me like a knife in the pit of the stomach. I felt as if I had been cheated! They should have warned me that it was a Catholic book! Then I would never have bought it. As it was, I was tempted to throw the thing out the window at the houses of Woodside—to get rid of it as something dangerous and unclean. Such is the terror that is aroused in the enlightened modern mind by a little innocent Latin and the signature of a priest. It is impossible to communicate, to a Catholic, the number and complexity of fearful associations that a little thing like this can carry with it. It is in Latin—a difficult, ancient and obscure tongue. That implies, to the mind that has roots in Protestantism, all kinds of sinister secrets, which the priests are supposed to cherish and to conceal from common men in this unknown language. Then, the mere fact that they should pass judgement on the character of a book, and permit people to read it: that in itself is fraught with terror. It immediately conjures up all the real and imaginary excesses of the Inquisition.

That is something of what I felt when I opened Gilson's book: for you must understand that while I admired Catholic *culture*, I had always been afraid of the Catholic Church. That is a rather common position in the world today. After all, I had not bought a book on medieval philosophy without realizing that it would be Catholic philosophy: but the imprimatur told me that what I read would be in full conformity with that fearsome and mysterious thing, Catholic Dogma, and the fact struck me with an impact against which everything in me reacted with repugnance and fear.

Now in the light of all this, I consider that it was surely a real grace that, instead of getting rid of the book, I actually read it. Not all of it, it is true: but more than I used to read of books that deep. When I think of the numbers of books I had on my shelf in the little room at Douglaston that had once been Pop's "den"—books which I had bought and never even read, I am more astounded than ever at the fact that I actually read this one: and what is more, remembered it.

And the one big concept which I got out of its pages was something that was to revolutionize my whole life. It is all contained in one of those dry, outlandish technical compounds that the scholastic philosophers were so prone to use: the word *aseitas*. In this one word, which can be applied to God alone, and which expresses His most characteristic attribute, I discovered an entirely new concept of God—a concept which showed me at once that the belief of Catholics was by no means the vague and rather superstitious hangover from an unscientific age that I had believed it to be. On the contrary, here was a notion of God that was at the same time deep, precise, simple and accurate and, what is more, charged with implications which I could not even begin to appreciate, but which I could at least dimly estimate, even with my own lack of philosophical training.

Aseitas—the English equivalent is a transliteration: aseity— simply means the power of a being to exist absolutely in virtue of itself, not as caused by itself, but as requiring no cause, no other justification for its existence except that its very nature is to exist. There can be only one such Being: that is God. And to say that God exists *a se*, of and by and by reason of Himself, is merely to say that God is Being Itself. *Ego sum qui sum*. And this means that God must enjoy "complete independence not only as regards everything outside but also as regards everything within Himself."

This notion made such a profound impression on me that I made a pencil note at the top of the page: "Aseity of God— God is being *per se*." I observe it now on the page, for I brought the book to the monastery with me, and although I was not sure where it had gone, I found it on the shelves in Father Abbot's room the other day, and I have it here before me.

I marked three other passages, so perhaps the best thing would be to copy them down. Better than anything I could say, they will convey the impact of the book on my mind.

When God says that He is being [reads the first sentence so marked] and if what He says is to have any intelligible meaning to our minds, it can only mean this: that He is the pure act of existing.

Pure act: therefore excluding all imperfection in the order of existing. Therefore excluding all change, all "becoming," all beginning or end, all limitation. But from this fulness of existence, if I had been capable of considering it deeply enough, I would soon have found that the fulness of all perfection could easily be argued.

But another thing that struck me was an important qualification the author made. He distinguished between the concepts of *ens in genere*—the abstract notion of being in general —and *ens infinitum*, the concrete and real Infinite Being, Who, Himself, transcends all our conceptions. And so I marked the following words, which were to be my first step towards St. John of the Cross:

Beyond all sensible images, and all conceptual determinations, God affirms Himself as the absolute act of being in its pure actuality. Our concept of God, a mere feeble analogue of a reality which overflows it in every direction, can be made explicit only in the judgement: Being is Being, an absolute positing of that which, lying beyond every object, contains in itself the sufficient reason of objects. And that is why we can rightly say that the very excess of positivity which hides the divine being from our eyes is nevertheless the light which lights up all the rest: *ipsa caligo summa est mentis illuminatio*.

His Latin quotation was from St. Bonaventure's *Itinerarium*.

The third sentence of Gilson's that I marked in those few pages read as follows:

When St. Jerome says that God is His own origin and the cause of His own substance, he does not mean, as Descartes does, that God in a certain way posits Himself in being by His almighty power as by a cause, but simply that we must not look outside of God for a cause of the existence of God.

I think the reason why these statements, and others like them, made such a profound impression on me, lay deep in my own soul. And it was this: I had never had an adequate notion of what Christians meant by God. I had simply taken it for granted that the God in Whom religious people believed, and to Whom they attributed the creation and government of all things, was a noisy and dramatic and passionate character, a vague, jealous, hidden being, the objectification of all their own desires and strivings and subjective ideals.

The truth is, that the concept of God which I had always entertained, and which I had accused Christians of teaching to the world, was a concept of a being who was simply impossible. He was infinite and yet finite; perfect and imperfect; eternal and yet changing—subject to all the variations of emotion, love, sorrow, hate, revenge, that men are prey to. How could this fatuous, emotional thing be without beginning and without end, the creator of all? I had taken the dead letter of Scripture at its very deadest, and it had killed me, according to the saying of St. Paul: "The letter killeth, but the spirit giveth life."

I think one cause of my profound satisfaction with what I now read was that God had been vindicated in my own mind. There is in every intellect a natural exigency for a true concept of God: we are born with the thirst to know and to see Him, and therefore it cannot be otherwise.

I know that many people are, or call themselves, "atheists" simply because they are repelled and offended by statements about God made in imaginary and metaphorical terms which they are not able to interpret and comprehend. They refuse these concepts of God, not because they despise God, but perhaps because they demand a notion of Him more perfect than they generally find: and because ordinary, figurative concepts of God could not satisfy them, they turn away and think that there are no other: or, worse still, they refuse to listen to philosophy, on the ground that it is nothing but a web of meaningless words spun together for the justification of the same old hopeless falsehoods.

What a relief it was for me, now, to discover not only that no idea of ours, let alone any sensible image, could delimit the being of God, but also that we *should not* allow ourselves to be satisfied with any such knowledge of Him.

The result was that I at once acquired an immense respect for Catholic philosophy and for the Catholic faith. And that last thing was the most important of all. I now at least recognized that faith was something that had a very definite meaning and a most cogent necessity.

If this much was a great thing, it was about all that I could do at the moment. I could recognize that those who thought about God had a good way of considering Him, and that those who believed in Him really believed in someone, and their faith was more than a dream. Further than that it seemed I could not go, for the time being.

How many there are in the same situation! They stand in the stacks of libraries and turn over the pages of St. Thomas's *Summa* with a kind of curious reverence. They talk in their seminars about "Thomas" and "Scotus" and "Augustine" and "Bonaventure" and they are familiar with Maritain and Gilson, and they have read all the poems of Hopkins—and indeed they know more about what is best in the Catholic literary and philosophical tradition than most Catholics ever do on this earth. They sometimes go to Mass, and wonder at the dignity and restraint of the old liturgy. They are impressed by the organization of a Church in which everywhere the priests, even the most un-gifted, are able to preach at least something of a tremendous, profound, unified doctrine, and to dispense mysteriously efficacious help to all who come to them with troubles and needs.

In a certain sense, these people have a better appreciation of the Church and of Catholicism than many Catholics have: an appreciation which is detached and intellectual and objective. But they never come into the Church. They stand and starve in the doors of the banquet—the banquet to which they surely realize that they are invited—while those more poor, more stupid, less gifted, less educated, sometimes even less virtuous than they, enter in and are filled at those tremendous tables.

When I had put this book down, and had ceased to think explicitly about its arguments, its effect began to show itself in my life. I began to have a desire to go to church—and a desire more sincere and mature and more deep-seated than I had ever had before. After all, I had never before had so great a need.

The only place I could think of was the Episcopal Church down the road, old Zion Church, among the locust trees, where Father had once played the organ. I think the reason for this was that God wanted me to climb back the way I had fallen down. I had come to despise the Church of England, the "Protestant Episcopal Church," and He wanted me to do away with what there was of pride and self-complacency even in that. He would not let me become a Catholic, having behind me a rejection of another church that was not the right kind of a rejection, but one that was sinful in itself, rooted in pride, and expressed in contumely.

This time I came back to Zion Church, not to judge it, not to condemn the poor minister, but to see if it could not do something to satisfy the obscure need for faith that was beginning to make itself felt in my soul.

It was a nice enough church. It was pleasant to sit there, in the pretty little white building, with the sun pouring through the windows, on Sunday mornings. The choir of surpliced men and women and the hymns we all sang did not exactly send me up into ecstasy: but at least I no longer made fun of them in my heart. And when it came time to say the Apostles' Creed, I stood up and said it, with the rest, hoping within myself that God would give me the grace someday to really believe it.

The minister sometimes called at our house. Pop addressed him as "Doctor," to his great embarrassment. He did not put himself forward, by any means, as a doctor of divinity. Nevertheless he had read a great deal and we used to get into conversations about intellectual matters and modern literary trends—even about D. H. Lawrence, with whom he was thoroughly familiar.

It seems that he counted very much on this sort of thing—considered it an essential part of his ministry to keep up with the latest books, and to be able to talk about them, to maintain contact with people by that means. But that was precisely one of the things that made the experience of going to his church such a sterile one for me. He did not like or understand what was considered most "advanced" in modern literature and, as a matter of fact, one did not expect him to; one did not demand that of him. Yet it was modern literature and politics that he talked about, not religion and God. You felt that the man did not know his vocation, did not know what he was supposed to be. He had taken upon himself some function in society which was not his and which was, indeed, not a necessary function at all.

When he did get around to preaching about some truth of the Christian religion, he practically admitted in the pulpit, as he did in private to anyone who cared to talk about it, that he did not believe most of these doctrines, even in the extremely diluted form in which they are handed out to Protestants. The Trinity? What did he want with the Trinity? And as for the strange medieval notions about the Incarnation, well, that was simply too much to ask of a reasonable man.

Once he preached a sermon on "Music at Zion Church" and sent me word that I must be sure to be there, for I would hear him make mention of my father. That is just about typical of Protestant pulpit oratory in the more "liberal" quarters. I went, dutifully, that morning, but before he got around to the part in which I was supposed to be personally interested, I got an attack of my head-spinning and went out into the air. When the sermon was being preached, I was sitting on the church steps in the sun, talking to the black-gowned verger, or whatever he was called. By the time I felt better, the sermon was over.

I cannot say I went to this church very often: but the measure of my zeal may be judged by the fact that I once went even in the middle of the week. I forget what was the occasion: Ash Wednesday or Holy Thursday. There were one or two women in the place, and myself lurking in one of the back benches. We said some prayers. It was soon over. By the time it was, I had worked up courage to take the train into New York and go to Columbia for the day.

ii

Now I come to speak of the real part Columbia seems to have been destined to play in my life in the providential designs of God. Poor Columbia! It was founded by sincere Protestants as a college predominantly religious. The only thing that remains of that is the university motto: *In lumine tuo videbimus lumen*—one of the deepest and most beautiful lines of the psalms. "In Thy light, we shall see light." It is, precisely, about grace. It is a line that might serve as the foundation stone of all Christian and Scholastic learning, and which simply has nothing whatever to do with the standards of education at modern Columbia. It might profitably be changed to *In lumine Randall videbimus Dewey*.

Yet, strangely enough, it was on this big factory of a campus that the Holy Ghost was waiting to show me the light, in His own light. And one of the chief means He used, and through which he operated, was human friendship.

God has willed that we should all depend on one another for our salvation, and all strive together for our own mutual good and our own common salvation. Scripture teaches us that this is especially true in the supernatural order, in the doctrine of the Mystical Body of Christ, which flows necessarily from Christian teaching on grace.

"You are the body of Christ and members one of another. . . . And the eye cannot say to the hand: I need not thy help: nor again the head to the feet, I have no need of you.

217

. . . And if one member suffer anything, all the members suffer with it; and if one member glory all the others rejoice with it."

So now is the time to tell a thing that I could not realize then, but which has become very clear to me: that God brought me and a half a dozen others together at Columbia, and made us friends, in such a way that our friendship would work powerfully to rescue us from the confusion and the misery in which we had come to find ourselves, partly through our own fault, and partly through a complex set of circumstances which might be grouped together under the heading of the "modern world," "modern society." But the qualification "modern" is unnecessary and perhaps unfair. The traditional Gospel term, "the world," will do well enough.

All our salvation begins on the level of common and natural and ordinary things. (That is why the whole economy of the Sacraments, for instance, rests, in its material element, upon plain and ordinary things like bread and wine and water and salt and oil.) And so it was with me. Books and ideas and poems and stories, pictures and music, buildings, cities, places, philosophies were to be the materials on which grace would work. But these things are themselves not enough. The more fundamental instinct of fear for my own preservation came in, in a minor sort of a way, in this strange, half-imaginary sickness which nobody could diagnose completely.

The coming war, and all the uncertainties and confusions and fears that followed necessarily from that, and all the rest of the violence and injustice that were in the world, had a very important part to play. All these things were bound together and fused and vitalized and prepared for the action of grace, both in my own soul and in the souls of at least one or two of my friends, merely by our friendship and association together. And it fermented in our sharing of our own ideas and miseries and headaches and perplexities and fears and difficulties and desires and hangovers and all the rest.

I have already mentioned Mark Van Doren. It would not be exactly true to say that he was a kind of nucleus around whom this concretion of friends formed itself: that would not be accurate. Not all of us took his courses, and those who did, did not do so all at the same time. And yet nevertheless our common respect for Mark's sanity and wisdom did much to make us aware of how much we ourselves had in common.

Perhaps it was for me, personally, more than for the others, that Mark's course worked in this way. I am thinking of one particular incident.

It was the fall of 1936, just at the beginning of the new school year—on one of those first, bright, crazy days when everybody is full of ambition. It was the beginning of the year in which Pop was going to die and my own resistance would cave in under the load of pleasures and ambitions I was too weak to carry: the year in which I would be all the time getting dizzy, and in which I learned to fear the Long Island Railroad as if it were some kind of a monster, and to shrink from New York as if it were the wide-open mouth of some burning Aztec god.

That day, I did not foresee any of this. My veins were still bursting with the materialistic and political enthusiasms with which I had first come to Columbia and, indeed, in line with their general direction, I had signed up for courses that were more or less sociological and economic and historical. In the obscurity of the strange, half-conscious semi-conversion that had attended my retreat from Cambridge, I had tended more and more to be suspicious of literature, poetry—the things towards which my nature drew me—on the grounds that they might lead to a sort of futile estheticism, a philosophy of "escape."

This had not involved me in any depreciation of people like Mark. However, it had just seemed more important to me that I should take some history course, rather than anything that was still left of his for me to take.

So now I was climbing one of the crowded stairways in Hamilton Hall to the room where I thought this history course was to be given. I looked in to the room. The second row was filled with the unbrushed heads of those who every day at noon sat in the *Jester* editorial offices and threw paper airplanes around the room or drew pictures on the walls.

Taller than them all, and more serious, with a long face, like a horse, and a great mane of black hair on top of it, Bob Lax meditated on some incomprehensible woe, and waited for someone to come in and begin to talk to them. It was when I had taken off my coat and put down my load of books that I found out that this was not the class I was supposed to be taking, but Van Doren's course on Shakespeare.

So I got up to go out. But when I got to the door I turned around again and went back and sat down where I had been, and stayed there. Later I went and changed everything with the registrar, so I remained in that class for the rest of the year.

It was the best course I ever had at college. And it did me the most good, in many different ways. It was the only place where I ever heard anything really sensible said about any of the things that were really fundamental—life, death, time, love, sorrow, fear, wisdom, suffering, eternity. A course in literature should never be a course in economics or philosophy or sociology or psychology: and I have explained how it was one of Mark's great virtues that he did not make it so. Nevertheless, the material of literature and especially of drama is chiefly human acts—that is, free acts, moral acts. And, as a matter of fact, literature, drama, poetry, make certain statements about these acts that can be made in no other way. That is precisely why you will miss all the deepest meaning of Shakespeare, Dante, and the rest if you reduce their vital and creative statements about life and men to the dry, matter-of-fact terms of history, or ethics, or some other science. They belong to a different order.

Nevertheless, the great power of something like *Hamlet*, *Coriolanus*, or the *Purgatorio* or Donne's *Holy Sonnets* lies precisely in the fact that they are a kind of commentary on ethics and psychology and even metaphysics, even theology. Or, sometimes, it is the other way 'round, and those sciences can serve as a commentary on these other realities, which we call plays, poems.

All that year we were, in fact, talking about the deepest springs of human desire and hope and fear; we were considering all the most important realities, not indeed in terms of something alien to Shakespeare and to poetry, but precisely in his own terms, with occasional intuitions of another order. And, as I have said, Mark's balanced and sensitive and clear way of seeing things, at once simple and yet capable of subtlety, being fundamentally scholastic, though not necessarily and explicitly Christian, presented these things in ways that made them live within us, and with a life that was healthy and permanent and productive. This class was one of the few things that could persuade me to get on the train and go to Columbia at all. It was, that year, my only health, until I came across and read the Gilson book.

It was this year, too, that I began to discover who Bob Lax was, and that in him was a combination of Mark's clarity and my confusion and misery—and a lot more besides that was his own.

To name Robert Lax in another way, he was a kind of combination of Hamlet and Elias. A potential prophet, but without rage. A king, but a Jew too. A mind full of tremendous and subtle intuitions, and every day he found less and less to say about them, and resigned himself to being inarticulate. In his hesitations, though without embarrassment or nervousness at all, he would often curl his long legs all around a chair, in seven different ways, while he was trying to find a word with which to begin. He talked best sitting on the floor.

And the secret of his constant solidity I think has always been a kind of natural, instinctive spirituality, a kind of inborn direction to the living God. Lax has always been afraid he was in a blind alley, and half aware that, after all, it might not be a blind alley, but God, infinity.

He had a mind naturally disposed, from the very cradle, to a kind of affinity for Job and St. John of the Cross. And I now know that he was born so much of a contemplative that he will probably never be able to find out how much.

To sum it up, even the people who have always thought he was "too impractical" have always tended to venerate him

—in the way people who value material security unconsciously venerate people who do not fear insecurity.

In those days one of the things we had most in common, although perhaps we did not talk about it so much, was the abyss that walked around in front of our feet everywhere we went, and kept making us dizzy and afraid of trains and high buildings. For some reason, Lax developed an implicit trust in all my notions about what was good and bad for mental and physical health, perhaps because I was always very definite in my likes and dislikes. I am afraid it did not do him too much good, though. For even though I had my imaginary abyss, which broadened immeasurably and became ten times dizzier when I had a hangover, my ideas often tended to some particular place where we would hear this particular band and drink this special drink until the place folded up at four o'clock in the morning.

The months passed by, and most of the time I sat in Douglaston, drawing cartoons for the paper-cup business, and trying to do all the other things I was supposed to do. In the summer, Lax went to Europe, and I continued to sit in Douglaston, writing a long stupid novel about a college football player who got mixed up in a lot of strikes in a textile mill.

I did not graduate that June, although I nominally belonged to that year's class: I had still one or two courses to take, on account of having entered Columbia in February. In the fall of 1937 I went back to school, then, with my mind a lot freer, since I was not burdened with any more of those ugly and useless jobs on the Fourth Floor. I could write and do the drawings I felt like doing for *Jester*.

I began to talk more to Lax and to Ed Rice who was now drawing better and funnier pictures than anybody else for the magazine. For the first time I saw Sy Freedgood, who was full of a fierce and complex intellectuality which he sometimes liked to present in the guise of a rather suspicious suavity. He was in love with a far more technical vocabulary than any of the rest of us possessed, and was working at something in the philosophy graduate school. Seymour used consciously to affect a whole set of different kinds of duplicity, of which he was proud, and he had carried the *mendacium jocosum* or "humorous lie" to its utmost extension and frequency. You could sometimes gauge the falsity of his answers by their promptitude: the quicker the falser. The reason for this was, probably, that he was thinking of something else, something very abstruse and far from the sphere of your question, and he could not be bothered to bring his mind all that way back, to think up the real answer.

For Lax and myself and Gibney there was no inconvenience about this, for two reasons. Since Seymour generally gave his false answers only to practical questions of fact, their falsity did not matter: we were all too impractical. Besides his false answers were generally more interesting than the truth. Finally, since we knew they were false anyway, we had the habit of seeing all his statements, in the common factual order by a kind of double standard, instituting a comparison between what he had said and the probable truth, and this cast many interesting and ironical lights upon life as a whole.

In his house at Long Beach, where his whole family lived in a state of turmoil and confusion, there was a large, stupid police dog that got in everybody's way with his bowed head and slapped-down ears and amiable, guilty look. The first time I saw the dog, I asked: "What's his name?"

"Prince," said Seymour, out of the corner of his mouth.

It was a name to which the beast responded gladly. I guess he responded to any name, didn't care what you called him, so flattered was he to be called at all, being as he knew an extremely stupid dog.

So I was out on the boardwalk with the dog, shouting: "Hey, Prince; hey, Prince!"

Seymour's wife, Helen, came along and heard me shouting all this and said nothing, imagining, no doubt, that it was some way I had of making fun of the brute. Later, Seymour or someone told me that "Prince" wasn't the dog's name, but they told me in such a way that I got the idea that his name was really "Rex." So for some time after that I called him: "Hey, Rex; hey, Rex!" Several months later, after many visits to the house, I finally learned that the dog was called nothing like Prince nor Rex, but "Bunky."

Moral theologians say that the *mendacium jocosum* in itself does not exceed a venial sin.

Seymour and Lax were rooming together in one of the dormitories, for Bob Gibney, with whom Lax had roomed the year before, had now graduated, and was sitting in Port Washington with much the same dispositions with which I had been sitting in Douglaston, facing a not too dissimilar blank wall, the end of his own blind-alley. He occasionally came in to town to see Dona Eaton who had a place on 112th Street, but no job, and was more cheerful about her own quandary than the rest of us, because the worst that could happen to her was that she would at last run completely out of money and have to go home to Panama.

Gibney was not what you would call pious. In fact, he had an attitude that would be commonly called impious, only I believe God understood well enough that his violence and sarcasms covered a sense of deep metaphysical dismay—an anguish that was real, though not humble enough to be of much use to his soul. What was materially impiety in him was directed more against common ideas and notions which he saw or considered to be totally inadequate, and maybe it subjectively represented a kind of oblique zeal for the purity of God, this rebellion against the commonplace and trite, against mediocrity, religiosity.

During the year that had passed, I suppose it must have been in the spring of 1937, both Gibney and Lax and Bob Gerdy had all been talking about becoming Catholics. Bob Gerdy was a very smart sophomore with the face of a child and a lot of curly hair on top of it, who took life seriously, and had discovered courses on Scholastic Philosophy in the graduate school, and had taken one of them.

Gibney was interested in Scholastic Philosophy in much the same way as James Joyce was—he respected its intellectuality, particularly that of the Thomists, but there was not enough that was affective about his interest to bring about any kind of a conversion.

For the three or four years that I knew Gibney, he was always holding out for some kind of a "sign," some kind of a sensible and tangible interior jolt from God, to get him started, some mystical experience or other. And while he waited and waited for this to come along, he did all the things that normally exclude and nullify the action of grace. So in those days, none of them became Catholics.

The most serious of them all, in this matter, was Lax: he was the one that had been born with the deepest sense of Who God was. But he would not make a move without the others.

And then there was myself. Having read *The Spirit of Medieval Philosophy* and having discovered that the Catholic conception of God was something tremendously solid, I had not progressed one step beyond this recognition, except that one day I had gone and looked up St. Bernard's *De Diligendo Deo* in the catalogue of the University Library. It was one of the books Gilson had frequently mentioned: but when I found that there was no good copy of it, except in Latin, I did not take it out.

Now it was November 1937. One day, Lax and I were riding downtown on one of those busses you caught at the corner of 110th Street and Broadway. We had skirted the southern edge of Harlem, passing along the top of Central Park, and the dirty lake full of rowboats. Now we were going down Fifth Avenue, under the trees. Lax was telling me about a book he had been reading, which was Aldous Huxley's *Ends and Means*. He told me about it in a way that made me want to read it too.

So I went to Scribner's bookstore and bought it, and read it, and wrote an article about it, and gave the article to Barry Ulanov who was editor of *Review* by that time. He accepted the article with a big Greek smile and printed it. The smile was on account of the conversion it represented, I mean the conversion in me, as well as in Huxley, although one of the points I tried to make was that perhaps Huxley's conversion should not have been taken as so much of a surprise.

Huxley had been one of my favorite novelists in the days

when I had been sixteen and seventeen and had built up a strange, ignorant philosophy of pleasure based on all the stories I was reading. And now everybody was talking about the way Huxley had changed. The chatter was all the more pleasant because of Huxley's agnostic old grandfather—and his biologist brother. Now the man was preaching mysticism.

Huxley was too sharp and intelligent and had too much sense of humor to take any of the missteps that usually make such conversions look ridiculous and oafish. You could not laugh at him, very well—at least not for any one concrete blunder. This was not one of those Oxford Group conversions, complete with a public confession.

On the contrary, he had read widely and deeply and intelligently in all kinds of Christian and Oriental mystical literature, and had come out with the astonishing truth that all this, far from being a mixture of dreams and magic and charlatanism, was very real and very serious.

Not only was there such a thing as a supernatural order, but as a matter of concrete experience, it was accessible, very close at hand, an extremely near, an immediate and most necessary source of moral vitality, and one which could be reached most simply, most readily by prayer, faith, detachment, love.

The point of his title was this: we cannot use evil means to attain a good end. Huxley's chief argument was that we were using the means that precisely made good ends impossible to attain: war, violence, reprisals, rapacity. And he traced our impossibility to use the proper means to the fact that men were immersed in the material and animal urges of an element in their nature which was blind and crude and unspiritual.

The main problem is to fight our way free from subjection to this more or less inferior element, and to reassert the dominance of our mind and will: to vindicate for these faculties, for the spirit as a whole, the freedom of action which it must necessarily have if we are to live like anything but wild beasts, tearing each other to pieces. And the big conclusion from all this was: we must practice prayer and asceticism.

Asceticism! The very thought of such a thing was a complete revolution in my mind. The word had so far stood for a kind of weird and ugly perversion of nature, the masochism of men who had gone crazy in a warped and unjust society. What an idea! To deny the desires of one's flesh, and even to practice certain disciplines that punished and mortified those desires: until this day, these things had never succeeded in giving me anything but gooseflesh. But of course Huxley did not stress the physical angle of mortification and asceticism—and that was right, in so far as he was more interested in striking to the very heart of the matter and showing the ultimate positive principle underlying the need for detachment.

He showed that this negation was not something absolute, sought for its own sake: but that it was a freeing a vindication of our real selves, a liberation of the spirit from limits and bonds that were intolerable, suicidal—from a servitude to flesh that must ultimately destroy our whole nature and society and the world as well.

Not only that, once the spirit was freed, and returned to its own element, it was not alone there: it could find the absolute and perfect Spirit, God. It could enter into union with Him: and what is more, this union was not something vague and metaphorical, but it was a matter of real experience. What that experience amounted to, according to Huxley, might or might not have been the nirvana of the Buddhists, which is the ultimate negation of all experience and all reality whatever: but anyway, somewhere along the line, he quoted proofs that it was and could be a real and positive experience.

The speculative side of the book—its strongest—was full, no doubt, of strange doctrines by reason of its very eclecticism. And the practical element, which was weak, inspired no confidence, especially when he tried to talk about a concrete social program. Huxley seemed not to be at home with the Christian term "Love" which sounded extraordinarily vague in his contexts—and which must nevertheless be the heart and life of all true mysticism. But out of it all I took these two big concepts of a supernatural, spiritual order, and the possibility of real, experimental contact with God.

Huxley was thought, by some people, to be on the point of entering the Church, but *Ends and Means* was written by a man who was not at ease with Catholicism. He quoted St. John of the Cross and St. Teresa of Avila indiscriminately with less orthodox Christian writers like Meister Eckhart: and on the whole he preferred the Orient. It seems to me that in discarding his family's tradition of materialism he had followed the old Protestant groove back into the heresies that make the material creation evil of itself, although I do not remember enough about him to accuse him of formally holding such a thing. Nevertheless, that would account for his sympathy for Buddhism, and for the nihilistic character which he preferred to give to his mysticism and even to his ethics. This also made him suspicious, as the Albigensians had been, and for the same reason, of the Sacraments and Liturgical life of the Church, and also of doctrines like the Incarnation.

With all that I was not concerned. My hatred of war and my own personal misery in my particular situation and the general crisis of the world made me accept with my whole heart this revelation of the need for a spiritual life, an interior life, including some kind of mortification. I was content to accept the latter truth purely as a matter of theory: or at least, to apply it most vociferously to one passion which was not strong in myself, and did not need to be mortified: that of anger, hatred, while neglecting the ones that really needed to be checked, like gluttony and lust.

But the most important effect of the book on me was to make me start ransacking the university library for books on Oriental mysticism.

I remember those winter days, at the end of 1937 and the beginning of 1938, peaceful days when I sat in the big living room at Douglaston, with the pale sun coming in the window by the piano, where one of my father's water-colors of Bermuda hung on the wall.

The house was very quiet, with Pop and Bonnemaman gone from it, and John Paul away trying to pass his courses at Cornell. I sat for hours, with the big quarto volumes of the Jesuit Father Wieger's French translations of hundreds of strange Oriental texts.

I have forgotten the titles, even the authors, and I never understood a word of what they said in the first place. I had the habit of reading fast, without stopping, or stopping only rarely to take a note, and all these mysteries would require a great deal of thought, even were a man who knew something about them to puzzle them out. And I was completely unfamiliar with anything of the kind. Consequently, the strange great jumble of myths and theories and moral aphorisms and elaborate parables made little or no real impression on my mind, except that I put the books down with the impression that mysticism was something very esoteric and complicated, and that we were all inside some huge Being in whom we were involved and out of whom we evolved, and the thing to do was to involve ourselves back in to him again by a system of elaborate disciplines subject more or less to the control of our own will. The Absolute Being was an infinite, timeless, peaceful, impersonal Nothing.

The only practical thing I got out of it was a system for going to sleep, at night, when you couldn't sleep. You lay flat in bed, without a pillow, your arms at your sides and your legs straight out, and relaxed all your muscles, and you said to yourself:

"Now I have no feet, now I have no feet . . . no feet . . . no legs . . . no knees."

Sometimes it really worked: you did manage to make it feel as if your feet and legs and the rest of your body had changed into air and vanished away. The only section with which it almost never worked was my head: and if I had not fallen asleep before I got that far, when I tried to wipe out my head, instantly chest and stomach and legs and feet all came back to life with a most exasperating reality and I did not get to sleep for hours. Usually, however, I managed to get to sleep quite quickly by this trick. I suppose it was a variety of auto-suggestion, a kind of hypnotism, or else simply

229

muscular relaxation, with the help of a little work on the part of an active fancy.

Ultimately, I suppose all Oriental mysticism can be reduced to techniques that do the same thing, but in a far more subtle and advanced fashion: and if that is true, it is not mysticism at all. It remains purely in the natural order. That does not make it evil, *per se*, according to Christian standards: but it does not make it good, in relation to the supernatural. It is simply more or less useless, except when it is mixed up with elements that are strictly diabolical: and then of course these dreams and annihilations are designed to wipe out all vital moral activity, while leaving the personality in control of some nefarious principle, either of his own, or from outside himself.

It was with all this in my mind that I went and received my diploma of Bachelor of Arts from one of the windows in the Registrar's office, and immediately afterwards put my name down for some courses in the Graduate School of English.

The experience of the last year, with the sudden collapse of all my physical energy and the diminution of the brash vigor of my worldly ambitions, had meant that I had turned in terror from the idea of anything so active and uncertain as the newspaper business. This registration in the graduate school represented the first remote step of a retreat from the fight for money and fame, from the active and worldly life of conflict and competition. If anything, I would now be a teacher, and live the rest of my life in the relative peace of a college campus, reading and writing books.

That the influence of the Huxley book had not, by any means, lifted me bodily out of the natural order overnight is evident from the fact that I decided to specialize in eighteenth century English Literature, and to choose my subject for a Master of Arts Thesis from somewhere in that century. As a matter of fact, I had already half decided upon a subject, by the time the last pile of dirty snow had melted from the borders of South Field. It was an unknown novelist of the second half of the eighteenth century called Richard Graves.

The most important thing he wrote was a novel called the *Spiritual Quixote*, which was in the Fielding tradition, a satire on the more excited kind of Methodists and other sects of religious enthusiasts in England at that time.

I was to work under Professor Tyndall, and this would have been just his kind of a subject. He was an agnostic and rationalist who took a deep and amused interest in all the strange perversions of the religious instinct that our world has seen in the last five hundred years. He was just finishing a book on D. H. Lawrence which discussed, not too kindly, Lawrence's attempt to build up a synthetic, home-made religion of his own out of all the semi-pagan spiritual jetsam that came his way. All Lawrence's friends were very much annoyed by it when it was published. I remember that in that year one of Tyndall's favorite topics of conversation was the miracles of Mother Cabrini, who had just been beatified. He was amused by these, too, because, as for all rationalists, it was for him an article of faith that miracles cannot happen.

I remember with what indecision I went on into the spring, trying to settle the problem of a subject with finality. Yet the thing worked itself out quite suddenly: so suddenly that I do not remember what brought it about. One day I came running down out of the Carpenter Library, and passed along the wire fences by the tennis courts, in the sun, with my mind made up that there was only one possible man in the eighteenth century for me to work on: the one poet who had least to do with his age, and was most in opposition to everything it stood for.

I had just had in my hands the small, neatly printed Nonesuch Press edition of the *Poems of William Blake*, and I now knew what my thesis would probably be. It would take in his poems and some aspect of his religious ideas.

In the Columbia bookstore I bought the same edition of Blake, on credit. (I paid for it two years later.) It had a blue cover, and I suppose it is now hidden somewhere in our monastery library, the part to which nobody has access. And that is all right. I think the ordinary Trappist would be only dangerously bewildered by the "Prophetic Books," and those who still might be able to profit by Blake, have a lot of other things to read that are still better. For my own part, I no longer need him. He has done his work for me: and he did it very thoroughly. I hope that I will see him in heaven.

But oh, what a thing it was to live in contact with the genius and the holiness of William Blake that year, that summer, writing the thesis! I had some beginning of an appreciation of his greatness above the other men of his time in England: but from this distance, from the hill where I now stand, looking back I can really appreciate his stature.

To assimilate him to the men of the ending eighteenth century would be absurd. I will not do it: all those conceited and wordy and stuffy little characters! As for the other romantics: how feeble and hysterical their inspirations seem next to the tremendously genuine and spiritual fire of William Blake. Even Coleridge, in the rare moments when his imagination struck the pitch of true creativeness, was still only an artist, an imaginer, not a seer; a maker, but not a prophet.

Perhaps all the great romantics were capable of putting words together more sensibly than Blake, and yet he, with all his mistakes of spelling, turned out the greater poet, because his was the deeper and more solid inspiration. He wrote better poetry when he was twelve than Shelley wrote in his whole life. And it was because at twelve he had already seen, I think, Elias, standing under a tree in the fields south of London.

It was Blake's problem to try and adjust himself to a society that understood neither him nor his kind of faith and love. More than once, smug and inferior minds conceived it to be their duty to take this man Blake in hand and direct and form him, to try and canalize what they recognized as "talent" in some kind of a conventional channel. And always this meant the cold and heartless disparagement of all that was vital and real to him in art and in faith. There were years of all kinds of petty persecution, from many different quarters, until finally Blake parted from his would-be patrons, and gave up all hope of an alliance with a world that thought he was crazy, and went his own way.

It was when he did this, and settled down as an engraver for good, that the Prophetic Books were no longer necessary. In the latter part of his life, having discovered Dante, he came in contact, through him, with Catholicism, which he described as the only religion that really taught the love of God, and his last years were relatively full of peace. He never seems to have felt any desire to hunt out a priest in the England where Catholicism was still practically outlawed: but he died with a blazing face and great songs of joy bursting from his heart.

As Blake worked himself into my system, I became more and more conscious of the necessity of a vital faith, and the total unreality and unsubstantiality of the dead, selfish rationalism which had been freezing my mind and will for the last seven years. By the time the summer was over, I was to become conscious of the fact that the only way to live was to live in a world that was charged with the presence and reality of God.

To say that, is to say a great deal: and I don't want to say it in a way that conveys more than the truth. I will have to limit the statement by saying that it was still, for me, more an intellectual realization than anything else: and it had not yet struck down into the roots of my will. The life of the soul is not knowledge, it is love, since love is the act of the supreme faculty, the will, by which man is formally united to the final end of all his strivings—by which man becomes one with God.

iii

On the door of the room in one of the dormitories, where Lax and Sy Freedgood were living in a state of chaos, was a large grey picture, a lithograph print. Its subject was a man, a Hindu, with wide-open eyes and a rather frightened expression, sitting cross-legged in white garments. I asked about it, and I could not figure out whether the answer was derisive or respectful. Lax said someone had thrown a knife at the picture and the knife had bounced back and nearly cut all their heads off. In other words, he gave me to understand that the picture had something intrinsically holy about it: that accounted for the respect and derision manifested towards it by all my friends. This mixture was their standard acknowledgment of the supernatural, or what was considered to be supernatural. How that picture happened to get on that door in that room is a strange story.

It represented a Hindu messiah, a savior sent to India in our own times, called Jagad-Bondhu. His mission had to do with universal peace and brotherhood. He had died not very long before, and had left a strong following in India. He was, as it were, in the role of a saint who had founded a new religious Order, although he was considered more than a saint: he was the latest incarnation of the godhead, according to the Hindu belief in a multiplicity of incarnations.

In 1932 a big official sort of letter was delivered to one of the monasteries of this new "Order," outside of Calcutta. The letter came from the Chicago World's Fair, which was to be held in the following year. How they ever heard of this monastery, I cannot imagine. The letter was a formal announcement of a "World Congress of Religions." I am writing this all from memory but that is the substance of the story: they invited the abbot of this monastery to send a representative to the congress.

I get this picture of the monastery: it is called Sri Angan, meaning "the Playground." It consists of an enclosure and many huts or "cells," to use an Occidental term. The monks are quiet, simple men. They live what we would call a liturgical life, very closely integrated with the cycle of the seasons and of nature: in fact, the chief characteristic of their worship seems to be this deep, harmonious identification with all living things, in praising God. Their praise itself is expressed in songs, accompanied by drums and primitive instruments, flutes, pipes. There is much ceremonial dancing. In addition to that, there is a profound stress laid on a form of "mental prayer" which is largely contemplative. The monk works himself into it, by softly chanting lyrical aspirations to God and then remains in peaceful absorption in the Absolute.

For the rest, their life is extremely primitive and frugal. It is not so much what we would call austere. I do not think there are any fierce penances or mortifications. But nevertheless, the general level of poverty in Hindu society as a whole imposes on these monks a standard of living which most Occidental religious would probably find unlivable. Their clothes consist of a turban and something thrown around the body and a robe. No shoes. Perhaps the robe is only for travelling. Their food—some rice, a few vegetables, a piece of fruit.

Of all that they do, they attach most importance to prayer, to praising God. They have a well-developed sense of the power and efficacy of prayer, based on a keen realization of the goodness of God. Their whole spirituality is childlike, simple, primitive if you like, close to nature, ingenuous, optimistic, happy. But the point is, although it may be no more than the full flowering of the natural virtue of religion, with the other natural virtues, including a powerful natural charity, still the life of these pagan monks is one of such purity and holiness and peace, in the natural order, that it may put to shame the actual conduct of many Christian religious, in spite of their advantages of constant access to all the means of grace.

So this was the atmosphere into which the letter from Chicago dropped like a heavy stone. The abbot was pleased by the letter. He did not know what the Chicago World's Fair was. He did not understand that all these things were simply schemes for accumulating money. The "World Congress of Religions" appeared to him as something more than the fatuous scheme of a few restless, though probably sincere, minds. He seemed to see in it the first step towards the realization of the hopes of their beloved messiah, Jagad-Bondhu: world peace, universal brotherhood. Perhaps, now, all religions would unite into one great universal religion, and all men would begin to praise God as brothers, instead of tearing each other to pieces.

At any rate, the abbot selected one of his monks and told him that he was to go to Chicago, to the World Congress of Religions.

This was a tremendous assignment. It was something far more terrible than an order given, for instance, to a newly ordained Capuchin to proceed to a mission in India. That would merely be a matter of a trained missionary going off to occupy a place that had been prepared for him. But here was a little man who had been born at the edge of a jungle told to start out from a contemplative monastery and go not only into the world, but into the heart of a civilization the violence and materialism of which he could scarcely evaluate, and which raised gooseflesh on every square inch of his body. What is more, he was told to undertake this journey *without money*. Not that money was prohibited to him, but they simply did not have any. His abbot managed to raise enough to get him a ticket for a little more than half the distance. After that heaven would have to take care of him.

By the time I met this poor little monk who had come to America without money, he had been living in the country for about five years, and had acquired, of all things, the degree of Doctor of Philosophy from the University of Chicago. So that people referred to him as Doctor Bramachari, although I believe that Bramachari is simply a generic Hindu term for monk—and one that might almost be translated: "Little-Brother-Without-the-Degree-of-Doctor."

How he got through all the red tape that stands between America and the penniless traveller is something that I never quite understood. But it seems that officials, after questioning him, being completely overwhelmed by his simplicity, would either do something dishonest in his favor, or else would give him a tip as to how to beat the various technicalities. Some of them even lent him fairly large sums of money. In any case he landed in America.

The only trouble was that he got to Chicago after the World Congress of Religions was all over.

By that time, one look at the Fair buildings, which were already being torn down, told him all he needed to know about the World Congress of Religions. But once he was there, he did not have much trouble. People would see him standing around in the middle of railway stations waiting for

Providence to do something about his plight. They would be intrigued by his turban and white garments (which were partly concealed by a brown overcoat in winter). They observed that he was wearing a pair of sneakers, and perhaps that alone was enough to rouse their curiosity. He was frequently invited to give lectures to religious and social clubs, and to schools and colleges, and he more than once spoke from the pulpits of Protestant churches. In this way he managed to make a living for himself. Besides, he was always being hospitably entertained by people that he met, and he financed the stages of his journey by artlessly leaving his purse lying open on the living room table, at night, before his departure.

The open mouth of the purse spoke eloquently to the hearts of his hosts, saying: "As you see, I am empty," or, perhaps, "As you see, I am down to my last fifteen cents." It was often enough filled up in the morning. He got around.

How did he run into Sy Freedgood? Well, Seymour's wife was studying at Chicago, and she met Bramachari there, and then Seymour met Bramachari, and Bramachari came to Long Beach once or twice, and went out in Seymour's sailboat, and wrote a poem which he gave to Seymour and Helen. He was very happy with Seymour, because he did not have to answer so many stupid questions and, after all, a lot of the people who befriended him were cranks and semi-maniacs and theosophists who thought they had some kind of a claim on him. They wearied him with their eccentricities, although he was a gentle and patient little man. But at Long Beach he was left in peace, although Seymour's ancient grandmother was not easily convinced that he was not the hereditary enemy of the Jewish people. She moved around in the other room, lighting small religious lamps against the intruder.

It was the end of the school year, June 1938, when Lax and Seymour already had a huge box in the middle of the room, which they were beginning to pack with books, when we heard Bramachari was again coming to New York.

I went down to meet him at Grand Central with Seymour, and it was not without a certain suppressed excitement that

I did so, for Seymour had me all primed with a superb selection of lies about Bramachari's ability to float in the air and walk on water. It was a long time before we found him in the crowd, although you would think that a Hindu in a turban and a white robe and a pair of Keds would have been a rather memorable sight. But all the people we asked, concerning such a one, had no idea of having seen him.

We had been looking around for ten or fifteen minutes, when a cat came walking cautiously through the crowd, and passed us by with a kind of a look, and disappeared.

"That's him," said Seymour. "He changed himself into a cat. Doesn't like to attract attention. Looking the place over. Now he knows we're here."

Almost at once, while Seymour was asking a porter if he had seen anything like Bramachari, and the porter was saying no, Bramachari came up behind us.

I saw Seymour swing around and say, in his rare, suave manner:

"Ah, Bramachari, how are you!"

There stood a shy little man, very happy, with a huge smile, all teeth, in the midst of his brown face. And on the top of his head was a yellow turban with Hindu prayers written all over it in red. And, on his feet, sure enough: sneakers.

I shook hands with him, still worrying lest he give me some kind of an electric shock. But he didn't. We rode up to Columbia in the subway, with all the people goggling at us, and I was asking Bramachari about all the colleges he had been visiting. Did he like Smith, did he like Harvard? When we were coming out into the air at 116th Street, I asked him which one he liked best, and he told me that they were all the same to him: it had never occurred to him that one might have any special preference in such things.

I lapsed into a reverent silence and pondered on this thought.

I was now twenty-three years old and, indeed, I was more mature than that in some respects. Surely by now it ought to have dawned on me that places did not especially matter. But no, I was very much attached to places, and had very definite likes and dislikes for localities as such, especially colleges, since I was always thinking of finding one that was altogether pleasant to live and teach in.

After that, I became very fond of Bramachari, and he of me. We got along very well together, especially since he sensed that I was trying to feel my way into a settled religious conviction, and into some kind of a life that was centered, as his was, on God.

The thing that strikes me now is that he never attempted to explain his own religious beliefs to me—except some of the externals of the cult, and that was later on. He would no doubt have told me all I wanted to know, if I had asked him, but I was not curious enough. What was most valuable to me was to hear his evaluation of the society and religious beliefs he had come across in America: and to put all that down on paper would require another book.

He was never sarcastic, never ironical or unkind in his criticisms: in fact he did not make many judgements at all, especially adverse ones. He would simply make statements of fact, and then burst out laughing—his laughter was quiet and ingenuous, and it expressed his complete amazement at the very possibility that people should live the way he saw them living all around him.

He was beyond laughing at the noise and violence of American city life and all the obvious lunacies like radio-programs and billboard advertising. It was some of the well-meaning idealisms that he came across that struck him as funny. And one of the things that struck him as funniest of all was the eagerness with which Protestant ministers used to come up and ask him if India was by now nearly converted to Protestantism. He used to tell us how far India was from conversion to Protestantism—or Catholicism for that matter. One of the chief reasons he gave for the failure of any Christian missionaries to really strike deep into the tremendous populations of Asia was the fact that they maintained themselves on a social level that was too far above the natives. The Church of England, indeed, thought they would convert the Indians by maintaining a strict separation—white men in one church, natives in a different church: both of them listening to sermons on brotherly love and unity.

But all Christian missionaries, according to him, suffered from this big drawback: they lived too well, too comfortably. They took care of themselves in a way that simply made it impossible for the Hindus to regard them as holy—let alone the fact that they ate meat, which made them repugnant to the natives.

I don't know anything about missionaries: but I am sure that, by our own standards of living, their life is an arduous and difficult one, and certainly not one that could be regarded as comfortable. And by comparison with life in Europe and America it represents a tremendous sacrifice. Yet I suppose it would literally endanger their lives if they tried to subsist on the standard of living with which the vast majority of Asiatics have to be content. It seems hard to expect them to go around barefoot and sleep on mats and live in huts. But one thing is certain: the pagans have their own notions of holiness, and it is one that includes a prominent element of asceticism. According to Bramachari, the prevailing impression among the Hindus seems to be that Christians don't know what asceticism means. Of course, he was talking principally of Protestant missionaries, but I suppose it would apply to anyone coming to a tropical climate from one of the so-called "civilized" countries.

For my own part, I see no reason for discouragement. Bramachari was simply saying something that has long since been familiar to readers of the Gospels. Unless the grain of wheat, falling in the ground, die, itself remaineth alone: but if it die, it bringeth forth much fruit. The Hindus are not looking for us to send them men who will build schools and hospitals, although those things are good and useful in themselves—and perhaps very badly needed in India: they want to know if we have any saints to send them.

There is no doubt in my mind that plenty of our missionaries are saints: and that they are capable of becoming greater saints too. And that is all that is needed. And, after all, St. Francis Xavier converted hundreds of thousands of Hindus

240

in the sixteenth century and established Christian societies in Asia strong enough to survive for several centuries without any material support from outside the Catholic world.

Bramachari was not telling me anything I did not know about the Church of England, or about the other Protestant sects he had come in contact with. But I was interested to hear his opinion of the Catholics. They, of course, had not invited him to preach in their pulpits: but he had gone into a few Catholic churches out of curiosity. He told me that these were the only ones in which he really felt that people were praying.

It was only there that religion seemed to have achieved any degree of vitality, among us, as far as he could see. It was only to Catholics that the love of God seemed to be a matter of real concern, something that struck deep in their natures, not merely pious speculation and sentiment.

However, when he described his visit to a big Benedictine monastery in the Mid-West he began to grin again. He said they had showed him a lot of workshops and machinery and printing presses and taken him over the whole "plant" as if they were very wrapped up in all their buildings and enterprises. He got the impression that they were more absorbed in printing and writing and teaching than they were in praying.

Bramachari was not the kind of man to be impressed with such statements as: "There's a quarter of a million dollars' worth of stained glass in this church . . . the organ has got six banks of keys and it contains drums, bells and a mechanical nightingale . . . and the retable is a genuine bas-relief by a real live Italian artist."

The people he had the least respect for were all the borderline cases, the strange, eccentric sects, the Christian Scientists, the Oxford Group and all the rest of them. That was, in a sense, very comforting. Not that I was worried about them: but it confirmed me in my respect for him.

He did not generally put his words in the form of advice: but the one counsel he did give me is something that I will not easily forget: "There are many beautiful mystical books written by the Christians. You should read St. Augustine's *Confessions,* and *The Imitation of Christ."*

Of course I had heard of both of them: but he was speaking as if he took it for granted that most people in America had no idea that such books ever existed. He seemed to feel as if he were in possession of a truth that would come to most Americans as news—as if there was something in their own cultural heritage that they had long since forgotten: and he could remind them of it. He repeated what he had said, not without a certain earnestness:

"Yes, you must read those books."

It was not often that he spoke with this kind of emphasis.

Now that I look back on those days, it seems to me very probable that one of the reasons why God had brought him all the way from India, was that he might say just that.

After all, it is rather ironical that I had turned, spontaneously to the east, in reading about mysticism, as if there were little or nothing in the Christian tradition. I remember that I ploughed through those heavy tomes of Father Wieger's with the feeling that all this represented the highest development of religion on earth. The reason may have been that I came away from Huxley's *Ends and Means* with the prejudice that Christianity was a less pure religion, because it was more "immersed in matter"—that is, because it did not scorn to use a Sacramental liturgy that relied on the appeal of created things to the senses in order to raise the souls of men to higher things.

So now I was told that I ought to turn to the Christian tradition, to St. Augustine—and told by a Hindu monk!

Still, perhaps if he had never given me that piece of advice, I would have ended up in the Fathers of the Church and Scholasticism after all: because a fortunate discovery in the course of my work on my M.A. thesis put me fairly and definitely on that track at last.

That discovery was one book that untied all the knots in the problem which I had set myself to solve by my thesis. It was Jacques Maritain's *Art and Scholasticism.*

The last week of that school year at Columbia had been rather chaotic. Lax and Freedgood had been making futile efforts to get their belongings together and go home. Bramachari was living in their room, perched on top of a pile of books. Lax was trying to finish a novel for Professor Nobbe's course in novel-writing, and all his friends had volunteered to take a section of the book and write it, simultaneously: but in the end the book turned out to be more or less a three-cornered affair—by Lax and me and Dona Eaton. When Nobbe got the thing in his hands he could not figure it out at all, but he gave us a B-minus, with which we were more than satisfied.

Then Lax's mother had come to town to live near him in the last furious weeks before graduation and catch him if he collapsed. He had to take most of his meals in the apartment she had rented in Butler Hall. I sometimes went along and helped him nibble the various health-foods.

At the same time, we were planning to get a ride on an oil barge up the Hudson and the Erie Canal to Buffalo—because Lax's brother-in-law was in the oil business. After that we would go to the town where Lax lived, which was Olean, up in that corner of New York state.

On "Class Day" we leaned out the window of Lax's room and drank a bottle of champagne, looking at the sun on South Field, and watching the people beginning to gather under the trees in front of Hamilton, where we would all presently hear some speeches and shake hands with Nicholas Murray Butler.

It was not my business to graduate that June at all. My graduation was all over when I picked up my degree in the registrar's office last February. However, I borrowed the cap and gown with which Dona Eaton had graduated from Barnard a year before, and went and sat with all the rest, mocking the speeches, with the edge of my sobriety slightly dulled by the celebration that had just taken place with the champagne in Furnald.

Finally we all got up and filed slowly up the rickety wooden steps to the temporary platform to shake hands with all the officials. President Butler was a much smaller man than I had expected. He looked intensely miserable, and murmured something or other to each student, as he shook hands. It was inaudible. I was given to understand that for the past six or seven years people had been in the habit of insulting him, on these occasions, as a kind of a farewell.

I didn't say anything. I just shook his hand, and passed on. The next one I came to was Dean Hawkes who looked up with surprise, from under his bushy white eyebrows, and growled:

"What are *you* doing here, anyway?"

I smiled and passed on.

We did not get the ride on the oil barge, after all, but went to Olean on a train, and for the first time I saw a part of the world in which I was one day going to learn how to be very happy—and that day was not now very far away.

It is the association of that happiness which makes upper New York state seem, in my memory, to be so beautiful. But it is objectively so, there is no doubt of that. Those deep valleys and miles and miles of high, rolling wooded hills: the broad fields, the big red barns, the white farm houses and the peaceful towns: all this looked more and more impressive and fine in the long slanting rays of the sinking sun after we had passed Elmira.

And you began to get some of the feeling of the bigness of America, and to develop a continental sense of the scope of the country and of the vast, clear sky, as the train went on for mile after mile, and hour after hour. And the color, and freshness, and bigness, and richness of the land! The cleanness of it. The wholesomeness. This was new and yet it was old country. It was mellow country. It had been cleared and settled for much more than a hundred years.

When we got out at Olean, we breathed its health and listened to its silence.

I did not stay there for more than a week, being impatient to get back to New York on account of being, as usual, in love.

But one of the things we happened to do was to turn off

the main road, one afternoon on the way to the Indian reservation, to look at the plain brick buildings of a college that was run by the Franciscans.

It was called St. Bonaventure's. Lax had a good feeling about the place. And his mother was always taking courses there, in the evenings—courses in literature from the Friars. He was a good friend of the Father Librarian and liked the library. We drove in to the grounds and stopped by one of the buildings.

But when Lax tried to make me get out of the car, I would not.

"Let's get out of here," I said.

"Why? It's a nice place."

"It's O.K., but let's get out of here. Let's go to the Indian reservation."

"Don't you want to see the library?"

"I can see enough of it from here. Let's get going."

I don't know what was the matter. Perhaps I was scared of the thought of nuns and priests being all around me—the elemental fear of the citizen of hell, in the presence of anything that savors of the religious life, religious vows, official dedication to God through Christ. Too many crosses. Too many holy statues. Too much quiet and cheerfulness. Too much pious optimism. It made me very uncomfortable. I had to flee.

When I got back to New York, one of the first things I did was to break away, at last, from the household in Douglaston. The family had really practically dissolved with the death of my grandparents, and I could get a lot more work done if I did not have to spend so much time on subways and the Long Island train.

One rainy day in June, then, I made a bargain with Herb, the colored taximan at Douglaston, and he drove me and all my bags and books and my portable vic and all my hot records and pictures to put on the wall and even a tennis racquet which I never used, uptown to a rooming-house on 114th Street, just behind the Columbia library.

All the way up we discussed the possible reasons for the mysterious death of Rudolph Valentino, once a famous movie

245

star: but it was certainly not what you would call a live issue. Valentino had died at least ten years before.

"This is a nice spot you got here," said Herb, approving of the room I was renting for seven-fifty a week. It was shiny and clean and filled with new furniture and had a big view of a pile of coal, in a yard by the campus tennis courts, with South Field and the steps of the old domed library beyond. The panorama even took in a couple of trees.

"I guess you're going to have a pretty hot time, now you got away from your folks," Herb remarked, as he took his leave.

Whatever else may have happened in that room, it was also there that I started to pray again more or less regularly, and it was there that I added, as Bramachari had suggested, *The Imitation of Christ* to my books, and it was from there that I was eventually to be driven out by an almost physical push, to go and look for a priest.

July came, with its great, misty heats, and Columbia filled with all the thousands of plump, spectacled ladies in pink dresses, from the Middle-West, and all the grey gents in seersucker suits, all the dried-up high-school principals from Indiana and Kansas and Iowa and Tennessee, with their veins shrivelled up with positivism and all the reactions of the behaviorist flickering behind their spectacles as they meditated on the truths they learned in those sweltering halls.

The books piled higher and higher on my desk in the Graduate reading room and in my own lodgings. I was in the thick of my thesis, making hundreds of mistakes that I would not be able to detect for several years to come, because I was far out of my depth. Fortunately, nobody else detected them either. But for my own part, I was fairly happy, and learning many things. The discipline of the work itself was good for me, and helped to cure me, more than anything else did, of the illusion that my health was poor.

And it was in the middle of all this that I discovered Scholastic philosophy.

The subject I had finally chosen was "Nature and Art in William Blake." I did not realize how providential a subject it actually was! What it amounted to, was a study of Blake's reaction against every kind of literalism and naturalism and narrow, classical realism in art, because of his own ideal which was essentially mystical and supernatural. In other words, the topic, if I treated it at all sensibly, could not help but cure me of all the naturalism and materialism in my own philosophy, besides resolving all the inconsistencies and self-contradictions that had persisted in my mind for years, without my being able to explain them.

After all, from my very childhood, I had understood that the artistic experience, at its highest, was actually a natural analogue of mystical experience. It produced a kind of intuitive perception of reality through a sort of affective identification with the object contemplated—the kind of perception that the Thomists call "connatural." This means simply a knowledge that comes about as it were by the identification of natures: in the way that a chaste man understands the nature of chastity because of the very fact that his soul is full of it—it is a part of his own nature, since habit is second nature. Non-connatural knowledge of chastity would be that of a philosopher who, to borrow the language of the *Imitation*, would be able to define it, but would not possess it.

I had learned from my own father that it was almost blasphemy to regard the function of art as merely to reproduce some kind of a sensible pleasure or, at best, to stir up the emotions to a transitory thrill. I had always understood that art was contemplation, and that it involved the action of the highest faculties of man.

When I was once able to discover the key to Blake, in his rebellion against literalism and naturalism in art, I saw that his Prophetic Books and the rest of his verse at large represented a rebellion against naturalism in the moral order as well.

What a revelation that was! For at sixteen I had imagined that Blake, like the other romantics, was glorifying passion, natural energy, for their own sake. Far from it! What he was glorifying was the transfiguration of man's natural love, his natural powers, in the refining fires of mystical experience: and that, in itself, implied an arduous and total purification,

247

by faith and love and desire, from all the petty materialistic and commonplace and earthly ideals of his rationalistic friends.

Blake, in his sweeping consistency, had developed a moral insight that cut through all the false distinctions of a worldly and interested morality. That was why he saw that, in the legislation of men, some evils had been set up as standards of right by which other evils were to be condemned: and the norms of pride or greed had been established in the judgement seat, to pronounce a crushing and inhuman indictment against all the normal healthy strivings of human nature. Love was outlawed, and became lust, pity was swallowed up in cruelty, and so Blake knew how:

> The harlot's cry from street to street
> Shall weave old England's winding-sheet.

I had heard that cry and that echo. I had seen that winding sheet. But I had understood nothing of all that. I had tried to resolve it into a matter of sociological laws, of economic forces. If I had been able to listen to Blake in those old days, he would have told me that sociology and economics, divorced from faith and charity, become nothing but the chains of his aged, icy demon Urizen! But now, reading Maritain, in connection with Blake, I saw all these difficulties and contradictions disappear.

I, who had always been anti-naturalistic in art, had been a pure naturalist in the moral order. No wonder my soul was sick and torn apart: but now the bleeding wound was drawn together by the notion of Christian virtue, ordered to the union of the soul with God.

The word virtue: what a fate it has had in the last three hundred years! The fact that it is nowhere near so despised and ridiculed in Latin countries is a testimony to the fact that it suffered mostly from the mangling it underwent at the hands of Calvinists and Puritans. In our own days the word leaves on the lips of cynical high-school children a kind of flippant smear, and it is exploited in theaters for the possibilities it offers for lewd and cheesy sarcasm. Everybody makes fun of virtue, which now has, as its primary meaning, an affectation of prudery practiced by hypocrites and the impotent.

When Maritain—who is by no means bothered by such trivialities—in all simplicity went ahead to use the term in its Scholastic sense, and was able to apply it to art, a "virtue of the practical intellect," the very newness of the context was enough to disinfect my mind of all the miasmas left in it by the ordinary prejudice against "virtue" which, if it was ever strong in anybody, was strong in me. I was never a lover of Puritanism. Now at last I came around to the sane conception of virtue—without which there can be no happiness, because virtues are precisely the powers by which we can come to acquire happiness: without them, there can be no joy, because they are the habits which coordinate and canalize our natural energies and direct them to the harmony and perfection and balance, the unity of our nature with itself and with God, which must, in the end, constitute our everlasting peace.

By the time I was ready to begin the actual writing of my thesis, that is, around the beginning of September 1938, the groundwork of conversion was more or less complete. And how easily and sweetly it had all been done, with all the external graces that had been arranged, along my path, by the kind Providence of God! It had taken little more than a year and a half, counting from the time I read Gilson's *The Spirit of Medieval Philosophy* to bring me up from an "atheist"—as I considered myself—to one who accepted all the full range and possibilities of religious experience right up to the highest degree of glory.

I not only accepted all this, intellectually, but now I began to desire it. And not only did I begin to desire it, but I began to do so efficaciously: I began to want to take the necessary means to achieve this union, this peace. I began to desire to dedicate my life to God, to His service. The notion was still vague and obscure, and it was ludicrously impractical in the sense that I was already dreaming of mystical union when I did not even keep the simplest rudiments of the moral law. But nevertheless I was convinced of the reality of the goal, and confident that it could be achieved: and whatever element of presumption was in this confidence I am sure God excused, in His mercy, because of my stupidity and helplessness, and because I was really beginning to be ready to do whatever I thought He wanted me to do to bring me to Him.

But, oh, how blind and weak and sick I was, although I thought I saw where I was going, and half understood the way! How deluded we sometimes are by the clear notions we get out of books. They make us think that we really understand things of which we have no practical knowledge at all. I remember how learnedly and enthusiastically I could talk for hours about mysticism and the experimental knowledge of God, and all the while I was stoking the fires of the argument with Scotch and soda.

That was the way it turned out that Labor Day, for instance. I went to Philadelphia with Joe Roberts, who had a room in the same house as I, and who had been through all the battles on the Fourth Floor of John Jay for the past four years. He had graduated and was working on some trade magazine about women's hats. All one night we sat, with a friend of his, in a big dark roadhouse outside of Philadelphia, arguing and arguing about mysticism, and smoking more and more cigarettes and gradually getting drunk. Eventually, filled with enthusiasm for the purity of heart which begets the vision of God, I went on with them into the city, after the closing of the bars, to a big speak-easy where we completed the work of getting plastered.

My internal contradictions were resolving themselves out, indeed, but still only on the plane of theory, not of practice: not for lack of good-will, but because I was still so completely chained and fettered by my sins and my attachments.

I think that if there is one truth that people need to learn, in the world, especially today, it is this: the intellect is only theoretically independent of desire and appetite in ordinary, actual practice. It is constantly being blinded and perverted by the ends and aims of passion, and the evidence it presents to us with such a show of impartiality and objectivity is fraught with interest and propaganda. We have become marvelous at self-delusion; all the more so, because we have gone to such trouble to convince ourselves of our own absolute infallibility. The desires of the flesh—and by that I mean not only sinful desires, but even the ordinary, normal appetites for comfort and ease and human respect, are fruitful sources of every kind of error and misjudgement, and because we have these yearnings in us, our intellects (which, if they operated all alone in a vacuum, would indeed register with pure impartiality what they saw) present to us everything distorted and accommodated to the norms of our desire.

And therefore, even when we are acting with the best of intentions, and imagine that we are doing great good, we may be actually doing tremendous material harm and contradicting all our good intentions. There are ways that seem to men to be good, the end whereof is in the depths of hell.

The only answer to the problem is grace, grace, docility to grace. I was still in the precarious position of being my own guide and my own interpreter of grace. It is a wonder I ever got to the harbor at all!

Sometime in August, I finally answered an impulse that had been working on me for a long time. Every Sunday, I had been going out on Long Island to spend the day with the same girl who had brought me back in such a hurry from Lax's town Olean. But every week, as Sunday came around, I was filled with a growing desire to stay in the city and go to some kind of a church.

At first, I had vaguely thought I might try to find some Quakers, and go and sit with them. There still remained in me something of the favorable notion about Quakers that I had picked up as a child, and which the reading of William Penn had not been able to overcome.

But, naturally enough, with the work I was doing in the library, a stronger drive began to assert itself, and I was drawn much more imperatively to the Catholic Church. Finally the urge became so strong that I could not resist it. I called up my girl and told her that I was not coming out that week-end, and made up my mind to go to Mass for the first time in my life.

The first time in my life! That was true. I had lived for several years on the continent, I had been to Rome, I had been in and out of a thousand Catholic cathedrals and churches, and yet I had never heard Mass. If anything had ever been going on in the churches I visited, I had always fled, in wild Protestant panic.

I will not easily forget how I felt that day. First, there was this sweet, strong, gentle, clean urge in me which said: "Go to Mass! Go to Mass!" It was something quite new and strange, this voice that seemed to prompt me, this firm, growing interior conviction of what I needed to do. It had a suavity, a simplicity about it that I could not easily account for. And when I gave in to it, it did not exult over me, and trample me down in its raging haste to land on its prey, but it carried me forward serenely and with purposeful direction.

That does not mean that my emotions yielded to it altogether quietly. I was really still a little afraid to go to a Catholic church, of set purpose, with all the other people, and dispose myself in a pew, and lay myself open to the mysterious perils of that strange and powerful thing they called their "Mass."

God made it a very beautiful Sunday. And since it was the first time I had ever really spent a sober Sunday in New York, I was surprised at the clean, quiet atmosphere of the empty streets uptown. The sun was blazing bright. At the end of the street, as I came out the front door, I could see a burst of green, and the blue river and the hills of Jersey on the other side.

Broadway was empty. A solitary trolley came speeding down in front of Barnard College and past the School of Journalism. Then, from the high, grey, expensive tower of the Rockefeller Church, huge bells began to boom. It served very well for the eleven o'clock Mass at the little brick Church of Corpus Christi, hidden behind Teachers College on 121st Street.

How bright the little building seemed. Indeed, it was quite new. The sun shone on the clean bricks. People were going in the wide open door, into the cool darkness and, all at once, all the churches of Italy and France came back to me. The richness and fulness of the atmosphere of Catholicism that I had not been able to avoid apprehending and loving as a child, came back to me with a rush: but now I was to enter into it fully for the first time. So far, I had known nothing but the outward surface.

It was a gay, clean church, with big plain windows and white columns and pilasters and a well-lighted, simple sanctuary. Its style was a trifle eclectic, but much less perverted with incongruities than the average Catholic church in America. It had a kind of a seventeenth-century, oratorian character about it, though with a sort of American colonial tinge of simplicity. The blend was effective and original: but although all this affected me, without my thinking about it, the thing that impressed me most was that the place was full, absolutely full. It was full not only of old ladies and broken-down gentlemen with one foot in the grave, but of men and women and children young and old—especially young: people of all classes, and all ranks on a solid foundation of working-men and -women and their families.

I found a place that I hoped would be obscure, over on one side, in the back, and went to it without genuflecting, and knelt down. As I knelt, the first thing I noticed was a young girl, very pretty too, perhaps fifteen or sixteen, kneeling straight up and praying quite seriously. I was very much impressed to see that someone who was young and beautiful could with such simplicity make prayer the real and serious and principal reason for going to church. She was clearly kneeling that way because she meant it, not in order to show off, and she was praying with an absorption which, though not the deep recollection of a saint, was serious enough to show that she was not thinking at all about the other people who were there.

What a revelation it was, to discover so many ordinary people in a place together, more conscious of God than of one another: not there to show off their hats or their clothes, but to pray, or at least to fulfil a religious obligation, not a human one. For even those who might have been there for no better motive than that they were obliged to be, were at least free from any of the self-conscious and human constraint which is

253

never absent from a Protestant church where people are definitely gathered together as people, as neighbors, and always have at least half an eye for one another, if not all of both eyes.

Since it was summer time, the eleven o'clock Mass was a Low Mass: but I had not come expecting to hear music. Before I knew it, the priest was in the sanctuary with the two altar boys, and was busy at the altar with something or other which I could not see very well, but the people were praying by themselves, and I was engrossed and absorbed in the thing as a whole: the business at the altar and the presence of the people. And still I had not got rid of my fear. Seeing the latecomers hastily genuflecting before entering the pew, I realized my omission, and got the idea that people had spotted me for a pagan and were just waiting for me to miss a few more genuflections before throwing me out or, at least, giving me looks of reproof.

Soon we all stood up. I did not know what it was for. The priest was at the other end of the altar, and, as I afterwards learned, he was reading the Gospel. And then the next thing I knew there was someone in the pulpit.

It was a young priest, perhaps not much over thirty-three or -four years old. His face was rather ascetic and thin, and its asceticism was heightened with a note of intellectuality by his horn-rimmed glasses, although he was only one of the assistants, and he did not consider himself an intellectual, nor did anyone else apparently consider him so. But anyway, that was the impression he made on me: and his sermon, which was simple enough, did not belie it.

It was not long: but to me it was very interesting to hear this young man quietly telling the people in language that was plain, yet tinged with scholastic terminology, about a point in Catholic Doctrine. How clear and solid the doctrine was: for behind those words you felt the full force not only of Scripture but of centuries of a unified and continuous and consistent tradition. And above all, it was a vital tradition: there was nothing studied or antique about it. These words, this terminology, this doctrine, and these convictions fell from the lips of the young priest as something that were most intimately part of his own life. What was more, I sensed that the people were familiar with it all, and that it was also, in due proportion, part of their life also: it was just as much integrated into their spiritual organism as the air they breathed or the food they ate worked in to their blood and flesh.

What was he saying? That Christ was the Son of God. That, in Him, the Second Person of the Holy Trinity, God, had assumed a Human Nature, a Human Body and Soul, and had taken Flesh and dwelt amongst us, full of grace and truth: and that this Man, Whom men called the Christ, was God. He was both Man and God: two Natures hypostatically united in one Person or suppositum, one individual Who was a Divine Person, having assumed to Himself a Human Nature. And His works were the works of God: His acts were the acts of God. He loved us: God, and walked among us: God, and died for us on the Cross, God of God, Light of Light, True God of True God.

Jesus Christ was not simply a man, a good man, a great man, the greatest prophet, a wonderful healer, a saint: He was something that made all such trivial words pale into irrelevance. He was God. But nevertheless He was not merely a spirit without a true body, God hiding under a visionary body: He was also truly a Man, born of the Flesh of the Most Pure Virgin, formed of her Flesh by the Holy Spirit. And what He did, in that Flesh, on earth, He did not only as Man but as God. He loved us as God, He suffered and died for us, God.

And how did we know? Because it was revealed to us in the Scriptures and confirmed by the teaching of the Church and of the powerful unanimity of Catholic Tradition from the First Apostles, from the first Popes and the early Fathers, on down through the Doctors of the Church and the great scholastics, to our own day. *De Fide Divina.* If you believed it, you would receive light to grasp it, to understand it in some measure. If you did not believe it, you would never understand: it would never be anything but scandal or folly.

And no one can believe these things merely by wanting to,

255

of his own volition. Unless he receive grace, an actual light and impulsion of the mind and will from God, he cannot even make an act of living faith. It is God Who gives us faith, and no one cometh to Christ unless the Father draweth him.

I wonder what would have happened in my life if I had been given this grace in the days when I had almost discovered the Divinity of Christ in the ancient mosaics of the churches of Rome. What scores of self-murdering and Christ-murdering sins would have been avoided—all the filth I had plastered upon His image in my soul during those last five years that I had been scourging and crucifying God within me?

It is easy to say, after it all, that God had probably foreseen my infidelities and had never given me the grace in those days because He saw how I would waste and despise it: and perhaps that rejection would have been my ruin. For there is no doubt that one of the reasons why grace is not given to souls is because they have so hardened their wills in greed and cruelty and selfishness that their refusal of it would only harden them more. . . . But now I had been beaten into the semblance of some kind of humility by misery and confusion and perplexity and secret, interior fear, and my ploughed soul was better ground for the reception of good seed.

The sermon was what I most needed to hear that day. When the Mass of the Catechumens was over, I, who was not even a catechumen, but only a blind and deaf and dumb pagan as weak and dirty as anything that ever came out of the darkness of Imperial Rome or Corinth or Ephesus, was not able to understand anything else.

It all became completely mysterious when the attention was re-focussed on the altar. When the silence grew more and more profound, and little bells began to ring, I got scared again and, finally, genuflecting hastily on my left knee, I hurried out of the church in the middle of the most important part of the Mass. But it was just as well. In a way, I suppose I was responding to a kind of liturgical instinct that told me I did not belong there for the celebration of the Mysteries as such. I had no idea what took place in them: but the fact was that Christ, God, would be visibly present on the altar in the

Sacred Species. And although He was there, yes, for love of me: yet He was there in His power and His might, and what was I? What was on my soul? What was I in His sight?

It was liturgically fitting that I should kick myself out at the end of the Mass of the Catechumens, when the ordained *ostiarii* should have been there to do it. Anyway, it was done.

Now I walked leisurely down Broadway in the sun, and my eyes looked about me at a new world. I could not understand what it was that had happened to make me so happy, why I was so much at peace, so content with life for I was not yet used to the clean savor that comes with an actual grace —indeed, there was no impossibility in a person's hearing and believing such a sermon and being justified, that is, receiving sanctifying grace in his soul as a habit, and beginning, from that moment, to live the divine and supernatural life for good and all. But that is something I will not speculate about.

All I know is that I walked in a new world. Even the ugly buildings of Columbia were transfigured in it, and everywhere was peace in these streets designed for violence and noise. Sitting outside the gloomy little Childs restaurant at 111th Street, behind the dirty, boxed bushes, and eating breakfast, was like sitting in the Elysian Fields.

v

My reading became more and more Catholic. I became absorbed in the poetry of Hopkins and in his notebooks—that poetry which had only impressed me a little six years before. Now, too, I was deeply interested in Hopkins' life as a Jesuit. What was that life? What did the Jesuits do? What did a priest do? How did he live? I scarcely knew where to begin to find out about all such things: but they had started to exercise a mysterious attraction over me.

And here is a strange thing. I had by now read James Joyce's *Ulysses* twice or three times. Six years before—on one of those winter vacations in Strasbourg—I had tried to read *Portrait of the Artist* and had bogged down in the part about his spiritual crisis. Something about it had discouraged, bored and depressed me. I did not want to read about such a thing: and I finally dropped it in the middle of the "Mission." Strange to say, sometime during this summer—I think it was before the first time I went to Corpus Christi—I reread *Portrait of the Artist* and was fascinated precisely by that part of the book, by the "Mission," by the priest's sermon on hell. What impressed me was not the fear of hell, but the expertness of the sermon. Now, instead of being repelled by the thought of such preaching—which was perhaps the author's intention—I was stimulated and edified by it. The style in which the priest in the book talked, pleased me by its efficiency and solidity and drive: and once again there was something eminently satisfying in the thought that these Catholics knew what they believed, and knew what to teach, and all taught the same thing, and taught it with coordination and purpose and great effect. It was this that struck me first of all, rather than the actual subject matter of their doctrine— until, that is, I heard the sermon at Corpus Christi.

So then I continued to read Joyce, more and more fascinated by the pictures of priests and Catholic life that came up here and there in his books. That, I am sure, will strike many people as a strange thing indeed. I think Joyce himself was only interested in rebuilding the Dublin he had known as objectively and vitally as he could. He was certainly very alive to all the faults in Irish Catholic society, and he had practically no sympathy left for the Church he had abandoned: but in his intense loyalty to the vocation of artist for which he had abandoned it (and the two vocations are not *per se* irreconcilable: they only became so because of peculiar subjective circumstances in Joyce's own case) he meant to be as accurate as he could in rebuilding his world as it truly was.

Therefore, reading Joyce, I was moving in his Dublin, and breathing the air of its physical and spiritual slums: and it was not the most Catholic side of Dublin that he always painted. But in the background was the Church, and its priests, and its devotions, and the Catholic life in all its gradations, from the Jesuits down to those who barely clung to the hem of the Church's garments. And it was this background that fascinated me now, along with the temper of Thomism that had once been in Joyce himself. If he had abandoned St. Thomas, he had not stepped much further down than Aristotle.

Then, of course, I was reading the metaphysical poets once again—especially Crashaw—and studying his life, too, and his conversion. That meant another avenue which led more or less directly to the Jesuits. So in the late August of 1938, and September of that year, my life began to be surrounded, interiorly, by Jesuits. They were the symbols of my new respect for the vitality and coordination of the Catholic Apostolate. Perhaps, in the back of my mind, was my greatest Jesuit hero: the glorious Father Rothschild of Evelyn Waugh's *Vile Bodies*, who plotted with all the diplomats, and rode away into the night on a motorcycle when everybody else was exhausted.

Yet with all this, I was not yet ready to stand beside the font. There was not even any interior debate as to whether I ought to become a Catholic. I was content to stand by and admire. For the rest, I remember one afternoon, when my girl had come in to town to see me, and we were walking around the streets uptown, I subjected her to the rather disappointing entertainment of going to Union Theological Seminary, and asking for a catalogue of their courses which I proceeded to read while we were walking around on Riverside Drive. She was not openly irritated by it: she was a very good and patient girl anyway. But still you could see she was a little bored, walking around with a man who was not sure whether he ought to enter a theological seminary.

There was nothing very attractive in that catalogue. I was to get much more excited by the article on the Jesuits in the *Catholic Encyclopaedia*—breathless with the thought of so many novitiates and tertianships and what not—so much scrutiny, so much training. What monsters of efficiency they must be, these Jesuits, I kept thinking to myself, as I read and reread the article. And perhaps, from time to time, I tried to picture myself with my face sharpened by asceticism, its pallor intensified by contrast with a black cassock, and every

259

line of it proclaiming a Jesuit saint, a Jesuit master-mind. And I think the master-mind element was one of the strongest features of this obscure attraction.

Apart from this foolishness, I came no nearer to the Church, in practice, than adding a "Hail Mary" to my night prayers. I did not even go to Mass again, at once. The following weekend I went to see my girl once again; it was probably after that that I went on the expedition to Philadelphia. It took something that belongs to history to form and vitalize these resolutions that were still only vague and floating entities in my mind and will.

One of those hot evenings at the end of summer the atmosphere of the city suddenly became terribly tense with some news that came out of the radios. Before I knew what the news was, I began to feel the tension. For I was suddenly aware that the quiet, disparate murmurs of different radios in different houses had imperceptibly merged into one big, ominous unified voice, that moved at you from different directions and followed you down the street, and came to you from another angle as soon as you began to recede from any one of its particular sources.

I heard "Germany—Hitler—at six o'clock this morning the German Army . . . the Nazis . . ." What had they done?

Then Joe Roberts came in and said there was about to be a war. The Germans had occupied Czechoslovakia, and there was bound to be a war.

The city felt as if one of the doors of hell had been half opened, and a blast of its breath had flared out to wither up the spirits of men. And people were loitering around the newsstands in misery.

Joe Roberts and I sat in my room, where there was no radio, until long after midnight, drinking canned beer and smoking cigarettes, and making silly and excited jokes but, within a couple of days, the English Prime Minister had flown in a big hurry to see Hitler and had made a nice new alliance at Munich that cancelled everything that might have caused a war, and returned to England. He alighted at Croydon and came stumbling out of the plane saying "Peace in our time!"

I was very depressed. I was beyond thinking about the intricate and filthy political tangle that underlay the mess. I had given up politics as more or less hopeless, by this time. I was no longer interested in having any opinion about the movement and interplay of forces which were all more or less iniquitous and corrupt, and it was far too laborious and uncertain a business to try and find out some degree of truth and justice in all the loud, artificial claims that were put forward by the various sides.

All I could see was a world in which everybody said they hated war, and in which we were all being rushed into a war with a momentum that was at last getting dizzy enough to affect my stomach. All the internal contradictions of the society in which I lived were at last beginning to converge upon its heart. There could not be much more of a delay in its dismembering. Where would it end? In those days, the future was obscured, blanked out by war as by a dead-end wall. Nobody knew if anyone at all would come out of it alive. Who would be worse off, the civilians or the soldiers? The distinction between their fates was to be abolished, in most countries, by aerial warfare, by all the new planes, by all the marvelous new bombs. What would the end of it be?

I knew that I myself hated war, and all the motives that led to war and were behind wars. But I could see that now my likes or dislikes, beliefs or disbeliefs meant absolutely nothing in the external, political order. I was just an individual, and the individual had ceased to count. I meant nothing, in this world, except that I would probably soon become a number on the list of those to be drafted. I would get a piece of metal with my number on it, to hang around my neck, so as to help out the circulation of red-tape that would necessarily follow the disposal of my remains, and that would be the last eddy of mental activity that would close over my lost identity.

The whole business was so completely unthinkable that my mind, like almost all the other minds that were in the same situation, simply stopped trying to cope with it, and refixed its focus on the ordinary routine of life.

I had my thesis to type out, and a lot of books to read, and I was thinking of preparing an article on Crashaw which perhaps I would send to T. S. Eliot for his *Criterion*. I did not know that *Criterion* had printed its last issue, and that Eliot's reaction to the situation that so depressed me was to fold up his magazine.

The days went on and the radios returned to their separate and individual murmuring, not to be regimented back into their appalling shout for yet another year. September, as I think, must have been more than half gone.

I borrowed Father Leahy's life of Hopkins from the library. It was a rainy day. I had been working in the library in the morning. I had gone to buy a thirty-five-cent lunch at one of those little pious kitchens on Broadway—the one where Professor Gerig, of the graduate school of French, sat daily in silence over a very small table, eating his Brussels sprouts. Later in the afternoon, perhaps about four, I would have to go down to Central Park West and give a Latin lesson to a youth who was sick in bed, and who ordinarily came to the tutoring school run by my landlord, on the ground floor of the house where I lived.

I walked back to my room. The rain was falling gently on the empty tennis courts across the street, and the huge old domed library stood entrenched in its own dreary greyness, arching a cyclops eyebrow at South Field.

I took up the book about Gerard Manley Hopkins. The chapter told of Hopkins at Balliol, at Oxford. He was thinking of becoming a Catholic. He was writing letters to Cardinal Newman (not yet a cardinal) about becoming a Catholic.

All of a sudden, something began to stir within me, something began to push me, to prompt me. It was a movement that spoke like a voice.

"What are you waiting for?" it said. "Why are you sitting here? Why do you still hesitate? You know what you ought to do? Why don't you do it?"

I stirred in the chair, I lit a cigarette, looked out the window at the rain, tried to shut the voice up. "Don't act on impulses," I thought. "This is crazy. This is not rational. Read your book."

Hopkins was writing to Newman, at Birmingham, about his indecision.

"What are you waiting for?" said the voice within me again. "Why are you sitting there? It is useless to hesitate any longer. Why don't you get up and go?"

I got up and walked restlessly around the room. "It's absurd," I thought. "Anyway, Father Ford would not be there at this time of day. I would only be wasting time."

Hopkins had written to Newman, and Newman had replied to him, telling him to come and see him at Birmingham.

Suddenly, I could bear it no longer. I put down the book, and got into my raincoat, and started down the stairs. I went out into the street. I crossed over, and walked along by the grey wooden fence, towards Broadway, in the light rain.

And then everything inside me began to sing—to sing with peace, to sing with strength and to sing with conviction.

I had nine blocks to walk. Then I turned the corner of 121st Street, and the brick church and presbytery were before me. I stood in the doorway and rang the bell and waited.

When the maid opened the door, I said:

"May I see Father Ford, please?"

"But Father Ford is out."

I thought: well, it is not a waste of time, anyway. And I asked when she expected him back. I would come back later, I thought.

The maid closed the door. I stepped back into the street. And then I saw Father Ford coming around the corner from Broadway. He approached, with his head down, in a rapid, thoughtful walk. I went to meet him and said:

"Father, may I speak to you about something?"

"Yes," he said, looking up, surprised. "Yes, sure, come into the house."

We sat in the little parlor by the door. And I said: "Father, I want to become a Catholic."

vi

I came out of the presbytery with three books under my arm. I had hoped that I could begin taking instructions at once, but the pastor had told me to read these books, and pray and think and see how I felt about it in a week or ten days' time. I did not argue with him: but the hesitation that had been in my mind only an hour or so before seemed to have vanished so completely that I was astonished and a little abashed at this delay. So it was arranged that I should come in the evenings, twice a week.

"Father Moore will be your instructor," said the Pastor.

There were four assistants at Corpus Christi, but I guessed that Father Moore was going to be the one whom I had heard preaching the sermon on the divinity of Christ and, as a matter of fact, he was the one who, in the designs of Providence, had been appointed for this work of my salvation.

If people had more appreciation of what it means to be converted from rank, savage paganism, from the spiritual level of a cannibal or of an ancient Roman, to the living faith and to the Church, they would not think of catechism as something trivial or unimportant. Usually the word suggests the matter-of-course instructions that children have to go through before First Communion and Confirmation. Even where it is a matter-of-course, it is one of the most tremendous things in the world, this planting of the word of God in a soul. It takes a conversion to really bring this home.

I was never bored. I never missed an instruction, even when it cost me the sacrifice of some of my old amusements and attractions, which had such a strong hold over me and, while I had been impatient of delay from the moment I had come to that first sudden decision, I now began to burn with desire for Baptism, and to throw out hints and try to determine when I would be received into the Church.

My desire became much greater still, by the end of October, for I made the Mission with the men of the parish, listening twice a day to sermons by two Paulist Fathers and hearing Mass and kneeling at Benediction before the Christ Who was gradually revealing Himself to me.

When the sermon on hell began, I was naturally making mental comparisons with the one in Joyce's *Portrait of the Artist* and reflecting on it in a kind of detached manner, as if I were a third and separate person watching myself hearing

264

this sermon and seeing how it affected me. As a matter of fact this was the sermon which should have done me the most good and did, in fact, do so.

My opinion is that it is a very extraordinary thing for anyone to be upset by such a topic. Why should anyone be shattered by the thought of hell? It is not compulsory for anyone to go there. Those who do, do so by their own choice, and against the will of God, and they can only get into hell by defying and resisting all the work of Providence and grace. It is their own will that takes them there, not God's. In damning them He is only ratifying their own decision—a decision which He has left entirely to their own choice. Nor will He ever hold our weakness alone responsible for our damnation. Our weakness should not terrify us: it is the source of our strength. *Libenter gloriabor in infirmitatibus meis ut inhabitet in me virtus Christi.* Power is made perfect in infirmity, and our very helplessness is all the more potent a claim on that Divine Mercy Who calls to Himself the poor, the little ones, the heavily burdened.

My reaction to the sermon on hell was, indeed, what spiritual writers call "confusion"—but it was not the hectic, emotional confusion that comes from passion and from self-love. It was a sense of quiet sorrow and patient grief at the thought of these tremendous and terrible sufferings which I deserved and into which I stood a very good chance of entering, in my present condition: but at the same time, the magnitude of the punishment gave me a special and particular understanding of the greatness of the evil of sin. But the final result was a great deepening and awakening of my soul, a real increase in spiritual profundity and an advance in faith and love and confidence in God, to Whom alone I could look for salvation from these things. And therefore I all the more earnestly desired Baptism.

I went to Father Moore after the sermon on hell and said that I hoped he was going to baptize me really soon. He laughed, and said that it would not be much longer. By now, it was the beginning of November.

Meanwhile, there had been another thought, half forming

itself in the back of my mind—an obscure desire to become a priest. This was something which I tended to hold separate from the thought of my conversion, and I was doing my best to keep it in the background. I did not mention it either to Father Ford or Father Moore, for the chief reason that in my mind it constituted a kind of admission that I was taking the thought more seriously than I wanted to—it almost amounted to a first step towards application for admission to a seminary.

However, it is a strange thing: there was also in my mind a kind of half-formed conviction that there was one other person I should consult about becoming a priest before I took the matter to the rectory. This man was a layman, and someone I had never yet seen, and it was altogether strange that I should be inclined so spontaneously to put the matter up to him, as if he were the only logical one to give me advice. In the end, he was the one I first consulted—I mean, the one from whom I first seriously asked advice, for I had long been talking about it to my friends, before I came around to him.

This man was Daniel Walsh, about whom I had heard a great deal from Lax and Gerdy. Gerdy had taken his course on St. Thomas Aquinas in the graduate school of Philosophy: and now as the new school year began, my attention centered upon this one course. It had nothing directly to do with my preparation for the exams for the M.A. degree in January. By now degrees and everything else to do with a university career had become very unimportant in comparison with the one big thing that occupied my mind and all my desires.

I registered for the course, and Dan Walsh turned out to be another one of those destined in a providential way to shape and direct my vocation. For it was he who pointed out my way to the place where I now am.

When I was writing about Columbia and its professors, I was not thinking of Dan Walsh: and he really did not belong to Columbia at all. He was on the faculty of the Sacred Heart College at Manhattanville, and came to Columbia twice a week to lecture on St. Thomas and Duns Scotus. His class was a small one and was, as far as Columbia was concerned, pretty much of an academic by-path. And that was in a sense an additional recommendation—it was off that broad and noisy highway of pragmatism which leads between its banks of artificial flowers to the gates of despair.

Walsh himself had nothing of the supercilious self-assurance of the ordinary professor: he did not need this frail and artificial armor for his own insufficiency. He did not need to hide behind tricks and vanities any more than Mark Van Doren did; he never even needed to be brilliant. In his smiling simplicity he used to efface himself entirely in the solid and powerful mind of St. Thomas. Whatever brilliance he allowed himself to show forth in his lectures was all thrown back upon its source, the Angel of the Schools.

Dan Walsh had been a student and collaborator of Gilson's and knew Gilson and Maritain well. In fact, later on he introduced me to Maritain at the Catholic Book Club, where this most saintly philosopher had been giving a talk on Catholic Action. I only spoke a few conventional words to Maritain, but the impression you got from this gentle, stooping Frenchman with much grey hair, was one of tremendous kindness and simplicity and godliness. And that was enough: you did not need to talk to him. I came away feeling very comforted that there was such a person in the world, and confident that he would include me in some way in his prayers.

But Dan himself had caught a tremendous amount of this simplicity and gentleness and godliness too: and perhaps the impression that he made was all the more forceful because his square jaw had a kind of potential toughness about it. Yet no: there he sat, this little, stocky man, who had something of the appearance of a good-natured prize fighter, smiling and talking with the most childlike delight and cherubic simplicity about the *Summa Theologica*.

His voice was low and, as he spoke, he half apologetically searched the faces of his hearers for signs of understanding and, when he found it, he seemed surprised and delighted.

I very quickly made friends with him, and told him all about my thesis and the ideas I was trying to work with, and he was very pleased. And one of the things he sensed at once

267

was something that I was far from being able to realize: but it was that the bent of my mind was essentially "Augustinian." I had not yet followed Bramachari's advice to read St. Augustine and I did not take Dan's evaluation of my ideas as having all the directive force that was potentially in it—for it did not even come clothed in suggestion or advice.

Of course, to be called "Augustinian" by a Thomist might not in every case be a compliment. But coming from Dan Walsh, who was a true Catholic philosopher, it was a compliment indeed.

For he, like Gilson, had the most rare and admirable virtue of being able to rise above the petty differences of schools and systems, and seeing Catholic philosophy in its wholeness, in its variegated unity, and in its true Catholicity. In other words, he was able to study St. Thomas and St. Bonaventure and Duns Scotus side by side, and to see them as complementing and reinforcing one another, as throwing diverse and individual light on the same truths from different points of view, and thus he avoided the evil of narrowing and restricting Catholic philosophy and theology to a single school, to a single attitude, a single system.

I pray to God that there may be raised up more like him in the Church and in our universities, because there is something stifling and intellectually deadening about textbooks that confine themselves to giving a superficial survey of the field of philosophy according to Thomist principles and then discard all the rest in a few controversial objections. Indeed, I think it a great shame and a danger of no small proportions, that Catholic philosophers should be trained in division against one another, and brought up to the bitterness and smallness of controversy: because this is bound to narrow their views and dry up the unction that should vivify all philosophy in their souls.

Therefore, to be called an "Augustinian" by Dan Walsh was a compliment, in spite of the traditional opposition between the Thomist and Augustinian schools, Augustinian being taken not as confined to the philosophers of that religious order, but as embracing all the intellectual descendants of St.

Augustine. It is a great compliment to find oneself numbered as part of the same spiritual heritage as St. Anselm, St. Bernard, St. Bonaventure, Hugh and Richard of St. Victor, and Duns Scotus also. And from the tenor of his course, I realized that he meant that my bent was not so much towards the intellectual, dialectical, speculative character of Thomism, as towards the spiritual, mystical, voluntaristic and practical way of St. Augustine and his followers.

His course and his friendship were most valuable in preparing me for the step I was about to take. But as time went on, I decided to leave the notion of becoming a priest out of the way for the time being. So I never even mentioned it to Dan in those days.

As November began, my mind was taken up with this one thought: of getting baptized and entering at last into the supernatural life of the Church. In spite of all my studying and all my reading and all my talking, I was still infinitely poor and wretched in my appreciation of what was about to take place within me. I was about to set foot on the shore at the foot of the high, seven-circled mountain of a Purgatory steeper and more arduous than I was able to imagine, and I was not at all aware of the climbing I was about to have to do.

The essential thing was to begin the climb. Baptism was that beginning, and a most generous one, on the part of God. For, although I was baptized conditionally, I hope that His mercy swallowed up all the guilt and temporal punishment of my twenty-three black years of sin in the waters of the font, and allowed me a new start. But my human nature, my weakness, and the cast of my evil habits still remained to be fought and overcome.

Towards the end of the first week in November, Father Moore told me I would be baptized on the sixteenth. I walked out of the rectory that evening happier and more contented than I had ever been in my life. I looked at a calendar to see what saint had that day for a feast, and it was marked for St. Gertrude.

It was only in the last days before being liberated from my

slavery to death, that I had the grace to feel something of my own weakness and helplessness. It was not a very vivid light that was given to me on the subject: but I was really aware, at last, of what a poor and miserable thing I was. On the night of the fifteenth of November, the eve of my Baptism and First Communion, I lay in my bed awake and timorous for fear that something might go wrong the next day. And to humiliate me still further, as I lay there, fear came over me that I might not be able to keep the eucharistic fast. It only meant going from midnight to ten o'clock without drinking any water or taking any food, yet all of a sudden this little act of self-denial which amounts to no more, in reality, than a sort of an abstract token, a gesture of good-will, grew in my imagination until it seemed to be utterly beyond my strength—as if I were about to go without food and drink for ten days, instead of ten hours. I had enough sense left to realize that this was one of those curious psychological reactions with which our nature, not without help from the devil, tries to confuse us and avoid what reason and our will demand of it, and so I forgot about it all and went to sleep.

In the morning, when I got up, having forgotten to ask Father Moore if washing your teeth was against the eucharistic fast or not, I did not wash them, and, facing a similar problem about cigarettes, I resisted the temptation to smoke.

I went downstairs and out into the street to go to my happy execution and rebirth.

The sky was bright and cold. The river glittered like steel. There was a clean wind in the street. It was one of those fall days full of life and triumph, made for great beginnings, and yet I was not altogether exalted: for there were still in my mind these vague, half animal apprehensions about the externals of what was to happen in the church—would my mouth be so dry that I could not swallow the Host? If that happened, what would I do? I did not know.

Gerdy joined me as I was turning in to Broadway. I do not remember whether Ed Rice caught up with us on Broadway or not. Lax and Seymour came after we were in church.

Ed Rice was my godfather. He was the only Catholic among

us—the only Catholic among all my close friends. Lax, Seymour, and Gerdy were Jews. They were very quiet, and so was I. Rice was the only one who was not cowed or embarrassed or shy.

The whole thing was very simple. First of all, I knelt at the altar of Our Lady where Father Moore received my abjuration of heresy and schism. Then we went to the baptistery, in a little dark corner by the main door.

I stood at the threshold.

"Quid Petis ab ecclesia Dei?" asked Father Moore.

"Fidem!"

"Fides quid tibi praestat?"

"Vitam aeternam."

Then the young priest began to pray in Latin, looking earnestly and calmly at the page of the *Rituale* through the lenses of his glasses. And I, who was asking for eternal life, stood and watched him, catching a word of the Latin here and there.

He turned to me:

"Abrenuntias Satanae?"

In a triple vow I renounced Satan and his pomps and his works.

"Dost thou believe in God the Father almighty, Creator of heaven and earth?"

"Credo!"

"Dost thou believe in Jesus Christ His only Son, Who was born, and suffered?"

"Credo!"

"Dost thou believe in the Holy Spirit, in the Holy Catholic Church, the Communion of saints, the remission of sins, the resurrection of the body and eternal life?"

"Credo!"

What mountains were falling from my shoulders! What scales of dark night were peeling off my intellect, to let in the inward vision of God and His truth! But I was absorbed in the liturgy, and waiting for the next ceremony. It had been one of the things that had rather frightened me—or rather, which frightened the legion that had been living in me for twenty-three years.

Now the priest blew into my face. He said: "*Exi ab eo, spiritus immunde*: Depart from him, thou impure spirit, and give place to the Holy Spirit, the Paraclete."

It was the exorcism. I did not see them leaving, but there must have been more than seven of them. I had never been able to count them. Would they ever come back? Would that terrible threat of Christ be fulfilled, that threat about the man whose house was clean and garnished, only to be reoccupied by the first devil and many others worse than himself?

The priest, and Christ in him—for it was Christ that was doing these things through his visible ministry, in the Sacrament of my purification—breathed again into my face.

"Thomas, receive the good Spirit through this breathing, and receive the Blessing of God. Peace be with thee."

Then he began again to pray, and sign me with Crosses, and presently came the salt which he put on my tongue—the salt of wisdom, that I might have the savor of divine things, and finally he poured the water on my head, and named me Thomas, "if thou be not already baptized."

After that, I went into the confessional, where one of the other assistants was waiting for me. I knelt in the shadows. Through the dark, close-meshed wire of the grille between us, I saw Father McGough, his head bowed, and resting on his hand, inclining his ear towards me. "Poor man," I thought. He seemed very young and he had always looked so innocent to me that I wondered how he was going to identify and understand the things I was about to tell him.

But one by one, that is, species by species, as best I could, I tore out all those sins by their roots, like teeth. Some of them were hard, but I did it quickly, doing the best I could to approximate the number of times all these things had happened—there was no counting them, only guessing.

I did not have any time to feel how relieved I was when I came stumbling out, as I had to go down to the front of the church where Father Moore would see me and come out to begin his—and my—Mass. But ever since that day, I have loved confessionals.

Now he was at the altar, in his white vestments, opening the book. I was kneeling right at the altar rail. The bright sanctuary was all mine. I could hear the murmur of the priest's voice, and the responses of the server, and it did not matter that I had no one to look at, so that I could tell when to stand up and kneel down again, for I was still not very sure of these ordinary ceremonies. But when the little bells were rung I knew what was happening. And I saw the raised Host—the silence and simplicity with which Christ once again triumphed, raised up, drawing all things to Himself—drawing me to Himself.

Presently the priest's voice was louder, saying the *Pater Noster*. Then, soon, the server was running through the *Confiteor* in a rapid murmur. That was for me. Father Moore turned around and made a big cross in absolution, and held up the little Host.

"Behold the Lamb of God: behold Him Who taketh away the sins of the world."

And my First Communion began to come towards me, down the steps. I was the only one at the altar rail. Heaven was entirely mine—that Heaven in which sharing makes no division or diminution. But this solitariness was a kind of reminder of the singleness with which this Christ, hidden in the small Host, was giving Himself for me, and to me, and, with Himself, the entire Godhead and Trinity—a great new increase of the power and grasp of their indwelling that had begun only a few minutes before at the font.

I left the altar rail and went back to the pew where the others were kneeling like four shadows, four unrealities, and I hid my face in my hands.

In the Temple of God that I had just become, the One Eternal and Pure Sacrifice was offered up to the God dwelling in me: the sacrifice of God to God, and me sacrificed together with God, incorporated in His Incarnation. Christ born in me, a new Bethlehem, and sacrificed in me, His new Calvary, and risen in me: offering me to the Father, in Himself, asking the Father, my Father and His, to receive me into His infinite and special love—not the love He has for all things that exist—for mere existence is a token of God's love, but the love of those creatures who are drawn to Him in and with the power of His own love for Himself.

For now I had entered into the everlasting movement of that gravitation which is the very life and spirit of God: God's own gravitation towards the depths of His own infinite nature, His goodness without end. And God, that center Who is everywhere, and whose circumference is nowhere, finding me, through incorporation with Christ, incorporated into this immense and tremendous gravitational movement which is love, which is the Holy Spirit, loved me.

And He called out to me from His own immense depths.

2

The Waters of Contradiction

How beautiful and how terrible are the words with which God speaks to the soul of those He has called to Himself, and to the Promised Land which is participation in His own life —that lovely and fertile country which is the life of grace and glory, the interior life, the mystical life. They are words lovely to those who hear and obey them: but what are they to those who hear them without understanding or response?

For the Land which thou goest to possess is not like the land of Egypt from whence thou camest out where, when the seed is sown, waters are brought in to water it after the manner of gardens. But it is a land of hills and plains, expecting rain from heaven.

And the Lord thy God doth always visit it, and His eyes are on it from the beginning of the year unto the end thereof.

If then you obey my commandments, which I command you this day, that you love the Lord your God and serve Him with all your heart, and with all your soul:

He will give to your land the early rain and the latter rain, that you may gather in your corn, and your wine, and your oil, and your hay out of the fields to feed your cattle, and that you may eat and be filled.

Beware lest perhaps your heart be deceived and you depart from the Lord and serve strange Gods and adore them: and the Lord being angry shut up heaven and the rain come not down, nor the earth yield her fruit, and you perish quickly from the excellent land which the Lord will give you . . .

I had come, like the Jews, through the Red Sea of Baptism. I was entering into a desert—a terribly easy and convenient desert, with all the trials tempered to my weakness—where I would have a chance to give God great glory by simply trusting and obeying Him, and walking in the way that was not according to my own nature and my own judgement. And it would lead me to a land I could not imagine or understand. It would be a land that was not like the land of Egypt from which I had come out: the land of human nature blinded and fettered by perversity and sin. It would be a land in which the work of man's hands and man's ingenuity counted for little or nothing: but where God would direct all things, and where I would be expected to act so much and so closely under His guidance that it would be as if He thought with my mind, as if He willed with my will.

It was to this that I was called. It was for this that I had been created. It was for this Christ had died on the Cross, and for this that I was now baptized, and had within me the living Christ, melting me into Himself in the fires of His love.

This was the call that came to me with my Baptism, bringing with it a most appalling responsibility if I failed to answer it. Yet, in a certain sense, it was almost impossible for me to hear and answer it. Perhaps it demanded a kind of miracle of grace for me to answer it at once, spontaneously and with complete fidelity—and, oh, what a thing it would have been if I had done so!

For it was certainly true that the door into immense realms was opened to me on that day. And that was something I could not help realizing however obscurely and vaguely. The realization, indeed, was so remote and negative that it only came to me by way of contrast with the triviality and bathos of normal human experience—the talk of my friends, the aspect of the city, and the fact that every step down Broadway took me further and further into the abyss of anticlimax.

Father Moore had caught us just as we were going out the door and rushed us into the rectory for breakfast, and that was a good thing. It had something of the character of my good Mother, the Church, rejoicing at having found her lost groat. We all sat around the table and there was nothing incongruous about the happiness I then felt at all this gaiety, because charity cannot be incongruous with itself: and certainly everybody was glad at what had been done, first of all myself and Father Moore, and then, in different degrees, Lax, Gerdy, Seymour and Rice.

But after that we went out, and discovered that we had nowhere to go: this irruption of the supernatural had upset the whole tenor of a normal, natural day.

It was after eleven o'clock, and nearly time for lunch, and we had just had breakfast. How could we have lunch? And if, at twelve o'clock, we did not have lunch, what was there for us to do?

And then once and for all, the voice that was within me spoke again, and I looked once again into the door which I could not understand, into the country that was meaningless because it was too full of meanings that I could never grasp. "The land which thou goest to possess is not like the land of Egypt from whence thou camest out . . . For my thoughts are not your thoughts, nor your ways my ways, saith the Lord . . . Seek the Lord while He may be found, call upon Him while He is near . . . Why do you spend money for that which is not bread and your labor for that which doth not satisfy you?"

I heard all this, and yet somehow I seemed not to be able to grasp or understand it. Perhaps, in a way, there was a kind of moral impossibility of my doing what I should have done, because I simply did not yet know what it was to pray, to make sacrifices, to give up the world, to lead what is called the supernatural life. What were the things I should have done and that it could not even occur to me to do?

I should have begun at once, in the first place, to go to Communion every day. That did occur to me, but at first I thought that was not generally done. Besides I believed you had to go to confession every time you wanted to go to Communion. Of course, the simple way out of that would have been to keep going to Father Moore and asking him questions.

277

That was the second thing I should have done: I should have sought constant and complete spiritual direction. Six weeks of instructions, after all, were not much, and I certainly had nothing but the barest rudiments of knowledge about the actual practice of Catholic life, and if I had not made the absolutely tragic assumption that now my period of training was finished and done with, I would not have made such a mess of that first year after my Baptism. Probably the very worst thing I could have done was to hesitate about asking questions that occurred to me, and to have been too ashamed of my weakness to approach Father Moore about the real, fundamental needs of my soul.

Direction was the thing I most needed, and which I was least solicitous to avail myself of. And as far as I remember I only got around to asking Father Moore some trivial questions—what was a scapular, what was the difference between a breviary and a missal, and where could I get a missal?

The idea of the priesthood had been put aside, for the time being. I had good enough motives for doing so: it was too soon, perhaps, to think of that. Nevertheless, when I ceased to think of myself explicitly as a possible candidate for a high and arduous and special vocation in the Church, I tended automatically to slacken my will and to relax my vigilance, and to order my acts to nothing but an ordinary life. I needed a high ideal, a difficult aim, and the priesthood provided me with one. And there were many concrete factors in this. If I were going to enter a seminary or a monastery some day, I would have to begin to acquire some of the habits of religious or seminarians—to live more quietly, to give up so many amusements and such worldliness, and to be very careful to avoid things that threatened to provoke my passions to their old riot.

But without this ideal, I was in real and constant danger of carelessness and indifference, and the truth is, that after receiving the immense grace of Baptism, after all the struggles of persuasion and conversion, and after all the long way I had come, through so much of the no-man's land that lies around the confines of hell, instead of becoming a strong and ardent and generous Catholic, I simply slipped into the ranks of the millions of tepid and dull and sluggish and indifferent Christians who live a life that is still half animal, and who barely put up a struggle to keep the breath of grace alive in their souls.

I should have begun to pray, really pray. I had read books all about mysticism, and what is more, at the moment of Baptism, had I but known it, the real mystical life—the life of sanctifying grace and the infused theological virtues and the gifts of the Holy Ghost—was laid open to me in all its fulness: I had only to enter in to it and help myself, and I would soon have advanced rapidly in prayer. But I did not. I did not even know what was ordinary mental prayer, and I was quite capable of practicing that from the start: but what is even worse, it was four or five months before I even learned how to say the Rosary properly, although I had one and used occasionally to say the *Paters* and *Aves* without knowing what else was required.

One of the big defects of my spiritual life in that first year was a lack of devotion to the Mother of God. I believed in the truths which the Church teaches about Our Lady, and I said the "Hail Mary" when I prayed, but that is not enough. People do not realize the tremendous power of the Blessed Virgin. They do not know who she is: that it is through her hands all graces come because God has willed that she thus participate in His work for the salvation of men.

To me, in those days, although I believed in her, Our Lady occupied in my life little more than the place of a beautiful myth—for in practice I gave her no more than the kind of attention one gives to a symbol or a thing of poetry. She was the Virgin who stood in the doors of the medieval cathedrals. She was the one I had seen in all the statues in the Musée de Cluny, and whose pictures, for that matter, had decorated the walls of my study at Oakham.

But that is not the place that belongs to Mary in the lives of men. She is the Mother of Christ still, His Mother in our souls. She is the Mother of the supernatural life in us.

Sanctity comes to us through her intercession. God has willed that there be no other way.

But I did not have that sense of dependence or of her power. I did not know what need I had of trust in her. I had to find out by experience.

What could I do without love of the Mother of God, without a clear and lofty spiritual objective, without spiritual direction, without daily Communion, without a life of prayer? But the one thing I needed most of all was a sense of the supernatural life, and systematic mortification of my passions and of my crazy nature.

I made the terrible mistake of entering upon the Christian life as if it were merely the natural life invested with a kind of supernatural mode by grace. I thought that all I had to do was to continue living as I had lived before, thinking and acting as I did before, with the one exception of avoiding mortal sin.

It never occurred to me that if I continued to live as I had lived before, I would be simply incapable of avoiding mortal sin. For before my Baptism I had lived for myself alone. I had lived for the satisfaction of my own desires and ambitions, for pleasure and comfort and reputation and success. Baptism had brought with it the obligation to reduce all my natural appetites to subordination to God's will: "For the wisdom of the flesh is an enemy to God: for it is not subject to the law of God, neither can it be. And they who are in the flesh, cannot please God . . . and if you live according to the flesh, you shall die: but if by the Spirit you mortify the deeds of the flesh, you shall live. For whosoever are led by the Spirit of God, they are the sons of God." *Spiritu ambulate, et desideria carnis non perficietis.*

St. Thomas explains the words of the Epistle to the Romans very clearly and simply. The wisdom of the flesh is a judgement that the ordinary ends of our natural appetites are the goods to which the *whole of man's life* are to be ordered. Therefore it inevitably inclines the will to violate God's law.

In so far as men are prepared to prefer their own will to

280

God's will, they can be said to hate God: for of course they cannot hate Him in Himself. But they hate Him in the Commandments which they violate. But God is our life: God's will is our food, our meat, our life's bread. To hate our life is to enter into death, and therefore the prudence of the flesh is death.

The only thing that saved me was my ignorance. Because in actual fact, since my life after my Baptism was pretty much what it had been before Baptism, I was in the condition of those who despise God by loving the world and their own flesh rather than Him. And because that was where my heart lay, I was bound to fall into mortal sin, because almost everything that I did tended, by virtue of my habitual intention to please myself before all else, to obstruct and deaden the work of grace in my soul.

But I did not clearly realize all this. Because of the profound and complete conversion of my intellect, I thought I was entirely converted. Because I believed in God, and in the teachings of the Church, and was prepared to sit up all night arguing about them with all comers, I imagined that I was even a zealous Christian.

But the conversion of the intellect is not enough. And as long as the will, the *domina voluntas*, did not belong completely to God, even the intellectual conversion was bound to remain precarious and indefinite. For although the will cannot force the intellect to see an object other than it is, it can turn it away from the object altogether, and prevent it from considering that thing at all.

Where was my will? "Where your treasure is, there will your heart be also," and I had not laid up any treasures for myself in heaven. They were all on earth. I wanted to be a writer, a poet, a critic, a professor. I wanted to enjoy all kinds of pleasures of the intellect and of the senses and in order to have these pleasures I did not hesitate to place myself in situations which I knew would end in spiritual disaster—although generally I was so blinded by my own appetites that I never even clearly considered this fact until it was too late, and the damage was done.

Of course, as far as my ambitions went, their objects were all right in themselves. There is nothing wrong in being a writer or a poet—at least I hope there is not: but the harm lies in wanting to be one for the gratification of one's own ambitions, and merely in order to bring oneself up to the level demanded by his own internal self-idolatry. Because I was writing for myself and for the world, the things I wrote were rank with the passions and selfishness and sin from which they sprang. An evil tree brings forth evil fruits, when it brings forth fruit at all.

I went to Mass, of course, not merely every Sunday, but sometimes during the week as well. I was never long from the Sacraments—usually I went to confession and Communion if not every week, every fortnight. I did a fair amount of reading that might be called "spiritual," although I did not read spiritually. I devoured books making notes here and there and remembering whatever I thought would be useful in an argument—that is, for my own aggrandizement, in order that I myself might take these things and shine by their light, as if their truth belonged to me. And I occasionally made a visit to a church in the afternoons, to pray or do the Stations of the Cross.

All this would have been enough for an ordinary Catholic, with a lifetime of faithful practice of his religion behind him: but for me it could not possibly be enough. A man who has just come out of the hospital, having nearly died there, and having been cut to pieces on an operating table, cannot immediately begin to lead the life of an ordinary working man. And after the spiritual mangle I have gone through, it will never be possible for me to do without the sacraments daily, and without much prayer and penance and meditation and mortification.

It took me time to find it out: but I write down what I have found out at last, so that anyone who is now in the position that I was in then may read it and know what to do to save himself from great peril and unhappiness. And to such a one I would say: Whoever you are, the land to which God has brought you is not like the land of Egypt from which

282

you came out. You can no longer live here as you lived there. Your old life and your former ways are crucified now, and you must not seek to live any more for your own gratification, but give up your own judgement into the hands of a wise director, and sacrifice your pleasures and comforts for the love of God and give the money you no longer spend on those things, to the poor.

Above all, eat your daily Bread without which you cannot live, and come to know Christ Whose Life feeds you in the Host, and He will give you a taste of joys and delights that transcend anything you have ever experienced before, and which will make the transition easy.

ii

The first morning of 1939 was a grey morning. It was to turn out a grey year—very grey. But now a cold wind was blowing in off the sea, where I walked, among the white empty houses to the naked place where stands the church of St. Ignatius Martyr. The wind did something to help me to wake up, but it did not improve my temper much. The new year was beginning badly.

The night before being New Year's Eve, we had had a party in the house of Seymour's mother-in-law, who was a doctor, in Long Beach. It had been a mixed-up, desultory affair, in which we remained in a place that served as the doctor's waiting-room, sitting on the floor, playing different kinds of drums and drinking I forget what. But whatever it was we drank it put me in a bad temper.

The only person in the place not more or less fed up with everything was Bramachari, who had taken his turban off and sat in a chair and did not mind the noise. Later on, however, John Slate, who was also in a bad mood, having had a tooth torn out of his head, tried to tie me up in Bramachari's turban so the monk quietly went home—that is, to Seymour's house —and slept.

Later on, I threw a can of pineapple juice at a street light and also went to bed. I was sleeping in the same room with

Bramachari, and consequently when it began to get light, he sat up and started chanting his morning prayers and I woke up. Since I could not get back to sleep even when his prayers trailed off into contemplation, I was going to an earlier Mass than I had expected. But it was a good thing. As usual, I found out that the only good thing about such days, or any other days, was Mass.

What a strange thing that I did not see how much that meant, and come at last to the realization that it was God alone I was supposed to live for, God that was supposed to be the center of my life and of all that I did.

It was to take me nearly a year to untangle that truth from all my disorganized and futile desires: and sometimes it seems to me that the hangovers I had while I was finding it out had something to do with what was going on in the history of the world.

For that was to be 1939, the year when the war that everybody had been fearing finally began to teach us with its inexorable logic that the dread of war is not enough. If you don't want the effect, do something to remove the causes. There is no use loving the cause and fearing the effect and being surprised when the effect inevitably follows the cause.

By this time, I should have acquired enough sense to realize that the cause of wars is sin. If I had accepted the gift of sanctity that had been put in my hands when I stood by the font in November 1938, what might have happened in the world? People have no idea what one saint can do: for sanctity is stronger than the whole of hell. The saints are full of Christ in the plenitude of His Kingly and Divine power: and they are conscious of it, and they give themselves to Him, that He may exercise His power through their smallest and seemingly most insignificant acts, for the salvation of the world.

But the world did not get very much of that out of me.

The end of January came. I remember, when I took my exams for the M.A., I went to Communion two days in a row, and both days I was very happy, and also I did quite well in the examinations. So after that I thought it was necessary for me to go to Bermuda for a week, and sit in the sun, and go swimming, and ride bicycles along those empty white roads, rediscovering the sights and smells that had belonged to a year of my early childhood. I met a lot of people who liked to ride around all night in a carriage singing: "Someone's in the kitchen with Dinah—strumming on the old banjo." The weather was so good that I came back to New York brown and full of health, with my pocket full of snapshots of the strangers with whom I had been dancing and sailing in yachts. And I was just in time to see Bramachari leave for India, at last, on the *Rex*. He was sailing with the Cardinals who were off to elect the new Pope.

Then I went to Greenwich Village and signed a lease for a one-room apartment and started work on my Ph.D. I suppose the apartment on Perry Street was part of the atmosphere appropriate to an intellectual such as I imagined myself to be and, as a matter of fact, I felt much more important in this large room with a bath and fireplace and French windows leading out on to a rickety balcony than I had felt in the little place ten feet wide behind the Columbia Library. Besides, I now had a shiny new telephone all my own which rang with a deep, discreet, murmuring sort of a bell as if to invite me suavely to expensive and sophisticated pursuits.

I don't, as a matter of fact, remember anything very important happening over that telephone, except that I used to make dates with a nurse who was stationed in one of the clinics out at the World's Fair which opened that year on Flushing Meadows. Also, it was the occasion of a series of furiously sarcastic letters to the telephone company because of various kinds of troubles, mechanical and financial.

The one I most talked to, over this phone, was Lax. He had a phone which did not even cost him anything, for he was living in the Hotel Taft, tutoring the children of the manager, and having access to an icebox full of cold chicken at all hours of the day and night. The two principal items of news which he communicated to me, from his point of vantage, were, first, the appearance of Joyce's *Finnegans Wake* and, second, the election of Pope Pius XII.

It was one of those first spring mornings when the new, warm sun is full of all kinds of delights, that I heard about the Pope. I had been sitting on the balcony in a pair of blue dungarees, drinking Coca-Cola, and getting the sun. When I say sitting on the balcony, I mean sitting on the good boards and letting my feet dangle through the place where the boards had broken. This was what I did a great deal of the time, in the mornings, that spring: surveying Perry Street from the east, where it ran up short against a block of brick apartments, to the west, where it ended at the river, and you could see the black funnels of the Anchor liners.

When I wasn't sitting on this balcony doing nothing, I was in the room, in the deepest armchair, studying the letters of Gerard Manley Hopkins and his Notebooks and trying to figure out various manuals on prosody and covering little white index cards with notes. For it was my plan to write a Ph.D. dissertation on Hopkins.

The typewriter that was always open on the desk was sometimes busy when I got a book to review: for I had been doing occasional reviews for the Sunday book sections of the *Times* and *Herald Tribune*. But what was better, I sometimes managed to grind out, with labor and anguish, some kind of a poem.

I had never been able to write verse before I became a Catholic. I had tried, but I had never really succeeded, and it was impossible to keep alive enough ambition to go on trying. I had started once or twice at Oakham, and I had written two or three miserable things at Cambridge. At Columbia, when I thought I was a Red, I got one stupid idea for a poem, about workers working on a dock and bombing planes flying overhead—you know: ominous. When it got on paper it was so silly that not even the magazines on the Fourth Floor would print it. The only other verse I had ever been able to turn out before my Baptism was an occasional line for the *Jester*.

In November 1938, I acquired a sudden facility for rough, raw Skeltonic verses—and that lasted about a month, and died. They were not much, but one of them took a prize which it did not deserve. But now I had many kinds of sounds ringing in my ears and they sometimes asked to get on paper. When their rhythms and tones followed Andrew Marvell, the results were best. I always liked Marvell; he did not mean as much to me as Donne or Crashaw (when Crashaw wrote well) but nevertheless there was something about his temper for which I felt a special personal attraction. His moods were more clearly my own than Crashaw's or even Donne's.

When I lived on Perry Street, it was hard to write poems. The lines came slow, and when it was all done, there were very few of them. They were generally rhymed iambic tetrameter, and because I was uneasy with any rhyme that sounded hackneyed, rhyming was awkward and sometimes strange.

I would get an idea, and walk around the streets, among the warehouses, towards the poultry market at the foot of Twelfth Street, and I would go out on the Chicken Dock trying to work out four lines of verse in my head, and sit in the sun. And after I had looked at the fireboats and the old empty barges and the other loafers and the Stevens Institute on its bluff across the river in Hoboken, I would write the poem down on a piece of scrap paper and go home and type it out.

I usually sent it at once to some magazine. How many envelopes I fed to the green mailbox at the corner of Perry Street just before you got to Seventh Avenue! And everything I put in there came back—except for the book reviews.

The more I failed, the more I was convinced that it was important for me to have my work printed in magazines like the *Southern Review* or *Partisan Review* or the *New Yorker*. My chief concern was now to see myself in print. It was as if I could not be quite satisfied that I was real until I could feed my ambition with these trivial glories, and my ancient selfishness was now matured and concentrated in this desire to see myself externalized in a public and printed and official self which I could admire at my ease. This was what I really believed in: reputation, success. I wanted to live in the eyes and the mouths and the minds of men. I was not so crude that I wanted to be known and admired by the whole world: there

287

was a certain naive satisfaction in the idea of being only appreciated by a particular minority, which gave a special fascination to this urge within me. But when my mind was absorbed in all that, how could I lead a supernatural life, the life to which I was called? How could I love God, when everything I did was done not for Him but for myself, and not trusting in His aid, but relying on my own wisdom and talents?

Lax rebuked me for all this. His whole attitude about writing was purified of such stupidity, and was steeped in holiness, in charity, in disinterestedness. Characteristically he conceived the function of those who knew how to write, and who had something to say, in terms of the salvation of society. Lax's picture of America—before which he has stood for twelve years with his hands hanging in helplessness at his sides—is the picture of a country full of people who want to be kind and pleasant and happy and love good things and serve God, but do not know how. And they do not know where to turn to find out. They are surrounded by all kinds of sources of information which only conspire to bewilder them more and more. And Lax's vision is a vision of the day when they will turn on the radio and somebody will start telling them what they have really been wanting to hear and needing to know. They will find somebody who is capable of telling them of the love of God in language that will no longer sound hackneyed or crazy, but with authority and conviction: the conviction born of sanctity.

I am not sure whether this conception of his necessarily implied a specific vocation, a definite and particular mission: but in any case, he assumed that it was the sort of thing that should be open to me, to Gibney, to Seymour, to Mark Van Doren, to some writers he admired, perhaps even to somebody who did not know how to talk, but could only play a trumpet or a piano. And it was open to himself also: but for himself, he was definitely waiting to be "sent."

In any case, although I had gone before him to the fountains of grace, Lax was much wiser than I, and had clearer vision, and was, in fact, corresponding much more truly to the grace of God than I, and he had seen what was the only important thing. I think he has told what he had to say to many people besides myself: but certainly his was one of the voices through which the insistent Spirit of God was determined to teach me the way I had to travel.

Therefore, another one of those times that turned out to be historical, as far as my own soul is concerned, was when Lax and I were walking down Sixth Avenue, one night in the spring. The street was all torn up and trenched and banked high with dirt and marked out with red lanterns where they were digging the subway, and we picked our way along the fronts of the dark little stores, going downtown to Greenwich Village. I forget what we were arguing about, but in the end Lax suddenly turned around and asked me the question:

"What do you want to be, anyway?"

I could not say, "I want to be Thomas Merton the well-known writer of all those book reviews in the back pages of the *Times Book Review*," or "Thomas Merton the assistant instructor of Freshman English at the New Life Social Institute for Progress and Culture," so I put the thing on the spiritual plane, where I knew it belonged and said:

"I don't know; I guess what I want is to be a good Catholic."

"What do you mean, you want to be a good Catholic?"

The explanation I gave was lame enough, and expressed my confusion, and betrayed how little I had really thought about it at all.

Lax did not accept it.

"What you should say"—he told me—"what you should say is that you want to be a saint."

A saint! The thought struck me as a little weird. I said:

"How do you expect me to become a saint?"

"By wanting to," said Lax, simply.

"I can't be a saint," I said, "I can't be a saint." And my mind darkened with a confusion of realities and unrealities: the knowledge of my own sins, and the false humility which makes men say that they cannot do the things that they *must* do, cannot reach the level that they *must* reach: the cowardice that says: "I am satisfied to save my soul, to keep out

289

of mortal sin," but which means, by those words: "I do not want to give up my sins and my attachments."

But Lax said: "No. All that is necessary to be a saint is to want to be one. Don't you believe that God will make you what He created you to be, if you will consent to let Him do it? All you have to do is desire it."

A long time ago, St. Thomas Aquinas had said the same thing—and it is something that is obvious to everybody who ever understood the Gospels. After Lax was gone, I thought about it, and it became obvious to me.

The next day I told Mark Van Doren:

"Lax is going around saying that all a man needs to be a saint is to want to be one."

"Of course," said Mark.

All these people were much better Christians than I. They understood God better than I. What was I doing? Why was I so slow, so mixed up, still, so uncertain in my directions and so insecure?

So at great cost I bought the first volume of the Works of St. John of the Cross and sat in the room on Perry Street and turned over the first pages, underlining places here and there with a pencil. But it turned out that it would take more than that to make me a saint: because these words I underlined, although they amazed and dazzled me with their import, were all too simple for me to understand. They were too naked, too stripped of all duplicity and compromise for my complexity, perverted by many appetites. However, I am glad that I was at least able to recognize them, obscurely, as worthy of the greatest respect.

iii

When the summer came I sub-let the apartment on Perry Street to Seymour's wife and went up-state, into the hills behind Olean. Lax's brother-in-law had a cottage, on top of a hill, from which you could see miles over New York and Pennsylvania—miles of blue hill-tops and wooded ridges, miles of forest smudged here and there, in the dry weeks, with smoke, and gashed open, in the neighboring valley, by the lumbermen. All day and all night the silence of the wood was broken by the coughing of oil-pumps, and when you passed through the trees you could see long metal arms moving back and forth clumsily in the shadows of the glade, because the hills were full of oil.

So Benjie, Lax's brother-in-law, gave us this place, and let us live there, trusting more than he should have in our ability to live in a house for more than a week without partially destroying it.

Lax and I and Rice moved in to the cottage, and looked around for places to put our typewriters. There was one big room with a huge stone fireplace and the works of Rabelais and a table which we presently ruined, feeding ourselves on it with hamburgers and canned beans and untold quarts of milk. There was a porch which looked out over the hills and where we eventually erected a trapeze. It was very pleasant to sit on the step of this porch, and look at the valley in the quiet evening, and play the drums. We had a pair of *bongós*, a Cuban double-drum, which is played two-handed and gives several different tones, depending where and how you hit it.

In order to make sure we would have plenty of books, we went down to the library at St. Bonaventure's College where this time, being baptized, I was no longer scared of the Friars. The librarian was Father Irenaeus, who looked up at us through his glasses and recognized Lax with ingenuous surprise. He always seemed to be surprised and glad to see everybody. Lax introduced us to him: "This is Ed Rice, this is Tom Merton."

"Ah! Mr. Rice. . . . Mr. Myrtle." Father Irenaeus took us both in, with the eyes of a rather bookish child, and shook hands without embarrassment.

"Merton," said Lax, "Tom Merton."

"Yes, glad to know you, Mr. Myrtle," said Father Irenaeus.

"They were at Columbia too," said Lax.

"Ah, Columbia," said Father Irenaeus. "I studied at the Columbia Library School," and then he took us into his own library and with reckless trust abandoned all the shelves to us.

It never occurred to him to place any limit upon the appetites of those who seemed to like books. If they wanted books, well, this was a library. He had plenty of books, that was what a library was for. You could take as many as you liked, and keep them until you were through: he was astonishingly free of red tape, this happy little Franciscan. When I got to know the Friars a little better, I found out that this trait was fairly universal. Those who love rigid and methodical systems have their life of penance all cut out for them if they enter the Franciscans, and especially if they become superiors. But as far as I know, Father Irenaeus has never been robbed of his books on a larger scale than any other librarian, and on the whole, the little library at St. Bonaventure's was always one of the most orderly and peaceful I have ever seen.

Presently we came out of the stacks with our arms full.

"May we take all these, Father?"

"Sure, sure, that's fine, help yourself."

We signed a vague sort of a ticket, and shook hands.

"Good-bye, Mr. Myrtle," said the Friar, and stood in the open door and folded his hands as we started down the steps with our spoils.

I still did not know that I had discovered a place where I was going to find out something about happiness.

The books we took back to the cottage were hardly opened all summer: but anyway, they were there, lying around, in case we needed something to read. But really they were not necessary: for we eventually found places that proved very suitable for our typewriters, and all started writing novels. Rice wrote a novel called *The Blue Horse*. It took him about ten days. It was about a hundred and fifty pages long, illustrated. Lax wrote several fragments of novels which presently coalesced into one called *The Spangled Palace*. But the thing I got started on grew longer and longer and longer and eventually it was about five hundred pages long, and was called first *Straits of Dover* and then *The Night Before the Battle*, and then *The Labyrinth*. In its final form, it was shorter, and had been half rewritten, and it went to several publishers but to my great sorrow never got printed—at least I was sorry about it in those days, but now I am full of self-congratulation at the fact that those pages escaped the press.

It was partly autobiographical, and therefore it took in some of the ground that this present book had covered: but it took in much more of the ground that I have avoided covering this time. Besides, I found the writing of it easier and more amusing if I mixed up a lot of imaginary characters in my own story. It is a pleasant way to write. When the truth got dull, I could create a diversion with a silly man called Terence Metrotone. I later changed him to Terence Park, after I showed the first draft of the book to my uncle, who abashed me by concluding that Terence Metrotone was a kind of an acrostic for myself. That was, as a matter of fact, very humiliating, because I had made such a fool of the character.

The mere pleasure of sitting on top of this wooded mountain, with miles of country and cloudless sky to look at, and birds to listen to all day, and the healthy activity of writing page after page of novel, out under a tree facing the garage, made those weeks happy ones, in a natural sort of a way.

We could have made even more of it than we did. I think we all had a sort of a feeling that we could be hermits up on that hill: but the trouble was that none of us really knew how and I, who was in a way the most articulate, as well as the least sensible, whenever it came to matters of conduct and decisions concerning good and evil, still had the strongest urges to go down into the valleys and see what was on at the movies, or play the slot machines, or drink beer.

The best we could do about expressing our obscure desire of living lives that were separate and in some sense dedicated was to allow our beards to grow, which they did more or less slowly. Lax ended up with the best. It was black and solemn. Rice's was rather ragged, but it looked fine when he grinned, because he had big teeth and slanting eyes like an Eskimo. I myself entertained the secret belief that I looked like Shakespeare. I was still wearing the thing when I went to New York, later, and I took it to the World's Fair. I was standing thus bearded in a side-show that had something to do with Africa, and a young man who was not an explorer, but wore a

293

white explorer's outfit, took me to be indeed an explorer because of the beard. Or at least he plied me with some knowing questions about central Africa. I think we were both trading on our knowledge of that wonderful movie, *Dark Rapture*.

The cottage would have made a good hermitage, and I now wish we had more exploited its possibilities. Lax was the only one who had the sense to get up, sometimes, very early in the morning, about sunrise. For my own part I usually slept until about eight, then fried a couple of eggs and swallowed a bowl of cornflakes and started at once to write. The closest I got to using the solitude for meditation was when I spent a few afternoons under a little peach tree in the high grass of what might have been a lawn, and read, at last, St. Augustine's *Confessions* and parts of St. Thomas's *Summa*.

I had accepted Lax's principle about sanctity being possible to those who willed it, and filed it away in my head with all my other principles—and still I did nothing about using it. What was this curse that was on me, that I could not translate belief into action, and my knowledge of God into a concrete campaign for possessing Him, Whom I knew to be the only true good? No, I was content to speculate and argue: and I think the reason is that my knowledge was too much a mere matter of natural and intellectual consideration. After all, Aristotle placed the highest natural felicity in the knowledge of God which was accessible to him, a pagan: and I think he was probably right. The heights that can be reached by metaphysical speculation introduce a man into a realm of pure and subtle pleasure that offers the most nearly permanent delights you can find in the natural order. When you go one step higher, and base your speculations on premises that are revealed, the pleasure gets deeper and more perfect still. Yet even though the subject matter may be the mysteries of the Christian faith, the manner of contemplating them, speculative and impersonal, may still not transcend the natural plane, at least as far as practical consequences go.

In such an event, you get, not contemplation, but a kind of intellectual and esthetic gluttony—a high and refined and even virtuous form of selfishness. And when it leads to no movement of the will towards God, no efficacious love of Him, it is sterile and dead, this meditation, and could even accidentally become, under certain circumstances, a kind of a sin—at least an imperfection.

Experience has taught me one big moral principle, which is this: it is totally impractical to plan your actions on the basis of a vast two-columned list of possibilities, with mortal sins on one side and things that are "not a mortal sin" on the other—the one to be avoided, the other to be accepted without discussion.

Yet this hopelessly misleading division of possibilities is what serves large numbers of Catholics as a whole moral theology. It is not so bad when they are so busy working for a living that the range of possibilities is more or less cut down and determined: but Heaven help them when they go on their vacation, or when Saturday night comes around.

Incomplete drunkenness is *per se* a venial sin. Therefore apply the two-column principle. You run your finger down the column of mortal sins *per se*. Going to a movie in which a man and woman maul each other at close range for hundreds of feet of film is not a mortal sin *per se*. Neither is incomplete drunkenness, nor gambling and so on. Therefore all these belong to the order of pursuits which are not illicit. Therefore they are licit. Therefore if anyone says, no matter with what qualifications, that you ought *not* to do these things—he is a heretic. If people are not careful, they get themselves into the position of arguing that it is virtuous to go to the movies, to gamble, to get half-drunk . . .

I know what I am talking about, because that was the way I was still trying to live in those days. Do you want to see the two-column principle in operation? Here is an example of a lot of things which were not mortal sins in themselves. What they were *per accidens* I am afraid to say: I leave them up to the mercy of God; but they were done by one whom He was calling to a life of perfection, a life dedicated to the joy of serving and loving Him alone . . .

A carnival came to Bradford. To us that meant a couple of Ferris wheels and a bingo game and the "Whip" and a man wearing a white uniform and a crash helmet being fired out of a cannon into a net. We got into the car and started out along the Rock City Road, through the dark woods alive with the drumming of the oil pumps.

It was a big carnival. It seemed to fill the bottom of a narrow valley, one of the zig-zag valleys in which Bradford is hidden, and the place blazed with lights. The stacks of the oil refinery stood up, beyond the lights, like the guardians of hell. We walked into the white glare and the noise of crazy electric music and the thick sweet smell of candy.

"Hey, fellows, come over this way if you please."

We turned our beards shyly towards the man in shirt sleeves, hatted with a felt hat, leaning out of his booth. We could see the colored board, the numbers. We approached. He began to explain to us that, out of the kindness of his big foolish heart, he was conducting this game of chance which was so easy and simple that it really amounted to a kind of public charity, a means for endowing intelligent and honest young men like ourselves with a handsome patrimony.

We listened to his explanation. It was not one of those games where you won a box of popcorn, that was evident. In fact, although it started at a quarter, the ante doubled at every throw: of course, so did the prize, and the prize was in dollars.

"All you have to do is roll the little ball into these holes and . . ."

And he explained just what holes you had to roll the little ball into. Each time you had to get a new and different combination of numbers.

"You put down a quarter," said our benefactor, "and you are about to win two dollars and fifty cents. If you should happen to miss it the first time, it will be all the better for you, because for fifty cents you'll win five dollars—for one dollar you'll take ten—for two you'll take twenty."

We put down our quarters, and rolled the little balls into the wrong holes.

"Good for you," said the man, "now you stand a chance of winning twice as much." And we all put down fifty cents.

"Fine, keep it up, you're getting ready to win more and more each time—you can't miss, it's in-ev-i-table!"

He pocketed a dollar bill from each of us.

"That's the way, men, that's the way," he exclaimed, as we all rolled the little ball into the wrong holes again.

I paused and asked him to go over the rules of the game a second time. He did, and I listened closely. It was as I thought. I hadn't the vaguest idea what he was talking about. You had to get certain combinations of numbers, and for my own part I was completely unable to figure out what the combinations were. He simply told us what to shoot for, and then rapidly added up all the numbers and announced:

"You just missed it. Try again, you're so close you can't fail." And the combination changed again.

In about two and a half minutes he had taken all our money except for a dollar which I was earnestly saving for the rest of the carnival and for beer. How, he asked us, could we have the heart to quit now? Here we were right on the point of cleaning up, getting back all our losses, and winning a sum that made us dizzy: three hundred and fifty dollars.

"Men," he said, "you can't quit now, you're just throwing away your money if you quit. It doesn't make sense, does it? You didn't come all the way out here just to throw away your dough? Use your heads, boys. Can't you see you've *got* to win?"

Rice got that big grin on his face that meant "Let's get out of here."

"We haven't any more money," someone said.

"Have you any traveller's checks?" the philanthropist inquired.

"No."

But I never saw anyone so absorbed and solemn as Lax was, at that moment, in his black beard, with his head bowed over all those incomprehensible numbers. So he looked at me and I looked at him, and the man said:

"If you want to run home and get a little more money, I'll hold the game open for you—how's that?"

We said: "Hold the game open, we'll be back."

We got into the car and drove, in the most intense silence, fifteen miles or whatever the distance was to the cottage, and fifteen miles back, with thirty-five dollars and all the rest of the money we had: but the thirty-five alone were for the game.

When the benefactor of the poor saw the three of us come through that gate again, he really looked surprised and a little scared. The expressions on our faces must have been rather frightening, and perhaps he imagined that we had gone home not only to get our money but our guns.

We walked up to the booth.

"You held this game open for us, huh?"

"Yes, indeed, men, the game is open."

"Explain it over again."

He explained it over again. He told us what we had to get to win—it seemed impossible to miss. We put the money down on the counter and Lax rolled the little ball—into the wrong holes.

"Is that all, boys?" said the prince of charity.

"That's all." We turned on our heels and went away.

With the money I had kept in my pocket we went into the other places we would have done well to keep out of, and saw all of the carnival, and then went into Bradford where, drinking beer in a bar, we began to feel better and started to assuage our wounds by telling a lot of fancy lies to some girls we met in the bar—they were maids who worked at the t.b. sanatorium at Rocky Crest, on the mountain about a mile and a half from the cottage.

I remember that as the evening went on, there was a fairly large mixed audience of strangers gathered around the table where we were holding forth about the amusement ring which we managed and controlled. It was called the Panama-American Entertainment corporation, and was so magnificent that it made the present carnival in Bradford look like a sideshow. However, the effect was somewhat spoiled when a couple of Bradford strong men came up with no signs of interest in our story, and said:

"If we see you guys around here again with those beards we are going to knock your heads off."

So Rice stood up and said: "Yeah? Do you want to fight?"

Everybody went out into the alley, and there was a great deal of talk back and forth, but no fight, which was a good thing. They were quite capable of making us eat those beards.

We eventually found our way home but Rice did not dare try to drive the car into the garage for fear he would miss the door. He stopped short in the driveway and we opened the doors of the car and rolled out and lay on the grass, looking blindly up into the stars while the earth rolled and pitched beneath us like a foundering ship. The last thing I remember about that night was that Rice and I eventually got up and walked into the house, and found Lax sitting in one of the chairs in the living room, talking aloud, and uttering a lot of careful and well-thought-out statements directed to a pile of dirty clothes, bundled up and ready for the laundry, which somebody had left in another armchair on the other side of the room.

iv

When we went back to New York, in the middle of August, the world that I had helped to make was finally preparing to break the shell and put forth its evil head and devour another generation of men.

At Olean we never read any newspapers, and we kept away from radios on principle, and for my own part the one thing that occupied my mind was the publication of the new novel. Having found an old copy of *Fortune* lying around Benjie's premises, I had read an article in it on the publishing business: and on the basis of that article I had made what was perhaps the worst possible choice of a publisher—the kind of people who would readily reprint everything in the *Saturday Evening Post* in diamond letters on sheets of gold. They were certainly not disposed to be sympathetic to the wild and rambling thing I had composed on the mountain.

And it was going to take them a good long time to get around to telling me about it.

For my own part, I was walking around New York in the

incomparable agony of a new author waiting to hear the fate of his first book—an agony which is second to nothing except the torments of adolescent love. And because of my anguish I was driven, naturally enough, to fervent though interested prayer. But after all God does not care if our prayers are interested. He wants them to be. Ask and you shall receive. It is a kind of pride to insist that none of our prayers should ever be petitions for our own needs: for this is only another subtle way of trying to put ourselves on the same plane as God— acting as if we had no needs, as if we were not creatures, not dependent on Him and dependent, by His will, on material things too.

So I knelt at the altar rail in the little Mexican church of Our Lady of Guadalupe on Fourteenth Street, where I sometimes went to Communion, and asked with great intensity of desire for the publication of the book, if it should be for God's glory.

The fact that I could even calmly assume that there was some possibility of the book giving glory to God shows the profound depths of my ignorance and spiritual blindness: but anyway, that was what I asked. But now I realize that it was a very good thing that I made that prayer.

It is a matter of common belief among Catholics that when God promises to answer our prayers, He does not promise to give us exactly what we ask for. But we can always be certain that if he does not give us that, it is because He has something much better to give us instead. That is what is meant by Christ's promise that we will receive all that we ask in His Name. *Quodcumque petimus adversus utilitatem salutis, non petimus in nomine Salvatoris.*

I think I prayed as well as I could, considering what I was, and with considerable confidence in God and in Our Lady, and I knew I would be answered. I am only just beginning to realize how well I was answered. In the first place the book was never published, and that was a good thing. But in the second place God answered me by a favor which I had already refused and had practically ceased to desire. He gave me back the vocation that I had half-consciously given up, and He opened to me again the doors that had fallen shut when I had not known what to make of my Baptism and the grace of that First Communion.

But before He did this I had to go through some little darkness and suffering.

I think those days at the end of August 1939 were terrible for everyone. They were grey days of great heat and sultriness and the weight of physical oppression by the weather added immeasurably to the burden of the news from Europe that got more ominous day by day.

Now it seemed that at last there really would be war in earnest. Some sense of the craven and perverted esthetic excitement with which the Nazis were waiting for the thrill of this awful spectacle made itself felt negatively, and with hundredfold force, in the disgust and nausea with which the rest of the world expected the embrace of this colossal instrument of death. It was a danger that had, added to it, an almost incalculable element of dishonor and insult and degradation and shame. And the world faced not only destruction, but destruction with the greatest possible defilement: defilement of that which is most perfect in man, his reason and his will, his immortal soul.

All this was obscure to most people, and made itself felt only in a mixture of disgust and hopelessness and dread. They did not realize that the world had now become a picture of what the majority of its individuals had made of their own souls. We had given our minds and wills up to be raped and defiled by sin, by hell itself: and now, for our inexorable instruction and reward, the whole thing was to take place all over again before our eyes, physically and morally, in the social order, so that some of us at least might have some conception of what we had done.

In those days, I realized it myself. I remember one of the nights at the end of August when I was riding on the subway, and suddenly noticed that practically nobody in the car was reading the evening paper, although the wires were hot with news. The tension had become so great that even this toughest of cities had had to turn aside and defend itself against

301

the needles of such an agonizing stimulation. For once everybody else was feeling what Lax and I and Gibney and Rice had been feeling for two years about newspapers and news.

There was something else in my own mind—the recognition: "I myself am responsible for this. My sins have done this. Hitler is not the only one who has started this war: I have my share in it too . . ." It was a very sobering thought, and yet its deep and probing light by its very truth eased my soul a little. I made up my mind to go to confession and Communion on the first Friday of September.

The nights dragged by. I remember one, when I was driving in from Long Island where I had been having dinner at Gibney's house at Port Washington. The man with whom I was riding had a radio in the car, and we were riding along the empty Parkway, listening to a quiet, tired voice from Berlin. These commentators' voices had lost all their pep. There was none of that lusty and doctrinaire elation with which the news broadcasters usually convey the idea that they know all about everything. This time you knew that nobody knew what was going to happen, and they all admitted it. True, they were all agreed that the war was now going to break out. But when? Where? They could not say.

All the trains to the German frontier had been stopped. All air service had been discontinued. The streets were empty. You got the feeling that things were being cleared for the first great air-raid, the one that everyone had been wondering about, that H. G. Wells and all the other people had written about, the one that would wipe out London in one night . . .

The Thursday night before the first Friday of September I went to confession at St. Patrick's Cathedral and then, with characteristic stupidity, stopped in at Dillon's, which was a bar where we went all the time, across the street from the stage-door of the Center Theater. Gibney and I used to sit there waiting for the show to end, and we would hang around until one or two in the morning with several girls we knew who had bits to play in it. This evening, before the show was out, I ran into Jinny Burton, who was not in the show, but could have been in many better shows than that, and she said she was going home to Richmond over Labor Day. She invited me to come with her. We arranged to meet in Pennsylvania Station the following morning.

When it was morning, I woke up early and heard the radios. I could not quite make out what they were saying, but the voices were not tired any more: there was much metallic shouting which meant something had really happened.

On my way to Mass, I found out what it was. They had bombed Warsaw, and the war had finally begun.

In the Church of St. Francis of Assisi, near the Pennsylvania Station, there was a High Mass. The priest stood at the altar under the domed mosaic of the apse and his voice rose in the solemn cadences of the Preface of the Mass—those ancient and splendid and holy words of the Immortal Church. *Vere dignum et justum est aequum et salutare nos tibi semper et ubique gratias agere, Domine sancte, Pater omnipotens, aeterne Deus* . . .

It was the voice of the Church, the Bride of Christ who is in the world yet not of it, whose life transcends and outlives wars and persecutions and revolutions and all the wickedness and cruelty and rapacity and injustice of men. It is truly meet and just always and in all things to give Thee thanks, Holy Lord, omnipotent Father, eternal God: a tremendous prayer that reduces all wars to their real smallness and insignificance in the face of eternity. It is a prayer that opens the door to eternity, that springs from eternity and goes again into eternity, taking our minds with it in its deep and peaceful wisdom. Always and in all things to give Thee thanks, omnipotent Father. Was it thus that she was singing, this Church, this one Body, who had already begun to suffer and to bleed again in another war?

She was thanking Him *in* the war, *in* her suffering: not for the war and for the suffering, but for His love which she knew was protecting her, and us, in this new crisis. And raising up her eyes to Him, she saw the eternal God alone through all these things, was interested in His action alone, not in the bungling cruelty of secondary causes, but only in His

303

love, His wisdom. And to Him the Church, His Bride, gave praise through Christ, through Whom all the angelic hierarchies praise Him . . .

I knelt at the altar rail and on this the first day of the Second World War received from the hand of the priest, Christ in the Host, the same Christ Who was being nailed again to the cross by the effect of my sins, and the sins of the whole selfish, stupid, idiotic world of men.

There was no special joy in that week-end in Virginia. On the Saturday afternoon when we started out from Richmond to go to Urbanna, where Jinny's family had a boat they were going to sail in a regatta, we got the news about the sinking of the *Athenia*, and then, that evening, I suddenly developed a pain in an impacted wisdom tooth. It raged all night and the next day I staggered off to the regatta, worn out with sleeplessness and holding a jaw full of pain.

Down at the dock where there was a gas-pump for the motor boats and a red tank full of Coca-Cola on ice, we stood out of the sun in the doorway of a big shed smelling of ropes and pitch, and listened to a man talking on the radio from London.

His voice was reassuring. The city had not yet been bombed.

We started out of the cove, and passed through the mouth into the open estuary of the Rappahannock, blazing with sun, and everybody was joking about the *Bremen*. The big German liner had sailed out of New York without warning and had disappeared. Every once in a while some high drawling Southern female voice would cry:

"There's the *Bremen*."

I had a bottle of medicine in my pocket, and with a match and a bit of cotton I swabbed the furious impacted tooth.

Nevertheless, when I got back to New York, it turned out that the war was not going to be so ruthless after all—at least so it seemed. The fighting was fierce in Poland, but in the west there was nothing doing. And now that the awful tension was over, people were quieter and more confident than they had been before the fighting had started.

I went to a dentist who hammered and chipped at my jaw until he got the wisdom tooth out of my head, and then I went back to Perry Street and lay on my bed and played some ancient records of Bix Beiderbecke, Paul Whiteman's trumpet player, and swabbed my bleeding mouth with purple disinfectant until the whole place reeked of it.

I had five stitches in my jaw.

The days went by. The city was quiet and confident. It even began to get gay again. Whatever happened, it was evident that America was not going to get into the war right away, and a lot of people were saying that it would just go on like this for years, a sort of state of armed waiting and sniping, with the big armies lined up in their impregnable fortified areas. It was as if the world were entering upon a strange new era in which the pretence of peace had defined itself out into what it was, a state of permanent hostility that was nevertheless not quite ready to fight. And some people thought we were just going to stay that way for twenty years.

For my own part, I did not think anything about it, except that the grim humor of Russia's position in the war could not help but strike me: for now, after a loud outcry and a great storm of crocodile tears over Chamberlain's betrayal of Czechoslovakia the year before, the Reds were comfortably allied with Germany and blessing, with a benign smile, the annihilation of Poland, ready themselves to put into effect some small designs of their own regarding the Finns.

The party line had evolved indeed, and turned itself into many knots since the days of the 1935 Peace Strike and the Oxford Pledge. We had once been led to believe that all wars were wars of aggression and wars of aggression were the direct product of capitalism, masking behind Fascism and all the other movements with colored shirts, and therefore no one should fight at all. It now turned out that the thing to do was support the aggressive war of the Soviets against Finland and approve the Russian support of German aggression in Poland.

The September days went by, and the first signs of fall were beginning to be seen in the clearing of the bright air.

The days of heat were done. It was getting on toward that season of new beginnings, when I would get back to work on my Ph.D., and when I hoped possibly to get some kind of job as an instructor at Columbia, in the College or in Extension.

These were the things I was thinking about when one night Rice and Bob Gerdy and I were in Nick's on Sheridan Square, sitting at the curved bar while the room rocked with jazz. Presently Gibney came in with Peggy Wells, who was one of the girls in that show at the Center Theater, the name of which I have forgotten. We all sat together at a table and talked and drank. It was just like all the other nights we spent in those places. It was more or less uninteresting but we couldn't think of anything else to do and there seemed to be no point in going to bed.

After Rice and Gerdy went home, Gibney and Peggy and I still sat there. Finally it got to be about four o'clock in the morning. Gibney did not want to go out on Long Island, and Peggy lived uptown in the Eighties.

They came to Perry Street, which was just around the corner.

It was nothing unusual for me to sleep on the floor, or in a chair, or on a couch too narrow and too short for comfort—that was the way we lived, and the way thousands of other people like us lived. One stayed up all night, and finally went to sleep wherever there happened to be room for one man to put his tired carcass.

It is a strange thing that we should have thought nothing of it, when if anyone had suggested sleeping on the floor as a penance, for the love of God, we would have felt that he was trying to insult our intelligence and dignity as men! What a barbarous notion! Making yourself uncomfortable as a penance! And yet we somehow seemed to think it quite logical to sleep that way as part of an evening dedicated to pleasure. It shows how far the wisdom of the world will go in contradicting itself. "From him that hath not, it shall be taken away even that which he hath."

I suppose I got some five or six hours of fitful sleep, and at

306

about eleven we were all awake, sitting around dishevelled and half stupefied, talking and smoking and playing records. The thin, ancient, somewhat elegiac cadences of the long dead Beiderbecke sang in the room. From where I sat, on the floor, I could see beyond the roofs to a patch of clear fall sky.

At about one o'clock in the afternoon I went out to get some breakfast, returning with scrambled eggs and toast and coffee in an armful of cardboard containers, different shapes and sizes, and pockets full of new packs of cigarettes. But I did not feel like smoking. We ate and talked, and finally cleared up all the mess and someone had the idea of going for a walk to the Chicken Dock. So we got ready to go.

Somewhere in the midst of all this, an idea had come to me, an idea that was startling enough and momentous enough by itself, but much more astonishing in the context. Perhaps many people will not believe what I am saying.

While we were sitting there on the floor playing records and eating this breakfast the idea came to me: "I am going to be a priest."

I cannot say what caused it: it was not a reaction of especially strong disgust at being so tired and so uninterested in this life I was still leading, in spite of its futility. It was not the music, not the fall air, for this conviction that had suddenly been planted in me full grown was not the sick and haunting sort of a thing that an emotional urge always is. It was not a thing of passion or of fancy. It was a strong and sweet and deep and insistent attraction that suddenly made itself felt, but not as movement of appetite towards any sensible good. It was something in the order of conscience, a new and profound and clear sense that this was what I really ought to do.

How long the idea was in my mind before I mentioned it, I cannot say. But presently I said casually:

"You know, I think I ought to go and enter a monastery and become a priest."

Gibney had heard that before, and thought I was fooling. The statement aroused no argument or comment, and anyway, it was not one to which Gibney was essentially unsympathetic. As far as he was concerned, any life made sense except that of a business man.

As we went out the door of the house I was thinking:

"I am going to be a priest."

When we were on the Chicken Dock, my mind was full of the same idea. Around three or four in the afternoon Gibney left and went home to Port Washington. Peggy and I sat looking at the dirty river for a while longer. Then I walked with her to the subway. In the shadows under the elevated drive over Tenth Avenue I said:

"Peggy, I mean it, I am going to enter a monastery and be a priest."

She didn't know me very well and anyway, she had no special ideas about being a priest. There wasn't much she could say. Anyway, what did I expect her to say?

I was glad, at last, to be alone. On that big wide street that is a continuation of Eighth Avenue, where the trucks run down very fast and loud—I forget its name—there was a little Catholic library and a German bakery where I often ate my meals. Before going to the bakery to get dinner and supper in one, I went to the Catholic library, St. Veronica's. The only book about religious Orders they seemed to have was a little green book about the Jesuits but I took it and read it while I ate in the bakery.

Now that I was alone, the idea assumed a different and more cogent form. Very well: I had accepted the possibility of the priesthood as real and fitting for me. It remained for me to make it, in some sense, more decisive.

What did that mean? What was required? My mind groped for some sort of an answer. What was I supposed to do, here and now?

I must have been a long time over the little book and these thoughts. When I came out into the street again, it was dusk. The side streets, in fact, were already quite dark. I suppose it was around seven o'clock.

Some kind of an instinct prompted me to go to Sixteenth Street, to the Jesuit Church of St. Francis Xavier. I had never been there. I don't know what I was looking for: perhaps I was thinking primarily of talking to some one of the Fathers there—I don't know.

When I got to Sixteenth Street, the whole building seemed dark and empty, and as a matter of fact the doors of the church were locked. Even the street was empty. I was about to go away disappointed, when I noticed a door to some kind of a basement under the church.

Ordinarily I would never have noticed such a door. You went down a couple of steps, and there it was, half hidden under the stairs that led up to the main door of the church. There was no sign that the door was anything but locked and bolted fast.

But something prompted me: "Try that door."

I went down the two steps, put my hand on the heavy iron handle. The door yielded and I found myself in a lower church, and the church was full of lights and people and the Blessed Sacrament was exposed in a monstrance on the altar, and at last I realized what I was supposed to do, and why I had been brought here.

It was some kind of a novena service, maybe a Holy Hour, I don't know: but it was nearly ending. Just as I found a place and fell on my knees, they began singing the *Tantum Ergo*. . . . All these people, workmen, poor women, students, clerks, singing the Latin hymn to the Blessed Sacrament written by St. Thomas Aquinas.

I fixed my eyes on the monstrance, on the white Host.

And then it suddenly became clear to me that my whole life was at a crisis. Far more than I could imagine or understand or conceive was now hanging upon a word—a decision of mine.

I had not shaped my life to this situation: I had not been building up to this. Nothing had been further from my mind. There was, therefore, an added solemnity in the fact that I had been called in here abruptly to answer a question that had been preparing, not in my mind, but in the infinite depths of an eternal Providence.

I did not clearly see it then, but I think now that it might have been something in the nature of a last chance. If I had hesitated or refused at that moment—what would have become of me?

But the way into the new land, the promised land, the land that was not like the Egypt where I persisted in living, was now thrown open again: and I instinctively sensed that it was only for a moment.

It was a moment of crisis, yet of interrogation: a moment of searching, but it was a moment of joy. It took me about a minute to collect my thoughts about the grace that had been suddenly planted in my soul, and to adjust the weak eyes of my spirit to its unaccustomed light, and during that moment my whole life remained suspended on the edge of an abyss: but this time, the abyss was an abyss of love and peace, the abyss was God.

It would be in some sense a blind, irrevocable act to throw myself over. But if I failed to do that . . . I did not even have to turn and look behind me at what I would be leaving. Wasn't I tired enough of all that?

So now the question faced me:

"Do you really want to be a priest? If you do, say so . . ."

The hymn was ending. The priest collected the ends of the humeral veil over his hands that held the base of the monstrance, and slowly lifted it off the altar, and turned to bless the people.

I looked straight at the Host, and I knew, now, Who it was that I was looking at, and I said:

"Yes, I want to be a priest, with all my heart I want it. If it is Your will, make me a priest—make me a priest."

When I had said them, I realized in some measure what I had done with those last four words, what power I had put into motion on my behalf, and what a union had been sealed between me and that power by my decision.

Part Three

1

Magnetic North

Once again, classes were beginning at the University. The pleasant fall winds played in the yellowing leaves of the poplars in front of the college dormitories and many young men came out of the subways and walked earnestly and rapidly about the campus with little blue catalogues of courses under their arms, and their hearts warm with the desire to buy books. But now, in this season of new beginnings, I really had something new to begin.

A year ago the conviction had developed in my mind that the one who was going to give me the best advice about where and how to become a priest was Dan Walsh. I had come to this conclusion before I had ever met him, or sat and listened to his happy and ingenuous lectures on St. Thomas. So on this September day, in 1939, the conviction was to bear its fruit.

Dan was not on the Columbia campus that day. I went into one of the phone booths at Livingston Hall and called him up.

He was a man with rich friends, and that night he had been invited to dinner with some people on Park Avenue, although there was certainly nothing of Park Avenue about him and his simplicity. But we arranged to meet downtown, and at about ten o'clock that evening I was standing in the lobby of one of those big, shiny, stuffy apartments, waiting for him to come down out of the elevator.

As soon as we walked out into the cool night, Dan turned to me and said: "You know, the first time I met you I thought you had a vocation to the priesthood."

I was astonished and ashamed. Did I really give that impression? It made me feel like a whited sepulchre, considering what I knew was inside me. On the whole, perhaps it would have been more reassuring if he had been surprised.

He was not surprised, he was very pleased. And he was glad to talk about my vocation, and about the priesthood and about religious Orders. They were things to which he had given a certain amount of thought, and on the whole, I think that my selection of an adviser was a very happy one. It was a good inspiration and, in fact, it was to turn out much better than I realized at first.

The quietest place we could think of in that neighborhood was the men's bar at the Biltmore, a big room full of comfortable chairs, hushed and panelled and half empty. We sat down in one of the far corners, and it was there, two being gathered together in His Name and in His charity, that Christ impressed the first definite form and direction upon my vocation.

It was very simply done. We just talked about several different religious Orders, and Dan suggested various priests I might consult and finally promised to give me a note of introduction to one of them.

I had read a little here and there about the Jesuits, the Franciscans, the Dominicans, the Benedictines, leafing through the *Catholic Encyclopaedia* in the reference library in South Hall, and shopping around in the stacks. I had put my nose into the Rule of St. Benedict and not derived much benefit from so cursory an acquaintance—all I remembered was that the saint seemed a little vexed at the fact that the monks of his day could not be persuaded to go without wine. I had looked into a little French book about the Dominicans, and there I met with a piece of information that gave me pause: it said they all slept together in a common dormitory, and I thought: "Who wants to sleep in a common dormitory?" The picture in my mind was that of the long, cold, green upstairs room in the Lycée, with row after row of iron beds and a lot of skinny people in nightshirts.

I spoke to Dan Walsh about the Jesuits, but he said he did not know any Jesuits, and for my own part, the mere fact that he did not seem to have any particular reaction, positive or negative, to that Order, did away with the weak and vague preference which I had hitherto given it in my own mind. I had instinctively turned that way first of all, because I had read the life of Gerard Manley Hopkins and studied his poems, but there had never been any real attraction calling me to that kind of a life. It was geared to a pitch of active intensity and military routine which were alien to my own needs. I doubt if they would have kept me in their novitiate —but if they had, they would probably have found me a great misfit. What I needed was the solitude to expand in breadth and depth and to be simplified out under the gaze of God more or less the way a plant spreads out its leaves in the sun. That meant that I needed a Rule that was almost entirely aimed at detaching me from the world and uniting me with God, not a Rule made to fit me to fight for God in the world. But I did not find out all that in one day.

Dan spoke of the Benedictines. In itself, the vocation attracted me: a liturgical life in some big abbey in the depths of the country. But in actual fact it might just mean being nailed down to a desk in an expensive prep-school in New Hampshire for the rest of my life—or, worse still, being a parish priest remotely attached to such a prep-school, and living in more or less permanent separation from the claustral and liturgical center which had first attracted me.

"What do you think of the Franciscans?" said Dan.

As soon as I mentioned St. Bonaventure's, it turned out that he had many friends there and knew the place fairly well; in fact they had given him some sort of an honorary degree there that summer. Yes, I liked the Franciscans. Their life was very simple and informal and the atmosphere of St. Bonaventure's was pleasant and happy and peaceful. One thing that attracted me to them was a sort of freedom from spiritual restraint, from systems and routine. No matter how much the original Rule of St. Francis has changed, I think his spirit and his inspiration are still the fundamental thing in Franciscan life. And it is an inspiration rooted in joy, because it is guided by the prudence and wisdom which are revealed only to the little ones—the glad wisdom of those who have had the grace and the madness to throw away everything in one uncompromising rush, and to walk around barefooted in the simple confidence that if they get into trouble, God will come and get them out of it again.

This is not something that is confined to the Franciscans: it is at the heart of every religious vocation, and if it is not, the vocation does not mean much. But the Franciscans, or at least St. Francis, reduced it to its logical limits, and at the same time invested it with a kind of simple thirteenth century lyricism which made it doubly attractive to me.

However, the lyricism must be carefully distinguished from the real substance of the Franciscan vocation, which is that tremendous and heroic poverty, poverty of body and spirit which makes the Friar literally a tramp. For, after all, "mendicant" is only a fancy word for tramp, and if a Franciscan cannot be a tramp in this full and complete and total mystical sense, he is bound to be a little unhappy and dissatisfied. As soon as he acquires a lot of special articles for his use and comfort and becomes sedate and respectable and spiritually sedentary he will, no doubt, have an easy and pleasant time, but there will be always gnawing in his heart the nostalgia for that uncompromising destitution which alone can give him joy because it flings him headlong into the arms of God.

Without poverty, Franciscan lyricism sounds tinny and sentimental and raw and false. Its tone is sour, and all its harmonies are somewhat strained.

I am afraid that at that time, it was the lyricism that attracted me more than the poverty, but really I don't think I was in a position to know any better. It was too soon for me to be able to make the distinction. However, I remember admitting that one of the advantages of their Rule, as far as I was concerned, was that it was easy.

After all, I was really rather frightened of all religious rules as a whole, and this new step, into the monastery, was not something that presented itself to me, all at once, as something that I would just take in my stride. On the contrary, my mind was full of misgivings about fasting and enclosure and all the long prayers and community life and monastic obedience and poverty, and there were plenty of strange spectres dancing about in the doors of my imagination, all ready to come in, if I would let them in. And if I did, they would show me how I would go insane in a monastery, and how my health would crack up, and my heart would give out, and I would collapse and go to pieces and be cast back into the world a hopeless moral and physical wreck.

All this, of course, was based on the assumption that I was in weak health, for that was something I still believed. Perhaps it was to some extent true, I don't know. But the fear of collapse had done nothing, in the past years, to prevent me from staying up all night and wandering around the city in search of very unhealthy entertainments. Nevertheless, as soon as there was question of a little fasting or going without meat or living within the walls of a monastery, I instantly began to fear death.

What I eventually found out was that as soon as I started to fast and deny myself pleasures and devote time to prayer and meditation and to the various exercises that belong to the religious life, I quickly got over all my bad health, and became sound and strong and immensely happy.

That particular night I was convinced that I could not follow anything but the easiest of religious rules.

When Dan began to talk about the one religious Order that filled him with the most enthusiasm, I was able to share his admiration but I had no desire to join it. It was the Order of Cistercians, the Cistercians of the Strict Observance. The very title made me shiver, and so did their commoner name: The Trappists.

Once, six years before—and it seemed much longer than that—when I had barely glanced at the walls of the Trappist monastery of Tre Fontane, outside Rome, the fancy of becoming a Trappist had entered my adolescent mind: but if it had been anything but a pure day-dream, it would not have got inside my head at all. Now, when I was actually and seriously thinking of entering a monastery, the very idea of Trappists almost reduced me to a jelly.

"Last summer," said Dan, "I made a retreat at a Trappist

monastery in Kentucky. It is called Our Lady of Gethsemani. Did you ever hear of it?"

And he began to tell me about the place—how he had been staying with some friends, and they had driven him over to the monastery. It was the first time they had ever been there. Although they lived in Kentucky, they hardly knew the Trappists existed. His hostess had been very piqued at the signs about women keeping out of the enclosure under pain of excommunication, and she had watched with awe as the heavy door closed upon him, engulfing him in that terrible, silent building.

(From where I sit and write at this moment, I look out the window, across the quiet guest-house garden, with the four banana trees and the big red and yellow flowers around Our Lady's statue. I can see the door where Dan entered and where I entered. Beyond the Porter's Lodge is a low green hill where there was wheat this summer. And out there, yonder, I can hear the racket of the diesel tractor: I don't know what they are ploughing.)

Dan had stayed in the Trappist monastery a week. He told me of the life of the monks. He told me of their silence. He said they never conversed, and the impression I got was that they never spoke at all, to anybody.

"Don't they even go to Confession?" I asked.

"Of course. And they can talk to the abbot. The retreat master talked to the guests. He was Father James. He said that it was a good thing the monks didn't have to talk—with all the mixture of men they have there, they get along better without it: lawyers and farmers and soldiers and schoolboys, they all live together, and go everywhere together and do everything together. They stand in choir together, and go out to work together and sit together in the same place when they read and study. It's a good thing they don't talk."

"Oh, so they sing in choir?"

"Sure," said Dan, "they sing the Canonical hours and High Mass. They are in choir several hours a day."

I was relieved to think that the monks got to choir and

exercised their vocal cords. I was afraid that so much silence would wither them up altogether.

"And they work in the fields," said Dan. "They have to make their own living by farming and raising stock. They grow most of what they eat, and bake their own bread, and make their own shoes . . ."

"I suppose they fast a lot," I said.

"Oh, yes, they fast more than half the year, and they never eat meat or fish, unless they get sick. They don't even have eggs. They just live on vegetables and cheese and things like that. They gave me a cheese when I was there, and I took it back to my friends' house. When we got there, they handed it to the colored butler. They said to him, 'Do you know what that is? That's monks' cheese.' He couldn't figure it out, and he looked at it for a while, and then he got an idea. So he looked up with a big smile and said: 'Oh, I know what you all mean: *monks!* Them's like goats.'"

But I was thinking about all that fasting. The life took my breath away, but it did not attract me. It sounded cold and terrible. The monastery now existed in my mind as a big grey prison with barred windows, filled with dour and emaciated characters with their hoods pulled down over their faces.

"They are very healthy," said Dan, "and they are big strong men. Some of them are giants."

(Since I came to the monastery I have tried to pick out Dan's "giants." I can account for one or two easily enough. But I think he must have seen the rest of them in the dark— or perhaps they are to be explained by the fact that Dan himself is not very tall.)

I sat in silence. In my heart, there was a kind of mixture of exhilaration and dejection, exhilaration at the thought of such generosity, and depression because it seemed such a drastic and cruel and excessive rejection of the rights of nature.

Dan said: "Do you think you would like that kind of a life?"

"Oh, no," I said, "not a chance! That's not for me! I'd never be able to stand it. It would kill me in a week. Besides, I have to have meat. I can't get along without meat, I need it for my health."

"Well," said Dan, "it's a good thing you know yourself so well."

For a moment it occurred to me that he was being ironical, but there was not a shadow of irony in his voice, and there never was. He was far too good and too kind and too simple for irony. He thought I knew what I was talking about, and took my word for it.

And so the conclusion of that evening was that I decided to go and see the Franciscans, and after all, we both agreed that they seemed to be the best for me.

So he gave me a note to his friend Father Edmund, at the monastery of St. Francis of Assisi on 31st Street.

ii

The Franciscan monastery on 31st Street, New York, is a grey unprepossessing place, crowded in among big buildings, and inhabited by very busy priests. Not the least busy of them in those days was Father Edmund, Dan Walsh's friend: and yet he was not too busy to talk to me practically any time I came around to see him. He was a big amiable man full of Franciscan cheerfulness, kind, disciplined by hard work yet not hardened by it, for his priesthood, which kept him close to Christ and to souls more than softened and humanized him.

From the first moment I met him, I knew I had a good friend in Father Edmund. He questioned me about my vocation, asking me how long it was since my Baptism, and what it was that attracted me to the Franciscans, and what I was doing at Columbia, and when I had talked to him for a while, he began to encourage me in the idea of becoming a Friar.

"I don't see any reason why you shouldn't eventually make application to enter the novitiate next August," he said.

Next August! That was a long way off. Now that my mind was made up, I was impatient to get started. However, I had not expected to be admitted immediately by any Order. But I asked him:

"Father, isn't there some chance of my entering sooner?"

"We admit all our novices together, in a group," he said. "They start out at Paterson, in August, then they go on together all the way through until ordination. It's the only way we can handle them. If you entered at any other time, you would miss out all along the line. Have you had much philosophy?"

I told him of Dan Walsh's courses, and he thought for a moment.

"Perhaps there might be a chance of starting you out in the novitiate in February," he said, but he did not seem to be very hopeful. No doubt what he was thinking of was that I might skip a half-year of philosophy and so catch up with the others at the house of studies up-state, where they would be sent after the year's noviceship.

"Are you living with your parents?" he asked me.

I told him they had long been dead, and that none of my family was left, except an uncle and a brother.

"Is your brother a Catholic too?"

"No, Father."

"Where is he? What does he do?"

"He goes to Cornell. He is supposed to get out of there next June."

"Well," said Father Edmund, "what about yourself? Have you got enough to live on? You aren't starving or anything, are you?"

"Oh, no, Father, I can get along. I've got a chance of a job teaching English in Extension at Columbia this year, and besides that they gave me a grant-in-aid to pay for my courses for the doctorate."

"You take that job," said the Friar; "that will do you a lot of good. And get busy on that doctorate, too. Do all the work you can, and study a little philosophy. Study won't hurt you at all. After all, you know, if you come into the Order you'll probably end up teaching at St. Bona's or Siena. You'd like that, wouldn't you?"

"Oh, sure," I said, and that was the truth.

I walked down the steps of the monastery into the noisy street, with my heart full of happiness and peace.

What a transformation this made in my life! Now, at last, God had become the center of my existence. And it had taken no less than this decision to make Him so. Apparently, in my case, it had to be that way.

I was still without any formal spiritual direction, but I went frequently to confession, especially at St. Francis' Church, where the Friars were more inclined to give me advice than secular priests had been. And it was in one of the confessionals at St. Francis' that a good priest one day told me, very insistently:

"Go to Communion every day, every day."

By that time, I had already become a daily communicant, but his words comforted and strengthened me, and his emphasis made me glad. And indeed I had reason to be, for it was those daily Communions that were transforming my life almost visibly, from day to day.

I did not realize any of this on those beautiful mornings: I scarcely was aware that I was so happy. It took someone else to draw my attention to it.

I was coming down Seventh Avenue one morning. It must have been in December or January. I had just come from the little church of Our Lady of Guadalupe, and from Communion, and was going to get some breakfast at a lunch wagon near Loew's Sheridan Theater. I don't know what I was thinking of, but as I walked along I nearly bumped into Mark who was on his way to the subway, going to Columbia for his morning classes.

"Where are you going?" he said. The question surprised me, as there did not seem to be any reason to ask where I was going, and all I could answer was: "To breakfast."

Later on, Mark referred again to the meeting and said:

"What made you look so happy, on the street, there?"

So that was what had impressed him, and that was why he had asked me where I was going. It was not where I was going that made me happy, but where I was coming from. Yet, as I say, this surprised me too, because I had not really paid any attention to the fact that I was happy—which indeed I was.

Now every day began with Mass and Communion, either at Our Lady of Guadalupe or St. Francis of Assisi Church.

After that I went back to Perry Street, and got to work rewriting the novel which had been handed back to me politely by one of those tall, thin, anxious young men with horn-rimmed glasses who are to be found in the offices of publishers. (He had asked me if I was trying to write in some new experimental style, and then ducked behind his desk as if I might pull a knife on him for his impertinence.)

About twelve I would go out to get a sandwich at some drug-store, and read in the paper about the Russians and the Finns or about the French sitting in the Maginot Line, and sending out a party of six men somewhere in Loraine to fire three rifle shots at an imaginary German.

In the afternoon I usually had to go to Columbia and sit in a room and hear some lecture on English Literature, after which I went to the library and read St. Thomas Aquinas' commentary on Aristotle's *Metaphysics* which I had reserved for me on my desk in the graduate reading room. This was a matter of great consternation to some Sisters of St. Joseph who occupied nearby desks and who, after a while, became timidly friendly when they learned that I was going to become a Franciscan in the summer.

At about three in the afternoon I was in the habit of going to Corpus Christi, or to Our Lady of Lourdes which was even closer, and doing the Stations of the Cross. This meditative and easy prayer provided me with another way, more valuable than I realized, of entering into participation in the merits of Christ's Passion, and of renewing within me the life that had been set alight by that morning's Communion.

In those days it took a little effort to walk to a church and go around the fourteen stations saying vocal prayers, for I was still not used to praying. Therefore, doing the Stations of the Cross was still more laborious than consoling, and required a sacrifice. It was much the same with all my devotions. They did not come easily or spontaneously, and they very seldom brought with them any strong sensible satisfaction. Nevertheless the work of performing them ended in a profound and fortifying peace: a peace that was scarcely perceptible, but which deepened and which, as my passions subsided, became more and more real, more and more sure, and finally stayed with me permanently.

It was also at this time that I first attempted any kind of mental prayer. I had bought a copy of the *Spiritual Exercises* of St. Ignatius many months before, and it had remained idle on the shelf—except that when I came back from Olean and took over the apartment from Seymour's wife, to whom I had sub-let it, I found a couple of little pencil marks in the margin opposite passages that might be interpreted as sinister and Jesuitical. One of them was about death, and the other had something to do with pulling all the blinds down when you wanted to meditate.

For my own part I had long been a little scared of the *Spiritual Exercises*, having somewhere acquired a false impression that if you did not look out they would plunge you head first into mysticism before you were aware of it. How could I be sure that I would not fly up into the air as soon as I applied my mind to the first meditation? I have since found out that there is very little danger of my ever flying around the premises at mental prayer. The *Spiritual Exercises* are very pedestrian and practical—their chief purpose being to enable all the busy Jesuits to get their minds off their work and back to God with a minimum of wasted time.

I wish I had been able to go through the *Exercises* under the roof of some Jesuit house, directed by one of their priests. However, I went about it under my own direction, studying the rules of procedure that were given in the book, and following them in so far as I managed to grasp what they were all about. I never even breathed a word about what I was doing to any priest.

As far as I remember I devoted a whole month to the *Exer-*

cises, taking one hour each day. I took a quiet hour, in the afternoon, in my room on Perry Street: and since I now lived in the back of the house, there were no street noises to worry me. It was really quite silent. With the windows closed, since it was winter, I could not even hear any of the neighborhood's five thousand radios.

The book said the room should be darkened, and I pulled down the blinds so that there was just enough light left for me to see the pages, and to look at the Crucifix on the wall over my bed. And the book also invited me to consider what kind of a position I should take for my meditation. It left me plenty of freedom of choice, so long as I remained more or less the way I was, once I had settled down, and did not go promenading around the room scratching my head and talking to myself.

So I thought and prayed awhile over this momentous problem, and finally decided to make my meditations sitting cross-legged on the floor. I think the Jesuits would have had a nasty shock if they had walked in and seen me doing their *Spiritual Exercises* sitting there like Mahatma Gandhi. But it worked very well. Most of the time I kept my eyes on the Crucifix or on the floor, when I did not have to look at the book.

And so, having prayed, sitting on the floor, I began to consider the reason why God had brought me into the world:

Man was created to this end: that he should praise God, Our Lord, and reverence and serve Him, and by doing these things, should save his soul. And all the other things on the face of the earth were created for man, to help him in attaining the end for which he was created. Whence it follows that man must use these things only in so far as they help him towards his end, and must withdraw himself from them in so far as they are obstacles to his attaining his end. . . . Wherefore it is necessary that we make ourselves indifferent to all created things, in so far as it is permitted to our free will . . . in such a way that, as far as we are concerned, we should not desire health rather than sickness, riches rather than

325

poverty, honor rather than ignominy, a long life rather than a short life, and so on, desiring and choosing only those things which more efficaciously lead us to the end for which we were created.

The big and simple and radical truths of the "Foundation" were, I think, too big and too radical for me. By myself, I did not even scratch the surface of them. I vaguely remember fixing my mind on this notion of indifference to all created things in themselves, to sickness and health, and being mildly appalled. Who was I to understand such a thing? If I got a cold I nearly choked myself with aspirins and hot lemonade, and dived into bed with undisguised alarm. And here was a book that might perhaps be telling me that I ought to be able to remain as cool as an icebox in the presence of a violent death. How could I figure out just what and how much that word "indifferent" meant, if there was no one to tell me? I did not have any way of seeing the distinction between indifference of the will and indifference of the feelings—the latter being practically a thing unknown, even in the experience of the saints. So, worrying about this big difficulty of my own creation, I missed the real fruit of this fundamental meditation, which would have been an application of its notions to all the things to which I myself was attached, and which always tended to get me into trouble.

However, the real value of the *Exercises* for me came when I got to the various contemplations, especially the mysteries of the life of Christ. I docilely followed all St. Ignatius' rules about the "composition of place" and sat myself down in the Holy House at Nazareth with Jesus and Mary and Joseph, and considered what they did, and listened to what they said and so on. And I elicited affections, and made resolutions, and ended with a colloquy and finally made a brief retrospective examination of how the meditation had worked out. All this was so new and interesting, and the labor of learning it engrossed me so much, that I was far too busy for distractions. The most vital part of each meditation was always the application of the senses (hearing the yelling of the damned in

326

hell, smelling their burning rottenness, seeing the devils coming at you to drag you down with the rest, and so on).

As far as I remember, there was one theological point that made a very deep impression on me, greater than anything else. Somewhere in the first week, after having considered the malice of mortal sin, I had turned to the evil of venial sin. And there, suddenly, while the horror of mortal sin had remained somewhat abstract to me, simply because there were so many aspects and angles to the question, I clearly saw the malice of venial sin precisely as an offense against the goodness and loving kindness of God, without any respect to punishment. I left that meditation with a deep conviction of the deordination and malice there is in preferring one's own will and satisfaction to the will of God for Whose love we were created.

In the big meditation on the "Two Standards," where you are supposed to line up the army of Christ in one field and the army of the devil in the other, and ask yourself which one you choose, I got into too much of a Cecil B. De Mille atmosphere to make much out of it, but in the considerations on a choice of a state in life which followed, a strange thing happened, which scared me a little. It was the only incident that savored of externally supernatural intervention in the retreat.

I had already made my choice of a state of life. I was going to be a Franciscan. Consequently, I embarked on these thoughts without too much personal concern. I was meandering around in considerations of what a man ought to do with his earthly possessions—a meditation that might have been useful to someone who really had some possessions to dispose of—when my doorbell rang. I pressed the button that opened the street-door below, and went to the head of the stairs, thinking that perhaps it was Gibney or somebody like that.

It was a little man in a mouse-colored overcoat, whom I had never before seen.

"Are you Thomas Merton?" he said to me, as he arrived on my landing.

327

I did not deny it, and he entered my room and sat down on the bed.

"Did you write that review of that book about D. H. Lawrence in the *Times* book section last Sunday?" he asked me.

I thought I was in for it. I had favorably reviewed a book on Lawrence by Tyndall, under whom I had done my thesis at Columbia. He had written just the kind of a book that was calculated to drive all the people who had made a Messiah out of Lawrence clean out of their wits with pain and rage. I had already got an angry letter in the mail for even reviewing such a book, and I thought that now somebody had come around to shoot me if I did not recant.

"Yes," I said, "I wrote the review. Didn't you like it?"

"Oh, I didn't read it," said the little man, "but Mr. Richardson read it, and he told me all about it."

"Who is Mr. Richardson?"

"You don't know him? He lives in Norwalk. I was talking to him about your review only yesterday."

"I don't know anybody in Norwalk," I said. I could not figure out whether this Mr. Richardson liked the review or not, and did not bother. It did not seem to have any bearing on the man's visit after all.

"I have been travelling around all day," he said, thoughtfully. "I was in Elizabeth, New Jersey; then in Bayonne, New Jersey; then in Newark. Then, when I was coming back on the Hudson Tube I thought of Mr. Richardson and how he had been talking about you, and I thought I would come and see you."

So there he was. He had been in Elizabeth and Bayonne and Newark and now he was sitting on my bed, with his mouse-colored overcoat and his hat in his hand.

"Do you live in New Jersey?" I said, out of politeness.

"Oh, no, of course not, I live in Connecticut," he said quickly. But I had opened out only an avenue to further confusion. He went into intricate geographical details about where he lived and how he happened to be associated with this Mr. Richardson of Norwalk, and then he said:

328

"When I saw the ad in the paper, I decided to go over to New Jersey."

"The ad?"

"Yes, the ad about the job I was looking for in Elizabeth, and didn't get. And now I haven't even enough money to get back to Connecticut."

I finally began to see what it was all about.

The visitor was stumbling around in a long, earnest and infinitely complicated account of all the jobs he had failed to get in New Jersey, and I, with a strange awe and excitement, began to think two things: "How much money have I got to give him?" and "How did he happen to walk in here just when I was in the middle of that meditation about giving all your goods to the poor? . . ."

The possibility that he might even be an angel, disguised in that mouse-colored coat, struck me with a force that was all the more affecting because it was so obviously absurd. And yet the more I think about it, the more I am convinced of the propriety of God sending me an angel with instructions to try and fool me by talking like a character in one of those confusing short stories that get printed in the *New Yorker*.

Anyway, I reached into my pockets and started emptying them, putting quarters and pennies and nickels on the desk. Of course, if the man was an angel, then the whole affair was nothing but a set-up, and I should give him everything I had on me, and go without supper. Two things restrained me. First, the desire of supper, and, second, the fact that the stranger seemed to be aware that I was somewhat moved with secret thoughts, and apparently interpreted them as annoyance. Anyway, figuring that I was in some way upset, he showed himself to be in a hurry to take the little I had already collected for him, as if that were plenty.

He hastened away, stuffing a dollar bill and the change into his pockets, leaving me in such a state of bewilderment that I positively could not sit down cross-legged and continue the meditation. I was still wondering if I should not run down the street after him and give him the other dollar which I still had.

But still, applying St. Ignatius' standard to the present circumstances, I had done fairly well. I had given him about three-fifths of my liquid capital.

Perhaps, in a way, it is better that I didn't give him everything and go without supper. I would have preened myself with such consummate and disgusting vanity—assuming I did not die of fear, and call up one of my friends to lend me something—that there would have been no merit in it at all. For all that, even if his story was disconnected and very silly, and even if he was not an angel, he was much more than that if you apply Christ's own standard about whatsoever you have done to the least of His little ones.

Anyway, it certainly put some point into that meditation.

iii

That was also the season in which, three nights a week, I taught a class in English composition, in one of the rooms in the School of Business at Columbia. Like all Extension classes, it was a mixture of all flesh. There was a tough and bad-tempered chemist who was a center of potential opposition, because he was taking the course under duress—it was required of all the students who were following a systematic series of courses in anything at all. There was an earnest and sensitive Negro youth who sat in the front row, dressed in a neat grey suit, and peered at me intently through his glasses all the time the class was going on. There was an exchange student from the University of Rome, and there was one of those middle-aged ladies who had been taking courses like this for years and who handed in neat and punctilious themes and occupied, with a serene and conscious modesty, her rightful place as the star of the class. This entitled her to talk more than anybody else and ask more unpredictable questions.

Once, after I had been insisting that they should stick to concrete and tangible evidence, in describing places and things, an Irishman called Finegan who had been sitting in bewilderment and without promise in one of the back rows, suddenly blossomed out with a fecundity in minute and irrelevant material detail that it was impossible to check. He began handing in descriptions of shoe factories that made you feel as if you were being buried under fifty tons of machinery. And I learned, with wonder and fear, that teachers have a mysterious and deadly power of letting loose psychological forces in the minds of the young. The rapidity, the happy enthusiasm with which they responded to hints and suggestions—but with the wrong response—was enough to make a man run away and live in the woods.

But I liked teaching very much—especially teaching this kind of a class, in which most of the students had to work for their living, and valued their course because they had to pay for it out of their own savings. Teaching people like that is very flattering: the class is always so eager to get anything you have to give them, and the mere fact that they want so much, is liable to give you the impression that you are capable of giving them all they want.

For my part I was left more or less free to go ahead and teach them according to my own ideas. Now if people are going to write, they must first of all have something to write about, and if a man starts out to teach English composition, he implicitly obliges himself to teach the students how to get up enough interest in things to write about them. But it is also impossible for people to learn to write unless they also read. And so a course in composition, if it is not accompanied somewhere along the line by a course in literature, should also take a little time to teach people how to read, or at least how to get interested in a book.

Therefore, I spent most of the time throwing out ideas about what might or might not be important in life and in literature, and letting them argue about it. The arguments got better when they also included discussion of the students' favorite ideas, as expressed on paper. It soon turned out that although they did not all have ideas, they all had a definite hunger for ideas and for convictions, from the young man who wrote a theme about how happy he had been one summer when he had had a job painting a church, to the quiet Catholic housewife who sat in one of the middle rows viewing me with a reassuring smile and an air of friendly complicity whenever the discussion got around near the borders of religion. So it was a very lively class, on the whole.

But it was only to last a term. And when January came around, they told me, down in the office, that they were going to give me a class in straight, unalleviated grammar in the spring session.

Grammar was something I knew absolutely nothing about, and only the most constant vigilance had kept it out of sight in the composition class. Besides, since I was entering the monastery in the summer, I assured myself that I ought to take a last vacation, and I was already leafing through books about Mexico and Cuba, trying to decide where I would spend the money that I was no longer going to need to support myself in the world.

I told the heads of my department that I could not teach grammar in the spring, because I wanted to prepare myself for life in the cloister. They asked me what made me want to do such a thing as that, and sadly shook their heads, but did not try to argue me out of it. They told me I could come back if I changed my mind—and it almost sounded as if they were saying: "We'll take you back when you've been disillusioned and given up this fantastic notion as a bad job."

Since I still had some money coming to me from the University on my "Grant-in-Aid" I signed up for two courses in the spring. One of them was a seminar on St. Thomas, with Dan Walsh, which ended up with two of us sitting and reading the *De Ente et Essentia* with Dan in his room, in a house run by an old lady who had made a kind of career for herself by harboring the New York Giants under her roof in the baseball season.

While I was still wondering whether I could afford to go to Mexico or only to Cuba, Lent came in sight, and so I put it off until after Lent. And then, one day, when I was working in the library, I suddenly began to get pains in my stomach, and to feel weak and sick. I put away my books, and went to see a doctor, who put me on a table, and poked at my stomach and said, without hesitation:

332

"Yes, you've got it."

"Appendicitis?"

"Yes. You'd better have that thing out."

"Right away?"

"Well, you might as well. What's the use of waiting? You would only get into trouble with it."

And immediately he called up the hospital.

I walked down the brownstone stairs of the doctor's house, thinking that it would be nice, in the hospital, with nuns to look after me: but at the same time I was already having visions of mishaps, fatal accidents, slips of the knife that would land me in the grave. . . . I made a lot of prayers to Our Lady of Lourdes and went home to Perry Street to get a toothbrush and a copy of Dante's *Paradiso*.

And so I started back uptown. In the Fourteenth Street subway station there was a drunk. And he was really drunk. He was lying prostrate in the middle of the turnstiles, in everybody's way. Several people pushed him and told him to get up and get out of there, but he could not even get himself up on his feet.

I thought to myself: "If I try to lift him out of there, my appendix will burst, and I too will be lying there in the turnstiles along with him." With my nervousness tempered by a nice warm feeling of smugness and self-complacency, I took the drunk by the shoulders and laboriously hauled him backwards out of the turnstiles and propped him up against the wall. He groaned feebly in protest.

Then, mentally congratulating myself for my great solicitude and charity towards drunks, I entered the turnstile and went down to take the train to the hospital on Washington Heights. As I looked back, over my shoulder, from the bottom of the stairs, I could see the drunk slowly and painfully crawling back towards the turnstile, where he once again flung himself down, prostrate, across the opening, and blocked the passage as he had done before.

It was night when I got out of the station uptown, and started to climb scores of monumental steps to the top of the bluff where St. Elizabeth's Hospital was. Ice was shining in

333

the branches of the trees, and here and there bright icicles would break off and fall and shatter in the street. I climbed the steps of the hospital, and entered the clean shiny hall and saw a crucifix and a Franciscan nun, all in white, and a statue of the Sacred Heart.

I was very sick when I came out of the ether, and I filled myself full of swords by taking a clandestine drink of water before I should have done so. But one of the nuns who was on night duty brought me a glass of what tasted like, and turned out to be, anisette. It braced me up considerably. After that, when I could eat again, I began to sit up and read Dante in bed, and the rest of the ten days were indeed a paradise.

Every morning, early, after I had washed my teeth and the nurse had fixed my bed, I would lie quiet, in happy expectancy, for the sound of the little bell coming down the hall which meant: Communion. I could count the doors the priest entered, as he stopped at the different rooms and wards. Then, with the nuns kneeling in the door, he came to my bedside with the ciborium.

"*Corpus Domini Nostri Jesu Christi custodiat animam tuam in vitam aeternam.*"

And he was gone. You could hear the bell disappear down the corridor. Under the sheet my hands folded quietly with my rosary between my fingers. It was a rosary John Paul had given me for Christmas: since he did not know the difference between one rosary and another, he had let himself be cheated in some pious store, and bought some beads that looked good but which fell to pieces in six months. It was the kind of rosary that was meant to be looked at rather than used. But the affection which it represented was as strong as the rosary itself was weak, and so, while the beads held together, I used them in preference to the strong, cheap, black wooden beads made for workmen and old washwomen which I had bought for twenty-five cents in the basement of Corpus Christi during the mission.

"You go to Communion every day?" said the Italian in the next bed. He had got himself full of pneumonia shovelling snow all night for the WPA.

334

"Yes," I said, "I am going to be a priest."

"You see this book," I said to him, later in the day. "That's Dante's *Paradiso*."

"Dante," he said, "an Italian." And he lay on the bed with his eyes staring at the ceiling and said nothing more.

This lying in bed and being fed, so to speak, with a spoon was more than luxury: it was also full of meaning. I could not realize it at the time—and I did not need to: but a couple of years later I saw that this all expressed my spiritual life as it was then.

For I was now, at last, born: but I was still only new-born. I was living: I had an interior life, real, but feeble and precarious. And I was still nursed and fed with spiritual milk.

The life of grace had at last, it seemed, become constant, permanent. Weak and without strength as I was, I was nevertheless walking in the way that was liberty and life. I had found my spiritual freedom. My eyes were beginning to open to the powerful and constant light of heaven and my will was at last learning to give in to the subtle and gentle and loving guidance of that love which is Life without end. For once, for the first time in my life, I had been, not days, not weeks, but months, a stranger to sin. And so much health was so new to me, that it might have been too much for me.

And therefore I was being fed not only with the rational milk of every possible spiritual consolation, but it seemed that there was no benefit, no comfort, no innocent happiness, even of the material order, that could be denied me.

So I was all at once surrounded with everything that could protect me against trouble, against savagery, against suffering. Of course, while I was in the hospital, there were some physical pains, some very small inconveniences: but on the whole, everybody who has had an ordinary appendix operation knows that it is really only a picnic. And it was certainly that for me. I finished the whole *Paradiso*, in Italian, and read part of Maritain's *Preface to Metaphysics*.

After ten days I got out and went to Douglaston, to the house where my uncle and aunt still lived and where they invited me to rest until I was on my feet again. So that meant two more weeks of quiet, and undisturbed reading. I could shut myself up in the room that had once been Pop's "den," and make meditations, and pray, as I did, for instance, on the afternoon of Good Friday. And for the rest my aunt was willing to talk all day about the Redemptorists whose monastery had been just down the street when she had been a little girl in Brooklyn.

Finally, in the middle of Easter week, I went to my doctor and he ripped off the bandages and said it was all right for me to go to Cuba.

I think it was in that bright Island that the kindness and solicitude that surrounded me wherever I turned my weak steps, reached their ultimate limit. It would be hard to believe that anyone was so well taken care of as I was: and no one has ever seen an earthly child guarded so closely and so efficiently and cherished and guided and watched and led with such attentive and prevenient care as surrounded me in those days. For I walked through fires and put my head into the mouths of such lions as would bring grey hairs even to the head of a moral theologian, and all the while I was walking in my new simplicity and hardly knew what it was all about, so solicitous were my surrounding angels to whisk the scandals out from the path of my feet, and to put pillows under my knees wherever I seemed about to stumble.

I don't believe that a saint who had been elevated to the state of mystical marriage could walk through the perilous streets and dives of Havana with notably less contamination than I seem to have contracted. And yet this absence of trouble, this apparent immunity from passion or from accident, was something that I calmly took for granted. God was giving me a taste of that sense of proprietorship to which grace gives a sort of a right in the hearts of all His children. For all things are theirs, and they are Christ's, and Christ is God's. They own the world, because they have renounced proprietorship of anything in the world, and of their own bodies, and have ceased to listen to the unjust claims of passion.

Of course, with me there was no question of any real detachment. If I did not listen to my passions it was because, in the merciful dispensation of God, they had ceased to make any noise—for the time being. They did wake up, momentarily, but only when I was well out of harm's way in a very dull and sleepy city called Camagüey where practically everybody was in bed by nine o'clock at night, and where I tried to read St. Teresa's *Autobiography* in Spanish under the big royal palms in a huge garden which I had all to myself.

I told myself that the reason why I had come to Cuba was to make a pilgrimage to Our Lady of Cobre. And I did, in fact, make a kind of a pilgrimage. But it was one of those medieval pilgrimages that was nine-tenths vacation and one-tenth pilgrimage. God tolerated all this and accepted the pilgrimage on the best terms in which it could be interpreted, because He certainly beset me with graces all the way around Cuba: graces of the kind that even a person without deep spirituality can appreciate as graces: and that is the kind of person I was then and still am.

Every step I took opened up a new world of joys, spiritual joys, and joys of the mind and imagination and senses in the natural order, but on the plane of innocence, and under the direction of grace.

There was a partial natural explanation for this. I was learning a thing that could not be completely learned except in a culture that is at least outwardly Catholic. One needs the atmosphere of French or Spanish or Italian Catholicism before there is any possibility of a complete and total experience of all the natural and sensible joys that overflow from the Sacramental life.

But here, at every turn, I found my way into great, cool, dark churches, some of them with splendid altars shining with carven retables or rich with mahogany and silver: and wonderful red gardens of flame flowered before the saints or the Blessed Sacrament.

Here in niches were those lovely, dressed-up images, those little carved Virgins full of miracle and pathos and clad in silks and black velvet, throned above the high altars. Here, in side chapels, were those *pietàs* fraught with fierce, Spanish drama, with thorns and nails whose very sight pierced the

337

mind and heart, and all around the church were many altars to white and black saints: and everywhere were Cubans in prayer, for it is not true that the Cubans neglect their religion —or not as true as Americans complacently think, basing their judgements on the lives of the rich, sallow young men who come north from the island and spend their days in arduous gambling in the dormitories of Jesuit colleges.

But I was living like a prince in that island, like a spiritual millionaire. Every morning, getting up about seven or half-past, and walking out into the warm sunny street, I could find my way quickly to any one of a dozen churches, new churches or as old as the seventeenth century. Almost as soon as I went in the door I could receive Communion, if I wished, for the priest came out with a ciborium loaded with Hosts before Mass and during it and after it—and every fifteen or twenty minutes a new Mass was starting at a different altar. These were the churches of the religious Orders—Carmelites, Franciscans, the American Augustinians at El Santo Cristo, or the Fathers of Mercy—everywhere I turned, there was someone ready to feed me with the infinite strength of the Christ Who loved me, and Who was beginning to show me with an immense and subtle and generous lavishness how much He loved me.

And there were a thousand things to do, a thousand ways of easily making a thanksgiving: everything lent itself to Communion: I could hear another Mass, I could say the Rosary, do the Stations of the Cross, or if I just knelt where I was, everywhere I turned my eyes I saw saints in wood or plaster or those who seemed to be saints in flesh and blood—and even those who were probably not saints, were new enough and picturesque enough to stimulate my mind with many meanings and my heart with prayers. And as I left the church there was no lack of beggars to give me the opportunity of almsgiving, which is an easy and simple way of wiping out sins.

Often I left one church and went to hear another Mass in another church, especially if the day happened to be Sunday, and I would listen to the harmonious sermons of the Spanish priests, the very grammar of which was full of dignity and mysticism and courtesy. After Latin, it seems to me there is no language so fitted for prayer and for talk about God as Spanish: for it is a language at once strong and supple, it has its sharpness, it has the quality of steel in it, which gives it the accuracy that true mysticism needs, and yet it is soft, too, and gentle and pliant, which devotion needs, and it is courteous and suppliant and courtly, and it lends itself surprisingly little to sentimentality. It has some of the intellectuality of French but not the coldness that intellectuality gets in French: and it never overflows into the feminine melodies of Italian. Spanish is never a weak language, never sloppy, even on the lips of a woman.

The fact that while all this was going on in the pulpit, there would be Cubans ringing bells and yelling lottery numbers outside in the street seemed to make no difference. For a people that is supposed to be excitable, the Cubans have a phenomenal amount of patience with all the things that get on American nerves and drive people crazy, like persistent and strident noise. But for my own part, I did not mind any of that any more than the natives did.

When I was sated with prayers, I could go back into the streets, walking among the lights and shadows, stopping to drink huge glasses of iced fruit juices in the little bars, until I came home again and read Maritain or St. Teresa until it was time for lunch.

And so I made my way to Matanzas and Camagüey and Santiago—riding in a wild bus through the olive-grey Cuban countryside, full of sugar-cane fields. All the way I said rosaries and looked out into the great solitary ceiba trees, half expecting that the Mother of God would appear to me in one of them. There seemed to be no reason why she should not, for all things in heaven were just a little out of reach. So I kept looking, looking, and half expecting. But I did not see Our Lady appear, beautiful, in any of the ceiba trees.

At Matanzas I got mixed up in the *paseo* where the whole town walks around and around the square in the evening coolness, the men in one direction and the girls in the other direction, and immediately I made friends with about fifty-one

339

different people of all ages. The evening ended up with me making a big speech in broken Spanish, surrounded by men and boys in a motley crowd that included the town Reds and the town intellectuals and the graduates of the Marist Fathers' school and some law students from the University of Havana. It was all about faith and morals and made a big impression and, in return, their acceptance of it made a big impression on me, too: for many of them were glad that someone, a foreigner, should come and talk about these things, and I heard someone who had just arrived in the crowd say:

"¿Es católico, ese Americano?"

"Man," said the other, "he is a Catholic and a very good Catholic," and the tone in which he said this made me so happy that, when I went to bed, I could not sleep. I lay in the bed and looked up through the mosquito netting at the bright stars that shone in upon me through the wide-open window that had no glass and no frame, but only a heavy wooden shutter against the rain.

In Camagüey I found a Church to La Soledad, Our Lady of Solitude, a little dressed-up image up in a shadowy niche: you could hardly see her. La Soledad! One of my big devotions, and you never find her, never hear anything about her in this country, except that one of the old California missions was dedicated to her.

Finally my bus went roaring across the dry plain towards the blue wall of mountains: Oriente, the end of my pilgrimage.

When we had crossed over the divide and were going down through the green valleys towards the Caribbean Sea, I saw the yellow Basilica of Our Lady of Cobre, standing on a rising above the tin roofs of the mining village in the depths of a deep bowl of green, backed by cliffs and sheer slopes robed in jungle.

"There you are, Caridad del Cobre! It is you that I have come to see; you will ask Christ to make me His priest, and I will give you my heart, Lady: and if you will obtain for me this priesthood, I will remember you at my first Mass in such a way that the Mass will be for you and offered through your hands in gratitude to the Holy Trinity, Who has used your love to win me this great grace."

The bus tore down the mountainside to Santiago. The mining engineer who had got on at the top of the divide was talking all the way down in English he had learned in New York, telling me of the graft that had enriched the politicians of Cuba and of Oriente.

In Santiago I ate dinner on the terrace of a big hotel in front of the cathedral. Across the square was the shell of a five-storey building that looked as if it had been gutted by a bomb: but the ruin had happened in an earthquake not so very long before. It was long enough ago so that the posters on the fence that had been put up in front of it had time to get tattered, and I was thinking: perhaps it is now getting to be time for another earthquake. And I looked up at the two towers of the cathedral, ready to sway and come booming down on my head.

The bus that took me to Cobre the next morning was the most dangerous of all the furious busses that are the terror of Cuba. I think it made most of the journey at eighty miles an hour on two wheels, and several times I thought it was going to explode. I said rosaries all the way up to the shrine, while the trees went by in a big greenish-yellow blur. If Our Lady had tried to appear to me, I probably would never even got a glimpse of her.

I walked up the path that wound around the mound on which the Basilica stands. Entering the door, I was surprised that the floor was so shiny and the place was so clean. I was in the back of the church, up in the apse, in a kind of oratory behind the high altar, and there, facing me, in a little shrine, was La Caridad, the little, cheerful, black Virgin, crowned with a crown and dressed in royal robes, who is the Queen of Cuba.

There was nobody else in the place but a pious middle-aged lady attendant in a black dress who was eager to sell me a lot of medals and so I knelt before La Caridad and made my prayer and made my promise. I sneaked down into the Basilica after that, and knelt where I could see La Caridad and where I could really be alone and pray, but the pious lady, impatient to make her deal, or perhaps afraid that I might get up to some mischief in the Basilica, came down and peeked through the door.

So, disappointed and resigned, I got up and came out and bought a medal and got some change for the beggars and went away, without having a chance to say all that I wanted to say to La Caridad or to hear much from her.

Down in the village I bought a bottle of some kind of *gaseosa* and stood under the tin roof of the porch of the village store. Somewhere in one of the shacks, on a harmonium, was played: *"Kyrie Eleison, Kyrie Eleison, Kyrie Eleison."*

And I went back to Santiago.

But while I was sitting on the terrace of the hotel, eating lunch, La Caridad del Cobre had a word to say to me. She handed me an idea for a poem that formed so easily and smoothly and spontaneously in my mind that all I had to do was finish eating and go up to my room and type it out, almost without a correction.

So the poem turned out to be both what she had to say to me and what I had to say to her. It was a song for La Caridad del Cobre, and it was, as far as I was concerned, something new, and the first real poem I had ever written, or anyway the one I liked best. It pointed the way to many other poems; it opened the gate, and set me travelling on a certain and direct track that was to last me several years.

The poem said:

> The white girls lift their heads like trees,
> The black girls go
> Reflected like flamingoes in the street.
>
> The white girls sing as shrill as water,
> The black girls talk as quiet as clay.
>
> The white girls open their arms like clouds,
> The black girls close their eyes like wings:
> Angels bow down like bells,
> Angels look up like toys,

Because the heavenly stars
Stand in a ring:
And all the pieces of the mosaic, earth,
Get up and fly away like birds.

When I went back to Havana, I found out something else, too, and something vastly more important. It was something that made me realize, all of a sudden, not merely intellectually, but experimentally, the real uselessness of what I had been half deliberately looking for: the visions in the ceiba trees. And this experience opened another door, not a way to a kind of writing but a way into a world infinitely new, a world that was out of this world of ours entirely and which transcended it infinitely, and which was not a world, but which was God Himself.

I was in the Church of St. Francis at Havana. It was a Sunday. I had been to Communion at some other church, I think at El Cristo, and now I had come here to hear another Mass. The building was crowded. Up in front, before the altar, there were rows and rows of children, crowded together. I forget whether they were First Communicants or not: but they were children around that age. I was far in the back of the church, but I could see the heads of all those children.

It came time for the Consecration. The priest raised the Host, then he raised the chalice. When he put the chalice down on the altar, suddenly a Friar in his brown robe and white cord stood up in front of the children, and all at once the voices of the children burst out:

"*Creo en Diós.* . . ."

"I believe in God the Father Almighty, the creator of heaven and earth . . ."

The Creed. But that cry, "*Creo en Diós!*" It was loud, and bright, and sudden and glad and triumphant; it was a good big shout, that came from all those Cuban children, a joyous affirmation of faith.

Then, as sudden as the shout and as definite, and a thousand times more bright, there formed in my mind an awareness, an understanding, a realization of what had just taken

343

place on the altar, at the Consecration: a realization of God made present by the words of Consecration in a way that made Him belong to me.

But what a thing it was, this awareness: it was so intangible, and yet it struck me like a thunderclap. It was a light that was so bright that it had no relation to any visible light and so profound and so intimate that it seemed like a neutralization of every lesser experience.

And yet the thing that struck me most of all was that this light was in a certain sense "ordinary"—it was a light (and this most of all was what took my breath away) that was offered to all, to everybody, and there was nothing fancy or strange about it. It was the light of faith deepened and reduced to an extreme and sudden obviousness.

It was as if I had been suddenly illuminated by being blinded by the manifestation of God's presence.

The reason why this light was blinding and neutralizing was that there was and could be simply nothing in it of sense or imagination. When I call it a light that is a metaphor which I am using, long after the fact. But at the moment, another overwhelming thing about this awareness was that it disarmed all images, all metaphors, and cut through the whole skein of species and phantasms with which we naturally do our thinking. It ignored all sense experience in order to strike directly at the heart of truth, as if a sudden and immediate contact had been established between my intellect and the Truth Who was now physically really and substantially before me on the altar. But this contact was not something speculative and abstract: it was concrete and experimental and belonged to the order of knowledge, yes, but more still to the order of love.

Another thing about it was that this light was something far above and beyond the level of any desire or any appetite I had ever yet been aware of. It was purified of all emotion and cleansed of everything that savored of sensible yearnings. It was love as clean and direct as vision: and it flew straight to the possession of the Truth it loved.

And the first articulate thought that came to my mind was:

"Heaven is right here in front of me: Heaven, Heaven!"

It lasted only a moment: but it left a breathless joy and a clean peace and happiness that stayed for hours and it was something I have never forgotten.

The strange thing about this light was that although it seemed so "ordinary" in the sense I have mentioned, and so accessible, there was no way of recapturing it. In fact, I did not even know how to start trying to reconstruct the experience or bring it back if I wanted to, except to make acts of faith and love. But it was easy to see that there was nothing I could do to give any act of faith that peculiar quality of sudden obviousness: that was a gift and had to come from somewhere else, beyond and above myself.

However, let no one think that just because of this light that came to me one day, at Mass, in the Church of St. Francis at Havana, I was in the habit of understanding things that clearly, or that I was far advanced in prayer. No, my prayer continued to be largely vocal. And the mental prayer I made was not systematic, but the more or less spontaneous meditating and affective prayer that came and went, according to my reading, here and there. And most of the time my prayer was not so much prayer as a matter of anticipating, with hope and desire, my entrance into the Franciscan novitiate, and a certain amount of imagining what it was going to be like, so that often I was not praying at all, but only day dreaming.

iv

The months passed quickly, but not quickly enough for me. Already it was June 1940: but the two months that remained until the date in August when the doors of the novitiate would open to receive thirty or forty new postulants seemed infinitely far away.

I did not stay long in New York when I came back from Cuba. I was there only a few days, in which I went to the monastery on 31st Street, and learned from Father Edmund that my application for admission had been accepted, and that some of the necessary papers had arrived. It was a very good thing that this was so, because postulants entering a religious Order need documents from every diocese where they have lived for a morally continuous year since their fourteenth year, as well as a birth certificate and a lot of other things as well.

But this was precisely the time when the German armies were pouring into France. At the moment when I stepped off the boat in New York, they had made their first great break through the French lines, and it had at last become obvious that the impregnable defence of the Maginot Line was a myth. Indeed, it was only a matter of very few days before the fierce armored divisions of the Nazis, following in the path broken out before them by the *Luftwaffe*, pierced the demoralized French army and embraced the betrayed nation in arms of steel. They had Paris within a fortnight, and then they were at the Loire, and finally the papers were full of blurred wirephotos of the dumb, isolated dining-car in the park at Compiègne where Hitler made the French eat the document on which the 1918 armistice had been written.

So, too, if my father and mother's marriage certificate from St. Anne's in Soho, London, had not come in that year, it might never have come at all. I don't know if the parish records of St. Anne's survived the blitzkrieg that was about to be let loose over the head of the huge, dark city full of sins and miseries, in whose fogs I had once walked with such wise complacency.

Everything seemed clear. A month would go by, and then another, and soon I would be walking, with my suitcase, up some drab, unimaginable street in Paterson, New Jersey, to a small brick monastery which I could not very well envisage. But the drabness of the city would be left behind at the door and I knew, although I had no special illusions about St. Anthony's novitiate either, that inside I would find peace. And I would begin my retreat, and after a month or so I would put on the brown robe and white cord of a friar and I would be walking in sandals with a shaved head, in silence, to a not too beautiful chapel. But anyway, there I would have God, and possess Him, and belong to Him.

Meanwhile, I would go upstate. The best thing I could think of was to join Lax and Rice and Gerdy and Gibney and the red-headed Southerner Jim Knight who were all living at the cottage on the hill over Olean. But on the way, I went through Ithaca to see my brother at Cornell.

Perhaps this was the last time I would see John Paul before I entered the novitiate. I could not tell.

This was the year he was supposed to graduate from Cornell, but it turned out that things had gone wrong, and he was not graduating after all. The bored, lost, perplexed expression that wrinkled his forehead, the restlessness of his walk, and the joyless noisiness of his laughter told me all I needed to know about my brother's college career. I recognized all the tokens of the spiritual emptiness that had dogged my own steps from Cambridge to Columbia.

He had a big second-hand Buick in which he drove up and down all day under the heavy-hanging branches of the campus trees. His life was a constant reckless peregrination back and forth between the college and the town in the valley below it, from his classes to Willard Straight Hall to sit on the terrace with the co-eds and drink sodas in the sun, and look at the vast, luminous landscape as bright and highly colored as a plate in the *National Geographic Magazine*. He wandered from the university library to his rooms in the town, and thence to the movies, and thence to all those holes in the wall whose names I have forgotten or never knew, where Cornell students sit around tables in a dull, amber semi-darkness and fill the air with their noise and the smoke of their cigarettes and the din of their appalling wit.

I only stayed with him at Ithaca a couple of days, and when I got up in the morning to go to Mass and Communion, he came down and knelt with me and heard Mass, and watched me go to Communion. He told me he had been talking to the chaplain of the Catholic students, but I could not make out whether his real attraction was the faith, or the fact that the chaplain was interested in flying. And John Paul himself, as it turned out, was going down most days to the Ithaca airport and learning to fly a plane.

347

After we had had breakfast, he went back to the campus to take an examination in some such subject as Oriental history or Russian Literature, and I got on a bus that would take me to Elmira where I would get the train to Olean.

The cottage was crowded, and that meant that there were far more dirty dishes piling up in the kitchen after those perilous meals of fried, suspicious meats. But everybody was busy with something and the woods were quiet and the sun was as bright as ever on the wide, airy landscape of rolling mountains before our faces.

Presently Seymour came from New York, with Helen his wife, and Peggy Wells came to the cottage, and later came Nancy Flagg who went to Smith and for whom Lax had written a poem in the *New Yorker*. Gibney and Seymour climbed into the tops of thirty-foot trees and built a platform there about ten feet long between the trees, reached by a ladder up the side of one of the trees. It was so high that Lax would not even climb it.

Meanwhile, in the early mornings, outside the room where the girls lived, you would see Peggy Wells sitting and reading one of those fancy editions of the Bible as literature out loud to herself. And when Nancy Flagg was there, she sat in the same sun, and combed her long hair, which was marvelous red-gold and I hope she never cut it short for it gave glory to God. And on those days I think Peggy Wells read the Bible out loud to Nancy Flagg. I don't know. Later Peggy Wells walked through the woods by herself puzzling over Aristotle's *Categories*.

Rice and Knight and Gerdy sat apart, mostly in or around the garage, typing or discussing novels or commercial short stories, and Lax grew his beard, and thought, and sometimes put down on paper thoughts for a story, or talked with Nancy Flagg.

For my own part, I found a good place where I could sit on a rail of the fence along the stony driveway, and look at the far hills, and say the rosary. It was a quiet, sunny place, and the others did not come by that way much, and you could not

348

hear the sounds of the house. This was where I was happiest, in those weeks in June.

It was too far from town to go down to Communion every morning—I had to hitch-hike down. And that was one reason why I asked one of my friends, Father Joseph, a Friar who had come to St. Bonaventure's from New York to teach summer school, if I could not come down there for a couple of weeks.

Seeing that I was going to enter the Order in August, it was not hard to persuade the Guardian to let me come down and stay in the big, dilapidated room in the gymnasium that was occupied by three or four poor students and seminarians who had odd jobs around the place as telephone operators and garage hands, for the summer.

At that time all the clerics from the different houses of studies in the Province came to St. Bonaventure's for the summer, and I suppose they are doing it again, now that the war is over. So in those weeks I really began to enter into Franciscan life, and get some taste of it as it is led in this country and to know some of its pleasant and cheerful and easy-going informality.

Summer school had not yet started, and the clerics had plenty of time to sit around on the steps of the library and gymnasium and tell me stories about how it had been with them in the novitiate. I began to get a picture of a life that was, in their estimation, somewhat severe, but was full of its own lighter moments.

St. Anthony's monastery, they said, was the hottest place they had ever seen, in the summer time, and the chapel was stuffy, and was filled with a sickening smell of wax from all the burning candles. Then there was a certain amount of work to be done. You had to scrub floors and wash dishes and work in the garden. But then you got some time to yourself and there was recreation too. I got dark hints of humiliations that were to be expected, here and there, but they all agreed that the novice master was a good sort of a fellow, and they liked him. They told me I would too.

The general impression I got was that all the unpleasantness and hardship was crowded into the year of the canonical novitiate, and that after that things opened out and became easy and pleasant as they were now: and certainly these clerics as I saw them were leading a life that could not by any stretch of the imagination be called hard. Here they were living at this college, among these beautiful green hills, surrounded by woods and fields, in a corner of America where the summer is never hot, and which they would leave long before the cold weather came. They had whole mornings and afternoons to read or study, and there were hours in which they could play baseball or tennis or go for walks in the woods, or even go in to town, walking two by two, solemnly in black suits and Roman collars.

They told me elaborate stories of the ways there were of getting around even the easy regulations that prohibited too much familiarity with seculars, and of course the good Catholic families in the town were falling over themselves in their anxiety to invite the young Franciscans to come and sit in their parlors and be made much of, with cookies and soft drinks.

For my part, I was already deciding in my mind that I would make use of all these opportunities to get away and read and pray and do some writing, when I was in my brown robe and wearing those same sandals.

Meanwhile, I got up when the clerics did—I suppose it was not much earlier than six in the morning—and went to Mass with them, and received Communion after them all, and then went to breakfast with the farm hands, where a little nun in a white and blue habit brought us cornflakes and fried eggs: for the cooking was done by some Sisters of one of those innumerable little Franciscan congregations.

After breakfast, I would walk over to the library, breathing the cold morning air as the dew melted on the lawns. Father Irenaeus gave me the key to the philosophy seminar room, and there I could spend the morning all alone reading St. Thomas, at my leisure, with a big, plain wooden crucifix at the end of the room for me to look at when I raised my eyes from the book.

I don't think I had ever been so happy in my life as I now

was in that silent library, turning over the pages of the first part of the *Summa Theologica,* and here and there making notes on the goodness, the all-presence, the wisdom, the power, the love of God.

In the afternoons, I would walk in the woods, or along the Alleghany River that flowed among the trees, skirting the bottom of the wide pastures.

Turning over the pages of Butler's *Lives of the Saints,* I had looked for some name to take in religion—indeed, that was a problem over which I had wasted an undue amount of time. The Province was a big one, and there were so many Friars in it that they had run out of all the names—and you could not take a name that was already taken by someone else. I knew in advance that I could not be a John Baptist or an Augustine or Jerome or Gregory. I would have to find some outlandish name like Paphnutius (which was Father Irenaeus' suggestion). Finally I came across a Franciscan called Bl. John Spaniard and I thought that would sound fine.

I considered the possibility of myself running around in a brown robe and sandals, and imagined I heard the novice master saying: "Frater John Spaniard, go over there and scrub that floor." Or else he would put his head out of his room and say to one of the other novices: "Go and get Frater John Spaniard and bring him here," and then I would come humbly along the corridor in my sandals—or rather *our* sandals—with my eyes down, with the rapid but decorous gait of a young Friar who knew his business: Frater John Spaniard. It made a pleasant picture.

When I went back to the cottage on the hill, and timidly admitted that I thought I might take the name of Frater John Spaniard, Seymour at least thought it was a good choice. Seymour had a weakness for anything that seemed to have some sort of dash about it, and maybe in the back of his mind he was thinking of Torquemada and the Inquisition, although I don't think the John Spaniard in question had much to do with that. But I have forgotten where that saint actually did belong in history.

All this fuss about choosing a fancy name may seem like

nothing but harmless foolishness, and I suppose that is true. But nevertheless I now realize that it was a sign of a profound and radical defect in the vocation which so filled my heart and occupied my imagination in those summer days of 1940.

It is true I was called to the cloister. That has been made abundantly clear. But the dispositions with which I was now preparing to enter the Franciscan novitiate were much more imperfect than I was able to realize. In choosing the Franciscans, I had followed what was apparently a perfectly legitimate attraction—an attraction which might very well have been a sign of God's will, even though it was not quite as supernatural as I thought. I had chosen this Order because I thought I would be able to keep its Rule without difficulty, and because I was attracted by the life of teaching and writing which it would offer me, and much more by the surroundings in which I saw I would probably live. God very often accepts dispositions that are no better than these, and even some that are far worse, and turns them into a true vocation in His own time.

But with me, it was not to be so. I had to be led by a way that I could not understand, and I had to follow a path that was beyond my own choosing. God did not want anything of my natural tastes and fancies and selections until they had been more completely divorced from their old track, their old habits, and directed to Himself, by His own working. My natural choice, my own taste in selecting a mode of life, was altogether untrustworthy. And already my selfishness was asserting itself, and claiming this whole vocation for itself, by investing the future with all kinds of natural pleasures and satisfactions which would fortify and defend my ego against the troubles and worries of life in the world.

Besides, I was depending almost entirely on my own powers and on my own virtues—as if I had any!—to become a good religious, and to live up to my obligations in the monastery. God does not want that. He does not ask us to leave the world as a favor to Himself.

God calls men—not only religious, but all Christians—to be

the "salt of the earth." But the savor of the salt, says St. Augustine, is a supernatural life, and we lose our savor if, ceasing to rely on God alone, we are guided, in our actions, by the mere desire of temporal goods or the fear of their loss: "Be ye not solicitous, therefore, saying what shall we eat, or what shall we drink or wherewith shall we be clothed? For after all these things do the heathens seek. For your Father knoweth that you have need of all these things." "And he said to all: If any man will come after me, let him deny himself and take up his cross daily, and follow me. For whosoever will save his life shall lose it; for he that shall lose his life, for my sake, shall save it."

No matter what religious Order a man enters, whether its Rule be easy or strict in itself does not much matter; if his vocation is to be really fruitful it must cost him something, and must be a real sacrifice. It must be a cross, a true renunciation of natural goods, even of the highest natural goods.

Since I was the person that I happened to be, and since I was so strongly attached to material goods, and so immersed in my own self, and so far from God, and so independent of Him, and so dependent on myself and my own imaginary powers, it was necessary that I should not enter a monastery feeling the way I did about the Franciscans.

The truth of the matter is simply this: becoming a Franciscan, especially at that precise moment of history, meant absolutely no sacrifice at all, as far as I was concerned. Even the renunciation of legitimate pleasures of the flesh did not cost me as much as it might seem. I had suffered so much tribulation and unrest on their account that I rejoiced in the prospect of peace, in a life protected from the heat and anguish of passion by the vow of chastity. So even this was a boon rather than a matter of pain—all the more so because I imagined, in my stupid inexperience, that the fight against concupiscence had already been won, and that my soul was free, and that I had little or nothing to worry about any more.

No, all I would have to do would be to enter the novitiate,

and undergo one year of inconveniences so slight that they would hardly be noticeable, and after that everything would be full of fine and easy delights—plenty of freedom, plenty of time to read and study and meditate, and ample liberty to follow my own tastes and desires in all things of the mind and spirit. Indeed, I was entering upon a life of the highest possible natural pleasures: for even prayer, in a certain sense, can be a natural pleasure.

Above all, it must be remembered that the world was at war, and even now, at the cottage, we sat around the fireplace at night and talked about the Selective Service Law that would soon be passed in Washington, wondering how it would be, and what we should do about it.

For Lax and Gibney this law involved a complicated problem of conscience. They were even asking themselves whether the war was licit at all: and if so, whether they could be justified in entering it as combatants. For my own part, no problems even arose, since I would be in a monastery, and the question would be settled automatically. . . .

I think it is very evident that such a vocation demanded more of a trial. God was not going to let me walk out of the miseries of the world into a refuge of my own choosing. He had another way prepared for me. He had several questions He wanted to ask me about this vocation of mine: questions which I would not be able to answer.

Then, when I failed to answer them, He would give me the answers, and I would find the problem solved.

It was a strange thing: I did not take it as a warning: but one night I was reading the ninth chapter of the Book of Job, and was amazed and stunned by a series of lines which I could not forget:

And Job answered and said: "Indeed I know that it is so, and that man cannot be justified compared with God. If He will contend with him, he cannot answer Him, one for a thousand. . . . He is wise in heart and mighty in strength: who hath resisted Him and hath had peace? . . . Who shaketh the earth out of her place, and the

354

pillars thereof tremble. Who commandeth the sun and it riseth not: and shutteth up the stars as it were under a seal."

It was a cool summer evening. I was sitting in the driveway outside the wide-open garage which had become a general dormitory, since we now had no car to put there. Rice and Lax and Seymour and I had all brought our beds out there to sleep in the air. With the book in my lap I looked down at the lights of the cars crawling up the road from the valley. I looked at the dark outline of the wooded hills and at the stars that were coming out in the eastern sky.

The words of the vulgate text rang and echoed in my heart: *"Qui facit Arcturum et Oriona . . ."* "Who maketh Arcturus and Orion and Hyades and the inner parts of the south. . . ."

There was something deep and disturbing in the lines. I thought they only moved me as poetry: and yet I also felt, obscurely enough, that there was something personal about them. God often talks to us directly in Scripture. That is, He plants the words full of actual graces as we read them and sudden undiscovered meanings are sown in our hearts, if we attend to them, reading with minds that are at prayer.

I did not yet have the art of reading that way, but nevertheless these words had a dark fire in them with which I began to feel myself burned and seared.

If He come to me, I shall not see Him: if He depart, I shall not understand. . . . If He examine me on a sudden who shall answer Him? Or who can say: why dost Thou so?

There was something in the words that seemed to threaten all the peace that I had been tasting for months past, a kind of forewarning of an accusation that would unveil forgotten realities. I had fallen asleep in my sweet security. I was living as if God only existed to do me temporal favors . . .

God whose wrath no man can resist, and under Whom they stoop that bear up the world.

What am I then, that I should answer Him and have
words with Him?

And if He should hear me when I call, I should not
believe that He had heard my voice.

For He shall crush me in a whirlwind and multiply
my wounds even without cause. . . .

"Even without cause!" And my uneasy spirit was already
beginning to defend itself against this unfair God Who could
not be unjust, could not be unfair.

If I would justify myself, my own mouth shall condemn me: if I would shew myself innocent He shall
prove me wicked.

. . . *and multiply my wounds even without cause.*

I closed the book. The words struck deep. They were more
than I would ever be able to understand. But the impression
they made should have been a kind of warning that I was
about to find out something about their meaning.

The blow fell suddenly.

I was within a few weeks of entering the novitiate. Already
I was receiving those last minute letters from the novice-
master, with the printed lists of things I was expected to bring
with me to the monastery. They were few enough. The only
perplexing item on the list was "one umbrella."

The list made me happy. I read it over and over. I began
to feel the same pleased excitement that used to glow in the
pit of my stomach when I was about to start out for camp in
the summer, or to go to a new school. . . .

Then God asked me a question. He asked me a question
about my vocation.

Rather, God did not have to ask me any questions. He knew
all that He needed to know about my vocation. He allowed
the devil, as I think, to ask me some questions, not in order
that the devil should get any information, but in order that I
might learn a thing or two.

There is a certain kind of humility in hell which is one of
the worst things in hell, and which is infinitely far from the

356

humility of the saints, which is peace. The false humility of hell is an unending, burning shame at the inescapable stigma of our sins. The sins of the damned are felt by them as vesture of intolerable insults from which they cannot escape, Nessus shirts that burn them up for ever and which they can never throw off.

The anguish of this self-knowledge is inescapable even on earth, as long as there is any self-love left in us: because it is pride that feels the burning of that shame. Only when all pride, all self-love has been consumed in our souls by the love of God, are we delivered from the thing which is the subject of those torments. It is only when we have lost all love of our selves for our own sakes that our past sins cease to give us any cause for suffering or for the anguish of shame.

For the saints, when they remember their sins, do not remember the sins but the mercy of God, and therefore even past evil is turned by them into a present cause of joy and serves to glorify God.

It is the proud that have to be burned and devoured by the horrible humility of hell. . . . But as long as we are in this life, even that burning anguish can be turned into a grace, and should be a cause of joy.

But anyway, one day I woke up to find out that the peace I had known for six months or more had suddenly gone.

The Eden I had been living in had vanished. I was outside the wall. I did not know what flaming swords barred my way to the gate whose rediscovery had become impossible. I was once more out in the cold and naked and alone.

Then everything began to fall apart, especially my vocation to the monastery.

Not that it occurred to me to doubt my desire to be a Franciscan, to enter the cloister, to become a priest. That desire was stronger than ever now that I was cast out into the darkness of this cold solitude. It was practically the only thing I had left, the only thing to cover me and keep me warm: and yet it was small comfort, because the very presence of the desire tortured me by contrast with the sudden hopelessness that had come storming up out of the hidden depths of my heart.

My desire to enter the cloister was small comfort indeed: for I had suddenly been faced with the agonizing doubt, the unanswerable question: Do I really have that vocation?

I suddenly remembered who I was, who I had been. I was astonished: since last September I seemed to have forgotten that I had ever sinned.

And now I suddenly realized that none of the men to whom I had talked about my vocation, neither Dan Walsh nor Father Edmund, knew who I really was. They knew nothing about my past. They did not know how I had lived before I entered the Church. They had simply accepted me because I was superficially presentable, I had a fairly open sort of a face and seemed to be sincere and to have an ordinary amount of sense and good will. Surely that was not enough.

Now the terrible problem faced me: "I have got to go and let Father Edmund know about all this. Perhaps it will make a big difference." After all, it is not enough merely to *desire* to enter the monastery.

An attraction to the cloister is not even the most important element in a religious vocation. You have to have the right moral and physical and intellectual aptitudes. And you have to be *accepted*, and accepted on certain grounds.

When I looked at myself in the light of this doubt, it began to appear utterly impossible that anyone in his right mind could consider me fit material for the priesthood.

I immediately packed my bag and started out for New York.

It seemed a long, long journey as the train crawled along the green valleys. As we were coming down the Delaware towards Callicoon, where the Franciscans had their minor seminary, the sky had clouded over. We were slowing down, and the first houses of the village were beginning to file past on the road beside the track. A boy who had been swimming in the river came running up a path through the long grass, from the face of the thunderstorm that was just about to break. His mother was calling to him from the porch of one of the houses.

I became vaguely aware of my own homelessness.

When we had gone around the bend and I could see the stone tower of the seminary on the hilltop among the trees, I thought: "I will never live in you; it is finished."

I got into New York that evening and called up Father Edmund, but he was too busy to see me.

So I went out to the house at Douglaston.

"When are you going to the novitiate?" my aunt asked me.

"Maybe I'm not going," I said.

They did not ask me any questions.

I went to Communion and prayed earnestly that God's will should be done—and it was. But I was far from being able to understand it then.

Father Edmund listened to what I had to say. I told him about my past and all the troubles I had had. He was very friendly and very kind.

But if I had had any hope that he would wave all my doubts aside with a smile, I was soon disappointed. He said:

"Well, Tom, listen: suppose you let me think it over and pray a bit. Come back in a couple of days. All right?"

"In a couple of days?"

"Come back tomorrow."

So I waited for another day. My mind was full of anguish and restlessness. I prayed: "My God, please take me into the monastery. But anyway, whatever You want, Your will be done."

Of course I understand the whole business now. My own mind was full of strange, exaggerated ideas. I was in a kind of a nightmare. I could not see anything straight. But Father Edmund saw clearly enough for all that.

He saw that I was only a recent convert, not yet two years in the Church. He saw that I had had an unsettled life, and that my vocation was by no means sure, and that I was upset with doubts and misgivings. The novitiate was full, anyway. And when a novitiate is crammed with postulants year after year it is time for somebody to reflect about the quality of the vocations that are coming in. When there is such a crowd, you have to be careful that a few who are less desirable do not float in on the tide with the rest. . . .

So the next day he told me kindly enough that I ought to write to the Provincial and tell him that I had reconsidered my application.

There was nothing I could say. I could only hang my head and look about me at the ruins of my vocation.

I asked a few faint-hearted questions, trying to feel my way and find out if my case were altogether hopeless. Naturally, Father did not want to commit himself or his Order to anything, and I could not even get what might seem to be a vague promise for the future.

There seemed to me to be no question that I was now excluded from the priesthood for ever.

I promised I would write at once, and that I would proclaim my undying loyalty to the Friars Minor in doing so.

"Do that," Father said. "The Provincial will be pleased."

When I walked down the steps of the monastery, I was so dazed I didn't know what to do. All I could think of was to go over across Seventh Avenue to the Church of the Capuchins, next to the station. I went inside the church, and knelt in the back and, seeing there was a priest hearing confessions, I presently got up and took my place in the short line that led to his confessional.

I knelt in the darkness until the slide snapped back with a bang and I saw a thin, bearded priest who looked something like James Joyce. All the Capuchins in this country have that kind of a beard. The priest was in no mood to stand for any nonsense, and I myself was confused and miserable, and couldn't explain myself properly, and so he got my story all mixed up. Evidently he decided that I was only complaining and trying to get around the decision that had been made by some religious Order that had fired me out of their novitiate, probably for some good reason.

The whole thing was so hopeless that finally, in spite of myself, I began to choke and sob and I couldn't talk any more. So the priest, probably judging that I was some emotional and unstable and stupid character, began to tell me in very strong terms that I certainly did not belong in the monastery, still less the priesthood and, in fact, gave me to understand that I was simply wasting his time and insulting the Sacrament of Penance by indulging my self-pity in his confessional.

When I came out of that ordeal, I was completely broken in pieces. I could not keep back the tears, which ran down between the fingers of the hands in which I concealed my face. So I prayed before the Tabernacle and the big stone crucified Christ above the altar.

The only thing I knew, besides my own tremendous misery, was that I must no longer consider that I had a vocation to the cloister.

2

True North

It was very hot on Church Street. The street was torn up, and the dust swirled in the sun like gold around the crawling busses and the trucks and taxis. There were crowds of people on the sidewalks.

I stood under the relatively cool, white walls of the new Post Office building. And then, suddenly, walking in the crowd I saw my brother who was supposed to be at Ithaca. He was coming out of the building, and walking with more of a purpose, more of a swing. He almost ran into me.

"Oh," he said, "hello. Are you going out to Douglaston? I'll give you a ride. I've got the car here, just around the corner."

"What are you doing here?" I said.

Under the arching door of the big building were placards about joining the Navy, the Army, the Marines. The only question in my mind was which one he had been trying to join.

"Did you read about this new Naval Reserve scheme they've got?" he said. I knew something about it. That was what he was trying to get into. It was practically settled.

"You go on a cruise," he said, "and then you get a commission."

"Is it as easy as that?"

"Well, I guess they're anxious to get men. Of course, you have to be a college man."

When I told him I was not going to enter the novitiate after all, he said: "Why don't you come in to the Naval Reserve."

"No," I said, "no, thanks."

Presently he said: "What's that package you've got under your arm? Buy some books?"

"Yes."

When he had unlocked the car, I ripped the paper off the package, and took out the cardboard box containing the set of four books, bound in black leather, marked in gold.

I handed him one of the volumes. It was sleek and smelled new. The pages were edged in gold. There were red and green markers.

"What are they?" said John Paul.

"Breviaries."

The four books represented a decision. They said that if I could not live in the monastery, I should try to live in the world as if I were a monk in a monastery. They said that I was going to get as close as possible to the life I was not allowed to lead. If I could not wear the religious habit, I would at least join a Third Order and would try my best to get a job teaching in some Catholic College where I could live under the same roof as the Blessed Sacrament.

There could be no more question of living just like everybody else in the world. There could be no more compromises with the life that tried, at every turn, to feed me poison. I had to turn my back on these things.

God had kept me out of the cloister: that was His affair. He had also given me a vocation to live the kind of a life that people led in cloisters. If I could not be a religious, a priest—that was God's affair. But nevertheless He still wanted me to lead something of the life of a priest or of a religious.

I had said something to Father Edmund about it, in a general way, and he had agreed. But I did not tell him about the Breviaries. It did not even occur to me to do so. I had said: "I am going to try to live like a religious."

He thought that was all right. If I was teaching, and living in a college, that would be all right, it would be fine. And he was glad I wanted to join the Third Order, although he did not seem to attach much importance to it.

For my own part, I was not quite sure what a Third Order secular amounted to in modern America. But thinking of the Franciscan Tertiaries of the Middle Ages, and of their great saints, I realized in some obscure way that there were, or at least should be, great possibilities of sanctification in a Third Order.

I did have a sort of a suspicion that it might turn out, after all, to be little more, in the minds of most of its members, than a society for gaining Indulgences. But in any case, I did not despise Indulgences either, or any of the other spiritual benefits that came with the cord and scapular. However, it was going to be a long time before I got them, and in the meantime I did not hesitate to shape out the new life I thought God wanted of me.

It was a difficult and uncertain business, and I was starting again to make a long and arduous climb, alone, and from what seemed to be a great depth.

If I had ever thought I had become immune from passion, and that I did not have to fight for freedom, there was no chance of that illusion any more. It seemed that every step I took carried me painfully forward under a burden of desires that almost crushed me with the monotony of their threat, the intimate, searching familiarity of their ever-present disgust.

I did not have any lofty theories about the vocation of a lay-contemplative. In fact, I no longer dignified what I was trying to do by the name of a vocation. All I knew was that I wanted grace, and that I needed prayer, and that I was helpless without God, and that I wanted to do everything that people did to keep close to Him.

It was no longer possible to consider myself, abstractly, as being in a certain "state of life" which had special technical relations to other "states of life." All that occupied me now was the immediate practical problem of getting up my hill with this terrific burden I had on my shoulders, step by step, begging God to drag me along and get me away from my enemies and from those who were trying to destroy me.

I did not even reflect how the Breviary, the Canonical Office, was the most powerful and effective prayer I could possibly have chosen, since it is the prayer of the whole Church, and concentrates in itself all the power of the Church's impetration, centered around the infinitely mighty

Sacrifice of the Mass—the jewel of which the rest of the Liturgy is the setting: the soul which is the life of the whole Liturgy and of all the Sacramentals. All this was beyond me, although I grasped it at least obscurely. All I knew was that I needed to say the Breviary, and say it every day.

Buying those books at Benziger's that day was one of the best things I ever did in my life. The inspiration to do it was a very great grace. There are few things I can remember that give me more joy.

The first time I actually tried to say the Office was on the feast of the Curé of Ars, St. John Vianney. I was on the train, going back to Olean—to Olean because the cottage was, for the time being, the safest place I could think of, and because anyway my best prospect for a job was at St. Bonaventure's.

As soon as the train was well started on its journey, and was climbing into the hills towards Suffern, I opened up the book and began right away with Matins, in the Common of a Confessor-non-pontiff.

"*Venite exultemus Domino, jubilemus Deo salutari nostro . . .*" It was a happy experience, although its exultancy was subdued and lost under my hesitations and external confusion about how to find my way around in the jungle of the rubrics. To begin with, I did not know enough to look for the general rubrics at the beginning of the *Pars Hiemalis* and anyway, when I did eventually find them, there was too much information in small-print and obscure canonical Latin for me to make much out of them.

The train climbed slowly into the Catskills, and I went on from psalm to psalm, smoothly enough. By the time I got to the Lessons of the Second Nocturn, I had figured out whose feast it was that I was celebrating.

This business of saying the Office on the Erie train, going up through the Delaware valley, was to become a familiar experience in the year that was ahead. Of course, I soon found out the ordinary routine by which Matins and Lauds are anticipated the evening of the day before. Usually, then, on my way from New York to Olean, I would be saying the Little Hours around ten o'clock in the morning when the train had passed Port Jervis and was travelling at the base of the steep, wooded hills that hemmed in the river on either side. If I looked up from the pages of the book, I would see the sun blazing on the trees and moist rocks, and flashing on the surface of the shallow river and playing in the forest foliage along the line. And all this was very much like what the book was singing to me, so that everything lifted up my heart to God.

Thou sendest forth springs in the vales: between the midst of the hills the waters shall pass. . . . Over them the birds of the air shall dwell, from the midst of the rocks they shall give forth their voices. Thou waterest the hills from Thy upper rooms: the earth shall be filled with the fruit of Thy works. . . . The trees of the field shall be filled and the cedars of Libanus which He hath planted: there the sparrows shall make their nests. The highest of them is the house of the heron. The high hills are a refuse for the harts, the rocks for the irchins. . . . All expect from Thee that Thou give them food in season. What Thou givest them they shall gather up: when Thou openest Thy hand they shall all be filled with good. . . . Thou shalt send forth Thy Spirit and they shall be created, and Thou shalt renew the face of the earth.

Yes, and from the secret places of His essence, God began to fill my soul with grace in those days, grace that sprung from deep within me, I could not know how or where. But yet I would be able, after not so many months, to realize what was there, in the peace and the strength that were growing in me through my constant immersion in this tremendous, unending cycle of prayer, ever renewing its vitality, its inexhaustible, sweet energies, from hour to hour, from season to season in its returning round. And I, drawn into that atmosphere, into that deep, vast universal movement of vitalizing prayer, which is Christ praying in men to His Father, could not help but begin at last to live, and to know that I was alive. And my heart could not help but cry out within me:

366

"I will sing to the Lord as long as I live: I will sing praise to my God while I have my being. Let my speech be acceptable to Him: but I will take delight in the Lord."

Truly, He was sending forth His Spirit, uttering His divine Word and binding me to Himself through His Spirit preceding from the Word spoken within me. As the months went on, I could not help but realize it.

Then, when I finished the Little Hours and closed the Breviary at the end of None reciting the *Sacrosancte,* and looked up out of the window to see the seminary of Callicoon momentarily appear on its distant hilltop, at the end of a long avenue of river, I no longer felt so much anguish and sorrow at not being in the monastery.

But I am getting ahead of my story. For in these days, in the late summer of 1940, it was not yet that way. The Breviary was hard to learn, and every step was labor and confusion, not to mention the mistakes and perplexities I got myself into. However, Father Irenaeus helped to straighten me out, and told me how the various feasts worked together, and how to say first Vespers for the proper feast, and all the other things one needs to find out. Apart from him, however, I didn't even speak of the Breviary to any other priest. I kept quiet about it, half fearing that someone would make fun of me, or think I was eccentric, or try to snatch my books away from me on some pretext. I would have been better off if I had been acting under the guidance of a director, but I had no understanding of such a thing in those days.

Meanwhile, I put on my best blue suit and hitch-hiked out to St. Bonaventure and spoke with Father Thomas Plassman, who was the president of the college, and the picture of benevolence. He listened kindly and soberly to my answers to his questions, filling a chair with his huge frame and looking at me through his glasses, out of a great kind face built on pontifical lines and all set for smiles paternal enough to embrace an archdiocese. Father Thomas would make a wonderful prelate, and, as a matter of fact, all the students and seminarians at St. Bonaventure held him in great awe for his learning and piety.

Back in Olean his reputation was even greater. Once I had someone whisper to me that Father Thomas was the third best educated man in America. I was not able to find out who were the other two ahead of him, or how it was possible to determine who was the best educated, or what that might precisely mean.

But in any case, he gave me a job at St. Bonaventure's, teaching English, for it fell out that Father Valentine Long, who wrote books and taught literature to the sophomores, had been transferred to Holy Name College, in Washington.

In the second week of September, with a trunkful of books and a typewriter and the old portable phonograph that I had bought when I was still at Oakham, I moved in to the little room that was assigned to me on the second floor of the big, red-brick building that was both a dormitory and a monastery. Out of my window I could look beyond the chapel front to the garden and fields and the woods. There was a little astronomical observatory out there behind the greenhouses, and in the distance you could tell where the river was by the line of trees at the end of the pasture. And then, beyond that, were the high, wooded hills, and my gaze travelled up Five Mile Valley beyond the farms to Martinny's Rocks. My eyes often wandered out there, and rested in that peaceful scene, and the landscape became associated with my prayers, for I often prayed looking out of the window. And even at night, the tiny, glowing light of a far farmhouse window in Five Mile Valley attracted my eye, the only visible thing in the black darkness, as I knelt on the floor and said my last prayer to Our Lady.

And as the months went on, I began to drink poems out of those hills.

Yet the room was not quiet, either. It was right on a corner next to the stairs, and when anybody on our floor was wanted on the telephone, someone would rush up the stairs and stick his head into the corridor right by my door and yell down the echoing hall. All day long I heard those voices bellowing, "Hey, Cassidy! Hey, Cassidy!" but I did not mind. It did not stop me from doing twice as much work in that room, in one year, as I had done in all the rest of my life put together.

It amazed me how swiftly my life fell into a plan of fruitful and pleasant organization, here under the roof with these Friars, in this house dedicated to God. The answer to this was, of course, the God Who lived under that same roof with me, hidden in His Sacrament, the heart of the house, diffusing His life through it from the chapel Tabernacle: and also the Office I recited every day was another answer. Finally, there was the fact of my seclusion.

By this time, I had managed to get myself free from all the habits and luxuries that people in the world think they need for their comfort and amusement. My mouth was at last clean of the yellow, parching salt of nicotine, and I had rinsed my eyes of the grey slops of movies, so that now my taste and my vision were clean. And I had thrown away the books that soiled my heart. And my ears, too, had been cleansed of all wild and fierce noises and had poured into them peace, peace—except for that yell, "Hey, Cassidy," which, after all, did not make much difference.

Best of all, my will was in order, my soul was in harmony with itself and with God, though not without battle, and not without cost. That was a price I had to pay, or lose my life altogether, so there was no alternative but wait in patience, and let myself be ground out between the upper and nether millstones of the two conflicting laws within me. Nor could I taste anything of the sense that this is really a martyrdom full of merit and pleasing to God: I was still too obsessed with the sheer, brute difficulty of it, and the crushing humiliation that faced me all the time. *Peccatum meum contra me est semper.*

Yet, in spite of all that, there was in me the profound, sure certitude of liberty, the moral certitude of grace, of union with God, which bred peace that could not be shattered or overshadowed by any necessity to stand armed and ready for conflict. And this peace was all-rewarding. It was worth everything. And every day it brought me back to Christ's altars, and to my daily Bread, that infinitely holy and mighty and

369

secret wholesomeness that was cleansing and strengthening my sick being through and through, and feeding, with His infinite life, my poor shredded sinews of morality.

I was writing a book—it was not much of a book—and I had classes to prepare. It was the latter work that had the most in it of health and satisfaction and reward. I had three big classes of sophomores, ninety students in all, to bring through English Literature from Beowulf to the Romantic Revival in one year. And a lot of them didn't even know how to spell. But that did not worry me very much, and it could not alter my happiness with *Piers Plowman* and the *Nun's Priest's Tale* and *Sir Gawain and the Green Knight:* I was back again in that atmosphere that had enthralled me as a child, the serene and simple and humorous Middle Ages, not the lute and goblin and moth-ball Middle Ages of Tennyson, but the real Middle Ages, the twelfth and thirteenth and fourteenth centuries, full of fresh air and simplicity, as solid as wheat bread and grape wine and water-mills and ox-drawn wagons: the age of Cistercian monasteries and of the first Franciscans.

And so, in my innocence, I stood up and talked about all these things in front of those rooms full of football players with long, unpronounceable names: and because they saw that I myself liked my own subject matter, they tolerated it, and even did a certain amount of work for me without too much complaint.

The classes were a strange mixture. The best elements in them were the football players and the seminarians. The football players were mostly on scholarships, and they did not have much money, and they stayed in at night most of the time. As a group, they were the best-natured and the best-tempered and worked as hard as the seminarians. They were also the most vocal. They liked to talk about these books when I stirred them up to argue. They liked to open their mouths and deliver rough, earnest and sometimes sardonic observations about the behavior of these figures in literature.

Also, some of them were strong and pious Catholics with souls full of faith and simplicity and honesty and conviction, yet without the violence and intemperance that come from mere prejudice. At Columbia it had been pretty much the fashion to despise football players as stupid: and I don't maintain that they are, as a class, geniuses. But the ones at St. Bona's taught me much more about people than I taught them about books, and I learned to have a lot of respect and affection for these rough, earnest, good-natured and patient men who had to work so hard and take so many bruises and curses to entertain the Alumni on the football field, and to advertise the school.

I wonder what has happened to them all: how many of them got shot up in Africa or the Philippines? What became of that black-haired, grinning Mastrigiacomo who confided to me all his ambitions about being a band-leader; or that lanky, cat-faced villain Chapman whom I saw one night, after a dance, walking around chewing on a whole ham? What have they done with that big, quiet Irishman Quinn, or Woody McCarthy with his long bulbous nose and eyebrows full of perplexity and his sallies of gruff wit? Then there was Red Hagerman who was not a Catholic, and who looked like all the big cheerful muscle-bound football players they believed in in the nineteen twenties. He went off and got himself married towards the end of that year. Another one called "Red" was Red McDonald, and he was one of the best students in the class, and one of the best people: a serious young Irishman with a wide-open face, all full of sincerity and hard work. Then there was the big round-faced Polish boy whose name I have forgotten, who grabbed hold of the tail of a cow which dragged him all around the pasture on the day of the sophomore beer-party at the end of the year.

The most intelligent students were the seminarians or the ones that were going to enter the seminary: and they were the quietest. They kept pretty much to themselves, and handed in neat papers which you could be relatively sure were their own original work. Probably by now they are all priests.

The rest of the class was a mixture of all kinds of people, some of them disgruntled, some of them penniless and hardworking, some of them rich and dumb and too fond of beer.

Some of them liked to play the drums and knew how. Others liked to play them and did not know how. Some of them were good dancers and danced a lot. Others just went uptown and played the slot machines until the last minute before midnight, when they came back to the college in a panic-stricken rush to get in before the time limit was up. One of them, Joe Nastri, thought he was a Communist. I don't suppose he had a very clear idea of what a Communist was. One day he went to sleep in class and one of the football players gave him the hotfoot.

Of all the crowd, it could not be said that they were very different from the students I had known in other colleges. With a few exceptions, they were probably no holier. They got drunk just as much, but they made more noise about it, and had less money to spend, and were handicapped by the necessity of getting back to the dormitory at a certain time. Twice a week they had to get up and hear Mass, which was a burden to most of them. Only very few of them heard Mass and went to Communion every day—outside of the seminarians.

However, most of them clung with conviction to the Catholic faith, a loyalty which was resolute and inarticulate. It was hard to tell just how much that loyalty was a matter of conscious faith, and how much it was based on attachment to their class and social environment: but they were all pretty definite about being Catholics. One could not say of them that, as a whole, they led lives that went beyond the ordinary level demanded of a Christian. Some of the most intelligent of them often startled me with statements that showed they had not penetrated below the surface of Catholicism and did not really appreciate its spirit . . . One, for instance, argued that the virtue of humility was nonsense, and that it sapped a man of all his vitality and initiative. Another one did not think there were any such things as devils. . . .

All of them were serene in their conviction that the modern world was the highest point reached by man in his development, and that our present civilization left very little to be desired. I wonder if the events of 1943 and the two following years did anything to change their opinions.

That winter, when I was talking about the England of Langland and Chaucer and Shakespeare and Webster, the war-machine of totalitarian Germany had turned to devour that island, and morning after morning when I glanced at the New York *Times* in the library, between classes, I read the headlines about the cities that had been cut to pieces with bombs. Night after night the huge dark mass of London was bursting into wide areas of flame that turned its buildings into empty craters and cariated those miles and miles of slums. Around St. Paul's the ancient City was devastated, and there was no acre of Westminster, Bloomsbury, Camden Town, Mayfair, Bayswater, Paddington that had not been deeply scarred. Coventry was razed to the ground. Bristol, Birmingham, Sheffield, Newcastle were all raided, and the land was full of blood and smoke.

The noise of that fearful chastisement, the fruit of modern civilization, penetrated to the ears and minds of very few at St. Bonaventure's. The Friars understood something of what was going on: but they lost themselves, for the most part, in futile political arguments if they talked about it at all. But the students were more concerned with the movies and beer and the mousy little girls that ran around Olean in ankle socks, even when the snow lay deep on the ground.

I think it was in November that we all lined up, students and secular professors, in De la Roche Hall and gave our names in to be drafted. The whole process was an extremely quiet and unmomentous one. The room was not even crowded. You didn't even have the boredom of waiting.

I gave my name and my age and all the rest, and got a small white card. It was quickly over. It did not bring the war very close.

Yet it was enough to remind me that I was not going to enjoy this pleasant and safe and stable life forever. Indeed, perhaps now that I had just begun to taste my security, it would be taken away again, and I would be cast back into the midst of violence and uncertainty and blasphemy and the play of anger and hatred and all passion, worse than ever before. It would be the wages of my own twenty-five years: this war was what I had earned for myself and the world. I could hardly complain that I was being drawn into it.

ii

If we were all being pulled into the vortex of that fight, it was being done slowly and gradually. I was surprised when my brother was cast back into the solid area of peace—relative peace. It was one rainy night in the fall that he appeared in Olean in a new shiny Buick convertible roadster with a long black hood and a chassis that crouched low on the road, built for expensive and silent speed. The thing was all fixed up with searchlights, and as for my brother, he was not in uniform.

"What about the Navy?" I asked him.

It turned out that they were not giving out commissions in the Naval Reserve as freely as he had supposed, and he had had some differences of opinion with his commanding officers and, at the end of a cruise to the West Indies and after an examination of some sort, both my brother and the Naval Reserve were mutually delighted to end their association with one another.

I was not sorry.

"What are you going to do now, wait until you are drafted?"

"I suppose so," he said.

"And in the meantime? . . ."

"Maybe I'll go to Mexico," he said. "I want to take some pictures of those Mayan temples."

And, as a matter of fact, that was where he went when the weather got cold: to Yucatan, to find out one of those lost cities in the jungle and take a pile of kodachromes of those evil stones, soaked in the blood that was once poured out in libation to the devils by forgotten generations of Indians. He did not get rid of any of his restlessness in Mexico or Yucatan. He only found more of it among those blue volcanoes.

Snow comes early to St. Bonaventure's, and when the snow

came, I used to say the Little Hours of the Breviary walking in the deep untrodden drifts along the wood's edge, towards the river. No one would ever come and disturb me out there in all that silence, under the trees, which made a noiseless, rudimentary church over my head, between me and the sky. It was wonderful out there when the days were bright, even though the cold bit down into the roots of my fingernails as I held the open Breviary in my hands. I could look up from the book, and recite the parts I already knew by heart, gazing at the glittering, snow-covered hills, white and gold and planted with bare woods, standing out bright against the blinding blue sky. Oh, America, how I began to love your country! What miles of silences God has made in you for contemplation! If only people realized what all your mountains and forests are really for!

The new year came, 1941. In its January, I was to have my twenty-sixth birthday, and enter upon my twenty-seventh, most momentous year.

Already, in February, or before that, the idea came to me that I might make a retreat in some monastery for Holy Week and Easter. Where would it be? The first place that came into my mind was the Trappist abbey Dan Walsh had told me about, in Kentucky. And as soon as I thought about it, I saw that this was the only choice. That was where I needed to go. Something had opened out, inside me, in the last months, something that required, demanded at least a week in that silence, in that austerity, praying together with the monks in their cold choir.

And my heart expanded with anticipation and happiness.

Meanwhile, suddenly, one day, towards the beginning of Lent, I began to write poems. I cannot assign any special cause for the ideas that began to crowd on me from every side. I had been reading the Spanish poet, Lorca, with whose poetic vein I felt in the greatest sympathy: but that was not enough, in itself, to account for all the things I now began to write. In the first weeks of Lent, the fasting I took on my-self—which was not much, but at least it came up to the standard required by the Church for an ordinary Christian, and did not evade its obligations under some privilege to which I was not entitled—instead of cramping my mind, freed it, and seemed to let loose the string of my tongue.

Sometimes I would go several days at a time, writing a new poem every day. They were not all good, but some of them were better than I had written before. In the end, I did not altogether reject more than half a dozen of them. And, having sent many of the others to various magazines, I at last had the joy of seeing one or two of them accepted.

Towards the beginning of March, I wrote to the Trappists at Gethsemani asking if I could come down there for a retreat during Holy Week. I had barely received their reply, telling me they would be glad to have me there, when another letter came.

It was from the Draft Board, telling me that my number was up for the army.

I was surprised. I had forgotten about the draft, or rather I had made calculations that put all this off until at least after Easter. However, I had thought out my position with regard to the war, and knew what I had to do in conscience. I made out my answers to the questionnaires with peace in my heart, and not much anticipation that it would make any difference to my case.

It was about eight years since we had all stood under the banner in the gymnasium at Columbia, and the Reds had shouted and stamped on the platform, and we had all loudly taken a pledge that we weren't going to fight in any war whatever. Now America was moving into position to enter a war as the ally of countries that had been attacked by the Nazis: and the Nazis had, as their ally, Communist Russia.

Meanwhile in those eight years, I had developed a conscience. If I had objected to war before, it was more on the basis of emotion than anything else. And my unconditional objection had, therefore, been foolish in more ways than one. On the other hand, I was not making the mistake of switching from one emotional extreme to the other. This time, as far as I was able, I felt that I was called upon to make clear my own position as a moral duty.

To put it in terms less abstract and stuffy: God was asking me, by the light and grace that He had given me, to signify where I stood in relation to the actions of governments and armies and states in this world overcome with the throes of its own blind wickedness. He was not asking me to judge all the nations of the world, or to elucidate all the moral and political motives behind their actions. He was not demanding that I pass some critical decision defining the innocence and guilt of all those concerned in the war. He was asking me to make a choice that amounted to an act of love for His Truth, His goodness, His charity, His Gospel, as an individual, as a member of His Mystical Body. He was asking me to do, to the best of my knowledge, what I thought Christ would do.

For a war to be just, it must be a war of defence. A war of aggression is not just. If America entered the war now, would it be a war of aggression? I suppose if you wanted to get subtle about it, you could work out some kind of an argument to that effect. But I personally could not see that it would be anything else than legitimate self-defence. How legitimate? To answer that, I would have had to be a moral theologian and a diplomat and a historian and a politician and probably also a mind-reader. And still I would not have had more than a probable answer. Since there was such strong probable evidence that we were really defending ourselves, that settled the question as far as I was concerned.

I had more of a doubt on the question of whether it was really necessary or not. Did we really have to go to war? A lot of people were asking themselves that question, and argument about it was rather hot among some of the Friars at St. Bonaventure's. As far as I could see, it was a question that no private individual was capable of answering: and the situation was getting to be grave enough for it to be necessary to leave the government to make its own choice. The men in Washington presumably knew what was going on better than we did, and if, in a situation as obscure as this one was, and as perilous, they thought war was getting to be necessary —what could we do about it? If they called us to the army, I could not absolutely refuse to go.

The last and most crucial doubt about the war was the morality of the means used in the fight: the bombing of open cities, the wholesale slaughter of civilians. . . . To my mind, there was very little doubt about the immorality of the methods used in modern war. Self-defence is good, and a necessary war is licit: but methods that descend to wholesale barbarism and ruthless, indiscriminate slaughter of non-combatants practically without defence are hard to see as anything else but mortal sins. This was the hardest question of all to decide.

Fortunately the draft law was framed in such a way that I did not have to decide it. For there was a provision made for those who were willing to help the country without doing any killing. As I say, I couldn't tell just how much those provisions would mean in actual practice, but they looked nice on paper, and the least I could do was take advantage of them.

And therefore I made out my papers with an application to be considered as a non-combatant objector: that is, one who would willingly enter the army, and serve in the medical corps, or as a stretcher bearer, or a hospital orderly or any other thing like that, so long as I did not have to drop bombs on open cities, or shoot at other men.

After all, Christ did say: "Whatsoever you have done to the least of these my brethren, you did it to me." I know that it is not the mind of the Church that this be applied literally to war—or rather, that war is looked upon as a painful but necessary social surgical operation in which you kill your enemy not out of hatred but for the common good. That is all very fine in theory. But as far as I could see, since the government was apparently holding out an opportunity to those who wanted to serve in the army without killing other men, I could avoid the whole question and follow what seemed to me to be a much better course.

After all, I might be able to turn an evil situation into a source of much good. In the medical corps—if that was where they put me—I would not be spared any of the dangers that fell upon other men, and at the same time I would be able to help them, to perform works of mercy, and to overcome

378

evil with good. I would be able to leaven the mass of human misery with the charity and mercy of Christ, and the bitter, ugly, filthy business of the war could be turned into the occasion for my own sanctification and for the good of other men.

If you set aside the practically insoluble question of cooperation that might be brought up, it seemed to me that this was what Christ Himself would have done, and what He wanted me to do.

I put down all my reasons, and quoted St. Thomas for the edification of the Draft Board and got the whole business notarized and sealed and put it in an envelope and dropped it in the wide-open mouth of the mailbox in the Olean post office.

And when it was done, I walked out into the snowy street, and an ineffable sense of peace settled in my heart.

It was a late, cold afternoon. The frozen piles of snow lay along the swept sidewalks, in the gutters, in front of the small, one-storey buildings on State Street. Presently Bob O'Brien, the plumber at the Olean house, who lived in Alleghany, and who used to fix the pipes when they went wrong up at the cottage, came by in his car. He stopped to give me a ride.

He was a big, jovial, family man, with white hair and several sons who served as altar boys at St. Bonaventure's Church in Alleghany, and as we passed out of town on the wide road, he was talking about peaceful and ordinary things.

The country opened out before us. The setting sun shone as bright as blood, along the tops of the hills, but the snow in the valleys and hollows was blue and even purple with shadows. On the left of the road, the antennae of the radio station stood up into the clean sky, and far ahead of us lay the red-brick buildings of the College, grouped in an imitation Italy in the midst of the alluvial valley. Beyond that, on the side of the hill were the redder buildings of St. Elizabeth's convent, past the high bridge over the railroad tracks.

My eyes opened and took all this in. And for the first time in my life I realized that I no longer cared whether I preserved

379

my place in all this or lost it: whether I stayed here or went to the army. All that no longer mattered. It was in the hands of One Who loved me far better than I could ever love myself: and my heart was filled with peace.

It was a peace that did not depend on houses, or jobs, or places, or times, or external conditions. It was a peace that time and material created situations could never give. It was peace that the world could not give.

The weeks went by, and I wrote some more poems, and continued to fast and keep my Lent. All I prayed was that God should let me know His will—and, if it pleased Him, there was only one other thing I asked for myself besides: if I had to go to the army, I begged Him at least to let me make a retreat with the Trappist monks before I went.

However, the next thing I got from the Draft Board was a notice to present myself for medical examination before the doctors in Olean.

I had not been expecting things to develop that way, and at first I interpreted this to mean that my request for consideration as a non-combatant had simply been ignored. There were three days before the examination, and so I got permission to go down to New York. I thought I might see the Draft Board and talk to them: but that was not possible. In any case, it was not necessary.

So the week-end turned out to be a sort of a festival with my friends. I saw Lax, who was now working for the *New Yorker*, and had a desk of his own in a corner of their offices where he wrote letters to pacify the people who complained about the humor, or the lack of it, in the pages of the magazine. Then we went out to Long Beach and saw Seymour. And then Seymour and I and Lax all together got in a car and went to Port Washington and saw Gibney.

The next day was St. Patrick's Day, and the massed bands of all the boys and girls in Brooklyn who had never had an ear for music were gathering under the windows of the *New Yorker* offices and outside the Gotham Book Mart. And I, an Englishman, wearing a shamrock which I had bought from a Jew, went walking around the city, weaving in and out of the crowds, and thinking up a poem called April, although it was March. It was a fancy poem about javelins and leopards and lights through trees like arrows and a line that said: "The little voices of the rivers change." I thought it up in and out of the light and the shade of the Forties, between Fifth and Sixth avenues, and typed it on Lax's typewriter in the *New Yorker* office, and showed it to Mark Van Doren in a subway station.

And Mark said, of the shamrock I was wearing:

"That is the greenest shamrock I have ever seen."

It was a great St. Patrick's Day. That night I got on the Erie train, and since I was so soon, I thought, to go to the army, I paid money to sleep in the Pullman. Practically the only other Pullman passenger was a sedate Franciscan nun, who turned out to be going to St. Elizabeth's: and so we got off at Olean together and shared a taxi out to Alleghany.

On Monday I prepared to go and be examined for the army. I was the first one there. I climbed the ancient stairs to the top floor of the Olean City Hall. I tried the handle of the room marked for the medical board, and the door opened. I walked in and stood in the empty room. My heart was still full of the peace of Communion.

Presently the first of the doctors arrived.

"You got here early," he said, and began to take off his coat and hat.

"We might as well begin," he said, "the others will be along in a minute."

So I stripped, and he listened to my chest, and took some blood out of my arm and put it in a little bottle, in a water-heater, to keep it cosy and warm for the Wassermann test. And while this was going on, the others were coming in, two other doctors to do the examining, and lanky young farm boys to be examined.

"Now," said my doctor, "let's see your teeth."

I opened my mouth.

"Well," he said, "you've certainly had a lot of teeth out!"

And he began to count them.

The doctor who was running the Medical Board was just

coming in. My man got up and went to talk to him. I heard him say:

"Shall we finish the whole examination? I don't see much point to it."

The head doctor came over and looked at my mouth.

"Oh, well," he said, "finish the examination anyway."

And he sat me down and personally took a crack at my reflexes and went through all the rest of it. When it was over, and I was ready to get back into my clothes, I asked:

"What about it, Doctor?"

"Oh, go home," he said, "you haven't got enough teeth."

Once again I walked out into the snowy street.

So they didn't want me in the army after all, even as a stretcher bearer! The street was full of quiet, full of peace.

And I remembered that it was the Feast of St. Joseph.

iii

There were still about three weeks left until Easter. Thinking more and more about the Trappist monastery where I was going to spend Holy Week, I went to the library one day and took down the *Catholic Encyclopaedia* to read about the Trappists. I found out that the Trappists were Cistercians, and then, in looking up Cistercians, I also came across the Carthusians, and a great big picture of the hermitages of the Camaldolese.

What I saw on those pages pierced me to the heart like a knife.

What wonderful happiness there was, then, in the world! There were still men on this miserable, noisy, cruel earth, who tasted the marvelous joy of silence and solitude, who dwelt in forgotten mountain cells, in secluded monasteries, where the news and desires and appetites and conflicts of the world no longer reached them.

They were free from the burden of the flesh's tyranny, and their clear vision, clean of the world's smoke and of its bitter sting, were raised to heaven and penetrated into the deeps of heaven's infinite and healing light.

382

They were poor, they had nothing, and therefore they were free and possessed everything, and everything they touched struck off something of the fire of divinity. And they worked with their hands, silently ploughing and harrowing the earth, and sowing seed in obscurity, and reaping their small harvests to feed themselves and the other poor. They built their own houses and made, with their own hands, their own furniture and their own coarse clothing, and everything around them was simple and primitive and poor, because they were the least and the last of men, they had made themselves outcasts, seeking, outside the walls of the world, Christ poor and rejected of men.

Above all, they had found Christ, and they knew the power and the sweetness and the depth and the infinity of His love, living and working in them. In Him, hidden in Him, they had become the "Poor Brothers of God." And for His love, they had thrown away everything, and concealed themselves in the Secret of His Face. Yet because they had nothing, they were the richest men in the world, possessing everything: because in proportion as grace emptied their hearts of created desire, the Spirit of God entered in and filled the place that had been made for God. And the Poor Brothers of God, in their cells, they tasted within them the secret glory, the hidden manna, the infinite nourishment and strength of the Presence of God. They tasted the sweet exultancy of the fear of God, which is the first intimate touch of the reality of God, known and experienced on earth, the beginning of heaven. The fear of the Lord is the beginning of heaven. And all day long, God spoke to them: the clean voice of God, in His tremendous peacefulness, spending truth within them as simply and directly as water wells up in a spring. And grace was in them, suddenly, always in more and more abundance, they knew not from where, and the coming of this grace to them occupied them altogether, and filled them with love, and with freedom.

And grace, overflowing in all their acts and movements, made everything they did an act of love, glorifying God not by drama, not by gesture, not by outward show, but by the very simplicity and economy of utter perfection, so utter that it escapes notice entirely.

Outside in the world were holy men who were holy in the sense that they went about with portraits of all the possible situations in which they could show their love of God displayed about them: and they were always conscious of all these possibilities. But these other hidden men had come so close to God in their hiddenness that they no longer saw anyone but Him. They themselves were lost in the picture: there was no comparison between them receiving and God giving, because the distance by which such comparison could be measured had dwindled to nothing. They were in Him. They had dwindled down to nothing and had been transformed into Him by the pure and absolute humility of their hearts.

And the love of Christ overflowing in those clean hearts made them children and made them eternal. Old men with limbs like the roots of trees had the eyes of children and lived, under their grey woolen cowls, eternal. And all of them, the young and the old, were ageless, the little brothers of God, the little children for whom was made the Kingdom of Heaven.

Day after day the round of the canonical hours brought them together and the love that was in them became songs as austere as granite and as sweet as wine. And they stood and they bowed in their long, solemn psalmody. Their prayer flexed its strong sinews and relaxed again into silence, and suddenly flared up again in a hymn, the color of flame, and died into silence: and you could barely hear the weak, ancient voice saying the final prayer. The whisper of the *amens* ran around the stones like sighs, and the monks broke up their ranks and half emptied the choir, some remaining to pray.

And in the night they also rose, and filled the darkness with the strong, patient anguish of their supplication to God: and the strength of their prayer (the Spirit of Christ concealing His strength in the words their voices uttered) amazingly held back the arm of God from striking and breaking at last the foul world full of greed and avarice and murder and lust and all sin.

384

The thought of those monasteries, those remote choirs, those cells, those hermitages, those cloisters, those men in their cowls, the poor monks, the men who had become nothing, shattered my heart.

In an instant the desire of those solitudes was wide open within me like a wound.

I had to slam the book shut on the picture of Camaldoli and the bearded hermits standing in the stone street of cells, and I went out of the library, trying to stamp out the embers that had broken into flame, there, for an instant, within me.

No, it was useless: I did not have a vocation, and I was not for the cloister, for the priesthood. Had I not been told that definitely enough? Did I have to have that beaten into my head all over again before I could believe it?

Yet I stood in the sun outside the dining hall, waiting for the noon Angelus, and one of the Friars was talking to me. I could not contain the one thing that filled my heart:

"I am going to a Trappist monastery to make a retreat for Holy Week," I said. The things that jumped in the Friar's eyes gave him the sort of expression you would expect if I had said: "I am going to go and buy a submarine and live on the bottom of the sea."

"Don't let them change you!" he said, with a sort of a lame smile. That meant "Don't go reminding the rest of us that all that penance might be right, by getting a vocation to the Trappists."

I said: "It would be a good thing if they did change me."

It was a safe, oblique way of admitting what was in my heart—the desire to go to that monastery and stay for good.

On the morning of the Saturday before Palm Sunday I got up before five, and heard part of a Mass in the dark chapel and then had to make a run for the train. The rain fell on the empty station straight and continuous as a tower.

All the way down the line, in the pale, growing day, the hills were black, and rain drenched the valley and flooded the sleeping valley towns. Somewhere past Jamestown I took out my Breviary and said the Little Hours, and when we got into Ohio the rain stopped.

We changed stations at Galion, and on the fast train down to Columbus I got something to eat, and in southern Ohio the air was drier still, and almost clearing. Finally, in the evening, in the long rolling hills that led the way in to Cincinnati, you could see the clouds tearing open all along the western horizon to admit long streaks of sun.

It was an American landscape, big, vast, generous, fertile, and leading beyond itself into limitless expanses, open spaces, the whole West. My heart was full!

So when we entered Cincinnati, in the evening, with the lights coming on among all the houses and the electric signs shining on the hills, and the huge freight yards swinging open on either side of the track and the high buildings in the distance, I felt as if I owned the world. And yet that was not because of all these things, but because of Gethsemani, where I was going. It was the fact that I was passing through all this, and did not desire it, and wanted no part in it, and did not seek to grasp or hold any of it, that I could exult in it, and it all cried out to me: God! God!

I went to Mass and Communion the next morning in Cincinnati, and then took the train for Louisville, and waited in Louisville all the rest of the day because I did not have the sense to take a bus to one of the towns near Gethsemani and buy a ride from there to the monastery.

It was not until after night fell that there was a train out to Gethsemani, on the line to Atlanta.

It was a slow train. The coach was dimly lighted, and full of people whose accents I could hardly understand, and you knew you were in the South because all the Negroes were huddled in a separate car. The train got out of the city into country that was abysmally dark, even under the moon. You wondered if there were any houses out there. Pressing my face to the window, and shading it with my hands, I saw the outline of a bare, stony landscape with sparse trees. The little towns we came to looked poor and forlorn and somewhat fierce in the darkness.

And the train went its slow way through the spring night,

branching off at Bardstown junction. And I knew my station was coming.

I stepped down out of the car into the empty night. The station was dark. There was a car standing there, but no man in sight. There was a road, and the shadow of a sort of a factory a little distance away, and a few houses under some trees. In one of them was a light. The train had hardly stopped to let me off, and immediately gathered its ponderous momentum once again and was gone around the bend with the flash of a red tail light, leaving me in the middle of the silence and solitude of the Kentucky hills.

I put my bag down in the gravel, wondering what to do next. Had they forgotten to make arrangements for me to get to the monastery? Presently the door of one of the houses opened, and a man came out, in no hurry.

We got in the car together, and started up the road, and in a minute we were in the midst of moonlit fields.

"Are the monks in bed?" I asked the driver. It was only a few minutes past eight.

"Oh, yes, they go to bed at seven o'clock."

"Is the monastery far?"

"Mile and a half."

I looked at the rolling country, and at the pale ribbon of road in front of us, stretching out as grey as lead in the light of the moon. Then suddenly I saw a steeple that shone like silver in the moonlight, growing into sight from behind a rounded knoll. The tires sang on the empty road, and, breathless, I looked at the monastery that was revealed before me as we came over the rise. At the end of an avenue of trees was a big rectangular block of buildings, all dark, with a church crowned by a tower and a steeple and a cross: and the steeple was as bright as platinum and the whole place was as quiet as midnight and lost in the all-absorbing silence and solitude of the fields. Behind the monastery was a dark curtain of woods, and over to the west was a wooded valley, and beyond that a rampart of wooded hills, a barrier and a defence against the world.

And over all the valley smiled the mild, gentle Easter moon, the full moon in her kindness, loving this silent place.

At the end of the avenue, in the shadows under the trees, I could make out the lowering arch of the gate, and the words: "*Pax Intrantibus.*"

The driver of the car did not go to the bell rope by the heavy wooden door. Instead he went over and scratched on one of the windows and called, in a low voice:

"Brother! Brother!"

I could hear someone stirring inside.

Presently the key turned in the door. I passed inside. The door closed quietly behind me. I was out of the world.

The effect of that big, moonlit court, the heavy stone building with all those dark and silent windows, was overpowering. I could hardly answer the Brother's whispered questions.

I looked at his clear eyes, his greying, pointed beard.

When I told him I came from St. Bonaventure's, he said drily:

"I was a Franciscan once."

We crossed the court, climbed some steps, entered a high, dark hall. I hesitated on the brink of a polished, slippery floor, while the Brother groped for the light switch. Then, above another heavy door, I saw the words: "God alone."

"Have you come here to stay?" said the Brother.

The question terrified me. It sounded too much like the voice of my own conscience.

"Oh, no!" I said. "Oh, no!" And I heard my whisper echoing around the hall and vanishing up the indefinite, mysterious heights of a dark and empty stair-well above our heads. The place smelled frighteningly clean: old and clean, an ancient house, polished and swept and repainted and repainted over and over, year after year.

"What's the matter? Why can't you stay? Are you married or something?" said the Brother.

"No," I said lamely, "I have a job . . ."

We began to climb the wide stairs. Our steps echoed in the empty darkness. One flight and then another and a third and a fourth. There was an immense distance between floors; it was a building with great high ceilings. Finally we came to the top floor, and the Brother opened the door into a wide room, and put down my bag, and left me.

I heard his steps crossing the yard below, to the gate house.

And I felt the deep, deep silence of the night, and of peace, and of holiness enfold me like love, like safety.

The embrace of it, the silence! I had entered into a solitude that was an impregnable fortress. And the silence that enfolded me, spoke to me, and spoke louder and more eloquently than any voice, and in the middle of that quiet, cleansmelling room, with the moon pouring its peacefulness in through the open window, with the warm night air, I realized truly whose house that was, O glorious Mother of God!

How did I ever get back out of there, into the world, after tasting the sweetness and the kindness of the love with which you welcome those that come to stay in your house, even only for a few days, O Holy Queen of Heaven, and Mother of my Christ?

It is very true that the Cistercian Order is your special territory and that those monks in white cowls are your special servants, *servitores Sanctae Mariae*. Their houses are all yours —Notre Dame, Notre Dame, all around the world. Notre Dame de Gethsemani: there was still something of the bravery and simplicity and freshness of twelfth-century devotion, the vivid faith of St. Bernard of Clairvaux and Adam of Perseigne and Guerric of Igny and Ailred of Rievaulx and Robert of Molesme, here in the hills of Kentucky: and I think the century of Chartres was most of all your century, my Lady, because it spoke you clearest not only in word but in glass and stone, showing you for who you are, most powerful, most glorious, Mediatrix of All Grace, and the most High Queen of Heaven, high above all the angels, and throned in glory near the throne of your Divine Son.

And of all things, it is the Rules of the Religious Orders dedicated to you, that are loudest and truest in proclaiming your honor, showing forth your power and your greatness obliquely by the sacrifices that love of you drives men to make. So it is that the Usages of the Cistercians are a Canticle for your glory, Queen of Angels, and those who live those Usages proclaim your tremendous prerogatives louder than the most exalted sermons. The white cowl of the silent Cistercian has got the gift of tongues, and the flowing folds of that grey wool, full of benediction, are more fluent than the Latin of the great monastic Doctors.

How shall I explain or communicate to those who have not seen these holy houses, your consecrated churches and Cistercian cloisters, the might of the truths that overpowered me all the days of that week?

Yet no one will find it hard to conceive the impression made on a man thrown suddenly into a Trappist monastery at four o'clock in the morning, after the night office, as I was the following day.

Bells were flying out of the tower in the high, astounding darkness as I groped half blind with sleep for my clothing, and hastened into the hall and down the dark stairs. I did not know where to go, and there was no one to show me, but I saw two men in secular clothes, at the bottom of the stairs, going through a door. One of them was a priest with a great head of white hair, the other was a young man with black hair, in a pair of dungarees. I went after them, through the door. We were in a hallway, completely black, except I could see their shadows moving towards a big window at the end. They knew where they were going, and they had found a door which opened and let some light into the hall.

I came after them to the door. It led into the cloister. The cloister was cold, and dimly lit, and the smell of damp wool astounded me by its unearthliness. And I saw the monks. There was one, right there, by the door; he had knelt, or rather thrown himself down before a *pietà* in the cloister corner, and had buried his head in the huge sleeves of his cowl there at the feet of the dead Christ, the Christ Who lay in the arms of Mary, letting fall one arm and a pierced hand in the limpness of death. It was a picture so fierce that it scared me: the abjection, the dereliction of this seemingly shattered monk at the feet of the broken Christ. I stepped into the cloister as if into an abyss.

The silence with people moving in it was ten times more gripping than it had been in my own empty room.

And now I was in the church. The two other seculars were kneeling there beside an altar at which the candles were burning. A priest was already at the altar, spreading out the corporal and opening the book. I could not figure out why the secular priest with the great shock of white hair was kneeling down to serve Mass. Maybe he wasn't a priest after all. But I did not have time to speculate about that: my heart was too full of other things in that great dark church, where, in little chapels, all around the ambulatory behind the high altar, chapels that were caves of dim candlelight, Mass was simultaneously beginning at many altars.

How did I live through that next hour? It is a mystery to me. The silence, the solemnity, the dignity of these Masses and of the church, and the overpowering atmosphere of prayers so fervent that they were almost tangible choked me with love and reverence that robbed me of the power to breathe. I could only get the air in gasps.

O my God, with what might You sometimes choose to teach a man's soul Your immense lessons! Here, even through only ordinary channels, came to me graces that overwhelmed me like a tidal wave, truths that drowned me with the force of their impact: and all through the plain, normal means of the liturgy—but the liturgy used properly, and with reverence, by souls inured to sacrifice.

What a thing Mass becomes, in hands hardened by gruelling and sacrificial labor, in poverty and abjection and humiliation! "See, see," said those lights, those shadows in all the chapels. "See Who God is! Realize what this Mass is! See Christ here, on the Cross! See His wounds, see His torn hands, see how the King of Glory is crowned with thorns! Do you know what Love is? Here is Love, Here on this Cross, here is Love, suffering these nails, these thorns, that scourge loaded with lead, smashed to pieces, bleeding to death because of your sins and bleeding to death because of people that will never know Him, and never think of Him and will never remember His Sacrifice. Learn from Him how to love

God and how to love men! Learn of this Cross, this Love, how to give your life away to Him."

Almost simultaneously all around the church, at all the various altars, the bells began to ring. These monks, they rang no bells at the *Sanctus* or the *Hanc igitur*, only at the Consecration: and now, suddenly, solemnly, all around the church, Christ was on the Cross, lifted up, drawing all things to Himself, that tremendous Sacrifice tearing hearts from bodies, and drawing them out to Him.

"See, see Who God is, see the glory of God, going up to Him out of this incomprehensible and infinite Sacrifice in which all history begins and ends, all individual lives begin and end, in which every story is told, and finished, and settled for joy or for sorrow: the one point of reference for all the truths that are outside of God, their center, their focus: Love."

Faint gold fire flashed from the shadowy flanks of the upraised chalice at our altar.

"Do you know what Love is? You have never known the meaning of Love, never, you who have always drawn all things to the center of your own nothingness. Here is Love in this chalice full of Blood, Sacrifice, mactation. Do you not know that to love means to be killed for glory of the Beloved? And where is your love? Where is now your Cross, if you say you want to follow Me, if you pretend you love Me?"

All around the church the bells rang as gentle and fresh as dew.

"But these men are dying for Me. These monks are killing themselves for Me: and for you, for the world, for the people who do not know Me, for the millions that will never know them on this earth . . ."

After Communion I thought my heart was going to explode.

When the church had practically emptied after the second round of Masses, I left and went to my room. When I next came back to Church it was to kneel in the high balcony in the far end of the nave, for Tierce and Sext and then None and the Conventual Mass.

And now the church was full of light, and the monks stood in their stalls and bowed like white seas at the ends of the psalms, those slow, rich, sombre and yet lucid tones of the psalms, praising God in His new morning, thanking Him for the world He had created and for the life He continued to give to it.

Those psalms, the singing of the monks, and especially the ferial tone for the Little Hours' Hymns: what springs of life and strength and grace were in their singing! The whole earth came to life and bounded with new fruitfulness and significance in the joy of their simple and beautiful chanting that gradually built up to the climax of the Conventual Mass: splendid, I say, and yet this Cistercian liturgy in Lent was reduced to the ultimate in simplicity. Therefore it was all the more splendid, because the splendor was intellectual and affective, and not the mere flash and glitter of vestments and decorations.

Two candles were lit on the bare altar. A plain wooden crucifix stood above the Tabernacle. The sanctuary was closed off with a curtain. The white altar cloth fell, at both ends, almost to the floor. The priest ascended the altar steps in a chasuble, accompanied by a deacon in alb and stole. And that was all.

At intervals during the Mass, a monk in a cowl detached himself from the choir and went slowly and soberly to minister at the altar, with grave and solemn bows, walking with his long flowing sleeves dangling almost as low as his ankles . . .

The eloquence of this liturgy was even more tremendous: and what it said was one, simple, cogent, tremendous truth: this church, the court of the Queen of Heaven, is the real capital of the country in which we are living. This is the center of all the vitality that is in America. This is the cause and reason why the nation is holding together. These men, hidden in the anonymity of their choir and their white cowls, are doing for their land what no army, no congress, no president could ever do as such: they are winning for it the grace and the protection and the friendship of God.

I discovered that the young man with black hair, in dunga-rees, was a postulant. He was entering the monastery that day. That evening, at Compline, we who were standing up in the tribune at the back of the church could see him down there, in the choir, in his dark secular clothes, which made him easy to pick out, in the shadows, among the uniform white of the novices and monks.

For a couple of days it was that way. Practically the first thing you noticed, when you looked at the choir, was this young man in secular clothes, among all the monks.

Then suddenly we saw him no more. He was in white. They had given him an oblate's habit, and you could not pick him out from the rest.

The waters had closed over his head, and he was submerged in the community. He was lost. The world would hear of him no more. He had drowned to our society and become a Cistercian.

Up in the guest house, somebody who happened to know who he was, told me a few facts about him, by way of a kind of obituary. I don't know if I got them straight or not: but he was a convert. He came from a rather wealthy family in Pennsylvania, and had gone to one of the big Eastern uni-versities, and had been on a vacation in the Bahama Islands when he had bumped into a priest who got to talking to him about the faith, and converted him. When he was baptized, his parents were so incensed that they cut him off, as the say-ing goes, without a penny. For a while he had worked as a pilot on one of the big air lines, flying planes to South America, but now that was all over. He was gone out of the world. *Requiescat in pace.*

The secular priest with the white hair was more of a mys-tery. He was a big, bluff fellow, with some kind of an accent which led me to place him as a Belgian. He was not entering the community, but it seemed he had been there in the guest house for some time. In the afternoons he put on a pair of overalls, and went about painting benches and other furniture, and he laughed and talked with the others.

As he talked, his talk seemed strange to me. In a place like this, you would expect someone to say something, at least indirectly, about religion. And yet that was a subject on which he seemed to be inarticulate. The only thing he seemed to know anything about was strength, strength and work. At the dinner table, he rolled up his sleeve and said:

"Huh! Look at dat mossel!"

And he flexed a huge biceps for the edification of the retreatants.

I found out afterwards that he was under ecclesiastical censure, and was in the monastery doing penance. The poor man, for some reason or another, had not lived as a good priest. In the end, his mistakes had caught up with him. He had come into contact with some schismatics, in a sect known as "the Old Catholics" and these people persuaded him to leave the Church and come over to them. And when he did so, they made him an archbishop.

I suppose he enjoyed the dignity and the novelty of it for a while: but the whole thing was obviously silly. So he gave it up and came back. And now here he was in the monastery, serving Mass every morning for a young Trappist priest who scarcely had the oils of his ordination dry on his hands.

As the week went on, the house began to fill, and the evening before Holy Thursday there must have been some twenty-five or thirty retreatants in the monastery, men young and old, from all quarters of the country. Half a dozen students had hitch-hiked down from Notre Dame, with glasses and earnest talk about the philosophy of St. Thomas Aquinas. There was a psychiatrist from Chicago who said he came down every Easter, and there were three or four pious men who turned out to be friends and benefactors of the monastery—quiet, rather solemn personages; they assumed a sort of command over the other guests. They had a right to. They practically lived here in this guest house. In fact, they had a kind of quasi-vocation all their own. They belonged to that special class of men raised up by God to support orphanages and convents and monasteries and build hospitals and feed the poor. On the whole it is a way to sanctity that is sometimes too much despised. It sometimes implies a more than ordinary humility in men who come to think that the monks and nuns they assist are creatures of another world. God will show us at the latter day that many of them were better men than the monks they supported!

But the man I most talked to was a Carmelite priest who had wandered about the face of the earth even more than I had. If I wanted to hear something about monasteries, he could tell me about hundreds of them that he had seen.

We walked in the guest house garden, in the sun, watching the bees fighting in the rich yellow tulips, and he told me about the Carthusians in England, at Parkminster.

There were no longer any pure hermits or anchorites in the world: but the Carthusians were the ones who had gone the farthest, climbed the highest on the mountain of isolation that lifted them above the world and concealed them in God.

We could see the Cistercians here going out to work in a long line with shovels tucked under their arms with a most quaint formality. But the Carthusian worked alone, in his cell, in his own garden or workshop, isolated. These monks slept in a common dormitory, the Carthusian slept in a hidden cell. These men ate together while someone read aloud to them in their refectory. The Carthusian ate alone, sitting in the window-alcove of his cell, with no one to speak to him but God. All day long and all night long the Cistercian was with his brothers. All day long and all night long, except for the offices in choir and other intervals, the Carthusian was with God alone. *O beata solitudo!* . . .

The words were written on the walls of this Trappist guest house, too. *O beata solitudo, o sola beatitudo!*

There was one thing the Cistercians had in their favor. The Carthusians had a kind of recreation in which they went out for walks together and conversed with one another, to prevent the possibilities of strain that might go with too uncompromising a solitude, too much of that *sola beatitudo*. Could there be too much of it, I wondered? But the Trappist with

396

his unbroken silence—at least as far as conversations were concerned—had one advantage!

And yet what did it matter which one was the most perfect Order? Neither one of them was for me! Had I not been told definitely enough a year ago that I had no vocation to any religious Order? All these comparisons were nothing but fuel for the fire of that interior anguish, that hopeless desire for what I could not have, for what was out of reach.

The only question was not which Order attracted me more, but which one tortured me the more with a solitude and silence and contemplation that could never be mine.

Far from wondering whether I had a vocation to either one, or from instituting a comparison between them, I was not even allowed the luxury of speculation on such a subject. It was all out of the question.

However, since the Carthusians were, after all, far away, it was what I had before my eyes that tortured me the most. The Carthusians were more perfect, perhaps, and therefore more to be desired: but they were doubly out of reach because of the war and because of what I thought was my lack of a vocation.

If I had had any supernatural common sense I would have realized that a retreat like this would be the best time to take that problem by the horns and overcome it, not by my own efforts and meditations but by prayer and by the advice of an experienced priest. And where would I find anyone more experienced in such matters than in a monastery of contemplatives?

But what was the matter with me? I suppose I had taken such a beating from the misunderstandings and misapprehensions that had arisen in my mind by the time that Capuchin got through with me, in his confessional, the year before, that I literally feared to reopen the subject at all. There was something in my bones that told me that I ought to find out whether my intense desire to lead this kind of a life in some monastery were an illusion: but the old scars were not yet healed, and my whole being shrank from another scourging.

That was my Holy Week, that mute, hopeless, interior

struggle. It was my share in the Passion of Christ which began, that year, in the middle of the night with the first strangled cry of the Vigils of Holy Thursday.

It was a tremendous thing to hear the terrible cries of Jeremias resounding along the walls of that dark church buried in the country. ". . . Attend and see if there be any sorrow like unto my sorrow . . . From above He hath sent fire into my bones, and hath chastised me: He hath spread a net for my feet, He hath turned me back, He hath made me desolate, wasted with sorrow all the day long."

It was not hard to realize Whose words these were, not difficult to detect the voice of Christ, in the liturgy of His Church, crying out in the sorrows of His Passion, which was now beginning to be relived, as it is relived each year, in the churches of Christendom.

At the end of the office, one of the monks came solemnly out and extinguished the sanctuary light, and the sudden impression froze all hearts with darkness and foreboding. The day went on solemnly, the Little Hours being chanted in a strange, mighty, and tremendously sorrowful tone, plain as its three monotonously recurring notes could possibly make it be, a lament that was as rough and clean as stone. After the *Gloria in Excelsis* of the Conventual Mass, the organ was at last altogether silent: and the silence only served to bring out the simplicity and strength of the music chanted by the choir. After the general Communion, distributed to the long slow line of all the priests and monks and brothers and guests, and the procession of the Blessed Sacrament to the altar of repose—slow and sad, with lights and the *Pange Lingua*—came the Maundy, the *Mandatum*, when, in the cloister, the monks washed the feet of some seventy or eighty poor men, and kissed their feet, and pressed money into their hands.

And through all this, especially in the *Mandatum*, when I saw them at close range, I was amazed at the way these monks, who were evidently just plain young Americans from the factories and colleges and farms and high-schools of the various states, were nevertheless absorbed and transformed in the liturgy. The thing that was most impressive was their absolute

398

simplicity. They were concerned with one thing only: doing the things they had to do, singing what they had to sing, bowing and kneeling and so on when it was prescribed, and doing it as well as they could, without fuss or flourish or display. It was all utterly simple and unvarnished and straightforward, and I don't think I had ever seen anything, anywhere, so unaffected, so un-self-conscious as these monks. There was not a shadow of anything that could be called parade or display. They did not seem to realize that they were being watched— and, as a matter of fact, I can say from experience that they did not know it at all. In choir, it is very rare that you even realize that there are any, or many, or few seculars in the house: and if you do realize it, it makes no difference. The presence of other people becomes something that has absolutely no significance to the monk when he is at prayer. It is something null, neutral, like the air, like the atmosphere, like the weather. All these external things recede into the distance. Remotely, you are aware of it all, but you do not advert to it, you are not conscious of it, any more than the eye registers, with awareness, the things on which it is not focussed, although they may be within its range of vision.

Certainly one thing the monk does not, or cannot, realize is the effect which these liturgical functions, performed by a group as such, have upon those who see them. The lessons, the truths, the incidents and values portrayed are simply overwhelming.

For this effect to be achieved, it is necessary that each monk as an individual performer be absolutely lost, ignored, overlooked.

And yet, what a strange admission! To say that men were admirable, worthy of honor, perfect, in proportion as they disappeared into a crowd and made themselves unnoticed, by even ceasing to be aware of their own existence and their own acts. Excellence, here, was in proportion to obscurity: the one who was best was the one who was least observed, least distinguished. Only faults and mistakes drew attention to the individual.

The logic of the Cistercian life was, then, the complete opposite to the logic of the world, in which men put themselves forward, so that the most excellent is the one who stands out, the one who is eminent above the rest, who attracts attention.

But what was the answer to this paradox? Simply that the monk in hiding himself from the world becomes not less himself, not less of a person, but more of a person, more truly and perfectly himself: for his personality and individuality are perfected in their true order, the spiritual, interior order, of union with God, the principle of all perfection. *Omnis gloria ejus filiae regis ab intus.*

The logic of worldly success rests on a fallacy: the strange error that our perfection depends on the thoughts and opinions and applause of other men! A weird life it is, indeed, to be living always in somebody else's imagination, as if that were the only place in which one could at last become real!

With all these things before me, day and night, for two days, I finally came to the afternoon of Good Friday.

After a tremendous morning of ten hours of practically uninterrupted chanting and psalmody, the monks, exhausted, had disappeared from the scene of their gutted church, with its stripped altars and its empty Tabernacle wide open to the four winds. The monastery was silent, inert. I could not pray, I could not read any more.

I got Brother Matthew to let me out the front gate on the pretext that I wanted to take a picture of the monastery, and then I went for a walk along the enclosure wall, down the road past the mill, and around the back of the buildings, across a creek and down a narrow valley, with a barn and some woods on one side, and the monastery on a bluff on the other.

The sun was warm, the air quiet. Somewhere a bird sang. In a sense, it was a relief to be out of the atmosphere of intense prayer that had pervaded those buildings for the last two days. The pressure was too heavy for me. My mind was too full.

Now my feet took me slowly along a rocky road, under the stunted cedar trees, with violets growing up everywhere between the cracks in the rock.

Out here I could think: and yet I could not get to any conclusions. But there was one thought running around and around in my mind: "To be a monk . . . to be a monk . . ."

I gazed at the brick building which I took to be the novitiate. It stood on top of a high rampart of a retaining wall that made it look like a prison or a citadel. I saw the enclosure wall, the locked gates. I thought of the hundreds of pounds of spiritual pressure compressed and concentrated within those buildings and weighing down on the heads of the monks, and I thought, "It would kill me."

I turned my eyes to the trees, to the woods. I looked up the valley, back in the direction from which I had come, at the high wooded hill that closed off the prospect. I thought: "I am a Franciscan. That is my kind of spirituality, to be out in the woods, under the trees . . ."

I walked back across the trestle over the sunny, narrow creek, embracing my fine new error. After all I had seen of the Franciscans, where did I get the idea that they spent their time under the trees? They often lived in schools in towns and in cities: and these monks, on the contrary, did go out every day and work in the very fields and woods that I was looking at.

Human nature has a way of making very specious arguments to suit its own cowardice and lack of generosity. And so now I was trying to persuade myself that the contemplative, cloistered life was not for me, because there was not enough fresh air. . . .

Nevertheless, back in the monastery I read St. Bernard's *De Diligendo Deo* and I read the life of a Trappist monk who had died in a monastery in France, ironically enough in my own part of France, near Toulouse: Father Joseph Cassant.

The Retreat Master, in one of his conferences, told us a long story of a man who had once come to Gethsemani, and who had not been able to make up his mind to become a monk, and had fought and prayed about it for days. Finally, went the story, he had made the Stations of the Cross, and at the final station had prayed fervently to be allowed the grace of dying in the Order.

"You know," said the Retreat Master, "they say that no petition you ask at the fourteenth station is ever refused."

In any case, this man finished his prayer, and went back to his room and in an hour or so he collapsed, and they just had time to receive his request for admission to the Order when he died.

He lies buried in the monks' cemetery, in the oblate's habit.

And so, about the last thing I did before leaving Gethsemani, was to do the Stations of the Cross, and to ask, with my heart in my throat, at the fourteenth station, for the grace of a vocation to the Trappists, if it were pleasing to God.

v

Back in the world, I felt like a man that had come down from the rare atmosphere of a very high mountain. When I got to Louisville, I had already been up for four hours or so, and my day was getting on towards its noon, so to speak, but I found that everybody else was just getting up and having breakfast and going to work. And how strange it was to see people walking around as if they had something important to do, running after busses, reading the newspapers, lighting cigarettes.

How futile all their haste and anxiety seemed.

My heart sank within me. I thought: "What am I getting into? Is this the sort of a thing I myself have been living in all these years?"

At a street corner, I happened to look up and caught sight of an electric sign, on top of a two-storey building. It read: "Clown Cigarettes."

I turned and fled from the alien and lunatic street, and found my way into the nearby cathedral, and knelt, and prayed, and did the Stations of the Cross.

Afraid of the spiritual pressure in that monastery? Was that what I had said the other day? How I longed to be back there now: everything here, in the world outside, was insipid and slightly insane. There was only one place I knew of where there was any true order.

Yet, how could I go back? Did I not know that I really had no vocation? . . . It was the same old story again.

I got on the train for Cincinnati, and for New York.

Back at St. Bonaventure's, where the spring I had already met in Kentucky finally caught up with me again, several weeks later, I walked in the woods, in the sun, under the pale blossoms of the wild cherry trees.

The fight went on in my mind.

By now, the problem had resolved itself into one practical issue: why don't I consult somebody about the whole question? Why don't I write to the abbot of Gethsemani, and tell him all about my case, and ask him his opinion?

More practical still, here at St. Bonaventure's there was one priest whom I had come to know well during this last year, a wise and good philosopher, Father Philotheus. We had been going over some texts of St. Bonaventure and Duns Scotus together, and I knew I could trust him with the most involved spiritual problem. Why did I not ask him?

There was one absurd, crazy thing that held me up: it was a kind of a blind impulse, confused, obscure, irrational. I can hardly identify it as it actually was, because its true nature escaped me: it was so blind, so elemental. But it amounted to a vague subconscious fear that I would once and for all be told that I definitely had no vocation. It was the fear of an ultimate refusal. Perhaps what I wanted was to maintain myself in an equivocal, indefinite position in which I would be free to dream about entering the monastery, without having the actual responsibility of doing so, and of embracing the real hardships of Cistercian life. If I asked advice, and was told I had no vocation, then the dream would be over: and if I was told I had a vocation, then I would have to walk right in to the reality.

And all this was complicated by that other dream: that of the Carthusians. If there had been a Carthusian monastery in America, things would have been much simpler. But there is still no such place in the whole hemisphere. And there was no chance of crossing the Atlantic. France was full of Germans and the Charterhouse in Sussex had been bombed flat to the ground. And so I walked under the trees, full of indecision, praying for light.

In the midst of this conflict, I suddenly got a notion which shows that I was not very far advanced in the spiritual life. I thought of praying God to let me know what I was going to do, or what I should do, or what the solution would be, by showing it to me in the Scriptures. It was the old business of opening the book and putting your finger down blindly on the page and taking the words thus designated as an answer to your question. Sometimes the saints have done this, and much more often a lot of superstitious old women have done it. I am not a saint, and I do not doubt that there may have been an element of superstition in my action. But anyway, I made my prayer, and opened the book, and put my finger down definitely on the page and said to myself: "Whatever it is, this is it."

I looked, and the answer practically floored me. The words were:

"Ecce eris tacens." "Behold, thou shalt be silent."

It was the twentieth verse of the first chapter of St. Luke where the angel was talking to John the Baptist's father, Zachary.

Tacens: there could not have been a closer word to "Trappist" in the whole Bible, as far as I was concerned, for to me, as well as to most other people, the word "Trappist" stood for "silence."

However, I immediately found myself in difficulties which show how silly it is to make an oracle out of books. As soon as I looked at the context, I observed that Zachary was being reproved for asking too many questions. Did the whole context apply to me, too, and was I also therefore reproved? And therefore was the news to be taken as ominous and bad? I thought about it a little, and soon found that I was getting completely mixed up. Besides, when I reflected, I realized that I had not put the question in any clear terms, so that, as a matter of fact, I had forgotten just what I had asked. I did not know whether I had asked God to tell me His will, or merely to announce to me what would happen in the future in point of fact. By the time I had got myself completely tied up in these perplexities, the information I had asked for was more of a nuisance, and a greater cause of uncertainty than my ignorance.

In fact, I was almost as ignorant as I was before, except for one thing.

Deep down, underneath all the perplexity, I had a kind of a conviction that this was a genuine answer, and that the problem was indeed some day going to end up that way: I was going to be a Trappist.

But as far as making any practical difference, there and then, it was no help at all.

I continued to walk in the woods, in the pastures, and in the old tank lots at the wood's edge, down towards the radio station. When I was out there alone, I would go about full of nostalgia for the Trappist monastery, singing over and over *Jam lucis orto sidere* on the ferial tone.

It was a matter of deep regret to me that I could not remember the wonderful *Salve Regina* with which the monks ended all their days, chanting in the darkness to the Mother of God that long antiphon, the most stately and most beautiful and most stirring thing that was ever written, that was ever sung. I walked along the roads, in Two Mile Valley, in Four Mile Valley, in the late afternoons, in the early evenings, in the dusk, and along the river where it was quiet, wishing I could sing the *Salve Regina*. And I could remember nothing but the first two or three neumes. After that, I had to invent, and my invention was not very good. It sounded awful. So did my voice. So I gave up trying to sing, humiliated and sorrowful, and complaining a little to the Mother of God.

The weeks went on, and the weather began to show signs of summer when John Paul suddenly arrived at St. Bonaventure's, on his way back from Mexico. The back seat of his Buick was full of Mexican records and pictures and strange objects and a revolver and big colored baskets, and he was looking relatively well and happy. We spent a couple of afternoons driving around through the hills, and talking, or just driving and not talking. He had been to Yucatan, as he had planned, and he had been to Puebla, and he had just missed being in an earthquake in Mexico City, and he had lent a lot of money to some gent who owned a ranch near St. Luis Potosi. On the same ranch he had shot, with his revolver, a poisonous snake some six feet long.

"Do you expect to get that money back?" I asked him.

"Oh, if he doesn't pay me, I'll have a share in his ranch," said John Paul without concern.

But at the moment he was heading back towards Ithaca. I could not be sure whether he was going to go to Cornell summer school, and finally get his degree, or whether he was going to take some more flying lessons, or what he was going to do.

I asked him if he had kept in touch with this priest he knew there.

"Oh, yes," he said, "sure."

I asked him what he thought about becoming a Catholic.

"You know," he said, "I've thought about that a little."

"Why don't you go to the priest and ask him to give you some instructions?"

"I think I will."

But I could tell from the tone of his voice that he was as indefinite as he was sincere. He meant well, but he would probably do nothing about it. I said I would give him a copy of the Catechism I had, but when I went to my room I couldn't find it.

And so John Paul, in the big shiny Buick built low on its chassis, drove off at a great speed, towards Ithaca, with his revolver and his Mexican baskets.

In the gay days of early June, in the time of examinations, I was beginning a new book. It was called *The Journal of My Escape from the Nazis* and it was the kind of book that I liked to write, full of double-talk and all kinds of fancy ideas that sounded like Franz Kafka. One reason why it was satisfying was that it fulfilled a kind of psychological necessity that had been pent up in me all through the last stages of the war because of my sense of identification, by guilt, with what was going on in England.

So I put myself there and, telescoping my own past with the air-raids that were actually taking place, as its result, I wrote this journal. And, as I say, it was something I needed to write, although I often went off at a tangent, and the thing got away up more than one blind alley.

And so, absorbed in this work, and in the final examinations, and in preparation for the coming summer school, I let the question of the Trappist vocation drop into the background, although I could not drop it altogether.

I said to myself: after summer school, I will go and make a retreat with the Trappists in Canada, at Our Lady of the Lake, outside Montreal.

3

The Sleeping Volcano

In the cool summer nights, when the road behind the power-house and the laundry and the garages was dark and empty, and you could barely see the hills, outlined in the dark against the stars, I used to walk out there, in the smell of the fields, towards the dark cow-barns. There was a grove along the west side of the football field, and in the grove were two shrines, one to the Little Flower and the other a grotto for Our Lady of Lourdes. But the grotto wasn't complicated enough to be really ugly, the way those artificial grottos usually are. It was nice to pray out there, in the dark, with the wind soughing in the high pine branches.

Sometimes you could hear one other sound: the laughter of all the nuns and clerics and Friars and the rest of the summer school students sitting in Alumni Hall, which was at the end of the grove, and enjoying the movies, which were shown every Thursday night.

On those nights, the whole campus was deserted and the Alumni Hall was crowded. I felt as if I were the only one in the place who did not go to the movies—except for the boy at the telephone switchboard in the Dormitory building. He had to stay there, he was being paid for that.

Even my friend Father Philotheus, who was editing fourteenth-century philosophical manuscripts, and who had taught me St. Bonaventure's way to God according to the *Itinerarium*, and with whom I had studied parts of Scotus' *De Primo Principio*, even he went to the movies in the hope that there would be a Mickey Mouse. But as soon as all the comedies were over, he left. He could not make anything much out of all those other dramas and adventures.

Oh, the gay laughter of the Sisters and the clerics in that old firetrap of a red-brick building! I suppose they deserved to have a little entertainment—at least the Sisters deserved it.

I know that many of them got some severe headaches from the course I was giving in "Bibliography and Methods of Research." The traditional way of teaching methods of research was to throw out a lot of odd names and facts to the class, without any clue as to where they came from, and tell them all to come back the next day with a complete identification. So I asked them things like: "Who is Philip Sparrow?" "What Oxford College has on its coat of arms a Pelican vulning herself proper?" To find out these things—which I only gave them because I already knew them myself—they had to break their heads over all kinds of reference books, and thus they got practical training in methods of research. But the Sisters always came back with the right answer, although they sometimes had circles under their eyes. The clerics had the right answer but no circles, because they had got the answer from the Sisters. In the back of the room sat a priest who belonged to some teaching Order in Canada and who seldom got the answers at all, even from the Sisters. He just sat there and gave me black looks.

So, on the whole, it was good that they should relax and laugh, and sit in those rows of ancient and uncomfortable chairs indulging their innocent and unsophisticated taste for carefully selected movies.

I walked along the empty field, and thought of their life—sheltered and innocent and safe. A number of them were, in many ways, still children—especially the nuns. They looked out at you from under various kinds of caps and coifs and blinkers and what not they had on, with round, earnest eyes; the sober, clear eyes of little girls. Yet you knew they had responsibilities, and many of them had suffered a lot of things you could only half guess: but it was all absorbed in quiet simplicity and resignation. The most you could observe even in the most harassed of them was that they looked a little tired: perhaps some of the older ones, too, were a trifle too tight-lipped, a trifle too grim. But even then, some of the old ones still had that little girl simplicity in their look, not yet altogether extinct.

Their life was secure. It was walled in by ramparts of order and decorum and stability, in the social as much as in the religious sphere. But they nevertheless all had to work hard—much harder than most of their relatives outside in the world. Most of the Sisters had long hours in their schoolrooms and then other things to do besides that. I suppose they had their fair share of cooking, and washing clothes, and scrubbing floors when they were in their proper communities. Yet even then, was not the relative comfort of their life apt to make them impervious to certain levels of human experience and human misery?

I wondered if they were aware of all the degrees of suffering and degradation which, in the slums, in the war zones, in the moral jungles of our century, were crying out to the Church for help, and to Heaven for vengeance against injustice. The answer to that would probably be that some of them were, and some of them were not: but that they all sincerely wanted to be doing something about these things, if they could. But, it was true, they were sheltered, protected, separated, in large measure, from the frightful realities that had a claim upon their attention if they loved Christ.

But then, why should I separate myself from them? I was in the same condition. Perhaps I was slightly more conscious of it than some of them: but all of us were going to have an occasion to remember this paradox, this accusing paradox that those who are poor for the love of Christ are often only poor in a purely abstract sense, and that their poverty, which is designed among other things to throw them into the midst of the real poor, for the salvation of souls, only separates them from the poor in a safe and hermetically-sealed economic stability, full of comfort and complacency.

One night there came to those nuns and to those clerics and to St. Bonaventure in general and myself in particular, someone sent from God for the special purpose of waking us up, and turning our eyes in that direction which we all tended so easily to forget, in the safety and isolation of our country stronghold, lost in the upstate hills.

It was right, of course, that my interior life should have been concerned first of all with my own salvation: it must be that way. It is no profit for a man to gain the whole world, and suffer the loss of his own soul, and anyway, one who is losing his own soul is not going to be able to do much to save the souls of others, except in the case where he may be giving out Sacraments which work, as they say, *ex opere operato*, without any intrinsic dependence on the sanctity of the one dispensing them. But now it was necessary that I take more account of obligations to other men, born of the very fact that I was myself a man among men, and a sharer in their sins and in their punishments and in their miseries and in their hopes. No man goes to heaven all by himself, alone.

I was walking around the football field, as usual, in the dark. The Alumni Hall was full of lights. It was not the night for movies. There was some speaker there. I had not paid much attention to the list of speakers that had been invited to come and stand on that platform and tell the clerics and Sisters all about some important topic. I knew there would be one from *The Catholic Worker*, and that David Goldstein, who was a converted Jew and ran an organization for street-preaching by laymen, was invited to speak, and I knew Baroness de Hueck, who was working among the Negroes in Harlem, was also going to come.

As far as I knew, this night was the one listed for David Goldstein, and I hesitated for a moment wondering whether I wanted to go and hear him or not. At first, I thought: "No," and started off towards the grove. But then I thought: "I will at least take a look inside the door."

Going up the steps to the second floor of the Hall, where the theater was, I could hear someone speaking with great vehemence. However, it was not a man's voice.

When I stepped in to the room, there was a woman standing on the stage. Now a woman, standing all alone on a stage, in front of a big lighted hall, without any decorations or costume or special lighting effects, just in the glare of the hall-lights, is at a disadvantage. It is not very likely that she will make much of an impression. And this particular woman was dressed in clothes that were nondescript and plain, even

411

poor. She had no artful way of walking around, either. She had no fancy tricks, nothing for the gallery. And yet as soon as I came in the door, the impression she was making on that room full of nuns and clerics and priests and various lay-people pervaded the place with such power that it nearly knocked me backwards down the stairs which I had just ascended.

She had a strong voice, and strong convictions, and strong things to say, and she was saying them in the simplest, most unvarnished, bluntest possible kind of talk, and with such uncompromising directness that it stunned. You could feel right away that most of her audience was hanging on her words, and that some of them were frightened, and that one or two were angry, but that everybody was intent on the things she had to say.

I realized it was the Baroness.

I had heard something about her, and her work in Harlem, because she was well known and admired in Corpus Christi parish, where I had been baptized. Father Ford was always sending her things they needed, down there on 135th Street and Lenox Avenue.

What she was saying boiled down to this:

Catholics are worried about Communism: and they have a right to be, because the Communist revolution aims, among other things, at wiping out the Church. But few Catholics stop to think that Communism would make very little progress in the world, or none at all, if Catholics really lived up to their obligations, and really did the things Christ came on earth to teach them to do: that is, if they really loved one another, and saw Christ in one another, and lived as saints, and did something to win justice for the poor.

For, she said, if Catholics were able to see Harlem, as they ought to see it, with the eyes of faith, they would not be able to stay away from such a place. Hundreds of priests and lay-people would give up everything to go there and try to do something to relieve the tremendous misery, the poverty, sickness, degradation and dereliction of a race that was being crushed and perverted, morally and physically, under the

412

burden of a colossal economic injustice. Instead of seeing Christ suffering in His members, and instead of going to help Him, Who said: "Whatsoever you did to the least of these my brethren, you did it to Me," we preferred our own comfort: we averted our eyes from such a spectacle, because it made us feel uneasy: the thought of so much dirt nauseated us—and we never stopped to think that we, perhaps, might be partly responsible for it. And so people continued to die of starvation and disease in those evil tenements full of vice and cruelty, while those who did condescend to consider their problems, held banquets in the big hotels downtown to discuss the "Race situation" in a big rosy cloud of hot air.

If Catholics, she said, were able to see Harlem as they should see it, with the eyes of faith, as a challenge to their love of Christ, as a test of their Christianity, the Communists would be able to do nothing there.

But, on the contrary, in Harlem the Communists were strong. They were bound to be strong. They were doing some of the things, performing some of the works of mercy that Christians should be expected to do. If some Negro workers lose their jobs, and are in danger of starving, the Communists are there to divide their own food with them, and to take up the defence of their case.

If some Negro is dying, and is refused admission to a hospital, the Communists show up, and get someone to take care of him, and furthermore see to it that the injustice is publicized all over the city. If a Negro family is evicted, because they can't pay the rent, the Communists are there, and find shelter for them, even if they have to divide their own bedding with them. And every time they do these things, more and more people begin to say: "See, the Communists really love the poor! They are really trying to do something for us! What they say must be right: there is no one else who cares anything about our interests: there is nothing better for us to do than to get in with them, and work with them for this revolution they are talking about. . . ."

Do the Catholics have a labor policy? Have the Popes said anything about these problems in their Encyclicals? The

Communists know more about those Encyclicals than the average Catholic. *Rerum Novarum* and *Quadrigesimo Anno* are discussed and analyzed in their public meetings, and the Reds end up by appealing to their audience:

"Now we ask you, do the Catholics practice these things? Have you ever seen any Catholics down here trying to do anything for you? When this firm and that firm locked out so many hundreds of Negro workers, whose side did the Catholic papers take? Don't you know that the Catholic Church is just a front for Capitalism, and that all their talk about the poor is hypocrisy? What do they care about the poor? What have they ever done to help you? Even their priests in Harlem go outside and hire white men when they want somebody to repaint their churches! Don't you know that the Catholics are laughing at you, behind the back of their hands, while they pocket the rent for the lousy tenements you have to live in? . . ."

The Baroness was born a Russian. She had been a young girl at the time of the October Revolution. She had seen half her family shot, she had seen priests fall under the bullets of the Reds, and she had had to escape from Russia the way it is done in the movies, but with all the misery and hardship which the movies do not show, and none of the glamour which is their specialty.

She had ended up in New York, without a cent, working in a laundry. She had been brought up a Roman Catholic, and the experiences she had gone through, instead of destroying her faith, intensified and deepened it until the Holy Ghost planted fortitude in the midst of her soul like an unshakeable rock. I never saw anyone so calm, so certain, so peaceful in her absolute confidence in God.

Catherine de Hueck is a person in every way big: and the bigness is not merely physical: it comes from the Holy Ghost dwelling constantly within her, and moving her in all that she does.

When she was working in that laundry, down somewhere near Fourteenth Street, and sitting on the kerbstone eating her lunch with the other girls who worked there, the sense of her own particular vocation dawned upon her. It was the call to an apostolate, not new, but so old that it is as traditional as that of the first Christians: an apostolate of a laywoman in the world, among workers, herself a worker, and poor: an apostolate of personal contacts, of word and above all of example. There was to be nothing special about it, nothing that savored of a religious Order, no special rule, no distinctive habit. She, and those who joined her, would simply be poor —there was no choice on that score, for they were that already —but they would embrace their poverty, and the life of the proletariat in all its misery and insecurity and dead, drab monotony. They would live and work in the slums, lose themselves, in the huge anonymous mass of the forgotten and the derelict, for the only purpose of living the complete, integral Christian life in that environment—loving those around them, sacrificing themselves for those around them, and spreading the Gospel and the truth of Christ most of all by being saints, by living in union with Him, by being full of His Holy Ghost, His charity.

As she spoke of these things, in that Hall, and to all these nuns and clerics, she could not help but move them all deeply, because what they were hearing—it was too patent to be missed—was nothing but the pure Franciscan ideal, the pure essence of the Franciscan apostolate of poverty, without the vows taken by the Friars Minor. And, for the honor of those who heard her, most of them had the sense and the courage to recognize this fact, and to see that she was, in a sense, a much better Franciscan than they were. She was, as a matter of fact, in the Third Order, and that made me feel quite proud of my own scapular, which was hiding under my shirt: it reminded me that the thing was not altogether without meaning or without possibilities!

So the Baroness had gone to Harlem. She stepped out of the subway with a typewriter and a few dollars and some clothes in a bag. When she went to one of the tenements, and asked to look at a room, the man said to her:

"Ma'am, you all don't want to live here!"

"Yes, I do," she said, and added, by way of explanation: "I'm Russian."

"Russian!" said the man. "That's different. Walk right in."

In other words, he thought she was a Communist. . . .

That was the way Friendship House had begun. Now they were occupying four or five stores on both sides of 135th Street, and maintained a library and recreation rooms and a clothing room. The Baroness had an apartment of her own, and those of her helpers who lived there all the time also had a place on 135th Street. There were more girls than men staying with her in Harlem.

When the meeting was over, and when the Baroness had answered all the usual objections like "What if some Negro wanted to marry your sister—or you, for that matter?" I went up and spoke to her, and the next day I ran into her on the path in front of the library, when I was going, with an arm full of books, to teach a class on Dante's *Divine Comedy*. These two times were the only chance I had to speak to her, but I said:

"Would it be all right if I came to Friendship House, and did a little work with you, there, after all this is over?"

"Sure," she said, "come on."

But seeing me with my arms full of all those books, maybe she didn't believe me.

ii

It was a hot day, a rainy day, in the middle of August when I came out of the subway into the heat of Harlem. There were not many people on the streets that afternoon. I walked along the street until I came to the middle of the block, and saw one or two stores marked "Friendship House" and "Bl. Martin de Porres Center" or some such title in big blue letters. There did not seem to be anyone around.

The biggest of the stores was the library, and there I found half a dozen young Negroes, boys and girls, high school students, sitting at a table. Some of them wore glasses, and it seemed they were having some kind of an organized intellectual discussion, because when I came in they got a little embarrassed about it. I asked them if the Baroness was there, and they said no, she had gone downtown because it was her birthday, and I asked who I should see, so they told me Mary Jerdo. She was around somewhere. If I waited she would probably show up in a few minutes.

So I stood there, and took down off the shelf Father Bruno's *Life of St. John of the Cross* and looked at the pictures.

The young Negroes tried to pick up their discussion where they had left off: but they did not succeed. The stranger made them nervous. One of the girls opened her mouth and pronounced three or four abstract words, and then broke off into a giggle. Then another one opened her mouth and said: "Yes, but don't you think . . . ?" And this solemn question also collapsed in embarrassed tittering. One of the young men got off a whole paragraph or so, full of big words, and everybody roared with laughter. So I turned around and started to laugh too, and immediately the whole thing became a game.

They began saying big words just because it was funny. They uttered the most profoundly dull and ponderous statements, and laughed at them, and at the fact that such strange things had come out of their mouths. But soon they calmed down, and then Mary Jerdo came along, and showed me the different departments of Friendship House, and explained what they were.

The embarrassment of those young Negroes was something that gave me a picture of Harlem: the details of the picture were to be filled in later, but the essentials were already there.

Here in this huge, dark, steaming slum, hundreds of thousands of Negroes are herded together like cattle, most of them with nothing to eat and nothing to do. All the senses and imagination and sensibilities and emotions and sorrows and desires and hopes and ideas of a race with vivid feelings and deep emotional reactions are forced in upon themselves, bound inward by an iron ring of frustration: the prejudice that hems them in with its four insurmountable walls. In

417

this huge cauldron, inestimable natural gifts, wisdom, love, music, science, poetry are stamped down and left to boil with the dregs of an elementally corrupted nature, and thousands upon thousands of souls are destroyed by vice and misery and degradation, obliterated, wiped out, washed from the register of the living, dehumanized.

What has not been devoured, in your dark furnace, Harlem, by marihuana, by gin, by insanity, hysteria, syphilis?

Those who manage somehow to swim to the top of the seething cauldron, and remain on its surface, through some special spiritual quality or other, or because they have been able to get away from Harlem, and go to some college or school, these are not all at once annihilated: but they are left with the dubious privilege of living out the only thing Harlem possesses in the way of an ideal. They are left with the sorry task of contemplating and imitating what passes for culture in the world of the white people.

Now the terrifying paradox of the whole thing is this: Harlem itself, and every individual Negro in it, is a living condemnation of our so-called "culture." Harlem is there by way of a divine indictment against New York City and the people who live downtown and make their money downtown. The brothels of Harlem, and all its prostitution, and its dope-rings, and all the rest are the mirror of the polite divorces and the manifold cultured adulteries of Park Avenue: they are God's commentary on the whole of our society.

Harlem is, in a sense, what God thinks of Hollywood. And Hollywood is all Harlem has, in its despair, to grasp at, by way of a surrogate for heaven.

The most terrible thing about it all is that there is not a Negro in the whole place who does not realize, somewhere in the depths of his nature, that the culture of the white men is not worth the dirt in Harlem's gutters. They sense that the whole thing is rotten, that it is a fake, that it is spurious, empty, a shadow of nothingness. And yet they are condemned to reach out for it, and to seem to desire it, and to pretend they like it, as if the whole thing were some kind of bitter cosmic conspiracy: as if they were thus being forced to work out, in their own lives, a clear representation of the misery which has corrupted the ontological roots of the white man's own existence.

The little children of Harlem are growing up, crowded together like sardines in the rooms of tenements full of vice, where evil takes place hourly and inescapably before their eyes, so that there is not an excess of passion, not a perversion of natural appetite with which they are not familiar before the age of six or seven: and this by way of an accusation of the polite and expensive and furtive sensualities and lusts of the rich whose sins have bred this abominable slum. The effect resembles and even magnifies the cause, and Harlem is the portrait of those through whose fault such things come into existence. What was heard in secret in the bedrooms and apartments of the rich and of the cultured and the educated and the white is preached from the housetops of Harlem and there declared, for what it is, in all its horror, somewhat as it is seen in the eyes of God, naked and frightful.

No, there is not a Negro in the whole place who can fail to know, in the marrow of his own bones, that the white man's culture is not worth the jetsam in the Harlem River.

That night I came back to Harlem, since Mary Jerdo told me to, and had dinner with them all, and congratulated the Baroness on her birthday, and we saw a play that was put on by the little Negro children in the recreation room of the group called the "Cubs."

It was an experience that nearly tore me to pieces. All the parents of the children were there, sitting on benches, literally choked with emotion at the fact that their children should be acting in a play: but that was not the thing. For, as I say, they knew that the play was nothing, and that all the plays of the white people are more or less nothing. They were not taken in by that. Underneath it was something deep and wonderful and positive and true and overwhelming: their gratitude for even so small a sign of love as this, that someone should at least make some kind of a gesture that said: "This sort of thing cannot make anybody happy, but it is a way of saying: 'I wish you were happy.'"

Over against the profound and positive and elemental reality of this human love, not unmixed with Christ's charity and almost obtrusively holy, was the idiotic character of the play itself. Some one of those geniuses who write one-act plays for amateur theatricals had thought up the idea of having King Arthur and his Knights appear in modern dress, running around in a country club.

Let me tell you, this piece of wit became so devastating that it nearly gave me grey hairs, watching its presentation by little Negro children in the midst of that slum. The nameless author, speaking in the name of twentieth-century middle-class culture, said: "Here is something very jolly." God, replying through the mouths and eyes and actions of these little Negro children, and through their complete incomprehension of what the jokes and the scene and the situations could possibly be about, said: "This is what I think of your wit. It is an abomination in my sight. I do not know you, I do not know your society: you are as dead to me as hell itself. These little Negro children, I know and love: but you I know not. You are anathema."

Two or three nights later there was another play put on in the parish hall by an older group. It was the same kind of a play, all about rich people having a good time, presented by poor hapless Negro youths and girls who had no means of knowing anything about a good time that was so inane and idiotic—or so expensive. The very zest and gaiety and enthusiasm with which they tried to make something out of this miserable piece of trash only condemned its author and his inspiration all the more forcibly. And you were left with the sense that these Negroes, even in Harlem, would have been able to give all the rich men on Sutton Place lessons in how to be happy without half trying: and that was why their imitation of the ruling class was all the more damning an indictment.

If the Baroness had tried to face the tremendous paradox of Harlem with no other weapons than these, I think Friendship House would have closed down in three days. But the secret of her success and of her survival in the teeth of this gigantic problem was that she depended not on these frail human methods, not on theatricals, or meetings, or speeches, or conferences, but on God, Christ, the Holy Ghost.

According to the plan of her vocation, the Baroness herself had come to Harlem, and had started to live there for God, and God had brought her quickly into contact with the others who were serving in His secret police in this enemy city: the saints He had sent to sanctify and purify, not Harlem, but New York.

On Judgement Day the citizens of that fat metropolis with its mighty buildings and its veins bursting with dollars and its brains overreaching themselves with new optimistic philosophies of culture and progress, will be surprised, astounded when they find out who it was that was keeping the brimstone and thunderbolts of God's anger from wiping them long since from the face of the earth.

Living in the same building as most of the Friendship House workers was an ageing Negro woman, thin, quiet, worn out, dying of cancer. I only saw her once or twice, but I heard a lot about her; for everyone said that she had visions of Our Lady. About that I know nothing, except that if Our Lady were to act according to her usual custom, Harlem would be one of the first and only places I would expect her to appear —Harlem, or some share-cropper's cabin in Alabama, or some miner's shack in Pennsylvania.

The only time I spoke to her and got a good look at her, I realized one thing: she possessed the secret of Harlem, she knew the way out of the labyrinth. For her the paradox had ceased to exist, she was no longer in the cauldron, except by the pure accident of physical presence, which counts for nothing since the cauldron is almost entirely of the moral order. And when I saw her and spoke to her, I saw in this tired, serene, and holy face the patience and joy of the martyrs and the clear, unquenchable light of sanctity. She and some other Catholic women were sitting on chairs by the doorsteps of the building, in the relatively cool street, in the early evening: and the group they made, there, in the midst of the turmoil of the lost crowd, astounded the passer-by with the sense of peace, of conquest: that deep, deep, unfathomable, shining peace that is in the eyes of Negro women who are really full of belief!

Seeing the boys and girls in the library, I had got some insight into the problem of Harlem. Here, just across the street, I saw the solution, the only solution: faith, sanctity. It was not far to seek.

If the Baroness, biding her time, letting the children put on plays, giving them some place where they could at least be off the street and out of the way of the trucks, could gather around her souls like these holy women and could form, in her organization, others that were, in the same way, saints, whether white or colored, she would not only have won her way, but she might eventually, by the grace of God, transfigure the face of Harlem. She had before her many measures of meal, but there was at hand already more than a little leaven. We know the way Christ works. No matter how impossible the thing may look, from a human angle, we may wake up one morning and find that the whole is leavened. It may be done with saints!

For my own part, I knew that it was good for me to be there, and so for two or three weeks I came down every night and ate dinner with the little community of them, in the apartment, and recited Compline afterwards—in English—all together, lined up in the narrow room in two choirs. It was the only time they ever did anything that made them look like religious, and there was not much that was really formally choral about it. It was strictly a family affair.

After that, for two or three hours, I devoted myself to the task of what was euphemistically called "looking after the Cubs." I stayed in the store that was their play-room, and played the piano as much for my own amusement as for anything else, and tried, by some sort of moral influence, to preserve peace and prevent a really serious riot. If a true fight had ever started, I don't know what would have happened. But most of the time everything was peace. They played ping-pong and monopoly, and for one little kid I drew a picture of the Blessed Virgin.

422

"Who is that?" he said.

"It is Our Blessed Mother."

Immediately his expression changed, became clouded over with a wild and strong devotion that was so primitive that it astonished me. He began crooning over and over: "Blessed Mother . . . Blessed Mother," and seized the picture and ran out into the street.

When August ended, and Labor Day came, the Baroness had to leave and go to Canada and I left to make the second Trappist retreat, which I had been promising myself ever since I returned from Gethsemani in the spring. But I did not have the time or the money to go to Canada. Instead, I had written to the monastery of Our Lady of the Valley, outside Providence, Rhode Island, and had received an answer to come the day after Labor Day.

Driving through Harlem with Seymour, the Saturday before Labor Day, I felt for Friendship House a little of the nostalgia I had felt for Gethsemani. Here I was, once again thrown back into the world, alone in the turmoil and futility of it, and robbed of my close and immediate and visible association with any group of those who had banded themselves together to form a small, secret colony of the Kingdom of Heaven in this earth of exile.

No, it was all too evident: I needed this support, this nearness of those who really loved Christ so much that they seemed to see Him. I needed to be with people whose every action told me something of the country that was my home: just as expatriates in every alien land keep together, if only to remind themselves, by their very faces and clothes and gait and accents and expressions, of the land they come from.

I had planned to spend the week-end before going to the monastery in somewhat the same way that everybody else in the country spends Labor Day week-end: trying to get some rest and recreation, which is certainly a very legitimate thing for them to do, at least in itself. But God, in order to remind me of my exile, willed that this plan of mine, which was primarily ordered to please no one but myself, should not be completely successful.

I had gone about it the way I had done things in the old days: I had decided just where I wanted to go, and just what I wanted to do, for my own pleasure and recreation. I would go, I thought, to Greenport, at the end of Long Island. There I would find some quiet place, and spend the days reading and writing and praying and meditating and swimming. After that I would cross the Sound on the New London Ferry, and go from there to Providence and to Our Lady of the Valley. And Lax thought that if he could get away from the *New Yorker* office in time, that Saturday afternoon, he would go to Greenport too. But he did not seem very definite about it.

I called up Seymour. Seymour said: "I will drive you to Greenport."

Having exacted some assurance that he meant what he said, I went out to Long Beach.

Seymour was at the station, with a lot of his friends and associates, people in Long Beach with whom he had once started a kind of an enterprise for turning the whole town into a Greek City State—the Athens of Pericles. We all started out in the car.

Having gone three blocks, we stopped, and everybody got out. And he said: "We are going to have lunch in this restaurant."

We took a few spoonfuls of bad food. Then, back into the car.

As I expected, Seymour turned the car around and started off in the direction, not of Greenport, but of his own house.

"I forgot my camera," he explained. Seymour never had a camera.

So we spent the afternoon in Seymour's sailboat, in the bay, and we landed on a sand-bar, and Seymour taught me some tricks in ju-jitsu. He had been learning ju-jitsu in a gymnasium on Broadway, considering that he would be able to use it in the war, if he got drafted: a little something to surprise the Japanese.

The next day, we started out for Connecticut. That was when we passed through Harlem. Seymour was going to find his wife, in Greenwich Village, and drive her to New Haven, where she was in a play at a summer theater. He did not find his wife in Greenwich Village, but somewhere in the Seventies where it was decided, after a long, secret argument, that she was not going to Connecticut that afternoon. Meanwhile, I tried to sneak away and take a train from Grand Central to somewhere where I would find the equivalent of the nice quiet room in Greenport.

(At that precise moment, although I did not know anything about it, Lax, having gone to Greenport, was searching for me in all the hotels and boarding houses and in the Catholic church.)

Finally, very late, Seymour and I sat in a traffic-jam on the Boston Post Road, and argued about the war.

He drove me all the way out to Old Lyme, and it got darker and darker, and everything I saw made me miserable. I could nowhere identify anything to suit my Labor-Day-Week-End dream.

Just before midnight I threw down my suitcase in a dirty little hotel back in New Haven, and finished saying the Office of that day. Seymour had vanished, silent and nervous, into the darkness, with his car, alleging that Helen was even now arriving in New Haven on the train.

As far as I knew, the plan was she would go to the summer theater and pick up some sewing or knitting or something, and then they would both drive back, at once, to New York.

"You see—" said Divine Providence—"you see how things are in the world where you are living. You see how it is with the plans and projects of men."

On the bright Tuesday morning when I rang the bell at the monastery gate, at Our Lady of the Valley, the sky was full of blue, and walking into that deep silence was like walking into heaven.

Kneeling in the tribune, with the sun pouring through the windows on to a great, curiously bloodless Crucifix, and with the chanting of the monks taking my heart home to God and rocking it in the peace of those majestic thoughts and cadences, I worked my way, or was led, rather, into a retreat that was serious and practical and successful—more than I realized. There were none of the great, overwhelming consolations and lights that had practically swamped me at Gethsemani: and yet when I came out again at the end of the week I was conscious of having acquired nourishment and strength, of having developed secretly in firmness and certitude and depth.

For I had come out of Harlem with what might well have been the problem of another vocation. Was it that? In these eight days, ending with the Feast of the Nativity of Our Lady, the matter had made itself more or less clear. If I stayed in the world, I thought, my vocation would be first of all to write, second to teach. Work like that at Friendship House would only come after the other two. Until I got some more definite light, I should stay where I was, at St. Bonaventure's. Had I been afraid, or perhaps subconsciously hoping, that the question of becoming a Trappist would once again become a burning issue here? It did not. That whole business remained in its neutral, indefinite state: relegated to the area which my mind could not quite perceive, because it was in darkness, and clouded with almost infinite uncertainties. One thing I knew, here at the Valley I was filled with the same unutterable respect for the Cistercian life, but there was no special desire to enter that particular monastery.

And so, once again, I was back in the world. The New Haven train sped through all those industrial towns, with occasional flashes of blue water and pale sand and greyish grass all along the line at the left. I read a story in the *New Yorker* about a boy who, instead of becoming a priest, got married, or at least fell in love or something. And the emptiness and futility and nothingness of the world once more invaded me from every side. But now it could not disturb me or make me unhappy.

It was sufficient to know that even if I might be in it, that did not compel me to have any part of it, or to belong to it, or even to be seriously begrimed with its sorry, unavoidable contact.

Back at St. Bonaventure's they gave me a room on the north side of the building, where you could see the sun shining on the green hillside which was a golf-course. And all day long you could hear the trains in the Olean freight-yards crying out and calling to one another and ringing their bells: the sound of journeys, sound of exile. I found that, almost without realizing it, I had little by little reorganized the pattern of my life on a stricter plan, getting up earlier in the morning, saying the Little Hours about dawn, or before it when the days got shorter, as a preparation for Mass and Communion. Now, too, I took three quarters of an hour in the morning for mental prayer. I was doing a lot of spiritual reading—Lives of Saints—Joan of Arc, St. John Bosco, St. Benedict. I was going through St. John of the Cross' *Ascent of Mount Carmel* and the first parts of the *Dark Night* for the second time in fact, but for the first time with understanding.

The big present that was given to me, that October, in the order of grace, was the discovery that the Little Flower really was a saint, and not just a mute pious little doll in the imaginations of a lot of sentimental old women. And not only was she a saint, but a great saint, one of the greatest: tremendous! I owe her all kinds of public apologies and reparation for having ignored her greatness for so long: but to do that would take a whole book, and here I have only a few lines to give away.

It is a wonderful experience to discover a new saint. For God is greatly magnified and marvelous in each one of His saints: differently in each individual one. There are no two saints alike: but all of them are like God, like Him in a different and special way. In fact, if Adam had never fallen, the whole human race would have been a series of magnificently different and splendid images of God, each one of all the millions of men showing forth His glories and perfections in an astonishing new way, and each one shining with his own particular sanctity, a sanctity destined for him from all eternity as the most complete and unimaginable supernatural perfection of his human personality.

If, since the fall, this plan will never be realized in millions of souls, and millions will frustrate that glorious destiny of theirs, and hide their personality in an eternal corruption of disfigurement, nevertheless, in re-forming His image in souls distorted and half destroyed by evil and disorder, God makes the works of His wisdom and love all the more strikingly beautiful by reason of the contrast with the surroundings in which He does not disdain to operate.

It was never, could never be, any surprise to me that saints should be found in the misery and sorrow and suffering of Harlem, in the leper-colonies like Father Damian's Molokai, in the slums of John Bosco's Turin, on the roads of Umbria in the time of St. Francis, or in the hidden Cistercian abbeys of the twelfth century, or in the Grande Chartreuse, or the Thebaid, Jerome's cave (with the lion keeping guard over his library) or Simon's pillar. All this was obvious. These things were strong and mighty reactions in ages and situations that called for spectacular heroism.

But what astonished me altogether was the appearance of a saint in the midst of all the stuffy, overplush, overdecorated, comfortable ugliness and mediocrity of the *bourgeoisie*. Thérèse of the Child Jesus was a Carmelite, that is true: but what she took into the convent with her was a nature that had been formed and adapted to the background and mentality of the French middle class of the late nineteenth century, than which nothing could be imagined more complacent and apparently immovable. The one thing that seemed to me more or less impossible was for grace to penetrate the thick, resilient hide of *bourgeois* smugness and really take hold of the immortal soul beneath that surface, in order to make something out of it. At best, I thought, such people might turn out to be harmless prigs: but great sanctity? Never!

As a matter of fact, such a thought was a sin both against God and my neighbor. It was a blasphemous underestimation of the power of grace, and it was an extremely uncharitable judgement of a whole class of people on sweeping, general and rather misty grounds: applying a big theoretical idea to every individual that happens to fall within a certain category!

I first got interested in St. Thérèse of Lisieux by reading Ghéon's sensible book about her—a fortunate beginning. If I had chanced on some of the other Little Flower literature that is floating around, the faint spark of potential devotion in my soul would have been quenched at once.

However, no sooner had I got a faint glimpse of the real character and the real spirituality of St. Thérèse, than I was immediately and strongly attracted to her—an attraction that was the work of grace, since, as I say, it took me, in one jump, clean through a thousand psychological obstacles and re-pugnances.

And here is what strikes me as the most phenomenal thing about her. She became a saint, not by running away from the middle class, not by abjuring and despising and cursing the middle class, or the environment in which she had grown up: on the contrary, she clung to it in so far as one could cling to such a thing and be a good Carmelite. She kept everything that was *bourgeois* about her and was still not incompatible with her vocation: her nostalgic affection for a funny villa called "Les Buissonnets," her taste for utterly oversweet art, and for little candy angels and pastel saints playing with lambs so soft and fuzzy that they literally give people like me the creeps. She wrote a lot of poems which, no matter how admirable their sentiments, were certainly based on the most mediocre of popular models.

To her, it would have been incomprehensible that anyone should think these things were ugly or strange, and it never even occurred to her that she might be expected to give them up, or hate them, or curse them, or bury them under a pile of anathemas. And she not only became a saint, but the great-est saint there has been in the Church for three hundred years—even greater, in some respects, than the two tremen-dous reformers of her Order, St. John of the Cross and St. Teresa of Avila.

The discovery of all this was certainly one of the biggest and most salutary humiliations I have ever had in my life. I do not say that it changed my opinion of the smugness of the nineteenth century *bourgeoisie*: God forbid! When something is revoltingly ugly, it is ugly, and that is that. I did not find myself calling the externals of that weird culture beautiful. But I did have to admit that as far as sanctity was concerned, all this external ugliness was, *per se*, completely indifferent. And, what is more, like all the other physical evil in the world, it could very well serve, *per accidens*, as an occasion or even as the secondary cause of great spiritual good.

The discovery of a new saint is a tremendous experience: and all the more so because it is completely unlike the filmfan's discovery of a new star. What can such a one do with his new idol? Stare at her picture until it makes him dizzy. That is all. But the saints are not mere inanimate objects of contemplation. They become our friends, and they share our friendship and reciprocate it and give us unmistakeable tokens of their love for us by the graces that we receive through them. And so, now that I had this great new friend in heaven, it was inevitable that the friendship should begin to have its influence on my life.

The first thing that Thérèse of Lisieux could do for me was to take charge of my brother, whom I put into her care all the more readily because now, with characteristic suddenness, he had crossed the border into Canada, and sent us word by mail that he was in the Royal Canadian Air Force.

Not that this was a very great surprise to anybody. As the time came closer for him to be drafted it began to be clear that he didn't care where he went so long as it was not into the infantry. Finally, just when he was about to be called, he had gone to Canada and volunteered as an airman. Since Canada was already long since actually at war, and since her fliers went relatively quickly into action, where they were badly needed, in England, it was at once evident that John Paul's chances of surviving a long war were very small. I suppose he was the only one who ignored this. As far as I could gather, he went into the air force as if flying a bomber were nothing more dangerous than driving a car.

So now he was in camp, somewhere near Toronto. He

wrote to me of some vague hope that, since he was a photographer, they might send him out as an observer, to take pictures of bombed cities and to make maps and so on. But meanwhile he was doing sentry duty, on the ground, along the length of a great wire fence. And I set the Little Flower as a sentry to look out for him. She did the job well.

But the things that happened in my own life, before two more months had passed, also bore the mark of her interference.

In October I was writing long letters, full of questions, to the Baroness, who was still in Canada—and getting letters just as long in return, full of her own vivid and energetic wisdom. It was good for me to get those letters. They were full of strong and definite encouragement. "Go on. You are on the right path. Keep on writing. Love God, pray to Him more. . . . You have arisen and started on the journey that seeks Him. You have begun to travel that road that will lead you to sell all and buy the pearl of great price."

To sell all! The thing had not bothered me so much, in September, and I had left it aside, to wait and see what would develop. It was beginning to develop now.

For now, in these days, I was often alone in the chapel, under those plain beams, watching the quiet Tabernacle, and things began to speak inside me. This time, it was a much deeper impulsion, the expression of a much profounder need. It was not a movement of love stretching out to grasp some external, tangible good, and to possess it: not a movement of appetite—intellectual if you like, but still of appetite towards some good that could be seen and felt and enjoyed: a form of life, a religious existence, a habit, a Rule. It was not a desire to see myself vested in this or that kind of a robe or cloak or scapular, and praying this way or that way, or studying here, or preaching there, or living in this or that kind of a monastery. It was something quite different.

I no longer needed to get something, I needed to give something. But here I was, day after day, feeling more and more like the young man with great possessions, who came to Christ, asking for eternal life, saying he had kept the Commandments, asking, "What is yet wanting to me?" Had Christ said to me: "Go, sell what thou hast, and give to the poor, and come, follow me"?

As the days shortened and grew darker, and the clouds were getting iron grey with the threat of the first snows, it seemed to me that this was what He was asking of me.

Not that I was a man of great possessions. Everybody on the staff at St. Bonaventure's was called a professor. That was in order that the title might compensate us all, more or less, for what we did not get in pay. The salary I got was quite sufficient to enable me to practice evangelical poverty.

The thought that first came into my mind was this. I still had some money that my grandfather had left me in a bank in New York. Perhaps what should be done was to give that away, to the poor.

That was as far as I had advanced, when I decided to make a novena, asking for grace to know what to do next.

On the third day of the novena, Father Hubert, one of the Friars, said: "The Baroness is coming. We are going to drive up to Buffalo and meet her train from Canada, and bring her down here. Do you want to come along?" Early in the afternoon we got in the car, and started north, up one of those long parallel valleys that slant down towards the Alleghany.

When the Baroness got off the train, it was the first time I had seen her with a hat on. But the thing that most impressed me was the effect she had on these priests. We had been sitting around in the station, bored, complaining of this and that situation in the world. Now they were wide awake and cheerful and listening very attentively to everything she had to say. We were in a restaurant having something to eat, and the Baroness was talking about priests, and about the spiritual life and gratitude, and the ten lepers in the Gospel, of whom only one returned to give thanks to Christ for having cured them. She had made what seemed to me to be certainly a good point. But I suddenly noticed that it had struck the two Friars like a bombshell.

Then I realized what was going on. She was preaching to them. Her visit to St. Bonaventure's was to be, for them and the Seminarians and the rest who heard her, a kind of a mission, or a retreat. I had not grasped, before, how much this was part of her work: priests and religious had become, indirectly, almost as important a mission field for her as Harlem. It is a tremendous thing, the economy of the Holy Ghost! When the Spirit of God finds a soul in which He can work, He uses that soul for any number of purposes: opens out before its eyes a hundred new directions, multiplying its works and its opportunities for the apostolate almost beyond belief and certainly far beyond the ordinary strength of a human being.

Here was this woman who had started out to conduct a more or less obscure work helping the poor in Harlem, now placed in such a position that the work which had barely been begun was drawing to her souls from every part of the country, and giving her a sort of unofficial apostolate among the priesthood, the clergy and the religious Orders.

What was it that she had to offer them, that they did not already possess? One thing: she was full of the love of God; and prayer and sacrifice and total, uncompromising poverty had filled her soul with something which, it seemed, these two men had often looked for in vain in the dry and conventional and merely learned retreats that fell to their lot. And I could see that they were drawn to her by the tremendous spiritual vitality of the grace that was in her, a vitality which brought with it a genuine and lasting inspiration, because it put their souls in contact with God as a living reality. And that reality, that contact, is something which we all need: and one of the ways in which it has been decreed that we should arrive at it, is by hearing one another talk about God. *Fides ex auditu.* And it is no novelty for God to raise up saints who are not priests to preach to those who are priests—witness the Baroness's namesake, Catherine of Siena.

But she had something to say to me, too.

My turn came when we were in the car, driving south along the shining wet highway.

The Baroness was sitting in the front seat, talking to everybody. But presently she turned to me and said:

433

"Well, Tom, when are you coming to Harlem for good?"

The simplicity of the question surprised me. Nevertheless, sudden as it was, the idea struck me that this was my answer. This was probably what I had been praying to find out.

However, it was sudden enough to catch me off my guard, and I did not quite know what to say. I began to talk about writing. I said that my coming to Harlem depended on how much writing I would be able to do when I got there.

Both the priests immediately joined in and told me to stop making conditions and opening a lot of loopholes.

"You let her decide about all that," said Father Hubert.

So it began to look as if I were going to Harlem, at least for a while.

The Baroness said: "Tom, are you thinking of becoming a priest? People who ask all the questions you asked me in those letters usually want to become priests. . . ."

Her words turned the knife in that old wound. But I said: "Oh, no, I have no vocation to the priesthood."

When the conversation shifted to something else, I more or less dropped out of it to think over what had been said, and it soon became clear that it was the most plausible thing for me to do. I had no special sense that this was my vocation, but on the other hand I could no longer doubt that St. Bonaventure's had outlived its usefulness in my spiritual life. I did not belong there any more. It was too tame, too safe, too sheltered. It demanded nothing of me. It had no particular cross. It left me to myself, belonging to myself, in full possession of my own will, in full command of all that God had given me that I might give it back to Him. As long as I remained there, I still had given up nothing, or very little, no matter how poor I happened to be.

At least I could go to Harlem, and join these people in their tenement, and live on what God gave us to eat from day to day, and share my life with the sick and the starving and the dying and those who had never had anything and never would have anything, the outcasts of the earth, a race despised. If that was where I belonged, God would let me know soon enough and definitely enough.

When we got to St. Bonaventure's, I saw the head of the English Department standing in the dim light under the arched door to the monastery, and I said to the Baroness:

"There's my boss. I'll have to go and tell him to hire somebody else for next term if I'm leaving for Harlem."

And the next day we made it definite. In January, after the semester was finished, I would come down to live at Friendship House. The Baroness said I would have plenty of time to write in the mornings.

I went to Father Thomas, the President, in his room in the Library, and told him I was going to leave.

His face became a labyrinth of wrinkles.

"Harlem," he said slowly. "Harlem."

Father Thomas was a man of big silences. There was a long pause before he spoke again: "Perhaps you are being a bit of an enthusiast."

I told him that it seemed to be what I ought to do.

Another big silence. Then he said: "Haven't you ever thought about being a priest?"

Father Thomas was a very wise man, and since he was the head of a seminary and had taught theology to generations of priests, one of the things he might be presumed to know something about was who might or might not have a vocation to the priesthood.

But I thought: he doesn't know my case. And there was no desire in me to talk about it, to bring up a discussion and get all mixed up now that I had made up my mind to do something definite. So I said:

"Oh, yes, I have thought about it, Father. But I don't believe I have that vocation."

The words made me unhappy. But I forgot them immediately, when Father Thomas said, with a sigh:

"All right, then. Go to Harlem if you must."

iv

After that, things began to move fast.

On the day before Thanksgiving I abandoned my Freshman

435

class in English Composition to their own devices and started to hitchhike south to New York. At first I was in doubt whether to make for New York or Washington. My uncle and aunt were at the capital, since his company was putting up a hotel there, and they would be glad to see me; they were rather lonely and isolated there.

However, the first ride I got took me on the way to New York rather than Washington. It was a big Standard Oil truck, heading for Wellsville. We drove out into the wild, bright country, the late November country, full of the light of Indian summer. The red barns glared in the harvested fields, and the woods were bare, but all the world was full of color and the blue sky swam with fleets of white clouds. The truck devoured the road with high-singing tires, and I rode throned in the lofty, rocking cab, listening to the driver telling me stories about all the people who lived in places we passed, and what went on in the houses we saw.

It was material for two dozen of those novels I had once desired to write, but as far as I was now concerned it was all bad news.

While I was standing on the road at the edge of Wellsville, just beyond a corner where there was a gas station, near the Erie tracks, a big trailer full of steel rails went past me. It was a good thing it did not stop and pick me up. Five or six miles further on there was a long hill. It led down to a sharp turn, in the middle of a village called I forget what—Jasper, or Juniper, or something like that. By the time I got another ride, and we came down the hill, my driver pointed to the bottom and said:

"Man, look at that *wreck!*"

There was a whole crowd standing around. They were pulling the two men out of the cab of the truck. I never saw anything so flat as that cab. The whole thing, steel rails and all, had piled up in an empty yard between two small houses. The houses both had glass store windows. If the truck had gone into one of those stores the whole house would have come down on top of them.

And yet, the funny thing was, the two men were both alive. . . .

A mile further on the man who had given me a lift turned off the road, and I started once again to walk. It was a big, wide-open place, with a sweep of huge fields all down the valley, and quails flew up out of the brown grass, vanishing down the wind. I took the Breviary out of my pocket and said the *Te Deum* on account of those two men who were not killed.

Presently I got to another village. Maybe that one was called Jasper or Juniper too. The kids were just getting out of school, at lunch time. I sat on some concrete steps that led down to the road from one of those neat white houses and started to say Vespers while I had a chance. Presently a big old-fashioned car, old and worn-out but very much polished, came along and stopped, and picked me up. It was a polite old man and his wife. They had a son who was a freshman at Cornell and they were going to bring him home for Thanksgiving. Outside of Addison they slowed down to show me a beautiful old colonial house that they always admired when they passed that way. And it was indeed a beautiful old colonial house.

So they dropped me at Horseheads and I got something to eat, and I broke a tooth on some nickel candy, and went walking off down the road reciting in my head this rhyme:

> So I broke my tooth
> On a bar of Baby-Ruth.

It was not so much the tooth that I broke as something a dentist had put there. And then a business man in a shiny Oldsmobile gave me a ride as far as Owego.

At Owego I stood at the end of the long iron bridge and looked at the houses across the river, with all their shaky old balconies, and wondered what it was like to live in such a place. Presently a car with a geyser of steam spouting over the radiator pulled up and the door opened.

It was a man who said he had been working on an all night shift in some war industry in Dunkirk that was operating twenty-four hours a day. And he said: "This car is running on borrowed time."

However, he was going all the way down to Peekskill for Thanksgiving.

I think it was on the day after Thanksgiving, Friday, the Feast of the Presentation, that I saw Mark. I had lunch with him at the Columbia Faculty Club. The main reason why I wanted to talk to him was that he had just read the book I had written that summer, the *Journal of My Escape from the Nazis,* and he had an idea that somebody he knew might publish it. That was what I thought was important about that talk, that day.

But Providence had arranged it, I think, for another reason.

We were downstairs, standing among a lot of iron racks and shelves and things for keeping hats and brief-cases, putting on our coats, and we had been talking about the Trappists.

Mark asked me:

"What about your idea of being a priest? Did you ever take that up again?"

I answered with a sort of an indefinite shrug.

"You know," he said, "I talked about that to someone who knows what it is all about, and he said that the fact you had let it all drop, when you were told you had no vocation, might really be a sign that you had none."

This was the third time that shaft had been fired at me, unexpectedly, in these last days, and this time it really struck deep. For the reasoning that went with this statement forced my thoughts to take an entirely new line. If that were true, then it prescribed a new kind of an attitude to the whole question of my vocation.

I had been content to tell everybody that I had no such vocation: but all the while, of course, I had been making a whole series of adjustments and reservations with which to surround that statement in my own mind. Now somebody was suddenly telling me: "If you keep on making all those reservations, maybe you will lose this gift which you know you have. . . ."

438

Which I knew I had? How did I know such a thing?

The spontaneous rebellion against the mere thought that I might definitely *not* be called to the monastic life: that it might certainly be out of the question, once and for all—the rebellion against such an idea was so strong in me that it told me all I needed to know.

And what struck me most forcibly was that this challenge had come from Mark, who was not a Catholic, and who would not be expected to possess such inside information about vocations.

I said to him: "I think God's Providence arranged things so that you would tell me that today." Mark saw the point of that, too, and he was pleased by it.

As I was taking leave of him, on the corner of 116th Street, by the Law School, I said:

"If I ever entered any monastery, it would be to become a Trappist."

It did not seem to me that this should have any effect on my decision to go to Harlem. If it turned out that I did not belong there, then I would see about the monastery. Meanwhile, I had gone down to Friendship House, and discovered that on Sunday they were all going to make their monthly day of retreat in the Convent of the Holy Child, on Riverside Drive.

Bob Lax went up with me, that Sunday morning, and together we climbed the steps to the convent door, and a Sister let us in. We were about the first ones there, and had to wait some time before the others came, and Mass began, but I think Father Furfey, their spiritual director, who was teaching philosophy at the Catholic University and running something like Friendship House in the Negro quarter of Washington, spoke to us first at the beginning of Mass. Everything he said that day made a strong impression on both me and Lax.

However, when I came back from receiving Communion, I noticed that Lax had disappeared. Later, when we went to breakfast, I found him there.

After we had all gone to Communion, he said he began

439

to get the feeling that the place was going to fall down on top of him, so he went out to get some air. A Sister who had noticed me passing the Missal back and forth to him and showing him the place, hurried out after him and found him sitting with his head between his knees—and offered him a cigarette.

That night when we left the convent, neither of us could talk. We just walked down Riverside Drive in the dusk, saying nothing. I got on the train in Jersey City and started back for Olean.

Three days went by without any kind of an event. It was the end of November. All the days were short and dark.

Finally, on the Thursday of that week, in the evening, I suddenly found myself filled with a vivid conviction:

"The time has come for me to go and be a Trappist."

Where had the thought come from? All I knew was that it was suddenly there. And it was something powerful, irresistible, clear.

I picked up a little book called *The Cistercian Life*, which I had bought at Gethsemani, and turned over the pages, as if they had something more to tell me. They seemed to me to be all written in words of flame and fire.

I went to supper, and came back and looked at the book again. My mind was literally full of this conviction. And yet, in the way, stood hesitation: that old business. But now there could be no delaying. I must finish with that, once and for all, and get an answer. I must talk to somebody who would settle it. It could be done in five minutes. And now was the time. Now.

Whom should I ask? Father Philotheus was probably in his room downstairs. I went downstairs, and out into the court. Yes, there was a light in Father Philotheus' room. All right. Go in and see what he has to say.

But instead of that, I bolted out into the darkness and made for the grove.

It was a Thursday night. The Alumni Hall was beginning to fill. They were going to have a movie. But I hardly noticed it: it did not occur to me that perhaps Father Philotheus might go to the movie with the rest. In the silence of the grove my feet were loud on the gravel. I walked and prayed. It was very, very dark by the shrine of the Little Flower. "For Heaven's sake, help me!" I said.

I started back towards the buildings. "All right. Now I am really going to go in there and ask him. Here's the situation, Father. What do you think? Should I go and be a Trappist?"

There was still a light in Father Philotheus' room. I walked bravely into the hall, but when I got within about six feet of his door it was almost as if someone had stopped me and held me where I was with physical hands. Something jammed in my will. I couldn't walk a step further, even though I wanted to. I made a kind of a push at the obstacle, which was perhaps a devil, and then turned around and ran out of the place once more.

And again I headed for the grove. The Alumni Hall was nearly full. My feet were loud on the gravel. I was in the silence of the grove, among wet trees.

I don't think there was ever a moment in my life when my soul felt so urgent and so special an anguish. I had been praying all the time, so I cannot say that I began to pray when I arrived there where the shrine was: but things became more definite.

"Please help me. What am I going to do? I can't go on like this. You can see that! Look at the state I am in. What ought I to do? Show me the way." As if I needed more information or some kind of a sign!

But I said this time to the Little Flower: "You show me what to do." And I added, "If I get into the monastery, I will be your monk. Now show me what to do."

It was getting to be precariously near the wrong way to pray—making indefinite promises that I did not quite understand and asking for some sort of a sign.

Suddenly, as soon as I had made that prayer, I became aware of the wood, the trees, the dark hills, the wet night wind, and then, clearer than any of these obvious realities, in my imagination, I started to hear the great bell of Gethsemani ringing in the night—the bell in the big grey tower, ringing

441

and ringing, as if it were just behind the first hill. The impression made me breathless, and I had to think twice to realize that it was only in my imagination that I was hearing the bell of the Trappist Abbey ringing in the dark. Yet, as I afterwards calculated, it was just about that time that the bell is rung every night for the *Salve Regina*, towards the end of Compline.

The bell seemed to be telling me where I belonged—as if it were calling me home.

This fancy put such determination into me that I immediately started back for the monastery—going the long way 'round, past the shrine of Our Lady of Lourdes and the far end of the football field. And with every step I took my mind became more and more firmly made up that now I would have done with all these doubts and hesitations and questions and all the rest, and get this thing settled, and go to the Trappists where I belonged.

When I came into the courtyard, I saw that the light in Father Philotheus' room was out. In fact, practically all the lights were out. Everybody had gone to the movies. My heart sank.

Yet there was one hope. I went right on through the door and into the corridor, and turned to the Friars' common room. I had never even gone near that door before. I had never dared. But now I went up and knocked on the glass panel and opened the door and looked inside.

There was nobody there except one Friar alone, Father Philotheus.

I asked if I could speak with him and we went to his room.

That was the end of all my anxiety, all my hesitation.

As soon as I proposed all my hesitations and questions to him, Father Philotheus said that he could see no reason why I shouldn't want to enter a monastery and become a priest.

It may seem irrational, but at that moment, it was as if scales fell off my own eyes, and looking back on all my worries and questions, I could see clearly how empty and futile they had been. Yes, it was obvious that I was called to the monastic life: and all my doubts about it had been mostly shadows. Where had they gained such a deceptive appearance of substance and reality? Accident and circumstances had all contributed to exaggerate and distort things in my mind. But now everything was straight again. And already I was full of peace and assurance—the consciousness that everything was right, and that a straight road had opened out, clear and smooth, ahead of me.

Father Philotheus had only one question:

"Are you sure you want to be a *Trappist?*" he asked me.

"Father," I answered, "I want to give God everything."

I could see by the expression on his face that he was satisfied.

I went upstairs like somebody who had been called back from the dead. Never had I experienced the calm, untroubled peace and certainty that now filled my heart. There was only one more question: would the Trappists agree with Father Philotheus, and accept my application?

Without any delay, I wrote to the Abbot of Gethsemani, asking permission to come and make a retreat at Christmas time. I tried to frame my request in words that hinted I was coming as a postulant, without giving them an opportunity to refuse me before I had at least put one foot inside the door. I sealed the envelope and took it downstairs and dropped it in the mailbox, and walked outside, once more, into the darkness, towards the grove.

Things were moving fast, now. But soon they began to move still faster. I had barely got a reply from Gethsemani, telling me that I was welcome to come there at Christmas, when another letter came in the mail. The envelope was familiar and frightening. It bore the stamp of the Draft Board.

I ripped it open and stood face to face with a notice that I was to report at once for a fresh medical examination.

It was not hard to see what that would mean. They had tightened up their requirements, and I would probably no longer be exempt from military service. For a moment it seemed to me that Providence had become deliberately cruel. Was this going to be a repetition of the affair of the year before, when I had had my vocation snatched out of my hands when I was practically on the doorstep of the novitiate? Was that going to start all over again?

Kneeling in the chapel, with that crumpled paper in my pocket, it took a certain amount of choking before I could get out the words "Thy will be done." But I was determined that my vocation would not fall in ruins all around me, the moment after I had recovered it.

I wrote to the Draft Board at once, and told them that I was entering a monastery, and asked for time to find out when and under what conditions I would be admitted.

Then I sat down to wait. It was the first week of December, 1941.

Father Philotheus, hearing about the sudden call from the Army, smiled and said: "I think that is a very good sign—I mean, as far as your vocation is concerned."

The week ended, with no news from the Draft Board.

Sunday, December the seventh, was the second Sunday in Advent. During High Mass the Seminarians were singing the *Rorate Coeli*, and I came out into the unusually warm sun with the beautiful Gregorian plaint in my ears. I went over to the kitchen, and got one of the Sisters to make me some cheese sandwiches and put them in a shoe-box, and started out for Two Mile Valley.

I climbed up the hillside, on the eastern slope of the valley, and reached the rim of the thick woods, and sat down in a windless, sunny place where there were a lot of brown dried ferns. Down the hill by the road was a little country school house. Further out, at the mouth of the little valley, near the Alleghany, were a couple of small farms. The air was warm and quiet, you could hear nothing but the pounding and coughing of a distant oil-pump, back in the woods.

Who would think there was a war anywhere in the world? It was so peaceful here, and undisturbed. I watched some rabbits come out and begin to play among the ferns.

This was probably the last time I would see this place. Where would I be in a week from that day? It was in the hands of God. There was nothing I could do but leave myself

444

to His mercy. But surely, by this time, I should have been able to realize that He is much more anxious to take care of us, and capable of doing so, than we could be ourselves. It is only when we refuse His help, resist His will, that we have conflict, trouble, disorder, unhappiness, ruin.

I started back in the afternoon towards the College. It was two or two and a half miles to the railway trestle over the river, then a half a mile home. I walked slowly along the tracks towards the red brick buildings of the College. The sky was getting cloudy, and it was not long before sunset. When I got to the campus, and was walking down the cement path towards the dormitory, I met two of the other lay-professors. They were talking animatedly about something or other, and as I approached they cried:

"Did you hear what happened? Did you hear the radio?"

America was in the war.

The next morning, the Feast of the Immaculate Conception, all the Sisters who worked in the kitchen and the laundry were at Mass in the College chapel. This was one of the rare occasions when they came out in public. It was their patronal feast. The front pews were full of blue and white habits, and after the Gospel, Father Conrad, a big burly Friar with a ruddy face, a professor of philosophy as stout as St. Thomas Aquinas, preached a sad little sermon, half hiding behind a corner of a buttress that held up the beam over the sanctuary. It was about Pearl Harbor.

When I left the chapel, and went to the Post Office, I found a letter from the Draft Board. They said the medical examination would be put off for one month.

I went to Father Thomas, and explained my situation, asked permission to leave at once, and asked, too, for a letter of recommendation. There was a meeting of the English Department, to share out my classes among my astonished confreres, for the remainder of the term.

I packed up most of my clothes, and put them in a big box for Friendship House and the Negroes of Harlem. I left most of my books on my shelf for Father Irenaeus and his library, and gave some to a friend in the Seminary, who had been reading Duns Scotus with me, under Father Philotheus. The rest I put in a box to take with me to Gethsemani. Apart from that, all my possessions fitted into one suitcase, and that was too much: except that the Trappists might not receive me in their monastery.

I took the manuscripts of three finished novels and one half-finished novel and ripped them up and threw them in the incinerator. I gave away some notes to people who might be able to use them, and I packed up all the poems I had written, and the carbon copy of the *Journal of My Escape from the Nazis*, and another *Journal* I had kept, and some material for an anthology of religious verse, and sent it all to Mark Van Doren. Everything else I had written I put in a binder and sent to Lax and Rice who were living on 114th Street, New York. I closed my checking account at the Olean bank, and collected a check, with a bonus, for my services in the English Department from the bursar who couldn't figure out why a man should want to collect his wages in the middle of the month. I wrote three letters—to Lax, the Baroness and my relatives—and some postcards, and by the afternoon of the following day, Tuesday, with an amazing and joyous sense of lightness, I was ready to go.

My train was in the evening. It was already dark when the taxi called for me at the College.

"Where you going, Prof?" said somebody, as I passed out of the building with my suitcase.

The cab door slammed on my big general good-bye, and we drove away. I did not turn to see the collection of heads that watched the parting cab from the shelter of the arched door.

When we got to town, there was still time for me to go to the church of Our Lady of the Angels, where I used to go to confession and where I often made the Stations of the Cross, when I was in Olean. The place was empty. There were one or two little candles burning out in front of the statue of St. Joseph, and the red sanctuary light flickered in the quiet shadows. I knelt there for ten or twelve minutes in the silence without even attempting to grasp or comprehend the im-

that made me happy, but where I was coming from. Yet, as I say, this surprised me too, because I had not really paid any attention to the fact that I was happy—which indeed I was.

Now every day began with Mass and Communion, either at Our Lady of Guadalupe or St. Francis of Assisi Church.

After that I went back to Perry Street, and got to work re-writing the novel which had been handed back to me politely by one of those tall, thin, anxious young men with horn-rimmed glasses who are to be found in the offices of publishers. (He had asked me if I was trying to write in some new experimental style, and then ducked behind his desk as if I might pull a knife on him for his impertinence.)

About twelve I would go out to get a sandwich at some drug-store, and read in the paper about the Russians and the Finns or about the French sitting in the Maginot Line, and sending out a party of six men somewhere in Loraine to fire three rifle shots at an imaginary German.

In the afternoon I usually had to go to Columbia and sit in a room and hear some lecture on English Literature, after which I went to the library and read St. Thomas Aquinas' commentary on Aristotle's *Metaphysics* which I had reserved for me on my desk in the graduate reading room. This was a matter of great consternation to some Sisters of St. Joseph who occupied nearby desks and who, after a while, became timidly friendly when they learned that I was going to become a Franciscan in the summer.

At about three in the afternoon I was in the habit of going to Corpus Christi, or to Our Lady of Lourdes which was even closer, and doing the Stations of the Cross. This meditative and easy prayer provided me with another way, more valuable than I realized, of entering into participation in the merits of Christ's Passion, and of renewing within me the life that had been set alight by that morning's Communion.

In those days it took a little effort to walk to a church and go around the fourteen stations saying vocal prayers, for I was still not used to praying. Therefore, doing the Stations of the Cross was still more laborious than consoling, and required a sacrifice. It was much the same with all my devotions. They did not come easily or spontaneously, and they very seldom brought with them any strong sensible satisfaction. Nevertheless the work of performing them ended in a profound and fortifying peace: a peace that was scarcely perceptible, but which deepened and which, as my passions subsided, became more and more real, more and more sure, and finally stayed with me permanently.

It was also at this time that I first attempted any kind of mental prayer. I had bought a copy of the *Spiritual Exercises* of St. Ignatius many months before, and it had remained idle on the shelf—except that when I came back from Olean and took over the apartment from Seymour's wife, to whom I had sub-let it, I found a couple of little pencil marks in the margin opposite passages that might be interpreted as sinister and Jesuitical. One of them was about death, and the other had something to do with pulling all the blinds down when you wanted to meditate.

For my own part I had long been a little scared of the *Spiritual Exercises,* having somewhere acquired a false impression that if you did not look out they would plunge you head first into mysticism before you were aware of it. How could I be sure that I would not fly up into the air as soon as I applied my mind to the first meditation? I have since found out that there is very little danger of my ever flying around the premises at mental prayer. The *Spiritual Exercises* are very pedestrian and practical—their chief purpose being to enable all the busy Jesuits to get their minds off their work and back to God with a minimum of wasted time.

I wish I had been able to go through the *Exercises* under the roof of some Jesuit house, directed by one of their priests. However, I went about it under my own direction, studying the rules of procedure that were given in the book, and following them in so far as I managed to grasp what they were all about. I never even breathed a word about what I was doing to any priest.

As far as I remember I devoted a whole month to the *Exer-*

cises, taking one hour each day. I took a quiet hour, in the afternoon, in my room on Perry Street: and since I now lived in the back of the house, there were no street noises to worry me. It was really quite silent. With the windows closed, since it was winter, I could not even hear any of the neighborhood's five thousand radios.

The book said the room should be darkened, and I pulled down the blinds so that there was just enough light left for me to see the pages, and to look at the Crucifix on the wall over my bed. And the book also invited me to consider what kind of a position I should take for my meditation. It left me plenty of freedom of choice, so long as I remained more or less the way I was, once I had settled down, and did not go promenading around the room scratching my head and talking to myself.

So I thought and prayed awhile over this momentous problem, and finally decided to make my meditations sitting cross-legged on the floor. I think the Jesuits would have had a nasty shock if they had walked in and seen me doing their *Spiritual Exercises* sitting there like Mahatma Gandhi. But it worked very well. Most of the time I kept my eyes on the Crucifix or on the floor, when I did not have to look at the book.

And so, having prayed, sitting on the floor, I began to consider the reason why God had brought me into the world:

Man was created to this end: that he should praise God, Our Lord, and reverence and serve Him, and by doing these things, should save his soul. And all the other things on the face of the earth were created for man, to help him in attaining the end for which he was created. Whence it follows that man must use these things only in so far as they help him towards his end, and must withdraw himself from them in so far as they are obstacles to his attaining his end. . . . Wherefore it is necessary that we make ourselves indifferent to all created things, in so far as it is permitted to our free will . . . in such a way that, as far as we are concerned, we should not desire health rather than sickness, riches rather than poverty, honor rather than ignominy, a long life rather than a short life, and so on, desiring and choosing only those things which more efficaciously lead us to the end for which we were created.

The big and simple and radical truths of the "Foundation" were, I think, too big and too radical for me. By myself, I did not even scratch the surface of them. I vaguely remember fixing my mind on this notion of indifference to all created things in themselves, to sickness and health, and being mildly appalled. Who was I to understand such a thing? If I got a cold I nearly choked myself with aspirins and hot lemonade, and dived into bed with undisguised alarm. And here was a book that might perhaps be telling me that I ought to be able to remain as cool as an icebox in the presence of a violent death. How could I figure out just what and how much that word "indifferent" meant, if there was no one to tell me? I did not have any way of seeing the distinction between indifference of the will and indifference of the feelings—the latter being practically a thing unknown, even in the experience of the saints. So, worrying about this big difficulty of my own creation, I missed the real fruit of this fundamental meditation, which would have been an application of its notions to all the things to which I myself was attached, and which always tended to get me into trouble.

However, the real value of the *Exercises* for me came when I got to the various contemplations, especially the mysteries of the life of Christ. I docilely followed all St. Ignatius' rules about the "composition of place" and sat myself down in the Holy House at Nazareth with Jesus and Mary and Joseph, and considered what they did, and listened to what they said and so on. And I elicited affections, and made resolutions, and ended with a colloquy and finally made a brief retrospective examination of how the meditation had worked out. All this was so new and interesting, and the labor of learning it engrossed me so much, that I was far too busy for distractions. The most vital part of each meditation was always the application of the senses (hearing the yelling of the damned in

mense, deep sense of peace and gratitude that filled my heart and went out from there to Christ in His Tabernacle.

Jim Hayes, who had taken over the main burden of my courses for me, was at the station, to present me with a note saying the English Department was having five Masses said for me. Then the Buffalo train came in through the freezing, sleety rain, and I got on, and my last tie with the world I had known snapped and broke.

It was nothing less than a civil, moral death.

This journey, this transition from the world to a new life, was like flying through some strange new element—as if I were in the stratosphere. And yet I was on the familiar earth, and the cold winter rain streaked the windows of the train as we travelled through the dark hills.

After Buffalo, we began to pass factory after factory, lit up with a blue glare in the rain, working all night on armaments: but it was like looking at something in an aquarium. The last city I remembered was Erie. After that I was asleep. We went through Cleveland and I knew nothing of it.

I had been getting up and saying the Rosary in the middle of the night, as a sort of a night office, for several months past. I asked God to wake me up at Galion, Ohio, so that I could do this, and so, in the middle of the night, I woke up, and we were just pulling out of Galion. I began to say the Rosary where our tracks crossed the Erie line, which was the way I had come there the first time, on my way to Gethsemani in the spring. Then I went back to sleep, rocked by the joyous music of the wheels.

At Cincinnati, where we arrived about dawn, I asked the Traveller's Aid girl the name of some Catholic churches, and got in a taxi to go to St. Francis Xavier's, where I arrived just as Mass was beginning at the high altar; so I heard Mass and received Communion and went back to the station and had breakfast and got on the train for Louisville.

And now the sun was up. It was shining on bare, rocky valleys, poor farm land, thin, spare fields, with brush and a few trees and willows growing along the creeks, and grey cabins, from time to time, along the line. Outside one of

447

the cabins a man was splitting a log with an axe and I thought: that is what I will be doing, if God wills it, pretty soon.

It was a strange thing. Mile after mile my desire to be in the monastery increased beyond belief. I was altogether absorbed in that one idea. And yet, paradoxically, mile after mile my indifference increased, and my interior peace. What if they did not receive me? Then I would go to the army. But surely that would be a disaster? Not at all. If, after all this, I was rejected by the monastery and had to be drafted, it would be quite clear that it was God's will. I had done everything that was in my power; the rest was in His hands. And for all the tremendous and increasing intensity of my desire to be in the cloister, the thought that I might find myself, instead, in an army camp no longer troubled me in the least.

I was free. I had recovered my liberty. I belonged to God, not to myself: and to belong to Him is to be free, free of all the anxieties and worries and sorrows that belong to this earth, and the love of the things that are in it. What was the difference between one place and another, one habit and another, if your life belonged to God, and if you placed yourself completely in His hands? The only thing that mattered was the fact of the sacrifice, the essential dedication of one's self, one's will. The rest was only accidental.

That did not prevent me from praying harder and harder to Christ and to the Immaculate Virgin and to my whole private litany, St. Bernard, St. Gregory, St. Joseph, St. John of the Cross, St. Benedict, St. Francis of Assisi, the Little Flower and all the rest to get me by hook or by crook into that monastery.

And yet I knew that if God wanted me to go to the army, that would be the better and the happier thing. Because there is happiness only where there is coordination with the Truth, the Reality, the Act that underlies and directs all things to their essential and accidental perfections: and that is the will of God. There is only one happiness: to please Him. Only one sorrow, to be displeasing to Him, to refuse Him

448

something, to turn away from Him, even in the slightest thing, even in thought, in a half-willed movement of appetite: in these things, and these alone, is sorrow, in so far as they imply separation, or the beginning, the possibility of separation from Him Who is our life and all our joy. And since God is a Spirit, and infinitely above all matter and all creation, the only complete union possible, between ourselves and Him, is in the order of intention: a union of wills and intellects, in love, charity.

I stepped on to the platform of Louisville station in the glory of that freedom, and walked out into the streets with a sense of triumph, remembering the time I had come that way before, the previous Easter. I was so happy and exultant that I didn't look where I was going and walked into the Jim Crow waiting room: whose shadows, full of Negroes, became somewhat tense with resentment. I hastened out again apologetically.

The Bardstown bus was half full, and I found a somewhat dilapidated seat, and we rode out into the wintry country, the last lap of my journey into the desert.

When I finally got off in Bardstown, I was standing across the road from a gas station. The street appeared to be empty, as if the town were asleep. But presently I saw a man in the gas station. I went over and asked where I could get someone to drive me to Gethsemani. So he put on his hat and started his car and we left town on a straight road through level country, full of empty fields. It was not the kind of landscape that belonged to Gethsemani, and I could not get my bearings until some low, jagged, wooded hills appeared ahead of us, to the left of the road, and we made a turn that took us into rolling, wooded land.

Then I saw that high familiar spire.

I rang the bell at the gate. It let fall a dull, unresonant note inside the empty court. My man got in his car and went away. Nobody came. I could hear somebody moving around inside the Gatehouse. I did not ring again. Presently, the window opened, and Brother Matthew looked out between the bars, with his clear eyes and greying beard.

449

"Hullo, Brother," I said.

He recognized me, glanced at the suitcase and said: "This time have you come to stay?"

"Yes, Brother, if you'll pray for me," I said.

Brother nodded, and raised his hand to close the window. "That's what I've been doing," he said, "praying for you."

4

The Sweet Savor of Liberty

The monastery is a school—a school in which we learn from God how to be happy. Our happiness consists in sharing the happiness of God, the perfection of His unlimited freedom, the perfection of His love.

What has to be healed in us is our true nature, made in the likeness of God. What we have to learn is love. The healing and the learning are the same thing, for at the very core of our essence we are constituted in God's likeness by our freedom, and the exercise of that freedom is nothing else but the exercise of disinterested love—the love of God for His own sake, because He is God.

The beginning of love is truth, and before He will give us His love, God must cleanse our souls of the lies that are in them. And the most effective way of detaching us from ourselves is to make us detest ourselves as we have made ourselves by sin, in order that we may love Him reflected in our souls as He has re-made them by His love.

That is the meaning of the contemplative life, and the sense of all the apparently meaningless little rules and observances and fasts and obediences and penances and humiliations and labors that go to make up the routine of existence in a contemplative monastery: they all serve to remind us of what we are and Who God is—that we may get sick of the sight of ourselves and turn to Him: and in the end, we will find Him in ourselves, in our own purified natures which have become the mirror of His tremendous Goodness and of His endless love. . . .

ii

So Brother Matthew locked the gate behind me and I was enclosed in the four walls of my new freedom.

And it was appropriate that the beginning of freedom should be as it was. For I entered a garden that was dead and stripped and bare. The flowers that had been there last April were all gone. The sun was hidden behind low clouds and an icy wind was blowing over the grey grass and the concrete walks.

In a sense my freedom had already begun, for I minded none of these things. I did not come to Gethsemani for the flowers, or for the climate—although I admit that the Kentucky winters were a disappointment. Still, I had not had time to plan on any kind of a climate. I had been too busy with the crucially important problem of finding out God's will. And that problem was still not entirely settled.

There still remained the final answer: would I be accepted into this monastery? Would they take me in to the novitiate, to become a Cistercian?

Father Joachim, the guest master, came out the door of the monastery and crossed the garden with his hands under his scapular and his eyes fixed on the cement walk. He only raised them when he was near me and then he grinned.

"Oh, it's you," he said. I suppose he had been doing some praying for me too.

I did not give him a chance to ask if I had come to stay. I said: "Yes, Father, this time I want to be a novice—if I can."

He just smiled. We went into the house. The place seemed very empty. I put the suitcase down in the room that had been assigned to me, and hastened to the church.

If I expected any grand welcome from Christ and His angels, I did not get it—not in the sensible order. The huge nave was like a tomb, and the building was as cold as ice. However, I did not mind. Nor was I upset by the fact that nothing special came into my head in the way of a prayer. I just knelt there more or less dumb, and listened to the saw down at the sawmill fill the air with long and strident complaints and the sound of labor.

That evening at supper I found that there was another postulant—an ancient, toothless, grey-haired man hunched up in a huge sweater. He was a farmer from the neighbor-

452

hood who had lived in the shadow of the abbey for years and had finally made up his mind to enter it as a lay brother. However, he did not stay.

The next day I found out there was still a third postulant. He arrived that morning. He was a fat bewildered youth from Buffalo. Like myself, he was applying for the choir. Father Joachim put the two of us to work together washing dishes and waxing floors, in silence. We were both absorbed in our own many thoughts, and I dare say he was no more tempted to start a conversation than I was.

In fact every minute of the day I was secretly congratulating myself that conversations were over and done with—provided always I was accepted.

I could not be quite sure whether someone would call me and tell me to go down for an interview with the Father Abbot, or whether I was expected to go down to him on my own initiative, but that part of the problem was settled for me towards the end of the morning work.

I went back to my room and started puzzling my head over the copy of the *Spiritual Directory* that Father Joachim had brought me. Instead of settling down quietly and reading the chapter that directly concerned me, the one that said what postulants were supposed to do while they were waiting in the Guest House, I started leafing through the two thin volumes to see if I could not discover something absolutely clear and definite as to what the Cistercian vocation was all about.

It is easy enough to say, "Trappists are called to lead lives of prayer and penance," because after all there is a sense in which everybody is called to lead that kind of a life. It is also easy enough to say that Cistercians are called to devote themselves entirely to contemplation without any regard for the works of the active life: but that does not say anything precise about the object of our life and it certainly does not distinguish the Trappists from any of the other so-called "contemplative Orders." Then the question always arises: "What do you mean by contemplation, anyway?"

From the *Spiritual Directory* I learned that "the Holy

453

Mass, the Divine Office, Prayer and pious reading which form the exercises of the contemplative life occupy the major part of our day."

It was a frigid and unsatisfying sentence. The phrase "pious reading" was a gloomy one, and somehow the thought that the contemplative life was something that was divided up into "exercises" was of a sort that would have ordinarily depressed me. But I think I had come to the monastery fully resigned to the prospect of meeting that kind of language for the rest of my life. In fact, it is a good thing that I was resigned to it, for it is one of the tiresome minor details of all religious life today, that one must receive a large proportion of spiritual nourishment dished up in the unseasoned jargon of transliterated French.

I had no way of saying what the contemplative life meant to me then. But it seemed to me that it should mean something more than spending so many hours a day in a church and so many more hours somewhere else, without having to go to the bother of preaching sermons or teaching school or writing books or visiting the sick.

A few lines further on in the *Directory* there were some cautious words about mystical contemplation which, I was told, was "not required" but which God sometimes "vouchsafed." That word "vouchsafe"! It almost sounded as if the grace came to you dressed up in a crinoline. In fact, to my way of interpreting it, when a spiritual book tells you that "infused contemplation is sometimes vouchsafed" the idea you are supposed to get is this: "infused contemplation is all right for the saints, but as for *you:* hands off!" The original French of the *Directory* is not so icy as the translation, and the book goes on to add that monks can ask God for these graces, if they do so with a right intention, and that the Cistercian life should normally be a perfect preparation for them. In fact, the French edition also adds that the Cistercian has the *duty* of leading the kind of life that would dispose him for mystical prayer.

And yet I was left with the impression that contemplation in a Trappist monastery was liable to be pretty much *secundum quid* and that if I had a secret desire for what the lingo of the pious manuals would call the "summits" I had better be cautious about the way I manifested it. Under other circumstances the situation might have disturbed me: but now it did not bother me at all. After all, it was largely a theoretical question anyway. All that I needed to worry about was to do God's will, to enter the monastery if I were allowed to do so, and take things as I found them, and if God wanted to do any of this "vouchsafing" He could go ahead and "vouchsafe." And all the other details would take care of themselves.

As I was laying aside the *Directory* to take up another small volume of pidgin English, someone knocked on the door.

It was a monk I had not seen before, a rather burly man with white hair and an extremely firm jaw, who introduced himself as the Master of Novices. I took another look at the determination in that jaw and said to myself: "I bet he doesn't take any nonsense from novices, either."

But as soon as he started to talk I found that Father Master was full of a most impressive simplicity and gentleness and kindness and we began to get along together very well from that hour. He was not a man that stood on ceremony and he would have nothing to do with the notorious technique of elaborately staged humiliations which have given La Trappe a bad name in the past. By those standards he should have walked into the room and slammed the door with an insult and then asked me if I were entering the monastery in order to get away from the police.

But he just sat down and said: "Does the silence scare you?"

I almost fell over myself in my eagerness to assure him that the silence not only did not scare me but that I was entranced with it and already felt myself to be in heaven.

"Aren't you cold in here?" he asked. "Why don't you shut the window? Is that sweater warm enough?"

I assured him with consummate bravery that I was as warm as toast but he made me shut the window anyway.

455

Of course, what had happened was that Brother Fabian, who worked in the Guest House that year, had been feeding me with horror stories about how cold it was when you got up in the morning and went creeping down to choir with your knees knocking together and your teeth chattering so loud that you could hardly hear the prayers. So I was trying to get myself in trim for the ordeal by sitting with the windows open, without a coat on.

"Have you ever learned any Latin?" asked Father Master. I told him all about Plautus and Tacitus. He seemed satisfied.

After that we talked about many other things. Could I sing? Did I speak French? What made me want to become a Cistercian? Had I ever read anything about the Order? Had I ever read the *Life of St. Bernard* by Dom Ailbe Luddy? —and a lot of other things like that.

It was such a pleasant conversation that I was getting to be more and more unwilling to unload the big shadowy burden that still rested on my conscience, and tell this good Trappist all the things about my life before my conversion that had once made me think I could not possibly have a vocation to the priesthood. However, I finally did so in a few sentences.

"How long is it since you were baptized?" said Father Master.

"Three years, Father."

He did not seem to be disturbed. He just said that he liked the way I had told him all that there was to be told, and that he would consult Father Abbot about it. And that was all.

I was still half expecting to be called down for a cross-examination by the First Superior, but that never came. The Fat Boy from Buffalo and I waxed floors for the next couple of days, and went down to church and knelt at the benches in front of St. Joseph's altar while the monks chanted the Office, and then came back to the Guest House to eat our scrambled eggs and cheese and milk. At what Brother Fabian would have described as our "last meal," he slipped us each a bar of Nestle's chocolate, and afterwards whispered to me:

456

"Tom, I think you are going to be very disappointed with what you see on the table when you go into the refectory this evening . . ."

That evening? It was the Feast of St. Lucy and a Saturday. I went back to the room and nibbled on the chocolate and copied out a poem I had just written by way of a farewell to Bob Lax and Mark Van Doren. Father Joachim came in and hid his face behind his hands to laugh when I told him what I was doing.

"A *poem?*" he said, and hastened out of the room.

He had come to get me to wax the floors some more, so presently the Fat Boy from Buffalo and I were on our knees again in the hall, but not for very long. Father Master came up the stairs and told us to get our things together and follow him.

So we put on our coats and got our bags and started downstairs, leaving Father Joachim to finish waxing the floor by himself.

The noise of our footsteps resounded in the great stair well. Down at the bottom of the flight, by the door, under the sign that said "God Alone" there were half a dozen local farmers standing around with their hats in their hands. They were waiting to go to confession. It was a kind of an anonymous, abstract delegation bidding us farewell in the name of civil society. As I passed one of them, a solemn polite old man with a four days' growth of beard, I suddenly got a somewhat melodramatic impulse and leaned over towards him whispering:

"Pray for me."

He nodded gravely that he was willing to do that, and the door closed behind us leaving me with the sense that my last act as a layman in the world still smacked of the old Thomas Merton who had gone around showing off all over two different continents.

The next minute we were kneeling by the desk of the man who had absolute temporal and spiritual authority over the monastery and everybody in it. This priest, who had been a Trappist for nearly fifty years, looked much younger

457

than he was because he was so full of life and nervous energy. They had been fifty years of hard work which, far from wearing him out, had only seemed to sharpen and intensify his vitality.

Dom Frederic was deep in a pile of letters which covered the desk before him, along with a mountain of other papers and documents. Yet you could see that this tremendous volume of work did not succeed in submerging him. He had it all under control. Since I have been in the monastery I have often had occasion to wonder by what miracle he manages to *keep* all that under control. But he does.

In any case, that day Father Abbot turned to us with just as much ease and facility as if he had nothing else whatever to do but to give the first words of advice to two postulants leaving the world to become Trappists.

"Each one of you," he said, "will make the community either better or worse. Everything you do will have an influence upon others. It can be a good influence or a bad one. It all depends on you. Our Lord will never refuse you grace . . ."

I forget whether he quoted Father Faber. Reverend Father likes to quote Father Faber, and after all it would be extraordinary if he failed to do so on that day. But I have forgotten.

We kissed his ring as he blessed us both, and went out again. His parting shaft had been that we should be joyful but not dissipated, and that the Names of Jesus and Mary should always be on our lips.

At the other end of the long dark hall we went into a room where three monks were sitting at typewriters, and we handed over our fountain pens and wristwatches and our loose cash to the Treasurer, and signed documents promising that if we left the monastery we would not sue the monks for back wages for our hours of manual labor.

And then we passed through the door into the cloister.

Now I began to see the part of the monastery I had never seen—the long wing beyond the cloister, in the back of the

458

building, where the monks actually live, where they gather in the intervals.

It was a contrast to the wide-open, frigid formality of the cloister itself. To begin with, it was warmer. There were notice boards on the walls, and there was a warm smell of bread coming from the bakery which was somewhere in those parts. Monks moved about with their cowls over their arms, waiting to put them on when the bell rang for the end of work. We stopped in the tailor shop and were measured for our robes, and then passed through the door to the novitiate.

Father Master showed us where the novitiate chapel was, and we knelt a moment before the Blessed Sacrament in that plain, whitewashed room. I noticed a statue of my friend St. Joan of Arc on one side of the door, and on the other was, of course, the Little Flower.

Then we went down to the basement where all the novices were milling around in the clatter of washbasins, groping for towels with their eyes full of soap and water.

Father Master picked the one who seemed to be the most badly blinded by suds and I heard him tell him to take care of me when we got to church.

"That's your guardian angel," Father explained, and added: "He used to be a Marine."

iii

Liturgically speaking, you could hardly find a better time to become a monk than Advent. You begin a new life, you enter into a new world at the beginning of a new liturgical year. And everything that the Church gives you to sing, every prayer that you say in and with Christ in His Mystical Body is a cry of ardent desire for grace, for help, for the coming of the Messiah, the Redeemer.

The soul of the monk is a Bethlehem where Christ comes to be born—in the sense that Christ is born where His likeness is reformed by grace, and where His Divinity lives, in a special manner, with His Father and His Holy Spirit, by charity, in this "new incarnation," this "other Christ."

The Advent Liturgy prepares that Bethlehem with songs and canticles of ardent desire.

It is a desire all the more powerful, in the spiritual order, because the world around you is dead. Life has ebbed to its dregs. The trees are stripped bare. The birds forget to sing. The grass is brown and grey. You go out to the fields with mattocks to dig up the briars. The sun gives its light, as it were, in faint intermittent explosions, "squibs," not rays, according to John Donne's conceit in his Nocturnal on St. Lucy's Day. . . .

But the cold stones of the Abbey church ring with a chant that glows with living flame, with clean, profound desire. It is an austere warmth, the warmth of Gregorian chant. It is deep beyond ordinary emotion, and that is one reason why you never get tired of it. It never wears you out by making a lot of cheap demands on your sensibilities. Instead of drawing you out into the open field of feelings where your enemies, the devil and your own imagination and the inherent vulgarity of your own corrupted nature can get at you with their blades and cut you to pieces, it draws you within, where you are lulled in peace and recollection and where you find God.

You rest in Him, and He heals you with His secret wisdom.

That first evening in choir I tried to sing my first few notes of Gregorian chant with the worst cold I had ever had in my life—the fruit of my experiment in preparing myself for the low temperature of the monastery before I was even inside the place.

It was the second vespers of St. Lucy and we chanted the psalms of the *Commune virginum*, but after that the *capitulum* was of the second Sunday of Advent, and presently the cantor intoned the lovely Advent hymn, *Conditor Alme Siderum*.

What measure and balance and strength there is in the simplicity of that hymn! Its structure is mighty with a perfection that despises the effects of the most grandiloquent secular music—and says more than Bach without even exhausting the whole range of one octave. That evening I saw how the measured tone took the old words of St. Ambrose and infused into them even more strength and suppleness and conviction and meaning than they already had and made them flower before God in beauty and in fire, flower along the stones and vanish in the darkness of the vaulted ceiling. And their echo died and left our souls full of peace and grace.

When we began to chant the *Magnificat* I almost wept, but that was because I was new in the monastery. And in fact it was precisely because of that that I had reason to weep with thanksgiving and happiness as I croaked the words in my dry, hoarse throat, in gratitude for my vocation, in gratitude that I was really there at last, really in the monastery, and chanting God's liturgy with His monks.

Every day, from now on, the office would ring with the deep impassioned cries of the old prophets calling out to God to send the Redeemer. *Veni, Domine, noli tardare: relaxa facinora plebis tuae.* And the monks took up the cry with the same strong voices, and armed with the confidence of grace and God's own presence within them, they argued with Him and chided Him as His old prophets had done before. What is the matter with You, *Domine?* Where is our Redeemer? Where is the Christ You have promised us? Are You sleeping? Have You forgotten us, that we should still be buried in our miseries and in the shadow of war and sorrow?

Yet if I had been stirred with a movement of feeling during that first evening in choir, I had little opportunity in those first days to enjoy what are commonly called "consolations." Consolations cannot get a good hold on you when you are half stupefied with the kind of cold I had. And then there was all the business of getting used to the thousand material details of monastic life.

Now I saw the monastery from within, from the church floor, so to speak, not from the visitor's gallery. I saw it from the novitiate wing, not from the shiny and well-heated Guest House. Now I was face to face with monks that belonged not to some dream, not to some medieval novel, but to cold and inescapable reality. The community which I had seen functioning as a unity, in all the power of that impressive and formal liturgical anonymity which clothes a body of men obscurely in the very personality of Christ Himself, now appeared to me broken up into its constituent parts, and all the details, good and bad, pleasant and unpleasant, were there for me to observe at close range.

By this time God had given me enough sense to realize at least obscurely that this is one of the most important aspects of any religious vocation: the first and most elementary test of one's call to the religious life—whether as a Jesuit, Franciscan, Cistercian, or Carthusian—is the willingness to accept life in a community in which everybody is more or less imperfect.

The imperfections are much smaller and more trivial than the defects and vices of people outside in the world: and yet somehow you tend to notice them more and feel them more, because they get to be so greatly magnified by the responsibilities and ideals of the religious state, through which you cannot help looking at them.

People even lose their vocations because they find out that a man can spend forty or fifty or sixty years in a monastery and still have a bad temper. Anyway, now that I was a part of Gethsemani I looked about me to see what it was really like.

I was in a building with huge thick walls, some painted green, some white and most of them with edifying signs and sentiments painted on them. "If any man think himself to be a religious, not bridling his tongue, that man's religion is vain." And so on. I never quite discovered the value of those signs, because for my own part as soon as I had read them once I never noticed them again. They are there before me all the time but they simply don't register on my mind. However, perhaps some people are still pondering on them after years in the house. In any case it is a Trappist custom. You find it practically everywhere in the Order.

What was important was not the thick, unheated walls, but the things that went on within them.

The house was full of people, men hidden in white cowls and brown capes, some with beards, the lay brothers, others with no beards but monastic crowns. There were young men

462

and old men, and the old ones were in the minority. At a rough guess, with all the novices we have in the house now I think the average age of the community cannot be much over thirty.

There was, I could see, something of a difference between the community proper and the novices. The monks and the professed brothers were more deeply absorbed in things that the novices had not yet discovered. And yet looking around at the novices there was a greater outward appearance of piety in them—but you could sense that it was nearer the surface.

It can be said, as a general rule, that the greatest saints are seldom the ones whose piety is most evident in their expression when they are kneeling at prayer, and the holiest men in a monastery are almost never the ones who get that exalted look, on feast days, in the choir. The people who gaze up at Our Lady's statue with glistening eyes are very often the ones with the worst tempers.

With the novices, their sensible piety was innocent and spontaneous, and it was perfectly proper to their state. As a matter of fact I liked the novitiate at once. It was pervaded with enthusiasm and vitality and good humor.

I liked the way they kidded one another in sign language, and I liked the quiet storms of amusement that suddenly blew up from nowhere and rocked the whole "scriptorium" from time to time. Practically all the novices seemed to be very enlightened and sincere about their duties in the religious life; they had been quick in catching on to the rules and were keeping them with spontaneous ease rather than hair-splitting exactitude. And the ingenuous good humor that welled up from time to time in the middle of all this made their faces all shine like the faces of children—even though some of them were no longer young.

You felt that the best of them were the simplest, the most unassuming, the ones who fell in with the common norm without fuss and without any special display. They attracted no attention to themselves, they just did what they were told. But they were always the happiest ones, the most at peace.

They stood at the mean between two extremes. On one

hand there were one or two who exaggerated everything they did and tried to carry out every rule with scrupulousness that was a travesty of the real thing. They were the ones who seemed to be trying to make themselves saints by sheer effort and concentration—as if all the work depended on them, and not even God could help them. But then there were also the ones who did little or nothing to sanctify themselves, as if none of the work depended on them—as if God would come along one day and put a halo on their heads and it would all be over. They followed the others and kept the Rule after a fashion, but as soon as they thought they were sick they started pleading for all the mitigations that they did not already have. And the rest of the time, they fluctuated between a gaiety that was noisy and disquieting, and a sullen exasperation that threw a wet blanket over the whole novitiate.

It was usually the ones that belonged to these two extremes that left and went back to the world. Those who stayed were generally the normal, good-humored, patient, obedient ones who did nothing exceptional and just followed the common rule.

On Monday morning I went to confession. It was Ember week, and the novices all went to their extraordinary confessor who was Father Odo that year. I knelt at the little open confessional and confessed with deep contrition that when Father Joachim had told me, one day in the Guest House, to go and tell the Fat Boy from Buffalo to go down to the church for the canonical office of None, I had failed to do so. Having unburdened my soul of this and other similar offences, I got so mixed up at the unfamiliar Cistercian ritual that I was all ready to leave the confessional and run away as soon as Father Odo had finished the first prayer and before he had given me any absolution.

In fact I was already on my feet and about to walk away when he started talking to me so I thought I had better stay.

I listened to the things he had to say. He spoke very kindly and simply. And the burden of it was this:

"Who knows how many souls are depending on your perseverance in this monastery? Perhaps God has ordained that

464

there are many in the world who will only be saved through your fidelity to your vocation. You must remember them if you are ever tempted to leave. And you probably will be tempted to leave. Remember all those souls in the world. You know some of them. Others you may never know until you meet them in heaven. But in any case, you did not come here alone . . ."

All the time I was in the novitiate I had no temptations to leave the monastery. In fact, never since I have entered religion have I ever had the slightest desire to go back to the world. But when I was a novice I was not even bothered by the thought of leaving Gethsemani and going to any other Order. I say I was not *bothered* by the thought: I had it, but it never disturbed my peace because it was never anything but academic and speculative.

I remember once how Father Master questioned me on that subject.

So I admitted: "I have always liked the Carthusians. In fact if I had had a chance I would have entered the Charterhouse rather than coming here. But the war made that impossible. . . ."

"You wouldn't get the penance there that we have here," he said, and then we began to talk of something else.

That did not become a problem until after profession.

The next morning Father Master called me in at the end of work and gave me an armful of white woolen garments, telling me to put them on. Postulants used to receive the oblate's habit a few days after their admission—one of those anomalous customs that grow up in isolated houses. It survived at Gethsemani until one of the recent visitations. And so within three days of my admission to the novitiate I was out of my secular clothing and glad to get rid of it for ever.

It took me a few minutes to figure out the complications of the fifteenth-century underwear that Trappists wear under their robes, but soon I was out of the cell in a white robe and scapular, and a white cloth band tied around my waist, with the white, shapeless oblate's cloak around my shoulders. And I presented myself to Father Master to find out my name.

I had spent hours trying to choose a name for myself when I thought I was going to become a Franciscan—and now I simply took what I got. In fact, I had been too busy to bother with such trivial thoughts. And so it turned out that I was to be called Frater Louis. The Fat Boy from Buffalo was Frater Sylvester. I was glad to be Louis rather than Sylvester, although I would probably never have dreamed of choosing either name for myself.

Still, it would seem that the only reason why God wanted me to remember all my life that I had first sailed for France on the twenty-fifth of August was in order that I should realize at last that it was the Feast of my patron saint in religion. That sailing was a grace. Perhaps ultimately my vocation goes back to the days I spent in France, if it goes back to anything in the natural order. . . . Besides, I remembered that I used rather frequently to pray at the altar of St. Louis and St. Michael the Archangel in the apse of St. Patrick's cathedral in New York. I used to light candles to them when I got in trouble in those first days of my conversion.

I went immediately into the scriptorium and took a piece of paper and printed on it "FRATER MARIA LUDOVICUS" and stuck it on the front of the box that was to represent all the privacy I had left: one small box, in which I would keep a couple of notebooks full of poems and reflections, and a volume of St. John of the Cross and Gilson's *Mystical Theology of St. Bernard,* and the letters I would receive from John Paul at his R.A.F. camp in Ontario, and from Mark Van Doren and from Bob Lax.

I looked out the window at the narrow rocky valley beyond the novitiate parapet, and the cedar trees beyond and the bare woods on the line of jagged hills. *Haec requies mea in saeculum saeculi, hic habitabo quoniam elegi eam!*

iv

In January the novices were working in the woods near the lake which the monks made by throwing a dam across a gulley. The woods were quiet and the axes echoed around

466

the sheet of blue-grey water sleek as metal among the trees.

You are not supposed to *pause* and pray when you are at work. American Trappist notions of contemplation do not extend to that: on the contrary you are expected to make some act of pure intention and fling yourself into the business and work up a sweat and get a great deal finished by the time it is all over. To turn it into contemplation you can occasionally mutter between your teeth: "All for Jesus! All for Jesus!" But the idea is to keep on working.

That January I was still so new that I had not flung myself into the complex and absurd system of meditation that I afterwards tried to follow out. And occasionally I looked up through the trees to where the spire of the abbey church rose up in the distance, behind a yellow hill skirted with cedars, and with a long blue ridge of hills for background. It was peaceful and satisfying, that scene, and I thought of a line from one of the gradual psalms: *Montes in circuitu ejus, et Dominus in circuitu populi sui.* Mountains are round about it, so the Lord is round about His people from henceforth, now and for ever.

It was true. I was hidden in the secrecy of His protection. He was surrounding me constantly with the work of His love, His wisdom and His mercy. And so it would be, day after day, year after year. Sometimes I would be preoccupied with problems that seemed to be difficult and seemed to be great, and yet when it was all over the answers that I worked out did not seem to matter much anyway, because all the while, beyond my range of vision and comprehension, God had silently and imperceptibly worked the whole thing out for me, and had presented me with the solution. To say it better, He had worked the solution into the very tissue of my own life and substance and existence by the wise incomprehensible weaving of His Providence.

I was now preparing for the reception of the habit of novice, which would make me canonically a member of the Order and start me out officially on my progress towards the vows. However, as my papers had not all come, no one knew exactly when I would be clothed in the white cloak. We were still waiting for a letter from the Bishop of Nottingham, whose diocese included Rutland and Oakham, my old school.

It turned out that I was to have a companion in the reception of the habit—and not the Fat Boy from Buffalo, either. He left the monastery at the beginning of Lent, after having slumbered peacefully through the choral offices for several weeks. He returned home to Buffalo and soon we heard that he was in the Army.

But no, my companion was to be, you might say, an old friend.

One day when we had come back from the lake and had taken off our work shoes and washed up, I was hurrying up the stairs from the basement when I ran into Father Master and a postulant coming around the corner.

The fact that I was hurrying and ran into people only indicates that I was much less of a contemplative than I thought I was.

In any case, the postulant was a priest, in a Roman collar, and when I took a second look at his face I recognized those bony Irish features and the dark rimmed spectacles, the high cheek bones and the ruddy skin. It was the Carmelite with whom I had had all those conversations in the Guest House garden on my retreat, the Easter before, when we had discussed the relative merits of the Cistercians and the Carthusians.

We both looked at each other with looks that said: "You—here!" I did not actually say the words, but he did. And then he turned to Father Master and said:

"Father, here is a man who was converted to the faith by reading James Joyce." I don't think Father Master had heard of James Joyce. I had told the Carmelite that reading Joyce had contributed something to my conversion.

So we received the habit together on the first Sunday of Lent. He received the name of Frater Sacerdos. We stood together in our secular clothes in the middle of the Chapter Room. There was an eighteen-year-old novice with us making simple profession. Behind us was a table stacked with the

468

books that were to be given out to the community as their formal "Lenten reading."

Father Abbot was ill. Everybody had become aware of that by the way he had struggled through the Gospel at the night office. He should have been in bed, because, as a matter of fact, he had a bad case of pneumonia.

However, he was not in bed. He was sitting on that rigid piece of woodwork euphemistically called a "throne," from which he presides in Chapter. Although he could hardly see us, he delivered an impassioned exhortation, telling us with deep conviction that we were making a big mistake if we came to Gethsemani expecting anything but the cross, sickness, contradictions, troubles, sorrows, humiliations, fasts, sufferings and, in general, everything that human nature hates.

Then we went up the steps to his throne one by one and he peeled off our coats (*Exuat te Dominus veterem hominem cum actibus suis* . . .) and helped by the cantor and Father Master, formally clothed us in the white robes we had been wearing as oblates, together with the scapulars and cloaks of full-fledged novices in the Order.

It cannot have been much more than two weeks after that that I was in the infirmary myself, not with pneumonia but with influenza. It was the Feast of St. Gregory the Great. I remember entering the cell assigned to me with a sense of secret joy and triumph, in spite of the fact that it had just been vacated two days before by Brother Hugh, whom we had carried out to the cemetery, lying in his open bier with that grim smile of satisfaction that Trappist corpses have.

My secret joy at entering the infirmary came from the thought: "Now at last I will have some solitude and I will have plenty of time to pray." I should have added: "And to do everything that I want to do, without having to run all over the place answering bells." I was fully convinced that I was going to indulge all the selfish appetites that I did not yet know how to recognize as selfish because they appeared so spiritual in their new disguise. All my bad habits, disinfected, it is true, of formal sin, had sneaked into the monastery with me and had received the religious vesture along with me: spiritual gluttony, spiritual sensuality, spiritual pride. . . .

I jumped into bed and opened the Bible at the Canticle of Canticles and devoured three chapters, closing my eyes from time to time and waiting, with raffish expectation, for lights, voices, harmonies, savors, unctions, and the music of angelic choirs.

I did not get much of what I was looking for, and was left with the vague disillusionment of the old days when I had paid down half a dollar for a bad movie. . . .

On the whole, the infirmary of a Trappist monastery is the worst place to go looking for pleasure. The nearest I came to luxury was in the purely material order, where I got plenty of milk and butter and one day—perhaps the Brother made some kind of a mistake—I even got one sardine. If there had been two or three I would have known it was a mistake, but since there was precisely one, I am inclined to think it was intentional.

I got up every morning at four and served Mass and received Communion and then the rest of the day I sat up in bed reading and writing. I said the office and went to the Infirmary chapel to do the Stations of the Cross. And in the late afternoon Father Gerard, the infirmarian, made sure that I did not forget to meditate on the volume of Father Faber I had received as a Lenten book.

But as soon as I began to get better, Father Gerard made me get up and sweep the infirmary and do other odd jobs and when the Feast of St. Joseph came, I was glad to go down to church for the night office and sing a lesson in the Jube.

It must have been a surprise for all those who thought that I had left the monastery: and when we were back in the infirmary, Father Gerard said: "You sure can sing *loud!*"

Finally, on the Feast of St. Benedict, I picked up our blankets and went back to the novitiate, thoroughly satisfied to get off with no more than nine days of what Brother Hugh had called "not Calvary but Thabor."

That was the difference between me and Brother Hugh—

between one who had just begun his religious life and one who had just finished his with signal success.

For, to judge by the way people keep mentioning him in sermons, Brother Hugh had been truly a success as a Cistercian. I had not known him, except by sight. And yet even that was enough to tell a great deal about him. I have never forgotten his smile—I don't mean the one he wore in the bier, but the one he had when he was alive, which was quite a different matter. He was an old Brother, but his smile was full of the ingenuousness of a child. And he had a great abundance of that one indefinite quality which everybody seems willing to agree in calling characteristically Cistercian: the grace of simplicity.

What that means is often hard to say: but in Brother Hugh and the others like him—and there are not a few—it meant the innocence and liberty of soul that come to those who have thrown away all preoccupation with themselves and their own ideas and judgements and opinions and desires, and are perfectly content to take things as they come to them from the hands of God and through the wishes and commands of their superiors. It meant the freedom of heart that one can only obtain by putting his whole life in the hands of another, with the blind faith that God wills to use our superiors, our directors, as instruments for our guidance and the formation of our souls.

From what I have heard, Brother Hugh had all that. And therefore he was also what they call a "man of prayer."

But this peculiar combination—a contemplative spirit and a complete submission to superiors who entrusted him with many distracting responsibilities around the monastery—sanctified Brother Hugh according to what is, as near as I can make out, the Cistercian formula.

For it seems to me that our monasteries produce very few pure contemplatives. The life is too active. There is too much movement, too much to do. That is especially true of Gethsemani. It is a powerhouse, and not merely a powerhouse of prayer. In fact, there is an almost exaggerated reverence for work in the souls of some who are here. Doing things, suffering things, thinking things, making tangible and concrete sacrifices for the love of God—that is what contemplation seems to mean here—and I suppose the same attitude is universal in our Order. It goes by the name of "active contemplation." The word active is well chosen. About the second half of the compound, I am not so sure. It is not without a touch of poetic license.

It is only in theory that our wills can be disinfected of all these poisons by the universal excuse of "obedience." Yet it has been the Cistercian formula ever since St. Bernard of Clairvaux and a score of Cistercian Bishops and Abbots in the Middle Ages. Which brings me back to my own life and to the one activity that was born in me and is in my blood: I mean writing.

I brought all the instincts of a writer with me into the monastery, and I knew that I was bringing them, too. It was not a case of smuggling them in. And Father Master not only approved but encouraged me when I wanted to write poems and reflections and other things that came into my head in the novitiate.

Already in the Christmas season I had half filled an old notebook that belonged to my Columbia days, with the ideas that came swimming into my head all through those wonderful feasts, when I was a postulant.

In fact, I had found that the interval after the night office, in the great silence, between four and five-thirty on the mornings of feast days, was a wonderful time to write verse. After two or three hours of prayer your mind is saturated in peace and the richness of the liturgy. The dawn is breaking outside the cold windows. If it is warm, the birds are already beginning to sing. Whole blocks of imagery seem to crystallize out as it were naturally in the silence and the peace, and the lines almost write themselves.

Or that was the way it went until Father Master told me I must not write poetry then. The Rule would keep that hour sacred for the study of Scripture and the Psalms. And as time went on, I found that this was even better than writing poems.

472

What a time that is for reading and meditation! Especially in the summer when you can take your book and go out under the trees. What shades of light and color fill the woods at May's end. Such greens and blues as you never saw! And in the east the dawn sky is a blaze of fire where you might almost expect to see the winged animals of Ezechiel, frowning and flashing and running to and fro.

For six years, at that time of the day, on feast days, I have been reading nothing but one or another of some three or four books. St. Augustine's Commentary on the Psalms, St. Gregory the Great's Moralia, St. Ambrose on some of the Psalms or William of St. Thierry on the *Song of Songs*. Sometimes I look at one or another of the Fathers, or else read Scripture *simpliciter*. As soon as I had entered into the world of these great saints, and begun to rest in the Eden of their writings, I lost all desire to prefer that time for any writing of my own.

Such books as these, and the succession of our offices, and all the feasts and seasons of the liturgical year, and the various times of sowing and planting and harvesting, and, in general, all the varied and closely integrated harmony of natural and supernatural cycles that go to make up the Cistercian year tend to fill a man's life to such overflowing satiety that there is usually no time, no desire for writing.

After the poems I wrote the first Christmas, and one or two in January, and one at the Purification, and one more in Lent, I was glad to be quiet. If there were no other reason for not writing, summer is too busy a season.

As soon as Paschal time was well begun, we were planting peas and beans, and when it ended we were picking them. Then in May they cut the first crop of alfalfa in St. Joseph's field, and from then on the novices were going out, morning and afternoon, in their long line, Indian file, straw hats on their heads, with pitchforks to hay fields in all quarters of the farm. From St. Joseph's we went to the upper bottom, in the extreme northeast corner of the property, in a hollow surrounded by woods, behind the knoll called Mount Olivet. After that we were down in the lower bottom, where I lifted up a shock of hay on the fork and a black snake tumbled out of it. When the big wagons were loaded, two or three of us would ride back and help unload them in the cow barn or the horse barn or the sheep barn. That is one of the hardest jobs we have around here. You get inside the huge, dark loft, and the dust begins to swirl and the ones on the wagon are pitching hay up at you as fast as they can, and you are trying to stow it back in the loft. In about two minutes the place begins to put on a very good imitation of purgatory, for the sun is beating down mercilessly on a tin roof over your head, and the loft is one big black stifling oven. I wish I had thought a little about that cow barn, back in the days when I was committing so many sins, in the world. It might have given me pause.

In June, when the Kentucky sun has worked up his full anger, and stands almost at the zenith, beating the clay furrows with his raging heat, it begins to be the season of the Cistercian's true penance. It is then that the little green flag begins to appear in the small cloister to announce that we no longer have to wear our cowls in the intervals and in the refectory. But even then, no matter how motionless you remain, out under the trees, everything you have on is soaked in sweat: and the woods begin to sizzle with a thousand crickets, and their din fills the cloister court and echoes around the brick walls and the tiled floors of the cloister and makes the monastery sound like a gigantic frying pan standing over a fire. This is the time when the choir begins to fill with flies, and you have to bite your lip to keep your resolution about never swatting them, as they crawl over your forehead and into your eyes while you are trying to sing. . . . And yet it is a wonderful season, fuller of consolations than it is of trials: the season of the great feasts: Pentecost, Corpus Christi—when we pave the cloister with whole mosaics of flowers—the Sacred Heart, St. John the Baptist, Sts. Peter and Paul.

This is when you really begin to feel the weight of our so-called active contemplation, with all the accidental additions that it acquires at Gethsemani. You begin to understand the

474

truth of the fact that the old Trappists of the eighteenth and nineteenth centuries saw in the "exercises of contemplation" —the choral office and mental prayer and so on—principally a means of penance and self-punishment. And so it is the season when novices give up and go back to the world—they give up at other times too, but summer is their hardest test.

My friend Frater Sacerdos had already left in May. I remember a few days before he vanished from our midst, the novices were dusting the church, and he was mooning around St. Patrick's altar with a woeful expression and great sighs and gestures. His former name, in religion, as a Carmelite, had been Patrick, and he was on the point of returning to the tutelage of the great apostle of Ireland.

But I had no desire to leave. I don't think I enjoyed the heat any more than anybody else, but with my active temperament I could satisfy myself that all my work and all my sweat really meant something, because they made me feel as if I were doing something for God.

The day Frater Sacerdos left we were working in a new field that had just been cleared over near the western limits of the farm, behind Aidan Nally's. And we came home in our long file over the hill past Nally's house, with the whole blue valley spread out before us, and the monastery and all the barns and gardens standing amid the trees below us under a big blue sweep of Kentucky sky, with those white, incomparable clouds. And I thought to myself: "Anybody who runs away from a place like this is crazy." But it was not as supernatural as I may have thought. It is not sufficient to love the place for its scenery, and because you feel satisfied that you are a spiritual athlete and a not inconsiderable servant of God.

Now, at the beginning of July, we were in the midst of the harvest, getting in the wheat. The big threshing machine was drawn up at the east end of the cow barn, and wagons loaded with sheaves were constantly coming in, from all directions, from the various fields. You could see the cellarer standing on top of the threshing machine, outlined against the sky, giving directions, and a group of lay brother novices were busily filling the sacks and tying them up and loading trucks as fast as the clean new grain poured out of the machine. Some of the choir novices were taking the grain down to the mill and unloading the sacks and spilling the wheat out on the granary floor: but most of us were out in the fields.

That year we had a phenomenal harvest: but it was always threatened with ruin by showers of rain. So practically every day the novices went out to the fields and dismantled the shocks and spread the damp sheaves around on the ground, in the sun, to dry before they began to get full of mildew: and then we would put them back together again and go home—and there would be another shower of rain. But in the end it was a good harvest, anyway.

How sweet it is, out in the fields, at the end of the long summer afternoons! The sun is no longer raging at you, and the woods are beginning to throw long blue shadows over the stubble fields where the golden shocks are standing. The sky is cool, and you can see the pale half-moon smiling over the monastery in the distance. Perhaps a clean smell of pine comes down to you, out of the woods, on the breeze, and mingles with the richness of the fields and of the harvest. And when the undermaster claps his hands for the end of work, and you drop your arms and take off your hat to wipe the sweat out of your eyes, in the stillness you realize how the whole valley is alive with the singing of crickets, a constant universal treble going up to God out of the fields, rising like the incense of an evening prayer to the pure sky: *laus perennis!*

And you take your rosary out of your pocket, and get in your place in the long file, and start swinging homeward along the road with your boots ringing on the asphalt and deep, deep peace in your heart! And on your lips, silently, over and over again, the name of the Queen of Heaven, the Queen also of this valley: "Hail Mary, full of grace, the Lord is with Thee. . . ." And the Name of her Son, for Whom all this was made in the first place, for Whom all this was planned and intended, for Whom the whole of creation was framed,

476

to be His Kingdom. "Blessed is the fruit of Thy womb, Jesus!"

"Full of grace!" The very thought, over and over, fills our own hearts with more grace: and who knows what grace overflows into the world from that valley, from those rosaries, in the evenings when the monks are swinging home from work!

It was a few days after the Feast of the Visitation, which is, for me, the feast of the beginning of all true poetry, when the Mother of God sang her *Magnificat*, and announced the fulfilment of all prophecies, and proclaimed the Christ in her and became the Queen of Prophets and of poets—a few days after that feast, I got news from John Paul.

For the last few months he had been at a camp in the plains of the Canadian west, in Manitoba. Day after day he had been making long flights and doing bombing practice, and now he had his sergeant's stripes and was ready to be sent overseas.

He wrote that he was coming to Gethsemani before he sailed. But he did not say when.

v

The Feast of St. Stephen Harding, the founder of the Cistercian Order, went by, and every day I was waiting to be called to Reverend Father's room, and told that John Paul had come.

By now the corn was high, and every afternoon we went out with hoes, to make war against our enemies, the morning-glories, in the cornfields. And every afternoon, I would disappear into those rows of green banners, and lose sight of everybody else, wondering how anybody would be able to find me if he were sent out there to bring me in with the news that my brother had come. Often you did not even hear the signal for the end of work, and frequently one or two of the more recollected novices would get left in the cornfield, hoeing away diligently in some remote corner, after everybody else had gone home.

But I have discovered from experience that the rule, in

these things, is that what you are expecting always comes when you are not actually expecting it. So it was one afternoon that we were working close to the monastery, within the enclosure, weeding a patch of turnips, that someone made me a sign to come in to the house. I had so far forgotten the object of my expectations that it took me a moment or two before I guessed what it was.

I changed out of work-clothes and went straight to Reverend Father's room and knocked on the door. He flashed the "Please wait" sign that is worked from a button at his desk, and so there was nothing for it but to sit down and wait, which I did, for the next half hour.

Finally Reverend Father discovered that I was there, and sent for my brother, who presently came along the hall with Brother Alexander. He was looking very well, and standing very straight, and his shoulders, which were always broad, were now completely square.

As soon as we were alone in his room, I began to ask him if he didn't want to get baptized.

"I sort of hoped I could be," he said.

"Tell me," I said, "how much instruction have you had, anyway?"

"Not much," he said.

After I had questioned him some more, it turned out that "not much" was a euphemism for "none at all."

"But you can't be baptized without knowing what it is all about," I said.

I went back to the novitiate before vespers feeling miserable.

"He hasn't had any instruction," I said gloomily to Father Master.

"But he wants to be baptized, doesn't he?"

"He says he does."

Then I said: "Don't you think I could give him enough instruction in the next few days to prepare him? And Father James could talk to him when he gets a chance. And of course he can go to all the conferences of the retreat."

One of the week-end retreats was just beginning.

478

"Take him some books," said Father Master, "and talk to him, and tell him everything you can. And I'll go and speak to Reverend Father."

So the next day I hurried up to John Paul's room with a whole armful of volumes purloined from the Novitiate Common Box—and soon he had a room full of all kinds of books that different people had selected for him to read. If he had wanted to read them all, he would have had to stay in the monastery for six months. There was an orange pamphlet with an American flag on the cover, called "The Truth About Catholics." There were, of course, *The Imitation of Christ* and a New Testament. Then my contribution was the Catechism of the Council of Trent, and Father Robert's suggestion was *The Faith of Millions* and Father James had come through with the *Story of a Soul*, the autobiography of the Little Flower. There were plenty of others besides, for Father Francis, who was guest-master that year, was also librarian. Perhaps he was the one who supplied the *Story of a Soul*, for he has great devotion to the Little Flower.

But in any case, John Paul looked them all over. He said: "Who is this Little Flower, anyway?" And he read the *Story of a Soul* all in one gulp.

Meanwhile, I spent practically the whole of the morning and afternoon work periods talking my head off about everything I could think of that had something to do with the faith. It was much harder work than my fellow novices were doing out there in the cornfield—and much more exhausting.

The existence of God and the creation of the world did not give him any difficulty, so we went over that in two sentences. He had heard something about the Holy Trinity at the Choir School of St. John the Divine. So I just said that the Father was the Father and the Son was the Father's idea of Himself and the Holy Ghost was the love of the Father for the Son, and that these Three were One nature, and that nevertheless they were Three Persons—and they dwelt within us by faith.

I think I talked more about faith and the life of grace than anything else, telling him all that I myself had found out by experience, and all that I sensed he wanted most to know.

He had not come here to find out a lot of abstract truths: that was clear enough. As soon as I had begun to talk to him, I had seen awaken in his eyes the thirst that was hiding within him, and that had brought him to Gethsemani—for he certainly had not come merely to see me.

How well I recognized it, that insatiable thirst for peace, for salvation, for true happiness.

There was no need of any fancy talk, or of elaborate argument: no need to try to be clever, or to hold his attention by tricks. He was my brother and I could talk to him straight, in the words we both knew, and the charity that was between us would do the rest.

You might have expected two brothers, at such a time as this, to be talking about the "old days." In a sense, we were. Our own lives, our memories, our family, the house that had served us as a home, the things we had done in order to have what we thought was a good time—all this was indeed the background of our conversation, and, in an indirect sort of way, entered very definitely into the subject matter.

It was so clearly present that there was no necessity to allude to it, this sorry, complicated past, with all its confusions and misunderstandings and mistakes. It was as real and vivid and present as the memory of an automobile accident in the casualty ward where the victims are being brought back to life.

Was there any possibility of happiness without faith? Without some principle that transcended everything we had ever known? The house in Douglaston, which my grandparents had built, and which they maintained for twenty-five years with the ice-box constantly full and the carpets all clean and fifteen different magazines on the living-room table and a Buick in the garage and a parrot on the back porch screaming against the neighbor's radio, was the symbol of a life that had brought them nothing but confusions and anxieties and misunderstandings and fits of irritation. It was a house in which Bonnemaman had sat for hours every day in front of a mirror, rubbing cold-cream into her cheeks as if she were going to the opera—but she never went to the opera, except, perhaps, the ones she saw before her in her dreams as she sat there, in peaceless isolation, among the pots of ointment.

Against all this we had reacted with everything our own generation could give us, and we had ended up doing, in the movies, and in the cheap, amber-lit little bars of Long Island, or the nosier ones, fixed up with chromium, in the city, all that she had been doing at home. We never went to our own particular kind of operas either.

If a man tried to live without grace, not all his works were evil, that was true, certainly. He could do a lot of good things. He could drive a car. That is a good thing. He could read a book. He could swim. He could draw pictures. He could do all the things my brother had done at various times: collect stamps, post-cards, butterflies, study chemistry, take photographs, fly a plane, learn Russian. All these things were good in themselves and could be done without grace.

But there was absolutely no need to stop and ask him, now, whether, without the grace of God, any of those pursuits had come anywhere near making him happy.

I spoke about faith. By the gift of faith, you touch God, you enter into contact with His very substance and reality, in darkness: because nothing accessible, nothing comprehensible to our senses and reason can grasp His essence as it is in itself. But faith transcends all these limitations, and does so without labor: for it is God Who reveals Himself to us, and all that is required of us is the humility to accept His revelation, and accept it on the conditions under which it comes to us: from the lips of men.

When that contact is established, God gives us sanctifying grace: His own life, the power to love Him, the power to overcome all the weaknesses and limitations of our blind souls and to serve Him and control our crazy and rebellious flesh.

"Once you have grace," I said to him, "you are free. Without it, you cannot help doing the things you know you should not do, and that you know you don't really want to do. But once you have grace, you are free. When you are baptized, there is no power in existence that can force you to commit a sin—nothing that will be able to drive you to it against your own conscience. And if you merely will it, you will be free forever, because the strength will be given you, as much as you need, and as often as you ask, and as soon as you ask, and generally long before you ask for it, too."

From then on his impatience to get to the Sacrament was intense.

I went to Reverend Father's room.

"We can't baptize him here, of course," he said. "But it might be done at one of the parishes near here."

"Do you think there is a chance of it?"

"I will ask Father James to talk to him and tell me what he thinks."

By Saturday afternoon I had told John Paul everything I knew. I had got to the Sacramentals and Indulgences and then gone back and given him an explanation of that notion, so mysterious to some outside the Church: "The Sacred Heart." After that I stopped. I was exhausted. I had nothing left to give him.

And he sat calmly in his chair and said: "Go on, tell me some more."

The next day was Sunday, the Feast of St. Anne. After Chapter, in the long interval before High Mass, I asked Father Master if I could go over to the Guest House.

"Reverend Father told me your brother might be going over to New Haven to get baptized."

I went to the novitiate chapel and prayed.

But after dinner I found out that it was true. John Paul was sitting in his room, quiet and happy. It was years since I had seen him so completely serene.

Then I realized, obscurely, that in those last four days the work of eighteen or twenty years of my bad example had been washed away and made good by God's love. The evil that had been done by my boasting and showing off and exulting in my own stupidity had been atoned for in my own soul, at the same time as it had been washed out of his, and I was full of peace and gratitude.

I taught him how to use a Missal and how to receive Communion, for it had been arranged that his First Communion would be at Reverend Father's private Mass the following day.

The next morning, all through Chapter, the obscure worry that John Paul would get lost and not be able to find his way down to the chapel of Our Lady of Victories had been haunting me. As soon as Chapter was over I hurried to the church ahead of Reverend Father, and entered the big empty building, and knelt down.

John Paul was nowhere in sight.

I turned around. At the end of the long nave, with its empty choir stalls, high up in the empty Tribune, John Paul was kneeling all alone, in uniform. He seemed to be an immense distance away, and between the secular church where he was, and the choir where I was, was a locked door, and I couldn't call out to him to tell him how to come down the long way 'round through the Guest House. And he didn't understand my sign.

At that moment there flashed into my mind all the scores of times in our forgotten childhood when I had chased John Paul away with stones from the place where my friends and I were building a hut. And now, all of a sudden, here it was all over again: a situation that was externally of the same pattern: John Paul, standing, confused and unhappy, at a distance which he was not able to bridge.

Sometimes the same image haunts me now that he is dead, as though he were standing helpless in Purgatory, depending more or less on me to get him out of there, waiting for my prayers. But I hope he is out of it by now!

Father Master went off to get him and I started lighting the candles on the altar of Our Lady of Victories and by the time the Mass started I could see, out of the corner of my eye, that he was kneeling there at one of the benches. And so we received Communion together, and the work was done.

The next day, he was gone. I went to see him off at the

Gate, after Chapter. A visitor gave him a ride to Bardstown. As the car was turning around to start down the avenue John Paul turned around and waved, and it was only then that his expression showed some possibility that he might be realizing, as I did, that we would never see each other on earth again.

The fall came, and the Great Tricenary in September when all the young monks have to recite ten psalters for the dead. It is a season of bright, dry days, with plenty of sun, and cool air, and high cirrus clouds, and the forest is turning rusty and blood color and bronze along the jagged hills. Then, morning and afternoon, we go out to cut corn. St. Joseph's field had long been finished—the green stalks had gone into the silo. Now we were working through the vast, stony fields in the middle and lower bottoms, hacking our way through the dry corn with each blow of the knife cracking like a rifle shot. It was as if those glades had turned into shooting galleries and we were all firing away with twenty-twos.

And behind us, in the wide avenues that opened in our wake, the giant shocks grew up, and the two novices that came last garrotted them with a big rope and tied them secure with twine.

Around November when the corn-husking was nearly finished, and when the fat turkeys were gobbling loudly in their pen, running from one wire fence to the other in dark herds, under the gloomy sky, I got news from John Paul in England. First he had been stationed at Bournemouth, from which he sent me a postcard that showed some boarding houses I recognized, along the West Cliff. It was only ten years since we had spent a summer there: but the memory of it was like something unbelievable, like another life—as if there were some such thing as the transmigration of souls!

After that he was sent somewhere in Oxfordshire. His letters arrived with little rectangles neatly cut out of them, here and there, but when he wrote: "I enjoy going into —— and seeing the —— and the bookstores," it was easy enough for me to insert "Oxford" in the first hole and "Colleges" in the other, since the postmark read "Banbury." Here he was still in training. I could not tell how soon he would get in to the actual fighting over Germany.

Meanwhile, he wrote that he had met a girl, whom he described, and it soon turned out that they were going to get married. I was glad on account of the marriage, but there was something altogether pathetic about the precariousness of it: what chance was there that they would ever be able to have a home and live in it, the way human beings were supposed to do?

Christmas came to the monastery bringing with it the same kind of graces and consolations as the year before, only more intense. On the Feast of St. Thomas the Apostle, Reverend Father had allowed me to make my vows privately to him, more than a year before public profession would be permissible. If I had been able to make ten different vows every day I would not have been able to express what I felt about the monastery and the Cistercian life.

And so 1943 began, and the weeks hastened on towards Lent.

Lent means, among other things, no more letters. The monks neither receive mail nor write it in Lent and Advent, and the last news I had, before Ash Wednesday, was that John Paul was planning to get married about the end of February. I would have to wait until Easter to find out whether or not he actually did.

I had fasted a little during my first Lent, the year before, but it had been broken up by nearly two weeks in the infirmary. This was my first chance to go through the whole fast without any mitigation. In those days, since I still had the world's ideas about food and nourishment and health, I thought the fast we have in Trappist monasteries in Lent was severe. We eat nothing until noon, when we get the regular two bowls, one of soup and the other of vegetables, and as much bread as we like, but then in the evening there is a light collation—a piece of bread and a dish of something like applesauce—two ounces of it.

However, if I had entered a Cistercian monastery in the twelfth century—or even some Trappist monasteries of the nineteenth, for that matter—I would have had to tighten my belt and go hungry until four o'clock in the afternoon: and there was nothing besides that one meal: no collation, no frustulum.

Humiliated by this discovery, I find that the Lenten fast we now have does not bother me. However, it is true that now in the morning work periods I have a class in theology, instead of going out to break rocks on the back road, or split logs in the woodshed as we did in the novitiate. I expect it makes a big difference, because swinging a sledge-hammer when you have an empty stomach is apt to make your knees a little shaky after a while. At least that was what it did to me.

Even in the Lent of 1943, however, I had some indoor work for part of the time, since Reverend Father had already put me to translating books and articles from French.

And so, after the Conventual Mass, I would get out book and pencil and papers and go to work at one of the long tables in the novitiate scriptorium, filling the yellow sheets as fast as I could, while another novice took them and typed them as soon as they were finished. In those days I even had a secretary.

Finally the long liturgy of penance came to its climax in Holy Week, with the terrible cry of the Lamentations once more echoing in the dark choir of the Abbey Church, followed by the four hours' thunder of the Good Friday Psalter in the Chapter Room, and the hush of the monks going about the cloisters in bare feet, and the long sad chant that accompanies the adoration of the Cross!

What a relief it was to hear the bells once more on Holy Saturday, what relief to wake up from the sleep of death with a triple "alleluia." Easter, that year, was as late as it could possibly be—the twenty-fifth of April—and there were enough flowers to fill the church with the intoxicating smell of the Kentucky spring—a wild and rich and heady smell of flowers, sweet and full. We came from our light, five hours' sleep into a church that was full of warm night air and swimming in this rich luxury of odors, and soon began that Easter invitatory that is nothing short of gorgeous in its exultation.

How mighty they are, those hymns and those antiphons of the Easter office! Gregorian chant that should, by rights, be monotonous, because it has absolutely none of the tricks and resources of modern music, is full of a variety infinitely rich because it is subtle and spiritual and deep, and lies rooted far beyond the shallow level of virtuosity and "technique," even in the abysses of the spirit, and of the human soul. Those Easter "alleluias," without leaving the narrow range prescribed by the eight Gregorian modes, have discovered color and warmth and meaning and gladness that no other music possesses. Like everything else Cistercian—like the monks themselves, these antiphons, by submitting to the rigor of a Rule that would seem to destroy individuality, have actually acquired a character that is unique, unparalleled.

It was into the midst of all this that news from England came.

There had been a letter from John Paul among the two or three that I found under the napkin in the refectory at noon on Holy Saturday. I read it on Easter Monday, and it said that he had been married more or less according to plan, and had gone with his wife to the English Lakes for a week or so, and that after that he had been stationed at a new base, which put him into the fighting.

He had been once or twice to bomb something somewhere: but he did not even give the censor a chance to cut anything out. You could see at once that there was a tremendous change in his attitude towards the war and his part in it. He did not want to talk about it. He had nothing to say. And from the way he said that he didn't want to talk about it, you could see that the experience was terrific.

John Paul had at last come face to face with the world that he and I had helped to make!

On Easter Monday afternoon I sat down to write him a letter and cheer him up a little, if I could.

The letter was finished, and it was Easter Tuesday, and we were in choir for the Conventual Mass, when Father Master came in and made me the sign for "Abbot."

487

I went out to Reverend Father's room. There was no difficulty in guessing what it was.

I passed the *pietà* at the corner of the cloister, and buried my will and my natural affections and all the rest in the wounded side of the dead Christ.

Reverend Father flashed the sign to come in, and I knelt by his desk and received his blessing and kissed his ring and he read me the telegram that Sergeant J. P. Merton, my brother, had been reported missing in action on April 17th.

I have never understood why it took them so long to get the telegram through. April 17th was already ten days ago—the end of Passion Week.

Some more days went by, letters of confirmation came, and finally, after a few weeks, I learned that John Paul was definitely dead.

The story was simply this. On the night of Friday the sixteenth, which had been the Feast of Our Lady of Sorrows, he and his crew had taken off in their bomber with Mannheim as their objective. I never discovered whether they crashed on the way out or the way home, but the plane came down in the North Sea. John Paul was severely injured in the crash, but he managed to keep himself afloat, and even tried to support the pilot, who was already dead. His companions had managed to float their rubber dinghy and pulled him in.

He was very badly hurt: maybe his neck was broken. He lay in the bottom of the dinghy in delirium.

He was terribly thirsty. He kept asking for water. But they didn't have any. The water tank had broken in the crash, and the water was all gone.

It did not last too long. He had three hours of it, and then he died. Something of the three hours of the thirst of Christ Who loved him, and died for him many centuries ago, and had been offered again that very day, too, on many altars.

His companions had more of it to suffer, but they were finally picked up and brought to safety. But that was some five days later.

On the fourth day they had buried John Paul in the sea.

Sweet brother, if I do not sleep
My eyes are flowers for your tomb;
And if I cannot eat my bread,
My fasts shall live like willows where you died.
If in the heat I find no water for my thirst,
My thirst shall turn to springs for you, poor traveller.

Where, in what desolate and smokey country,
Lies your poor body, lost and dead?
And in what landscape of disaster
Has your unhappy spirit lost its road?

Come, in my labor find a resting place
And in my sorrows lay your head,
Or rather take my life and blood
And buy yourself a better bed—
Or take my breath and take my death
And buy yourself a better rest.

When all the men of war are shot
And flags have fallen into dust,
Your cross and mine shall tell men still
Christ died on each, for both of us.

For in the wreckage of your April Christ lies slain,
And Christ weeps in the ruins of my spring:
The money of Whose tears shall fall
Into your weak and friendless hand,
And buy you back to your own land:
The silence of Whose tears shall fall
Like bells upon your alien tomb.
Hear them and come: they call you home.

Epilogue

Meditatio Pauperis in Solitudine

Day unto day uttereth speech. The clouds change. The seasons pass over our woods and fields in their slow and regular procession, and time is gone before you are aware of it.

Christ pours down the Holy Ghost upon you from heaven in the fire of June, and then you look about you and realize that you are standing in the barnyard husking corn, and the cold wind of the last days of October is sweeping across the thin woods and biting you to the bone. And then, in a minute or so, it is Christmas, and Christ is born.

At the last of the three great Masses, celebrated as a Solemn Pontifical High Mass with Pontifical Tierce, I am one of the minor ministers. We have vested in the Sacristy, have waited in the sanctuary. In the thunder of the organ music, Reverend Father has come with the monks in procession through the cloister, and has knelt a moment before the Blessed Sacrament in the Chapel of Our Lady of Victories. Then Tierce begins. After that the solemn vesting and I present the crozier with the suitable bows, and they go to the foot of the altar and the tremendous introit begins, in the choir, summing up with the splendor of its meaning the whole of Christmas. The Child born on earth, in lowliness, in the crib, before the shepherds, is born this day in heaven in glory, in magnificence, in majesty: and the day in which He is born is eternity. He is born forever, All-Power, All-Wisdom, begotten before the daystar: He is the beginning and the end, everlastingly born of the Father, the Infinite God: and He Himself is the same God, God of God, Light of Light, True God of True God. God born of Himself, forever: Himself His own second Person: One, yet born of Himself forever.

He it is also that is born each instant in our hearts: for this unending birth, this everlasting beginning, without end, this everlasting, perfect newness of God begotten of Himself, issuing from Himself without leaving Himself or altering His one-ness, this is the life that is in us. But see: He is suddenly born again, also, on this altar, upon that cloth and corporal as white as snow beneath the burning lights, and raised up above us in the hush of the consecration! Christ, the Child of God, the Son, made Flesh, with His All-power. What will You say to me, this Christmas, O Jesus? What is it that You have prepared for me at Your Nativity?

At the *Agnus Dei* I put aside the crozier and we all go to the Epistle side, together, to receive the kiss of peace. We bow to one another. The salutation passes from one to the other. Heads bow. Hands are folded again. Now we all turn around together.

And suddenly I find myself looking straight into the face of Bob Lax. He is standing at the benches that are drawn up, there, for visitors. He is so close to the step of the sanctuary, that if he were any closer he would be in it.

And I say to myself: "Good, now he'll get baptized too."

After dinner I went to Reverend Father's room and told him who Lax was, and that he was an old friend of mine, and asked if I might speak to him. We are ordinarily only allowed to receive visits from our own families, but since I had practically nothing left of my family, Reverend Father agreed that I might speak to Lax for a little while. And I mentioned that I thought he might be ready to be baptized.

"Isn't he a Catholic?" said Reverend Father.

"No, Reverend Father, not yet."

"Well, in that case, why was he taking Communion last night at the midnight Mass? . . ."

Up in the Guest House, Lax told me how the Baptism had come about. He had been at the University of North Carolina teaching some earnest young men how to write radio plays. Towards the end of Advent he had got a letter from Rice which said, in so many words, "Come to New York and we will find a priest and ask him to baptize you."

All of a sudden, after all those years of debating back and forth, Lax just got on the train and went to New York. Nobody had ever put the matter up to him like that before.

494

They found a Jesuit in that big church up on Park Avenue and he baptized him, and that was that.

So then Lax had said: "Now I will go to the Trappists in Kentucky and visit Merton."

Bob Gibney told him: "You were a Jew and now you are a Catholic. Why don't you black your face? Then you will be all the three things the Southerners hate most."

The night had already fallen, Christmas Eve, when Lax got to Bardstown. He stood by the road to hitch a ride to the monastery. Some fellows picked him up, and while they were driving along, they began talking about the Jews the way some people talk about the Jews.

So Lax said that he was not only a Catholic but a converted Jew.

"Oh," said the fellows in the car, "of course, you understand we were talking about *orthodox* Jews."

From Lax I heard the first scraps of information about all the friends I had not forgotten: about Bob Gerdy who was in England in the army, after having been baptized into the Church in September. Rice was working on one of those picture magazines. Gibney had got married, and soon he and Lax would also be working on another picture magazine—a new one that had started since I came to the monastery, called *Parade* or *Fanfare* or something like that. I don't know if Peggy Wells had already gone to Hollywood, but she went soon and is there still. Nancy Flagg was working either on *Vogue* or *Harper's Bazaar*. Somehow, too, I have the impression that all the people who had lived in the cottage at Olean the summer I did not enter the Franciscans, had at one point got themselves jobs on the magazine *House and Garden*. The whole thing is very obscure and mysterious. Perhaps it is something I dreamed. But for those three or four months, or however long it was, *House and Garden* must have been quite a magazine! Surely nothing like the old *House and Garden* I used to yawn over in the doctor's office.

And Seymour was in India. He was in the army. He had not yet, as far as I knew, found any practical application for his jujitsu. In India his chief task was to edit a paper for the

495

boys in the army. So one day he walked in to the printing press, where all the typesetters working for him were Hindus, nice peaceful fellows. And Seymour, in the middle of the printing press and in full view of all his native staff, swatted a fly with a report that rang through the shop like a cannon. Instantly all the Hindus stopped work and filed out on strike. I suppose that was the time Seymour had leisure enough to travel to Calcutta and pay a visit to Bramachari.

When Lax went back to New York he took with him a manuscript of some poems. Half of them had been written since I entered the novitiate. The other half went back, mostly, to the days at St. Bonaventure. It was the first time I had looked at them since I had come to Gethsemani. Getting these poems together and making a selection was like editing the work of a stranger, a dead poet, someone who had been forgotten.

Lax took this collection to Mark Van Doren, and Mark sent it to James Laughlin at New Directions, and just before Lent I heard he was going to print it.

The exceedingly tidy little volume, *Thirty Poems,* reached me at the end of November, just before we began the annual retreat, in 1944.

I went out under the grey sky, under the cedars at the edge of the cemetery, and stood in the wind that threatened snow and held the printed poems in my hand.

ii

By this time I should have been delivered of any problems about my true identity. I had already made my simple profession. And my vows should have divested me of the last shreds of any special identity.

But then there was this shadow, this double, this writer who had followed me into the cloister.

He is still on my track. He rides my shoulders, sometimes, like the old man of the sea. I cannot lose him. He still wears the name of Thomas Merton. Is it the name of an enemy?

He is supposed to be dead.

But he stands and meets me in the doorway of all my prayers, and follows me into church. He kneels with me behind the pillar, the Judas, and talks to me all the time in my ear.

He is a business man. He is full of ideas. He breathes notions and new schemes. He generates books in the silence that ought to be sweet with the infinitely productive darkness of contemplation.

And the worst of it is, he has my superiors on his side. They won't kick him out. I can't get rid of him.

Maybe in the end he will kill me, he will drink my blood.

Nobody seems to understand that one of us has got to die.

Sometimes I am mortally afraid. There are the days when there seems to be nothing left of my vocation—my contemplative vocation—but a few ashes. And everybody calmly tells me: "Writing is your vocation."

And there he stands and bars my way to liberty. I am bound to the earth, in his Egyptian bondage of contracts, reviews, page proofs, and all the plans for books and articles that I am saddled with.

When I first began to get ideas about writing, I told them to Father Master and Father Abbot with what I thought was "simplicity." I thought I was just "being open with my superiors." In a way, I suppose I was.

But it was not long before they got the idea that I ought to be put to work translating things, writing things.

It is strange. The Trappists have sometimes been definite, even exaggerated, in their opposition to intellectual work in the past. That was one of the big battle cries of De Rancé. He had a kind of detestation for monkish dilettantes and he took up arms against the whole Benedictine Congregation of Saint Maur in a more or less quixotic battle that ended in a reconciliation scene between De Rancé and the great Dom Mabillon that reads like Oliver Goldsmith. In the eighteenth and nineteenth centuries, it was considered a kind of a monastic sin for a Trappist to read anything but Scripture and the lives of the saints: and I mean those lives that are a chain of fantastic miracles interspersed with pious platitudes. It was considered a matter worthy of suspicion if a monk developed too lively an interest in the Fathers of the Church.

But at Gethsemani I had walked into a far different kind of a situation.

In the first place, I entered a house that was seething with an energy and a growth that it had not known for ninety years. After nearly a century of struggle and obscurity, Gethsemani was suddenly turning into a very prominent and vital force in the Cistercian order and the Catholic Church in America. The house was crowded with postulants and novices. There was no longer any room to hold them all. In fact, on the Feast of St. Joseph, 1944, when I made my simple profession, Father Abbot read out the names of those who had been chosen for the first daughter house of Gethsemani. Two days later, on the Feast of St. Benedict, the colony left for Georgia and took up its abode in a barn thirty miles from Atlanta, chanting the psalms in a hayloft. By the time this is printed there will have been another Cistercian monastery in Utah and another in New Mexico, and still another planned for the deep South.

This material growth at Gethsemani is part of a vaster movement of spiritual vitality that is working throughout the whole Order, all over the world. And one of the things it has produced has been a certain amount of Cistercian literature.

That there should be six Cistercian monasteries in the United States and a convent of nuns soon to come: that there should also be new foundations in Ireland and Scotland, all this means a demand for books in English about the Cistercian life and the spirituality of the Order and its history.

But besides that, Gethsemani has grown into a sort of a furnace of apostolic fire. Every week-end, during the summer, the Guest House is crowded with retreatants who pray and fight the flies and wipe the sweat out of their eyes and listen to the monks chanting the office and hear sermons in the library and eat the cheese that Brother Kevin makes down in the moist shadows of the cellar that is propitious for that kind of thing. And along with this retreat movement, Gethsemani has been publishing a lot of pamphlets.

There is a whole rack of them in the lobby of the Guest House. Blue and yellow and pink and green and grey, with fancy printing on the covers or plain printing—some of them even with pictures—the pamphlets bear the legend: "A Trappist says . . ." "A Trappist declares . . ." "A Trappist implores . . ." "A Trappist asserts . . ." And what does a Trappist say, declare, implore, assert? He says things like this: It is time you changed your way of looking at things. Why don't you get busy and go to confession? After death: what? and things like that. These Trappists, they have something to tell laymen and laywomen, married men and single men, old men and young men, men in the army and men who have just come out of the army and men who are too crippled up to get into the army. They have a word of advice for nuns, and more than a word for priests. They have something to say about how to build a home, and about how to go through four years of college without getting too badly knocked about, spiritually, in the process.

And one of the pamphlets even has something to say about the Contemplative Life.

So it is not hard to see that this is a situation in which my double, my shadow, my enemy, Thomas Merton, the old man of the sea, has things in his favor. If he suggests books about the Order, his suggestions are heard. If he thinks up poems to be printed and published, his thoughts are listened to. There seems to be no reason why he should not write for magazines. . . .

At the beginning of 1944, when I was getting near the time for simple profession, I wrote a poem to Saint Agnes on her feast in January, and when I had finished it my feeling was that I did not care if I never wrote another poem as long as I lived.

At the end of the year, when *Thirty Poems* were printed, I still felt the same way, and more so.

So then Lax came down again for another Christmas, and told me I should be writing more poems. I did not argue about it. But in my own heart I did not think it was God's will. And Dom Vital, my confessor, did not think so either.

Then one day—the Feast of the Conversion of Saint Paul, 1945—I went to Father Abbot for direction, and without my even thinking of the subject, or mentioning it, he suddenly said to me:

"I want you to go on writing poems."

iii

It is very quiet.

The morning sun is shining on the gate-house which is bright with new paint this summer. From here it looks as though the wheat is already beginning to ripen on St. Joseph's knoll. The monks who are on retreat for their ordination to the diaconate are digging in the Guest House garden.

It is very quiet. I think about this monastery that I am in. I think about the monks, my brothers, my fathers.

There are the ones who have a thousand things to do. Some are busy with food, some with clothing, some with fixing the pipes, some with fixing the roof. Some paint the house, some sweep the rooms, some mop the floor of the refectory. One goes to the bees with a mask on and takes away their honey. Three or four others sit in a room with typewriters and all day long they answer the letters of the people who write here asking for prayers because they are unhappy. Still others are fixing tractors and trucks, others are driving them. The brothers are fighting with the mules to get them into harness. Or they go out in the pasture after the cows. Or they worry about the rabbits. One of them says he can fix watches. Another is making plans for the new monastery in Utah.

The ones who have no special responsibility for chickens or pigs or writing pamphlets or packing them up to send out by mail or keeping the complicated accounts in our Mass book—the ones who have nothing special to do can always go out and weed the potatoes and hoe the rows of corn.

When the bell rings in the steeple, I will stop typing and close the windows of this room where I work. Frater Sylvester will put away that mechanical monster of a lawn-mower and his helpers will go home with their hoes and shovels. And I will take a book and walk up and down a bit under the trees, if there is time, before the Conventual Mass. And most of the others will sit in the scriptorium and write their theological conferences or copy things out of books on to the backs of envelopes. And one or two will stand around in a doorway that leads from the Little Cloister to the monks' garden, and twine their rosaries around in their fingers and wait for something to happen.

After that we will all go to choir, and it will be hot, and the organ will be loud, and the organist, who is just learning, will make a lot of mistakes. But on the altar will be offered to God the eternal Sacrifice of the Christ to Whom we belong, and Who has brought us here together.

Congregavit nos in unum Christi amor.

America is discovering the contemplative life.

There are paradoxes in the history of Christian spirituality and not the least of them is the apparent contradiction in the way the Fathers and modern Popes have looked at the active and contemplative lives. Saint Augustine and Saint Gregory lamented the "sterility" of contemplation, which was in itself, as they admitted, superior to action. Yet Pope Pius XI came out in the constitution "Umbratilem" with the clear statement that the contemplative life was *much more* fruitful for the Church (*multo plus ad Ecclesiae incrementa et humani generis salutem conferre . . .*) than the activity of teaching and preaching. What is all the more surprising to a superficial observer is the fact that such a pronouncement should belong to our energetic times.

Practically anyone who realizes the existence of the debate can tell you that Saint Thomas taught that there were three vocations: that to the active life, that to the contemplative, and a third to the mixture of both, and that this last is superior to the other two. The mixed life is, of course, the vocation of Saint Thomas's own order, the Friars Preachers.

But Saint Thomas also comes out flatly with a pronouncement no less uncompromising than the one we read from "Umbratilem." *Vita contemplativa,* he remarks, *simpliciter est melior quam activa* (the contemplative life in itself, by its very nature, is superior to the active life). What is more, he proves it by natural reason in arguments from a pagan philosopher—Aristotle. That is how esoteric the question is! Later on he gives his strongest argument in distinctly Christian terms. The contemplative life directly and immediately occupies itself with the love of God, than which there is no act more perfect or more meritorious. Indeed that love is the root of all merit. When you consider the effect of individual merit upon the vitality of other members of the Mystical Body it is evident that there is nothing sterile about contemplation. On the contrary Saint Thomas's treatment of it in this question shows that the contemplative life establishes a man in the very heart of all spiritual fecundity.

When he admits that the active life *can* be more perfect under certain circumstances, accidentally, he hedges his statement in with half a dozen qualifications of a strictness that greatly enhances what he has already said about contemplation. First, activity will only be more perfect than the joy and rest of contemplation if it is undertaken as the result of an overflow of love for God (*propter abundantiam divini amoris*) in order to fulfill His will. It is not to be continuous, only the answer to a temporary emergency. It is purely for God's glory, and it does not dispense us from contemplation. It is an added obligation, and we must return as soon as we morally can to the powerful and fruitful silence of recollection that disposes our souls for divine union.

First comes the active life (practice of virtues, mortification, charity) which prepares us for contemplation. Contemplation means rest, suspension of activity, withdrawal into the mysterious interior solitude in which the soul is absorbed in the immense and fruitful silence of God and learns something of the secret of His perfections less by seeing than by fruitive love.

Yet to stop here would be to fall short of perfection. According to Saint Bernard of Clairvaux it is the comparatively weak soul that arrives at contemplation but does not overflow with a love that must communicate what it knows of

God to other men. For all the great Christian mystics without exception, Saint Bernard, Saint Gregory, Saint Theresa, Saint John of the Cross, Blessed John Ruysbroeck, Saint Bonaventure, the peak of the mystical life is a marriage of the soul with God which gives the saints a miraculous power, a smooth and tireless energy in working for God and for souls, which bears fruits in the sanctity of thousands and changes the course of religious and even secular history.

With this in mind, Saint Thomas could not fail to give the highest place to a vocation which, in his eyes, seemed destined to lead men to such a height of contemplation that the soul must overflow and communicate its secrets to the world.

Unfortunately Saint Thomas's bare statement "the religious institutes which are ordered to the work of preaching and teaching hold the highest rank in religion" is, frankly, misleading. It conjures up nothing more than a mental image of some pious and industrious clerics bustling from the library to the classroom. If it meant no more than this the solution would be hardly comprehensible to a Christian. Yet the tragedy is that many—including members of those "mixed" Orders—cannot find in it any deeper significance. If you can give a half-way intelligent lecture applying some thoughts from scholastic philosophy to the social situation, that alone places you very near the summit of perfection. . . .

No, we keep our eyes on those flaming words which lay down the conditions under which it is valid to leave contemplation for action. First of all *propter abundantiam divini amoris.* The "mixed life" is to be rated above that of the pure contemplatives only on the supposition that their love is *so much more vehement, so much more abundant* that it has to pour itself out in teaching and preaching.

In other words Saint Thomas is here teaching us that the so-called mixed vocation can only be superior to the contemplative vocation if it is itself *more contemplative.* This conclusion is inescapable. It imposes a tremendous obligation. Saint Thomas is really saying that the Dominican, the Franciscan, the Carmelite must be supercontemplatives. Either that or he is contradicting everything he said about the superiority of the contemplative.

Whether the "mixed" Orders today in America are actually as contemplative as this program would demand is a question I have no intention of answering. But at any rate it seems that most of them have reached, in practice, a sort of compromise to get out of the difficulty. They divide up their duties between their nuns and their priests. The nuns live in cloisters and do the contemplating and the priests live in colleges and cities and do the teaching and preaching. In the light of *"Umbratilem"* and the doctrine of the Mystical Body this solution is at least possible, if conditions leave them with no other way out. Saint Thomas, however, envisaged a program that was far more complete and satisfactory, for the individual and for the Church!

But what about the contemplative Orders? Their rules and usages at least grant them all they need to dispose themselves for contemplation and if their members do not reach it, it is not because of any difficulty inherent in their actual way of life. Granting that they are, or can be, as contemplative as they were meant to be by their founders: are they anything else?

The fact is, there does not exist any such thing as a purely contemplative Order of men—an Order which does not have, somewhere in its constitution, the note of *contemplata tradere*. The Carthusians, with all their elaborate efforts to preserve the silence and solitude of the hermit's life in their monasteries, definitely wrote into their original "Customs" the characteristic labor of copying manuscripts and writing books in order that they might preach to the world by their pen even though their tongues were silent.

The Cistercians had no such legislation, and they even enacted statutes to limit the production of books and to forbid poetry altogether. Nevertheless they produced a school of mystical theologians which, as Dom Berlière says, represents the finest flower of Benedictine spirituality. I just quoted what Saint Bernard, the head of that school, had to say on the subject, and in any case even if the Cistercians never wrote anything to pass on the fruit of their contemplation to the Church at large, *contemplata tradere* would always be an essential element in Cistercian life to the extent that the abbot and those charged with the direction of souls would always be obliged to feed the rest of the monks with the good bread of mystical theology as it comes out in smoking hot loaves from the oven of contemplation. This was what Saint Bernard told the learned cleric of York, Henry Murdach, to lure him from his books into the woods where the beeches and elms taught the monks wisdom.

And these "purely active" Orders, what about them? Do any such things exist? The Little Sisters of the Poor, the nursing sisterhoods cannot truly fulfil their vocations unless there is something of that *contemplata tradere*, the sharing of the fruits of contemplation. Even the active vocation is sterile without an interior life, and a deep interior life at that.

The truth is, in any kind of a religious Order there is not only the possibility but even in some sense the obligation of leading, at least to some extent, the highest of all lives—contemplation, and the sharing of its fruits with others. Saint Thomas's principle stands firm: the greatest perfection is *contemplata tradere*. But that does not oblige us to restrict this vocation, as he does, to the teaching Orders. They only happen to be the ones that seem to be best equipped to pass on the knowledge of God acquired by loving Him—if they have acquired that knowledge in contemplation. Yet others may perhaps be better placed for acquiring it.

In any case, there are many different ways of sharing the fruits of contemplation with others. You don't have to write books or make speeches. You don't have to have direct contact with souls in the confessional. Prayer can do the work wonderfully well, and indeed the fire of contemplation has a tendency to spread of itself throughout the Church and vivify all the members of Christ in secret without any conscious act on the part of the contemplative. But if you argue that Saint Thomas's context limits us at least to some sort of visible and natural communication with our fellow men (though it is hard to see why this should be so) nevertheless even in that event there exists a far more powerful means of sharing the mystical and experimental knowledge of God.

Look in Saint Bonaventure's *Itinerarium* and you will find one of the best descriptions ever written of this highest of all vocations. It is a description which the Seraphic Doctor himself learned on retreat and in solitude on Mount Alvernia. Praying in the same lonely spot where the great founder of his Order, Saint Francis of Assisi, had had the wounds of Christ burned into his hands and feet and side, Saint Bonaventure saw, by the light of a supernatural intuition, the full meaning of this tremendous event in the history of the Church. "There," he says, "Saint Francis 'passed over into God' (*in Deum transiit*) in the ecstasy (*excessus*) of contemplation and thus he was set up as an example of perfect contemplation just as he had previously been an example of perfection in the active life in order that God, through him, might draw all truly spiritual men to this kind of 'passing over' (*transitus*) and ecstasy, *less by word than by example*."

Here is the clear and true meaning of *contemplata tradere*, expressed without equivocation by one who had lived that life to the full. It is the vocation to transforming union, to the height of the mystical life and of mystical experience, to the very transformation into Christ that Christ living in us and directing all our actions might Himself draw men to desire and seek that same exalted union because of the joy and the sanctity and the supernatural vitality radiated by our example—or rather because of the secret influence of Christ living within us in complete possession of our souls.

And notice the tremendously significant fact that St. Bonaventure makes no divisions and distinctions: Christ imprinted His own image upon Saint Francis in order to draw not some men, not a few privileged monks, but *all* truly spiritual men to the perfection of contemplation which is nothing else but the perfection of love. Once they have reached these heights they will draw others to them in their turn. So any man may be called at least *de jure*, if not *de facto*, to become fused into one spirit with Christ in the furnace of contemplation and then go forth and cast upon the earth that same fire which Christ wills to see enkindled.

This means, in practice, that there is only one vocation. Whether you teach or live in the cloister or nurse the sick, whether you are in religion or out of it, married or single, no matter who you are or what you are, you are called to the summit of perfection: you are called to a deep interior life perhaps even to mystical prayer, and to pass the fruits of your contemplation on to others. And if you cannot do so by word, then by example.

Yet if this sublime fire of infused love burns in your soul, it will inevitably send forth throughout the Church and the world an influence more tremendous than could be estimated by the radius reached by words or by example. Saint John of the Cross writes: "A very little of this pure love is more precious in the sight of God and of greater profit to the Church, even though the soul appear to be doing nothing, than are all other works put together."

Before we were born, God knew us. He knew that some of us would rebel against His love and His mercy, and that others would love Him from the moment that they could love anything, and never change that love. He knew that there would be joy in heaven among the angels of His house for the conversion of some of us, and He knew that He would bring us all here to Gethsemani together, one day, for His own purpose, for the praise of His love.

The life of each one in this abbey is part of a mystery. We all add up to something far beyond ourselves. We cannot yet realize what it is. But we know, in the language of our theology, that we are all members of the Mystical Christ, and that we all grow together in Him for Whom all things were created.

In one sense we are always travelling, and travelling as if we did not know where we were going.

In another sense we have already arrived.

507

We cannot arrive at the perfect possession of God in this life, and that is why we are travelling and in darkness. But we already possess Him by grace, and therefore in that sense we have arrived and are dwelling in the light.

But oh! How far have I to go to find You in Whom I have already arrived!

For now, oh my God, it is to You alone that I can talk, because nobody else will understand. I cannot bring any other man on this earth into the cloud where I dwell in Your light, that is, Your darkness, where I am lost and abashed. I cannot explain to any other man the anguish which is Your joy nor the loss which is the Possession of You, nor the distance from all things which is the arrival in You, nor the death which is the birth in You because I do not know anything about it myself and all I know is that I wish it were over—I wish it were begun.

You have contradicted everything. You have left me in no-man's land.

You have got me walking up and down all day under those trees, saying to me over and over again: "Solitude, solitude." And You have turned around and thrown the whole world in my lap. You have told me, "Leave all things and follow me," and then You have tied half of New York to my foot like a ball and chain. You have got me kneeling behind that pillar with my mind making a noise like a bank. Is that contemplation?

Before I went to make my solemn vows, last spring, on the Feast of Saint Joseph, in the thirty-third year of my age, being a cleric in minor orders—this is what it looked like to me. It seemed to me that You were almost asking me to give up all my aspirations for solitude and for a contemplative life. You were asking me for obedience to superiors who will, I am morally certain, either make me write or teach philosophy or take charge of a dozen material responsibilities around the monastery, and I may even end up as a retreat master preaching four sermons a day to the seculars who come to the house.

And even if I have no special job at all, I will always be on the run from two in the morning to seven at night.

Didn't I spend a year writing the life of Mother Berchmans who was sent to a new Trappistine foundation in Japan, and who wanted to be a contemplative? And what happened to her? She had to be gate-keeper and guest-mistress and sacristan and cellaress and mistress of the lay sisters all at the same time. And when they relieved her of one or two of those jobs it was only in order to give her heavier ones, like that of Mistress of Novices.

Martha, Martha, sollicita eris, et turbaberis erga plurima . . .

When I was beginning my retreat, before solemn profession, I tried to ask myself for a moment if those vows had any condition attached to them. If I was called to be a contemplative and they did not help me to be a contemplative, but hindered me, then what?

But before I could even begin to pray, I had to drop that kind of thinking.

By the time I made my vows, I decided that I was no longer sure what a contemplative was, or what the contemplative vocation was, or what my vocation was, and what our Cistercian vocation was. In fact I could not be sure I knew or understood much of anything except that I believed that You wanted me to take those particular vows in this particular house on that particular day for reasons best known to Yourself, and that what I was expected to do after that was follow along with the rest and do what I was told and things would begin to become clear.

That morning when I was lying on my face on the floor in the middle of the church, with Father Abbot praying over me, I began to laugh, with my mouth in the dust, because without knowing how or why, I had actually done the right thing, and even an astounding thing. But what was astounding was not my work, but the work You worked in me.

The months have gone by, and You have not lessened any of those desires, but You have given me peace, and I am beginning to see what it is all about. I am beginning to understand.

Because You have called me here not to wear a label by which I can recognize myself and place myself in some kind of a category. You do not want me to be thinking about what I am, but about what You are. Or rather, You do not even want me to be thinking about anything much: for You would raise me above the level of thought. And if I am always trying to figure out what I am and where I am and why I am, how will that work be done?

I do not make a big drama of this business. I do not say: "You have asked me for everything, and I have renounced all." Because I no longer desire to see anything that implies a distance between You and me: and if I stand back and consider myself and You as if something had passed between us, from me to You, I will inevitably see the gap between us and remember the distance between us.

My God, it is that gap and that distance which kill me.

That is the only reason why I desire solitude—to be lost to all created things, to die to them and to the knowledge of them, for they remind me of my distance from You. They tell me something about You: that You are far from them, even though You are in them. You have made them and Your presence sustains their being, and they hide You from me. And I would live alone, and out of them. *O beata solitudo!*

For I knew that it was only by leaving them that I could come to You: and that is why I have been so unhappy when You seemed to be condemning me to remain in them. Now my sorrow is over, and my joy is about to begin: the joy that rejoices in the deepest sorrows. For I am beginning to understand. You have taught me, and have consoled me, and I have begun again to hope and learn.

I hear You saying to me:

"I will give you what you desire. I will lead you into solitude. I will lead you by the way that you cannot possibly understand, because I want it to be the quickest way.

"Therefore all the things around you will be armed against you, to deny you, to hurt you, to give you pain, and therefore to reduce you to solitude.

"Because of their enmity, you will soon be left alone. They will cast you out and forsake you and reject you and you will be alone.

"Everything that touches you shall burn you, and you will draw your hand away in pain, until you have withdrawn yourself from all things. Then you will be all alone.

"Everything that can be desired will sear you, and brand you with a cautery, and you will fly from it in pain, to be alone. Every created joy will only come to you as pain, and you will die to all joy and be left alone. All the good things that other people love and desire and seek will come to you, but only as murderers to cut you off from the world and its occupations.

"You will be praised, and it will be like burning at the stake. You will be loved, and it will murder your heart and drive you into the desert.

"You will have gifts, and they will break you with their burden. You will have pleasures of prayer, and they will sicken you and you will fly from them.

"And when you have been praised a little and loved a little I will take away all your gifts and all your love and all your praise and you will be utterly forgotten and abandoned and you will be nothing, a dead thing, a rejection. And in that day you shall begin to possess the solitude you have so long desired. And your solitude will bear immense fruit in the souls of men you will never see on earth.

"Do not ask when it will be or where it will be or how it will be: On a mountain or in a prison, in a desert or in a concentration camp or in a hospital or at Gethsemani. It does not matter. So do not ask me, because I am not going to tell you. You will not know until you are in it.

"But you shall taste the true solitude of my anguish and my poverty and I shall lead you into the high places of my joy and you shall die in Me and find all things in My mercy which has created you for this end and brought you from Prades to

Bermuda to St. Antonin to Oakham to London to Cambridge to Rome to New York to Columbia to Corpus Christi to St. Bonaventure to the Cistercian Abbey of the poor men who labor in Gethsemani:

"That you may become the brother of God and learn to know the Christ of the burnt men."

SIT FINIS LIBRI, NON FINIS QUAERENDI

Index

515

516

517

OTHER IMAGE BOOKS

OTHER IMAGE BOOKS

Since its first publication, this autobiography of an exceptional man has been read by millions and has become one of the greatest spiritual classics of our time. Some of the tremendous praise accorded THE SEVEN STOREY MOUNTAIN is indicated below:

"It is a rare pleasure to read an autobiography with a pattern and meaning valid for all of us. THE SEVEN STOREY MOUNTAIN is a book one reads with a pencil so as to make it one's own."
Graham Greene

"THE SEVEN STOREY MOUNTAIN is essentially the odyssey of a soul. As such it stands as a more human document than the comparable 'Apologia Pro Vita Sua' of John Henry Newman. It has warmth and gusto and Augustinian wit."
Saturday Review of Literature

"The autobiography of Thomas Merton is a Twentieth Century form of the *Confessions of St. Augustine.*"
Bishop Fulton J. Sheen

"THE SEVEN STOREY MOUNTAIN is a book that deeply impresses the mind and the heart for days. It fills one with love and hope and shame—shame for one's self."   *Commonweal*

"It is to a book like this that men will turn a hundred years from now to find out what went on in the heart of man in this cruel century."   Clare Boothe Luce

"I found THE SEVEN STOREY MOUNTAIN more than merely interesting, because it deals, as do so few modern autobiographies (or indeed books of any sort), not with what happens *to* a man, but what happens inside him—that is, inside his soul. It should hold the attention of Catholic and non-Catholic alike."   Clifton Fadiman

Books by Thomas Merton

THE SEVEN STOREY MOUNTAIN

THE SIGN OF JONAS

THE ASCENT TO TRUTH

THE WATERS OF SILOE

SEEDS OF CONTEMPLATION

BREAD IN THE WILDERNESS

EXILE ENDS IN GLORY

WHAT ARE THESE WOUNDS?

THE LAST OF THE FATHERS

NO MAN IS AN ISLAND

Verse

THE TEARS OF THE BLIND LIONS

A MAN IN THE DIVIDED SEA

FIGURES FOR AN APOCALYPSE

THIRTY POEMS